Prince of Foxes

BY SAMUEL SHELLABARGER

Introduction by
JONATHAN YARDLEY

Bridge Works Publishing Company
BRIDGEHAMPTON, NEW YORK

Published by Bridge Works Publishing Company, Bridgehampton, New York, a
member of the Rowman & Littlefield Publishing Group.

Distributed in the United States by National Book Network, Lanham, Maryland.
For descriptions of this and other Bridge Works books, visit the National Book
Network website at www.nbnbooks.com.

First Bridge Works Publishing Edition 2002

The characters and events in this book are fictitious. Any similarity to actual
persons, living or dead, is coincidental and not intended by the author.

Library of Congress Cataloging-in-Publication Data

Shellabarger, Samuel, 1888–1954.
    Prince of foxes / by Samuel Shellabarger : introduction by Jonathan
Yardley.— 1st Bridge Works Pub., ed.
       p.   cm.
    ISBN 1-882593-65-0 (alk. paper) — ISBN 1-882593-64-2 (pbk. : alk.
paper)
    1. Italy—History—1492–1559—Fiction.   2. Borgia, Cesare,
1476?–1507—Fiction.   I. Title.
PS3537.H64 P75   2002
813'.52—dc21   2002071714

10 9 8 7 6 5 4 3 2 1

To my daughter Marianne

CONTENTS

Scale of Miles

0 10 20 30 40 50 60 70 80

L. Como

L. Maggiore

L. Garda

Oglio R.

L O M B A R D Y

Milan

Ticino R.

Mantua

P I E D M O N T

Po R.

Po R.

Tanaro R.

Trebbia R.

Secchia R.

L I G U R I A

Genoa

Gulf of Genoa

Ligurian

Sea

Pisa

Arno R.

T U S C

CAPRAJA

ELBA

GIGLIO

F R A N C E

SWITZERLAND   TYROL   KINGDOM
                                  OF
           VENETIA   HUNGARY
    LOMBARDY   Venice   CROATIA
PIEDMONT Ferrara
                           OTTOMAN
     Bologna   EMPIRE
              Ravenna
   Florence   Urbino
   TUSCANY Città   Ancona
           del Monte
        UMBRIA
CORSICA Viterbo
              ABRUZZI
              Rome
                         Biseglia
Area shown in large map   APULIA
              CAMPANIA
           Naples

SARDINIA   Tyrrhenian
              Sea

Mediterranean
    Sea   SICILY   Ionian
                          Sea

ITALY ~ 1500   Miles
                       0 50 100

Adriatic Sea

VENETIAN REPUBLIC

R. Lenz

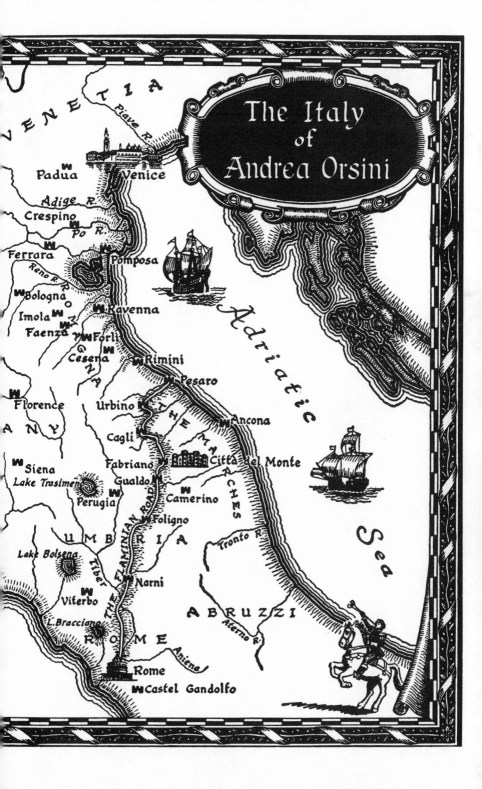

INTRODUCTION

Jonathan Yardley

THERE ARE many reasons for reading *Prince of Foxes*—not least, as some reviewers like to say, that it's just about impossible to put down once you start it—but I would like to put it forward as a textbook example of what Americans were reading during the golden age of American popular fiction. This period lasted for about three decades, from the early 1930s to the late 1950s, during which much of the commercial fiction that millions of Americans read for pleasure—fiction that made the best-seller lists—was work of considerable literary skill and stylistic distinctiveness.

That stands in sharp contrast to the popular fiction that Americans now read. In the fall of 2001 my colleague at the *Washington Post*, Linton Weeks, wrote a feature story in which he argued that commercial, mass-market American fiction had become characterized by "the No-Style style," in which one writer is utterly indistinguishable from every other. The prose of today's pop writers—Tom Clancy, Mary Higgins Clark, John Grisham, Jonathan Kellerman, Stephen Coonts, Robin Cook, et al.—might as well roll off an assembly line. It is flat, lifeless, reportorial, matter-of-fact, with occasional attempts at fine or evocative prose that merely serve to underscore how bad it is. Whether it is written *by* people who don't know how to write or *for* people who don't know how to read is open to argument, but any way you slice it, it's dead.

Consider by contrast the popular fiction that Americans read during the golden age. I'm not talking about the occasional novel by a writer of real literary distinction—Ernest Hemingway, John P. Marquand, Katherine Anne Porter—that made it onto the best-seller lists, but about novels written with the mass readership plainly in mind, with commercial rather than literary expectations foremost in their authors' minds. Among those who wrote such books were

Thomas B. Costain, Herman Wouk, Marjorie Kinnan Rawlings, Kenneth Roberts, Edna Ferber, Sholem Asch, Ben Ames Williams, Frederic Wakeman, Frances Parkinson Keyes, Irwin Shaw, Budd Schulberg, Hamilton Basso, and, of course, Samuel Shellabarger. Whatever one might say about the individual merits of their many books, it certainly can be said that they had *style*. It wasn't always particularly good style, but it was real, the work of writers who were trying to sound like themselves rather than mere replications of everybody else.

This isn't just nostalgia talking, though of course one must always be alert against that. Then as now the literati resented commercial success and were quick to find fault with those who achieved it, so most of the writers mentioned above came in for their share of whacks in book-review sections and literary journals. My own parents were discriminating readers, and I can recall disparaging words they uttered about Ferber and Keyes and Schulberg, to name three. Yet it seems to me no exaggeration to say that, whatever the shortcomings of these writers in the literary beauty contest, they had in common one essential characteristic of writers: They could *write*.

None wrote better than Shellabarger. Over ten years, beginning in late 1944, he published four remarkable historical romances: *Captain from Castile*, *Prince of Foxes*, *The King's Cavalier*, and *Lord Vanity*. All spent time on the best-seller lists. The first two were sold to the movies and made into wonderful films, full of action and romance and spectacular scenery; it is a measure of how high Shellabarger stood in the world of popular entertainment that the lead role in each picture—Pedro de Vargas in *Captain from Castile*, Andrea Orsini in *Prince of Foxes*—was played by Tyrone Power, the Tom Cruise or Brad Pitt of the day and a huge box-office draw.

Shellabarger did not become a well-known writer until he was in his mid-fifties. Born in Washington, D.C., in 1888, he grew up surrounded by books.[1] His family was well established and apparently

---

1. For biographical information about Shellabarger, I am indebted to a website assembled by Jesse F. Knight: http://uts.cc.utexas.edu/~soon/histfiction/shellabarger-bio.html.

of a somewhat conservative bent; he himself was a life-long Republican and Episcopalian. At age fifteen he toured Europe and later wrote that "the impressions of London, Paris, and Rome at the turn of the century became indelible in my mind and have left a nostalgia for the past which has colored my historical writing." He did undergraduate work at Princeton, got a Ph.D. from Harvard, served in the Intelligence Corps during World War I, taught English at Princeton for a few years, then decided to become a full-time writer. His books (some written under pen names) included mysteries, romances, and scholarly works; perhaps the most notable of the latter was a biography of Lord Chesterfield, published in 1935.

During and after World War II, Shellabarger combined his scholarly and literary interests, serving as headmaster of a girls' school in Ohio for nearly a decade—which strikes a personal note with me, as my own father served as headmaster of a girls' school in Virginia for two decades—while writing short stories for popular magazines, notably *McCall's* and *Cosmopolitan*, which in those days were considerably more than mere "women's magazines." But it was during the war that Shellabarger began work on *Captain from Castile*, the book that changed his life. It and his three other historical novels made him wealthy, but they did more than that: they brought him an avid following and critical respect. His sudden death after a heart attack in March 1954 was widely mourned as ending a distinguished career far too prematurely.

Prince of Foxes, like Shellabarger's other historical novels, is notable as much for its solid history as for its adventure and romance. As with *Captain from Castile*—a new edition of which has been published by Bridge Works as a companion to this edition of *Prince of Foxes*—his fictitious characters are surrounded by actual ones drawn from history, to such an extent that one would have to be steeped in the history of Renaissance Italy and its city-state wars to know with absolute certainty which of the many people in this book are Shellabarger's inventions and which are real. His purpose in doing this obviously was to give his novels as much verisimilitude as possible—which every writer of historical fiction tries to do—but it went deeper than that. Shellabarger was an educator by training and inclination, and he wanted readers to learn from his novels as well as be entertained by them.

To say that you will learn a lot about Renaissance Italy from *Prince of Foxes* is if anything an understatement. Cesare Borgia and his sister Lucretia, their father Pope Alexander VI, Alphonso d'Este, Duke Ercole d'Este . . . these and innumerable other men and women in Shellabarger's cast are right out of history, and he has researched them with care. His portraits are often swiftly drawn miniatures, but they rest in fact. Thus Alexander, the philandering, power-hungry churchman, is depicted at age seventy as abounding "in vigor and animal spirits," yet his "courtly grace and charm of manner [disguise] a certain rankness, a brutal quality." Born Rodrigo Borgia, he is Borgia to the core:

> In him the Vicar of Christ had declined into a temporal sovereign. Alexander ruled over provinces and cities, had armies in his pay, contracted alliances with or against kings and emperors; the House of Borgia concerned him rather than the Household of Faith. Victim as well as exploiter of a relatively brief historical epoch, he was no more typical of the Papacy than is a fungus typical of the mighty oak to which it may be attached. Contemporary and modern Catholic historians of the Church have adequately condemned him. Sensual, shallow, and greedy, he merits no defense except as the creature of his times, which contributed to his sins and made them possible.

That paragraph is typical of Shellabarger. He knew his history as well as the people who made it, and he wasn't in the least hesitant about expressing his opinions about it and them. He was steeped in the literature and language of the times about which he wrote. "Like Rafael Sabatini," according to Jesse F. Knight, "Shellabarger believed that the best research for the historical writer was not to read histories, but to read works actually written during the time [about which] one wishes to write." The dialogue in *Prince of Foxes* certainly seems authentic, never more so than when it is the dialogue of flattery, which is essential to the book.

That is because *Prince of Foxes* is at its core a book about politics as practiced in the time of Nicolo Machiavelli and his *Prince*, whose traits as he defined them were deeply influenced by Cesare Borgia. "Trick and countertrick, betrayal and double-dealing, were not only commonplaces of the political game, they were the texture of it," Shellabarger writes. "In current practice, they were to be expected, and, if successful, they were even to be admired." Flattery—flowery, oily, transparent, surpassingly cynical—was the language of politics then even more than it is now, and Shellabarger employed it with skill as well as self-evident delight.

No one speaks it more skillfully in *Prince of Foxes* than Andrea Orsini. He is if anything an even more interesting character than Pedro de Vargas in *Captain from Castile*, because he has more to overcome: a low birth, which he has disguised by taking on an assumed name, but—and this is what makes him so interesting—a most imperfect character. He has grace, warmth, tact, and vitality, but he is also unscrupulous, crafty, manipulative, and self-interested. He loves art and is an uncommonly gifted painter, but he is no less skilled at darker arts and has no compunctions about practicing them. The young and beautiful Camilla degli Baglioni finds him enchanting, "*un cortigiano eminente*," to which her friend Lorenzo da Pavia replies: "Aye, an eminent courtier. I have rarely met anyone more finished. But think: a soldier who knows art, a Neapolitan who speaks like a Florentine, an Orsini unrelated to the Orsini, a servant of the Borgia in the service of the Borgia's enemies. A contradiction. He has too many faces."

Thus Andrea's story is the exact opposite of Pedro de Vargas's. The latter is, as *Captain from Castile* begins, a strong but wholly innocent young man who is to receive in the next few years a hard if necessary education in the world's cruelties, vanities, and betrayals. By contrast Andrea is, at the outset of *Prince of Foxes*, a strong but wholly cynical young man who is about to undergo a process of moral replenishment and growth. Inasmuch as he is besotted with Camilla upon first seeing her and grows ever more so with each further encounter, one would assume that she is the chief agent of this rebirth, but the story is vastly more complicated and surprising than that. Much to his confusion, Andrea finds himself confronted by a man of genuine goodness who at first seems to be an obstacle in the way of richness and happiness—in other words, someone to be gotten out of the way—but eventually becomes an exemplar whom Andrea is determined to emulate, at whatever cost.

Though the story of Andrea Orsini is set in Renaissance Italy, it is quintessentially American. What Orsini seeks is at the heart of the American dream—"a new life"—and what he seeks for Italy is American as well: ". . . that the states of Italy should be brought together under one rule is in itself desirable and worthy of support." No doubt this helps explain why *Prince of Foxes*, like Shellabarger's other historical novels, was so warmly received by so many American readers; he was writing about matters of which they had prior understanding, in their own history and in their shared ideals.

Precisely why it is that Shellabarger's novels fell out of popular favor is a mystery I cannot hope to explain. It is easy (and tempting) to blame this, along with just about everything else, on television, and in one important respect it may indeed be a prime suspect: Television has accustomed people to entertainment that can be enjoyed without concentration or intellectual effort. Shellabarger's novels, by contrast, demand the reader's attention and engagement. They are not difficult—far from it—but they are demanding. They make you think, which is reason enough to read them, but I am confident that a reading of *Prince of Foxes* will persuade you that they offer many, many other rewards.

Jonathan Yardley is the book critic and a columnist for the Washington Post. *He is the author of six books and the recipient of a Pulitzer Prize for Distinguished Criticism.*

PART ONE

Ferrara

CHAPTER I

IT WAS to be a lute this time, a lute fit for an angel. Perfect. Incomparable. While Lorenzo da Pavia's pencil, sensitive as a moth's antenna. hovered above the drawing board, the thought of the famous instrument designer passed thirstily from imagined curve to curve, each lovelier than the last. If now and then his gaze drifted through the spacious Venetian room, with its timbered ceiling dappled by reflections of the near-by canal, he was unconscious of the many instruments which decorated it, those he had formerly made: viols, lutes, theorbos, and clavichords. They belonged to yesterday. Fragments of beauty not now completely satisfying. He followed today's vision of a more perfect achievement.

He thought of color and materials — ebony and ivory — of a lady's shapely hands, of her costume embroidered with golden musical notes; but these were secondary elements blending into the supreme synthesis of form — the instrument's lines and curves — abstract and thrilling as music. "Yes," he dreamed, "*nella forma sta il tutto.*"

His homely, patient face darkened with concentration. Then suddenly his pencil stole to the paper and swept a slender, triumphant arc, foreshadowing the sounding board. And now the vault of the back —

A cough startled him and he looked up dazed. An apprentice from the downstairs shop stood humbly awaiting his attention.

"If the Master pleases."

Enraged, the Master could find no words for a moment.

"A stranger below, a Roman gentleman, one Andrea Orsini, seeking audience. *Un gran signore* by the looks of him. Shall he be shown up?"

Lorenzo slammed his drawing board down on the table, rose to his feet, and called on God.

"Exactly! Did it ever fail? I say, did it ever fail, when I was on the point of achieving some notable work, that I must be broken in on!

3

Ahimè, Madonna! I had it almost in my grasp, a divine shape. But no! A big lord drops in, and art can wait!" Then, as if the name had registered for the first time, "You say, Andrea Orsini?"

"*Sì.*"

"Ah!"

Master Lorenzo had a quick memory, and the name of the caller now sank home. He had heard yesterday somewhere of this Orsini. In what connection? Not a pleasant one, he remembered. Yes — it came back to him — messenger from the Pope's Holiness and from Cesare Borgia to the Doge's Serenity. A shadow attended any messenger of the Borgias, whose crimes and invasion of the Romagna had set the whole of Italy on guard. Yes, and he recalled the gossip that Orsini did not belong to the great Roman family but to a Neapolitan branch that Lorenzo had thought extinct. A curious resurrection. In any case he ranked as one of the leading captains of Duke Valentino, as Cesare Borgia was called, and had held a prominent command in the recent campaign against Forlì. But Lorenzo da Pavia was an artist and tradesman, therefore professionally neutral towards war and politics.

"Shall I send him away?" suggested the apprentice, used to the Maestro's temperament.

"*Canchero!* What good would that do now? I might just as well talk with this Orsini as twiddle my thumbs. Let him come up." And with a farewell sigh toward his drawing board, Lorenzo added bitterly: "Tell His Magnificence it grieves me that he should have had to wait."

The apprentice lingered. "Master, I'm not sure whether he comes to buy or sell. It is good to be prepared."

"Sell?"

"He has a page boy with him, a blackamoor, who carries a roll of canvas under one arm."

Known as a collector, who frequently made purchases of art pieces for favored clients or for himself, Lorenzo was not too much surprised. But why a soldier like Orsini —

"Hm-m," he nodded. "Well, bring the gentleman up."

He had been working in his doublet but now slipped on a wide-sleeved gown, proper to the reception of a caller. Then, adjusting his black velvet cap and smoothing out his beard, he advanced to the head of the stairs, composed for the civilities of welcome.

He looked what he was, a distinguished craftsman, the friend of princes, artists, and scholars, one of the notables of Venice. Popes, dukes, and marquises wrangled for one of his masterpieces, a lute or a clavichord; or they turned to him for advice on items of beauty. His

4

profession was beauty, the unacknowledged religion of his age; and he held a place among its high priests.

It was with no sense of inferiority that he waited for the noble captain to present himself, even if the name was as illustrious as Orsini. He merely felt curious as to what sort of person the camp of Borgia produced. Besides, the man was fresh from the south and would have news.

Presently he heard a light tread on the stairs, then a tall figure appeared on the landing. At once Messer Lorenzo felt pleasantly surprised. He had expected brawn, scars and swagger, but he encountered grace and deference. He liked the stranger's smile, his big mouth and bold, triangular nose. He liked the play of his dark eyes and the abundant vitality in them. The restraint, too, of his dress was pleasing: complete black, except for the tawny collar of marten's fur on the mantle, a costume that set off vividly the flame of his crimson cap. But, most of all, Messer Lorenzo was struck by an overtone of charm, the supreme quality either in a person or in a work of art, indefinably mysterious. Perhaps Orsini's young manhood had something to do with it, for he could not have been older than twenty-six.

At the heels of the caller appeared a fat little Negro boy, black as midnight and wearing a turban of varicolored silk with a tall aigret that matched the white of his eyeballs. As the apprentice had reported, he carried a roll of cloth or canvas longer than his own height, and as soon as his master was seated he took his stand beside him like a midget halberdier.

"*Maestro mio*," bowed Orsini with just the right manner, "I can say in all truth that I have long aspired to throw myself at the feet of one whose fame is so sweetly published through all Italy, not only on men's lips but in the tones of your divine instruments. It seems hardly possible that I am actually in your presence."

Lorenzo relished the neat turn of the compliment and replied in the same manner. True or false, well-polished and courteous phrases were admirable in themselves.

"Your Magnificence embarrasses me. That an illustrious captain of the sublime Duke, my lord Cesare Borgia, should condescend to visit so obscure an artisan as I, is honor enough without the kind but ex-cessive praise which Your Magnificence bestows. You flatter but, of course, you please me, Messer Andrea, and incline me in all ways to your service."

Yes, Lorenzo approved of his caller, who was evidently a man of parts, but this did not mean in the least that he trusted him and was not on guard. Like master, like man perhaps. However attractive he

5

might appear, an officer of the sublime Duke was probably as great a rascal as the Duke himself.

"You are but recently come to Venice?" he added.

"Only two days ago. I had business with the Serenity of the Doge. But as soon as I could free myself, I hastened to present my homage to you. This in itself would not have warranted the intrusion, Messer Lorenzo, but I bear a message that justifies it, as I think you will allow."

Drawing a rectangle of paper from his belt pouch, Orsini presented it; and, at the sight of the Papal arms, Master Lorenzo dropped to one knee and kissed the seal. Then, breaking it reverently, he began to read, while the messenger, getting up from his chair, walked over to a rack of instruments near by and stood admiring them. From outside, beyond the sun-warmed curtains, sounded the distant calls of boatmen — *a-òel . . . sia stali . . . premi* — and the creak of oars against tholes.

Pope Alexander VI gave greeting and apostolic blessing to his *diletto figlio*, Lorenzo da Pavia, and wanted an organ for his private chapel. It should be the finest organ on earth, corresponding to Lorenzo's fame and to the dignity of the Pope's Holiness. Moreover, it was desired without delay; the Master should put off all other work to furnish it at the earliest moment. He should set his own price; but let him create a perfect thing. And it would be to his great advantage and earn the pontifical gratitude. *Datum Rome apud Sanctum Petrum die xx Augusti, 1500, Pontificatus Nostri anno octavo.*

Humph! chafed Lorenzo. It was always that way! These great people expected you to drop everything at their bidding and hurried the soul out of your body. Did they think that fine things were created like penny whistles! By God, he would do the organ, if ever, when he chose. And so, having kissed the letter more reverently than before, he looked up to find that his caller had taken down one of the lutes, drawing his hands caressingly over its velvet surface. The Master noticed that the hands were long and sensitive, although muscular. Orsini made a fine picture, standing in the sun glow of the curtain, with his crimson cap and square-cut, slightly curling hair.

"I see you like the feel of it," Lorenzo said.

"Yes, eye and ear are not enough to appreciate your work, Master. It requires touch."

Orsini restored the lute carefully to its place but stood lingering a moment before he returned to his chair.

"As to the Holiness of Our Lord," continued Lorenzo, "I kiss his pontifical feet. He shall be served at once — *subito!* I shall make him

6

an organ unequaled in the world." (These promises cost nothing but breath.) "And when Your Nobility returns to Rome, you will be good enough to carry my humble letter of submission to His Beatitude."

To the Master's surprise, Orsini shook his head. "No, sir, alas. I am not returning to Rome. It may interest you that, with the delivery of this letter, my term of service with the House of Borgia expires. I belong now to the most illustrious House of Este and leave tomorrow for Ferrara. As you know, in my profession, one sells one's sword as advantage prompts. The ambassador of this Republic will no doubt carry your letter."

"Ah," said Lorenzo, nodding; but he drew his own conclusions. There had been much talk of Borgian designs on Ferrara — perhaps of a marriage to be forced between the heir apparent of that uneasy duchy and the notorious Madonna Lucrezia, whose second husband her brother, Cesare, had newly murdered. It did not need great shrewdness to suspect that Andrea Orsini at Ferrara would be serving two masters, the old and the new.

However, such dark matters were none of Lorenzo's business. He shrugged almost disdainfully but viewed his caller in a new light. He felt there was something opaque about the young soldier in spite of his charm and frank smile — an impression that renewed Lorenzo's interest.

"You will find His Excellence Duke Ercole d'Este different, I imagine, from the magnificent and glorious prince you have just left," he remarked casually.

"No doubt." Aware of the sarcasm, Orsini did not conceal the twinkle in his eyes. "No doubt. There are few who can match the divine genius of my lord Cesare."

"Of course," Lorenzo agreed. He would have liked to add, "Fratricide! Assassin! Bandit!" but he said merely, "Divine genius is well put."

"And let me tell you," smiled Orsini, "that he is not the monster that you people of Venice make him. Is not gossip the mother of monsters, Maestro? He has great ends and lets nothing distract him. Perhaps merely he's too consistent. Hard, if necessary; selfish, yes (and who isn't?); but able, of great *virtù* and splendor. A valiant prince. . . . I wager you'd love him, Messer Lorenzo, unless you stood in his way."

"Probably," said Lorenzo, doubting it. "I rejoice to learn about him."

"Look you" — Orsini leaned forward — "if he were a painter, he would use rich colors. Life is his canvas."

Per Bacco, thought the instrument maker of his guest, an unusual

7

young man! "And does your admiration extend to Madama Lucrezia Borgia?" he ventured.

"Her Excellence's slave! What hair of gold! What perfect eyes! What sweetness! And to see her dance, you would think Venus had returned to earth. If you love beauty, sir, you'll find nowhere a more triumphant lady."

Lorenzo was impressed. Madonna Lucrezia might be known in some quarters as the greatest whore in Italy; but, to an artist, morals did not matter. He was aware of a growing fellow feeling with his guest. Apparently they looked at life from the same angle.

"Which reminds me," Orsini went on. He turned to the little blackamoor. "Seraph, hand me that roll." Then, slipping out an innermost canvas, together with four strips of molding to form an impromptu frame, he joined the latter together. . . . "I have here, *Maestro mio*, a portrait of the divine Signora done by a painter in Rome. It may interest you."

He unrolled the canvas, while keeping it turned away from Lorenzo; attached it to the molding; and, having selected the proper light, used a chair as an easel.

"*Ecco!*" he said, stepping aside with a gesture. "Behold the lady!"

"By God! By God!" exclaimed Lorenzo.

He found himself facing a masterpiece. It was this fact, rather than the fair-haired beauty in crimson and cloth of gold, that absorbed him; the fundamental design, the harmony of colors, the drawing, the brushwork. He stepped back and forth, admiring, one hand in his beard. . . . "*Domineddio!*"

"You like it?" Orsini asked intently. "You like it?"

"*Santa Maria benedetta!* Do I like it! A marvel!"

"The hands, eh? The foreshortening of the forearm?"

"Yes, yes." Lorenzo drew closer, looked for the signature. "It is unsigned. Who painted it?"

"Guess."

Lorenzo pondered. "Francia? Perugino? Yet it has something Florentine. Not my good friend Leonardo da Vinci, but — You know, it reminds me of work once shown me in Florence, done by a youth of great promise, whose name I forget. He perished at the time of the French invasion. Messer Leonardo acquired it. He used to say that if the boy had lived — Nay, I am at a loss, Your Magnificence."

Orsini sighed. "Well, I can't help you, sir. The portrait was given me by Madama herself, but not the name of the painter. I hoped you could inform me, though it hardly matters."

8

"Is it for sale?" murmured the other.

"No, it accompanies me to Ferrara for certain reasons."

Once again Lorenzo thought of opaqueness, of deep water with a play of ripples on the surface. . . . "You have another painting?"

"Indeed. A fine piece if you care to see it."

Lorenzo felt the collector's fever mounting. He did not reflect until afterwards how cleverly Orsini had managed it. His appetite, stimulated by the portrait, was impatient for the next dish.

"A part of my profit from the intaking of Forlì," the young soldier explained, readjusting the strips of molding for a larger canvas. "It seemed unfair that d'Allègre's French mercenaries should have all. There was no sack, you understand, but a certain interest in souvenirs." Orsini smiled happily. "I took this along to preserve it from the *hommes d'armes*. Ah, *Maestro caro*, is it not a wonder?"

And stepping back again dramatically, he revealed the painting.

Lorenzo's eyes glowed. His admiration this time was speechless. He tasted the fine qualities of the work with the silent reverence of an epicure enjoying a great wine. It represented the Triumph of Virtue, a delightful grouping of allegorical figures beneath a pergola. When Lorenzo found his tongue, it was to sympathize with the painting's former owner, Caterina Sforza of Forlì, who had been deprived of it.

"*Quella poverina di signora!*" he muttered. "She must have taken pride in this. A cruel fortune."

Orsini nodded sentimentally. "My heart bleeds for her. Alas, that her loss should be my gain! . . . But, Master, note that this canvas too is unsigned."

"It does not have to be signed. The whole of it is one signature writ large for any fool to read. No, my son, we are on firm ground here. That effect of sculpture, that drawing, that classic edge — Mantegna. One of his best. Softer than most and, therefore, to me more pleasing." Lorenzo suddenly altered his tone to a drier key. "Do you think of selling it?"

"Perhaps. At a price worthy of Mantegna."

Lorenzo stroked his beard. The collector's fever did not prevent him from driving a bargain. "Too bad, of course, that it is unsigned. I might be able to offer fifty ducats. A great sum, but, because of you, Messer Andrea, I should make an effort."

"*Va bene, Maestro.* A hundred and fifty, you said?"

"No, fifty. Or perhaps sixty as an outside offer."

Andrea lifted his arms, let them fall to his sides. "Ah, Messer Lorenzo da Pavia, I had thought better of you. . . . Well, Seraph, roll up the painting. In any case, I intended to offer it at Ferrara. The signori of that illustrious court will value it properly." He raised his arms again in an access of indignation. "Behold those flesh tints! Behold that space of heaven above the arches of the pergola! Sixty ducats! Seraph, I weep."

The black boy rolled his eyeballs and spat in sympathy.

"Sixty ducats!" Andrea repeated, snapping his fingers. "Look at those breasts of Lady Virtue! It lacks little but you could cup them in your hands. Take down the painting, Seraph."

"Your Magnificence, one moment," put in Lorenzo, admiring Orsini's fine acting and flow of language. "For your sake, I offer seventy-five — my last word."

He had already thought of a purchaser. Isabella d'Este of Mantua, the patroness of Mantegna, would welcome this treasure for her studio. But Madama was a shrewd buyer and did not fling her money out of the window.

"Seventy-five ducats!" returned Orsini. "Another outrage! A slight upon the genius of a great artist! I laugh! . . . Messer Lorenzo, for love of you, my lowest price is one hundred ducats. A gift from heaven."

"Your Nobility, I cannot."

"Roll up the painting, Seraph."

"No," came an imperious voice from the landing of the stairs behind them. "Signore, I shall buy your painting. By God, it is a thing of excellence and worth a hundred ducats. Let it stand there, boy. I want to look at it."

And as they turned, a young woman in brown velvet and gold crossed the room and stood gazing at the picture.

CHAPTER II

ANDREA ORSINI could tell at once that the newcomer was a great lady, *una illustrissima*, not merely a noble woman. The assurance of her bearing, the unconscious haughtiness of her mouth, showed it, even if Messer Lorenzo had not confirmed the opinion by the profound deference of his bow.

She wore a velvet cap embroidered in spirals of gold, like her dress, and with a green plume drooping to one side. This and her small head and short curled hair gave a boyish impression, which was enhanced rather than diminished by the wide sleeves and the pelisse of russet fur worn over one shoulder. She had brown, tawny eyes and a piquant nose. She was young, perhaps eighteen or nineteen, slender and of small stature, but very erect and light.

"*Iddio!*" Lorenzo exclaimed. "*Madama mia!* What a surprise, delight and honor! Your Signory drops, like an angel, from heaven and does not permit your servant even to welcome you. I lay my excuses at your feet."

Still gazing at the painting, she held out her hand to him. "No, my friend, I beg pardon myself. I wouldn't let your people announce me. 'By God,' I told them, 'have I not the right of entrée with this great Master at all times?' So I tripped upstairs alone and found you and this cavalier. . . . What do you think of my purchase?"

"A glorious thing."

"And worth its price? Tell me truly, Messer Lorenzo."

"No doubt it is — if beauty has a price, if genius can be valued. But I sought to acquire it for a client, Her Signory of Mantua, and —"

"Then it's her loss," the lady exulted. "I hope you tell her about it. If you don't, I'll write her myself. Her Excellence snaps up everything. Am I proud to overreach her for once! And it's your punishment for being so niggardly." She turned a radiant smile on Orsini. "Sir, you will let me have it for a hundred ducats? You'll not deny me?"

A flush had crept up under the gentleman's tan. It was good sport to bargain, but he regretted that such an exalted lady had overheard him. It took a moment to compose himself. Then he bowed.

"Your Highness must not deny *me.*"

"*Che cosa?*" she said uncertainly.

"A painting, even of Mantegna, is overwhelmed by Your Excellence's approval. No artist could desire more — certainly not gold. Extend but your favor to Mantegna and me, Madonna, and accept this as a humble gift, a tribute of admiration."

It should be confessed that Andrea did not expect his gesture to be taken seriously, but he hoped that it would efface the bargaining episode. He was startled by the answer.

"Really, sir? Indeed? You would give me this beautiful thing?"

"If Your Highness will honor me," he assured her, managing to keep dismay out of his voice.

11

"*Dio mio!*" she sighed. "Did you hear that, Master Lorenzo? And he does not even know me. What gallantry! What greatness of soul!"

Her face revealed only innocence and delight; but, sensing the mischief behind it, Orsini felt like a fly on a pin.

Lorenzo played up to her. "One could expect no less from His Magnificence."

"And he shall be treated with magnificence," she went on. "My lord husband often declares that it takes no less generosity to accept a gift nobly than to present one. Sir, I know it would offend you if I did not accept your painting with due appreciation. I shall hang it in one of my chief *stanze*. It will always recall our meeting and Your Lordliness."

Andrea had the rare gift of viewing himself objectively, and at this absurd moment he confessed that he looked like an ass. Instead of the chagrin which the fair brigand, ambushed behind her gratitude, no doubt expected, she encountered a provocative smile.

She looked down, biting her lips, but a flick of laughter slipped out. "Well, sir, are you tongue-tied? Have you nothing appropriate to say?"

"A great deal, Your Excellence. At the moment, I was thinking with admiration of your lord husband, whom I haven't the honor of knowing, and how superbly Your Signory practises his noble precepts. I was wishing for an opportunity to see whether I could practise them myself. And I was deploring that, while Your Highness has a memento of our meeting, I have nothing."

"My God, sir," she retorted, trying to keep her lips straight, "it can't be that you're hinting at a gift in return."

"Hinting is not the word for it, Madonna."

At that, she broke down and burst out laughing, until her eyes filled. She looked like a page boy in masquerade, and her laughter was so catching that Lorenzo and Orsini joined in.

"Well, then," she went on at last, drawing off her glove and slipping a diamond ring from her finger, "here is your opportunity. And what now?"

An expert like Andrea could tell that the ring was worth a hundred and fifty ducats if it was worth a marchetto. He kissed it devoutly.

"I can do no better than copy Your Excellence," he returned. "It would offend you, Madonna, if I did not accept this glorious ring, which I shall keep as a saint's relic in memory of the divine hand that wore it." And he perched it on the end of his little finger.

"Isn't it about time, Master," she said, turning to Lorenzo, "that you presented this gentleman?"

"*Il Magnifico* Andrea Orsini," pronounced Lorenzo, "late captain of His Lordship, Cesare Borgia, the Duke Valentino, and now in the service of Ferrara."

"Then I know your kinsmen," she exclaimed: "the Cardinal, the Duke of Gravina, my lord Giangiordano."

"Distant kinsmen," he answered. "My family is of Naples. My great-uncle was Raimondo Orsini, Count of Nola."

"Indeed?" she said politely and vaguely. "But you haven't the accent of Naples. I'd have thought you were from Lombardy or the Veneto, if not from Tuscany itself."

"I have traveled much, Your Excellence. I attended the University of Padua."

"That accounts for it. . . . And now, since Master Lorenzo does not present me, let me tell you that Camilla degli Baglioni, wife to His Excellence Marc' Antonio Varano, lord of Città del Monte, is very much at your service."

She curtsied slightly to his bow and did not notice the startled expression that crossed his face before he could control it. Not that she belonged to the turbulent and bloodstained family that ruled Perugia; not that her elderly husband had been a famous *condottiero* — there was nothing surprising in this — but her name brought back a recent scene which flashed across his mind, even as he bowed in front of her with hands wide and knee half bent.

For this was the woman that Cesare Borgia had promised him!

He could still see the exquisite shape of the Borgia's hand which concealed the viselike strength of it, the long forefinger shifting from place to place on the map over which they were leaning. "You perceive, Andrea, there are two ways an army can take to enter the Marches: *here* across the mountains from Foligno and *here* through Fabriano. But at this last point Città del Monte blocks the way, and another Varano. These Varano wasps! We must burn their nests if we are to hold the region. But this particular wasp, this doddering Marc' Antonio, should give no trouble. And hark you — " The Duke straightened up. Orsini could still see before him the deadly white beauty of his face, like a cameo brought to life by the splendor of his eyes. "Hark you, Andrea, his widow is worth having, the Baglione bud he married. Talk of Spring in the lap of Winter! Maybe she's still a virgin. There's a prize for you! There's the plum you've been looking for! Well, do our business in Ferrara — win over this mule of an Alfonso d'Este to the alliance with our sister — and you shall have the Baglione girl and Città del Monte to boot. You can count on it."

13

Orsini could not keep a certain intentness out of his eyes when he had made his bow. If, always alert to the present moment, he had admired the lady before, he now studied her.

"But to those who love me, I'm known as Milla," she was saying. "Camilla's too long."

"Madonna Milla," he ventured — "it is music in words."

"Thank you so much," she half-teased him.

He reflected that the Duke had been right in calling her a girl. Certainly marriage and rank had not sobered her. She reminded him of a bird on the wing — as swift and light and unpredictable. Until then, his bargain with Borgia had seemed only a bargain; now —

"And His Signory, my lord Marc' Antonio?" Lorenzo asked. "I trust he is well."

"If he was not well, do you think I should be here, Master?" she retorted, a softer light in her eyes. "No, thank God, His Excellence is in good health. He is at present visiting our dear friends in Urbino. Wasn't it kind of him to let me go jaunting to Venice! I tell you he spoils me."

Andrea Orsini pondered the overtones of this. Could it be that she actually loved a man old enough to be her grandfather? It sounded strangely like it. Andrea recalled that Marc' Antonio's two sons by a former marriage had fallen at Fornuovo. Left alone in his tiny mountain state, the old lord, now close upon seventy, had no doubt taken this bride partly for her dowry and the Baglione interest, and partly to warm his hands one last time before the fire of life. Of course he would indulge her, buy her gratitude; perhaps, even, her affection. But there was more than this in the warmth of her voice. What she needed, thought Andrea confidently, was experience.

"*Com'è carino!*" exclaimed Camilla on another topic, her eyes caressing the little blackamoor, Seraph. "What a love! Adorable! Is he yours? Where did you get him?"

"At dice from the Cardinal Farnese, Madonna, six weeks past. . . . Kneel to Her Excellence, Seraph."

"*Carino! Bambolone mio!*" She drew her forefinger over the plump black cheek. "If you stripped him, he'd look like an ebony cherub, a jet Cupid. What a partner he would make for my pet dwarf, Alda! She's white as a lily. Can't you see them dancing a *moresca* together on the table! I've always wanted a blackamoor page. *Dear* Messer Andrea," she begged, "let me have him. I'll pay you anything I can afford, good Your Magnificence."

"I'll lend him to you, Madama, if that will serve. Without compliment, I should be glad to place him, for he's more in my way than a help. We can settle the price later if he pleases you."

"Poor gentleman!" She laid a repentant hand on his sleeve. "I rob you of everything. You did not expect so disastrous an afternoon."

"No, I did not expect it." Her eyes faltered before the fire in his, and he added casually, "You hear, Seraph. You are now in the service of Her Highness. Be a good boy; practise the virtues you have seen in me; avoid spitting and thieving — and God bless you."

"Or beware!" said Camilla with a lifted forefinger. "And now, Messer Lorenzo, to the business for which I called on Your Worship. I would have a theorbo full-toned for my collection, a lovely thing such as only you can furnish. . . ."

Somehow Andrea felt that she had drawn back within herself. Perhaps his eyes had revealed more than he intended. There was a note of exclusion and dismissal in her conference with the instrument maker. But, refusing to accept it, Orsini managed to linger while he rolled up the portrait of Madonna Lucrezia. Now that Seraph had left his service, he would arrange to have the painting delivered at his lodgings by one of Lorenzo's apprentices. This meant a word with the Master and a pretext for delay. He could not permit his meeting with Camilla Baglione to end so casually.

He listened to the discussion about the theorbo. Characteristically Lorenzo regretted that he had nothing worthy of Her Illustrious Excellence at the moment. He could offer only a poor thing of little value if she deigned to look at it. But Madonna Milla, for her part, expressed enchantment at the beautiful instrument of Spanish walnut enlivened with graceful designs of tarsia work.

"You always depreciate what you have done, Maestro."

"Because I always dream of doing better."

She intended the theorbo for a favorite singer at Città del Monte. Deftly tuning the multiple strings, she hummed a snatch from a song; but, since the theorbo is a bass lute, it did not fit her voice.

"If I could hear someone," she began and was once more aware of Andrea.

He needed no further invitation. "If Your Signory will forgive a poor voice," he suggested, "and listen only to the tone of the instrument."

She handed it to him with a trace of the constraint he had noticed after their exchange of glances; but, overlooking this and undeterred, he adjusted the pegs of the diapason strings on the forward curving neck. He could have found no better occasion for a dramatic finale, and he intended to make the most of it.

15

"Perhaps you know this sonnet of the divine Petrarch, Madonna Milla: '*In qual parte del cielo, in quale idea . . .*' "

Then with one foot on a stool, the instrument cradled in his arm, his crimson cap at an angle, he sang. He had a strong, deep, compelling voice. She could not resist it and looked up, and he held her eyes, while the ardor in his own interpreted the song.

> *In what celestial sphere, by whom inspired,*
> *Did Nature find the cast from which she drew*
> *This lovely face wherein she hath aspired*
> *To manifest below what Heaven can do? . . .*

The momentary chill was forgotten. She listened with parted lips.

> *Of Godly beauty he is unaware*
> *Who hath not gazed into my lady's eyes,*
> *Nor gathered her sweet glances here on earth;*
> *He knoweth not Love's Hell nor Paradise*
> *Who never heard her sighs as light as air,*
> *The gentle music of her speech and mirth.*

He repeated softly the last line, "*e come dolce parla e dolce ride,*" letting the mental echoes die away, and still gazing at her.

She drew a sharp breath when he had finished, but said merely: "A rich tone, Messer Lorenzo. I've never heard finer. Even you must admit that it's a perfect instrument."

"The voice is the better part of it," returned the Master, who had uttered an emphatic "*Bravo!*" as Andrea ended.

Orsini did not wait for compliments. Reserve is best countered by reserve. Having struck the proper note, he knew that he must avoid anticlimax. He handed the theorbo back to Camilla with a bow.

"And so — many thanks, Your Highness. Master, may I beg you to return the portrait here to my lodgings at the Star on the Riva degli Schiavoni?"

The maneuver succeeded. "But, sir," Camilla put in, "what manners! You do not even offer to wait on us. We are stopping at the Ca' Contarini."

By a flash of insight, Andrea resisted the temptation. Finesse meant restraint. At a later meeting, it would strengthen his position.

"Alas, Madama, I am not my own master. I leave tomorrow for Ferrara, and until then — " He left the excuse hanging.

"Ah?" she said, piqued. "I regret. We are ourselves returning through Ferrara after some days. It would have been pleasant to make the journey together."

Again he felt tempted — perhaps he was overplaying his game — but a journey up the Po in a hot, horse-drawn barge did not lend itself to gallantry. There were fairer settings in Ferrara.

"Pleasant, indeed!" he sighed. "Your Excellence understates Paradise." He let the warmth of his voice and manner soften the evasion. "But I am restored to life, Signora, by the thought that soon again I may have the honor, as now, of proclaiming myself Your Highness's slave. . . . Farewell, Madonna Milla."

His cap described a low arc before her. Though bowing deeply, he was still aware, from her heightened color, that he had made the impression he intended.

"Farewell, Your Magnificence."

When his footsteps had died away on the stairs, she turned to Lorenzo.

"How long have you known this gentleman?"

"Only today."

"You are a man of experience, Master. What do you make of him?"

The other fingered his beard. "What do you make of him yourself, my lady? That's more important."

"Why?"

"Your Excellence will be seeing him again."

"Well, I should say attractive, *un cortigiano eminente*."

"Aye, an eminent courtier. I have rarely met anyone more finished. But think: a soldier who knows art, a Neapolitan who speaks like a Florentine, an Orsini unrelated to the Orsini, a servant of the Borgia in the service of the Borgia's enemies. A contradiction. He has too many faces."

"I find him interesting."

Lorenzo was silent a moment. "I hope you may not find him dangerous, Madonna."

She laughed. "Not to me at least. He would not even call on me."

"Your Excellence, it is not usually the obvious that is dangerous."

CHAPTER III

STILL somewhat in a haze of lyrical feeling, Andrea Orsini found himself in the Merceria, the great shopping street of Venice. It deserved his notice that afternoon of early autumn, when the gold and languor of summer still rested upon the city, and the lengthening rays of the sun both darkened the shadows of the street and at the same time kindled its riches to a blaze. The autumn fleet from the Levant had just unloaded its cargoes, which, subdivided among the merchant adventurers of the shopping district, filled the air with an Eastern pungency or flashed in textiles and gems.

Always keenly perceptive, Orsini feasted his senses on color and smell; now pausing to admire the purples, saffrons, azures, greens, and golds of the fabrics of Coromandel, Bengal, or Cashmere, the brocades of Cambay, the Damascus steel of Nirmul, the ivories of Zanzibar; now inhaling the odor of spices from the Moluccas, spikenard from Nepal, musk from Tibet, balsam and frankincense from Zeila, Berbera, and Shehr; now absorbed by antique marbles from Rhodes and the Greek Islands, or by jewels from Ceylon or Golconda. But, invisible, behind everything else, lending an added aura of splendor and pride, he could feel the vibration of Venice herself, the triumphant city with its tentacles of trade that these things represented, reaching to the uttermost seas.

The throng in the street — patricians in their rich gowns, flaming gallants, substantial merchants, bearded soldiers and seamen, courtesans with bronze-dyed hair — differed from a similar throng in Rome or Florence. These people reflected the arrogance of the city, as its canals reflected the splendor of its domes and palaces. The thousand-year-old crescendo of its history exalted them, as it exalted even strangers like Orsini with a sense of human achievement and power. No need to analyze the inspiration; but he knew that it was good to be in Venice and to be young and to have met an enchanting lady and to be on the threshold of a golden career.

In front of a jewel shop, he remembered Camilla's ring and stopped to deliberate. Sentimentally, he would have liked to enlarge it for his own finger. It symbolized their meeting and his expectations — really a betrothal ring if the lady had known. Aside, too, from its connection with her, the diamond would add to his prestige at the Ferrarese court.

But the brutal fact was that he could not afford a ring worth a hundred and fifty ducats. He needed the money more than sentiment and prestige. So, with a sigh, he entered the shop and by masterly bargaining secured ten ducats more than he expected. Then, drifting with the crowd, he followed the Merceria to the Piazza San Marco.

By this time, only the basilica dome and the summit of the campanile remained in sunlight; beneath them, the soft amethyst of evening was setting in, though the four unbridled horses of Saint Mark still reflected a golden gleam. One by one, the indolent pigeons of the Piazza withdrew to their nesting places. Venice turned from business to pleasure, its great square gradually filling with people in multicolored dress appropriate to the night's diversions.

Seating himself near the door of a *trattoria* under the arcade on the northern side, Andrea ordered bread, cheese, and wine, stretched his legs, and viewed the unceasing pageant with absent-minded contentment. The kaleidoscope of costumes against the background of matchless architecture, the drifting of footsteps through the arcade and murmur of voices diffused by space, lulled him into pleasant reflections.

Talk of a prize, a plum, or, in choicer language, a pearl of great price! For the sake of Città del Monte and its revenues, he would have put up with a crone or a humpback; but, aside from all else, Camilla was dowry enough in herself. Such good fortune was incredible. Her lightness and boyish figure completely satisfied his aesthetic taste. He loved the swift, the elusive, the ethereal. Donatello for him, or Botticelli!

The varied riches of the Merceria, still gleaming in his imagination, imparted something of their opulence to his dreams. But the dreams, though daring, were entirely practical. He was the kind of man, and they were the kind of dreams, that make history. The passers-by, seeing a handsome young patrician trifling away a half hour over his wine, would have been startled if they could have read beneath the apparent idleness of his gaze resting upon the Piazza. Actually it rested upon Italy and his own role on that confused stage. He thought in large terms, keenly, intuitively balancing one against the other: the political drift of the age, the rivalry of states and personalities, the soaring career open to himself when he had once acquired Città del Monte as a springboard.

A pretty girl, who thought that she had attracted his notice, swung her hips and drooped her eyes at him; then tossed her head and trudged on. He did not see her.

Take the world tide for instance. It was plainly set toward unification and strong central governments. England, France, and Spain, under the leadership of able princes, had rid themselves of the clutter of small independencies and become nations. Only Italy, more civilized and, in every other respect, more modern than any, clung to its patch quilt of jealous little states, undercutting each other. So, France was encroaching from the north, while Spain reached up from the south; and the candles of Italy, which, united, would have made a proud, free torch, were going out one by one or timidly burning at the pleasure of these foreign powers.

It made a man sick! Milan and Genoa already lopped off. Florence clinging to the French skirts yet still plaguing Pisa. Venice with a knife out for everybody. Ferrara tightrope-walking. Rome intriguing. Naples waiting to be raped and quarreled over by the French and Spaniards. The countless little signories scampering about to keep from being trampled on. The foreign mercenaries, hired to defend people who wouldn't defend themselves, swaggering everywhere. . . .

Orsini drew out a jeweled toothpick from the small case at his belt and used it thoughtfully.

There wasn't much time; Italy would have to hurry. But the way was clear. Unification. Perhaps the process had already begun. The subject gave plenty of scope for dreams.

Suppose the right sort of man, himself, for instance, backed the right prince, the right state; suppose that by courage, adroitness, and luck, he gained control of one or the other (it had been done by the Sforzas in Milan); suppose that little by little, cajoling, expanding, annexing by force or diplomacy, as had happened in France, he reached the summit and held a block of power so great that it exacted the respect of foreign states, then a new nation would have been born, the nation of Italy.

What a career! From the rung of the ladder which Andrea had reached, it seemed a long climb, but possible and irresistibly fascinating.

As for the right prince to back, who wouldn't bet on the genius, courage, and luck of Cesare Borgia? Financed by his father, the Pope, supported by the leading captains of venture in Italy, favored by the French king, he was successfully snapping up the little lordships of Romagna and the Marches and he would doubtless bring them all under his government. Give him time, and he would control Tuscany. So there was the nucleus of your nation on a platter.

Andrea returned the toothpick to its case, sipped his wine, gazed absently at the shifting throng of the Piazza.

Yes, Cesare Borgia was the prince for anybody's money, and Andrea stood high in his favor. But shrewdness and distrust of the obvious were as equally characteristic of Orsini as promptness and daring. He sensed uneasily a taint of impermanence about the glamorous Duke. Today Borgia enjoyed the wealth of the Church, which his unprincipled father diverted to him. But the Pope was old. Tomorrow another, an enemy, like the fierce Cardinal Juliano, might be elected. What then? Everybody knew what had happened in the case of Cesare's uncle, Don Pedro Luis, who had embarked on a like course under the protection of the first Borgia Pope: at first success, and then ruin. Today, France smiled; but smiles veered with the political weather. Today, it was easy for Cesare to gather the small states of Central Italy into his basket; but, mutually hostile and in part devoted to their old lords, would they stay gathered? Meanwhile Borgia was making scores of enemies for tomorrow. It was the Duke's ruthlessness that Andrea most disliked. If it led to the unifying of Italy, that end probably justified any means. But distrust and hatred did not make good political cement. . . .

Orsini sprang to his feet and bowed low to a benevolent-looking old gentleman with a white beard, who paused to greet him. It was Messer Aldobrandino di Guidone, the Ambassador of Ferrara to Venice. He wore a broad gold chain on his breast and an expensive fur collar on his mantle. His secretary and several gentlemen attended him. Andrea had dined at his palace two days before.

"So you're leaving tomorrow morning for Ferrara, Captain Orsini? A pleasant journey to you, and my humblest salutations to the Duke's Excellence. It grieves me that I am otherwise engaged this evening, or I should have insisted on your company. Pray forgive me."

Andrea expressed eternal gratitude for the consideration he had already received from the Ambassador. He wondered if he might serve him in any way.

Aldobrandino smiled. "Perhaps I may take advantage of Your Magnificence's good nature to the extent of asking you to carry a letter to the Duke." The Ambassador was afflicted by a slight wheeze in his speech and paused now to cough. "It may be. If the letter is finished in time, I shall see to it that it is delivered to you here or in Chioggia."

"Your Lordship's servant."

"*Your* servant, Messer Andrea, believe me, your most affectionate well-wisher. May your career in Ferrara be long and prosperous! God bless you!"

With parting flourishes on both sides, the Ambassador wheezed on, and Andrea reseated himself at the table. The interruption turned his thoughts to Ferrara, though it did not break the thread of them.

He had heard good things of the twenty-four-year-old Alfonso d'Este, heir apparent of the duchy. Men spoke of him as shrewd, practical, and an expert in the manufacture of cannon. As an alternative, he might serve the purposes of Andrea's ambition for Italy and for himself if Borgia failed. Ferrara was a long-established state in a key position. The House of Este ranked almost as royal and had great connections and prestige.

But one point was certain. Orsini must accomplish his present mission to Ferrara. He must serve Duke Cesare until he had secured Camilla and Città del Monte as the next big step up the ladder. Afterwards, he could look around. Thoroughly modern, he set no store by loyalty that led nowhere. As to Camilla's present husband, the poor old lord cast barely a shadow. Andrea could even piously assume that he would die a natural death.

He dropped back from the future a moment to observe a man who must have seated himself at the near-by table during his talk with the Ambassador. Unusual faces held an intense fascination for him. Eying this one over his wine cup, he concluded that he had never seen anybody so ugly: a disaster of a man, the spitting image of Judas Iscariot, if an artist, painting a "Last Supper," were in search of a model. That beak of a nose, the half-bald head, shifty eyes and cunning lips, the secretive smile, the vicious lines of the face — exceptional! Objectively considering him as a grotesque, Orsini felt extreme interest. But he was struck by something else: a hint of breeding — the way he sat and handled his cup — which, together with the scar on his forehead, the width of his shoulders and carelessness of his stare, suggested not only the soldier but the nobleman. He might be one of the many mercenary captains in the pay of Venice, who had returned from the wars with the autumn fleet. At a third or fourth glance, it gave Orsini an almost uncanny sensation to discover that, in spite of his baldness, the man was not much older than himself. Youth peered cynically through the mask of age.

"*Fuoco!*" Andrea thought. "There's a tragedy! I wonder what hell's college *he* attended." Then, refilling his goblet, he forgot the man.

His immediate task at Ferrara absorbed him. It would take a good deal of management. Andrea had no illusions about his position at that court. Venetian influence at the Pope's request, coupled with Cesare Borgia's insistence, had procured him the reluctant appointment to the Duke of Ferrara's guard, an appointment that fooled nobody. He would be received with politeness and held at arm's length. His mission was to intrigue for Lucrezia Borgia's marriage with

Don Alfonso against the hatred and pride of the House of Este, who scorned an alliance with the Borgian upstarts as beneath its honor and age-old name. He must ingratiate himself with the proposed bridegroom and incline him to a woman, the Pope's bastard, already stained by two tragic marriages and the slander of all Italy, when Alfonso had counted on a bride from the friendly and royal House of France.

To promote such a marriage was extremely difficult, all the more as it so obviously revealed Borgia's future ambitions. If Andrea was successful, he would fully deserve the high reward that had been promised.

His glance turned again toward the man at the near-by table, but he was surprised to find him gone as suddenly as he had appeared.

"Who was that one?" he asked a serving boy, jerking his head toward where the other had sat. "I suppose you don't know."

"But yes. It was Messer Mario Belli. He teaches swordplay."

"Belli!" Andrea laughed. "*Diàscolo!* He's well-named. I never saw anyone prettier."

The boy did not smile. "A regular customer, sir."

Amethyst had yielded to azure in the square, the deep azure of Venetian night, which has its own starry radiance. Torches began flaring on the Piazza. An echo of music sounded from the lagoon.

Orsini got up at last and strolled to the Columns of St. Mark, where the gondola lanterns bobbed up and down like tethered fireflies. He deliberated on the evening. Of course he would be welcome at the Papal Legate's, but he had called there that morning and wound up his official business. An excellent establishment in the Giudecca, kept by a certain Mona Giulia, had been recommended to him if he required a *buona compagna;* but he reflected that he must leave at dawn for Chioggia, the starting point for Ferrara, and he was in no mood for a white night.

Selecting a gondola and settling down in the cushions, he instructed the boatman: "Anywhere, friend. The Canal Grande — an affair of an hour — then back to the Riva degli Schiavoni."

They glided away through the spangled water, and he filled his lungs with the haunting sea air. Other gondolas slipped past with lovers or merrymakers. A delicious languor filled the night, lapping of water, wandering of music. He felt a longing, sweeter than possession, for the indescribable, the unattainable. He would return here someday with *her;* he would occupy one of these palaces; they would live in terms of color — sapphire and silver — in terms of a casement open on the sea-scented night.

23

In front of the Contarini Palace, he had the boatman hold his oar a moment. The windows blazed with light, and two torches, set in brackets flanking the doors, revealed the livery of retainers and gondoliers awaiting their masters. Evidently the Contarini were holding a banquet in honor of their guest, Camilla Baglione. Regretting now his policy of restraint and burning with desire for her, he at last waved the boatman on.

What with the beauty of the night, Andrea put off his return from hour to hour. It had grown late when finally the gondola, following the Riva degli Schiavoni, glided into the Rio della Pietà, upon which the entrance of the tavern, the Star, opened. Having paid his fare, Orsini stood a moment, drawing a last breath of the sea breeze and watching the lantern of the gondola until it disappeared beyond the next curve of the canal. Half drowsily he realized that it was a night he would always remember, the more perhaps because he had spent it alone. Then, turning back into the dank passage between house walls that led to the front of the inn, he found that the lamp marking the tavern door had been allowed to go out.

He groped his way through the pitch darkness, cursing the carelessness of the inn servants; but he could see vaguely the space between the mouth of the alley and the inn, which stood in a tiny *campiello* surrounded by houses. The scuttle of a rat startled him as if it had been a footstep, and he was glad to reach the end of the passage. He determined to have a word with the landlord about that lamp.

A metal click sounded, and at the same moment he was dazzled by the light of a dark lantern turned full against his eyes.

"*Gran Dio!*" he exclaimed. "What's up?"

"*This,*" answered a voice, coupled with the ripping, stinging blow of a knife.

CHAPTER IV

IF ANDREA ORSINI had not sold Madonna Camilla's ring that afternoon, he would probably not have survived this attack. It shows the logic of luck that, being conscious of the gold in his purse as he groped through the darkness, he had been therefore subconsciously on guard. Quick as was the flash of the dark lantern and the accompanying blow, his own reaction was still quicker, at least to the extent of a couple of inches, so that the knife, aimed professionally low and jerked upward, ripped his doublet and his skin without penetrating deeper. And in the next instant, gripping the wrist of his assailant, he drove his fist into the man's face.

The lantern clattered down, renewing the complete darkness, which, however, was not quite so black as in the passageway. At any rate, Andrea got in several vaguely directed blows, and, snatching out his own poniard, aimed it at his adversary's chest.

He might just as well have struck at a stone wall. The blade snapped against the other's steel undershirt; and, simultaneously, with a revolving movement of the body, the man freed his wrist from Andrea's grasp.

But by now, surprise had given way in Orsini to white rage. He had not spent years in the motley camps of adventure up and down Italy without learning the tricks of such encounters as this. Bare survival meant knowing them, and the command of men required even greater expertness. He met the renewed onslaught with a kick at the robber's groin that threw him back a step; then, crouching low, he grappled him about the knees, put his shoulder into it, and, lifting him clear of the ground, crashed him to the pavement on his back. And in the same breath, he dropped, pinning the fellow beneath him, his hand gripping the dagger arm.

Probably it was no ruse that the other lay as if stunned, though Andrea took no chances. Feeling along the outflung arm, he secured the knife. But when he lifted the weapon for a final blow, a congested voice gasped:

"Don't be a fool."

"Ha, whoreson!" Andrea breathed. "Fool to kill you? *Corpo di Cristo*, you have one wink left for an Ave Maria."

"I say, don't be a fool. Dead men can't talk."

"That's one of their merits."

"Not in this case. If you kill me, you'll never know why I attacked you."

"Bah! With a rascal like you, *ladrone*, the reason isn't far to seek!"

"I'm not a thief." The voice gathered strength. "I resent the insult."

"Oh, you do! Well, talk then. What have you to say?"

"Nothing, with you on top of me. Let me up. This is no place for conversation."

Andrea seethed again. "Brother, if you take me for a donkey, it's your last mistake. Speak up, and I'll decide what to do with you. If not, *sia con Dio!*"

"Wait, Magnifico!" Then, after a moment, the voice added, "Ever hear of His Excellence, the Duke Ercole d'Este?"

If Andrea repressed a start, he was unable to cover up the pause that followed, while his mind adjusted itself to this unexpected possibility. And that it was very possible, he admitted at once. Really these illustrious princes of Ferrara lost no time! Since they were expecting him, why wait, after all, until the unwelcome agent of the Borgias reached their city? To assassinate him after his arrival would mean suspicions and explanations. It was easier to deal with him beforehand. Orsini felt ashamed that he had not foreseen this enlightened move. Such dullness disgraced his training.

"Yes, I've heard of His Lordship," he said carelessly.

"Well then, is it worth your while to hear more?"

Andrea reflected aloud. "If I let you up, and you take to your heels, what's that to me? You deserve to die, but so do most people — and I owe you for a useful hint. If, on the contrary, you come up to my room and tell me something valuable, it might be as much worth your while as if you had killed me."

"It's strange that I had the same idea," came the dry voice out of the darkness. "Besides, I give you my word of honor that I won't escape."

"Your word of honor clinches it," scoffed Orsini. "That's all that's needed."

He got up, alert and with the knife still in hand. "Perhaps you'll be good enough to recover the lantern," he suggested. "We need light in this pit. I suppose it was you who put out the door lamp, eh?"

The dark bulk of the man heaved itself up. There was a sound of brushing.

"Perhaps I did."

He fumbled with his foot, located the lantern, and, striking fire from a tinderbox, lighted the wick.

"Let's have a look at you," said Andrea.

Without a word the man raised the lantern level with his own face. Then, out of the darkness leaped the unforgettable grotesque Orsini had admired at the *trattoria*, the evil countenance of Mario Belli. If he had looked like Judas Iscariot in daylight, he now appeared so singularly devilish in the chiaroscuro of the lantern that instinctively Andrea crossed himself.

26

"Yes, you've seen me before," said the other, lowering the lantern. "I suppose you want me to go ahead with the light."

"Courtesy to guests," Andrea murmured, with a wave of the knife. "Precede me by all means."

So, through the door of the inn, past a drowsy porter who nodded at the sound of Orsini's voice, then up the stairs and along a gallery, they continued to Andrea's quarters.

Across the table, lighted by a couple of candles, the two men faced each other in a game of wits and of mutual appraisal. Andrea wondered whether anyone could be quite so wicked as Belli looked, and he came to the sudden conviction that it was impossible. Experience taught him that one can tell very little about people from their faces. He had known too many handsome devils to jump at conclusions. Still, he had to admit that, if Mario Belli were only one quarter as bad as his appearance, he could, as the saying went, have made sauce for Satan. Meanwhile, what Belli was wondering lay deep beneath his crafty eyes and constant, razor-thin smile.

"Your Magnificence has blood on your hands," he observed, as Andrea, having felt gingerly between belt and midriff, decided that the wound was no more than a scratch. "I hope I didn't go too far."

"No, not at all, I thank you, Messer Mario."

The other's eyebrows lifted at the mention of his name, but he said merely, "Congratulations! I don't often fail."

Andrea bowed. "I'm quick to believe it. You give every token of an excellent craftsman in your art. Have you practised it long?"

"A good while — at intervals." Belli paused a moment. "But I'm not often called on to deal with a man of prowess like Your Lordship. Success in art depends so much on the materials one has to work with. By God, the Bull of the Borgias must have lent you his thews."

"You have the advantage of me," Andrea smiled. "You know whom I have been serving and in whose service I now am. Tell me something about yourself."

The other shook his head. "Too long a story, Magnifico. Why rake over lost games? Hold me excused."

Andrea, surveying his would-be assassin more carefully, noticed to his surprise that Belli's hands were as beautiful as his face was ugly. They were well-shaped, sensitive. He noticed too that, although Belli spoke perfect Italian, it was with a French intonation, an accent so slight as to be perhaps misleading. He might come from Turin.

27

Orsini experimented. "Well, I know your name's Belli, and I perceive that you're from beyond the Alps."

"Indeed?"

"And that you're of gentle birth."

Belli's eyes leveled in sudden anger. "What the devil has my birth to do with you? Why are we wasting time?"

"I like to know something about the people I deal with. If you have information to give, the value of it depends a little on who you are."

"I see. Well, then, Your Lordship guessed near enough. I'm from Savoy. My family have a coat of arms. Will that do?"

Orsini nodded. "As you please. . . . Now about this business. Who employed you? Duke Ercole himself?"

"*Piano un poco!*" The other jerked his head back in a silent laugh. "Before I hand over my wares, how much do I get for them?"

Andrea showed his most winning smile. "How much is your life worth?"

Nothing could have sounded more casual, but Belli's grin froze.

"My life? Why?"

"Because you'll live, if you speak up. What's that worth to you?"

Complete silence fell. Belli's stare concentrated on Andrea's smile, and what it read was illuminating.

"Understand me," Orsini added. "You're unarmed, and I'm not squeamish. You're in no state to haggle. Who employed you in this business?"

It was clear that Andrea had made an impression, though the other's face expressed admiration rather than fear.

"I can see that the illustrious Valentino picks men after his own image. So, then, I have no choice, though Your Worship led me to expect handsomer terms. . . . I was employed by Messer Aldobrandino di Guidone, Ambassador of Ferrara to this Signory of Venice."

The old, whited sepulchre! Andrea recalled their recent parting: the Ambassador's benevolent smile and wheezing benedictions. With this hired assassin in the background! But Belli's statement sounded authentic. The princes of Ferrara were removed from any direct contact with the crime.

"And Messer Aldobrandino acted on the Duke's orders?"

"To tell you the truth, that is my personal theory. It's plain that he did not act on his own hand. But whether his orders come from the Serenity of Duke Ercole himself or from the very humane Don Alfonso or from the Most Reverend Cardinal Ippolito d'Este makes no difference as far as I can see. The Estes are one in all that concerns their House."

28

Andrea agreed. "Not much difference. When did the Ambassador engage you?"

"Day before yesterday at noon."

"And I had dinner with him that evening. He was all smiles and caresses. Ah, Messer Mario, the wickedness of the world makes me weep. The corruption of this age is unbelievable."

"Very bad," Belli assented, shaking his head.

"And yet," Andrea continued, "the noble Aldobrandino showed good management. I have known others who would have poisoned me at dinner and would thus have implicated their prince. He chose the wiser course, even if it failed. An able man."

"So able," nodded the other, "that having disappointed him, I shall be leaving Venice at dawn." He coughed, and probed Andrea with one of his needlelike glances. "It takes money to travel fast. A debonair gentleman, like Your Magnificence, should be happy to stake me fifty ducats to the border for saving his life."

Andrea laughed. "That's what you call next-to-murder, eh?"

"Your Nobility knows what I mean. Thanks to me — or rather this timely warning — you may survive Ferrara. Notice, I'm frank as gospel. I say *may:* the chances are slim. You're distinctly not wanted in Ferrara."

Leaning back, Orsini slipped two fingers into his belt purse and clinked the gold coins in it, a siren music to fix the other's attention. Meanwhile, he thought hard. He had anticipated trouble in Ferrara, but he had not supposed that the Estes' antagonism to his mission had reached so hot a pitch. At this rate, in one way or another, he would be silenced before he could even gain a hearing.

"How much do you know?" he asked Belli.

"A good deal. It's my specialty to know things."

"Ah?"

"Look you, sir." Belli hitched his chair closer to the table and stuck his evil face forward. "Don't blunder by taking me for nothing but a ruffian. A sharp guesser like you should know better. Yes, I've come down in the world perhaps, but I've not yet reached the point of cutting throats without knowing whose or why. I'm not a market-place hireling. If I cared to swagger, I might say that by profession I'm a confidant of dangerous secrets, and I've had my finger in a good many pies. Big pies, the sort that are baked in private by His Excellency this and His Signory that. Well then, it isn't strange if I know a number of things that concern you."

"Such as?" Andrea prodded the coins in his purse.

"How about the fifty ducats I suggested, Magnifico? You can spare that much from the sale of Madonna's ring."

Orsini kept his face blank at this disclosure of Belli's knowledge. "How about twenty-five to begin with? The next twenty-five depend on you."

Belli shrugged acceptance; and, coin by coin, Andrea flicked the required sum across the table.

"So then?"

"Well, sir, I don't envy you the job in Ferrara. Swing a dead rat beneath the noses of these lords of Este, and you'd please 'em better than to press a marriage between Don Alfonso and Lucrezia Borgia." Belli's exact information about Andrea's mission was immediately impressive.

"Strong words!" frowned Orsini.

"But true ones. Consider. The rat would afflict their stomachs: this thing blisters their pride. Lord knows I'm not dainty nor a sovereign prince, but even I can sympathize with them on that score. The lady's had too public a career; the Estes know too much about her. *Vieux jeu*, as the French say."

"Lies, for the most part, " Andrea put in.

"Granted." Belli tipped his shapely fingers together. "But Your Dignity will agree that there's some warrant for them. *Pasques dieu!* Look at her. Brought up in the company of her father's mistress, La Bella Julia. Betrothed at eleven to a Spanish lord. Betrothed next year to another Spaniard. Then unbetrothed. Tongues busy. Then married next year to Giovanni Sforza of Pesaro, a cut higher in the scale. Lives with him till the Pope spies a better move, and the marriage is off. More stench. Then married to the young prince from Naples, whom *Somebody* recently murdered. And now a widow at twenty, ready to be played in the Pope's and her brother's next game. All of which is truth — not lies — and, from the standpoint of her next bridegroom, the truth's sorry enough without the rumors and hints that go with it."

Yes, Andrea reflected, the man was certainly more than a commonplace bravo. His knowledge was accurate and complete, not the sort to be picked up in taverns. At every point, he showed courtly experience.

"It makes a cheap impression in Ferrara," Belli went on — "like the Borgia family itself. Spanish parvenus whom nobody ever heard of until fifty years ago. Church climbers. Who are they to mate with the House of Este under any circumstances? . . . So, there's part of Your Magnificence's problem. I wish you well of it."

Since Belli showed himself so fully informed of the attitude at Ferrara, it would be useful to pump him further. Andrea nodded. "Thanks. You speak of *part*. What next?"

"Fear. Quiet the Este pride, and you've still their fear to deal with. Do you think these maneuvers of Cesare Borgia in the Romagna fool anybody? *Gran Dio*, it's plain he plans the conquest of Central Italy. And this marriage is a move in that direction. It's a marriage at the sword's point: Borgia's troops at Imola are very close. Take yourself, for instance. Your Lordship knows as well as I that you would never have had a captaincy in Ferrara except for pressure that couldn't be denied. And that's the reason for putting you out of the way. It's easier than to quarrel about you. . . . Yes, fear. Princes don't like marriages *and* captains that are crammed down their throats."

Orsini pumped again. "So these illustrious lords look to France for protection. Know anything about that?"

"Something. I know that Duke Ercole d'Este has fixed his hopes on a French bride for Don Alfonso, Madame d'Angoulême or Mademoiselle de Foix. And I know that a French delegation from Lombardy is expected in Ferrara — Louis d'Ars with a squadron of his company. Informal, of course; but the marriage will be discussed. Another complication for Your Lordship to handle if you live that long."

Here was real news. Andrea had not heard of this French mission, and he began to feel that his twenty-five ducats were well placed. D'Ars, with his gentlemen-at-arms, welcomed and courted in Ferrara, would make it harder than ever for Orsini to promote the Borgian interest, even if, as Belli put it, he lived long enough to begin.

"I remember d'Ars," he remarked, "in the invasion of Naples six years ago. He's a soldier, not a man of affairs. Do you know him?"

Belli turned his head and spat suddenly. His lips wrinkled against his teeth. Then, controlling the grimace, he said: "Yes, he commands de Ligny's company. There aren't many Frenchmen of that rank I don't know."

Wondering at the hatred in the other's face, Andrea asked, "Can he be bought?"

For an instant, Belli seemed to be weighing the point. Every cunning line in his face showed. But at last, with evident regret, he shook his head. "No, he's an honorable ass. One of the old-fashioned breed. Christ!" He stared vacantly a moment at something in his own mind, shrugged. "But I take Your Lordship's meaning. No, not d'Ars; but the King of France could be bought."

They exchanged a glance of mutual understanding. It was unnecessary to elaborate. Louis XII wanted Naples: and could the Borgias or the Estes help him most in that enterprise? Make him a sufficient offer of troops, and the French bride for Alfonso might not be forthcoming. Andrea knew that the Borgian agents at the court of France were working on this move, and he could do as much with d'Ars in Ferrara. Another strand in the delicate spider web of crisscrossing politics.

But Orsini's thought turned to Belli. He found himself increasingly impressed by the man's knowledge of affairs; a valuable man. An odd notion, absurd at first and then not so absurd, rose in Andrea's mind.

"I can see you're no fool, Messer Mario. In my place, how would you open the game at Ferrara?"

Belli smiled, tipped his fingers together. "I should be a fool, indeed, to instruct Your Dignity. And I'm thankful not to be in your place. However, as I see it, Duke Ercole d'Este himself is your main concern. He wants no truck with the Borgias. As to Cardinal Ippolito, they tell me he's a vain donkey, full of himself and of his House; but, being in the Church, I should think he might be open to inducements from the Pope. He's dangerous, cruel — and no doubt greedy. As to Don Alfonso, I shouldn't be surprised if he listened to you. They say he has a mind of his own. Has a hobby for making cannon and works like a blacksmith; lets the court fops chatter. He's the sort of man who ought to be taken by a pretty woman like Madonna Lucrezia. But I speak from hearsay. I've had no personal dealings with these lords."

"You've not been to Ferrara?"

"No. I've seen the Estes at a distance only. However, their kinsman, the Marquis of Mantua, was my patron."

"Indeed?" Orsini murmured. There was no better listening post in North Italy than the court of Mantua. "And you say you're familiar with the French captains?"

Again something flickered behind Belli's ugly mask. "It was this that endeared me to the illustrious Marquis."

Andrea leaned back, revolving the notion that now took definite shape in his mind. Here was a man out of employment and out of funds, a desperate man, a skillful, informed, experienced agent, handy with sword and wit, versed in the deadly underworld of political action — a tool in a million! If he could count on him, even to a limited extent, Orsini could use such a man not only in Ferrara but in the bigger schemes beyond. Belli's knowledge of the French might be particularly useful.

32

Without comment, Andrea handed another twenty-five ducats across the table and noted the other's start of surprise.

"I rejoice," said Belli, "that Your Magnificence is pleased. If I could serve you further —"

"Perhaps you could, Messer Mario. Let us consider. We're both leaving Venice tomorrow, and, I take it, your plans are vague. Why not come with me? It's only fair that having caused you the loss of one employment, I should offer you another. You can have my patronage for what it's worth (perhaps it will be worth more in time), also Duke Valentino's favor. What do you say?"

For once, Belli forgot his smile. After a pause, he muttered, "What's the game?"

"No game. Perhaps it amuses me to enter Ferrara with the man who had been hired to kill me. Perhaps, when it gets around, these exalted lords of Este will put water in their wine. Then, too, I'm superstitious. Were we brought so intimately together merely to part? I believe the stars forbid it. I feel strangely drawn to you."

"*O cacasangue!*" jeered Belli. "I kiss your hand!"

"Don't be cynical," Orsini retorted. "I've a theory about you, Messere, that I'd like to test. I think you're more honest than you look — that is, up to a point."

"What point?"

"If you gave me your word, I think you'd keep it."

"Really?"

"Yes. . . . Do you accept my offer?"

Silence followed. Belli's eyes glinted and the tip of his nose twitched. At last he queried, "What will happen to me in Ferrara, when this gets around, as Your Lordship says?"

"No more than may happen to me. We'll live or die together, and I intend to live."

"Is it permitted to ask how?"

"Certainly. We'll leave Venice, not at dawn but at noon tomorrow. That will give me time to call on Aldobrandino di Guidone."

"Call on — " Belli sat staring. "*Call on whom?*"

"The Ambassador, your ex-patron. Yes, Messere, you see I hope to convert him from thoughts of murder, and through him, the Estes. I hope to persuade him that your success tonight would have been a blunder on his part, and that your failure was a blessing in disguise. He looks like a man of intelligence. If he agrees with me, why should there be any enmity against you? I have no doubt that he'll write to

33

Ferrara. In that case, we'll both live easier, at least for a while, though there's some risk. . . . Well, does that answer your question?"

Belli's sinister face glowed. He rapped the table. "By God, sir, you're a bold man. Calling on Aldobrandino's the last thing I should have thought of. But you're right. A shrewd stroke! My lord, I perceive you're a man with a future. It will be an honor to serve you."

"You accept then?"

"With humble thanks — but on one condition. While d'Ars and these particular Frenchmen are in Ferrara, I must keep to our quarters. They and I know each other, and they bear me a grudge."

"It's as bad as that?"

"Worse."

A shiver twitched Belli's shoulders, and the hunger of hatred looked out of his eyes. Andrea took note of it: hatred could be used as well as love.

"I understand," he nodded. "So, from now on you're with me?"

"Heart and soul. But in what capacity: Your Lordship's valet, secretary, ensign?"

"My ally," bowed Orsini.

Belli flung out his arm in exaggerated reverence. "You overwhelm me. Your ally in opening the world's oyster — if I judge Your Magnificence correctly." Leaning forward, he extended his beautiful hand across the table and leered like a devil. "I'll bear you stout service, while the bond lasts, and warn you when I'm quitting. Is that enough?"

Andrea's manner revealed none of his skepticism. He shook hands cordially. "It's quite enough. We'll meet then in Chioggia at noon tomorrow and take a barge from there. Meanwhile, you'll wish to pack. *A rivederci*, my friend."

"I have nothing to pack." Belli's mouth gave a wry twist. "I'll not return to my lodgings. One of Aldobrandino's people will be waiting there for a report, and he had better go on waiting. Could I sleep here?"

"As you please."

Orsini indicated a pallet. Then casually, as if it meant nothing, he handed back the other's knife. And still casually, exposing a perfect target to attack, he stripped off his doublet and shirt.

"I'll have a look at that scratch. . . . You see, nothing to speak of."

If he was on the alert, he gave no hint of it. A smear of dried blood showed against the white of the skin. Pouring out some water from the ewer on the night table, he washed the wound, the muscles of arms and torso standing out in the flicker of the candles.

34

Belli grinned in appreciation of the bravado and gripped the hilt of his dagger.

"*Lead us not into temptation,*" he commented. "By God, I still don't understand this offer of yours."

Andrea squeezed out the washrag. "You're too modest, then. A man of your abilities! But there's something more. Your face is your fortune, if you only knew it. As a lover of art, I can't forgo keeping it near me. It deserves to be immortalized."

CHAPTER V

THE hot Venetian morning, cloudless over the lagoons, held two shocks in store for Messer Aldobrandino di Guidone, Ambassador from Ferrara. The first occurred almost with the drawing of his bed curtains and before he had finished the cup of spiced milk which served as an eye opener. Having called for Emilio, one of his confidential servants, he adjusted his nightcap, straightened himself against the pillows of the bed, and, eying the man above the rim of his cup, he asked:

"Well?"

"I spent the night at Mario Belli's lodgings."

"Yes. Well?"

"He did not return."

"He did not return?" faltered the Ambassador.

"No, sir. Then, although it was not included in Your Grace's command, but knowing your concern" (Emilio coughed) "for the health of the Magnifico Orsini, I took the liberty of calling at his inn to make inquiries."

"Quite properly, my good Emilio. . . . Yes?"

The servant lifted his shoulders. "Sir, it appears that Captain Orsini and Messer Mario passed the night together. I learned from the inn boy that His Magnificence seems well and blithe this morning. Messer Mario departed early, but in what direction no one knew."

The Ambassador managed to guide his shaking cup down to the

silver tray on his knees. He leaned back against the pillows and closed his eyes a moment, then he opened them to stare blankly at the servant. He was an old man and not up to sudden reverses. He stared not so much at Emilio as at his own ruin. His orders had been peremptory and explicit. He was to take the proper measures to prevent Captain Andrea Orsini from appearing at the court of Ferrara, and he was to engage whatever agents were necessary to put this order into effect. The Duke attached extreme importance to it as concerning both the welfare and the honor of the duchy. And let the noble Aldobrandino take care that this thing be done without fail, but let him act with discretion, so that the Serenity of the Duke might not be involved. The official seal on the letter dangled before the Ambassador's thought. His mind echoed one word, like a refrain: "Sold!"

But how could he have done better? He had selected the best man in Venice for the job, a most highly recommended man with a sterling reputation for success in commissions of that kind. Entrust an affair to Mario Belli, informants had told him, and it was as good as finished. Aldobrandino had slept soundly in full confidence.

"Passed the night together?" he wheezed feebly after a pause.

The sympathetic Emilio nodded. "So they say."

In a panic, the Ambassador swung his gouty legs out of bed, as if there were something he could do; but there was so obviously nothing that he sat motionless with his feet dangling. It took time to hire other bravos, and by that time Orsini would be gone. But even if they had been available, no attack could be carried out in broad daylight within the limits of Venice. For an instant the Ambassador thought of pursuit along the Po, but again there was no time to arrange it.

At last his feelings overflowed in language, animated by twinges of the gout and a seizure of asthma. He denounced the crookedness of men and of Mario Belli in particular. He pointed out the injustice of Fortune, which had deserted him in his old age.

"So there's the end of your master," he said. "I'll have to write to Ferrara. God help me!"

The second shock occurred an hour later, when he was seated at his desk, quill in one hand and twisting his beard with the other. An untrained footman (or perhaps he had been bribed) opened the door and announced without warning, "The Magnifico Orsini."

In the whole of Aldobrandino's eventful career, he had never been so thoroughly startled. Last night's proposed victim, cap in hand, advanced upon him down the long room. At the same moment, the Ambassador realized that he was alone and cut off from the door.

While he scrambled to his feet, the other made a low bow, which, under the circumstances, looked ironic.

"Good morning to Your Excellence."

Aldobrandino faltered. "Noble Captain! What a surprise and pleasure!"

"I grant the surprise; the pleasure flatters me."

Andrea resumed his cap, setting it at the proper tilt, and smiled happily, though, to the older man, the smile looked even more threatening than the bow. Orsini then plucked out his shirt cuff, which had slipped a trifle into the sleeve of his doublet.

"To what do I owe — " The Ambassador felt that his legs were giving way, and he sat down suddenly. "I thought Your Magnificence had left early."

"Such was my intention." Unbidden, Andrea drew up a chair. "But Your Grace will recall that last evening you spoke of a letter to Ferrara which I might have the honor of carrying." He glanced at the sheet on the writing table. "Since the delay of an hour or so is a small matter, I thought I should once more offer my services. It was also a temptation to renew my respects to Your Excellence."

Aldobrandino's heart thumped heavily. He was no infant to be lulled by fine words. He knew that Orsini was leading up to something, and he felt like a man in the presence of a suave tiger. At the same time, if he could hold the fellow in play a moment and communicate with his servants, last night's failure could be retrieved and the Duke's orders carried out; Orsini would not leave the Ca' Este alive. This surprising visit was not only a threat but an unhoped-for opportunity.

"Your Nobility's favor touches me more than I can express," he chattered, "more than I can express. As it happens, I was even now on the point of finishing this letter to the Duke's Excellence, and I should be more than beholden if you would be good enough to deliver it." Was it by chance that Andrea's hand strayed to his dagger hilt? The Ambassador's heart labored faster. He mopped his forehead. "*Dio mio*, it's a hot day. If Your Lordship will excuse me a moment — "

He started to get up but found Orsini's hand on his shoulder.

"No, Your Grace, that won't do. You can speak to your people later. Besides, on a hot day, it's best to remain seated. Relax, sir. You look on the point of a stroke." Drawing out his handkerchief, Andrea waved it in front of the other's face. "There! That's better."

Aldobrandino gripped the arms of his chair. "Perhaps," he stammered, "if Your Lordship would explain — I mean, frankness is always a good policy. At least, I've always found it a good policy."

37

"Bravo!" Orsini approved. "I hail the sentiment. I should expect nothing less from a statesman of your mark. Like Your Excellence, I too believe in frankness and forthrightness. So let's be open. I suppose you know what happened last night."

The Ambassador's face was a picture of embarrassed deprecation. Since he had clamped his teeth together, to keep them from chattering, he could manage only a vague "Hm-m."

"But perhaps," Andrea continued, "you don't know all of it. Let me say at the start that Mario Belli did everything that a brave and skillful assassin could do. Luck was against him." Orsini outlined the course of the fight. He added: "The best of us slip up at times — don't we, Your Excellence? And you can't blame anyone short of a martyr for preferring life to three inches of steel in the weasand. Even Your Grace" — Andrea squinted at the other's collapsed countenance — "might have weakened under the circumstances."

"Hm-m, hm-m," said the Ambassador.

"And I must tell you next," Orsini went on, "that Your Lordship grossly mistakes me if you believe me capable of harboring any personal grudge against you on this account. *Il cielo mi guardi!* We are both men of business and take a detached view of such affairs. Your Grace would be equally tolerant, I'm sure, if it should seem expedient for me at this moment to plant my dagger in your heart. You would consider it a purely objective move — though perhaps ill-considered. *Non è vero?*"

The other roused himself to speech. "Indeed, yes — Unworthy of Your Greatness. You wouldn't — "

"Precisely," Orsini interrupted. "I would not. And my reproach to you, Messer Aldobrandino, is entirely on that score. To copy your words, it was unworthy of Your Greatness and of Duke Ercole's noted finesse. I'm disillusioned, sir. I expected discernment and sound policy; but instead, I'm shocked by a blunder. Do I make myself clear? No grudge at all, but disappointment."

Aldobrandino began to revive. Since Orsini took so dispassionate a view of the matter, it ought to be possible to content him until he could be eased into the hands of the servants. The Ambassador gazed wistfully at a bell cord on the opposite wall and out of reach. Then, combing his beard, he expressed agreement with his caller's attitude.

"Messer Andrea, you have a rare spirit. The world would be a happier place if most men could divorce emotion from politics and realize that there is only one true test of a political action; is it intelligent or is it stupid? I rejoice that Your Lordship is of this opinion; but it grieves me that the illustrious Duke Ercole, not to speak of my humble self, should incur your criticism. Speaking frankly — Remember, we were to speak frankly."

"That was the plan, Your Excellence."

"Well, then, frankly, a gentleman of your enlightenment ought to recognize the equivocal position you occupy with regard to the House of Este. . . . Mind you, I do not admit for a moment that the lamentable Belli attacked you on my orders, let alone on those of the Duke. I reject his statements to you with the scorn they deserve. Aware that Your Lordship is in the service of Ferrara, he trumped up this charge against me to cover his attempt on your purse. That's clear."

Since it was clear that any right-minded ambassador must repudiate his secret agents, Andrea nodded. "I agree with Your Excellence. The man's a rogue. . . . But you referred to my equivocal position."

"Yes, speaking frankly now, and theoretically, I cannot conceive how a man so gifted as Your Magnificence could miss the point of view of my lord Duke or tax him with a blunder in policy if — I say *if* — he took means to relieve himself of an officer whom he has every reason to regard as the agent of another prince. No blunder in that. If the illustrious Cesare Borgia wished to send an envoy to the court of Ferrara, he was entirely free to do so; but that he should press for your appointment to the guard of my lord Duke makes a strange impression, all the more because of his military operations on the borders of the duchy. You see what I mean."

It did no harm to speak openly for once. In an ironical fashion, Aldobrandino was now enjoying himself. He had remembered an abandoned well with a heavy stone cover in the courtyard of the palace, an ideal place for disposing of a body. When Andrea, duly appeased and reassured, took his leave, the Ambassador would escort him outside. A half-word would be enough to close the palace doors. Then Orsini would disappear completely.

"And yet a blunder," the latter was saying. "Who am I to instruct a minister of your experience or to reflect on the sagacity of the exalted Duke? But let me tell you how I should have met the problem, and Your Grace will see what *I* mean."

Aldobrandino's attention wandered. A timid man who disliked bloodshed, he regretted the messiness of a fight. But recalling that a crossbow rather than steel could be used, he took comfort and leaned back.

"I'm all ears, my lord."

"In the Duke's place," said Orsini, "I should have regarded my appointment to his guard as a priceless opportunity. . . . Of course I do not admit for a moment that I am an agent of the illustrious Cesare Borgia. I reject the insinuation with the same scorn that Your Grace feels toward the reckless charges of Belli. . . . But, speaking theoretically, *if* I were an agent of said magnificent Signor, I should think that Duke Ercole would have welcomed me. The reason is plain. Since Borgia could have no excuse for insisting on my appointment to the Duke's household except to place me on a freer and more intimate footing than would be accorded to an envoy, it should be to the Duke's advantage to play the game on those terms. As an officer in his pay, am I not specially open to inducements? Might it not be possible to persuade me to shift my allegiance in fact as well as in name? Since my lord Cesare need not be informed of this conversion, should I not be valuable to the sublime Duke of Ferrara as a source of information concerning the Borgian plans?"

Aldobrandino had no longer any difficulty in keeping his mind on the conversation. His chief concern was to hide amazement and admiration at this boldly original line of thought. The more he considered the possibilities involved in Orsini's suggestions, the more promising they seemed. He felt almost humble — like a novice in the presence of a master.

"Ha — hm-m," he pondered.

Orsini added. "Your Excellence will recall that this is pure theory."

"Of course, of course."

"Now, if I were the Duke," Andrea went on, "I should point out to Captain Orsini that the fortunes of Cesare Borgia — depending in large measure on the life of his father, the Pope — are a hot fire of straw, but that Ferrara is rooted in the heart of Italy. And I should take counsel with said Orsini as to how I might best fall heir to Borgia's gains in the Romagna and thus double the size of my duchy — nay, raise it to a kingdom. But, alas, instead of these fascinating and creative things, you and the accomplished Prince, your master, can think of no wiser move than to assassinate me. *Al corpo di Dio*, it's complete childishness. I have no words for it."

"But look you," put in the Ambassador, "is it not your mission to promote the marriage of the lady Lucrezia with our Don Alfonso?"

"Most certainly. And I should do it as a well-wisher of Ferrara. Think. Where else will he find a wife to bring him one hundred thousand ducats cash, not to speak of other assets that can be squeezed from the Vatican? Will he find one in France? Bah! And let me tell you that

40

a hundred thousand ducats should cover sundry objections in the eyes of a prudent prince. Or am I wrong?"

"Ha — hm-m," wheezed the Ambassador.

"But if I am wrong, Duke Ercole had only to refuse. The bare proposal should not dismay him. . . . So, I repeat, my death would have been a blunder. Mark you, I said nothing of other considerations: that the forces of my lord Cesare are now in Imola, and that this is no time to murder one whom he has especially recommended to the Duke of Ferrara's protection. I would not threaten, but if, for example, Your Grace were so ill-advised as to pursue the blunder and have me dispatched before I leave this palace, Messer Mario Belli, who is now in my service, would deliver a letter I have written into the Borgia's hands. It might amuse Your Grace to speculate how long you would live afterwards."

A chill crept down Aldobrandino's spine. He had been so close, so close to an irretrievable mistake. More than ever, he felt like a novice.

"What a horrible idea!" he babbled. "That I should ever dream of lifting a finger against Your Lordship! That you should think —" The Ambassador's voice tangled with his asthma, but he got out, "You say Mario Belli's in your service?"

"Yes, I consider him useful. He is aware that, since he has failed Your Excellence, you would probably reject his services; and therefore, though regretting your patronage and with high regard for your person, he turns to me. A mutually convenient arrangement. I trust that Your Grace would not believe me capable of luring away another man's servant and will view the matter in its true light."

But whatever the true light was, Aldobrandino at the moment could not focus it. The disarray of his mind did not permit him to work out the implications of this move on the part of his terrible caller. He felt and looked stricken.

Andrea picked up his gloves, which he had laid on the writing table beside him.

"And now, my lord Ambassador, I turn to you for advice. We have talked frankly, and I believe we understand each other. I shall be governed entirely by you. Shall I proceed to Ferrara in the service of the illustrious Ercole d'Este, or shall I return to my former patron, Duke Valentino, and report that such and such circumstances make it impossible for me to enter upon this service? Heaven forbid that a gentleman of my House should inflict himself upon a prince who does not welcome him. I have my own pride, after all, and, with due respect to humility, I know my worth."

By this time, Aldobrandino had reached a state of fog that reduced foresight to nothing. But he knew, at least, that a decision in this case did not lie with him. Only Duke Ercole could judge of Andrea Orsini. Had the latter *really* suggested that he might betray the Borgian interests? In that case, Aldobrandino had no right to deprive his master of such an opportunity. Did Orsini actually know the figure of Madonna Lucrezia's dowry? If so, the Duke should be informed of it. Was it possible that this talented, resourceful man had measures to propose that would benefit the duchy? The lords of Este would want to hear of them. In the last ten minutes, the Ambassador's opinion of Captain Orsini had reversed itself. He admired almost as much as he feared him, and he thanked his stars that last night's attempt had failed. A divine intervention! He would write to Ferrara on that tone.

"My dear lord," he protested, "what a question! That it should even cross your mind! You should of course fulfill your agreement with my lord Duke. He will receive you as one of your birth and attainments so richly deserves."

"I have a fondness for living," Andrea hinted — "if Your Grace understands what I mean."

"Pooh, sir! Do not permit the lies of the infamous Belli to darken your mind. You have my definite assurance. I confess that I once had some doubts regarding Your Lordship's position in Ferrara, but our talk has completely erased them. You see here the marvelous results of frankness. Let men but reveal their hearts to each other, as we have done, and difficulties vanish. I shall forward the gist of our interview to the Duke, who will be happy to receive it. But, as the writing will take time, I should prefer to send it by courier tomorrow rather than that Your Magnificence should wait. It will reach Ferrara early enough, believe me."

Thinking it over, Andrea agreed. Any letter entrusted to him would be conditioned by the thought that he might open it. A confidential letter for the Duke's information would, in any case, be sent by special courier. There was no use forcing the Ambassador to write twice. But that he would now write favorably seemed probable.

"I am touched by Your Grace's consideration. . . . Well, then, I shall follow your advice and proceed to Ferrara. You inspire me with confidence, my lord, all the more as I believe that your advantage and mine are closely related." (It was just as well to put in this half threat, half enticement; and Orsini noticed that the point struck home.) "So, therefore, I take my leave with all humble respect and obedience."

He rose and drew on his gloves, set his mantle to rights, and gave an extra tilt to his cap. Aldobrandino accompanied him effusively down the room. But Orsini paused to admire an example of Murano glass, an iridescent vase with golden lights. "Such form, Your Excellence, outrivals nature. By Bacchus, a marvelous thing!" He paused again on the landing above the courtyard to comment on the exquisite sense of proportion displayed by the Byzantine architects of Ca' Este, which had anciently belonged to the family of Pesaro. "By God, I've never seen finer. We of the new age cannot surpass it. The spacing of the arches — irregular but subtler than music. Ah, progress! Is it an illusion?" He shook his head and tripped down the steps, the Ambassador wheezing beside him.

Emilio, lounging in one of the arcades, started and gaped. He half expected a signal from his master; but Aldobrandino escorted the caller to the outer doors of the palace and saw him installed in a gondola.

"Farewell, noble Captain!"

Leaning back, Andrea reflected. Without committing himself in any way, he had secured a measure of safety in Ferrara — at least, for a while — and had opened approaches to the future.

CHAPTER VI

UNDER an ultra-blue sky, the barge, drawn by two heavy-headed horses in single file, made a steady but almost imperceptible progress between the limitless meadows bordering the Po. As befitted his rank, Andrea Orsini traveled luxuriously, having rented the entire barge for Belli and himself. But, except for privacy, little could be said for the comforts of the boat, harried by flies, exposed to the relentless late September sun, and pinned, as it were, to the green flatness of the plain. The tattered awning, spread over the waist of the barge, radiated heat; and the straw-filled cushions swarmed with fleas, annoying even to such case-hardened cavaliers as Andrea and Belli. Behind, on the poop, the bargee, Toni Vecchio, dozed over his steering oar;

43

the horse boy dozed on the crupper of one of the horses; the two passengers dozed or at times chatted beneath the awning.

Conversation, such as it was, remained impersonal; but Andrea found Belli an interesting companion. The latter's observations on characters and events, on cities and states, on mankind in general, though colored by cynicism, confirmed Orsini's opinion of the man's shrewdness and experience. Bitter experience, exclusive familiarity with the sham behind appearances, with deceit and greed, with selfishness and treason, that blossom into bloodshed. Belli's mind, steeped in this, could not be expected to believe in the reality of anything else. Andrea wondered what had befallen him, what self-defeat accounted for the bitterness of his denial. But probing, however tactful, led only to elusiveness. Belli talked fluently on objective matters; he kept his intimate concerns to himself.

Orsini concluded that this was just as well. On his own side, he had no intention of making the man his confidant except when necessary. Besides, the tight-lipped habit in a secret agent was most desirable. But Andrea considered one disquieting point. Belli might be an expert in double-dealing and murder, but he gave no indication of drunkenness or lechery. A more complete reprobate would be easier to understand and, therefore, to manage. No, the mainspring of evil in him seemed to be protest, hatred, a vendetta against life. That sort of man takes watching at all times.

When the sun declined and swallows began circling, Andrea shook off the day's languor and began paying attention to the countryside, though there was still no change in its featureless monotony. Since, because of the late start from Chioggia, it was impossible to reach Ferrara before evening, he had stipulated with the bargeman that they spend the night at Crespino, a village several leagues from the city downstream, and complete the journey next morning. "Your Lordship seems to know the country," Toni Vecchio had remarked, when they discussed possible stopping places. "Why, yes," Orsini replied, "there're few regions of Italy I haven't crossed one time or another. I remember the Polesine from my school days in Padua. Crespino had a passable inn at that time."

Now, as the afternoon grew late, he stepped up to the poop beside the boatman, while Belli, still outstretched on the cushions, looked as if he were meditating some special villainy and stared into space. The raised finger of a campanile broke the distance far off, indicating the location of a village.

"That should be Crespino," Andrea observed.

44

"Right, *padrone*," returned the boatman. "We'll be there in an hour."

"A rich country — fat soil, good harvests — only too prone to floods and war. Sad loss to Ferrara, when it fell to Venice in '84."

"Aye, sir, but who wouldn't exchange the rule of our Saint Mark for the damned bloodsucking Estes? It was a big gain for the farmers. Being a poor man" — Toni slapped his chest — "I sympathize with them. I was born not far from here; though, *per la Dio mercè*, my parents were Venetians."

"Born here, you say?"

"Yes, in old Niccolo d'Este's time. They were only Marquises of Ferrara then."

"You've had a long life," Andrea remarked. "That's sixty years ago."

He continued to gaze out across the plain toward the point of the distant campanile.

"By the way," he added after a while, "since you were born here, did you ever know of a family by the name of Zoppo?"

"Did I ever! You mean Giovanni Zoppo, nicknamed Braccioforte, the blacksmith, on the road from Crespino to Rovigo?"

"It may be. I had a friend from these parts, one Andrea Zoppo, in Padua. We were good comrades at that time. I remember now: he said his father was a blacksmith."

Toni Vecchio released his oar to lift both hands in astonishment. "*A le guagnele di San Zaccaria!* So Your Magnificence knew Andrea Zoppo?"

Orsini nodded. "He was a boy of parts, I recall, though poor as Job. Tall, for his age, and managed a dagger well. He was gifted too with the brush, spent more time on paints and drawing than on Latin. He used to be called *Il Dipintore*."

The old man looked excited. "And does Your Honor know where he is, what happened to him?"

"How should I? It's been ten years since those days. He crossed my mind with the name of that village there. What's the to-do about him? Where is he, and what happened?"

"Ah, *mio padrone*," answered Toni, with the look of a gossip happy in an audience, "I hoped you knew. If you did, his mother, the widow Mona Costanza, would give the shirt off her back for word of him. He's the talk of the countryside. He disappeared, and yet not altogether, if you take me."

"No," Andrea smiled, "I do not. You mean he's become a phantom?"

45

"No, my lord." Toni spat into the water. "It's the case of a boy raised above his station — though perhaps the blood in him accounts for it."

Since a question was expected, Orsini asked, "What blood?"

"I can't tell for sure; I repeat only rumors. It's said that the Marquis Niccolò d'Este, who took women where he found them and had as many as Solomon, once cast his eyes on a wench of Crespino, a certain Nanna Morelli, when he rode through there hawking, and that the child she bore nine months afterwards was his. At any rate, this child was Mona Costanza Zoppo's mother, and therefore grandmother of Your Magnificence's friend. I say the Este blood addled him."

Orsini's lip curled. "A devil of a thin trickle. How did he suffer from it?"

"Or," hedged Toni, "it may have been his upbringing. He was an only child, the apple of his parents' eyes. The other Zoppo children perished of the plague twenty years back, but this *sciagurato* survived. It is so in life; the good are taken, the wicked flourish."

"By God's cross," put in a voice dry as a file, "isn't that the truth!" Unnoticed by Andrea and the boatman, Mario Belli had stepped up beside them. "It's what I've always said. To be alive is a reflection on one's character. Which makes me wonder how you and I happen to have been spared, Messer Andrea."

The boatman, startled by this interruption and Belli's ugly face, shrank away and stuck out his first and little fingers in the form of horns to avert the evil eye. Belli tipped back his head in one of his silent displays of merriment.

"*Orsù, Vecchio,*" prompted Orsini, "get on with your story."

"Well, Messere," the old man continued with a sidelong glance at Belli, "the said Mona Costanza and the said Braccioforte, blacksmith, spoiled their son past belief. It is true that he was promising — at least so I'm told, for I never saw him — and they had that much excuse for their folly. But you can't make a rose of a turnip. They sent him to school to the parish priest, then squandered their savings to send him to Padua, where he wasted his time daubing paint on canvas, as Your Nobility remarked. There, too, the frequenting of lads of great houses like Your Magnificence went to his head. I'm told that it was not enough for him to become a man of law or a doctor of medicine as his worthy parents hoped; he must be a gentleman, a *cavaliere*, though why, in that case, he stained his noble hands with paint, I'm unable to guess."

"I can tell you why," Orsini interrupted. "The painter's craft is a passion. He could resist it no more than a drunkard can resist drink. As you say, he aped the manners of his betters until he was almost accepted on an equal footing. But then he would slink off to the workshop of Master So-and-so and grind colors and work on designs like the other artisans. By God, I felt sorry for him."

"What an ass!" exclaimed Belli. "I could never paint a stroke myself, but if I could — be damned to the dirty profession of gentleman or cavalier!"

Andrea eyed his henchman curiously a moment, as if appraising this new facet of him; but he only said, "Well, then?" to the boatman.

"Well, then, Your Honor, the family scrapings gave out. The young rascal, who had learned neither law nor medicine and was ashamed to come back to his father's forge, apprenticed himself to a painter and ended up in Florence. They say he did some fine things there, much admired by the masters. Indeed, he sent home a Madonna in red and blue, the pride of Mona Costanza, who has made a shrine for it."

Andrea laughed. "*Via*, friend, I can see no great wickedness in this. Would you rather have him stink in a smithy than paint Madonnas?"

"My lord, wait. You have not heard the end. When the French bandits swarmed into Italy six years ago and passed through Florence, young Zoppo followed them. Afterwards, corrupted by these barbarians, he became a brigand down south in the Regno. His father, the good Braccioforte, died of grief. *Ecco*, Messere" — Toni struck an attitude — "behold the end!"

"Too bad," Orsini nodded. "How did the news get back? He'd hardly write home that he had turned thief. One of his victims, maybe?"

"No, he writes home that he is well and happy. But when a starveling wastrel sends a hundred ducats to his mother, not once but several times, when he can fit her out with lands, repair the village church, and buy enough masses for his father's soul to get Barabbas into Paradise, what must people think? If he came by the money honestly, why not say how and let his mother glory?"

"What does *she* think?"

"Signore, you know mothers. She will hear no evil of him. But she keeps her thoughts to herself and she keeps the money, though I hear that Don Procopio, the priest, exhorts her to redeem the rascal's sins by giving all to God. Why, only last week, when I had a fare from Chioggia, they were talking in Crespino of a fat purse she had but then received. So, as I told Your Magnificence, the wicked flourish,

47

while an honest man" — Toni slapped his chest again — "earns not enough to live and too much to starve."

"Ha!" Orsini muttered. "It's a strange case — What do you think, Mario?"

"Think what?" retorted Belli. "That this friend of your youth is a rogue? Of course I do. What of it in a world of rogues?"

"Hm-m," Andrea meditated. And after a while, during which the barge made a number of furlongs and the distant campanile showed nearer, he added: "A fat purse. I hope Mona Costanza keeps her ducats in a safe place."

"Ah, my lord," returned the boatman, with a sigh as if the same thought were familiar to him, "you do not know Mona Costanza, a woman of great decision. She is a host in herself. Besides, she has stout doors and two dogs of a fierceness that it is a dread to speak of. A prudent woman."

"I'm glad to hear it," said Orsini, "all the more as her house must stand at some distance from Crespino, and without many neighbors, eh?"

"So it is."

"She sleeps alone, I dare say, and the farm hands in one of the barns."

"*Sì, padrone.*"

Belli's eyes narrowed a second, but then looked as innocent as it was possible for them to look.

That evening, Belli was hardly surprised when, after supper in their room at the Crespino inn, his patron renewed the topic.

"You know, whether this Mona Costanza has doors and dogs or not, it is tempting Providence for a lone woman to keep a hoard of gold ducats in her *cassetta*."

The other's tight smile opened enough to show some teeth. "Whom do you mean by Providence, Messere?"

Orsini dismissed the insinuation with a wag of the head. "I need to stretch my legs after today in the boat. I'll sleep better for it."

He got up, standing undecided a moment. "I believe I'll call on Mona Costanza — it can't be far. Have a talk about Andrea, warn her not to keep too much gold in the house."

"Kindly thought," Belli murmured.

Having buckled on his sword belt, Orsini took down his cloak from a peg behind the door. When Belli started to do the same, he said: "No, two of us would frighten the woman. I'll go alone."

The other bowed with a hand on his heart. "What an honor Your Nobility is to the profession!"

"What profession?"

"Gentleman and cavalier."

But after Andrea had gone out, Belli stood for a while dreaming. "You can learn something from this lord, Mario," he whispered at last.

Several minutes later, he drew on his cloak.

"Yes, and you can learn more by overlooking the game."

He snuffed the candle with his fingers and stole out into the night.

CHAPTER VII

THE moon had not yet risen; but the stars were bright, and the outline of the hedges, broken here and there by a ghostly poplar, sufficiently indicated the highway to Rovigo. There had been little rain that month, so that Andrea did not have mud to contend with and could make good progress over the thick, soft dust, which drifted back from him in a mist somewhat paler than the darkness. It also deadened his footsteps and those of Belli, following at a distance. Even the farm dogs, as he passed, could not be sure that they heard anything and gave tongue only occasionally and uncertainly.

Beyond the village, houses grew rarer, and the vast loneliness of the plain increased until, after a half hour, Orsini reached a crossroads and could make out, some hundred yards off, a squat huddle of buildings to the right of the highway. By this time, a sliver of moon added more luminance to the night, so that he could distinguish details.

The buildings formed a U — a one-story house in the center, with two higher and more spacious projecting barns, enclosing three sides of an open cobblestone courtyard. In the middle stood a fountain or a drinking trough that supplied water both to the farm hands and to the livestock. It looked a prosperous, solid, well-equipped farm, better off than many others in that region. The smell of hay, cows, pigs, and chickens breathed from it. As Andrea approached, he was aware, too, of the sound of sleep and the loud trickle of the fountain.

49

He stopped for a moment at the entrance of the courtyard, as if to take his bearings. The wing to the right had the wide doors of a smithy; but a wealthy manure pile, now standing close to them, indicated that the forge had been turned into a barn. He could hear a confused munching, grunting, and shifting of animals inside. The opposite wing to his left was no doubt reserved for poultry, to judge by the sourer odor in that direction. Yes, a well-to-do farm that showed the effect of the vagabond son's ducats.

But the peace and silence of the courtyard lasted no longer than Orsini's first steps on the cobblestones. Instantly an explosion greeted him from a kennel in front of the dwelling house; and the clanking and jerking of a chain accompanied the outburst, as a huge, black body leaped from side to side and stood on its hind legs. Then a similar uproar began inside the house, where smaller but no less furious voices joined in. A fluttering, neighing, bellowing, and stamping issued from the barns, until the whole place vociferated. Only the farm hands, deep in sleep, gave no sign of waking.

Belli, following at a distance, watched Andrea disappear into the courtyard. Then, under cover of the turmoil, he stole carefully up to the barn and, keeping in the shadow of it, peered around the corner. The upper panel of the house door had now been thrown back, and a light showed.

"Who's there?" came a firm, contralto voice.

Belli heard Andrea call back: "I seek Mona Costanza Zoppo, with a message from her son."

"Quiet!" ordered the voice, and the barking subsided, while the chained watchdog half drew back into his kennel. "Now, listen," the voice continued. "Messages from my son come by daylight and are brought by honest carriers. Your trick has been tried before. Step over here. I'll speak to you through the door. If I find you're lying, I'll loose the dogs. *Hai compreso?*"

The voice was so assured and uncompromising that Belli held his breath as Andrea crossed the courtyard. But, to his amazement, he heard the bolts drawn back almost at once; the door opened, and Orsini disappeared inside.

"*Mort de ma vie!*" hissed the eavesdropper to himself in French. "Is this lord a conjurer?"

For a couple of minutes he stood uncertain, aching to know what was going on behind the shuttered windows and blank walls. To reconnoiter the house from the front meant rousing again the still unappeased watchdog. So after a while he turned and, following the wall of the barn, crept behind the house, alert for any glimmer of light. On this side, too, the windows were covered by shutters, and, as the ground fell away, his head was no higher than the sills. But, undefeated, he continued to lurk and peer.

Andrea and Mona Costanza faced each other beyond the door. The candle, which she held in one hand, cast its flicker upon both of them; and, if Belli could have seen, he would have been struck at once by their odd resemblance: the same high-bridged, angular nose; the same big mouth and shape of eyes. He would have noticed too that, though barefoot and dressed only in a smock that revealed her brown arms and legs, she did not conform to the peasant type. Something in the poise of her head, the restraint of her lips, her slenderness, hinted of breeding and spirit. She stood almost as tall as Andrea; and her hair, equally dark, showed no touch of gray. As she stared at him, her hand, which held the smock together at her throat, did not conceal the excited rise and fall of her breasts.

Then, with a "*Domineddio!*" she put her candlestick down on a ledge, threw her arms around Andrea's neck, and smothered him with kisses.

"Son! *Figliol mio!*"

"*Mamma! Mamma mia dolce!*"

She drew back to look, then caught him to her again.

"Jesus, help!" he exclaimed. "Let me get my breath! *Mammina!* You haven't changed at all. You're as beautiful as ever!"

"Beautiful? Ah, Madonna! But you, my soul — talk about change! With a sword! With fur on his collar! And a red hat!" Her welcome took the form of imprecations. "Scoundrel! *Traditore!* What do you mean with your message from my son! With your Mona Costanza! Surprising the breath from my body! After eight years! Eight years! How could you treat me so, *ladro e truffatore che tu sei!*"

Several minutes passed before Belli discovered a chink in the shutter two feet above his head. Gripping the sill and chinning himself, he managed to bring his eyes on a level with the crack and peered through. He could see the woman, whose back was towards him, setting out food on a rough-hewn table — bread, cheese, a billet of sausage, a pitcher of wine — while Andrea, seated on a bench with the dogs at his feet, followed her with his eyes. Both were talking at full tilt, though Belli could not hear what was said. Now and then, the woman paused to gesticulate, and Orsini answered with equal passion. The spy wondered that the topic of the lost son should absorb his patron to such

51

an extent. "Marvelous actor!" he thought. "Probably working up to a loan." But the strain on his arms proved too great, and, muttering, he lowered himself to the ground.

"Why?" demanded Mona Costanza. "For what reason? You with your good mind! That you go on clinging to this folly!"

She spoke the dialect of the Polesine, but not entirely with the peasant modulation. Her voice corroborated her curious distinction.

"Folly?" Andrea repeated. "To rise in the world? Come now, *Mammina*, who encouraged me in folly, as you call it? Who persuaded my good father, when he would have kept me at the forge — when everybody cried out against sending me to Padua? Wasn't it you perhaps?"

Instinctively he glanced about the room, as if inviting it to confirm him. It represented the past, what he had emerged from. For a moment the recognition of its half-forgotten details swept him back in time: the closeness of garlic, cheese, and oil; the cupboardlike bedstead forming one corner, with utensils stored on its wooden top, a wicker cradle beneath it; the canopied fireplace, with spits, pans, and brick oven on one side; the rustic ladder up to the loft; litter and jumble of clouts, brooms, kettles, milk buckets, odds and ends; the little shrine, strangely apart, with a Madonna in red and blue.

"Yes," Mona Costanza admitted, "I — and your father, who agreed with me in the end. We had only to look through your eyes into the spirit behind them. You weren't born to hammer iron, and nothing else. But we encouraged you to what, *figliol mio?* To become a man of thought, as God intended — yes, or a master painter. We accepted that, too, when you showed your skill; for the painter's craft is honorable, and you had a divine gift. Were we not proud of your works in Florence and of the praise of Messer Leonardo and the good Master Filippino you wrote us about! I don't call that folly, Andrea. But this is folly."

She made a circle with her hand that somehow included and denounced the trappings of Andrea's gentility.

"You could have done anything you pleased," she went on, "*anything* — either with your hands or your head. You were good even at the forge. The bellows you designed were the best ever seen hereabouts. You knew the secrets of metal. You could paint pictures, make music, write verses. You could have been as great as this Leonardo da Vinci or any other master. But that wouldn't do." Again the scornful, invisible circle. "You didn't want the real things: you wanted show."

He tried to smile, as one who knows the ways of the world smiles at another who can have no comprehension of them; but he did not succeed. It was hard to patronize his mother in this room where he had spent his boyhood and where every object reasserted the past. It is always hard to patronize truth. Another set of values, once his own, challenged the newer ones he had adopted and put him on the defensive.

To gain time, he reached for the sausage, hacked off a slice, and poured himself a cup of wine. Having emptied it, he remarked: "*Deh, Mammina!* I wouldn't exchange your *vernaccia* for the best malmsey I ever drank. And no one can make sausage like you."

She sat down opposite him, leaning forward with her elbows on the table, her eyes absorbing him.

"Then eat, *Andrea mio*. Would God I always had the tending of you! My life's empty." Reaching out, she took his hand, fondling it with her brown fingers. "To think it's really you! But you've grown too old; I can see it in your eyes. . . . There! You're right. We won't argue. Nothing matters except that I have you again."

But the insistent topic could not be dismissed. It overshadowed small talk and endearments, like an implacable presence that demanded attention. Andrea surrendered at last and pushed away his plate.

"You see, *Mammina*, it started years ago before my first breeches. Your talk of the Marquis Niccolò d'Este and Grandmother — remember?"

"Bah!" she protested. "Bedtime tales when you sat on my knee. I've never known the real truth. Grandmother babbled in her old age."

He retorted: "True or false — what difference? It's not the drop or two of Este blood I may have but the wings you gave to my spirit that have lifted me. Or perhaps it wasn't that; perhaps it was the cavaliers riding past on the road to Rovigo, with hawks and hounds. And I, privileged to hold the hoof of a magnifico's horse in my apron, honored to pick up the coin he flung and knuckle my forehead — I, his better at every point except gold and birth. The same in Padua, in Florence. Poverty, subservience. Painters — even the greatest — are artisans, remember that. The successful are honored, but never as equals of the lord who hires them. The others starve. And I was young and poor and unknown. I starved — and dreamed."

He looked up from the table to meet his mother's eyes, and they both gazed steadily at each other before he went on.

"*Your* dreams. I tired of starving. You say I could do what I pleased

53

with head or hands. I think that's true. Well then, I pleased to try another art, one that could make me the equal of count or cavalier. . . . The French passed through Florence. Andrea Zoppo went with the storm, but he kept his eyes open. . . . And now *eccomi*." A flourish of the hand asserted cap and mantle, sword and brocaded doublet. "Not bad. While friends of mine in Florence still grind their masters' paints and eat their masters' leavings." He broke off, smiling. "Tell me how many golden ducats has my folly sent home?"

She shrugged. "Enough to make people call me the mother of a robber. They say you're one of the band of Giambattista Carrero, that bandit in the south. He's an artist too — in his way. It's not hard to get money, son, at the cost of honesty."

"You believe such talk?" He clenched his fist on the table.

"What am I to believe? Granting you turned soldier — a mistake, I say, to squander your gifts in such a trade, but since you have — why this mystery? Don't I love you? Wouldn't I give the last drop of my blood for you? When people asked me, 'Where is he living? What is he doing?' what could I answer?"

"Answer that I serve a great lord, that the money I sent was part of my gains."

"What great lord?"

He hesitated, but the pain and suspense in her face decided him. "Why, the lord Cesare Borgia, if you must have it, the Duke Valentino."

"Well!" exclaimed Mona Costanza, relieved. "I'm glad of that at least. Men call him a mighty prince, though false and cruel. Why not tell me before?"

"Because I know you, *Mammina*. You would have had Father Procopio write a letter for you to Andrea Zoppo in Rome, and it would not have reached him."

"Why not?"

"Then," Andrea continued, "you would have taken the money I sent and come in search of me. But you wouldn't have found Andrea Zoppo. I bear another name now. And it's too early for others to know that it isn't mine. Understand?"

She kept silent a moment, searching him with her eyes. For the first time, he noticed the stamp of the years under them; their wistfulness disconcerted him.

She shook her head. "No, I don't understand. I wasn't brought up that way. Nor was your father. We haven't dealt in lies."

"I wouldn't call it that."

"What else?"

"Policy."

The word touched off an explosion. "Policy! *Al corpo di messer san Buovo!* To be ashamed of your name — the sure mark of a rascal! To drop it for another! To tell people you are Ser So-and-so! That's not a lie, eh? No! That's policy."

At the moment, with the impressions of boyhood upon him, he did not have the force to withstand her. She was right from her standpoint — perhaps from any standpoint. He felt suddenly small. The earlier side of his dual self took control for an instant.

"No, I'll admit that lying and policy belong to the same litter. But the world isn't so straight and simple as the road to Rovigo." He took to explaining. "You see, every art has its own approach. To open certain doors, I needed a talisman, and Zoppo isn't one. Names are important. Don't worry. 1 robbed nobody. I'm simply keeping a dead branch of a family alive. And who cares? But the name I took carries further than Zoppo. It's been done before."

"What name?"

He shook his head. "I'll tell you someday. Listen. It's a long time that I've left *ser* behind. I'm *messere* now and *captain*, at home in a great many palaces. But that's nothing; there are bigger stakes on the board. What do you say to *signore?* To a great marriage? To founding a princely house? What do you say to that?"

He looked at her expectantly and flushed a little when she laughed.

Getting up, she rounded the table and laid her hand on his shoulder. "*Figliol mio,* remember the man who built his house on the sand. That's your case. . . . Look." She pointed to the enshrined Madonna, which he had sent her from Florence years ago. "There's something real, something that grew out of you. When you painted that, you weren't depending on luck or favor, but on yourself and on the light God gave you. As a painter, you were yourself. As a *gran signore*, you are a straw man. And the higher you climb, the farther you fall. Look to it; I speak the truth."

Oddly enough, he did not rebel. His eyes were on the little Madonna, whom he had painted between two lilies. In the vague candlelight, she seemed to hover like a delicate, luminous ghost, independent of the drab surroundings — like an artist's soul, Andrea reflected, even if he lives in a cellar. Yes, there was reality. He could see that clearly in the presence of the one person who loved him and in this familiar place. Not good or evil — he did not think in those terms — but real or false, the two sides of him which he was in danger of forgetting.

"I say look to it," repeated Mona Costanza. "You're a painter in your own right; you'll be a *gran signore* by right of sham and trick. Isn't it so? Have done with it!"

He did not answer for a moment, his gaze still on the picture. It brought back, in a gust of nostalgia, the old enthusiasms, the passion for beauty that still at times possessed him to the exclusion of everything else.

Then he thought of Camilla Baglione, the ambitions beyond, the tangle of great events he was involved in.

He sighed. "A man in a millrace can't swim upstream. You don't understand, *Mammina*. . . . But what if I become a great lord in my own right?"

"That's different," she returned sadly. "Miracles are always different."

Mario Belli lifted himself again to peer through the crack in the shutter. He saw Mona Costanza's face for the first time and caught his breath. She was standing next to Andrea; bending down, she laid her cheek against his. Mario's eyes widened, narrowed. "*Mort dieu!*" he breathed, his supple mind adjusting itself. "*Mort dieu!*" He stared long enough to make sure, then lowered himself noiselessly. "So that's it! I ought to have guessed. I wouldn't take a thousand ducats for this." He stood gazing into the darkness. "Who'll pay me most, and when shall I sell? . . . The reverse of me, eh? Lackey to lord, lord to lackey. Hm-m!"

The shadow of the house covered him. He emerged an instant in the moonlight beyond the barn; the dust muffled his footsteps. Then, keeping close to the hedge, he stole back to Crespino.

When Andrea returned to the inn sometime after midnight, he found Belli asleep. But the latter wakened and sat up.

"Well?" he asked.

Andrea nodded. "An enjoyable evening. An unusual woman."

"*Senti!*" yawned the other. "And a peasant at that! I hope she was duly impressed by the condescension of Your Lordship."

CHAPTER VIII

FROM the ducal chambers in the Castle of Ferrara, a convenient stairway led upward to the battlements of the northeast tower, known as the Tower of the Lions. From this vantage point, Duke Ercole d'Este liked to view the city — especially that part of it which he had created — and point out its beauties to newcomers at court. One did not have to stand unusually high in the Duke's favor to merit this attention, since the topic absorbed him, and he wanted only an audience. Nor did Andrea Orsini, the new captain of crossbowmen, overvalue the honor when, being on duty ten days after his arrival, he attended the Duke to the battlements and followed the pointing of the great man's finger.

Tall, though a little bent, clean-shaven, hatchet-faced, a fringe of gray locks showing under his black velvet cap, Ercole d'Este reminded Andrea of nothing so much as of the white eagle that formed the center of the Este arms. His piercing eyes and thin lips strengthened the comparison. Still poised and alert in spite of his sixty-nine years, he looked out over his domain watchfully, complacently.

To a man of intelligence and imagination like Andrea, the view was thrilling. Behind him, to the south, lay the past — the medieval town with its haphazard, narrow streets; in front of him, to the north, stretched the future — something absolutely new in the world, the first modern city. Interested, like most men of his age, in new developments, Andrea at once acclaimed what he saw. With wholehearted admiration, he realized that Duke Ercole was not only a gifted diplomat (everybody admitted this) but a creator and pioneer, just as the great Leonardo or the Spanish admiral, Colombo, were innovators in other fields.

"This is a marvelous thing, Your Serenity," he exclaimed. "This is beyond praise."

For what he saw was the beauty of mathematics expressed in design, architecture, and landscaping on a canvas of several square miles. From the Padiglione gardens, which replaced the old walls on the north of the castle, a stately avenue, the Street of Angels, stretched off into distance, forming a cross midway with an equally wide thoroughfare that connected two opposite city gates. There were other intersections at regular, but not too regular, intervals; and one could make

57

out the pattern of aligned palaces and gardens, some new and some unfinished, interspersed here and there by the rising walls of churches and monasteries. Beyond all this, far off, veiled by distance, lay another glory of Ferrara, the impregnable city walls, and still further, beyond these, other gardens and hunting grounds of the Duke. Indeed, the prevailing impression was not so much of streets and architecture, splendid as these were, but of lordly gardens. And the perfume of their flowers reached up even to the gap-toothed battlements of the castle.

"A herculean labor," Orsini bowed, with obvious reference to the Duke's name.

"Yes, we call it the Herculean Addition." Detecting the ring of sincerity in Andrea's voice, Ercole smiled. "So you admire our city, Messer Captain? I am delighted that you should, for you have seen much of Italy. Tell me, in your opinion how does it compare with other cities?"

"Your Excellence knows that there is no comparison. Rome is a tangle of ruins. Naples is a lovely slattern. Florence and Milan have fine sections, but none are equal in scope and design to this. Venice" (he paused, recalling the splendor of it) "is Venice; but it would be hard to picture her without the waterways. . . . No, Your Sublimity, not until my good fortune and your ducal condescension permitted me to enter this right splendid city of Ferrara did I learn of what grandeur art is capable in the planning of cities. The world, my lord, will seek instruction from Your Signory."

Ercole was visibly pleased, though he let his eyes rove again over the distance.

"Few princes," Andrea went on, "would be able to meet the charges of so great an enterprise. Any other lord than Your Excellence could hardly support the burden of it."

He intended a compliment but was met by a sharp glance. If Orsini was prying into the financial state of Ferrara, he would not find the Duke napping.

"Perhaps. But we have loyal subjects, Messere — a hundred thousand of them." And Ercole went on to point out the wide Piazza Nuova to the right, where an equestrian statue of him was to be set up on a specially imported column. "The new palace yonder belongs to the Strozzi family. It has a most elegant *cortile*. And that one near it was built by the lords Bevilacqua."

Orsini's mind lingered a moment on the plight of the Duke's loyal subjects. The prisons were full of debtors; the streets of beggars. One did not have to be a spy to know the cost of grandeur. But somehow the top-heavy state maintained itself from generation to generation. That was the supreme achievement of the Estes. The citizens of Ferrara might starve, but they could take pride in their princes.

"I believe you have not yet made a circuit of the walls," the Duke was saying. "You should do so on the first occasion. Our fortifications merit your attention."

The voice had a dry flavor to which Andrea had grown accustomed. If Ercole and his sons had concealed their surprise and chagrin when the man who was to have been eliminated in Venice presented himself at court, and if Ambassador Aldobrandino's letter had given them food for thought, they still did not permit Orsini to believe that they took him at face value.

It was not surprising when the Duke added: "Your former patron, the illustrious Duke Valentino, for whom I have the warmest esteem and devotion, would enjoy a description of our walls, Messer Andrea — I mean as one who delights in the profession of arms. Pray have no hesitation in sending him one. We shall be glad to supply you with drawings if you wish. There is no one whom I would so gladly serve as him."

Stripped of diplomatic verbiage, the meaning of this could not be clearer. Ercole might just as well have said: I know you are the agent of Cesare Borgia, whose guts I hate and who wants to devour Ferrara as he is gobbling up the Romagna at this moment. Well, show him our walls as a reminder that it won't be easy. And a pox on him!

But Orsini bowed low. "Your Signory honors me above my deserts. However, the walls of Ferrara are so justly famous that the magnanimous prince whom I formerly served is already familiar with them. He was at pains to procure a complete set of plans, so that he might study the engineering principles involved. I have often heard him express the warmest admiration."

"A complete set of plans, eh?"

"Down to the smallest details. Indeed, he employed the architect, Master Bramante, to make him a table model of these walls for the instruction of his captains. Of course it is purely an academic interest, since my lord Cesare's perfect love and respect for Your Serenity excludes any hostile purpose."

"As does mine for him," returned the Duke, "as does mine for him! Ah, Messer Andrea, if there is any lord in Italy to whom I feel drawn by natural affection, it is this renowned and gracious prince. *A la fè di Dio*, the chief ornament of our age!"

Since this was his first private conversation with the Duke, Andrea did not intend to lose any opening. He sighed. "Far be it from me to meddle in such high matters, but how often have I heard my lord Cesare wish that the ties between Your Sublimity and the House of Borgia were confirmed before God and the world by an even closer and dearer relationship! The Holiness of the Pope himself and the divine Lady Lucrezia have the same desire. It would be a blessing for Italy."

Both the Duke and Andrea enjoyed the exhilaration of seeing through each other's game. Ercole had not missed the veiled threat of that complete set of plans nor the hint that a marriage between his son and Lucrezia Borgia was better than war. But he countered skillfully, with a sigh as deep as Orsini's.

"Indeed, the thought you express lies close to my own heart. But what would you have? It's my son Don Alfonso's marriage, not mine. While wholly valuing the beauty and virtues of that chaste and excellent Madonna whom you mention" (Andrea could not detect the faintest irony in this), "my son expects a princess from the House of France. As you know, Ferrara enjoys the protection of the Most Christian King, and such an alliance is natural."

Yes, skillfully countered. It was the mailed fist of France, rather than Ferrara's walls, that checked the Borgia's ambition. But Andrea wondered whether the Duke knew of talks he had already had with Louis d'Ars, the newly arrived French envoy to Ferrara, to whom he had suggested that the King of France, with his designs on Naples, could hardly afford to alienate the support of the Borgias by sponsoring a French marriage to the detriment of Madonna Lucrezia, a point which the Pope's legate was now pressing at the French court in Blois. The French princess might not be forthcoming.

"Perhaps," continued Ercole, "there is also something of *this* in Don Alfonso's thought." He pointed to the Estensian coat-of-arms carved into the rampart of the battlement, the Lilies of France quartered with the Double Eagle of the Empire, the Papal arms emblazoned above the White Eagle of Este. It was a famous shield, heavy with history. Beside it, the Ox of Borgia would look like a squire's crest. "Something of this, Messer Andrea. For five hundred years, our House has ruled in Italy."

Orsini bowed again. "*Oimè, Vostra Signoria,* if the very glorious and excellent Don Alfonso seeks a bride equal in nobility to himself, what princess in Europe is worthy of his condescension? That in his extreme youth he was married to the late, ever-lamented Madama Anna Sforza has perhaps given reason for belief in some quarters that he would consider merit and beauty as well as blazonry."

To have argued this point, that Lucrezia Borgia was as well born as Alfonso's child wife now dead, the great-granddaughter of the upstart, Muzio Sforza, would have been beneath the Duke's dignity. He merely raised his eyebrows and remarked: "Well, sir, you have my leave to discuss the matter with Don Alfonso. Perhaps you may convert him."

"And if I do, my lord?"

"If you do, I should be surprised. Meanwhile, if by chance" (again the dry note in Ercole's voice) "you should write to this renowned prince, the Duke Valentino, you might tell him of our personal regrets and of our high regard for him."

Then, changing the subject abruptly, the Duke fell once more to discussing details of the new Ferrara. "Consider these waterworks . . ."

But, though outwardly attentive, what Andrea considered at the moment were his cards in the diplomatic game. Since his arrival in Ferrara, he had not done badly. He had put the aforesaid bee in the bonnet of the Frenchman, Louis d'Ars; he had even made progress with the hoped-for bridegroom, Don Alfonso. So far, so good. But Alfonso was not the only one concerned. How to win over the House of Este as a whole: Alfonso's brothers, the haughty Cardinal Ippolito in chief, let alone this proud old autocrat, their father? Yes, and keep alive while he was winning them? For the breathing space gained by Aldobrandino's letter might be cut short at any moment.

"Perfect!" Orsini agreed absently, as the Duke paused. "A perfect city!" But he was startled into renewed attention by the reply.

"No, not perfect. Ferrara lacks one thing."

"I cannot conceive what Your Excellence means."

"Ha!" exulted the Duke. "Then I shall tell you. It lacks holiness, Messer Captain. And for that reason I desired this talk with you, for it seems to me that you can help me."

Andrea could not hide a stare of vulgar amazement. That holiness should rank with streets and waterworks in the Duke's schemes for city promotion was odd enough; but that he, Andrea, should be called on to assist in the matter was still more extraordinary. He managed to stammer, "Indeed?" and reckoned that His Excellence showed the effects of age.

"Aye, sir, indeed, in very deed," rejoined the Duke. "You see this fair city which is in the making. But beauty is not always the counterpart of Christian faith. Not that I would suggest that Ferrara is worse in respect to religion than Venice or Milan, but the moral tone is low. I grieve to confess it. 'Swounds, do we build a city only for display, and neglect its soul? For cities are living things, my friend, and the soul of a city is its life."

Though a little breathless, Andrea could now follow the transition. He perceived that the Duke was again speaking as an artist; and what he said made excellent sense.

"True," Orsini murmured. "It is not only design and color that make a painting live, but something more."

Ercole pointed upward solemnly. "That something more is God, the Divine Spirit. . . . Well, then, to speak of our city, I am afflicted by its sins. As I said before, it has everything but holiness. *Per Dio, per Dio,* you would never believe the amount of cursing that goes on in this fair-seeming place. As for fornication, sodomy, drunkenness, gluttony, and murder — in short, the whole scale of sins — we are no whit better than other cities. And the point is we *must* be better. We must be a holy city. Ferrara is my offering to God."

Andrea remembered that the Duke had an unusual reputation for piety. He was a great founder of churches. His voice and manner now gave every evidence of sincerity.

"Our Lord could have no finer offering, Your Excellence. It is worthy of an emperor. But deign to instruct me as to how this right heavenly virtue of holiness is to be acquired."

Ercole nodded. "In this way. Look you, we have imported learned men for our university, skilled engineers and architects for our public works, valiant captains, like yourself, for our army; but with respect to one class necessary to a complete and prosperous city, we are bone bare. We have not a single saint. We must import at least one saint."

Struggling again with astonishment, Orsini murmured: "To be sure! Your Grandeur thinks of everything."

"A saint," the Duke continued triumphantly, "whose merits before God will atone for all the sins of Ferrara. This is sound and sober policy. Besides, it will bring us fame and luster. Why should Mantua, Perugia, Viterbo, and other towns crow over us in this respect? By God, they shall not."

"They shall not indeed." It was Andrea's proper cue at the moment to catch fire. "I am dazzled by Your Signory's wisdom. But has a saint been selected for this honor?"

"Of course," returned the Duke. "And it is in this holy business that I would employ you."

Orsini made an effort not to look bewildered. "At your command, my lord."

"Well, then, Messer Andrea, to the point. Have you heard of that holy maiden, that bride of Christ and favorite of Saint Catherine's, Suor Lucia Brocadelli da Narni?"

"She of the stigmata, who lives in Viterbo?"

"The same. Is it not a proof of the Divine love that in these evil days of unspeakable corruption, God manifests Himself in so many pious and religious persons, especially of the feminine sex? I can tell you, sir, that it is better than a book of sermons only to read of the ecstasies of this same venerable Suor Lucia. I need only refer to that miracle of miracles, that four years ago she received the wounds of Our Lord, and that the cloths wrapping her hands and feet are endowed with the power of healing. Is not this the person appointed by God's grace to remove the reproach of Ferrara?"

Andrea crossed himself. "Truly a saint, Your Excellence. To think that these heavenly honors should have been paid to one so young! I hear that she has not passed twenty-four. When will she adorn this city?"

"Aye, when!" snapped the Duke. "There's the hitch. We have offered to build a convent for her; we have paid her uncle, Antonio Mei, the price — and a stiff one — for his consent; we have got her mother on our side; we have the support of the Pope and of the General of the Dominicans; we have spent money like water; the holy Lucia herself is eager to come. But it's all to no avail, and our salvation founders in the quagmire."

"How so, Your Signory?"

"Because of the mule-headed people of Viterbo. May an apoplexy strike them! They refuse to let her leave. They keep her prisoner in their cursed town. Selfish pigs! They want this heaven's treasure for themselves, and nothing will move them. I sent your colleague, Captain Alessandro da Fiorano of my guard, to carry her off by force of arms when she left Viterbo to make her devotions at the shrine of the Madonna della Quercia; but these devils got wind of it and shut the gates. He is still at Narni, close to Viterbo; but he effects nothing. . . . Now, sir, do you see what you are to do?"

Andrea was beginning to see, but he gained time by replying, "Not quite, Your Serenity."

"You are to go to Viterbo. You are to succeed where Captain Alessandro failed. By hook or by crook, you are to secure me this jewel, which I value more highly than any other thing. And I can tell you,

Messer Andrea Orsini, that, if you can render us this service, we shall make our gratitude to you manifest before the world."

Clever! There could be no doubt of the Duke's sincerity in desiring Suor Lucia as a crowning perfection for Ferrara; the cleverness consisted in appointing Andrea as his agent. After all, it might not be wise to assassinate him — Aldobrandino had reasoned well on that point — but there was another way of disposing of Cesare Borgia's unofficial representative. Send him on a wild-goose chase to Viterbo. If he succeeded, it would be so much to the good. Meanwhile, and in any case, he would be out of the way.

Seeing this clearly, Andrea had not the faintest intention of complying; but the sweep of his hand, the inclination of his shoulders, were submission itself.

"Your Excellence's slave. I cannot adequately express my thanks for this mark of favor. That I should be chosen for this holy mission exceeds any office I had dared to hope for. And by the help of the saints, I shall pluck this rose of heaven for Your Excellence."

"You speak well," approved the Duke, "very well — as I should expect one of the House of Orsini to speak."

"But is it not the very tyranny of fortune," Andrea continued, "is it not a vexation beyond words that I cannot leave at once for Viterbo?"

Ercole's smile vanished. "What do you mean?"

"Alas, Your Highness, I mean a wound, newly received in Venice. I had not meant to trouble Your Signory with such a trifle."

If the Duke was embarrassed, he did not show it. "*Per Bacco!* A wound?"

"Yes, *Signor mio*. The robber who attacked me failed, but his knife struck in. I was left weak, my lord, and inclined to fever. A thing of no moment, except that the long journey to Viterbo takes strength. I should be glad to lay down my life for Your Sublimity, but that would hardly serve to accomplish the desired mission. Grant me a delay of ten days long."

And ten days could be spun out longer, and something else might turn up. Meanwhile, it spoke volumes that the Duke accepted Andrea's almost fictitious wound.

Glance encountered glance, both so limpid and both impenetrable. "Gladly, Messer Captain. Your misadventure grieves me."

"I humbly thank Your Excellence."

A page, his cap brushing the pavement, had appeared from below.

"His Eminence, the Cardinal Ippolito, bids me inform Your Serenity that the right noble and exalted madonna, Camilla degli Baglioni

64

of Città del Monte, entered Ferrara by the Porta Po an hour since. When she has changed her attire at the Palazzo Varano, she will hasten to pay her respects, if it would please Your Excellence to receive her."

Duke Ercole nodded. Then, before turning to the stairway, he leveled his gaze once more at Andrea Orsini. Yes, by God, looking closely, it seemed to him now that his captain of the guard did actually show signs of fever.

CHAPTER IX

To A clatter of hoofs on the drawbridge, a ruffle of drums, flourish of trumpets, grounding of halberds, Camilla Baglione rode through the tunnel-like portal into the sun-drenched courtyard of the castle. She rode a richly caparisoned roan mule, and she was escorted by Don Sigismondo, the youngest of the Duke's sons, on a big bay horse. Her hair, showing a tinge of bronze in the sunlight, stood out like an aura around the edges of her small velvet cap studded with garnets. She wore a costume of crimson velvet striped with gold bands. At her stirrup trotted the black page, Seraph, with a new turban of cloth of gold. Behind her rode several of her ladies and a number of Don Sigismondo's gentlemen.

Duke Ercole omitted no touch of pageantry when he received a distinguished guest. The center of a brilliant semicircle, he stood at the foot of the great outside stairway leading to the halls above; but he hastened forward as Camilla slipped from her mule, and he met her deep curtsy with a deep bow. His welcome left nothing to be desired. There might have been more parade if the consort of a greater lord had entered the castle, but not much more. After all, she represented two of the most prominent families in Italy, the Baglioni and Varani; her husband ranked as an independent ruler, however small his state. Besides, he was an old friend of the House of Este.

With the Duke were his sons, who now repeated the welcome: Don Alfonso, burly and handsome in his black satin, with leonine head and blond beard; Cardinal Ippolito, a tall young man of twenty-one, who, except for his red biretta perched at an angle on his curls and the red mantle hung carelessly from one shoulder, displayed few signs of the churchman; Don Ferrando, unimpressive in spite of his fine clothes and eclipsed by his two brothers; Don Giulio, the bastard, a handsome youth with magnificent eyes.

Members of the court followed — gentlemen and ladies who happened to be in waiting — Count this, Madonna that, vassals of the duchy, Contrari, Romei, Costabili, Bevilacque, and others. A mingling of colors: black and gold, crimson, azure, violet, and silver.

To Andrea Orsini in the background, Camilla, though only a few yards off, seemed miles away. Being on duty that afternoon, he had seen to the ordering of the ducal guards and the flourish of trumpets. Now, as little better than an adjunct and stage property, he stood with his line of halberdiers at the angle of the stairs. Surprised at his own flutter, he was unable to determine whether the sight of Camilla in these circumstances gave him more pleasure or bitterness. Since his career depended on the brazen virtue of assurance, a sense of inferiority rarely troubled him. But now, he recalled the wayside farm near Crespino, the mud and manure; he could feel the grip of the soil on his heels. What had Mona Costanza told him not two weeks since? And, outwardly rigid in front of the halberdiers, he writhed inwardly.

Camilla had not seen him or, if so, had given no sign. The Duke, presenting his arm, upon which she rested her gloved hand, led her toward the stairs, while the graceful cortege made way with a shimmering of colors and regrouped behind. She came nearer; Andrea could see her tawny eyes, with the well-remembered spark of mischief in them, tilted up politely toward His Highness, who was finishing off a compliment. And suddenly it became a matter of life and death to Orsini that she should look at him, as if destiny depended on that look, and he would be able to read the future in it.

Nearer. No, she did not see him. Nearer. Then, worst of all, her glance passed over him casually without recognition. His heart turned to lead.

"*Eh, Dio mio!*" He found her eyes on him again; they widened, kindled. She stopped. "*Per mia fè!* Messer Andrea?"

He collected himself just in time to sweep off his cap. "Illustrious Signora!"

"You know this gentleman?" put in the Duke. But his voice sounded thin against the music in Andrea's veins.

"We met in Venice. I am much beholden to the Lord Orsini for a

66

painting, a page and" — the word came more slowly — "a song. . . . I am happy to see you again, Magnifico."

She passed on up the steps; the train of courtiers followed; Andrea stood at attention. But the world was clothed in rainbow. He had expected at most a word and a smile, not such an accolade. His dreams blazed up. And, to cap it all, Camilla's greeting had not fallen on thin air. He could hear the whisper of the court: "Orsini . . . Her Signory." One more feather in the cap of this unwelcome officer at whom the Ferrarese gentry, taking their cue from the Este princes, looked askance. In spite of themselves, during the past two weeks, they had envied his dress and manners and the hint of power that went with the Borgia backing. He might be distrusted, but he was not overlooked. Now they had something else to envy him for.

In the great reception hall at the top of the stairway, with its gilded beams and vivid frescoes, people moved to and fro, forming groups that dissolved again in new combinations of color. Mature courtiers, perfumed fops, foreign representatives (notably the privileged and arrogant Frenchmen), ladies with jeweled headdresses, in silks and brocades of every hue, drifted here and there. Pages, like flashing minnows, whipped in between. A buffoon or two angled for attention. The beloved little monsters of the court, dwarfs and other human curios, trotting about in attire no less eccentric than themselves, added the gargoyle touch. Alone stationary, at the doors of the hall and at intervals along the walls, stood the ducal guards, stiff as their partisans, in the Este livery of white and red.

The ceremony of welcome over, Andrea mounted the stairs in his turn, eager to renew his bow to Camilla. From the doorway, he could see her at the opposite end of the hall in a group that included Alfonso d'Este and his brother the Cardinal, together with the French envoy, Captain Louis d'Ars, and a couple of Ferrarese ladies. By one of those curious lulls that sometimes interrupt the babble of a company, Andrea found himself walking the length of the hall in a kind of hush, and he could feel an escort of glances on either side of him.

Sure of his appearance and with renewed self-confidence, he turned the moment to profit. He wore a gold chain worth two hundred ducats, as any courtier could see. If it represented a good part of his fortune, that was his own secret. The gold medal on his black velvet cap, depicting Europa and the Bull, had been a gift of the Pope himself. As to dress, he equaled anyone present. His doublet, stiff with golden arabesques, glittered sufficiently in the opening of his wide-sleeved, knee-length mantle, which was also of black velvet edged with gold. His black hose revealed a perfect leg. And the scrollwork on the scabbard of his sword, which he wore by virtue of his military office, reflected the design of the doublet. Handsome, tall, dark, and erect, he made a distinguished impression. That he was conscious of it and full of himself did not lessen him in the eyes of the court. The self-assertive individualists there expected a man to put his best foot forward.

But Camilla Baglione disconcerted him. As he came up, she drew back her head, advanced one shoulder and then the other in the faint imitation of a strut, and finally drove the point home with a friendly but impish smile. It completely upset his intended flourish.

"Ah!" she exclaimed. "Yes! There you are, Messer the laggard! Don't try to propitiate me with your noble airs. Traitor!" She appealed to the group. "Signori, in Venice this man declared that until I reached Ferrara life to him would not be worth living. Was he at the landing to help me from my barge? No. Did he even meet me at the city gate? No. Or at the drawbridge of this castle? Alas! I had to pluck him out of the crowd, looking like a statue, looking as if he had never seen me. And now, last of all, he comes sauntering in! *Ahi!* But you men are wind harps and mockers!"

She spoke quickly, her words like the bubbles of new wine. They had the same effect on Andrea.

"And you ladies have every virtue but justice." He flung his arms wide, hands clenched. "Behold me, wretch that I am! When every breath I have drawn has been in memory of Your Ladyship! Is it my fault that Madonna comes to Ferrara unheralded? Is it my fault that, in the service of this illustrious Duke, I must stand at attention while others pay court? Alas, the injustice of beautiful ladies!"

"No," put in the Cardinal d'Este. (There was something of the tiger and something of the tall gamecock about him, with his red biretta, round, hot eyes, and masterful nose.) "I'm on your side, Madama. A true cavalier, expecting so lovely a lady, would have spent his days and nights on the river landing rather than miss the first glimpse of her."

"Why, this man," she went on wickedly, "refused even to escort me to Ferrara. He left me high and dry in Venice, alleging duty as an excuse. He put his office before gallantry — to the lasting shame of Italian gentlemen."

But this was too much for honest Louis d'Ars, who had been following the banter with some difficulty and growing disapproval. His sense of humor did not extend to Italian dramatics, which he was apt to take literally, and his flat-nosed, battle-scarred face looked bewildered.

"*Ma foi, madame*," he rumbled, "you are main hard on the Seigneur d'Orsini, to my thinking. *Nous autres français* — I say we Frenchmen rate duty higher than that. Let me catch one of my lances neglecting his charge for the sake of a woman's eyes, and I would drum him out of camp. *Vive dieu!* What has this gentleman done to deserve your reproach? He has merely obeyed the orders of his prince. You should respect him for it. Nay, Madame, forgive him."

Ippolito d'Este coughed to hide his amusement. Even the burly Don Alfonso smiled. The Ferrarese ladies tittered.

Camilla, wicked to the end, looked down. "*Ecco!*" she murmured. "I hadn't thought of it that way, Monseigneur d'Ars. You are an irresistible peacemaker. Well then, for your sake, I forgive him." Her eyelid flickered at Andrea. "But only for your sake. And here's my hand on it."

Don Alfonso stifled a yawn. Court chatter bored him. "Since that's the case, Captain Orsini, you'll join us in persuading Her Excellence to put off leaving Ferrara until after next week's hunt. . . . We'll show you good sport, Madama."

"And my lord husband," Camilla protested, "who's waiting for me in Urbino? I haven't seen him for" — she counted on her fingers — "one, two, three, four — four weeks."

Andrea wondered again at the softer note in her voice when she spoke of her husband.

"In Urbino," put in Julia Costabili, one of the ladies, "he will not miss even you, *Signora mia dolce*. It's so pleasant a court. Stay with us for the hunting."

"If you'll stay," urged the Cardinal, "I'll get off a rider to Urbino for His Signory your husband's permission. He won't refuse *me*."

Camilla hesitated. Andrea fancied that her eyes lingered a moment on him.

"Give me leave until tomorrow, my lords. I'll decide then. I'm confused by Your Lordships' hospitality and torn between two desires."

Others joined the group. Don Alfonso, whose hobby was the forging of cannon, discussed his newer models with Captain d'Ars and upheld the future of artillery; while the other maintained that no guns under heaven could turn back the charge of the French horse. Cardinal Ippolito rallied the ladies in his hot fashion. For an instant Orsini could exchange a word with Camilla.

69

"You'll stay, Madonna? You'll give a poor little week to Ferrara?"

"Persuade me this evening, Messere. I shall expect you at the Palazzo Varano. After all, I hardly know you, do I? Strange that you should seem an old friend."

CHAPTER X

ACROSS a richly carved Venetian table, empty except for a salver of fruit, a pitcher of wine, and two goblets, Ercole d'Este and his son Ippolito faced each other an hour later in the Duke's cabinet. There was a strong family likeness between them, the same purposeful mouth, arrogant nose, and alert eyes; but the Duke showed the frost of age as compared with his son's flush and fire. Perhaps they were too much alike to be congenial — their relations were never of the happiest — but they shared a common interest: devotion to their House.

"So he tells me," said Ercole, "that he was wounded in the Venetian affair and begs off from Viterbo — which brings us no further than we were."

The Cardinal snorted. "Precisely. Saddled with a Borgian spy. Content even to pay him wages. Forced to coddle the adder. I marvel at Your Signory's patience when there's so quick a way to dispose of him. God help Ferrara if we have grown so weak that we must boggle at such a straw! Leave Orsini to me."

Letting his head sink back against the upper cushion of his chair, the Duke regarded his son beneath drooping eyelids. "*Cavolo!*" he remarked, ironically mild. "God help Ferrara if Your Reverence held the rudder! How do you expect to grow great, particularly in the Church, when you reason so hotly? Learn one thing: passion doesn't help in politics. As for straws, this Orsini happens to be important."

"Indeed?" Ippolito reached out to the salver for a grape and tossed it into his mouth. "Important to whom?"

"Important to us. Important in himself." The Duke nodded emphatically. "A man of talent. I say, *most* promising. A skillful negotiator.

70

In the course of my life I've seen few more admirably endowed for great affairs. It will be a pity, as our Aldobrandino urges, if such gifts have to be sacrificed; though, I confess, should everything else fail, we may be forced back to our first plan."

"Everything else? What's Your Excellence's meaning?"

"I mean our Ambassador's hint that Messer Andrea is open to proposals. I should like to win him to our service in fact as well as in name. He would be a minister without peer in Italy. On that account, I urged the mission to Viterbo, which would have kept him out of mischief until I had leisure to seduce him. I think he made a mistake."

The Cardinal spat a grape skin into the palm of his hand. "Does Your Signory want to know what I think?"

Again the scornful drooping of the eyelids. "Pray instruct me."

"Why, then, I admit Orsini has a smooth tongue. And he made a fool of my lord Ambassador. He knew that he wouldn't live long in Ferrara unless he muddied the water. So what does he do? Suggests a pretty little game of double-face. Intimates how valuable he could be to us if he sold out Valentino. Expresses doubt of the said Duke's future. Hints of a scheme to our profit. Thirsts to devote himself to us. And what's the upshot? Leisure, as Your Signory puts it; leisure for us to seduce him if we can; leisure for him to carry out Borgia's orders — and thumb his nose at us."

Ercole nodded again. "Rudimentary."

"I beg your pardon?"

"Yes, rudimentary. Didn't I call him talented? Why waste time pointing out what's obvious? I understand his motives for calling on Aldobrandino. . . . A bold stroke, however, and well-conceived! . . . I know that at present he's playing the Borgian game, and that we'll have to block it. But, reverend son, look a shade deeper. Don't be superficial."

The Cardinal eyed his father with sullen bewilderment. "Superficial, how?"

"Can't you see that his suggestions to our ambassador, whether or not they were sincere at the moment, showed his turn of mind? A noble simpleton would have been incapable of making them. Only the trained politician, steeped in his trade, could have proposed so crafty and fertile a scheme for tricking Valentino. Maybe he *was* sincere. In any case, a good idea worth developing if we have time for it. I know politicians and how to buy them."

"The question is," retorted the Cardinal, "whether Your Excellence does, or does not, desire this Borgian marriage."

71

"You know I abominate it."

"Well, then, to my limited apprehension" (Ippolito consumed another grape) "it would appear that Your Excellence has no time for subtleties. This admirable Orsini is making good use of his leisure. As, for example, *primo*" — the Cardinal checked off his points with the shapely forefinger of one hand on the fingers of the other — "they tell me he's furnished Alfonso with a portrait of Madonna Lucrezia that would corrupt Saint Anthony; that our brother keeps it in his cabinet to moon over. He's a man of flesh and blood, with plenty of both. And Messer Cupid plays a part even in the marriages of princes. If you don't believe me, ask Alfonso himself. You'll find that Orsini's made progress."

The Duke nodded but brushed off the trifle with a wave of the hand. "Yes. . . . Well?"

"*Secondo*, he assures me that the Pope loves none of his cardinals as he does me, that he longs to make me Archpriest of St. Peter's — under certain conditions. A fat benefice. To be considered as part of the dowry."

Ercole made no comment. The two realists pondered the matter in silence.

"*Terzo*. Orsini has paid his respects more than once to Monseigneur d'Ars. And what they talked about needs no guessing."

This time the Duke's nod showed concern. "Indeed, I've noticed that d'Ars shies off from discussing the French bride. That wasn't so at first. Perhaps you're right. . . ."

"Then, I say again, leave the fellow to me."

Ercole took a sip of wine before replying. His answer, when it came, was apparently unrelated to the subject, but Ippolito did not miss the connection. "Borgia already holds Cesena and Forlì. He's out now for his second rape in the Romagna. I've had word that he crossed the mountains last week at Gualdo. He'll take Rimini, Pesaro, and Faenza — perhaps Bologna. If so, we'll have him next door. *With* six hundred lances and ten thousand foot. I hope Your Reverence follows me." The Duke sipped his wine and then sat eying the embossed silver-gilt figures on the goblet. But probably the Triumph of Bacchus, which the goldsmith had designed, did not absorb him at the moment. "For that reason alone," he added, "Messer Andrea deserves consideration."

The Cardinal's ever-ready anger frothed over. He pushed his chair back and sprang up for the freer use of his hands. "Then why debate? Throw up the game! Double the spy's wages! Marry our brother to the Borgian girl! If we've come to the point of cringing at Valentino's power — "

"Silence!"

"Farewell, honor! Farewell, Ferrara!"

"Silence!" The unaccustomed loudness of the Duke's voice took Ippolito by surprise, and he let his extended arm sink. "You talk like a muleteer. You disgrace the priesthood and offend me. You're as featherheaded as a woman. Learn the use of words, for one thing. Agent and spy have two different meanings. You've called Orsini a spy, not once but twice — "

"And I call him so again. Will Your Signory have patience?"

"If God gives it to me."

"Then mark this. As Your Signory directed, we've had Orsini watched since the day he reached Ferrara. Put my man, Ombra, on the scent, and he's seldom at fault. I don't think our Magnifico or the traitor, Belli, has taken a step without our knowledge — except twice. Twice they have disappeared."

"Disappeared?" The Duke shot a glance at his son and lowered the goblet to the table. "Disappeared, how?"

"My people lost them in the marshes east of the city, when they rode out on two separate occasions."

"Well, what's suspicious in a jaunt?"

"A jaunt that lasts overnight," the Cardinal retorted, "looks more like a rendezvous. With whom? The Venetians? Valentino's men? Perhaps both? He's not likely to be keeping a wench in the marshes. As Your Excellence points out, Borgia follows the coast. How do we know that from Rimini he will strike first at Faenza? How do we know that he and the Venetians have not reached an agreement which would put him in Ravenna? Perhaps these marriage proposals are only a blind to cover a surprise attack. That's Valentino's way. And this Orsini has been well planted to keep him informed of our strength or even to open our gates."

It was significant of the ticklish situation in Italy at the moment, and particularly in Ferrara, that Duke Ercole's face grew darker at each of these suggestions. He might consider them improbable; but they were not impossible and hence had to be taken seriously. Trick and counter trick, betrayal and double-dealing, were not only commonplaces of the political game, they were the texture of it. In current practice, they were to be expected, and, if successful, they were even to be admired. The Duke remembered that detailed study of

73

Ferrara's walls which Orsini had mentioned. He recalled, too, that, as a soldier, Orsini was, in the Cardinal's phrase, well planted.

"Why haven't I known of this?"

Ippolito shrugged. "I wanted proof."

"Well, then, get it." Ercole's eyes shifted from annoyance to anger. "Track him down. Find out where he goes. *Prove* that he's plotting against this state, and you can have the hanging and quartering of him in the teeth of the Borgias. There's a limit to caution. We'll have no traitor among us at anyone's bidding."

"By God, I rejoice to hear it!" crowed the other.

"And I grant you this," Ercole went on, "regarding Orsini's practice with Don Alfonso and the French, that in any case he must be got out of the way. We shall not have this dirty marriage. Even if he is no spy, but will not leave Ferrara for Viterbo or elsewhere, why then, the worse for him. But take no action without word from me."

The hot young Cardinal chafed at even this touch of the curb. "More caution!" he grumbled. "And this cutthroat, Belli, this whoreson villain, whom he had the unspeakable impudence to bring with him — No taste! No sense of decency! *Per Cristo*, at least you'll let me deal with *him*, I hope."

"Yes," nodded Ercole. "In time. But consider. The man who sold us to Orsini will sell Orsini to us. So, buy him, *figliolo mio*, if you want to learn the truth about his master. Treat him gently at present. Afterwards — " The Duke finished with a wave of the hand.

"Excellent!" agreed the Cardinal. "I hadn't thought of that. We'll set about it. I applaud Your Signory's wisdom."

And Ippolito d'Este tossed off a cup, as if to put out the ever-burning fire in him.

CHAPTER XI

RETURNING that afternoon from the castle, Andrea Orsini had stopped at a perfumer's, a haberdasher's, and a goldsmith's; and now, by candlelight in his quarters at the Angel, with the aid of a newly purchased Venetian hand mirror and of comments by Mario Belli, he made ready for the evening. His appointment with Camilla at the Varano Palace demanded his utmost. It would not do to appear in the same attire which he had worn that day at court, so he changed to his very best — a gorgeous creation of black and cloth of gold. He was careful also to change the medal on his velvet cap. A medal is a symbol; and, for a first call, the Bull carrying off Europa might seem indelicate.

"Crude," nodded Belli. "Keep it for a future evening when you can wear it appropriately. But for tonight" — he probed with his forefinger in the small jewel box and found what he wanted — "wear this. Saint George is propriety itself."

"It's only gilt," Andrea objected.

"Like most propriety. But what of that? The badge is well cut and makes a fine show. The lady won't bite it to test the metal. I wager she'll be taken in by it. She'll note the resemblance."

"What resemblance?"

"Between Saint George and Your Greatness." Belli gave his two-edged grin and stuck his tongue in his cheek.

The grin faded suddenly. Below them, in the common room of the tavern, a rumble of voices, which had been going on for some time, now gathered itself into song; and, as the bass predominated, it shook the house like a roll of thunder. They were the voices of the French archers belonging to Captain Louis d'Ars and the gentlemen lances who had attended him from Lombardy. Since the arrival of their troop six days ago, they had behaved like all such barbarians. The gentlemen, bronzed and arrogant young bloods, flirted outrageously with the Ferrarese ladies and took no trouble to hide their scorn of Italian men. They were jealous of their honor, which consisted in fighting at the twitch of an eyelid; and, as several of them, notably Pierre de Bayard and Pierre de Bellabre, had already won fame in duels, people were careful in their company. The plebeian archers, on their side, swaggered and rollicked as they pleased to the dread of peaceful citizens. And in all this insolence, the Frenchmen were encouraged by Duke Ercole himself, who attached such importance to their visit as to let it be known through Ferrara that a quarrel with these guests was an affront to him.

Belli had taken cover in his room as soon as the French appeared and since then had remained secluded except on the two excursions mentioned by Ippolito d'Este, when he had accompanied Andrea out of the city at dawn. It did not help him that the French used the Angel as a headquarters and that they were generally to be found in the public rooms and corridors. But, though he was out of circulation, his advice on the character and foibles of Louis d'Ars, whom he seemed to know intimately, had been of great use to Andrea in his interviews with that captain.

Now, while the lusty French song roared through the tavern, the raillery in Belli snuffed out, leaving his ugly face more venomous than usual, and he stood wrapped up in himself like a dreaming vulture.

Orsini, turning away, applied several drops of essence to his hair. Then, deciding for Saint George, he pinned the medal on his cap and slipped a couple of rings on his fingers, including a large intaglio for the thumb with the Orsini arms. The poniard he had just purchased, with an ivory hilt representing Medusa, would look well at his belt when he sat down and the mantle opened up. His sword hilt, though not so notable, was rich enough; and he could always take comfort in the authentic clink of his gold chain, which he spread out carefully on his shoulders.

By this time the singing below had died down, and he could make himself heard.

"Lend a hand, Mario. Link me this bracelet on my left wrist."

It was a broad band of filigree work, its rosettes pricked out with seed pearls, which, by tightening the sleeve of his doublet, expressed the white fullness of the shirt cuff.

"Admirable!" pronounced Belli, whose smirk reappeared. "When Her Excellency spies that, she'll be struck by the verse of Holy Writ."

"Ha?"

"That Solomon in all his glory was not arrayed like Your Magnificence." Belli stood hunched over the back of a chair. "I return to my point," he added. "Gilt or not, you and Saint George are twins, Messere. I refer to the medal of course."

Directing a last glance at the hand mirror, Andrea laid it down. Sometimes Belli's remarks struck too close to be comfortable.

"Well, Messer Mario," he smiled, "thanks for the compliment, however it's intended. I leave you now to the French Sickness."

"Not bad," Belli murmured in reference to the pun. "But don't flatter me. I have no traffic with women. . . . Here's a riddle, Magnifico," he went on. "One man, like you, has good features and an agreeable person: so, for him, trysts with the ladies, the applause of men. While I — while another man, by a trick of birth — d'you see? — because he's a goblin from the cradle, can suck his thumb in the corner, for all the world cares. Eh?"

"Well?"

"*Why?* What justice? That's the riddle."

76

Andrea was aware of himself in his cloth of gold contrasted with the gargoyle leaning over the back of the chair, a distressing contrast. He was aware, too, that for once Belli had given him a glimpse of whatever self he had below the surface, the bitter self that might explain him. If Orsini had lived up to his pose and his costume, he would have laughed. To an authentic lord, Belli's outburst would seem comic. Andrea revealed more than he knew by taking it seriously. That he said nothing was perhaps more than Belli expected.

"Yes," observed the latter, "I see Your Magnificence hasn't the answer. And who has?"

Detaching himself from the chair, he handed Andrea the long outer cloak and the velvet mask worn in the streets at night by gentlemen on private errands. Then, opening the door to an inner room, he notified Giuseppe, the lantern boy, that His Lordship was ready, and bade him lead on with his light.

"Good fortune, Messere, and safe return!"

Having descended the stairs, Andrea passed the clamor of voices in the common room on his right and emerged, with the evening before him, into the hot closeness of the Via San Romano.

The older section of Ferrara, trailing southeast from the castle, like an ancient, patched cloak, had none of the modern planning that distinguished Duke Ercole's northern extension. Though the Varano Palace and the Angel Tavern were actually not far from each other in a straight line, the tangle of streets between them doubled the distance.

Threading his way through the tunnel of arcades built under projecting houses, Andrea, with the lantern bearer, proceeded toward the cathedral. As usual in an Italian city during the hot season, numbers of young men were prowling out of doors, and an obscure throng in the arcades made progress slow. Occasional lanterns pricked the darkness, or a torch flared, or windows released limited zones of light; but on the whole, circulation ran invisible and blind along the street level. The smell of old walls, sour wine, and garlic mingled with the scent of roasting chestnuts, harbingers of autumn.

Orsini drew a breath of relief when the narrow street opened out into the market place. Since his adventure with Belli two weeks before, he did not relish close and unlighted passageways. Perhaps it was this experience which gave him the almost constant sense of being watched and shadowed since his arrival in Ferrara. He glanced back sharply now; but it was impossible, among the shadowy loiterers in the *piazza*, to determine whether any one of them was on his traces.

77

A rising moon glanced on the marble columns of the loggia, that half-concealed the flank of the cathedral facing him across the square. It lighted up the stately figures of the lords of Este on their pedestals; it cast a flattering ray on the bell tower recently heightened by the present Duke; it rested discreetly on the scaffold not yet removed since the last execution. Turning east and crossing the *piazza* lengthwise, Andrea could feel at every step the shadow of the great Ferrarese House, and instinctively he looked back again at the sound of footsteps. It was only a company of youths on a lark, their red caps and parti-colored hose vivid in the light of torches. One of them struck up on a lute.

Andrea drew aside for a couple of French men-at-arms steering a straight course down the square and giving way to no one. The Frenchmen collided with the group of singers, shouldered them out of the way.

With a shrug, Andrea strode on. Although a soldier, he viewed his profession as a trade and had an Italian scorn for the French delight in combat, the silly honor they were always flourishing.

Beyond the Piazza dell' Erbe, he plunged again into the closer darkness of streets; but on this side they were less pent in than to the south. He passed the Contrari Palace on his left, then other mansions fronting each other along the winding lane, their grimmer sides turned outward; but here and there a lonely cypress stood against the moon, implying a hidden garden. The air grew softer with the smell of moss and late roses. Somewhere a nightingale throbbed in the darkness, and now and then sounded the plash of a fountain.

Guided by the boy, whose lantern revealed the windings of the street, Andrea followed the Via Contrari, the Via del Saraceno, and, turning up the Via Praisolo, he could make out the silhouette of a church against the sky and of lower buildings adjoining it — probably a convent.

"The community of Corpus Domini," Giuseppe explained. "The Palazzo Varano opens on the same street."

But upon rounding the corner of the Via Campo Franco, Andrea's heart sank. A crowd of torchbearers, escorting several gentlemen on horseback, surrounded the portal of the mansion, and a parley was going on with a doorkeeper who stood in the entrance.

Other callers on Madama of Città del Monte. As might have been expected. It was true that she had declined the routine state dinner at the Ducal Palace (the dinner offered to any visiting potentate) on the plea of fatigue after her journey; but good manners required, and her own charms encouraged, a paying of respects on the part of the House of Este and the court. Andrea had realized that his hope of finding Camilla Baglione alone was a very slim one; and yet he had clung to it, partly because something in the tone of her invitation that afternoon had hinted at privacy.

"*Va bene*," he gloomed, "it can't be helped. But when shall I ever be able to see this illustrious madonna except in a crowd of chatterers! If she leaves tomorrow, it may not be for months — not until I have finished with my business and claim her of the Duke. But I would rather have courted and won her myself. By God, she mustn't leave tomorrow!"

Meanwhile, there seemed to be some hitch in the proceedings at the main door. The gentlemen still sat their horses; the doorkeeper still addressed them. It actually looked as if the callers were not being received. And, in that case, would Andrea himself be received?

Bidding Giuseppe darken his lantern, and keeping within the shadow of the wall, Orsini drew nearer to the palace entrance. As he approached, he could distinguish the mounted figures more clearly, especially one in a red cloak and cap, who towered from his saddle above the torches. The flaring lights brought out the color of his dress until he seemed incarnate flame. Andrea started: it was none other than the Cardinal Ippolito d'Este.

The latter's voice now interrupted his chamberlain, who had been speaking with the doorman. "And have you told Her Highness *who* it is who gives himself the honor of waiting on her?"

"My lord, she has been informed. But Her Signory pleads the fatigue of the day. She hopes, however, that Your Eminence and these gentlemen will take such poor refreshment as the Palazzo Varano affords."

"Which means then," returned the Cardinal, "that Her Excellence cannot receive us?"

"Not in person — to her deep distress. But she attends my lord in spirit."

"Well, *per Dio*," laughed the Cardinal, "not being a spirit myself, I don't know what to do in the circumstances. Here's a coin for you, fellow. Assure Madama that we remain her slaves and hope for better luck in the future."

"If Your Greatness will enter — "

"No, not tonight. . . . Come, signori, there are other ladies we know of in Ferrara who are not fatigued. *Avanti!*"

He turned his horse and set off down the street to a rattle of hoofs and flickering of torches. The odor of musk blew back from his red robe.

When the street was empty, Andrea removed his mask and walked to the door with some trepidation. If a Prince of Este had been denied, there was small likelihood that a mere captain would be admitted.

Probably Camilla's invitation had been a casual polite remark, which she had promptly forgotten. But nothing was lost by venturing, and he modestly rattled the bronze ring that served as knocker.

"Messer Andrea Orsini," he answered to the challenge from inside, "at the command and service of Her Highness."

To his surprise, the door swung open. The doorman bowed low.

"The Signora awaits Your Lordship."

Still hardly believing his good fortune, Andrea was ushered into the courtyard of the palace. He had a moonlight impression of arcades surmounted by balconies and of a lion-mouth fountain gurgling near by.

Then, without warning, a voice at one side exclaimed, "Ha! *Ecco!* There you are!" And he turned to see Camilla, dressed in glimmering white satin, with a black-clad servant beside her.

Outside the main door, Giuseppe, the lantern bearer, propped himself against the wall and vacantly waited. But he had not waited long when a voice at his elbow startled him. A shadowy nondescript of a man had come up with no more sound than a shadow.

"You attend the lord Orsini, don't you?"

"Yes, sir."

"Who has but now entered the Palazzo Varano?"

"Yes, sir."

"I thank you."

And rapidly, but with the silence of a ghost, the dark figure moved on in the direction taken by Ippolito d'Este. The boy followed him with his eyes but a second later saw no one.

Giuseppe's scalp prickled; he crossed himself.

"*Oimè!*" he whispered. "I wonder what he wanted, that specter."

CHAPTER XII

IT WAS too much to expect that a great lady, the wife of Marc' Antonio Varano, would receive a gentleman alone, unattended by her waiting women. But the loggia, overlooking a small, enclosed garden behind the palace, was long; and Mona Emilia, together with Mona Agnoletta and the blackamoor page, Seraph, remained at one end of it, while, almost out of earshot, their mistress conversed with Captain Orsini. Seraph, sprawling on a cushion, went to sleep, with his turban on Mona Emilia's knees; the two women chatted together in low voices. So, in comparative privacy, Andrea could take his bearings and feel his way in that most uncertain element, a woman's opinion. For, in its first stages, love is only a form of reconnaissance.

The place and the hour lent themselves to this purpose. Vibrations of moonlight that flooded the loggia; odors of evergreens, verbena, and roses, exhaling from the garden; bird notes, like drops of music, scattered upon distance; emanations of the past brooding over the old city: all these cast their reflection on the mind to irradiate it.

"You speak well, Messere."

"It is the spirit of the night that speaks, Madonna — its beauty, your beauty."

And for once he did not flatter. The impression Camilla made upon him exceeded words. Even in the more congenial medium of paint and canvas, he knew that he could not have expressed, let alone flattered, her. As they talked, his imagination, instinctively active with line and color and chiaroscuro, straining towards a new technique, admitted despair. How to reproduce the shimmer of moonlight on the satin of her gown, the mingling of pearl and shadow that molded her face, the magic background of the night? And even that would be far easier to catch and interpret than the essential point, Camilla's youth and charm, that gave significance to everything else. No, he concluded, not words or paint, but the art of music, was in some way adequate to express her.

"I'm in doubt of you, Messer Andrea."

"In doubt?"

"Yes — and, let me tell you, Master Lorenzo da Pavia feels the same."

"Doubt regarding what?"

"Whether you're really a soldier."

"Why not, Madonna?"

"Because you speak like a poet, an artist."

"Can I help it — in your presence?"

"Now, now," she protested, lifting a finger, "no compliments. Tell me your secret."

"Is a soldier forbidden to love beauty?"

"You don't answer my question."

81

He shrugged. "Why, then, in all truth, Madama, a soldier. If you doubt it, ask your illustrious husband, my lord Marc' Antonio. He may have heard of me."

To his surprise, she answered: "I *have* asked him. After our meeting in Venice, I wrote him in full. His letter reached me three days since. He speaks well of you, Messere — of a certain bridge in the Regno, whose name I forget, which you and a handful of others held nobly in the teeth of the enemy; of your gallantry at the capture of Forlì. . . . And yet I doubt. I say tell me your secret."

She leaned forward, smiling but intent, her curiously exciting voice stirring his pulses.

"My kinsmen are all soldiers," she went on. "To rule in Perugia, one must fight or die. Yes, and the Baglioni love beauty, which is the wine of life. But none of them speak like you. It is a matter of tone, Messere, something deeper than words. *Eh, davvero!* I agree you have no doubt fought, as my husband tells me, with the French against Naples, with the Barons against the Church, with the Church against Forlì, and that you are now in the service of Ferrara. But what of it? By God, I still say you're an artist, not a soldier."

Andrea hovered between relief and uneasiness. Though noted among the younger captains of venture in Italy, it might well have happened that Marc' Antonio would not have heard of him, and he breathed freer that he had. On the other hand, Camilla's shrewd guesswork was both troubling and stimulating. She had the gift in conversation, rarer than wit, of drawing one out to the best advantage.

He found himself saying: "Perhaps. But a man may be an artist as well as a soldier."

"*Ma che!* A creator as well as a destroyer?"

"Of course. A destroyer in order to create."

She laughed. "I'm not sure I follow Your Lordship. We were speaking of art."

"And am I not speaking of it? The art of the statesman, who uses the sword instead of pen or brush. Does Your Signory restrict the word only to poets, sculptors, and painters? Is government not an art?"

"And is Messer Andrea Orsini not a quibbler?" she murmured. "But have it your way. Soldier or artist, you know I find you unusual."

It was queer, he thought suddenly, how, on an occasion like this, talk bore no relationship to the real issue at hand. Let them talk of King Solomon's beard, but the overtones and undertones followed an utterly different theme, played a separate accompaniment. Not what was said, but the curve of Camilla's lips, the moon-bright aura of her hair, the trimness of her hand, were important. And yet, on the level of speech, this underflow imparted its passion to his thoughts.

"No, not unusual. Our age is unusual, Madonna. Do you not feel it? The future rises upon us like the sun. Mankind has been long asleep, bound by dreams; now he is waking, is conscious of his power, glories in life, and pays God the tribute, long withheld, of finding creation good. Nay, more, by His grace we take it upon ourselves to make creation better. And dawn has come first to Italy. So, then, we Italians are especially artists, in all ways building the new world. But I say again there is much to be destroyed before it is possible to build."

Could he have pleaded his cause any better if he had spoken of love? No — or if, at that moment, he had amused her with trifles. There are times when a woman is courted best by not courting her at all.

Camilla leaned forward. "Destroying what? Building what?"

"Madama, I bare my mind to you. Destroying states, building a nation — the nation of Italy."

It was not a new dream; but he expressed it well, and she listened with parted lips. Plainly, too, she agreed with him and, as a well-read woman educated in courts, easily grasped the vision he outlined. Overshadowed as it was by local loyalties, the memory of the Roman Empire still engrossed the imagination of cultivated people. The city-state — Venice, Florence, Milan, Perugia — might come first; but with many, Italy at least came second.

"Away with the barbarians, Madonna!" Orsini gave a sweep of his right arm. "Away with Frenchmen, Spaniards, Switzers, Germans — *insieme, insieme!* Are we to give up our women to rape, our cities to pillage? Is the sacred soil of Italy to be parceled out by foreign bandits?" His extended arms appealed to Camilla, dropped to his sides, gathered strength again. "And why? Because, by God, Milan, Venice, Florence, Naples, the Papacy, call in these foreign wolves to help them cut the throats of other Italians! And be themselves enslaved! *Ahi, che Dio le perdoni!* Is there no cure? Yes! It stares us in the face. *Eccola!* Union. A central state. A nation strong to defend itself. That — or ruin, death. But he, the statesman-artist, who would bring salvation, must destroy the little before he can build the great."

"*Bravo!*" she admired. "I wish my lord husband could hear you. I think he would agree, even if it cost us our holdings. But, Messere, how? What city could take the lead in this? What city is strong enough or enough beloved?"

"No city. It must be a man, a prince."

"And where to find him?"

"Aye, where?" He did not go beyond this point, but let the spirit of the night, vague and passionate, interpret him. It was one of those hours when imagination lends wings, when the difficult is easy, the dubious, certain. He could not tell her that, if fortune served, if ambition, tenacity, ruse and daring, meant anything, he was the man who intended to play the role he had outlined. Nor could he tell her of the part reserved for her in that plan and how admirably she would fill it. No, only reconnaissance tonight. But perhaps some emanation of his dream, more compelling than words, would express the mood of what had been left unspoken.

He did not know that somehow this happened, that suddenly she perceived him with new eyes, absorbed and yet afraid, was oddly conscious of peril more dangerous because of its attraction.

When he spoke again, it was as if he had been revealing himself to her. "Your Excellence will not betray me? I should have been more discreet."

She answered impulsively by leaning forward and placing her hand a moment on his knee. The touch passed through him like an electric spark.

"Betray you?" But she dropped the personal note at once and added: "Yes, there's the problem: the man." She fell silent a moment, gazing out into the night. "You know, my lord husband could have been such a man, if he had cared for power and if his sons had lived."

Andrea made a show of interest, though the reference to Marc' Antonio chilled him. "*Per Dio*, yes! No lord is more renowned than His Signory."

"He is strong and bold," she went on, "but he is true and merciful. Men follow him because they love him. How shall I say? He has serenity and nobleness of mind. And let me tell you, sir, that I am a right good judge of this, after the feuds and passions of us Baglioni in Perugia, God mend us! Since I was first given to my lord, he has been my hero. He would have built a nation founded on loyalty and justice. I wish you could speak with him."

No relationship between what was said and the true pulse of the night. No hint of disturbing thoughts in her mind that contrasted white and dark hair, an old and a young face.

"I yearn for that honor," bowed Andrea. He thought sardonically of Borgia's promise. "Will His Signory spend the winter in Città del Monte?"

"Yes, after our return from Rome."

The word left Orsini numb for a moment. He doubted his hearing.

84

"*Rome?*"

"It's the Year of Jubilee, isn't it?" she said casually. "We shall pay our devotions at the shrines, like other good Christians."

Rome! She might just as well have said Tophet, as far as she and Varano were concerned. Talk of putting one's head in the lion's mouth! Such simplicity was wicked. Decidedly, thought Andrea, the illustrious Duke Valentino played in luck. He did not even have to pursue his victims: they came to him. But what could Orsini do about it? Indeed, what did he wish to do? It was certainly to his advantage that Varano be eliminated as soon as possible. Considered from that standpoint, the pilgrimage to Rome was a great stroke of good fortune. It meant that Borgia could pay his debt to Andrea as soon as the mission in Ferrara had been successfully completed. It meant Città del Monte and the greater career beyond. Andrea himself would not even be involved; he had only to let events take their course.

And yet something foolish and irrational blurted out, "Is that safe, Madonna?"

"Why not?"

"Because of rumors that a certain prince has designs against all the lords of the Romagna and the Marches."

She tossed her head. "Marc' Antonio Varano is no fledgling. Do you think he would put himself into Valentino's power if he were not sure of him? No, Messere. The Pope's Holiness and the Duke himself have written letters so kind and loving that better could not be imagined. It's hinted that my lord will even receive the Golden Rose at the hands of His Beatitude. We shall visit Rome not only in safety but in honor."

This was not simplicity; it was lunacy. As if such kind and loving letters meant anything more than trap bait! Well, be it on their own heads. Andrea had warned her. He smiled inwardly at the drollness of it.

But another thought sobered him. How could he blame the Varani for trusting the Borgia's honey, when he was doing no less himself? True, the Duke was known as a faithful paymaster to those who served him; but, after all, how could Andrea be sure that the plum of Città del Monte would not fall nearer the tree; that is, to someone in Rome, while he was forgotten in Ferrara? If Camilla and her husband were mad enough to venture into the lions' den, ought not Orsini be there to protect his interests?

With more than casual politeness, he asked, "When do Your Lordships plan this journey?"

"Within the month."

Well, he reflected, by that time he might have won his suit in Ferrara; but even then he would need an excuse to leave. . . . By Bacchus! He had one. This saint whom Ercole d'Este prattled about, the girl in Viterbo. Viterbo was close to Rome. Marvelous how at times everything fell into the right pattern.

The appearance of a servant with comfits and wine reminded Orsini of the hour. His heart sank; he had said none of the thousand things he wanted to say. And when would he again have such an opportunity? But he toyed helplessly with the sugared almond paste and sipped his muscatel, while the moments slipped by.

"Madonna Milla, I count myself the ambassador of the court to you in one urgent matter."

"Indeed, Magnifico? What should concern the court so urgently?"

"That Your Highness may condescend to give the next few days to Ferrara and take part in the hunt day after tomorrow. Far be it from Your Grace's courtesy to deny so many cavaliers and ladies their request — to you at worst an inconvenience, to them an incalculable boon! Let me be a herald of good tidings to the court."

She *must* stay! He set his will upon her answer as if to compel her consent.

To his joy, she hesitated. "You know, my friend, I think you could persuade Messer Saint Peter at the gates of heaven . . ."

"Then show yourself no more forbidding than that saint, Madonna Milla. Grant the request!"

"On one condition."

He set down his goblet of wine on the salver, raised his hand in triumph. "*Any* condition!"

"That you wear the ring I gave you in Venice!"

The blow struck home. Not even the moonlight concealed the imp behind her mock-serious expression, though he could not know that the imp was a screen for something else.

"Yes, Messere, I confess that it grieves me not to find the ring on your finger, in view of your kind remarks when I gave it to you — as if Your Magnificence disdains such a trifle."

The pitfall did not catch Andrea entirely unprepared. He had given much thought to that ring.

"How does Your Signory, guided by what ill star, happen to touch upon the tragedy I had hoped to conceal, the disaster that befell me on the very day we met? Alas, Madonna Milla!"

She followed his lead. "Jesus help us! Disaster?"

86

"Indeed—and worse! Stolen! *Sozzi cani! Che gli vengano mille accidenti!*"
His voice and gestures denounced the imaginary thieves. For a moment, he almost believed in them himself. "I can only cast myself upon the mercy of Your Signory."

"But, sir, how can I know that what you tell me is true, that you haven't given the ring away — to some woman perhaps?"

On this safer ground, he could be as sincere as the Recording Angel. "*Ah, meschino me!* That I should be so accused!"

"Well, the condition stands. You will either wear that ring, or I leave tomorrow for Urbino."

He slipped from his chair to one knee and bowed his head. "Madonna Milla, is not my loss great enough without a double punishment?"

Camilla was not the only one favored by the moonlight. It glanced from the medal of Saint George on his cap to his dark hair, softened his features, transmuted the gold of his mantle to silver.

"I'm afraid you're a sad rogue, Magnifico," she said gently. "I insist on my condition. You must wear my ring. Here it is again."

She slipped something hard into his hand. Spreading out the palm, he found the selfsame ring which she had given him in Venice, the diamond surrounded by pearls; but for once he did not find his voice.

"I came upon it in a jewel shop on the Merceria," she went on, her words edged by laughter. "No doubt the merchant bought it from the thief, eh, Messere?"

"No doubt, Madonna."

Their eyes met, and suddenly they both laughed, laughed so that Seraph raised his heavy turban from Mona Emilia's knees. It was a laughter of understanding, more intimate than a caress.

"Guard it carefully this time, *amico mio.*"

"With my life."

And this time he meant what he said.

"Remember to wear it," she added. "Remember my condition."

He pressed the ring to his lips. "May I wait on you tomorrow?"

"If you will."

When he had taken leave, she stood against one of the pillars of the loggia and gazed across the garden.

At first she was conscious only of the echoes of Andrea's voice lingering in her mind. Intonations and turns of phrase repeated themselves. She laid her cheek against the column and drew a deep breath, inhaling the fragrance of the night. Sensations she had never before experienced vibrated through every nerve of her body. She felt an almost physical change, over which she had no control, taking place in herself. The life of yesterday seemed to her amazingly far off and featureless, as if the past hour had carried her into a new existence expressible only in terms of springtime and dawn — or love? Was this love, this irresistible force? At least it was not love as she had known it.

Then slowly, as thought replaced feeling, the mood changed. A breath of uneasiness chilled her. She recalled Lorenzo da Pavia's warning in the Venetian shop: *Too many faces, Madonna.* And tonight, beneath Andrea Orsini's lovable charm, beneath his eloquence — indeed, the more because of this — had she not been troubled by the same misgiving? What was the real man behind the many faces? She could not find him. She could find only ambition, inspiring enough, as he expressed it, but ruthless even on his own terms. This talk of destroying — but what of those who were destroyed? She could imagine Andrea's recent patron, Cesare Borgia, the statesman and murderer, speaking like that. A suggestive comparison.

And with uneasiness came a growing sense of insecurity, of menace, even of panic. A few minutes ago, she had wondered about love. Now, her straightforwardness faced the truth. Suddenly she realized that she feared Andrea Orsini. She feared him not only for herself. Dismay took possession of her. . . . Something in his voice when he had spoken of her husband, of Rome — she recalled that vividly now. . . . Danger. She could not have explained the intuition, but it had the cogency of fact. Danger to her husband. And she had been on the verge . . .

"Emilia *mia*, Agnoletta," she called out, "see to our packing and give orders. We leave at dawn for Urbino. Make haste. We haven't too much time."

"But I thought Your Ladyship promised the lord Orsini for tomorrow and for the hunt."

"Yes, but I'd forgotten, Emilia. Something important — more important than anything else. *Orsù, andate!*"

CHAPTER XIII

THE Cardinal Ippolito d'Este, with his gentlemen and torchbearers, had not yet reached the Palazzo Bevilacqua, where he hoped to compensate himself for his unsuccessful call at the Palazzo Varano, when, happening to look down, he discovered a drab-looking fellow gliding along next to his right stirrup.

"By God, Ombra," he exclaimed irritably, "if I didn't know that you were flesh and blood, I'd think you were nothing but a nightmare. Can't you announce yourself, man? Do you have to pop up at me like a goblin?"

A cringing voice answered: "Forgive, Your Eminence! I could only wait until it pleased you to glance at me."

"Well, then, what news?"

"If I might speak with Your Excellence apart."

"*A la croce di Dio!* Am I to have no rest day or night!" But Ippolito held up his arm as a sign to halt and, with Ombra at his side, rode some paces forward out of the torchlight. "Well?" he repeated.

"Your Eminence might care to learn that you had hardly left the Via Campo Franco when Captain Andrea Orsini knocked at the Varano Palace and was immediately received."

A moment of heavy silence fell. The Cardinal's hand tightened on his riding whip. Ombra edged back a step.

"Body of Christ!" choked Este. "You have the insolence to tell me that when *I* — when *I* was turned away — "

To save his own skin and his master from a stroke, the other ejaculated, "A political meeting no doubt."

The tension passed: Ippolito, who had risen in his saddle, sank back. Politics. Of course! That could be the only explanation. None other was tolerable. A political plot might be sinister, but it was not a personal affront.

"Humph!" he nodded. "Yes. But keep it to yourself. If I hear any tittering at court about this, it will be the worse for you. . . . Well, His Ducal Excellency will be interested in a link between the Varani and Borgia. . . . I suppose Orsini was attended by his bravo, the man Belli?"

"No, Your Eminence. Except for a linkboy, he was alone. Belli remained at the inn."

"Which means," Ippolito speculated, "a good time to have speech with him, as my lord father suggested. . . . Hark you, Ombra. Take some men and fetch me this same Belli to the palace. At once, *subito*, understand? I'll meet you there. And, by the way, have a couple of varlets from the prison in readiness with their questioning tools. They may be needed."

So it happened not an hour later that Mario Belli, unwashed and unshaven, appeared forcibly before His Eminence in the Ducal Palace behind the castle. He looked so devilish that the armed escort who brought him in could not have treated a tiger with greater respect; and Ombra, reporting to the Cardinal, urged caution on the latter before ushering him into the great man's presence.

Seating himself in a high-backed chair with crimson arm and head cushions, while a page saw to his footstool, Este looked down the bridge of his nose at the door with arrogant curiosity and a dash of suppressed uneasiness. When Mario Belli entered, dark in the light of the flambeaux, the Cardinal's hand stole instinctively to the amulet he wore as a protection against the evil eye. The man was not deformed, Ippolito reflected; he merely gave the impression of deformity. The individual features were not bad; it was their union that clashed, and the expression of the eyes. Not easily deceived by appearances, the Cardinal noted the courtly bow, the delicacy of hand. Here was no common cutthroat. Clearly this man had made a pact with Satan and exhaled hell. Ippolito thought of Andrea Orsini. It must take steady nerves to live with such a familiar. Or was it perhaps fundamentally a case of like master like man?

"By God, I have never seen a fouler face than yours," remarked Este with perfect frankness.

"Alas!"

Something in Belli's voice stung like a nettle. "*Cospetto!* Do you sneer at *me*, rascal!"

Belli sank to his knees. "What shall I say?" he returned with a thin smile. "If Your Sanctity would only deign to instruct me how I have merited Your Eminence's displeasure!"

"*How?*" Aware of Ombra and other attendants at the door, Ippolito dismissed them with a wave of the hand. "*How?*" he repeated when they were gone. "Are you an idiot?"

"Plainly, Your Eminence, and worthy of compassion."

The man expressed himself like a courtier; there was no doubt of that. His accent piqued Este's curiosity.

"Where do you come from?"

"From Savoy, mighty lord."

"And are all *savoiardi* like you: hideous, villains, traitors, and imbeciles?"

"How shall I answer, when I cannot guess what it is that calls down Your Signory's anger upon so obscure an insect as I? Could I have dreamed that Your Eminence had even heard of me? It is said that lightning does not strike at cabbages."

Ippolito d'Este might be a cardinal and a prince, but that did not insure him against the limitations of youth. He began to suspect uncomfortably that he was being jockeyed, though he could not have told just how. For Belli's humility left nothing to be desired; he cringed in the proper way. And yet the twitch at the corner of his mouth, the exaggerated whine of his voice, implied mockery. As if the fellow were unafraid! As if, like a veteran fencer with an amateur, he felt humorously sure of himself! And to this, the Cardinal had no rejoinder but rage and the brute force of his position. It was infuriating to be somehow reminded that he was only twenty-one and overheated.

"You can't guess, eh?" Ippolito clenched his fist on the arm of his chair. "I'll stir up your wits then. . . . Ever hear of Messer Aldobrandino di Guidone, the Ambassador of Ferrara in Venice?"

Belli's face lighted up with enthusiasm. "A noble gentleman. My revered patron."

"Who engaged you," boiled the Cardinal, "for a certain business — yes, and paid you good money for it in advance."

It startled Este that the other, without a sign of embarrassment, merely wagged his head. "Twenty-five ducats. I ask Your Eminence whether that was a sum proportionate to the affair."

"Blast you!" the Prince retorted, off balance. "What have I to do with your twenty-fives? I was saying that you engaged with our ambassador for a sum of money to carry out a certain thing, and that — What are you muttering?"

Belli's jaw was set. "If Your Eminence will bear with me, I demanded fifty; I received — "

"You'll receive five hundred — "

"I thank Your Lordship."

— "lashes on your bare carcass! Will you listen to me, whoreson? You agreed with Messer Aldobrandino for a certain sum."

"Twenty-five beggarly ducats on account!"

"Did you or did you not agree?"

"Ah, my lord, you who have never felt the bite of poverty, how shall I describe — "

"Who asks you to? In short, you agreed?"

"In short, Your Excellence — " A glance at Este's convulsed face showed that the limit had been reached. "In short, I agreed."

"*Finalmente!*" The Cardinal leaned back in his chair. He felt a little tired, and his memory blurred an instant. What the devil was he getting at? Yes, Andrea Orsini. But at this speed it would take all night. He glared at the still kneeling Belli and thought of a fox and thought of a rat. Extraordinary fellow! It would be a saving of time to hand him over at once to the torturers. But, making another scornful effort, he went on. "And then? You carried out the agreement, eh?"

Belli looked complacent. "What a question, my lord! Of course I did."

To such effrontery as this, Ippolito could find no answer at the moment beyond a startled oath.

"Your Sublimity's patience!" Belli added. "I shall explain all. It was not the fee, it was the zeal I cherished for the magnanimous House of Este, the desire I have long had to put my talents at the service of princes so inclined to appreciate them — "

"Ha!" breathed the Cardinal.

"Is it Your Reverence's pleasure to hear what happened?"

"Go on." Ippolito told himself that he would let the rascal exhibit his impudence to the end and then annihilate him. But he began to feel bewildered. Belli's reptilian eyes had a confusing effect. A slight dizziness occurred, and it grew harder to bear in mind what they were talking about.

"Well, then, full of devotion to the glorious House which Your Eminence adorns, I took every proper step for sending the Magnifico Orsini to heaven. The choice of time and place, the choice of tools (for the right knife had to be selected, as Your Reverence knows), the careful observation of Messer Andrea's movements — nothing was overlooked. I felt certain of a neat performance . . ."

The Cardinal found himself distracted by a sort of swaying movement on the part of Belli, who kept shifting from knee to knee, as if the floor were too hard. Negligible at first, the motion gradually affected Este, so that he felt tempted to sway with it, and the effort it cost him not to do so rasped his nerves.

92

"Damn you," he interrupted, "keep still. Do you have to rock like a cradle? Are you drunk?"

"Forgive it, sublime lord. I have an ailment of the joints that makes kneeling painful after a time."

"Well, then, stand up, in God's name!"

"Far be it from Your Highness's slave to address Your Signory except on his knees!"

Belli sagged to the right; the Cardinal wavered in that direction.

"Stand up! Am I to be dazzled by your antics? Up!"

"Since Your Lordship permits."

Belli rose without effort and brushed off his knees. The other stared at him absently.

"What the devil were you saying?"

"About Messer Andrea's midriff."

The Cardinal took a deep breath and exhaled. "Orsini's midriff! Yes, I am mad. What has his midriff to do with anything?"

Belli's eyes were two black points. "But I was telling Your Signory. I say behold his midriff, strip it, finger the scab on it. There's my signature. There's the proof that I kept my word to the noble Aldobrandino. By God, was it my fault that the knife snapped on Messer Andrea's ribs, that he bears a charmed life, that he has the strength of ten lions, that after valor surpassing Gawain or Lancelot, I went down in defeat? Was it my fault, Your Eminence?"

"I suppose not," returned Este, hypnotized.

The other bowed. "I felt sure that Your Eminence would agree with me."

But the Cardinal rallied. Shaking off the spell, he burst out: "Agree nothing, you false rogue! You're safe enough with Orsini's midriff: I'm no scab picker. As for Lancelot and Gawain, I take 'em with salt. The truth is that, paid for killing a man, you sell out to him, pocket both wages, and have the infernal gall to turn up here under our very noses in his service. Talk yourself out of that, scoundrel!"

Belli's face, ugly enough before, turned uglier in its expression of sorrow. He said at last, "Wretch that I am! To be misunderstood!"

"Misunderstood? What is there to misunderstand?"

"My motives, cruel lord."

"Mountebank!"

"No, my lord, far from it. Not mountebank. Hear me. Was not honorable surrender to Orsini my only course? That Your Eminence could think for a moment that I was false in this affects me — " Belli

93

paused — "affects me deeply. Is it not plain that everything I did was governed by zeal and duty and good faith?"

The Cardinal drew his hand across his forehead.

"If I had not surrendered," Belli went on, "if I had lost my life, then indeed Your Eminence could have accused me. As it was, intent on duty, I used my wits. I live and am in the way to carry out the commands of Your Lordship, all the more as Orsini now trusts me."

Once again Ippolito collected his thoughts. He had known wicked men in his time and had few qualms himself; but Belli's depravity impressed him. However, let the fellow settle his own accounts with the devil. Interest required that he be made the most of.

"I'm to believe, then, that you did not sell us out? That you shifted employment only to keep your bargain with Messer Aldobrandino?"

Again the razor-sharp smile. "Obviously, my lord."

"And I can count on you?"

"Like hilt on blade."

"*Molto bene!*" nodded the Cardinal. "*Benissimo!* I am pleased with you. Appearances were misleading. . . . Well, then, take no steps for the moment against the life of Andrea Orsini. We want only a statement about him."

Belli's sinister face lighted up. "I see. Your Divine Sanctity does not wish me to kill him — *for the moment* — only betray him."

"You are a man of intelligence, Ser Mario. . . . It imports us to learn where, on two separate occasions, you and Messer Andrea passed the night after riding out from Ferrara. You were last seen headed eastward through the marshes. Our solicitude for Messer Andrea, which has watched over him day and night, suffered a shock; and the backs of the men who lost touch with you suffered even worse. I'm depending on you to clear up the matter." And when Belli hesitated, coughing a little and squinting at his finger tips, the Cardinal added: "What's more, I expect a straight answer. There're people waiting outside, who have tools to open oysters."

To Este's surprise, Belli laughed. "Well put, Your Highness! It was not that I demurred at answering Your Lordship's question: I burn to tell all I know about Messer Andrea. But a train of thought crossed my mind." He eyed his finger tips again and bit reflectively at the side of one of them.

"What train of thought?"

"May I be frank?"

"Get on with it."

94

"I was thinking of Messer Aldobrandino's twenty-five ducats. The information desired by Your Eminence is important."

The Cardinal gave a resounding *faugh*. "Your thirty pieces of silver, eh, Judas?"

"Make them gold, mighty lord. Nothing like gold to buy a golden servant."

"Hell!" But with Duke Ercole's advice that afternoon in mind, the Cardinal got up, jerked open the drawer of a cabinet, found a purse, and threw it scornfully at Belli, who scooped it out of the air with the ease of a ballplayer.

"*Mille grazie*, noble prince!"

"Now then, where did Orsini ride to?"

"Pomposa."

"The Abbey of Santa Maria in Pomposa?"

"The same, Your Eminence."

Ippolito digested this a moment. The once famous but now desolate monastery on the shore of the Adriatic seven leagues from Ferrara was one of the Cardinal's own benefices. As Abate Commendatario, he enjoyed whatever revenues could still be squeezed from its fishing rights and waterlogged fields. But he seldom visited there. In the tangle of shallow lagoons that made an island of it, mosquitoes and fever diminished its inhabitants and value year by year. A lonely, spectral place haunted by memories. No wonder Ippolito's people had lost track of Orsini in those marshes. What opportunities it offered for a secret rendezvous! Agents of Venice or of Borgia could put in from the sea unsuspected.

"Pomposa? To meet whom?"

"Various men from different parts of Italy."

"Venice? Rome?"

"No doubt, Your Grace."

"Their names?"

"I don't know."

"The purpose of this meeting? What was discussed?"

Belli shrugged. "Your Excellence will allow that the Magnifico Orsini is a prince of foxes. Small likelihood that I should be admitted to his secret parleys. But in the refectory, in my presence, there was much talk of traitors and Judas Iscariots. I did not catch all the drift."

"Hm-m," growled Este. He would have liked to know more, but he already knew enough. An officer of the Duke of Ferrara's guard, plotting with Venetians and Romans on Ferrarese soil. Belli's testimony would suffice. But the latter's next remark doubled Ippolito's pleasure.

"I can put Your Eminence in the way of catching Messer Andrea at the next meeting."

"*Per Bacco!* You can? So there's to be a next meeting? When?"

"Day after tomorrow, the day of the hunt, unless Madonna Camilla Baglione delays things. We were to detach ourselves from the chase, when it scatters, and ride for Pomposa. Your Grandeur might take a full bag that day."

"By God! By God!" Este exulted. "If I don't, call me no huntsman! . . . Ser Mario, I see you are worth your money. You are a fellow of value."

Belli made a leg and a gesture of the hands. "I live to obey Your Mightiness. Are there any orders?"

"Yes. Get back to your inn before Orsini returns. You'll breathe no word of your summons here. If he hears of it, fob him off. Keep me in touch with the plans for Pomposa."

"Have no fear of that, *signor mio.*"

"And, by the way — " in his exuberance, the Cardinal almost laid his hand on Belli's shoulder, but drew it back in time, as if he had been about to touch a snake — "by the way, good Ser Mario, speaking of Madonna Camilla, what can you tell me of Orsini's relations with her? Love or politics?"

The end of Belli's curved nose twitched, as if he were picking up a trail.

"Your Eminence, Messer Andrea is as full of stratagems as an egg is of meat. He lives and breathes politics. Consider the location of Città del Monte in the Marches and Duke Valentino's ambitions. But whether Orsini treats Madama as a dupe or an ally or both, how can I say? Talk about oysters!"

"Well," muttered Este, "we'll open him too, before long. . . . Ser Mario, I thank you. Be faithful in this matter, and you'll not regret it; betray us, and, by God, you'll long for death before it comes. *Hai compreso?*"

Belli cast up his eyes. "The very thought of betraying Your Signory!"

Summoning a page, the Cardinal bade him escort Belli to the gates of the palace. As the lad obeyed, in some awe of his sinister-looking companion, he wondered what pleasant topic had been discussed in the cabinet. For Belli's furtive mouth wrinkled with smiles, and at one point he startled the page by a sound which might have been a dry cough but was curiously like a laugh or — to use the proper term — a snicker.

CHAPTER XIV

To REGAIN his inn, Belli had only to cross the *piazza* and walk south a
few minutes through the pitch-black arcades of the Via Santo Romano.
As he approached the Angel, his recent smiles faded; he moved more
tensely; and, upon reaching the doorway of the tavern, he paused to
listen and peer before going in.

The French carousal was still at full blast; but as far as Belli could
see, the hallway outside the common room was empty, so that he
ought to have no trouble in reaching the stairs to the upper floors without being noticed. His luck had been equally good an hour earlier,
when he had left the inn with the Cardinal's guards. A drunken archer
or two, lounging in the doorway, had paid no attention, all the more
as Belli had kept his face down in the folds of his mantle.

Having reconnoitered, he slipped through the door, with his cap
pulled low and his cloak drawn up. But he would have done better
without these precautions; for he had hardly crossed the threshold
when a couple of burly Frenchmen, taken with the need of relieving
themselves, emerged from the taproom and almost collided with him.
If he had not looked so furtive and muffled-up, they would probably
have passed by, all the more as the lantern hanging from a beam in the
hallway cast only a dim light; but his appearance stirred up the sub-
conscious reactions of drunkenness. Before he could dodge them and
reach the stairs, a broad hand gripped his shoulder and a voice bawled:
"*Seigneur Dieu!* Here's a stinking thief! *Par Saint Jean, vien ça, que je te
donne un tour de peigne!* He nips in to rifle our luggage. Italian dog! Let's
have a look at you!"

Belli did the proper thing. He stood quiet and answered in French:
"Italian dog yourself, comrade! *Nom de dieu!* Can't a gentleman of
Savoy enter his own inn without being called a thief? What courtesy
is this!"

Startled at hearing French, the archer dropped his hand and at
once bubbled over with good feeling. "Cry you pardon, *mon ami!* No
offense!" He turned to his companion. "Hear that, Blaise? The gentleman is one of us, a true heart. Join us, Monsieur. We'll drink a glass
to Savoy. Come along, by God!"

"Gladly," said Belli, on pins and needles. "Permit me to go to my
room, and I'll be with you in a moment."

And during that moment, tipsy as they were, they would forget him, he hoped.

But another soldier now stood in the doorway of the taproom. He was tall, lean, and well-dressed. Even in the poor light, Belli recognized him as Pierre Terrail de Bayard, nicknamed "Spur," one of Count de Ligny's best-known lances.

"Who speaks of Savoy?" he asked in a pleasant, hearty voice. "*Fête dieu!* I've spent some of my happiest years there. Anyone from Savoy—" He stopped suddenly, his eyes dilating. "*Marius de Montbel!*"

And he had hardly spoken when Belli leaped toward the street door.

He would have made it, except for Blaise the archer, who blocked the way and grappled with him. Belli rammed the yeoman with his head and sent in a blow to the chin that half lifted the fellow from his feet. But Blaise did not lose his grip, and the other archer pitched in, locking his arm from behind around Belli's throat. Overpowered, the latter found himself once more facing the scornful eyes of Bayard.

"Marius de Montbel!"

By this time, others were pushing out from the taproom, forming a circle, while the name Montbel passed in crescendo through the group. A ring of lowering faces surrounded Belli. Evidently the gentlemen lances, in the interests of good-fellowship, had been drinking that evening with the archers; for most of the contingent that had escorted Captain d'Ars to Ferrara was present.

An odd change came over Belli, one that submerged the craftiness in his face, the meaner lines of it, by an overlay of black hatred. A sort of fierce nobility confronted Bayard and returned stare for stare.

"*Par dieu!*" he burst out. "Yes, Marius de Montbel. And what of it? I can still look *you* between the eyes." His glance stabbed round the circle. "Any of you. Ha, Messeigneurs, you've come down in the world since we last met. Chicken livers? You see me unarmed; but even so, your lackeys hang on to me." With a tremendous effort, he wrenched himself from the archers and took a step forward, fists on hips. "Lend me a sword. Who cares to step up first? Or do you want to do your butcher's work together? *Je m'en fous!*" He spat. "There lies my gage. Who'll pick it up?"

If there was policy in this, the policy of despair, the hope of a clean death, Belli was disappointed. An answering growl arose, but Pierre de Bayard's voice struck in.

"Will anyone here forget that this man has lost the right of arms? No cavalier crosses swords with a traitor." He blazed at the archers: "Who told you to release the prisoner? Pinion his wrists. Bring him into the common room and guard the door. We have a job to finish."

It was one thing to match wits with the Cardinal d'Este — in that case sophistication fenced with sophistication — but it was another thing to match wits with simple minds like those of the French lances. From Belli's standpoint, they had no wits that he could appeal to. They represented an immemorial code of values as elemental as a force of nature. They were medieval; he had become a modern; and there was no bridge between. Now, standing bound in front of a long table, behind which the lances seated themselves, while the archers formed a half-circle on either side of him, he realized that he was a dead man.

It would have been easier if he had not known his judges so well. Their familiar faces emphasized and reviewed the long rebellion of his life. They rekindled the hatred he felt for each of them, hatred of a misfit for the caste to which he belonged by a trick of birth, but which had despised and made sport of him. He kept his head up, though desperately conscious of the ignoble figure he cut in the cold blue eyes of Pierre de Pocquières, lord of Bellabre. The latter sat next to his friend Bayard, already the beau ideal of French chivalry. And there was Antoine de la Villette, Jacques de Monteynart, Georges de Saint-Gilles — good lances all, popular and Olympian. Belli must not let them see that he feared them.

"I observe that our friend hasn't improved in appearance since he left us," observed Jacques de Monteynart. He laughed. "*Cré dieu!* Who will tell me that treason pays! It looks as if he sleeps in the gutter with the other rats. Wouldn't you expect him at least to scrape the soup from his doublet? You know, gentlemen, I shouldn't have recognized him, except that there're not two such faces under the sun, thank God!" He kept his bold, dark eyes on Belli as he spoke, and enjoyed the effect. "Yes, *mon bel,*" he jibed, punning on the name, "I'm referring to you."

Belli knew that he ought to ignore him, but he could not. He hissed back, "Whoreson and coward!"

And Monteynart laughed.

"Have done!" Bayard exclaimed. "It's unfitting to mock even a condemned dog who has no means of defense. And I tell you frankly, Monsieur de Monteynart, that I'll have no liberties taken with the name of my good friend, Jacques de Montbel, this man's brother."

"*Corps dieu!*" Monteynart retorted inevitably. "When I need a lesson in manners, perhaps I'll ask you for it, Monsieur de Bayard. Until then, I'll decide for myself what's unfitting."

99

"Gentlemen!" soothed Bellabre. "For love of me, do not elaborate this affair. As I see it, no point of honor is involved. You know what Captain Louis d'Ars thinks of needless quarrels in the company. *Eh bien, mes amis!* Your hands on it!"

Anger passed; a handshake was given; good form had been preserved.

And Belli, with the straps cutting into his wrists, did not know which he hated most, Monteynart's taunts or Bayard's intervention. "Idiots!" he thought passionately.

"Comrades," said Bayard, when harmony had been restored, "for the sake of those among us who were not present at the battle of Fornuovo, it is only right that the charges against this man, Marius de Montbel, be rehearsed before we do justice upon him, as is our duty and the King's command. But because of my friendship with his brother, let Monsieur de Bellabre speak on this point."

Bellabre nodded. "If you wish. . . . Messieurs, six years ago, on the march north from Florence, when it pleased the late King Charles to return to France, after having valiantly conquered the kingdom of Naples, we were hard beset for two reasons. First, we had left overmany men behind us in garrison to uphold His Majesty's right; and second, as you know, the Venetians, leagued with Milan, barred our passage. We had no trouble up to Florence. What concerned His Majesty and the captains was to cross the mountains beyond. . . . You've heard all that. Most of you have heard too, for it was common knowledge, that this man, a member of our company" — Bellabre pointed his ringed forefinger at Belli — "out of sheer villainy and black spite, sought to betray His Majesty's army into the hands of the Marquis of Mantua, at that time Venetian general. Letters from him to my lord Marquis were intercepted, laying bare the whole of his practice with said lord: our poor numbers and poorer supplies, the ordering of our force. By the aid of the Devil, he escaped arrest, or he would have been hanged on the line of march for all men to see. He took refuge with the Marquis; but, not content with one treason, he plotted a second and worse."

Bellabre withdrew his hard eyes from Belli a moment to glance around the group.

"And let me tell you, my friends, that this is no gossip or secondhand chatter. Monsieur de Comines had it direct from the Marquis himself, when that lord found it wiser to shift from Saint Mark to Saint Denis. Who was it, on the field of Fornuovo, where only a miracle of God saved France — I say who was it that directed the full heat of the

Venetians against our good King and this company, which had the honor of guarding him? When His Majesty, by a chance of battle, found himself alone in the melee, who was it that pointed him out to the Italian cavaliers and himself joined in the attack? . . . By God, gentlemen, except for the King's own prowess and his horse, Savoy, that would have been a sorry day for us! And who was the traitor and Judas?" Languid with scorn, Bellabre flicked his hand toward Belli. "This ugly cur. Look at him if you can keep your gorge down. To lift his dirty hand against the Majesty of France, shame our company, disgrace the name of cavalier!"

Upon Belli, the closeness of the room, the dim and smoky oil lamps, the ring of implacable faces, the intense silence that, so to speak, framed in Bellabre's words, produced an effect of nightmare. In the circumstances, it was hard to keep up a front. The scornful circle of eyes, directed by Bellabre's hand, riveted into him. A bead of sweat, following the lines of his face, dripped from his chin.

"Therefore, Messieurs, he was degraded from noblesse and hanged in effigy. The order was given to all companies of *gens d'armes* that, if luck served and if anywhere he fell into French hands, he should be hanged in person. And, sirs, our captain-in-chief, the Lord Louis de Luxembourg, Count of Ligny, made a special vow to wipe out the disgrace that Montbel had brought upon our company by once belonging to it. . . . Is this a true statement, Messeigneurs?"

The lances nodded grimly. Bayard asked: "Has the man anything to say in his own defense? If so, let him speak." And the silence weighed heavier than before.

Belli struggled with the dryness of his throat. "Nothing that would count with you. But I'll say this. I'd die happier if any one of you noble obscenities will point out one reason I ever had not to hate you and France and the tripping little King. Betray what? Love and friendship? Go on, tell me how much I had of that with you, how you cherished me, eh! Think over some of the good jokes you played on the Baboon of Montbel. You laughed until I taught some of you, my noble brother included, that the Baboon had teeth. And then you hated. *Sang dieu!* The good King Charles, the Majesty of France! Betray him, who used to call me the court abortion? Betray my name and family? *Merde!* What allegiance did I owe to my father's whip and boot?"

"Is it necessary," put in Saint-Gilles, "to listen to this blasphemy?"

"Speak to the point," said Bellabre. "Did you or did you not commit the crimes I have charged against you?"

"No crimes." Belli put all his strength into a last stare. "Good deeds. My only regret is that they failed."

A shifting and rustling passed through the group, such as marks the end of a court session. Bellabre instructed two of the archers to fetch a leading rope and cast it over one of the upper beams.

"Crimes?" Belli repeated. "What of yourselves? What right do you have over me in the Duke of Ferrara's dominions — or anywhere else? Without trial? Without warrant — "

"No crime," Monteynart mimicked, "a good deed. As for the Duke, he'll approve. You're no subject of his."

And the truth was, as everyone realized, that, whether or not the Duke approved, he would overlook.

Bayard interrupted. "One moment. We've forgotten something. For his body, yes, we have right enough; but we have no right upon his soul. He should be given space to reconcile himself with God. Let someone fetch a priest."

"Why?" demanded Belli. "What do I owe God?" And with a sneer at the circle of startled faces, he added: "*Dea!* As I consider my life, there's more reason that God should reconcile Himself with me!"

The gentlemen crossed themselves. A couple of archers present vowed afterwards that they saw Belli's eyes light up red at the moment, as the demon peered through.

In a cold silence, preparations were now made. The rope was flung over a beam and securely anchored. The noose was knotted at shoulder-high distance above a bench, which would be kicked away under Belli's feet. Bellabre gave a signal. The archers hustled their victim under the makeshift gallows, lifted him to the bench.

Returning from his call on Camilla, Andrea Orsini encountered the frightened landlord of the Angel in the doorway of the inn. The latter, Raffaelo Rosso, was so agitated that every part of him twitched and quivered.

"*Iddio ci aiuti!*" he babbled. "Alas, Your Magnificence! *Ahimè!*"

"What the devil!" Andrea freed himself from Rosso's clutch. "What's wrong with you? Stop cackling!"

"Ser Mario!"

"Well?"

"They're hanging him in there. This very minute — now. I could see through the taproom shutter. I hastened — "

"The French lords?"

"Yes."

Indecision was not one of Andrea's faults. Grasping Rosso by the shoulder, he bestowed a steadying slap on his cheek.

"Listen!" Orsini's black eyes dominated the man. "Run to the Ducal Palace. Find Captain Louis d'Ars — he's lodged there. Tell him what's happened. He may hold these scatterbrains in check. Say that I, an officer of the Duke's, am doing what I can. Quick!"

"But, *signor mio*, why not call on the Duke's guards?"

"That would lead to a riot, bloodshed — trouble with France. Besides, your house would be ruined. Quick!"

"They won't let you in. They're holding the doors."

"They'll let me in." Hitching forward the pommel of his sword, Andrea hammered it against the panel of the taproom door and shouted, "In the Duke's name! . . . *Orsù!*" he repeated to Rosso. "Quick!"

The innkeeper hurried out. The round knob on the pommel of the sword crashed again, cracking the door panel.

"Open in the Duke's name!"

Suddenly Orsini found himself confronting two archers. "Stand back," one of them growled. "Here's none of your business, or the Duke's either."

They might as well have challenged a battering-ram. Driving his shoulder into one of them and straight-arming the other, Andrea burst past them into the room.

CHAPTER XV

A GLANCE informed Orsini that he had arrived in the nick of time. But the same glance made it equally clear that he had thrust himself into a tangle which would require all his wits if he was to get out of it with a whole skin himself, let alone rescue Belli.

Greeted by a blast of amazed and profane indignation, he had no time to think and could only act on impulse.

"*Olà*, Messeigneurs! One word, if you please!"

103

Instinctively he used the French idiom and tone, which he had picked up during the campaigns of the past six years. This, together with his splendid appearance — his stature, the cloth of gold, chain, and medal — delayed attack. Then the Frenchmen recognized him. During the last few days, he had met Bayard, Bellabre, and the others repeatedly at court. They knew him as a man of station and authority.

"*Pour grâce*," he went on, "what outrage is this, that you lay hands on my ensign without word to me? *Ventre Saint Quenet!* I am amazed! Is this the deportment to be looked for from gentlemen of France? I demand an explanation."

Boldness, not humility, was the right tack. His eyes shifted, challenging, from one face to the other. Tension slackened. For the first time, he exchanged glances with Belli and noted the vague conjecture in the latter's face.

Bayard spoke for the others. "So the man's your ensign, is he? *Fête dieu*, Monsieur d'Orsini, you are villainously squired. How well do you know this ensign?"

"Well enough to protect him until I hear of what he is accused."

"Then I hope you do not know that Marius de Montbel is a notable traitor to the King of France. I should be loath to think that a cavalier of your reputation wittingly enlisted such vermin in his service." Bayard rapidly reviewed the charges against Belli. He added: "These are proved, nor does he deny them. We are hanging him at the command of His Majesty and according to our vow. *Eh bien*, Monsieur, there's your explanation. Have the goodness to stand back and allow us to proceed."

Andrea thought fast, but he could see no way out of the dilemma. With no reflection on his courage, prudence and sound policy required that he stand back. A brawl with these gamecocks would land him nowhere except in the grave and would not help Belli. Even if he survived, he would have offended the French and, through them, the Duke of Ferrara, who had been downright in forbidding any quarrel with them. To accomplish his mission, he must keep on the good side of both parties. He would be a fool to risk his future for a rascal like Belli, who might be useful but was not indispensable. Outnumbered twenty to one, it was no disgrace to accept the fact with a shrug of the shoulders.

The devil of it was that something deeper than policy pleaded for Belli at that moment. Perhaps the peasant, perhaps the modern in Andrea ranged him against the cocksure aristocrats behind the table. Glancing from their haughty, conventional faces at Belli's embittered ugliness, Andrea, as an artist, could perfectly understand the conflict between them. He remembered Belli's passionate riddle earlier that evening and the self-revelation it implied. "What justice? That's the riddle." It was too bad that Andrea had to witness the last scene of this fundamental injustice and could do nothing about it. Well, no: there was at least something. He could try to gain time.

"You force a hard decision upon me, Messeigneurs."

Jacques de Monteynart rapped out: "What decision? I can't see that you have any to make, except to remain here or leave, as you choose. *We*'ve made the decision."

The man's tone was a blow in the face. Frenchman to Italian, master to underling. Andrea's blood boiled, but he kept his head.

"Indeed? I think you misunderstand me, Monsieur de Monteynart. I happen to be an officer of the Duke's Excellence. You and these gentlemen have taken the Duke's law into your own hands. But also you are His Signory's guests. I repeat, you force me to a hard decision."

"Meaning," scoffed the other, "that you might seek to prevent us from doing what we please? Oh, gentle Monsieur d'Orsini, think better of it." He winked at Antoine de la Villette. "Think better of it."

The temperature in Andrea's veins rose higher. Something else was now involved beyond the fate of Belli: dignity, self-respect, all the usual pretexts for a fight. But it served no purpose to fight and get beaten; he meant, if possible, to keep these barbarians for once from doing what they pleased. And that took wit. On this level, as an Italian, he felt superior.

He shrugged. "I crave advice, my lords. In my present position, I could find no better guidance than yours. Put yourselves in my place. How should I act? If I uphold the law of Ferrara against you single-handed, I lose my life; if, as an officer of the Duke's, I fail to uphold it, I lose my honor."

It was the master word for these men. Andrea knew that the ears of all five lances pricked up as if at the sound of a trumpet. If he could start a debate on the point of honor, it might take a good while.

The gentlemen's reactions varied. "That's your business," declared Monteynart. "You forced yourself into the pickle and can get out of it as you please. Of course everyone knows what a French cavalier would do in the circumstances. Given a choice between life and honor, he would not ask advice. I say a *French* cavalier. But honor with us has a special value. In Italy it rates lower. So, act like an Italian, *mon ami*, and enough said. . . . Archers, get on with the job. We'll finish Montbel, while his master decides whether to live or die."

Bellabre interrupted. "Not so fast. We have all known good men in Italy, who yield to none in the pursuit of honor. Certes that, too, is the reputation of Monseigneur d'Orsini. He turns to us for advice, as a fellow cavalier, and deserves consideration. There must be some way —"

Once again Andrea caught the eye of Belli. The latter's lips twitched in a faint smile, as if he recognized the red herring which Orsini had drawn across the trail and took comfort in the French pursuit of it.

Their fool honor! thought Andrea. By Bacchus, yes, it rated lower in enlightened Italy, thank heaven! Honor of cut and thrust, brawn and muscle! Schoolboy nonsense!

Bayard was saying: "I agree with Pierre de Bellabre. We should lower the honor of French men-at-arms if we did not respect it in the cavaliers of other nations. Monseigneur d'Orsini speaks well and boldly; I have no doubt he would back his words. We must, therefore, accommodate him in this matter. He should be given every means of maintaining his honor, with an even chance of his life."

An eager wistfulness showed in Bayard's voice and began to kindle in the eyes of the others. They sniffed with delight what he was getting at.

He addressed Orsini. "My lord, you spoke of engaging us all single-handed. But surely you would not put such an affront upon French chivalry as to imagine that we would take the advantage of our numbers against you. No, sir, I propose a fairer course. Let one of us, chosen by lot, uphold our right to hang the traitor, Montbel. Do you, on your side, maintain your duty as an officer of Ferrara. If you kill or disable your opponent, then let Montbel be handed over to your Duke for judgment. In that case, you will have honorably acquitted yourself. If, on the other hand, unfortunately, you should be killed or disabled, Montbel must hang; but you will still have a clear conscience. Do you agree, sir?" He turned to the others. "Do you agree, gentlemen?"

The cavaliers nodded enthusiastically. Excitement whipped through them; this was better sport than they had looked for. Saint-Gilles smacked the back of one hand into the palm of the other. "Trust Spur to hit the nail on the head!" The archers growled applause.

Orsini bowed. "Monseigneur de Bayard, a most gentle and generous proposal! I can only thank Your Lordship."

With this respite over, he could think of no other pretext to gain time and he raged inwardly at the stupidity of the whole thing. What, to these northern fire-eaters, was a thrilling chance to win honor seemed to Andrea a clumsy defeat. He ought to have been able to outtalk such idiots without coming to blows. But subtlety made no impression on them. If only the cursed innkeeper would arrive with Captain Louis d'Ars!

"We'll dice for it," shouted La Villette. "Dice here! The one of us who throws the highest main wins. In case of a tie, cast again."

A rattle and clicking sounded. Heads together, the men-at-arms bent over the table. Prayers to the saints and oaths accompanied the roll of the dice. Intensely interested, the archers crowded round; even the two who were guarding Belli forgot him and craned their necks in the same direction. "Five and four, by Saint John!" came the voice of Monteynart. "Best yet! Ten candles to Our Lady of Paris if I win!"

Andrea noted that Belli's haggard expression had been replaced by a look of deep concentration; and, observing a slight movement, he guessed the cause. Belli's hands, pinioned behind his back, were no doubt plucking at the cord that bound them. In view of the lack of time, this was probably useless. But a stroke of Andrea's poniard would do the trick. Eying the two archers on either side of Belli, he calculated the chances and decided against it. He could not effect Belli's escape that way without ruining himself.

A roar rose from the group at the table. Bayard had thrown two sixes and won. Bellabre clapped him on the back, but several of the others gloomed. "It isn't fair," Monteynart sulked. "Why should you have all the luck? Every time there's a chance for honor, you manage to get it. If you'll let me take your place against Orsini, I'll give you my horse, Rohan."

Bayard's rugged face was glowing. He had already slipped off his mantle and was loosening his doublet across the chest for greater ease of movement. "*Nenni, mon ami!* Ask me anything but that. You can take my wench or my purse if you like, but not Monseigneur d'Orsini." He kicked aside one of the benches. "Clear a space, archers. Jacques, hand me my sword."

Talk about luck! thought Andrea. Talk about honor! He detested both.

With his mind on the innkeeper, he slowly removed his cloak and mantle and took time with the upper lacing of his doublet. Bayard, impatient to begin, tapped the floor with the point of his sword. Meanwhile, the center of the room had been cleared and a circle formed. Belli, removed by his guards to one side, kept the same dogged and remote expression.

"May I ask, my lord," said Orsini, "what rules govern our encounter? Is the poniard allowed?"

"To my thinking," returned Bayard, "anything is allowed. Our meeting is irregular and does not admit of rules. I shall use my poniard if I need it. . . . But, sir, let me suggest that time is passing. I beg you to show me the color of your steel."

Andrea unsheathed with a flourish and, as if in answer to Bayard's hint, the light ran blue along the blade.

For a moment, the two men eyed each other. In regard to stature and build, they looked a good match. But although, by Italian standards, Orsini was reckoned an accomplished swordsman, he considered himself a novice in contrast to the single-minded French professional. If he had been faced by any other of the men-at-arms, he would have felt less concern; but this was Bayard, who even at that time bore the proud qualification, soon to become world-famous, of *without fear and without reproach.*

"I'll give five to one on Spur," said Bellabre. And he found no takers.

Smoothly, almost casually, the Frenchman stepped in. But when, at the same moment, Andrea thought to catch him off guard by a sudden flick of his blade in quarte, Bayard parried and smiled and whipped back a riposte, which, though parried in its turn, jarred Andrea's arm from wrist to shoulder.

"Not bad," approved Bayard, with a shift from cut to thrust at Orsini's throat, that the latter avoided only in a split second by leaping back. "Not bad, Monsieur. You have a good eye. . . . How's this?" A feint, a slash in sixte, a dazzling moulinet, as the blade wheeled and came down in prime. All parried, though at the cost of extreme effort and tingling muscles. "Excellent! You delight me! *Fête dieu,* I see I have my work cut out."

Bayard's eyes sparkled; he balanced gaily, as if at a dance, his whole being rising, as a wave rises, toward a crest, a surge of joy and power. He lived for moments like these, with honor as the prize: one more deed of arms to be told and retold around the campfires. If he died, it was the death he sought; if he conquered, it was the best that life could give him. His advantage over Orsini was largely a psychological advantage. For while Andrea stubbornly parried the shower of blows, he was not fighting for honor but for life. To die in a common taproom, relinquish his career, the affairs of state, his dreams of the future, for such balderdash as this was a bitterness beyond words. His fury against it nearly equaled in intensity Bayard's rapturous enthusiasm.

Then, to Andrea's surprise, the French cavalier stepped back out of range and lowered his weapon.

"*Halte-là!* One moment! I did not at first perceive the difference in our swords."

Andrea held onto his breath. "What difference?"

"*Cré dieu*, the length. I outreach you by a quarter of a span. I'll not accept the advantage."

"It's a small matter."

"Small matter nothing. You promise me a good bout, Monsieur d'Orsini. You're a man of worth. If by luck I should win, do you think I want it said that I had the reach of you by two inches of steel? No honor in that! . . . La Villette, *mon ami*, lend me the new blade you bought in Milan. I think it will serve." And when the sword was handed over, Bayard insisted on laying the flat of it upon Orsini's. . . . "There," he nodded. "The same length — point to hilt. That's better."

His sportsmanship was contagious. Andrea protested, "You have the disadvantage of a strange sword."

"Think nothing of it. I frequently change weapons for the sake of practice."

But already, indeed, Andrea was thinking of something else. His eye, trained to the forge, had noted a small speck on the new blade. Probably it meant nothing more than a surface dimple; but specks like that sometimes betrayed an inner flaw, the lurking fragment of dross ambushed in the steel. If it did in this case, it might make all the difference between life and death.

"*A vous*, Monseigneur!"

Bayard sprang in again. Cut and thrust alternating; quarte, sixte, septime, prime, faster — faster. But this time Andrea, parrying desperately, hammered as much as possible above the center of the blade, where the possible flaw lay. In vain. Nothing happened. The tempo of Bayard's attack quickened, as if his speed had no limit; and meanwhile Andrea realized that he had reached the end. He could not stand the pace. His arm felt numb, leaden; sweat blinded him; his breath was gone. He wondered, indeed, that he had been able to survive thus far.

He was dimly conscious of the bystanders, the roar and stamping that greeted some particular turn of the fight; but, for the most part, consciousness narrowed itself to the immediate second. Now, at close quarters, steel grinding steel; now, leaping back or to the side, twisting, circling; now, in again.

He foresaw the last cut but knew that he could not stop it. A weak parry succeeded only in deflecting the blow, which flashed down upon the gilded lead medal of Saint George on his cap, severed it, bit through the velvet beneath —

A miracle happened. It would remain forever a miracle to the simple men-at-arms who witnessed it.

Something clattered to the floor. Bayard stepped back, staring at the mere stump of his sword. A groan went up, as Andrea, rallying to what had happened, lurched forward with his blade in hand.

He had every right to use his advantage. No rules had been stipulated. He had disarmed his opponent and could not be condemned for imposing death or surrender. But foolishly he withheld. Perhaps the look in Bayard's eyes stopped him.

"Take another sword, Monseigneur," he gasped.

"I will not," returned Bayard, breathing hard himself. "I will not, by God — when my lord Saint George intervenes against me for maiming his image. It demands penance."

"Then you admit defeat?"

"I do not." He whipped out his dagger. "I spoke of penance acceptable to a cavalier like Monseigneur Saint George. He does not stomach cravens. Kill me if you can. I would rather die than forfeit honor in this affair — "

A shout of protest rose from the lances and archers. Bellabre, leaping forward, locked his arms around his friend. The others crowded in. No point of honor was involved. Bayard should take another sword, as the gallant Monsieur d'Orsini permitted; or he should concede the fight. Who was he to defy the saints? What discredit attached to a gentleman for accidentally provoking heaven? Nay, by God, such a miracle demanded submission from a good Christian. And ought a brave and loyal cavalier aimlessly throw away his life for the sake of a traitor like Montbel? . . . The room heaved with tumult.

"Let me alone," stormed Bayard. He shook off the restraining arms of Bellabre, shouldered the others back. "I'll decide for myself, by your leave! Throw away my life? Pooh! I'll certainly not throw away this chance for honor in fighting Monseigneur d'Orsini at a trifling disadvantage — though I thank him for his courtesy. I'd fight him with my bare hands — "

A great voice thundered from the doorway: "You'll put your bare hands in your breeches, sir, or I'll have them hacked off. *Mort dieu!* Do you break the laws of this good Duke, His Majesty's friend and ally? Do you disobey my orders? Did I appoint you from our company to brawl in taverns or to help me support His Majesty's interests in Ferrara? You pack of puppies! *Foi de gentilhomme!* I'll have you cashiered for this — the lot of you. Wait till I report your doings to the Viceroy in Milan!"

Andrea gave a sigh of relief and leaned back against a table to catch his breath. Louis d'Ars's burly figure strode through to the center of the room, his eyes blazing, his face grim. He apparently turned a deaf ear to the babble of explanations. It was only at the name of Montbel that his attention quickened.

"Ha? Well, there's sense in that at least. So you've got him, have you? Still, you should have brought him to me. . . . Where is the bastard?"

"Here, Your Worship."

A stricken silence followed. Faces lengthened. Empty glances ranged here and there.

Belli had disappeared.

CHAPTER XVI

WHEN Captain Louis D'Ars had finished reviling the evening's performance of his young subalterns, honor cut a poor figure. Having laid their hands on the scoundrel Montbel, they had let him slip through their fingers to the grief of God. They had broken the Ferrarese laws and prejudiced the King's business. As for Andrea Orsini, his credit had correspondingly risen. What honor there was belonged to him. Even Jacques de Monteynart admitted that no French cavalier could have borne himself better.

But from Andrea's standpoint, this was only froth. It was clear enough that his connection with Mario de Montbel remained suspect in the eyes of d'Ars and the others. His next interview with the French Captain on the subject of Borgian aid in Naples, as a return for King Louis's co-operation in blocking the Este hopes of a French marriage, would be more constrained than the last. And that was not the worst. It would not help him when the news of the fracas reached Duke Ercole, as reach him it would, when the French demanded a hue and cry after Belli. Nothing at the moment so concerned the Duke as pleasing the

French envoys. By this luckless fight, Orsini had given Ercole d'Este every pretext he needed to imprison, execute, or banish him, a pretext that Cesare Borgia himself would be forced to approve.

Disconsolately, he bade the French cavaliers good night and started for his room. Bayard accompanied him to the door.

"Monseigneur d'Orsini, it grieves me that you should have been cheated of complete victory in our pleasant encounter by" — he lowered his voice — "an unhappy interruption. If it would please you at any time to renew the debate on the same terms — I mean your sword against my dagger — I should be more than glad, I should be honored, to oblige you."

Holy Saints, thought Andrea, if ever these donkeys cornered him again might the devil take him and them together! But he managed to smile.

"Your valor, my lord, is only exceeded by your courtesy. You know as well as I that you're the better man, and I count myself fortunate to have escaped on such easy conditions. Believe me, I'm more than satisfied."

The other looked disappointed. "You're quite sure?"

"Quite, Monseigneur."

"Well, then, I take your word for it. But *I'm* not satisfied. Your gallantry in offering me another sword, when you had so clear an advantage, leaves a debt upon my honor. Sir, I'm not a man of fine words; but, without compliments, I remain your servant. If on any occasion, in war or peace, you should need my help, and I am within reach, I beg you to call on me. Saving only my duty to the King, my sword and purse are yours to command. Monseigneur, I mean what I say, believe it."

His muscular hand clasped the cross hilt of his poniard, confirming the promise. At another time, the old-fashioned phrases might have amused Orsini; but now he felt touched. It was unlikely that he would ever turn to Bayard for help, but the latter's directness and manhood were refreshing. At the moment, in contrast to his own complexities, Andrea found them enviable.

"None of your monkey tricks, Spur!" boomed d'Ars from the center of the room. "We'll have no more fighting."

"God forbid, *mon capitaine!*" Bayard grinned.

Andrea warmly shook the hand outstretched to him and then plodded upstairs.

Worn out, and with every muscle slack, he sat dully on the edge of his bed, too tired to undress or even to kindle a light. The events of the evening drifted back and forth through his mind. He found it impossible to think of tomorrow. Let come what would, Andrea could now do nothing about it. Indeed, could anybody do much about anything? What was the use of foresight, of policy, when luck ruled the game as it pleased? How could he have avoided the entanglement that drew him into the silly duel with Bayard? Only by keeping out of the common room and letting Belli hang. That one impulsive step across the threshold, and the rest followed inevitably.

Through the window facing him drifted an occasional breath of air that felt late as the hour. The wakeful city had at last gone to sleep, and Andrea was conscious of almost complete silence. Little by little, the throb of his pulses, the jumble in his mind, faded out. His head drooped.

Then, suddenly alert again, he found himself staring at the black torso of a man, who had popped up outside the window, blocking it. At the same moment, a leg appeared over the sill, and, quiet as a cat, the apparition slithered in.

Orsini sprang to his feet; but as the figure straightened up, its silhouette against the faint light of the window revealed the beaked nose and jutting chin of Mario Belli.

"What the devil! You?"

"Yes, who else? Your Lordship didn't think I'd sleep without thanking my deliverer?"

"But, man, if you're taken! The Frenchmen are still downstairs."

"Not likely they'll look for me here," returned Belli. "The safest hiding place is always under the constable's bed. But I grant that dawn shouldn't find me in Ferrara. So I came back to bid Your Magnificence farewell and, as I said before, to thank you."

Andrea's bitterness overflowed. "A fine pickle you got me into! I'll fare to purgatory in the company of other ghosts down under the castle, or, at best, I'll fare out of Ferrara and out of my office. That's about what you've cost me!"

A full minute passed before Belli answered.

"Your Lordship overlooks a certain point, I believe."

"What?"

"The pride of the French. They're not apt to complain against you. On the contrary, they'll sing your praises. They may not like your connection with me, but they'll paint you up to Duke Ercole as a second Roland. It wouldn't do to have one of their best lances come off short in a fight of his own choosing and then accuse you for fighting him. Honor forbid! No, they'll make much of both you and Bayard: a glorious, inconclusive battle. If the Duke took measures against you now on that score, he'd offend more than he pleased them. So, as far as the duel's concerned, I think he'll do nothing for the moment. Your Lordship may have time to finish your business."

Chewing this over, Andrea felt a little easier. There was a good chance that Belli might be right. He was usually right in forecasts involving the French.

After a pause, Belli added, "You have an audience tomorrow with Don Alfonso, haven't you?"

"Yes, in the cannon shop, to look at his bombards."

"Then make the most of it, Messere. Aside from the fight, my guess is that at best you haven't too much time."

How Belli had arrived at this opinion, whether by special knowledge or instinct, it was hard to judge. In any case, Andrea shared it himself. He had a strong feeling that the success or failure of his mission in Ferrara would be settled in the next day or two.

"Know anything definite?" he asked.

"How should I? Call it a sixth sense." Belli's form, shapeless in the darkness, detached itself from the stool. "It's time I took the road."

"Where are you going?"

"That's what I'm waiting to hear. . . . Where Your Lordship commands, of course."

Andrea started. "What have my commands to do with it? Go where you please."

"How! I don't quite grasp — " Belli's voice expressed shock. "Does it mean — can Your Greatness mean that you *dispense with my services?* Are you so devoted to the French as to exclude me from your favor because I hate them? Surely not, my services — "

"For God's sake, what services? How can you serve me when you have to leave Ferrara?"

The answer was prompt. "In Pomposa, signore. You've not yet finished there."

"Humph! Yes. But — "

"And is it wise," Belli hinted, "to dismiss me at the very moment when you wish that great work to be kept secret?"

Andrea recalled the old legend of the devil. Once give him house-room, and he remains forever.

"Besides," the other went on, "I'm convinced that Your Magnificence will soon be traveling — for one reason or another. Well, sir, I can help you anywhere better than here: in Viterbo, if it seems wise to kidnap that saint His Signory spoke to you of; in Città del Monte, if you wish to — "

"One moment." Andrea leaned forward, his hand, invisible to Belli, on the Medusa hilt of his knife. "What do you know about Città del Monte and my wishes?"

"Nothing, nothing at all." Belli did not need to see Andrea's hand. "I meant only that Your Lordship's regard for Madonna Camilla made a visit likely, and that I — "

"Keep your thoughts from her," said Orsini.

"As my lord desires. . . . Then there's Rome. Am I permitted to suppose that you'll be returning there in the not too distant future? Now, Rome is a city of quicksands, where a man of enterprise, like Your Greatness, might need my talents, now especially devoted — "

"Why *especially?*" Andrea put in.

"Can you ask? Let me say that no one on earth would have done for poor Mario Belli what Your Lordship did tonight. Have I no gratitude? Do I cling to your service for any other reason?"

Andrea could not see, but he could imagine, the shifty smile that contradicted the words. And yet he imagined, too, that they were perhaps not wholly false.

"Remember how I said," continued Belli, "that you and Saint George are twins. After the conduct of Your Magnificence tonight, who could deny it? Few gentlemen of my trade have the privilege of serving so triumphant a captain."

Andrea burst out laughing. "I'll admit this much, that the lead medal you recommended saved my life more surely than if it had been true gold."

"A moral reflection, of deep significance, my lord! Have the wisdom to cherish another lead medal, named Mario Belli, which I am also recommending. Gilded or not, it might serve its turn."

A silence of hesitation fell. Then Andrea said, "*Va bene.* Wait for me at Pomposa."

"Pomposa it is," approved Belli. "My humble thanks!"

A moment later, he had swung out through the window. Ippolito d'Este's gold purse weighed heavier in his pocket than on his conscience.

CHAPTER XVII

IT DID not improve Andrea's spirits next morning to be awakened by a page in the Varano livery, who handed him a polite note of farewell from Camilla. With a lengthening face, he read that, on second thought, she felt compelled to rejoin her husband in Urbino, while regretting the pleasure which the hunt and Orsini's company would have afforded her. She hoped that they would meet again and that her husband would be favored by his acquaintance. Nothing more.

Propped up against the backboard of his bed, he gazed blankly at the letter.

"When did Madonna leave?" he asked the page.

"At dawn, sir."

"What road?"

"To Ravenna. Her Excellence follows the coast through Rimini and Pesaro, then cuts in toward the mountains by the valley of the Foglia."

Orsini swung a leg over the edge of the bed. If he rode fast, he could easily overtake Camilla and her escort before they had gone two leagues. Perhaps he could persuade her to return; at least he could bid a proper farewell. But a sobering afterthought checked him. He could not afford to miss the all-important audience that morning with Don Alfonso at the castle. Too much depended on it.

"*Dolente a me!*" he chafed. And addressing the page, "I suppose you'll be rejoining Her Ladyship."

"By the time she reaches Argenta, God willing."

"You are fortunate, my friend. Tell Her Signory from me that I dare not face the court with the news of her departure, and that my heart is as broken as her promise. . . . Wait a moment: hand me my tablets there."

Balancing a letter case across his knees, he labored with his quill. Having sanded and sealed the paper, he handed it over to the page.

When the boy was gone, he stared moodily out of the window at the neighboring chimneypots; but what he saw was Camilla's little cortege on the broad highway to the coast. He could almost hear the tinkle of the bells on her mule's bridle. His thought strained after her toward the south. Why had she so abruptly changed her mind after their parting last night? He reviewed every minute of the hour he had spent at the palace, but he could find no cause for the sudden reversal of her agreement to spend that week in Ferrara. Possibly it was his lie about the ring that had offended her. But it seemed to him that the laugh they had had together afterwards had more than atoned for it.

From his purse on the bedside table, he drew out the ring and sat turning it between his fingers. His first act that morning would be to get it enlarged at a goldsmith's. But he no longer thought of the added éclat the diamond would give him, as he had in Venice. The ring now implied something much deeper than vanity, something that he did not quite understand himself and for which he felt an odd disquietude.

Until now, he would have said that he knew as much about love as most men. It had been one of the condiments of living, like wine and food. From the sweetheart he had had in his teens up to his latest and most distinguished affair last June involving Angela Borgia, the enchanting cousin of Duke Cesare and Madonna Lucrezia, he could look back on a considerable number of conquests. But suddenly it occurred to him that until now he had never known love at all, this ferment of the mind as well as of the senses. He found himself torn between its imperious attraction and the fear of what it might entail. He could lose his heart, but he dared not lose his head if he was to reach his political goal. He realized all at once that ambition and love might not make good bedfellows, that a choice between them might be necessary.

Well, what were brains for but to use at such a pinch? Meanwhile, by God, he was in love! He was more in love every moment. The thought of Camilla absorbed him, as he dressed for his appointment at the castle.

Alfonso d'Este had set up his cannon smithy on a lower floor of the Tower of the Lions. Here, without cloak or doublet, sweaty, sooty, and shoulder to shoulder with common workmen, he superintended the manufacture of his guns, laid hand to tongs or hammer if he felt inclined, and knew more about forging and welding than most of his smiths. At court or on diplomatic missions for the duchy, he moved in a strait jacket of policy and ceremonial; but here he could roar and joke, unleash his muscles, and be concerned with no other conventions than the laws of manipulating iron. The hobby gave scope for his creative urge, his absorbing interest in the development of the new tool of war. Upstairs, the poets sang of Roland and Oliver and medieval glamour; downstairs, in the same castle, were being made the cannon that would help blow medievalism out of the world. The Este guns would turn the tide at Ravenna and proclaim the supremacy of fire power; they would break the ranks of the invincible pikemen at Mari-gnano; they would drive back the Venetians from Ferrara. For, if his father built the modern city, Alfonso built cannon to save it. But indeed, like others of his time, he was building more than he guessed: for good or evil, a new age.

"It comes back to powder," he shouted at Andrea above the din of the anvils, "always powder. Solve me that problem, and you'll make your fortune. If cannon could stand the right charge of hand-gun powder instead of our having to use this obscenity serpentine, look you what would follow. *Range*, in the first place. I'll bet you the day will come when you can train cannon at a thousand yards — maybe two thousand."

Andrea registered astonishment, but he took the prophecy with a grain of salt. Allowance had to be made for Alfonso's enthusiasm.

"Then, there's the shot. An iron ball's worth three of stone; but ram me in enough of this serpentine to throw iron, and you risk your gun. We have to do it, of course, in siege work — and foot the bill. Powder again, you see. And for the same reason, I'm forced to fiddle with wrought iron, which takes time but is stronger than bronze or iron casting. Though we'll come to that; we'll come to it soon."

They were looking down at a bombard built of wrought-iron bars welded together to form a barrel and reinforced on the outside by iron hoops, shrunk on and forming a second barrel. In principle, it was not unlike the modern built-up gun.

Andrea, attracted by anything new in art or science, followed the Prince's remarks intently. He forgot temporarily Alfonso's rank and even forgot the ulterior purpose of this interview. For the moment, they were only two minds fascinated by a scientific problem.

The Prince spat thoughtfully. "Of course I'm stressing but one mem-ber of the equation. There's the question of metal on the other side: the resistance of metal to equal the pressure of the charge."

"What of design?" put in Andrea, roaring in his turn. "Why not the resistance of metal plus design to equal the pressure of the charge?"

Alfonso fingered his still youthful beard and nodded. "Yes, there's much to that. You know, Messer Andrea, as compared with some of our court, you don't talk like an ass. Design surely. What did you have in mind?"

"Reinforcing the breech," Orsini shouted. "In the case of a casting, wouldn't that offset the softness of bronze or the brittleness of cast iron? You'd then have an elongated cone instead of a cylinder. Or why not cast your piece and then reinforce, as now, with wrought iron? Thus."

Stooping down, he sketched out both suggestions in the soot of the floor.

"I've thought of it. Look here." Este led him over to a cabinet against one of the walls and drew out papers covered with the designs of several molds. "There's beauty, eh? And much according to your thought. I said we would come to casting soon. We plan to name that cannon 'the Earthquake.' . . . Tell me, sir, how did you learn about the properties of metal? I'll wager there's not one in ten of our gentlemen who knows the difference between wrought and cast iron, not to speak of the ingredients of bronze. Sometimes you talk like a craftsman. Your company pleasures me."

Andrea improvised. "The lord Fabrizio Orsini took great interest in the forging of iron, and I learned much from him. As to bronze, I had the privilege of frequenting the learned Master Antonio Pollaiuolo when I was last in Florence. The progress of any craft interests me, but especially of this right subtle craft which Your Signory favors. The future of war may depend on it."

"*Will* depend on it," amended Este; "and upon war, the future of history. Look you, sir, I have a liking for you. You are a man of intelligence and enterprise. I can talk with you. Consider these guns." He pointed out the rows of cannon, culverins, falcons, and smaller pieces. "These are toys compared with what shall be. Look you . . ."

He began dreaming aloud, his heavy voice, appropriate to his whole leonine appearance, rising above the clanging of hammers and bustle of the workshop. He dealt with the future of ordnance; with the development of precision in aiming; with the development of fuses that might make possible an explosive shell against troops; with the improvement of the *baricado* or *orgue*, a contrivance of small pieces arranged, like organ pipes, for rapid fire. As he followed his thought from one subject to the next, stopping at times to discuss some question raised by Andrea, his stature grew in the latter's opinion. It might very well be that Alfonso d'Este, with his guns, fitted the role of Italy's supreme prince better than the half-Spanish Borgia. He would be more acceptable to native prejudices. The feasibility of shifting from one to the other had to be borne in mind.

Meanwhile, Andrea paid court by proving an excellent listener. It was not often that Alfonso found anyone to talk to about his hobby on such even terms, and his cordiality grew. When noon arrived, he insisted that Andrea accompany him back to the San Francesco Palace, his official residence at that time near the church of the same name.

"No, Messere," he declared, drawing together his shirt laces over his broad chest, "we'll not part yet. You'll bear me company at table, I hope. There're still several matters. . . . You say you have skill with the pencil?"

"Very indifferent, my lord."

"I doubt that. But in any case, I want you to see some drawings of a new bombard carriage. You might improve on them. The profile's all right, but I need a cross section. Keep your modesty in your pocket."

He resumed his doublet and mantle with a sigh, roared a hearty *a rivederci* to his workmen, and sallied out with Andrea into the uncongenial world of court gossip.

The tensions of it made themselves felt at once. Behind the bows of gentlemen and servants that greeted the heir apparent to the duchy, behind the polite smiles, Orsini sensed the mental whispering, the exchanged glances, which were to translate themselves into words. Within a half hour the discreet ripple would reach Duke Ercole's ears that Don Alfonso and Captain Orsini had ridden off side by side to the Palace of San Francesco. His Ducal Excellence would judge from that what progress the Borgian agent was making in the Prince's confidence, and His Signory would consider what steps should be taken accordingly.

What would those steps be? Andrea wondered about them, as he rode with Alfonso through the streets of Ferrara. The court was already buzzing with the French reports of last night's duel; glances, admiring and speculative, had greeted his arrival that morning at the Castle. But although, as Belli had prophesied, Duke Ercole so far appeared to ignore the matter, Orsini's instinct warned him that the kettle was on the point of boiling; and now this public demonstration of Alfonso's favor would raise the heat that much further. He realized that the impending conversation in Don Alfonso's palace might easily determine his success or failure and, with it, his future. No other such chance would be forthcoming.

He braced himself for the gamble; and in spite of good nerves his pulses beat faster as he dismounted in the great pillared *cortile* of the palace.

CHAPTER XVIII

NOT until after meat and after a prolonged discussion of the new bombard carriage, during the course of which Andrea amazed the Prince by drawing an excellent cross section, did Orsini reconnoiter the topic of Lucrezia Borgia.

He approached it indirectly with a remark on the beauties of this triumphant palace of San Francesco, and how it needed only a princess worthy of His Illustrious Highness to give it the final touch. By this time, they had come in from the garden balcony to Alfonso's private chamber, where Andrea's quick eye distinguished a curtained portrait of about the same dimensions as the one he had brought from Rome. To his surprise, Alfonso now walked over to it, twitched the curtain aside, and waved a complacent hand at the crimson and gold canvas.

"Why beat about the bush, Messere? I know what you're after. My lord father and reverend brother gnash their teeth at the thought (to put it baldly) of harboring a pimp of Madama Lucrezia's at our court, but not I. You've listened to me for a good while and made me a fine drawing; it's only fair I should listen to you. Tell me about the jade."

And, seating himself in an armchair, with his big legs stuck out straight in front of him, the Prince half closed his eyes.

"Well, then?" he prodded.

Andrea considered the factors of the problem. He had before him a full-blooded young man with the appetites of a blacksmith. Alfonso might be a genius of sorts, but his talents expressed themselves in material terms. For the rest, he had close affinities with the workmen of his shop, with the horses he raced and the animals he hunted. Subtle refinements would be useless here. Andrea reckoned that the best ally he had was Nature herself, the heat in Este's veins.

"The picture speaks for itself, Your Grace. I glory to pimp, as you say, for a second Venus."

"The painter fellow hasn't overdrawn her then? He's kept to a reasonable likeness? She was only a child when I saw her in Rome eight years ago. But, if the painting's true, I'll say she's personable. *Per Bacco*, yes! Personable enough to put a strain on my *braguette!*"

"Who could overdraw her, Your Excellence! As to the likeness, it's as like as the reflection of a goddess in dull water."

"Speaking of goddesses," Alfonso chuckled, "I wish she'd been painted in the same costume as that one on a shell by Master Botticelli. The clothes are pretty no doubt, but who's to know what's beneath them — if you follow me?"

Andrea joined in the Prince's laugh. He protested that the eyes of any artist, not to speak of his peace of mind, could hardly survive the splendor of the unveiled charms of Madonna Lucrezia. But fortunately those charms did not have to be taken on faith. Andrea himself had had the privilege of hearing her late husband, the Duke of Biselli, describe them over the cups to several of his gentlemen, and, by God, it was a ravishment to listen.

"Her *very* late husband," Alfonso grunted. "How long since they murdered him?"

"His Excellence died two months ago." Andrea did not choose to get off on that slippery subject. "I especially recall some of his expressions concerning Her Signory: *soft fire, a rose warmed in the sun, contours of peach marble.*"

The diversion worked. Alfonso's eyes lingered on the portrait.

"Beautiful!" he muttered. "Most beautiful! . . . Tell me, sir, would you call her plump or slender — I mean without these satins and brocades? It's hard to determine — "

Andrea thought quickly. He wished he knew what type of woman Este preferred, for Lucrezia could fit almost any description. "Speaking of goddesses," he ventured, "and with all reverence, I believe that Her Highness is less angular than the Venus of Botticelli."

Evidently he had guessed right. Alfonso nodded approval. "*Bellissima!*" he repeated.

A long pause followed. Andrea could sense the growth of desire in the Prince's mind, like an expanding ripple. Lucrezia was, indeed, her own best advocate. The provocative eyes of the portrait, spirited and gay but with a faint shadow in the depths of them, rested on Alfonso, half-challenging, half-inviting. It was a young face, but it did not express innocence so much as an amused acquiescence in the world and the ways of men, combined with an odd wistfulness. It implied neither good nor evil but a pagan tolerance, warm and gracious — the more so because it smiled on human frailty. A face vividly young and immemorially old. Andrea could not help comparing it with the neighboring portrait of the Prince's sister, Isabella d'Este. Both revealed the same paganism, but the intellectual arrogance of the Lady of Mantua was absent in Lucrezia: Pallas Athene compared with Aphrodite Pandemos.

In the end, Alfonso shrugged and flung out a hand. "But what nonsense! How old is the girl? Twenty?"

"Aye, my lord."

"And twice married — not to speak of lovers, not to speak of other scandal! The goods are shopworn."

"Shopworn by Venetian slander, for the most part, as Your Excellence should know. But, admitting that, Madama still deserves to be pitied. With all humble respect to the Holiness of Our Lord, her father, and to the renowned Duke, her brother, she has been more used than are most ladies in the service of her House. She merits a better fortune. If I may speak boldly, she regards Your Signory as a second Perseus, for whom she reserves her entire obedience and love. In your arms, my lord, let her find lasting covert! And wear her as the brightest jewel among the jewels of Ferrara!"

With the tempting portrait in front of them, it was not bad play to strike the protective note in Alfonso's mind. A hint of misfortune, of dependence, makes a pretty woman still more appetizing. But there was an objection to this that Este did not overlook.

"It's an odd chance," he remarked, "that the Pope's Beatitude and my lord Cesare Borgia share her eagerness that I should save her from them — in the covert of my arms, as you so neatly put it. Do you suppose they regard it in that light? To their minds, isn't the same lady serving the same House? So all three are happy. Don't be too poetic, Captain."

Andrea admitted that, of course, the Pope and the Duke desired this marriage above everything else, and that they considered it essential to their interests — as, indeed, it might be of equal advantage to Ferrara. If they had opposed the marriage, Madonna Lucrezia was too completely in their hands to have asserted herself. But it was nonetheless true that for once their policy offered her escape and sanctuary from constant vicissitudes. This was the dragon from which she hoped that the Este Perseus might deliver her, and in so doing he would win a prize "more lovely than Andromeda, more beautiful than Helen, more enchanting than Venus."

"In brief," Alfonso returned, but with his gaze still on the portrait, "you're simple enough to propose that for the sake of love and a pretty wench, I should neglect the interests of my own House, forgo the advantages of an alliance with France, and merge my line with that of these Spanish upstarts." He added moodily, "Princes don't marry for love. Perhaps you didn't know that."

They had reached the nub of the matter. Andrea had prepared his approaches: he had won Alfonso's liking; he had fanned the flame which the portrait had kindled. But unless this stubborn central point could be carried, everything else was useless; and he made ready for the crucial effort.

"Let my devotion to Your Lordship and my hope for your favor and protection absolve me for speaking on a subject so far above my knowledge and scope. If Madonna Lucrezia, however desirable, were a lady of small station and of trivial dowry, without backing and without support, I should indeed be worse than a fool to plead her cause to Your Signory. Ignorant as I am of great affairs, I know well that princes must at all times subordinate liking to interest and bear in mind the welfare of the state. But, my lord, the daughter of His Beatitude, Pope Alexander VI, the sister of the Duke de Valentinois, whose deeds ring through Italy, and who at this moment tames the Romagna — such a princess, bringing a dowry greater than France could offer, is not a wren to be disdained even by the Eagle of Este."

"By God," put in Alfonso, "what a fellow you are! Well spoken!"

Orsini made a disclaiming gesture. "If I speak warmly, may Your Highness forgive! It is the subject that speaks, not I. But since you permit, let me say that I have never heard that princes are *forbidden* to love when love does not clash with interest. Is it a law that Your Excellence must take to wife some pale northern girl, with bad teeth and a foul breath, simply because you do not love her, and must turn away from the most triumphant lady in Europe because she brings love and delight and beauty to your bed? I cannot endure the thought of it. . . . And as to alliance with the House of Borgia, Your Grace will recall that the Most Christian King himself did not consider it beneath his dignity to offer Mademoiselle de Foix, his niece, to Cesare Borgia, and that that lord has married the sister of the King of Navarre."

"What's this about stinking breath and bad teeth?" Alfonso interrupted.

Andrea's face expressed surprise. "A matter of common knowledge, sir. These unfortunate girls who have been brought up by Anne of Brittany have no more juice in them than dry grape skins. They have been so laced and berated by the good Queen that they are fitter for heaven than this world. Blessed martyrs, my lord, with corns on their knees from kneeling at prayer and watery eyes from reading their hours. Since every care has been spent on their morals and none on their persons, the result is that they wash seldom and have a breath like a church crypt. Sink me all such! Though doubtless if a man wishes to go to bed to one, it's an acceptable penance."

Humorously overdone as it was, the picture had enough grains of truth in it to please Italian prejudice, and the Prince laughed. "How many of Queen Anne's ladies have you had the squiring of?"

"None. But Madonna Angela Borgia, cousin and lady in waiting to Madama Lucrezia, has known several and makes a report of them which I dare not repeat to the delicate ears of Your Highness."

"Don't mind me! I've heard that Lady Angela has a spicy tongue."

However, as Este's eyes had wandered back to the portrait, Andrea left well enough alone. He felt that his sally against the Frenchwomen had not been amiss. Alfonso would be comparing the caricature of the prim, gothic ladies of Anne of Brittany's court with Lucrezia's piquant beauty. Let the ripple spread.

And when the Prince spoke again, it was on a reassuring note of hesitation. "This dowry you mentioned — you think that His Holiness would be inclined to generosity? Some such figure as a hundred thousand ducats, wasn't it? I must have more."

"In a matter so close to his heart, he would do all in his power to satisfy Your Highness. It should be remembered, too, that Madama's dowry will consist not only of gold but of steel, the lances and *condottas* of Duke Cesare, who will maintain the rights of Ferrara" — Orsini nodded toward the north and Venice — "against any state. Since this lord will soon hold the Marches to the south, is such an alliance not worth more than French help from Milan, which may or may not be forthcoming?"

The reverse of the coin did not need to be stated: that, if the proposed marriage did not occur, these same lances and *condottas* might just as handily join with Venice for the partition of the duchy.

"It's reached my ears," said the Prince, "that you think Valentino can't last. What of his *condottas* then?"

Andrea shrugged. "In that case, the gold that Madonna brings with her will purchase all the troops that Your Highness needs. But I make bold to repeat that the supreme dowry of this divine lady is herself, her beauty and the love she bears Your Excellence."

In his indecision, the Prince exclaimed: "Folderol! What love? She's only seen me once when she was little more than an infant. How can she bear me love?"

"My lord, childhood's impressions are the lasting ones. I did not speak at random. She cherishes vivid memories of your visit to Rome. And if Your Signory admires this portrait of her, she no less admires the still finer portrait of Your Grace, copied from one by the late Master Ercole de' Roberti."

"Indeed?"

"If Your Lordship does not believe it, I have the proof at hand."

It was time for Orsini to play his leading trump. He drew forth and presented with a bow an unmistakably feminine letter, sealed with a Captive Cupid.

"You have it there. So hot is Madama that she sets at defiance all the proprieties to unveil her heart to Your Grace. Let her own words justify me."

The alloy in this did not concern Orsini. That the letter had been prompted by Cesare Borgia himself; that it was not written in Lucrezia's hand but in that of her cousin, Angela; that the two ladies had composed it together as a pastime; and, finally, that it bore no signature beyond a phrase which revealed its writer as one devoted to Alfonso, were in large part necessary precautions. Este would not learn of them, and, in any case, the seal was Lucrezia's. But if the letter should fall into wrong hands, it could never be fixed on her. A great lady, however bold, dared not outrage the conventions by writing openly to a prince not yet designated as her future husband. That she did not sign the letter would not surprise him.

Alfonso's handsome face grew flushed; he read with parted lips. Orsini, who knew the letter by heart, could gauge the effect of each well-calculated phrase.

When he had finished, the Prince drew a deep breath and gazed again, more possessively than before, at the portrait. If he looked remotely like a fish who has swallowed a bait, it was not to his discredit. Flattered by an attractive woman, the shrewdest man in the world becomes a fool, and Alfonso was only twenty-four.

Suddenly he slapped his knee and stood up. "This letter requires an answer, and it shall have one. I'm sick of whores and of the *mal francese*. My late wife (God be with her) had the temperament of a carrot. Why, as you say, should I marry a frost-bitten, flabby-skinned, long-nosed female, when I can have such a *bellezza*" — his gesture embraced the portrait — "to be wife and mistress in one?"

"Why, indeed, my lord?"

"Without too much loss by the bargain, remember. The Pope will have to unbuckle. I'll take nothing less than two hundred thousand ducats. But a man needs some pleasure in life. . . . Is it true that my father is sending you on a mission to that saint in Viterbo?"

Andrea caught the twinkle in the Prince's eye and smiled. "That is His Signory's desire."

"Then execute it, sir. You have no reason for delay. You shall carry a letter from me to the divine Lucrezia and please both my father and me on the same errand. His Wisdom won't know that he got rid of you too late."

The two men eyed each other with perfect understanding.

"Mind you, I make no promises," Alfonso added. "My lord father has set his heart on the French marriage, and I must seem to play his game. I'll balk and protest even more than he. It's the only way. But, by the aid of Cupid and the House of Borgia together, we won't be able to help ourselves. . . . Do you get the point?" Alfonso winked. "I believe we may count on it."

Joy rang its carillon in Orsini's mind. He thought of Camilla on the road south. She would see him again before she expected. The future had come much nearer in the last ten minutes. With Ferrara nearly in the bag, he was already plotting the move beyond. Cesare Borgia had crossed the Apennines. He would report to him on the way south and renew his claim to Città del Monte.

"We hunt tomorrow," Este pondered. "I shall have letters ready for you the day after. . . . And, Messere, a word. Until then be careful — particularly of cardinals, if you take me. And don't fight any more Frenchmen. I say again that, after the hunt, you will have no reason for delay. Don't be caught napping. I should grieve if promise like yours were lost to the world unnecessarily."

While the Prince was speaking, Andrea's thought turned to Pomposa. Would he dare to disappear from tomorrow's hunt, as he had planned? That sideway was becoming dangerous.

"A small loss, Your Grace," he said absently. But Alfonso's answer fixed his attention.

"No, Messere — at least not to me. If you want my favor, you can have it."

Here was an opening that had to be evaded. Andrea bowed. "Could I possibly want anything so much? My utmost hope is that I may enjoy Your Signory's condescension."

CHAPTER XIX

AN HOUR after midnight, the brazen hunting horns, winding through the city streets, proclaimed that the Princes of Este would ride out that morning to the chase and invited the court to take part.

Torches flickered, dogs barked, horses neighed; the streets grew louder with the rattle of hoofs and creaking of carts. The courtyards of palaces, taverns, and public stables each furnished its complement of well-dressed riders and well-groomed horses, with their attendants on foot, carrying spears or leaning back against the leashes of the dogs. Wagons were heaped up with hunting nets, extra spears, and other tools of the chase. And while one stream, formed of these separate trickles, pressed toward the main assembly place in the courtyard of the castle, another stream was already rolling out through the Porta degli Angeli toward the east and the distant woodlands. For there was much to prepare against the coming of the hunt.

In the dark courtyard of the inn, Andrea waited while the hostler gave a last polish to the flanks of his horse and meanwhile listened, half-amused, to the uproar of the French lances, who, as usual, monopolized everything.

"But I keep telling you, *mon ami*, that this hunt of theirs resembles a *battue*, not a chase. They have no art of venery as we Frenchmen know it. The fine points of hunting, they've never heard of. One has to be born in France for that. No, Monseigneur, they fence you in a certain space of marsh and forest with their nets, block all the paths, and then proceed to butcher every living beast in said space. *Quelle pailliardise! Ma foi*, I laugh."

"Don't laugh too high," crowed another voice. "It's a battle, not a hunt, depending on what you find inside the nets. I hear it's seldom they don't rouse a bear or a wild ox, not to speak of boar, wolves, elk, and deer. *Fête dieu!* In my opinion, it's a fair chance to win honor. And I make my vow to dismount, if Our Lady sends me a bear or urus, and fight him foot to foot. . . . Ha! Monseigneur d'Orsini, if I'm not mistaken. Your servant, sir."

And Andrea was drawn into the whirlpool of talk until at last, mounted, he rode out with the Frenchmen to join the torch-spangled stream flowing down the Via San Romano toward the Ducal Palace and the castle.

Within the precincts of the great pile, a dense throng of men, horses, and dogs was gathering. Gradually, as the darkness paled, faces became distinct, and at last, out of a cloudless sky, sunrise renewed the miracle of color.

And what color! The court had put on its gala clothes in honor of the hunt: purple, vermilion, azure, saffron, emerald, black or white velvets. The sun rays kindled the fire in gold and gems, played along the glossy flanks of the horses or on the magnificent saddle housings or on jeweled bridles, flashed on sword hilts and on the tips of spears. A dazzlement, from the Princes of Este, who outshone everybody else, to the clashing, parti-colored hose of the spearmen.

Groups formed: around the Duke in his purple cloak, belted with gold, who sat a tall black, with a white star in the forehead; around Alfonso d'Este, wearing a double fillet of pearls on his cap and the eagle of the House pendent on his breast chain; around some court lady, who was riding out to view the sport, and whose crimson-stockinged leg and jeweled garter showed alluringly from the sidesaddle; around one of the great hunting dogs, in charge of their keepers; the Duke's tawny favorite, Breakleash, Cardinal Ippolito's Albino, Mirandola's spotted mastiff, Leopard; a half dozen others, majestic among the common fry of hounds; beast killers and man killers, too, if they got out of hand, their chests and necks protected with chain mail.

As one of the aides of Ippolito d'Este, who acted as master of the hunt, Andrea assisted in straightening out the crowd in some order of precedence. Then, finally, the trumpets sounded; the horses reared and pranced; the Duke, erect and all the more commanding because of his white hair, rode to the front, making his horse curvet from side to side.

Through the great portal of the castle, across the drawbridge, the cavalcade emerged, glittering and glowing. Down the long Street of the Angels it flowed, through the gate of that name, out into the flat country beyond, some hundreds strong, followed by a train of servants and townsfolk, while the trumpets kept rollicking, and the sky darkened to a deeper blue, and the first chill of autumn set the horses dancing more than the spur. Viewed from the crowded city walls, the column showed vividly against the green fields, and a light breeze carried off to one side the dust of the march.

Andrea, riding next to Bianca Torelli, one of the ladies of the court, bowed low when the Cardinal d'Este did him the honor to draw rein alongside. Ippolito had left off today any sobering reminder of the Church. He wore a green cloak and a small green cap embroidered with jewels, half submerged in the thickness of his hair. An ivory horn hung on his back. His face had a quizzical expression that set Orsini at once on guard.

"Too bad," observed the Cardinal, "that Madonna Camilla saw fit to shake the dust of Ferrara so quickly from her feet. How do you account for it, sir?"

"How should anyone account for the whims of beautiful women?" Andrea gave a flattering glance to Bianca.

"But I thought *you* might," returned Este. "You know, I suspect that call of yours the other evening had something to do with it. You weren't too impulsive, were you — too hot, eh? No tact, Magnifico?"

Without blinking an eye, Andrea reflected how well-informed about his doings Ippolito was. The Prince's warning of yesterday gained point.

"An impersonal discussion only, Your Eminence."

"So *that* was the trouble? Too impersonal. You talked politics" — Ippolito's voice sounded overcasual — "when she expected compliments. I thought you were a better courtier. Learn that there is a middle line between the impersonal and the too personal, the one I should have followed in your place."

"Would that Your Signory had been there to give me an example! . . . Madonna Bianca, be my instructress. Teach me this line, and I shall prove your devoted scholar."

"That's right," nodded Este. "Keep him at your side, Madonna. I'll ask you how well you succeeded, after the hunt."

And with a last ambiguous smile, the Cardinal spurred his horse and cantered off.

On the surface, this exchange had been nothing but court chitchat. Double-tongue chitchat, however, thought Andrea, as he recalled its undertones.

The chase was in the direction of Mesola, whose forest at that time reached closer to Ferrara than now. By the time the court arrived, a rough square of woodland had been netted off; and now, with horns blaring and dogs baying, the huntsmen with their spearmen rode into the wooded enclosure, spreading out to form a thin circle, that would gradually narrow on whatever beasts had been trapped.

Making a show of eagerness, Andrea detached himself from Bianca Torelli, who, with other spectators, remained on a small rise of land. He had hardly left when she whispered to a page, who set out in search of Cardinal Ippolito.

Meanwhile, Orsini plunged off down a glade leading toward the far side of the netted area. Luckily a fine stag, that emerged from a covert ahead of him and raced off down the same glade, gave him a pretext of riding hard in that direction. But, even so, he caught glimpses of the hunt: a boar at bay against the dogs and spear of Alfonso d'Este; a she-wolf pierced by an arrow and gnashing at the shaft, her cubs about her; the dog Albino, with the Cardinal whooping him on, as he clung to the throat of a urus, his great bulk pendent from the ox and slowly pulling it down. Here and there, horns sounded a kill; and at one moment Orsini distinguished the vaunting flourish of French trumpets, announcing that some one of the lances had fulfilled his vow.

Having reached the eastern limit of the enclosure, Andrea paused for a final decision. After all, was it wise to desert the hunt? Instead of returning for this last time to Pomposa, would he not do better to join in the chase, take part in the open-air banquet that followed, and then ride back with the court to Ferrara? He could somehow get word to Belli to meet him on the road south.

But although he pondered, like a toper at the door of a wineshop, he knew already how he would decide. The work at Pomposa was too important to give up.

Finding an opening between the nets, he paused a moment to peer and listen before guiding his horse through; but he saw no one and heard only the distant sounds of the hunt. Then, making his way out of the enclosure, he headed through the forest in a southeastern direction. After about a mile, he stopped again in the cover of a thicket and remained motionless long enough to determine that no one was following. Reassured at length by the unbroken rustle of the forest, he rode on as fast as the tangle of the woods permitted.

Nearer the sea, the forest thinned out into sparse pines, then into swampy undergrowth. Splashing through shallow pools, finding a way between the marshes, making good speed for a while along some higher ridge, he finally emerged from the reeds upon the thin margin of land that seemed almost one with the still expanse of the lagoon beyond it. To his left, a half mile off, rose the walls of the monastery of Pomposa, guarded by its lonely campanile. Except for these, he confronted the vacancy of blue sky and hazy water and the interminable southern reach of the coast.

Dismounting in the shelter of the rushes, he stripped off the fine court suit he had been wearing and exchanged it for a much soberer costume, carried in one of his saddlebags; for he was not known as Andrea Orsini at the monastery. Then, leading his horse to the firmer sand at the edge of the water, he stood lingering awhile, with his eyes on the horizon.

The golden languor of high autumn lay upon sea and land, merging everything into mellow harmony. The solitude and remoteness of the place, the silence of the distant abbey, seemed dedicated to reminiscence. Transmuted by the mind, the very smell of the lagoon became a haunting of memories rich with associations. Once this water, empty and listless now in its autumn haze, had been thronged with the colored sails of the crusades. Here Barbarossa had passed, and Boniface had done penance. Damiani lived here, and Dante had paused for a night from his wayfaring. For centuries the now desolate coast had pulsed with human life flowing back and forth between Venice and Ravenna. Soldiers, merchants, scholars, saints, men and women. Long ago. Now, forgotten behind the marshes, but golden in the light of an eternal sunset, Pomposa dreamed of human glory and impermanence.

But to Andrea, who had a touch of the philosopher, the scene was not merely commemorative: it symbolized a dead past and a dying faith. Like humanity itself, even the ocean, which had once embraced Pomposa, had now receded, leaving her behind. The campanile still pointed to heaven, but men preferred to look around them on the earth. The bells, calling to prayer, repeated the old promise and the old renunciation to a world that had rediscovered another creed.

After a while, he led his horse the remaining distance to the abbey.

"Peace to you, *Padre mio*," he greeted the porter at the gate.

"And to you, peace."

An observer, stationed some distance off behind a screen of reeds, nodded with satisfaction and, mounting his horse, set off through the marshes in the direction of the hunt.

CHAPTER XX

THE news that Andrea Orsini had gone to earth in Pomposa filled Ippolito d'Este with exulting delight. Mario Belli had been well worth the fifty ducats paid him. Except for that invaluable traitor, no one could have guessed that Orsini would use the half-forgotten monastery as a hatching place of foreign plots against Ferrara. The circumstance that he had changed his clothes and entered the abbey in disguise was itself enough to convict him and completely sustained Belli's report.

It was late afternoon when, accompanied by his gentlemen and the dog Albino, Este halted outside the monastery and gave instructions to his small force. Prudence required that he keep them in the dark as long as possible. What if the foreign members of Orsini's plot turned out to be really great lords, fish too big for the net? It was even not impossible that Duke Valentino himself might have come north for a secret interview with his agent. In that case, the less court gossip there was, the better. And in that case, too, the whole procedure would necessarily be different than if obscure nobodies were involved. So, with a hint merely that unexpected arrivals from abroad were lodged at Pomposa and that they ought to receive a proper welcome, Ippolito had whetted the curiosity of his gentlemen and left himself freedom of action. He now ordered them to wait for him outside the abbey either until they were called or until (and this spurred their pulses) he sounded his horn. In that event, they were to rejoin him at once. Then, with his huge mastiff on a leash beside him, he walked up to the porter's gate and demanded entrance.

Although Santa Maria in Pomposa was one of the Cardinal's benefices, and although he held the title there of Commandatory Abbot, he so seldom visited the place that the good monk on duty, a relative newcomer, had never even seen him. Roused from his breviary by the sound of horses' hoofs and by voices outside, he had been examining these arrivals through the sliding panel of his gate with increasing alarm. Bloodstained from the chase, their horses and accouterments splashed with mire, they had every appearance of a troop of gaudy robbers. Nor did their spokesman, accompanied by his devilish dog, look reassuring.

"Peace to *you!*" snapped Ippolito in reply to the ostiary's stammer from within. "Open up here! And fetch the Abbot at once. I want a word with him."

"But, sir, who are you? Who shall I say — "

"*Who am I?*" roared the Cardinal. "I like that! Do I have to explain myself to you, perhaps, and cool my heels at the gate of my own abbey until you decide to admit me?"

"God save me!" the gateman ejaculated. "Your own abbey! Sir, let me tell you that this house is governed by the reverend Abbot Giovanni da Spoleto under the command and protection of the holy Cardinal of Este, and I advise you for your own good to leave us in peace or else to give me your worshipful name — "

133

Ippolito's mounting ire cooled. "Well, who do you think I am but the said Cardinal of Este? Now, open here . . ."

Whatever doubts might have remained as to the identity of the fire-breathing swordsman and the holy Cardinal were swept away by the assurance of Ippolito's manner. Only a great prince could speak so roundly.

Within a minute, Abbot Giovanni, attended by a couple of the older monks, appeared, full of apologies and profuse in welcome. But Ippolito cut the reception short. "I'd have a word in private with you, Father Giovanni, and at once."

"The scriptorium will be empty," murmured the Abbot, and he nervously conducted his young overlord a few paces along the cloisters. "Your Eminence comes most appropriately dressed to Pomposa in emulation of our blessed patron, Saint Eustace, that holy hunter."

Este banged shut the door of the writing room. "Yes. Do you know what game I'm hunting? Among other foxes, a false monk named Giovanni da Spoleto, who harbors traitors and enemies to Ferrara in the abbey entrusted to him, who sells himself to Venice and Rome, and who, *per Dio*, shall answer it before I've finished with him. You look guilty plain enough. Don't imagine that you can fool *me!*"

The Abbot's cheeks had turned white as his beard; his blank eyes expressed guilt or amazement. Ippolito could read what he liked in them.

"Traitors? Enemies to Ferrara? Here?"

"At this very minute. Hatching their plots, while — "

"No, my lord!"

"Will you deny what my people have seen with their own eyes?"

"Seen what? Seen what?"

"Men of Rome and Venice — perhaps others — in council with Messer Andrea Orsini, a captain of the Duke's archers at the court of Ferrara."

"Andrea Orsini?" gaped the Abbot. "As I hope for salvation, I've never heard of the man until this moment."

"Don't lie to me. He was seen entering here not five hours ago."

The Abbot extended his clasped hands. "That may be true, but *I* did not see him. Men come to Pomposa: peasants, artisans from Codigoro. We're repairing the walls, redecorating the church and refectory. But as to evil plotters — Hear me, Your Eminence. The abbey is yours. Have the goodness to search, and if you find any such, punish me as you will. I can say no more."

"Agreed," snapped the Cardinal. "And you'll come *with* me. And no tricks. You see this dog?"

Since, roused by the conversation, Albino was straining at the leash with all teeth bared, it would have been difficult for Father Giovanni to see anything else, and he nodded faintly.

Like tempest incarnate, Ippolito swept through the monastery, accompanied by the padding dog and the breathless Abbot. The buildings were not too extensive for a rapid survey, and the small community of monks, greatly reduced since the prosperous days of the abbey, could be easily accounted for. But, except for these and the novices and a few obvious workmen engaged on masonry and decoration, the Cardinal discovered no one. He swept through the church, climbed the campanile, glanced into the sacristy, the library, the refectory, the Abbot's hall of justice. Doors banged, cells were entered.

"But I tell you, this Orsini, riding a bay horse, was admitted here not long before noon."

The frightened ostiary, being summoned, confirmed that Ser Beppo Lenti, the Paduan worker in colors, had arrived about sext on a horse of that color.

"Oho! Where is the fellow?"

"But Your Eminence saw him," panted the Abbot — "at work on a *cenacolo* in the refectory."

"Pooh! That scrub!"

"Might it be," ventured the Abbot, "that Your Eminence's servant was mistaken in the person he saw entering?"

"Yes, damn him! And if he was, he'll hang. . . . Hark you, Father, is the name Mario Belli known to you?"

The Abbot shook his head. "No, my lord."

"A hideous man, one to be remembered?"

"There's a certain Greek — " Father Giovanni pondered.

"No, the fellow's from Savoy."

A devastating suspicion, which had so far only brushed the Cardinal's mind, now exploded in it. Sold! He recalled his interview with Belli, remembered the sense he had had of being outplayed and overreached. The rat! He had made up this entire Pomposa story as a blind and had got paid for it to boot. He had had the unparalleled insolence to make a fool out of the Cardinal Prince of Este.

When a young man of twenty-one has spent most of his life in positions for which he has no qualification except the accident of birth — archbishop at eight, cardinal at fourteen, possessor of rich benefices whose revenues alone interested him — his ego fills up the void and becomes gigantic. To offend it in any way is like pinching a gouty toe. The agony suffered by the Cardinal at that moment was so extreme, and his face turned so purple, that the good Abbot, fearful of a stroke, suggested a chair for His Eminence and ventured a word or two of sympathy.

This brought relief, like the lancet of a surgeon, by pricking the boil of Ippolito's vocabulary. The simple monks had never before experienced the blasting drive of Italian at such white heat. The Cardinal damned the Abbot's chair and sympathy. He damned Pomposa. He damned the idiots who served him and had put him to the labor of riding leagues through marshes to this unprintable place. But he used his supreme efforts in denouncing his own fate that condemned a life intended for pleasure to the sorrow of dealing with reptiles like Mario Belli and Andrea Orsini. Launching out upon a further description of them, words at last failed even him, and he demanded a drink.

Since they were close to the refectory, Father Giovanni opened the door. "If Your Eminence will but enter, wine and a collation would refresh Your Signory."

"By God, I'm in need of it!"

Este flung himself down on a bench, while the Abbot hastened to fill a goblet for him with his own hands.

Meanwhile, Ser Beppo Lenti, the Paduan worker in colors, painted on at his *cenacolo* in the corner of the large room. So absorbed was he in the work that he did not even look around. His bent shoulders and muffled-up appearance suggested an old man; the frayed cap, drawn down to his ears, and the general seediness of his costume, reflected poverty. The Cardinal, eying him over his cup, hardly saw him.

It was only when a ray of the setting sun, through the wide casement, made vivid the painting itself that Este glanced back and then glanced again. He was no patron of art and, in his present mood, was even less receptive to it than usual; still, like most of that age, he responded to beautiful things, and the painting compelled a second glance.

It revealed the Saviour at the head of the board, with Saints John and Peter on either hand, excellently drawn and with a wonderful radiance of light. The two rows of Apostles, seated opposite each other at the U-shaped table, formed a perspective that drew the eye at once to the central figure of the Christ. But, though subordinate, none of the faces already finished were vague or conventional; they were individual portraits of ecclesiastics such as might have attended a conclave. All but one at the end, all but Judas . . .

The Cardinal sprang to his feet with an oath, his extended arm pointing. "There's the viper!"

So startling were the gesture and tone of voice that Albino, whose leash was fortunately attached to the leg of the table, reared upright with a soul-chilling snarl; and the poor Abbot, seeing His Eminence apparently glaring into space, became more convinced than ever that he had to do with a madman.

"Where, my lord?" he asked soothingly.

"There, curse him! Judas Iscariot yonder!"

Relieved that Este was, at least, pointing at something, Father Giovanni nodded. "Yes, an excellent portrait of the Greek servant of Ser Beppo, of whom I was telling — "

"Greek, nothing! The villain, Mario Belli!"

And Ippolito strode down the room toward the painting; but his eyes were now fixed on the Paduan artist, whose back was still toward him. Grasping one shoulder, he swung the man around and faced Andrea Orsini.

"*Diàscolo!*" the Cardinal burst out. "What the devil do you mean by this mummery?"

"No mummery, my lord. I did not wish to present myself at Pomposa as a captain of His Excellence's guard. Beppo Lenti was more appropriate."

"But why present yourself at all? Why sneak off from Ferrara?"

"To paint." Andrea glanced ruefully at the unfinished work. "Truly, sometimes I need art more than bread."

"Nonsense! Do you take me for a fool? Does a courtier and cavalier daub with paint? He leaves that to craftsmen."

"What daub?" Andrea's voice stiffened. "Will Your Signory call this a daub? I'd dare submit it to the judgment of any masters in Italy. If Your Eminence thinks it's easy to give that impression of depth — "

But Ippolito would not be put off. "And if you must daub, why not in Ferrara? Why do you travel here through the marshes?"

"Because, as Your Lordship implies, I am a courtier. People would not understand. Here I could be unknown and please both the reverend fathers and myself."

The truth made a thinner impression than a flat lie would have made. The Cardinal's skepticism expressed itself in a sneer.

"Listen, friend Orsini, for a man of your parts, you're not doing well. You founder like a horse in a bog. Let me help you. I agree that you come to Pomposa to practise art. But what art? There's a difference between painting and the art of treason, in which, I admit, you're a master of rank. To be plain, you come here to meet agents of Rome and Venice and to plot against us. You see, I'm informed of your doings. Don't lie more than you can help."

Andrea was so much humiliated at being caught out of his lordly and military role in the humble masquerade of a traveling painter that he almost welcomed this fantastic charge. High treason conferred more dignity than painting, though, of course, it had to be denied.

"I grieve that Your Eminence thinks so ill of me. Let my lord Abbot bear witness that the only Venetians and Romans I have met at Pomposa are the reverend monks, who sat to me as models of the Holy Apostles. And let him inform Your Grace whether or not I have worked too hard at this canvas to leave much time for treasonable practices."

"On my conscience," Father Giovanni agreed, "Ser Beppo — or, I should say, this gentleman — speaks the truth. Consider the size of his work, which will beautify the end of the refectory. . . . Did Your Eminence speak?"

Ippolito shook his head. He had merely cursed at the recollection of Mario Belli. These men of Rome, Venice, and other parts of Italy, with whom Andrea foregathered in the refectory! This talk of Judas Iscariots! In the present light, it all made damnably good sense. A hoax! The fellow had dared to make merry at Ippolito's expense — and had profited from it. Saints!

The Cardinal's arm shot out again toward Belli's leering countenance in the painting. "That scoundrel! Where is he? Bring him here. I'll have him torn limb from limb."

"If I can find him," said the Abbot, hurrying out, while Andrea gathered from Este's verbal explosions what had happened.

In his first heat against Belli, Orsini agreed that hanging and quartering would be too good for him. Then the humor of the case began to appeal, and he bit his lips. Strangely enough, Belli had always ridiculed Andrea's shamefaced concealment of his art, and to him it meant nothing that his master's talents should be discovered. If he could lead Ippolito on a fool's chase through forest and swamp, and touch him for a good sum besides, it would seem to him only a capital joke. Andrea had no fear that the Abbot would find him. Belli had slipped out shortly after Orsini's arrival at the abbey and would now have a long start toward Ravenna, which he and Andrea had decided would be their first stop on the road south.

The Abbot returned. "He has taken flight, Your Eminence. But perhaps if a pursuit were ordered — "

"No," gulped the Cardinal. Instinctively he knew that Belli would not be taken, and he had had enough. But, as it was, he determined to get something out of this.

"It will be a pleasure to inform the court of your unsuspected abilities,

Messere," he scoffed, at the same time noting the flush on Orsini's cheeks. "One doesn't expect a gentleman of your House and profession to be so handy with the paintbrush. I wonder if it will help you in your career and whether my lord Cesare Borgia knows that he sponsored an artisan to be captain in our guard."

Andrea protested. "I should prefer that Your Eminence kept this matter secret."

"A good thing like that? Indeed not, my magnificent friend. I shall even take pains to publish it." Ippolito seemed to hesitate. "Except, perhaps, on one condition."

"What condition?"

"That you'll take yourself out of this court. That you'll do my father's mission in Viterbo. In that case, we may forget Ser Beppo Lenti."

Andrea's heart expanded, though he gave no sign of relief. Better let Ippolito flatter himself on his victory. But, aside from Orsini's own advantage, it was droll to consider with what unanimous benediction of friends and enemies he would now be riding south — Alfonso's, the Duke's, the Cardinal's. All omens were with him.

"I accept the condition, Your Eminence. I shall leave tomorrow."

That night at his inn Andrea packed for the journey and cast up his accounts. He had had an interview with the Duke and received his orders. He could congratulate himself on his success at Ferrara. He had accomplished the mission for Borgia and had secured Alfonso d'Este's favor. But, although the gates to the future lay wide open, he was realist enough to know that he had only crossed the threshold. Beyond lay Città del Monte and beyond that the still dizzier summit of his ambition. The foothills were past; the real climb was about to begin.

PART TWO

Viterbo

CHAPTER XXI

WRITING from the lonely castle at Nepi to her factor, Vincenzo Giordano, in Rome, Lucrezia Borgia finished the letter and, having signed herself *The Most Unhappy Princess of Salerno,* she allowed a tear to dim the sparkling blue of her eyes. But nonetheless — and indeed, perhaps, the more because of it — she looked entrancingly lovely even to her envious cousin, Angela Borgia, who had come up from Rome on a week's visit. Angela reflected that black was most becoming to Lucrezia: it brought out the fine spun-gold effect of her hair, enhanced the luster of her skin, chastened her figure to an exquisite slenderness. It was almost worth losing a husband in order to be able to put on a mourning costume. And tears, if not overdone, were piquant.

However, Lucrezia's signature to the letter expressed sincere feeling. During the past three months, she had been as unhappy as her buoyant and adaptable nature permitted. She had been fond of her late husband, the handsome young prince from Naples; but she was fond of her brother, Cesare, who had had him strangled in the Vatican in spite of her entreaties; and she was fond of her indulgent father, the Pope, who, though annoyed by the murder, had afterwards condoned it. The trouble was she was fond of almost everybody. That the people she loved should suffer or commit such horrid things confused and depressed her. When life could be so pleasant and amusing, why did men have to spoil it by killing each other? Reasons of state. From the cradle, she had been brought up to accept that as the final word for everything tedious or hateful. But there are limits sometimes to what a woman can stand without a tear.

Besides, she began to feel bored at Nepi and longed for Rome. She could mourn her husband completely for a month or even two months; but she was not the kind to mourn indefinitely, and with the third month sorrow tended to become merely official. The castle at Nepi, so spick-and-span modern that it still smelled of mortar, provided every comfort; but it could not supply the familiar conveniences of her own palace of Santa Maria in Portico near the Vatican. As to surroundings, nothing, to Lucrezia's taste, could be more dismal than Nepi with its wide view over the desolate Campagna, the gloomy chasms beneath it, the cheerless, cold mountains in the distance. No sound but of wind and torrents and the sad bleating of sheep on the uplands. No spectacle except the meaningless colors of sunset flaming in through the recessed windows. Everything reminded her of grief, and there was nothing to do but grieve with her ladies and gentlemen until grief went stale. She missed the come-and-go of St. Peter's Square, its whirlpool of news, the equipages of the cardinals, the brilliant companies and excitement of Rome. If Angela had not arrived several days ago with the latest gossip of the city, the routine of sorrow would have been too much to bear.

"Don't," observed the latter, looking up again from her embroidery to note that Lucrezia had applied the tip of a forefinger to the corner of her eye. "We're alone. You don't have to mourn with *me*."

Lucrezia half smiled. "I'd like to see you in my place. It's easy to be resigned when all you have to do is ride your mule back to Rome. You're not banished and forgotten, while the rest of the world enjoys itself." She stretched her arms. "O-ho, I'm sick of things, Angeletta."

"So *that's* it! I thought it might be something else."

Lucrezia used the tip of her forefinger again. "Of course my late lord — of course that, too. . . . How long do you think His Holiness will keep me here? You'd suppose it was I who had done wrong instead of my lord brother. I'm the one who's punished. It *was* wrong to kill His Highness. I told them so at the time; I say it again. Wrong! Unjust!"

She tossed back her hair, which was confined only by the fillet of a jeweled ribbon, and lifted her head with a look of girlish independence. Angela, impressed by such daring, glanced instinctively about the room, to make sure they were alone.

"Hush, *cara mia!* I quite agree, of course, but don't talk so loud. Yes, it was very wrong, but — "

She left the sentence unfinished and examined the frame of needlework at arm's length.

The two young women were of about the same age and showed a strong family likeness. They both had the Borgia corn-gold hair and delicacy of features. The taste of the time preferred blue eyes; and in this respect, Lucrezia had the best of her cousin, whose dark Spanish eyes suggested a trace of Moorish blood somewhere in her veins. But the defect was almost counterbalanced by the contrast with the blondness of her hair and skin. For the rest, they were alike in elegance of dress and polish of grooming, the well-schooled grace of fashionable women.

"But what?"

Angela still appraised her embroidery. "I understand my lord Cesare's point, don't you? Nothing had come of your marriage to His late Highness — I mean no advantage to our House. It seemed best to sever relations with Naples. It was important to make Your Signory available for a more useful marriage — in Ferrara if possible. Since the Prince of Salerno had given you a son, there were no grounds for divorce, as in the case of your first husband. Well, then, look at it sensibly, my love. What better move could the lord Cesare make than to solve all problems at once by the death of your dear lord? Sad for you, yes; wrong, in a way; but, from the standpoint of our House, advantageous. You can't deny that. And my lord Cesare does not let scruples influence policy; he knows what he wants and where he is going. Quite a man!"

Lucrezia got up from her writing desk. "Yes, but isn't there such a thing as God?"

In reply to this naïve question, Angela could only stare. Then she smiled. "I'm not very good at theology, darling. I see what you mean; but, as far as that goes, isn't the Pope God's viceroy on earth? Doesn't he hold the two keys? I shouldn't think you'd deny that he had the power to absolve my lord Cesare in this affair."

Overcome by the argument, Lucrezia shook her head. "No, that's true. I don't understand these things." She added wistfully: "My mind gets lost. Only I still *feel* it was wrong. Strange how thinking and feeling are different."

This was too deep for Angela, who resumed her needlework.

Her cousin went on: "I mean you wouldn't talk so coolly, if you had been there when my lord came into the Vatican after that first attack on him in front of St. Peter's. Covered with blood, dragging himself to His Holiness's rooms. I thought he was dying. I almost died myself at the look of him. *Ahi, Madonna!* The death in his eyes, with the candlelight on them! Shall I ever forget it? I loved him: we loved each other."

Angela nodded sympathetically and drew a piece of thread between her lips.

"We thought we had saved him. He was getting well. Sancia and I nursed him every minute. We cooked his food. . . . You can be cool about it! You weren't there when my brother called that day and stood by the bed, looking down at him. You know Cesare's smile. 'What

wasn't finished at noon can be finished at night,' he said. And my dear
lord staring up. He knew it was the end. I wish I could stop remembering!"

"Dreadful," murmured Angela.

"Then Captain Michelotto came. He forced us out of the room.
We ran downstairs to His Holiness for help. When we got back,
Michelotto was gone; my lord was dead. He was beautiful even in
death. I kissed him on the lips. . . . Wouldn't you think they would
seal up that cursed room in the Vatican forever?"

"*I should say so, my love!* I wouldn't sleep there for the world!"

"That's what I *mean* by feeling. You can bring out all the arguments
you want, but I still say it was wrong and unjust and cruel."

"Don't say it." Angela lowered her embroidery. "Not if you wish to
leave Nepi. There's the trouble. You were too outspoken. His Holiness
doesn't want you reproaching and lamenting in the Vatican. It's as if
you weren't loyal to the family. Besides, you angered your brother by
talking too much, and his word is law. So, they say, if you want to
mourn, you shall mourn where no one can hear you. A word to the
wise, *carissima*."

Lucrezia's brief independence faded. Her eyes fell. "How long?"

"Oh, not too long." Angela smiled reassuringly. "I should suppose
it depended on two things: your discretion and how soon they need
you for the next move. I told you there was some talk of the Duke of
Gravina."

"But Alfonso d'Este?"

Angela shrugged. "You know as much as anyone. When I left Rome,
His Holiness told me that there had been no word from the lord Andrea
Orsini." Her eyes softened. "If anyone can snare your eagle, he's the
man. Heigh-o, I miss him. What a galliard! What good company!"

She sank into reflection, smiling from time to time; while Lucrezia,
standing in front of the hearth, held out her hands to the fire. It was
late October, and the autumn chill made itself felt toward evening.

The latch rattled; a page, entering, announced gravely, "The illustrious Duke of Biselli," and Lucrezia whirled around with outstretched
arms. Carried by his wet nurse, the illustrious Duke, a year old, approached his mother with a solemn baby look that changed suddenly
to an almost toothless smile. He wore a tight-fitting hood of red velvet,
pricked out with jewels, and was wrapped in brocaded cloth, from
which his tiny slippers stuck out stiffly like a doll's.

"*Bambino mio!*" Lucrezia caroled. "Come to Mother."

The baby held out his miniature hands and babbled his own language.

146

Lucrezia hugged him. "Of course, my Blessing! So, you missed *Mammina?* . . . Hear that, Angela? He speaks already like a little orator. My Rodrigo! Come, let's see you walk."

She kneeled down and balanced the child on his feet, holding her hands slightly away from his sides.

Mona Teresa, the nurse, a full-bosomed Roman girl, laughed. "No need to worry! His Highness walks like a lion. *Dio!* What a little captain!"

Lucrezia backed away on her knees, and the baby tottered a step or two after her.

"See, Angeletta? See? It's a true miracle the way he learns. Just as the astrologer, Master Simone, predicted. . . . There, *piccino!* I caught you!"

Rodrigo collapsed against his mother, who took him in her arms again. "Want to see Cousin Angela?" But, as the baby vigorously declined this suggestion and turned his back, Lucrezia carried him over to the deep-set window, rich with the purples and ambers of sunset. "Behold, my treasure! See the pretty flag on the tower?" Standing in that play of light on the raised platform of the window niche, she looked like an enshrined Madonna against a background of stained glass.

"By the Seven Churches," admired the nurse, "Your Signory is as beautiful as the Blessed Mother herself!"

"Nonsense, Teresa! . . . Listen, *carino*. Someone is crossing the drawbridge. On a pretty horse perhaps. *Eccolo!*"

The window overlooked the courtyard, from which at that moment sounded the challenge of a guard and then a rattle of hoofs suddenly stopping.

"See, the fine horse." But at the same instant, Lucrezia caught her breath. "Angela! It's a messenger." Her voice faded. "He's wearing my brother's livery. God spare me!"

In a flash, Angela crossed the room to her cousin's side and looked down.

"Yes, Duke Cesare's colors. I wonder — "

They walked back to the hearth, Lucrezia still holding her little son; but her eyes were on the door. A vague sound of footsteps and voices came from below, grew louder on the stairs. The door opened.

A page's young voice announced, "The noble Captain Medrano on the part of His Exalted Excellence, the Duke de Valentinois."

And a thick-set, swarthy man in red and yellow, his high boots gray with dust, his spurs jingling, crossed the floor, dropped to one knee, and bowed his head.

"At the command of Your Signory."

He was one of the Spanish adventurers who followed Cesare Borgia, and Lucrezia vaguely remembered that she had seen him in Rome. She remembered, too, that he was the fast friend of Michelotto di Coriglia, her husband's assassin.

Pale to the lips and clasping the baby closer in her arms, she faltered, "Rise, sir. You bring news from my brother? I hope all goes well with him."

"A second Mars, Your Grace. He sweeps from victory to victory. He holds Pesaro and Rimini; he plans the leaguer of Faenza. I left him at Pesaro in high contentment with the progress of the campaign. But this letter" — the captain presented a sealed paper — "will speak for him. . . . And now may Your Excellence permit me to take leave. I have letters for His Holiness, and it's twenty miles to Rome. I kiss Your Grace's feet — "

Lucrezia breathed more freely, but the hand holding the letter still trembled.

"You'll take some refreshment."

"I dare not. My men are waiting for me below this place; and we must ride hard, for the message is urgent. I beg your forbearance — "

She murmured her thanks, gave him her hand. The jingle of his spurs had not died away before she returned the child to Teresa, and, breaking the seal of the letter, began reading it. Angela stood on tiptoe with curiosity. A letter from Cesare Borgia to his sister, with whom he had recently been at outs, might mean anything.

Then slowly the tenseness of Lucrezia's face relaxed and was followed by a wave of color. Her eyes danced. "Glorious!" she exclaimed. "Blessed Madonna!"

"What is it?" Angela urged. "Tell me! I can't wait!"

"Listen. . . . Such happiness! *Oh, Angela mia dolce!* . . . Here, listen. He writes: 'This day the talented and ingenious Messer Andrea Orsini has been with me, and in all ways he has managed the business at Ferrara according to our hopes. He is now riding to Viterbo on some errand of the illustrious Duke Ercole; but this is no more than a pretext to bring him south. He bears letters to Your Excellence from the illustrious Don Alfonso, than which, though unsigned, I have never read any more loving and full of promise. Captain Orsini has quite won over this illustrious prince to an alliance with our House, and he has worked subtly upon Monseigneur d'Ars of France, now at the court of Ferrara, to induce His French Majesty rather to aid than to hinder our desire. In short, though much yet remains to negotiate, and thougn the illustrious Don Alfonso cannot as yet publicly declare himself, the chief points have been gained. And I felicitate Your Signory upon the happy outcome of our endeavors. You know that I am not one to predict success without cause. . . . As for the lord Andrea, we are right well pleased with his devotion and we have promised him the signory of Città del Monte in due time. He deserves your favor for his diligence. . . . And now, dearest sister, the night of your sorrow is past. Though it was natural that you should mourn the late illustrious Duke, your husband, it is still more natural that you should rejoice in the glorious and triumphant future. With these, I have written to His Holiness urging your speedy recall to Rome — ' "

Lucrezia waved the letter above her head and then kissed it. "Here, Angela, you can read the rest. Duchess of Ferrara! The most brilliant court in Italy! Lucrezia d'Este!" In her jubilation, she snatched her little son from the arms of his nurse and, setting him on his feet, with her hands half lifting him, she danced in a circle before the hearth, while the baby laughed with delight. "*Bambino mio*, shall we go to Ferrara? Shall we be free and happy? No dark old Vatican any more! Dance, baby, dance!" Her black gown, edged with the firelight, half revealed the graceful contours beneath it.

In the words of the letter, it was very natural. Angela and the nurse shared Lucrezia's joy. There would be a great wedding, marvelous new clothes. It was a marriage lofty enough to dazzle anyone. Of course, Lucrezia, at times, would remember her late husband with a sigh. But sighs and family grudges are no use; a pleasure-loving woman takes life as it comes and makes the best of it. Quite natural.

And it was natural as well that the excitement proved too great for little Rodrigo. Certain signs appeared on the floor; the dance broke off. Bleak nods were exchanged between Lucrezia and the nurse, who resumed possession of the child and bore him solemnly away. The illustrious Duke needed to be changed.

Alone with her cousin, Lucrezia drew a long breath. "*Dolce vita*, what news!"

Angela was still intent on the letter. "Congratulations," she murmured. "How lucky you are!" But her mind was apparently on something else. "Città del Monte's a fine signory," she remarked.

"Yes," said Lucrezia, preoccupied.

A long minute passed. The figured wall-hangings rippled to the draft behind them, as if stirred by ghosts. The two ladies dreamed before the fire. Finally Angela leaned forward.

"Dearest cousin, I have a favor to ask of the Duchess of Ferrara. Promise you'll grant it."

"If I can, dearest."

"Pooh! No doubt about that, now that you're back in favor with the Duke and His Holiness. Only a trifle anyway. You know how I feel toward Andrea Orsini."

Lucrezia smiled. "Mm-m. A little. I thought he had got you in bad trouble last summer."

"By God, and so did I!" Angela laughed at the recollection. "But the old Jew Isacco's herbs pulled me through. Well, in short, I dote on the lord Andrea. My dear, what a lover!"

She sighed and leaned back in her chair. At times, Lucrezia, sensitive to such things, was conscious of a certain grossness in her cousin. It revealed itself perhaps in the hot quality of Angela's voice or perhaps in her hands and the prominence of her thumbs.

Lucrezia's eyes widened. "God pardon you! What of your betrothal to the young della Rovere?"

"Politics. I give *that* for my betrothal." Angela snapped her fingers. "You ought to know how easily betrothals are broken when they've served their purpose. And mine will have served in another year, by the time my Andrea is seated in Città del Monte. His Holiness will absolve me at a mere little word from you."

Always inclined to generosity, Lucrezia agreed. "Why, of course, my love, you shall have that word and all that I can do. There was some gossip about giving Orsini the Baglione girl, wife to old Varano of Città del Monte, after that lord has been dealt with. But naturally he'd prefer you on every count: yourself, the alliance with our House. And we owe him our favor. . . . Rest assured, you shall have your prince of lovers."

Springing up from her chair, Angela made a low court curtsy. "I'll hold Your Signory to that promise."

CHAPTER XXII

As ANDREA ORSINI had expected, he found Mario Belli awaiting him at a roadside tavern not more than a safe league beyond the limits of Ferrara. And, as Belli had expected, it did not take long to absolve himself for the practical joke he had played on Ippolito d'Este.

"Sir," he explained, "a few temptations are beyond my power to resist, and a donkey in a cardinal's hat is one of them. I like to encourage asses in their folly, for how else could a man of my profession live? And Your Magnificence will mark that I did no more than that. No untruth, not the shadow of a lie. His Asininity had great sport while it lasted. I had my fee and a laugh — "

"Fine," interjected Andrea. "You seem to forget that I was betrayed and embarrassed."

Belli wagged his head. "Betrayed? To be recognized as one of the lights of Italy in painting! Embarrassed? To be the known creator of a priceless masterpiece! . . . I'll bet you one thing. The next time you're in Ferrara, you'll find the Duke has robbed Pomposa of that picture and taken it for himself. More embarrassment."

"It wasn't finished," Andrea objected.

"The Duke will have it finished by one of his men — that's my belief."

Forgetting his grievance against Belli, Andrea clenched his fists. "I'll have no bungler tampering with my work. Saint Peter's head needed retouching. The color must be deepened behind Our Lord's aureole to bring out the light. By God, if I believed you, I'd return this moment to Pomposa and either destroy the painting or finish it to my liking."

He looked back up the road and did not observe the shrewd smile that flickered under Belli's nose, or the cunning droop of one of his eyelids.

"But there's nothing to that," Andrea concluded. "The illustrious Ippolito couldn't tell a work of art from his horse's rump. My painting will stay in Pomposa."

Thus reconciled, the two allies, followed by a boy with a pack mule, continued on to Rimini and then took the coast road south to Pesaro, which, by good chance, they reached on October 27th, the same day that witnessed Cesare Borgia's triumphant entry into the city. After the interview, which Borgia reported in his message to Lucrezia, Andrea and Belli, richer in funds and further rewarded by the great man's favor, turned west to the mountains and up the Flaminian Road to Urbino, where Andrea hoped to find Camilla. His reception at the court of the young Duke Guidobaldo and the Duchess Elisabetta was worthy of his name and position; but he learned at once that Camilla, in company with her husband, had departed two days earlier for Città del Monte.

The disappointment was great, but it provided also an opportunity. Since Città del Monte lay only a few leagues to the southeast, and not far off the main road, he had now every excuse to visit and reconnoiter his future domain en route to Viterbo. So, having dispatched a messenger with his respects to the lord Varano and Camilla, and begging permission to wait upon them, he continued south next morning along the Via Flaminia.

Toward the close of the Jubilee Year, 1500, there was plenty to see on the great highway, which for centuries has been one of the chief veins along the leg of Italy. During the daytime, a faint canopy of dust marked its windings between the steep mountains; a murmur of voices and click of hoofs, now louder, now swallowed up behind projecting cliffs, added a human stir to the lonely rush of torrents along the ravine-like valleys. Since not much time was left to take advantage of the spiritual benefits earned by those who paid their devotions at the Roman shrines, all the laggards were trudging south; while a north-bound stream of absolved people, who had fulfilled their Christian duties, met and tangled with them in narrower sections of the road or on humpbacked bridges arching the wider chasms.

Pilgrims, with their long staffs and rosaries, wearing the scallop shell on their hats, drifted in both directions. Some were beggars by profession and some for the good of their souls; but they all whined for alms — *una santa elemosina* — and extracted a trickle of copper along the line of travel. Peasants, on foot or on donkey, in the costume of their separate villages; mendicant friars, bearded and burly; carriers, shepherding their mules; two-wheeled wine carts with their rows of casks; occasional horsemen jogging through the dust; still more occasional fine ladies in back-breaking coaches; rarest of all, an arrogant great lord or prelate with his following; whores and bandits on vacation; rich men, poor men, beggar men: everybody journeyed down to, or up from, Rome.

"'Sblood!" coughed Belli. "We're traveling in religious company, my patron. When do we leave it?"

"*Occhio!* Take care!" warning voices shouted in front. And a herd of oxen, driven north to Borgia's army, plunged by, half seen through the dust, their branching horns like a moving thicket above them. Andrea and Belli each wheeled to his side of the road and disappeared from sight till the avalanche had passed.

"I say when do we leave it?"

"God knows, at this rate."

The steady beat of a marching drum reached beyond the turn of the road, then grew louder, as the vanguard of a band of Swiss pikemen came into view. A huge fellow in parti-colored hose carried the banner of Zurich, blue and silver, in front. Rank upon rank of blond-bearded giants followed him, some of them shouldering eighteen-foot pikes, others two-handed swords, all of them veteran mercenaries, proud of their self-imposed, invincible discipline. The walls of the valley echoed with the tramp of the company and the beat of the drum.

Once again Andrea drew to the side, but the Swiss captain, on horseback at the left of the column, suddenly halted.

"*Grüss Gott*, Herr Orsini," he bellowed. "What are you doing out of camp? You remember me from Forlì?"

"Captain Jacob Meiss?"

"The same, and glad to see you. Have you quit Valentino's service?" He spoke as one military artisan to another, discussing business.

Andrea explained that he held a command under the Duke of Ferrara.

"How's the pay?" Meiss demanded.

"Pretty good."

The other shook his head. "Then that's not good enough for us. It's only pretty good with Valentino. It'll have to be something special to keep us south of the Alps when our engagement with him runs out come December. We're sick for the Cantons. . . . Where're you bound?"

"Viterbo."

"Well, see that you keep to the main road, that's my advice. No short cuts. *Herr Gott Donnerwett'*! I'll wager that all the brigands in Italy are nosing this line of march for stragglers. Two of our boys went foraging close to Narni and had their throats cut. We burned the nearest village and did some hanging, but that won't bring back Willi and Fritzi. God's pity on them! . . . What's this I hear about you and Pierre de Bayard? A courier from the Duke — that Spanish fellow, Medrano — was telling us about it only yesterday at Gualdo. Sounded like a good fight."

Andrea shrugged and deprecated. Quick as news traveled, it amazed him that his recent duel in Ferrara should have already been reported so far south. But sports items of that kind spread fast in military circles.

"Ach, modesty!" chuckled Meiss. Leaning over, he smote Andrea on the back. "Congratulations, all the same. Bayard's a stout man-at-arms."

The baggage carts of the company had now passed, and Meiss gathered his reins. "Well, sir, *auf Wiederlug!* We'll be meeting again, no doubt, on one side or the other."

He raised his gauntlet and spurred off to catch up with his men. Perhaps for Andrea's benefit, the Swiss fifers, a moment later, striking up, shrilled back down the road an air of the Cantons.

Andrea gazed after them. "Lord!" he sighed, "if it were only possible to raise troops like that in Italy! To keep these blood merchants out. Until then, what hope have we? You can't make bricks out of sand. . . . *Burned a village, did some hanging!* Christ!"

Belli's eyes narrowed at this outburst; but he said nothing, and the two riders, trailed by their pack mule, pressed on as fast as possible through the circulation on the road until at length, in a valley between mountain pyramids, they caught sight of the walls and campaniles of Fabriano.

Here they stopped long enough for a meal and to put on steel caps and corselets. The Swiss Captain's advice regarding brigands was too sound to overlook. Banditry, always rife in these mountains, would no doubt be still more active in view of the Jubilee pilgrimage; and the eastward road from Fabriano, less frequented than the Flaminian Way, led through the wildest country. Aside from their horses and personal equipment, Orsini's and Belli's purses, well lined by the gold of Cesare Borgia and Ippolito d'Este, offered a rich prize to robbers. It could be expected, too, that scouts would inform the bandit chiefs of any travelers off the main highway.

But in spite of this, Andrea was not too much concerned. After Fabriano, he and Belli would be riding almost at once in Varano territory, and the reputation of Marc' Antonio did not suggest that he would tolerate brigandage in his signory. Besides, it was only a few miles to Città del Monte, a distance that could be covered in little more than an hour.

"You know," remarked Belli, as the walls of the town disappeared behind a spur of cliffs, "I wouldn't mind a brush with a few rogues. It's been a long time since I've had my tuck out of its scabbard. But the devil of it is, losels like that aren't apt to come to grips. They'll plant you a crossbow shaft in your horse and one in your throat before you can lay an eye on them and then pick your bones at leisure. Saints! What country for an ambush!"

He turned an experienced gaze on the steep wooded slopes right and left, with an outcropping of scattered boulders that gave excellent cover to marksmen. Above the forest towered craggy summits half-concealed by clouds. The road looked almost furtive, as it threaded between the walls of beeches and pine; and it seemed doubly lonesome after the throngs on the Roman highway.

"There you are," Andrea pointed. "I don't believe it's healthy for bandits in this region. Look at that."

They had come out upon a sort of crossroads formed by intersecting valleys. Hanging from the outstretched limb of an oak, two grisly skeletons with only tatters of clothes still adhering to them swung gently back and forth in a light wind. Nailed to the trunk of the tree appeared a statement of names and crimes with a bold signature at the end and the Varano seal.

Belli sniffed. "Yes, and rather recent. The ravens make quick work of carcasses. . . . These Varani," he went on, "I knew a couple of gallants by that name who were killed at the Battle of the Taro."

"Marc' Antonio's sons. He had no other heirs."

"Sad. An old family, they say."

"They've held their lands a hundred years or more, one branch at Camerino and one at Città del Monte. I've heard nothing but evil of those at Camerino and nothing but good of this lord. He was friend and comrade of the late Duke Federigo of Urbino. But *he* has no heirs, while his rascal cousins flourish."

"Precisely," Belli agreed. "My favorite thesis."

Orsini hesitated. "By the way, friend Mario, I shall be occupied at Città del Monte, while you may have time on your hands. Give heed to the town and castle, its approaches, the strength and weakness of the walls, the temper of the townsfolk. It's well to improve one's knowledge. And a certain prince is interested."

Belli's face was inscrutable as ever. "You can count on me. I believe I understand what you want. It's a privilege — " He broke off. "My lord, if that wasn't a lookout I saw dodge behind that cliff up there, call me blind."

They stared upward at a crag naked against the sky.

"A man's head, on my honor," Belli muttered. "Shall we turn or ride on?"

"Some shepherd perhaps." Orsini tightened his reins. "We'll ride for it. If it's nothing, we'll be there the sooner. If it's an ambush we may get by." He shouted to the mule boy to hurry and quickened his pace toward the next turn of the road.

But in an instant several horsemen rounded the elbow of the woods just in front. They carried crossbows at the ready. Others on foot, similarly armed, emerged from behind the trees. Though in the same moment Orsini's sword was out, he knew that resistance would be fatal. Wheeling his horse for flight in the opposite direction, he saw that the mule was already surrounded and the road blocked by another group of *balestrieri*. He was too experienced a campaigner not to accept hard facts. Resheathing his sword and with a nod to Belli to do the same, he turned his horse again and rode toward the mounted party in front.

"What's the meaning of this, sirs? What's your will?"

A rider with a black patch over one eye advanced to meet him.

"Think it over," said the horseman. "Maybe you can answer those questions yourself."

CHAPTER XXIII

THE bandit leader was clean-shaven and wore a round, high-crowned, purple hat, which would have been fashionable a generation earlier. Except for the black patch on his left eye, he looked weathered and hearty rather than sinister. His craggy nose and massive face, but, above all, the heavy-lidded, keen eye, at that moment surveying Andrea, made a straightforward, soldierly impression. He was apparently in the middle fifties. Unlike most robbers who could boast of such a following as this, he wore no flashy colors or finery, but a plain leather doublet smudged here and there by the rust stains of armor. On the other hand, his horse, a fine Barb stallion, no doubt stolen in some lucky snatch, would have graced a prince.

"What's your name?" he demanded.

"Andrea Orsini, captain in the service of the renowned Duke Ercole d'Este."

"Orsini? What branch?"

"Of Naples. The House of Raimondo Orsini, Count of Nola."

"That's a lie. The Count you speak of had no sons. His line died with him."

"Ever hear of the bar sinister, Messer Bandit?"

"Oho! I see. Well, beg your pardon. I've known as many great lords who were bastards as those who weren't; and, speaking of Ferrara, the Duke Borso d'Este, for one. But learn the proper phrase. *Baton* sinister, not *bar*. False usage."

Andrea bit his lips.

"I take it, then, you're the grandson of Count Raimondo. Who's this — " the robber's good eye wondered at Belli — "this fellow?"

"My ensign, Mario Belli."

They were encircled now by the other horsemen, tattered ruffians with dirty faces. Like their leader, they were well mounted and showed a kind of rakehell grace in the saddle.

"Signori," said the chief, "we can do one of three things with these men: kill and strip them; strip them and let them go; or, if it's worth our while, hold them to ransom. Which shall it be?"

A confused mutter answered. Several spoke up for a short shrift; some were for mercy; but about half contended that ransom offered the bigger profit.

To Andrea's surprise, Belli laughed. "You have other alternatives, signori. Suppose we joined you? Your profession's attractive — the world to rob. Eh, Your Magnificence?"

"Who invites you to join us, Merry Andrew?" the leader burst out. "And hide that grin if you want to live."

"Messer Bandit," soothed Andrea, "my friend's tongue runs away with him at times. He wishes only to make himself agreeable — "

The leader ignored this remark and turned to the business at hand. "Let's see if you're worth a ransom. An officer of Duke Ercole ought to have a jewel or so on his person, rings and the like. Take off your glove."

Andrea drew off his gauntlet slowly. Camilla's diamond ring showed on his little finger.

"*Madonna!*" breathed the chief. "That's not bad. Give it over."

Andrea folded his arms. "Not so fast. You can take the ring from my dead body. Or if it's ransom you're thinking of, you'll be paid for it. But, Messer Cutthroat, don't imagine that I'll hand it over to you or anybody else."

"Love token, ha?"

Orsini's temper rose higher. "That's not your business."

Under ordinary circumstances, he would have realized that he was acting like a fool. The ring wasn't worth dying for. But his recent promise to Camilla and what the ring now meant to him outweighed prudence.

"Very well, my son," the leader grinned, "we'll hack off that finger and send it to your lady as a keepsake, if you'll give us the address. She'll treasure your fidelity; we'll treasure the ring. Everybody pleased. How's that?"

"*How's this?*"

For a moment it looked like an explosion. Andrea spurred his horse, which reared against the bandit's stallion. Unable to free his sword in the narrow space, he snatched out his dagger, thrusting at the man on his right who tried to grapple with him. Shouts, yells, and dust filled the road. Steel flickered. The entire band closed in on the tossing center of the fight.

Andrea's idea, as far as he had one, was to break through and plunge into the woods. But his jaded horse could not deliver the effort. In a few seconds, wedged between the more powerful steeds of his opponents, his dagger wrenched out of his hand, his bridle in the grip of a robber, he sat once more confronting the old chieftain's inexorable eye. Except that the purple hat tilted on one side, the bandit looked as unruffled as before.

"Pretty good," he remarked. "Lad of spirit. Makes me think Duke Ercole might not care to lose you." He glanced around at the others. "Signori, we'll hold these men to ransom. If the Duke pays a fat sum, well; if he doesn't, we're no worse off. . . . As for you, sir, take your choice! Give me your word to attempt no escape, and you can ride along with us free and easy; if not, we'll truss you up. Though it's little consideration you deserve after your capers," he added.

Andrea gave in. "*Va bene,* you have my word." He noticed that the ring had been momentarily forgotten.

The robber fulfilled his part of the bargain. Orsini's dagger and bridle reins were handed back to him and he was apparently left unguarded. Riding between the leader and another horseman, he might have been one of the band as far as appearances were concerned.

Orsini expected that they would now cut back at once into the mountains toward whatever camp the robbers maintained; but, with perfect assurance, the entire troop kept up the road toward Città del Monte. It spoke volumes for the collapse of law in that district. High time the doddering old Varano was replaced by a younger lord. Andrea thought of Julius Caesar and the pirates and vowed, if he survived this case and got possession of the signory, to hang his swaggering captors the length of the road to Fabriano. Meanwhile, he pitied Camilla, forced to live in such a disreputable region.

"Messer Bandit," he remarked at last to the one-eyed chieftain on

158

his right, "since we're apt to be spending some time together, may I have the favor of your name? It's awkward to address you only with reference to your profession. You may even consider it impertinent —"

"*Non importa*," returned the other. "Call me anything you like. I'm generally known as the Old Soldier. I've belonged to that trade, too. Not much difference."

"Well, then, Messer Old Soldier, can you inform me how it is that you and your men ride the highways of this state in such security? Have you come to an understanding with the lord Varano, or how?"

"Something like that," nodded the chief. "The old fellow spends so much on his young wife that he's forced to swell his revenues one way or another. She junkets to Venice, buying paintings, lutes, blackamoor urchins, and God knows what rubbish, while the old lord sweats at home to make ends meet. So, we've struck a bargain. You'll grieve to hear that the better part of your ransom will pass into His Excellence's strongbox. But, in return, we have the freedom of the road. Understand?"

Andrea digested this in silence. Except that he had heard better things of the lord of Città del Monte, it did not too much surprise him. The Varani of Camerino had a reputation for harboring bandits, and they were by no means the only tyrants in Italy so accused. Andrea noted, too, the correct report of Camilla's acquisitions in Venice: the painting, the theorbo, and Seraph.

"You speak slightingly of Madama," he probed.

"That hussy? Who wouldn't?" Old Soldier shook his head. "That traipsing gadabout, up to every devilment under heaven! If I didn't hate old Varano so well, by Bacchus I'd pity him. They tell me she's just planted a fresh pair of horns on his head with some young captain up in Ferrara. Perhaps you've heard of it."

Andrea boiled. "Let me tell you, sir, I know Madama Camilla and reverence her. We'll talk of something else, if you please. I'll endure no disrespect to her."

"Messere, Messere, you sound like a hooked fish. She'll play one of her tricks on you, mark my word."

By this time, the wooded valley they were following had opened up into a wider landscape. Though hills billowed in every direction, their slopes had been cleared for pasture or vine or olive groves. Farmhouses could be seen, and a near-by village; while in the distance, covering a summit that overlooked the highway, Città del Monte, with its walls and campaniles and the dominating mass of its palace castle, stood out, delicately tinted by the rays of the declining sun. As a whole, the view

159

gave an impression of serene, secluded contentment. It suggested also a rich yield of oil, wine, and flocks.

Andrea, scanning the country, found it better than he had expected, a right choice domain, an ideal springboard for the future. Of course, it should be linked to Fabriano, whose excellent paper works would bring in additional revenue; and he wondered at the Varani's lack of ambition in not having laid hands on the neighboring town by some hook or crook. No doubt, too, the little state could be extended to the east; he was not quite sure of its frontiers in that direction. With Cesare Borgia in his present good humor, it ought to be possible to secure a larger grant than the first offered. The more, the better. Scheme merged with scheme.

They now began to pass country folk, either on the road or in the adjoining fields, well-set-up mountaineers who would make excellent recruits for a levy when the time came. But it disgusted Andrea that, far from being disturbed at the appearance of the robbers, they greeted them with a kind of affectionate deference, grinning and doffing their caps, while Old Soldier waved a fatherly hand.

Roads zigzagged everywhere between the hills; and, at any moment, Andrea imagined that his kidnapers would turn off from the main valley. However, the town on the hill came steadily closer. When the final side road had been passed, it seemed evident that the bandits would continue along the highway to the east under the very walls of Città del Monte itself.

Orsini examined the approaching town with sarcastic interest. In the circumstances, it would not surprise him if the guards on the walls waved to the robbers and bade them Godspeed. He could see dots, representing men, along the ramparts; and he could make out clearly features of the city, in particular the overshadowing palace castle, that looked like a smaller version of the one in Urbino. But when, instead of following the eastern highway, the bandit captain turned into the cobblestone road leading directly uphill to the town gate, Andrea's jaw dropped.

"What now, sir! By God — "

He found himself staring at the robber's altered appearance. He had two perfect eyes, the black patch was gone.

"I . . ." he stammered. "What . . ."

A rattle of hoofs on the cobblestones in front brought his eyes back in that direction. Down from the gate rode Camilla Baglione, a plume fluttering on her hat, her white palfrey caracoling.

And at the roar of laughter from behind, he turned to see the band

160

of riders undergoing transformation, their tatters and headdresses disintegrating, their features released from the make-up of patches and false hair, until — while his head swiveled back and forth between them and Camilla — he saw a typical company of court gentlemen in the highest spirits and finest clothes, rollicking at his expense.

"Wonderful!" cheered Camilla, stretching up in her stirrups and waving a gloved hand above her head. "That's what I call a triumph! Ah, Messere, were you really taken in for once? Didn't you like your reception? Poor Magnifico!"

The troop formed a circle of stamping horses and gleeful men, with Camilla, Orsini, and the delighted ex-bandit, Varano, at the center. Andrea's cheeks burned. It did not help to see Belli leering at him like a hyena, in the background. He had taken part in many such court pranks himself and ought to have seen through this one. If it hadn't been for Jacob Meiss and his chatter about brigands, he wouldn't have been so easily fooled. This jest, from now on, with all kinds of additions, would be told of Andrea Orsini by every scribbler and court anecdotist up and down Italy; for the practical joke or *beffa* was the best-loved sport of the times. He would never live it down.

"It's all the fault of that little devil," Varano proclaimed, with admiring eyes on Camilla. "She staged everything." He had taken off his purple hat and was swinging it around a forefinger. Andrea noticed that he looked much older without it. "That ensign of yours almost spoiled the game. He's sharper than you are." He looked over at Belli and nodded. "But, gentlemen, don't blame me for carrying out Madonna's orders; she always gets her way."

► Andrea knew enough to join in the merriment; but the effort hurt, and his face was red.

Varano's heavy-lidded, dark eyes relented. He stopped twirling his hat and, bending forward in the saddle, laid a broad hand on Andrea's shoulder. "Only fun, sir. I'm sure you'll take it in good part. Hark you, Messere, aside from the joke, I'm right glad of this means of knowing you — without court patter and smooth talk. You showed up well. Forgive us, and welcome to Città del Monte."

Andrea glanced at Camilla. She smiled back, impish as always. "Isn't it something of an honor to be kidnaped, Captain? We don't usually take so much trouble for guests. Besides, when you kidnap that saint in Viterbo, as is rumored, you'll know how it's done."

There were presentations to the gentlemen of the cortege, more compliments and laughter. Andrea's embarrassment vanished. With a strangely warm feeling toward Varano and more charmed by Camilla than ever, he rode between them at the head of the company through the cool arches of the city gate. Even Belli was forgiven.

"How did you know?" he demanded later, when he and Belli were alone in the spacious apartment which had been assigned them.

"The fruit of a misspent life, Your Magnificence. If I couldn't tell false rogues from true ones by this time, I'd peddle chestnuts. Bandits on Arab horses, discussing your ancestry, shocked by *bars* and demanding *batons*, overdressed in rags. *Voilà!*"

"You might have given me a hint!"

"Hint! I did what I could. And the joke? Would it have served better to have spoiled it?"

"Perhaps not."

"Be assured not. My lord, to disarm people, let them sometimes overreach you." Belli gave one of his silent laughs. "For once, thanks to me, you were clever without knowing it."

CHAPTER XXIV

THE resemblance of the palace castle at Città del Monte to the much larger and more sumptuous residence of the Dukes of Urbino was in no way accidental. Just as the latter represented the versatile tastes of the great Federigo da Montefeltro, so the smaller palace at Città del Monte reflected the lifelong devotion of Marc' Antonio Varano to that famous captain and prince. Younger than his patron by eight years, Varano had followed the Duke's standard in war and supported his policies in peace. He had emulated his character and copied his virtues. As one of the Duke's most trusted lieutenants, he had shared, too, in the rich fees paid by Church, king, or city for the hire of Federigo's mercenary troops and leadership. It was natural, then, that the palace at Città del Monte, so far as difference in location and smaller resources allowed, should have been modeled on that of Urbino. The same architects, Luziano Lauranna and Baccio Pontelli of Florence, had a hand in both; and Varano had consulted with the Duke while both palaces were in the course of building.

With the keen eye of an artist and of a future proprietor, Andrea Orsini admired the tasteful parallels of design. There was the same pillared courtyard as at Urbino, surrounded by two-storied buildings and entered through a main gate flanked by wings containing Varano's library. There was the same generous stairway leading to the reception rooms above, the same impression of lofty corridors connecting the various parts of the building. Gilded doors with sculptured frames, delicate moldings, panels of tarsia mosaic, rich furnishings, gave variety and interest. The difference from Urbino consisted in smaller dimensions and in less of everything, as befitted a lord who was content not to play the prince. The steepness of the hill on which the palace stood and the squat medieval castle connected with one wing of it prevented architectural symmetry; but this was more than counter-balanced by structural details, that took advantage of location and of the wide mountain panorama beyond the rambling walls.

Eagerly appraising, Andrea congratulated himself on his good luck and on Cesare Borgia's liberality. He found Città del Monte more to his liking than Urbino. It was less formal, more smiling. A spirit of peace, kindliness and leisure, seemed to emanate from the place like a delicate aroma: the result in part, no doubt, of Varano's generous personality. One could not help liking the old man. It seemed almost a pity, even though self-interest required it, to deprive him of his state and probably of his life in case he refused to die soon in a natural way.

Later, in an anteroom adjacent to the dining hall, gilded orange slices and cups of malmsey were served while the little court gathered for dinner. There were the local gentry and their wives from the town and *contado* in addition to the chief officers of Varano's household: Master Paolo, the astrologer, without whom no enterprise could be undertaken, and who looked professionally important and mysterious; Master Pipo of Florence, the court painter and architect; Master Gentile Filelfo, librarian and humanist; Captain Galeazzo Branca of the guard; Don Procopio, the chaplain; Master Giulio Lenti, Varano's secretary; and about fifteen gentlemen and ladies in waiting. These were the elect who ate at Varano's table. They formed the lesser part of his establishment. Unincluded, of course, was the retinue that served the palace: major-domo and apothecary, steward of the buttery, dancing master, pages, musicians, chamber attendants, table waiters, cooks, purveyors of the stable, master armorers — to mention only some of the many departments.

Standing with Varano and Camilla in front of the blazing hearth, Andrea focused attention. His dark, bold face, his stature, the black court suit he had had made in Ferrara, his worldly manner, set him off from the others. There was still some laughter about the prank of the afternoon; but it was edged with deference due an Orsini, an officer of Ferrara, a former captain of Borgia's, a duelist undefeated by Bayard himself. He brought news from the north, had talked recently with Valentino in person, could report the latter's progress in Romagna, knew the latest gossip of a half-dozen courts. Sipping his wine, and with an orange segment between his courtesy fingers, he spoke engagingly about this and that.

"Your Magnificence doesn't say when we can expect Valentino here in the Marches," queried Captain Branca, putting into words the question on everybody's lips. He was a brawny, blustering man with a red face and watery eyes. "We belong as much to the Patrimony of the Church as Pesaro or Rimini. Since that Patrimony is to be made a dukedom for this Pope's son, what's our place in the order of business?"

Andrea cocked an eyebrow. "Good Lord! Captain Branca, if I knew Borgia's schemes, I could sell 'em for my weight in gold. That he should have his eye on the Marches is possible; but I'm inclined to believe that at present Bologna offers him more at an easier price."

"Easier is right!" Branca expanded his chest. "He'd find how easy it is to operate in these mountains. By God, we'd cut him to pieces. We'd swallow him alive."

"Bravo, Captain! Just like this, eh?" Andrea popped the orange piece into his mouth. "Well, in that case, you've nothing to worry about."

He glanced at Camilla. She was listening with rapt attention, her lips parted. Upon meeting his eyes, she colored and looked away, but at the same time drew closer to Varano. Her teasing expression of the afternoon had disappeared. He sensed that it had only been a mask to cover up something else. She looked very young and slight by the side of Varano. His rough-hewn face brought out the delicacy of hers; his short white hair contrasted with the reddish brown of her curls. She wore them up this evening in a smooth line crowned by a knot of pear-shaped pearls, which, with the fillet of pearls around them, suggested an exquisite little cap. Against the dark velvet of her husband's mantle, the gray brocade of her gown reflected the light of the flambeaux in tones of silver. Andrea worshiped the perfect lines of her neck and throat, the modeling of her small hand that rested on Varano's arm.

"Dangerous talk," said the latter in his clipped style. "The less of it, the better. War's a slippery business. Your true fighting cock crows after the victory, not before. Besides, talk of the Devil and he shows up; the same with war. God shield us from it! I've had my fill of it." He slipped his arm around Camilla. "All I ask is to end my days in peace with Madonna here."

She nestled against him. The father-daughter relationship, thought Orsini; but he could take no comfort from the reflection. It had been natural at Venice or Ferrara to expect an easy conquest. A young girl married to an aged husband oughtn't to be hard to seduce. Now, seeing them together, he was not so sure. Their personalities did not fit the program. Whatever their relationship might be, it looked discouragingly devoted. Varano might be seventy, but he looked fifty-five; Camilla might be eighteen, but she obviously loved him. Orsini was not so sure that, even with youth and Nature helping him, she could be easily won over; that, if her husband were sacrificed, her resentment might not outweigh practical considerations. True, if they went to Rome against his warning, Andrea himself would not seem involved in Varano's death. There was hope in that. But he would have liked to win her before rather than afterwards.

"How well I understand the hope of Your Excellence!" he said devoutly, with a smile at Camilla. "Your Lordship's many laurels —"

He broke off with a start that shook the wine in his cup. Happening to look down, he realized that his vision was playing him a trick. Camilla had shrunk to little higher than his knee. Instead of facing her on about the same level, he now stared down at the pear-shaped pearls on the top of her head, and met her eyes, proportionately smaller, gazing up at him. Face, hands, the dressing of her hair, the gray gown, had all at once become minute. Or had he become gigantic? It made the impression of a crazy dream.

"*Benedicite!*" he exclaimed. "Ha!" But, glancing up again, he found Camilla, in her proper stature, at the side of Varano; and looking down once more — there she was in miniature beneath him. "What the devil!"

A midget! He caught himself in time to turn his astonishment into a compliment. Indeed, he would not have been startled at all if the little creature had not been gotten up at every point to look like Camilla. Even the color of the hair was the same.

"What a beautiful poppet, Madama! I took it to be the reflection of Your Signory."

"Thanks, Messere." She glanced down at the tiny lady. "Isn't he a flatterer, Alda?" And, stooping, she raised the midget easily to a seat in the crook of her arm. "I present the Princess dei Nani to the Magnifico Orsini."

With his courtliest bow, Andrea raised the little hand to his lips. "Your Highness's slave."

The brown doll-eyes fluttered at him. He was taken aback when a perfectly normal and charming voice said, "I perceive that the praise I have heard of Your Magnificence is nothing more than the barest justice, sir. I am glad to accord you my protection and the leave to serve me."

It was the professional quip to be expected of a dwarf, but the tones of voice expressed something else, something forlorn, that touched Andrea more than it amused him.

"Naughty little coquette!" laughed Camilla. "Be careful of her, Messere. She's two years older than I and twice as clever. She'll wind you around her finger as she does me. . . . Where's your bodyguard, Alda? Where's Seraph?"

The Princess tossed her head. "That imp? I marvel that Your Excellence attaches so little importance to my safety that you leave me in the care of a blackamoor baby without courage, who could not defend me from a sparrow. Instead, I must defend him — as today from Your Signory's ruffianly spaniel who fastened on the seat of his breeches. Madama, I ask, is it right to embarrass me in this way? Am I to have no other cavalier at table tonight than this juvenile Moor?"

Andrea was surprised when a familiar voice put in: "I should be honored if Your Mightiness would accept my arm and give me the privilege of your company at table. Indeed, as a guest, I make bold to claim Your Highness's consideration."

It was Mario Belli, who, as Andrea's ensign, had been invited to appear at supper by Varano himself. Otherwise, he would have eaten alone, too obscure to be included among the courtiers, too obviously well-born to be ranked with menials. He had taken some pains for the occasion, had put on his best clothes and newest cap; but the effect was to make him look uglier than ever. Andrea had noticed how both men and women in the anteroom melted away from him, and that he had been standing by himself, with his usual oblique grin turned on the company. Yet now, as he hooked his knee before the dwarf and swept his cap, every gesture showed breeding. Varano's keen eyes studied him, evidently at a loss.

To the astonishment of everybody, Princess Alda clapped her hands.

"There's gallantry, my lords! It takes a stranger to appreciate me. . . . Noble sir, I am pleased to grant your request. Give me your arm at once."

The tiny lady was transferred to Belli's arm, her feet crossed and pointed, her miniature face overshadowed by his beetling nose and crooked mouth. The contrast was too bizarre for any smile except Belli's.

"Heavy?" she asked, looking up at him.

"Heavy as a violet," he answered. "It's been a long time since I carried a nosegay."

The pages now brought scented water and napkins for the washing of hands before supper. The turban of the dilatory Seraph showed up among them. He flashed his teeth and rolled his eyes in greeting to Andrea.

"You come take me with you, Master? I pretty tired. Too much work here, *per Dio!*"

"Work to carry your fat, eh, Seraph? I believe you. You're twice as plump as in September."

Camilla smiled. "I think I ought to hate you for lending him to me. He's more of a cherub and less of an angel every day. . . . Seraph, haven't I told you never to leave Madonna Alda out of your sight? Where have you left her?"

The boy hung his head. "She so quick, Mistress, she fly round like a mouse. Up, down! The trouble I have looking after that lady!" Then, catching sight of the Princess on Belli's arm, his face cleared. "See, there she is. Up." And, keen for duty, he drifted off to take his station as Alda's bodyguard next to Belli.

The trumpets sounded from the dining hall; the gilded doors were thrown back. Led by Varano, Camilla, and Orsini, the little procession of gentlemen and ladies, in order of their rank, flowed through to supper, with Belli at the end, carrying his living doll. Last of all, solemn and composed, the small blackamoor swaggered along, one hand on his toy scimitar, like an infant sultan.

CHAPTER XXV

A LINE of candelabra, suspended from the great gilded beams of the ceiling down the length of the hall and equipped with many candles, gave a sparkling though subdued light, which was reinforced by the great hearth fire burning in the sculptured chimney place at one end. It was a light flattering to dresses and jewels. It brought out the richness of slashes, the tones of brocade and satin, the gems in the ladies' hair, the medals on the gentlemen's hats. It glittered on trenchers, goblets, and ewers, and wakened the shadowy figures of hunting scenes on the wall tapestries.

The room was not large enough to engulf the fifty guests present; but half of it contained them easily at an L-shaped table on trestles along the end and one side away from the hearth. On the opposite side stood a mighty serving board loaded with wines to suit various tastes, and beyond this were carving tables for the endless joints and fowls that made up most of the repast. Everybody faced the center of the room. Between the walls and the diners, a space was left for pages, who refilled cups and presented silver basins of rose water for hand-washing between courses. Knife and spoon would not do for everything and had to be supplemented by generous use of the fingers. Inside the L, waiters circulated, bringing food and removing trenchers.

From where he sat between Varano and Camilla on a slightly raised dais, Andrea looked diagonally at Belli, who, with Alda, occupied the extreme end of the table along the side wall. Cushions raised the midget to a level with the board, so that her head came almost to Belli's shoulder. She handled a miniature soup spoon, which the attendant Seraph had provided, and looked up at Belli with flattering attention. They were deep in talk.

"Where did you find her, Madonna?" Orsini asked. "If she's as perfect without her clothes as in them, she's a marvel. Dwarfs are usually deformed somehow. But, except for her voice, everything seems proportioned."

"Yes," Camilla agreed, "she was a wedding gift from my cousin, Giampaolo Baglione. I have trouble keeping her. My lady of Urbino and the Marchesana of Mantua want her at any price. Even the Pope's Holiness wrote that he would be pleased to buy her for the lady Lucrezia. She'll become a state issue, and that won't help her conceit.

I'll show you the majolica figurine I had made of her without clothes. Quite perfect. . . . My lord is waiting to drink your health, Messere."

Turning to Varano, Andrea raised his goblet and lifted his hat. There were similar pledges along the table. A swarm of waiters removed the soup bowls and replaced them with trenchers, then presented meat pasties of various kinds. According to custom, one trencher served two people, and Orsini was given the honor of eating from the same plate with Madonna herself. He admired her skillful use of knife and bread in disposing of a pigeon without leaving a drop of gravy on her lips and nothing to speak of on her fingers. It was enchanting to watch.

Varano motioned a page to refill his goblet. "Tell us something of your errand to Viterbo, Captain Orsini, if you're permitted to speak of it. What's all this about kidnaping saints, that my lady here mentioned? She came back from Ferrara with a pouchful of gossip. What saint?"

"The holy Lucia da Narni, my lord. You will have heard of her. But kidnaping's hardly the word. Our mission is to deliver her out of the hands of selfish admirers in Viterbo, who would keep her shut up to the profit of their town and deny Ferrara the blessing it covets, which she would be glad to give if she were free."

Orsini described Duke Ercole's enlightened plans for Ferrara and his conviction that holiness must be added to crown his perfected city. "So Mario Belli and I are humble instruments in this great enterprise, signori, and I hope, with the aid of Saint Catherine, to bring it to a good issue."

If Andrea's tongue was slightly in his cheek, he gave no sign of it, leaving cynicism to his hearers. But the lord Varano banged his cup down on the table in approval.

"Thank God, sir, there lives such a prince in this depraved time! How wise to perceive that the art of government includes spiritual leadership, that riches and military power are worse than useless to maintain a state if its soul is gross! There's our trouble in Italy. We sow tares and expect corn. Duke Ercole's thought is right. He would have Ferrara great in the eyes of God. As to the means he uses, I don't know. But it is something, that a chief of state dares to proclaim the truth and strive toward it."

Varano turned his keen gaze full on Orsini. "Messer Andrea, Madonna informs me that you are an ambitious man, interested in government. If Italy is ever to become a nation, as I understand is your hope, believe me it will not be by force of arms alone, or clever schemes. Reverence for God and honest dealing must play the bigger part. It may be that the journey to Viterbo will teach you more than you think. Your health again, sir, and success!"

Andrea was struck by this. Until now, he had somewhat impatiently considered the errand to Viterbo a silly mission that, however, gave him an excuse to push his fortunes in Rome. Now he could see that, instead of being an episode, it might fit very much into his future.

"What are you thinking of, Messere?" asked Camilla.

"Of you, Madonna. The color of your eyes, the gold light in them. The tones of your hair. . . . In short, of you. What a needless question!"

"What a false answer!" But she could not keep a softer note out of her voice. "Shall I tell you what you were thinking of? Future things, expedients, policies."

"Which shows how simple and transparent I am," he replied. "But I answered truly in the present tense. When you speak to me and I look at you, then, like your mirror, my mind reflects only you. How else should I have answered?"

She shook her head. "There's no catching you, my lord. I envy the saint at Viterbo. Have you decided how to woo her? Will it be something like this?" Camilla's small face lengthened in a droll approximation of Andrea's; her eyes grew solemn; she contrived a hint of his voice. "Most reverend Lucia, I kneel to a rose of heaven. Words fail to express my admiration, my devotion. With me Ferrara kneels before Your Reverence — "

"Excellent!" Orsini put in. "I'll remember that." He smiled at her over the rim of his goblet.

A new tide of food swept into the hall: swans natural as life in mimic glass pools on the top of rolling tables; peacocks with a magnificence of spreading tails; a furious boar, tusks white, back bristling. And so in procession around the open L of the tables to the racketing of trumpets. Then the carvers performed their magic. The lifelike skins of bird and beast were stripped off; knives flashed; and freshly heaped trenchers appeared before the guests. The scent of rose water mingled with the steam of spiced meat.

In an undercurrent of thought, while he chatted, now with Camilla, now with Varano, Andrea compared the banquet with others he had attended — at the Vatican or in the palaces of cardinals and great lords at Rome or elsewhere. They were more flamboyant, colorful, and imperial; but the difference consisted not so much in display as in a spiritual contrast. To anyone who enjoyed irony and passion, those other banquets were infinitely more intriguing. The lustful, envious, arrogant egos appraising each other behind courtly smiles and experienced eyes gave off a heat of life not to be found in this secluded mountain hold. But there were compensations here in a more delicate scale of values — trust, innocence, and loyalty.

That was Varano's creation. Not only the palace but the spirit within it was a projection of him. It was fascinating to reflect how one man, as if inevitably, could mold a state in the features of his own mind and character. Andrea wondered how, by what processes. He found it hard to imagine a state molded after the mind and character of Cesare Borgia or of Alfonso d'Este, no — or of Andrea Orsini, for that matter.

"What policy," he asked, "does Your Excellence follow in the levying of taxes?"

This was the bone of contention in most of the Italian states: the many squeezed to support the few. The promise of lower taxes had been used successfully by Cesare Borgia in his recent conquests; and considering the size and expensiveness of this palace, it might be effective to propose it here before Città del Monte was attacked.

"No policy," said Varano, "except justice. I love my people, and they know it. They pay me a tenth, which seems reasonable. But I take nobody by the throat. As you've probably heard, I didn't build this house out of the sweat of peasants but from the proceeds of service to various states in the days of Duke Federigo. Ah, Messere, there was a man. My beloved master! My captain! I was with him to the end."

Launched on his favorite topic, Varano described incidents from the life of his hero, while Andrea digested the tax situation in Città del Monte. Except for the case of Urbino, it was unique. No chance to stir up a revolt on that pretext. A tenth! Andrea expected to wring three times that sum out of the domain when he got it. Città del Monte would be a hard nut to crack. Fired with devotion to Varano, it would fight to the last ditch against Borgia's troops. But, even when taken, how to hold and exploit it, with a rebellious peasantry harking back to a Golden Age when they had been taxed no more than a tenth? Of course, to marry Camilla would help; but, beyond expectation, the whole game was infinitely complicated because Varano's people loved him. And, to a statesman, there was food for thought in that.

A page, with basin and ewer, waited until Varano had finished the anecdote he was telling. Then hands were washed and wiped again; the broken meats were removed; and, high on wheels, a cake castle, filled with confections, made the triumphal round of the tables. Sweeter wine from Cyprus and Malaga was served. The musicians in their gallery tuned their instruments to softer music; and Lucio, the singer, for whom Camilla had bough* the theorbo in Venice, sang of love.

> Donna, contra a la mia voglia
> Mi convien da te partire . . .

It was a popular *canzona* of the time and a favorite with Cesare Borgia, whom Andrea had heard render it in a lighter moment. With the reminiscent power of music, it brought to mind a small dinner in Angela Borgia's apartment at Rome in early summer; the dank, sweet night air through the open casement, the heavy perfume of roses. Orsini had been sitting next to his hostess, while Duke Cesare sang in a conventional languishing voice, thinly disguising an undercurrent of scorn.

> Donna, contra a la mia voglia . . .
> *Lady, though against my will,*
> *From thee I needs must part . . .*

Andrea breathed the refrain to himself, lost for a moment. He had not thought of Angela recently.

"I like your voice better than Lucio's," said Camilla.

Orsini came to himself with a start. "Because I'm not singing?"

She tossed her head. "Remember that day in Venice? Petrarch's sonnet?"

"Shall I ever forget it!"

"And I!" Her voice faltered, then steadied itself. "You sang as if you had written the verses. That's the difference between you and a professional like Lucio. Are you a poet, too, my lord-of-all-trades?"

"Perhaps — at your inspiration." Raising his goblet, he held her eyes.

Without looking down, she reached for her cup, hesitated a moment, then lifted it to her lips.

"Madama," came the voice of Varano, "isn't it about time to gratify our worthy dancing master? He's been waiting for a sign from you. He would be heartbroken if he couldn't show the *moresca* of your midget and Seraph. . . . Come here, Maestro Tifi."

A long-necked thin man, with a tuft of beard, who had been waiting at the door of the hall, now minced forward, pointing his toes, and obviously relieved at the summons. He executed an elaborate bow in front of the dais and swept the floor with his cap.

"Good Master," said Camilla, "the crowning delight of any feast at Città del Monte is a sample of your art. Oblige the Magnifico and us with some droll or graceful dance you have invented, such as the one you lately showed us of Madonna Alda and the blackamoor. *Prego, maestro mio.*"

The thin man skipped into another bow. "When my lady solicits what she has a right to command, she lends wings to her servant. I was in dread Your Grace had forgotten me. I usually come on with the comfits. But poor Tifi must be content with better late than never."

He gave a sniff of reproach and then, having expressed his temperament, took charge of things. Tables were set up in the open section of the L. Waiters, hounded by the capering Tifi, bustled off with the remains of the feast. . . . "No clashing of plates," he directed. "You all but ruined my last *moresca* with your gross noises. Where is my background?" Several varlets carried in uprights connected by a broad width of brocaded cloth, and set them up behind the makeshift platform, which began to look like a doll's theater. Alda, detached from her conversation with Belli but proud to show off, rode on Tifi's shoulder to the stage and waved a kiss at the tables. Seraph, hand on scimitar, strutted behind, was also lifted to the platform. "Musicians," called Tifi, with a jut of his beard toward the gallery, "sound off!"

"He teaches dancing to the pages," whispered Camilla. "The vainest he on two feet. But artists have to be humored." She nodded toward the little stage. "Original, isn't it?"

Small as Seraph was, he seemed an elephant beside the gazelle-like figure of Alda. He pivoted in one spot, pumping his chubby legs up and down, snapping his fingers and flashing his teeth, while she swept around him in circles of gray brocade. They mutually showed each other off: black and blond, plump and slender, awkward and airy. Master Tifi was an artist in contrasts, and Andrea forgot himself in appreciation. Bravo! Here was an inspiration for something quite new in the field of humor. Andrea leaned forward absorbed, his fingers itching for a pencil and a sheet of note paper.

Alda, availing herself of a dwarf's privilege, showed more of her garters and legs than she ought — but who could be shocked by a figurine? She swept in and out around the gamboling Seraph, now hand in hand with him, now pirouetting under his arm, now dizzying him with mothlike spirals. . . . *"Bravissima!"* roared the audience. . . . Was it nature or art that the little sultan swayed and tottered and staggered and tripped, with his turban careening in all directions, while the ecstatic Tifi beat time to the climax, as if he were whipping eggs in the air? *"Bravissima! Bravo!* L'Alda! Serafino! Ah-ha!" . . . Madonna Alda sank in a curtsy that amounted to a split; Seraph's behind struck

173

the stage in a resounding period. Master Tifi accepted the laurels of applause with bows in all directions.

But his hour of importance was not over. The table platform being removed, several of the pages presented a graceful square dance under his watchful eye, with much flickering of parti-colored hose and swinging of mantles. Then six of the court ladies, whom he had coached, rose from table and delighted the company with an elegant pavane.

Andrea noticed that Camilla's eyes sparkled, and her hand moved slightly to the rhythm of the violins and flutes.

"I'll wager Your Signory is a most triumphant dancer," he hinted. "More accomplished than the divine Lucrezia herself. Her *romanesca* is the high point of any feast at the Vatican. Show us your skill, Madonna."

"Will you dance against me?"

"I'd prove an indifferent partner," he deprecated. "But as a foil to you, like Seraph to Alda, I should be happy to try, if that would persuade you."

Leaning forward, Varano added his request. "Favor us, Madama, for love of me. And you, Messer Andrea, do us the kindness. By God, in my young days, there's nothing I liked better than a galliard with a pretty lady. She wouldn't have had to ask me twice."

"A *romanesca*, then?" challenged Camilla.

Orsini rose. "If it pleases Your Excellence."

The court dancing at that period had not yet reached its later formality. There could still be frolic and speed in it and a closer approximation to popular steps. A page flew to bring a tambourine; the tables buzzed; the musicians tuned up. Camilla and Orsini made their way around to the open space in front.

She faced him with a faint smile, her foot tapping the measure as the music began. He bowed, she half curtsied. Then they were off to the rapid, staccato rhythm, marked by the beat of her tambourine, as they circled each other, now in one direction, now in the opposite direction, hands above head or planted on hips. He was a practised dancer, but any thought of his own performance was lost in admiration of her. She seemed to him an embodiment of the cadenzas of the music, light and effortless as they. Her cheeks were flushed; her small head with its chaplet of pearls bobbed enticingly close and was tilted back, as if to provoke the kiss he could not give. The fragrance of her possessed him. His pulses beat hotter. The racing bells of her tambourine made carnival in his mind.

174

Then suddenly another element was added to the dance, though at the moment he had no leisure to consider it. They were dancing in front of Varano, and at a given point Andrea became aware of him and of the curious expression on his face. Suspicion, resentment, jealousy were to be expected; they would have added fuel to gaiety. But Orsini was not prepared for what he saw: compassion, love; a serene, reminiscent look, as if it embraced the past and the future.

It was only a glimpse, but one that somehow became entangled in the dance, lending a tenderer note to the insistent rhythm. As the final figure reached its end, and Andrea sank to one knee before Camilla, while the storm of applause rose from the tables, it was odd that what he had read on Varano's face he now expressed in words.

"Love and its eternal *romanesca!*"

"You were saying, my lord?" asked Camilla.

"Only my homage to Your Signory, whose dancing surpasses any I have seen."

CHAPTER XXVI

How to be alone with Camilla? Orsini's pulses beat to the syllables of that apparently hopeless question. The palace had a thousand ears, a thousand eyes. Unfamiliar with its plan and habits, Andrea could do nothing to effect a meeting; Camilla herself must provide the opportunity. And of this, if he could judge the situation correctly, there was not the smallest likelihood. Give him time — but time was running out. He had no excuse to prolong his visit beyond tonight.

It took all his suavity to disguise ill-humor when the company dispersed after dinner and he bade Camilla good night. The pressure of his lips on her fingers, the declaration of a glance, were but crumbs to his hunger for something more. And it did nothing to cheer him when, instead of that something more, Varano requested an interview in his private cabinet. Failing the impossible moment with Camilla, he would rather have dreamed of her alone than sit up with her husband.

"I beg you will wait for me in my room," said Varano. "Our chamberlain, Ser Mario Giusti, is ill, and I promised to look in on him. Make yourself at ease. I'll rejoin you shortly."

Preceded by two servants bearing torches, Andrea followed the windings of the corridor to that section of the palace nearest the castle. But, as he went, his moroseness gradually gave way to a different order of thought. Uneasy conscience suggested that if Marc' Antonio Varano had any inkling of his designs on both Camilla and Città del Monte, this was an excellent opportunity for action. Indeed, according to the ethics of the time, he would be stupid to forgo it. Familiar with sinister practices as Andrea was, it did not take much imagination to see a trap in Varano's casual invitation to his room, nor how the affair might be handled. All the earmarks of a stroke in the Borgian style were present: cordial welcome at the palace; high honor at table; the dance that confirmed Varano's jealousy, however benevolent he seemed; and then, in this remote part of the palace, the secret finale — strangling cord or dagger. No questions would be asked. The fate of Andrea Orsini would remain a surmise to the outside world. Who could tell what Varano had heard or what he feared? If he knew only a fragment of the truth, it would be enough to justify extreme measures.

Nor did the bleak stone chamber into which Andrea was finally ushered reassure him. The conical fireplace, several suits of armor along the walls, a writing desk, a *prie-dieu*, and some straight-backed chairs, gave the impression of a courtroom. Compared with the sumptuousness of the palace as a whole, it was like a secret hair shirt under satin. Except for a zone in front of the hearth, where some olive logs crackled, the place felt chill and smelled damp.

Having fixed their torches into side brackets, the servants withdrew, leaving Orsini to warm his back uneasily in front of the fire. As far as he could judge, the room was probably next to the castle end of the palace. He noticed a door opposite to the one he had entered, that no doubt opened upon a passageway leading to the keep. If the misgivings that had begun to preoccupy him had any basis except in fancy, it was likely enough through this door that an attack would be made. His eyes kept returning to it. He even imagined footsteps on the other side and then the kind of silence as of someone listening.

Probably it was nothing, the effect of his own self-knowledge that ascribed the same knowledge to others. But the more he considered the time and place and Varano's pretext for keeping him waiting, the more uneasily alert he became.

And, by God, he was right! Someone was standing on the other side of the door. A lock turned, the latch rattled. Then noiselessly the door swung back upon a dark opening and a dim figure beyond the threshold.

Legs wide, hand on dagger, Andrea braced himself. They would not take him like a sheep. "Well?" he challenged.

"Well, Messere," echoed a voice. "What's wrong? Did I startle you?" And in the same instant, the figure, advancing, resolved itself into Camilla Baglione.

"You!" he stammered. "Madama!"

"Yes." She came forward toward the hearth. "You looked at me as if I were a nightmare." Then she added with a smile, "Guilty conscience, Captain?"

The question was too close for comfort. "Perhaps," he murmured, readjusting himself to this undreamed-of good fortune. "But the nightmare turned to a vision of heaven."

She shook her head so impatiently that the scarf she was wearing fell to her shoulders. "We haven't time for pretty words. My Lord should be here in a few minutes. I hurried to see you before he came."

Andrea's heart beat high. She had shared his need for a moment together; she had made it possible.

"Yes, Madonna?"

"He wants to discuss our journey to Rome. You warned me against it in Ferrara. Since then, I have often thought of what you said. . . . Messer Andrea, was it only caution, or do you know of something, some danger to him? If you do, please tell me or tell my lord himself. I came to ask it of you."

"And for no other reason?" His triumph sagged. Her husband again! Always Varano! "I hoped for something better, Madonna Milla."

"I don't understand."

"Not after the dance? Not, when you must know how much I love you?" The word was out in spite of him. "I love you," he repeated. "I would die for you! *Vita della mia vita!* Forgive! I had to speak. What I feel is stronger than I."

He raised her hand to his lips. She freed it gently, and, drawing nearer to the hearth, stared down into the fire.

"You haven't answered my question," she said finally — "about Rome. Whether you know of any danger to my lord."

Only a few moments had passed since she had first asked him that; but, during them, their whole relationship had changed. It was not so easy now to evade and equivocate. The mills of the gods were beginning to grind, and he squirmed a little.

"What danger? We all know that Duke Cesare is bent on unifying the States of the Church into one domain under himself, and that this signory, as well as Camerino, is exposed. Do you imagine, if Caterina Sforza had visited Rome on the eve of the attack against Forlì, that she would have been safe? Or, at this moment, the young Astorre Manfredi of Faenza? You see what I meant."

"Then you knew of nothing certain?" Camilla drew a sigh of relief. "I explained why my lord needs to have no fear of the Pope or Cesare Borgia — You're sure there was nothing beyond what you said?"

Counterattack, at this point, was better than dodging. "Why do you press me so, Madonna? Can you doubt me?"

She made a helpless movement of the hands. "What shall I say? Do you know why I left Ferrara?" Her gold-brown eyes looked up at him, half searching, half entreating. "I was afraid. Perhaps of this." She broke off. "But not only that. . . . It's hard for me to speak. . . . Something in you. Something I can't understand that isn't you. Cold. Hidden. Perhaps your ambition. As if you threatened my lord Varano, whom I love."

"Your fancy," he muttered.

"Promise me something," she urged. "Promise."

"Anything, Madonna."

"That you will protect him if you can. That, if you hear of danger to him, you will do all in your power for his safety. He has the heart of a child. He is so true himself that he believes good of everyone. Perhaps some day you could help. Promise it, for the peace of my soul."

The mills of the gods were grinding too small. What a strange love meeting this was! Promise that he would protect the man who stood between him and her? Between him and his goal? Promise to sacrifice love for the sake of love? Nonsense! That sort of thing belonged to poetry.

Perhaps she could read something of this in his eyes. "Because if harm should come to him through you," she added, "then I should hate you to the death. I should spit upon myself and hate you." Her face grew suddenly hard. "You have heard how we Baglioni can hate."

"Or love," he retorted, "which is the twin of hate."

"You have not promised."

"Madonna, your least word is my law. I promise. . . . Enough of this! I leave tomorrow, but we shall meet in Rome if you make the pilgrimage. If not — "

"Listen!" she whispered. The tread of approaching footsteps sounded along the outer corridor. "I must go."

178

She crossed the room, opened the door to the passageway, and slipped out. It seemed to Andrea that her "good night" still lingered in the air when Varano entered.

The old Lord's broad shoulders filled the doorway. He came forward with his long horseman's stride.

"I'm sorry to have kept you," he began. "Our chamberlain — " Then, breaking off, he added, "But I see that the time hasn't hung heavy."

"No, sir," Andrea faltered. "I — What does Your Lordship mean?"

"Only," said Varano, "that you have a pretty scarf to keep you company."

Following the other's glance, Andrea looked down thunderstruck at Camilla's scarf, which had fallen unnoticed to the floor.

CHAPTER XXVII

ORSINI's cheeks flamed. The silly mischance caught him unprepared. He had no time to think.

To his complete surprise, Varano gave a hearty laugh. "Wait till I joke my wife about this! The little plotter! She watches over me like a hawk. Afraid of our Roman journey. Thinks you know more than you told her in Ferrara. She's been filling my ears with suspicions ever since she got back. I'll wager she wanted to pump you." He scooped up the scarf with a chuckle and draped it fondly over the back of a chair. "Never get married, Captain, if you don't want to be managed behind your back."

Andrea grinned with relief. "Your Excellence hits the nail on the head. Her Grace is concerned for your safety in Rome, as am I. But she didn't wish you to think her meddlesome."

"She couldn't help being meddlesome to save her neck. . . . Sit down, Messere."

Drawing up a chair before the hearth, Varano seated himself and waved Orsini into the one opposite. The latter reflected on his host's simplicity. One had to admit that he was lovable. No wonder Camilla cared for him.

"As to Rome," Varano went on, "my mind's made up, though I promised Madonna to talk things over with you. What have you to say?"

With a clear conscience, Orsini repeated the warning he had expressed to Camilla. It was cogent enough and true to the facts.

"Yes, yes," the other nodded, "to be sure." Stooping over, he picked up a bowl of nuts from the hearth, offered it to Andrea, who declined, and then, placing it between his knees, cracked a shell between his square thumb and forefinger. "There's nothing new in any of that. But note three things. First. No one should neglect his Christian duties for the sake of his own skin. I'm as much in need of God's indulgence as the next man. I travel to Rome for my soul's good and in God's keeping. Second. The stars are favorable. Master Paolo, the astrologer, foresees no harm in the journey. Third. Without prejudice to my cousins of Camerino, against whom you believe His Holiness and Duke Valentino are hatching plans, my case is different. You'll recall my long service to the Church under Federigo of Urbino. Unlike others, my tribute has been paid year by year in full and on the dot. All this has been acknowledged recently in letters by the Pope himself. Well then, sir, I'm not one to expect evil at the hands of those whom I have never harmed and who express friendship for me. I'm not made that way; I can't breathe that sort of air." He shelled a hazelnut and tossed it into his mouth. "So you see how I stand."

Poor old fellow! thought Orsini. Mixing up God, the stars, and the Borgias in a guarantee of safety! As if past services and good faith meant anything in politics when they stood in the way of ambition!

"I bow to Your Excellence's wisdom," Andrea murmured. "It's to be hoped, however, that you'll visit Rome incognito."

Varano cracked another nut. "Pooh! . . . Why?"

"To be on the safe side."

"Well, perhaps for Madonna's sake," the other conceded. "If there's any risk — which I don't believe — I won't have her involved. Besides, if we went officially, there'd be invitations, and we're not in Rome to amuse ourselves. I'll take your advice. If incognito's the thing, so be it."

The fire crumbled on the hearth. Varano, getting up, replenished it with another log. But his next remark stiffened Andrea in his chair.

"A word about my wife, Messere. It's easy to see that she's much taken with you."

"With me, my lord?" A prickle of cold chilled Orsini's spine. Perhaps his host was not so simple after all. "What an honor!"

"And it's equally plain that you're in love with her."

Andrea's every nerve sounded an alarm. "Only with the deepest respect, Your Signory. Who could help — "

"Words!" interrupted the other.

"I regret that Your Lordship thinks ill of me. For what reason?"

Varano shook his head. "Life. I've lived seventy years. But I don't think ill of you." He stretched his feet out toward the fire and tipped his fingers together. "Hark you, sir, in spite of the poets, youth isn't the happiest season. I'm sorry for you and Madonna because you are young and have a long road ahead."

Orsini recalled Varano's expression during the dance.

"Let me tell you something," the old man continued. "In the first place, when I married Madonna two years ago, I did not fool myself. I didn't believe I was turning back the hands of the clock. We met in Perugia. Her father, an old comrade of mine, was dead. Her kinsmen had betrothed her to a dolt she hated. I loved her at first sight for what she is. She loved me, a little, perhaps, because of her father. The old story. I offered escape to her, and to the Baglione lords the better bargain. But before we married, we had a talk. . . . About love, Messere." Varano glanced sideways at Andrea and smiled. "You're a subtle man. Perhaps you can imagine what was said. I leave that to you."

By this time, Orsini wasn't so sure that he could imagine it. The superior attitude toward his host began to fade. In the case of a blunt old lord like this, the talk with Camilla had probably not been conventional.

"But here's the point," Varano added. "Love's a word with a great many meanings. My wife and I use it in one sense; you and she may use it in another. *With all respect*, eh? So I'm not jealous and I shall never be jealous of you or any man."

In his bewilderment, Andrea expressed admiration of His Lordship's tolerance.

"Tolerant, nothing — not of anything that affects her honor or reputation! But the certainty I have of Madonna excludes jealousy, suspicion, and such claptrap. Notice, I speak of certainty."

"Of course," Orsini bowed. "It's the only word possible in connection with Her Ladyship."

Varano nodded. "Yes, certainty. In what way? Because I think her a saint? No. She's a Baglione. Her blood's hot enough. She's as capable of going to the devil as others of her House. But I'm certain of this: if she did go, she wouldn't sneak about it. If she betrayed me — to use the cant phrase — I should hear of it first from her. There's my certainty and — let me add — my pride, because I love frankness, Captain."

That this opinion of Camilla was true came to Orsini with the force of revelation. He had not thought of it before; but, when stated by Varano, it was immediately obvious. Impossible to picture Camilla in the role of the two-faced wife, tripping discreetly between husband and lover. If she chose the lover, it would be openly. . . . But she loved her husband.

Varano stood up. "And finally remember this: because we are frank, she and I are both free. Is subtlety worth its price? I wonder. You think me a simple old man. . . . Oh, yes, you do. Don't protest. . . . But I assure you that simplicity has clearer eyes than you believe." He held out his hand. "Well, sir, I shan't detain you longer. If you must leave tomorrow, it's a hard journey to Viterbo, and you need rest. By the way, what plans have you made for capturing your saint?"

With half his mind still on the late discussion, Andrea explained that his colleague in Duke Ercole's guard, Captain Alessandro da Fiorano, who had vainly attempted to carry off the reverend Lucia by force of arms, awaited him at Narni, and that they would there confer as to the best plan of accomplishing the holy mission.

"So then," said Varano, "you don't need my help, though I should gladly furnish it for the love I bear the illustrious House of Este." Crossing to the door, he clapped his hands for torchbearers to escort his guest. "Good night, sir. I shall bid you farewell in the morning." And, taking up Camilla's scarf, he smiled again. "I'll return this to Madonna. You ought to have it as a token, but no doubt you'd rather receive it from her."

Having made his bow, with due thanks for Varano's hospitality, Orsini once more followed the flaring lights along the otherwise dark corridor. His mind was in a fog. He could deal with force or ruse — they fitted naturally into the cynical conventions of his life — but straightforwardness bewildered him. He realized that his conception of love had been widened this evening and perhaps enriched; but he was suddenly glad to be leaving Città del Monte, at least for a time.

He found Belli in his room, dreaming in front of the fire. The ensign was apparently in one of his most taciturn moods. For a while, neither spoke, Andrea absently warming his hands at the hearth, Belli motionless on his stool.

Finally the latter said: "I stayed up to make my report."

"About what?"

"Your Lordship recalls that you asked me to reconnoiter this place. Before dinner I took a stroll, but there wasn't much time. The western wall's the weakest; it oughtn't to be hard to breach. In general, the fortifications aren't above average difficult. They're not the main obstacle to an attack."

"What d'you mean?"

"I mean what Your Lordship must have gathered by now: the people's love for Varano. After viewing the walls, I made a round of the wineshops, passed the time of day. Same story everywhere: God bless His Signory! There're your walls. The thickest walls on earth are human breasts, if they have the heart to fight in them. So I'd warn this prince whom you say is interested that he might burn his fingers on Città del Monte."

"Humph!" mused Andrea. "Anything else?"

"Scraps merely. Nothing to interest the prince you spoke of." A pale smile flickered on Belli's lips. "Gossip about Madama. The dwarf girl was a mine of information."

"So that's why you courted her?"

Belli was silent a moment. "Of course. Always intent on Your Lordship's service."

Curiosity got the better of Orsini. "What gossip?"

"That, for one thing, Her Ladyship's still a virgin. An interesting detail, but of no political significance."

Andrea thought of the talk that Varano had had with Camilla before marriage. He began to see more clearly the point of his host's reference to it.

"His Signory and Her Grace sleep apart," murmured Belli. "Her room is not far from this."

Andrea said nothing.

"The dwarf girl chattered about the love of Madonna for Your Magnificence."

Orsini exploded. "Hold your tongue! Who asked you to meddle?"

In reply, Belli raised his shoulders to his ears, gave a toss of the hand, and laughed. A long pause followed.

Then Belli said: "If I meddle, it is to earn my pay. Why do you employ me? Isn't it obvious that you have only one thing to do? We'll talk straight for a moment. Your remedy's easy. Varano. Remove him, and this town will fall at the crook of a finger; the lady will drop in your net. He's going to Rome; so are we. Well, then, give me a nod when we're there; the rest is my business."

Andrea held out his hands again to the fire. "Thank you," he said.

"I'm beholden to you. We'll see how things look in Rome. Until then, remember the text: *Sufficient unto the day is the evil thereof*."

"Quite so," agreed Belli. "I should even say *more than sufficient*."

"And meanwhile," Andrea added, "we must take thought to our holy mission in Viterbo. I'm relying on your talents to help win this saint for Ferrara."

CHAPTER XXVIII

IN THE tavern of the Dove at Narni, Captain Alessandro da Fiorano related to Andrea Orsini and Mario Belli, stiff from two days in the saddle, the vexatious story of his defeat. After months of effort, he was still as far as ever from robbing Viterbo of its saint in the interest of his master, Duke Ercole.

"*Che bella tresca!*" he complained. "A mess, sirs, if there ever was one! Give me a plain job that takes stomach and military management, and I don't believe I'd be lacking. But why His Excellence ever appointed me to this to-do, I can't see. I'm only a soldier."

While Andrea thoughtfully picked his teeth and Belli twitched his nose, Captain Alessandro went on to describe the present situation. It appeared that the venerable Lucia was under as tight a guard at Viterbo as a mouse in a hole with the cat outside. Even her mother and kinsfolk from Narni were denied access to her. The people of Viterbo had no regard for the authority of Rome or for human decency. They maintained that, since the blessed signs of Our Lord's Passion had been accorded Lucia in their town, they had the first claim on her. It was as much as a man's life was worth to poke into that wasps' nest.

"I wish you good luck," Alessandro concluded.

"Look you," said Andrea, "if news were sent that the reverend Lucia's mother lies at the point of death and calls for her daughter, who would have the heart to deny so urgent a request?"

The Captain grinned. "We tried that and lost a round sum by it. I paid the Sister's uncle, Antonio Mei, to carry that very news to Viterbo. But what happened? One of the busybody nuns discovered the trick; she roused the town; they arrested and kicked him out. It's the kind of luck I've had all along. I thought the game was in the bag that time when Sister Lucia got leave to visit the shrine of the Madonna della Quercia outside the walls. I was there with my men-at-arms to snap her up. Some cursed rascal betrayed me — and there you are."

"Well," Orsini pondered, "we'll look around in Viterbo. A couple of pilgrims the more won't make a stir at this season. Something may turn up. But, hark you, sir, as between friends, this saint — what's your opinion of her?"

"Pure gold," Alessandro declared, "if that's your meaning. No hocus-pocus. A real saint. By God, only touch one of the bandages on her blessed hands, and you can feel power go through you like a spark." The Captain crossed himself. "Everybody speaks of her cures. But, sir, look into her eyes, and you'll see God's peace there. That's proof enough for me."

Following Alessandro's example, Andrea and Belli made the sign of the cross. They would not have belonged to their age if they had not felt impressed.

"Wonderful," Andrea agreed. "Rest assured, if it's humanly possible, that we'll pry her loose from the clutches of Viterbo for the glory of Ferrara. So, keep saddled, Messer Captain. I imagine, if we turn the trick, that we'll hand her over to you without much warning, and it then behooves you to get her across the mountains in haste. I sorrow only that because of this letter" — he tapped a sheet of paper sealed with the Este arms — "I shall not be able to accompany you back to Ferrara and share your honor."

For there was other news, personally more important than the mission to Viterbo that had awaited Andrea at Narni. It was a message from Duke Ercole, which had missed him on the road because of the side visit to Città del Monte. His Excellence commanded that when the lord Orsini had successfully finished his enterprise at Viterbo, he should proceed to Rome and report to Monsignor Felino Sandeo, a Ferrarese prelate of the Curia, who would give him further instructions.

Andrea found food for amusement in this letter. Indeed, he had half expected to receive it. Clearly, from Ercole d'Este's standpoint, the too adroit agent of Cesare Borgia should be kept away from Ferrara until the discreditable marriage with Lucrezia had been successfully avoided. Behind that could be seen the hand of Don Alfonso, who wanted his love letter to Lucrezia delivered in Rome and contrived this pretext to enable Orsini to carry it. In any case, somehow or other Andrea would have managed to reach Rome; now he could go there officially.

Having spent the night at Narni, lulled by the roar of the Nera below the town, Orsini and Belli turned west from the Flaminian Road, passed through Amelia, crossed the Tiber, and, reaching the Via Cassia south of Lake Bolsena, continued on to Viterbo. It was an eight-hour ride, and the golden haze of afternoon clung to the towers and walls of the city, as the two horsemen approached it across the hill-girdled plain.

They wore cockleshells on their hats in token of pilgrimage; and, as the road they followed was the main highway from Florence, the direction tallied with the Tuscan names they gave, when forced to identify themselves at the town gate. Undistinguished amid the steady southern flow of pilgrims, they passed in without further challenge and obtained cramped quarters at a small tavern on the Piazza di San Tomaso. This location had two advantages: it was close to the house occupied by the Dominican sisterhood to which Lucia Brocadelli belonged, and it was near the Porta San Pietro, the southern gate of the city, if a quick departure became advisable.

When they had dusted their clothes and washed their faces, they sauntered out to reconnoiter, though with due regard to their roles as sightseers. The ancient city, with its forest of towers, Lombard walls, and many fountains, offered numerous points of interest to strangers; and they were not the only pilgrims, in the cool of the afternoon, who threaded the arcades, tossed a glance or a word to pretty women, or stopped to admire the Palace of Justice and the Fontana Grande. They even paid their devotions at the shrine of Saint Mary of Truth, where Andrea lingered in delight over the frescoes of Lorenzo da Viterbo. But if anyone had followed the two sightseers, he would have observed that they confined themselves to the southeastern part of the town and paid careful attention to distances, the lay of the streets, and location of city gates.

"When we leave this place," remarked Andrea, "I have a notion that it may be in a hurry, with not much time for getting lost. How's your sense of direction, Mario?"

"Excellent, my lord. I usually leave places in a hurry."

The feel of the south was in the air, the last mellowness of autumn, which had not yet been replaced by the winter damp. Having completed their tour, the two Florentine gentlemen loitered awhile in the little piazza outside their inn. If they paid unusual attention to the blank exterior of the house that contained the sisterhood, it was not apparent to a watchman obviously on guard in front of the door. He

186

was equally unaware that the strangers had studied the back premises of the house, with the garden wall surrounding them. Nor did he find it odd that, strolling about, they finally stopped to pass the time of day.

They were pleasant gentlemen. It flattered the watchman that Florentines like them admired Viterbo and were eager to hear of its monuments and points of interest. He liked even the ugly cavalier, who smiled all the time and had such a droll way of jerking back his head.

"What's your job, friend?" asked the latter in due course. "Why does the city put a guard at this door? House of importance, eh?"

The watchman swelled. "Sirs, of the greatest importance. I'm set here to guard the abode of the Sisters of Penitence, Dominican Tertiaries, who follow the rule of Saint Catherine of Siena and enjoy her favor. A rich treasure in a plain casket, signori, the richest in Viterbo."

"Ha!" exclaimed the handsomer of the two men. "I've heard of these same Sisters. They have much in common with our Friar Girolamo Savonarola, who was also a Dominican. You find them elsewhere in Italy — am I right? They seek to redeem our age as the Holy Catherine sought to redeem hers. And our Lord God blesses them with sublime visions and miracles. Truly a heartening sign! . . . But why guard them? Surely — "

"Because," the watchman interrupted, with a dramatic wave of the arm, "here dwells the blessèd Sister Lucia da Narni, who, on a second Thursday in Lent, while in the choir at matins between Sister Diambra, the Prioress, and Sister Leonarda, received the divine stigmata of our Lord Christ in her hands, feet, and side. Here in this very house, sirs. And here she endures the anguish of the heavenly wounds, which bleed afresh every Wednesday and Friday and on all feasts sacred to Our Lord's Passion."

The tone of the watchman's voice indicated that he often conveyed this information to strangers. Andrea and Belli, with all devoutness, uncovered, bent a knee, and crossed themselves.

"But still," put in the former, "why do you guard her? One would think — "

"Exactly, Messer the Florentine, one would think that human villainy had limits. Not at all. The whoreson lords of Este, who regard nothing but their own fame and profit, would steal this pearl of Viterbo and impoverish our city, if we didn't keep an eye open. Listen."

The watchman plunged into an account of the Este outrages, while the two supposed Florentines stared and sympathized. . . . "So it is, gentlemen. And here I am!" the watchman added.

187

"*Canaglia! Bestioni!*" exclaimed Andrea. "That there should be men alive capable of such wickedness!" His indignation, coupled with Belli's, warmed the watchman's heart.

"But to think, Mario," Orsini went on, "that you and I are standing on this holy ground! What shall we not be able to tell the people at home on our return! . . . Friend Watchman, you see before you two sinners. You have it in your power to enrich our souls. If it were possible for us to see this rose of heaven only for a moment, to crave her blessing, to kiss her feet?" The watchman shook his head. "Do not say no, sir, I beg. Give us cause to celebrate the glory of Viterbo in our city. The Florentines believe that the blessed Sister Colomba of Perugia and the venerable Sister Osanna of Mantua are the only living saints — "

"They do, eh?" muttered the watchman. "*Ignoranti!* As if Suora Lucia didn't bear away the bell from any of them!"

"No doubt. But what report can I make of her except *they say, I have been told?* Sir, be considerate for the sake of her fame and of Viterbo's, if not for our sake, though I, for one, have taken an extreme liking to you."

"Hm-m," the watchman pondered. He was assailed by local pride and by a growing fondness for the strangers. He was assailed now, too, by something else, upon perceiving a bright, new, gold ducat between Andrea's thumb and forefinger. . . . "It's against my orders, signori, as long as this threat of the Estes continues. But there's no harm in your case. The venerable Sister is glad to receive honest visitors. . . . I'll see what can be done."

He turned to the house and knocked. Then, after an interchange with a portress through the sliding panel of the door, he beckoned triumphantly to Andrea and Belli. "The reverend Sister will see Your Worships, though only for a few minutes. It's close upon vespers."

Andrea slipped him the coin; the door opened; and the two callers were ushered into a chilly, clean, bare parlor. Since the Monache della Penitenza were not a cloistered order but rather a group of religious devoted to following the example of Saint Catherine, the formal restrictions of some convents with regard to receiving guests did not apply here. Besides, as directress of the house, Suora Lucia apparently enjoyed certain privileges. In any event, Orsini congratulated himself that he would be able to speak with her unhampered.

But as he and Belli stood shifting from foot to foot on the naked flagging of the parlor and confronted the black crucifix above the door, he felt conscious of an uneasy suspense, a growing awe. The mission which he had undertaken so nonchalantly seemed now all at once fearsome and dangerous. What was he doing here, a schemer meddling in sacred things? He rubbed the palms of his hands nervously against the sides of his breeches. Even Belli had stopped smiling and shot furtive glances here and there, as if seeking an escape.

Then a slow approaching step became audible in the long corridor outside the room. It was a light step and yet faltering, as though from weariness or pain. Since the corridor was very long and the house completely silent, the time seemed endless while the two men listened to the strange footfall drawing nearer. Belli caught his breath; Andrea's scalp stirred.

A last ray of the afternoon sun, striking through the barred window, made a pool of light across the threshold of the door. And suddenly it illumined the tall figure of a young woman in black, who paused before entering. The vivid effect of the light lent her an unearthly beauty.

A calm, musical voice filled the room.

"Peace to you, my brothers."

Andrea and Belli sank to their knees with bowed heads.

CHAPTER XXIX

THE beauty of Lucia Brocadelli — as Andrea realized, when he had collected himself enough to look up at her — consisted solely in the magnificence of her eyes. Large, gray, and translucent, they compelled attention to the exclusion of her other features: the thin, waxlike face, insignificant nose, and austere mouth. One gazed as if into immeasurably deep pools of water filled with a mysterious, serene light. They brought to memory a glimmering of associated loveliness: thrill of an April dawn, lark notes at Angelus, the peace of a cloistered garden. They were utterly innocent but also searching, like the eyes of a young child.

She gave both her hands to Andrea and Belli, whose lips reverently touched the thin linen bandages that covered the sacred wounds. And, as Captain Alessandro had foretold, they felt, or imagined, a strange current of power passing through them.

"Why do you kneel, my brothers, unless you kneel to that sweet Lord whose handmaid I am? No, I entreat you, rise. What is your errand? In what way can I serve you?"

She spoke a cultivated Italian, and Andrea recalled that she was of noble birth. Except for this accent of breeding and the grace with which she induced her callers to be seated in two stiff chairs at one side of the room, there was nothing about her to suggest worldly distinction. Since the religious order to which she belonged had not yet obtained the privilege of wearing wimple and scapular, she was dressed in a dark robe and hood that might have served any poor woman of the laity who had taken vows. As she seated herself, Andrea was struck by her extreme emaciation. Her body had become little more than the palpable outline of indwelling spirit. She did not make the impression of a skeleton but of a wraith. And once more he forgot everything else in the incomparable beauty of her eyes.

"How can I serve you?" she repeated.

Constraining himself, Andrea at last found his tongue. "To be received by Your Reverence," he said with perfect sincerity, "is already a greater boon than we deserve. We hope, rather, to be permitted to serve you or, indeed, God through you." He lowered his voice. "Have the goodness to read this."

It was a brief note, which he had written at the inn, outlining his mission to Viterbo. In the event that he obtained an audience with Sister Lucia, but in the presence of others, he had hoped somehow to deliver it unnoticed. Even now it was possible that someone might be eavesdropping. A bare mention of Ferrara would sound the alarm.

She glanced over the slip of paper without a trace of surprise and then returned it. Her calm rebuked his strain.

"I see. You are the one of whom Saint Catherine told me."

"Saint Catherine?" he faltered.

"Yes. She appears to me often. It was last week. She promised that someone would soon release me from this place to do God's will in Ferrara. . . . Why do you start?"

Andrea glanced significantly toward the door.

Her eyes smiled. "There's no one listening. And, if there were, who can withstand the will of God? Do not be fearful, my brother. Until now it was not intended that I should leave, but now the time has come. I have longed for this hour because Our Lord has made known to me that I must serve Him in Ferrara. But I sorrow to leave the sisters here whom I love. Do you think that Duke Ercole will let some of them come to me later?"

Andrea assured her that His Illustrious Lordship waited only to satisfy her least desire; that he planned to build a convent in her honor which should be the pride of Ferrara; and that she had only to select the nuns who would reside there.

"He is a righteous prince," said Lucia. "I consider him my lord and father, and I pray continually to that sweet Jesus that He may preserve him in this mortal world with health of soul and body. . . . What plans have you made for our departure?"

"None, Your Reverence. It was necessary first for my friend and me to see you and learn of any thoughts or wishes you might have in regard to the matter."

She made a slight movement of her bandaged hands. "I have no skill in these things. I know only that, since God wills it, a way of escape from the good but mistaken people who keep me here will be found. It is not for me to decide but to follow. I shall pray Our Lord that He may enlighten you."

Andrea suppressed a sigh. He thought of the impractical Mary, whom Christ had commended, and of the practical Martha whom He had rebuked. He thought, too, of the Maid of Orleans, whose faith, similar to Lucia's, had wrought miracles in France seventy years before. These were strange, uncharted waters. Glancing at Belli, he was struck by the rapt expression on the latter's face.

"Has Your Reverence access to the garden?" Orsini asked.

"Certainly."

"If the need arose, could Your Reverence leave through the garden gate?"

Lucia shook her head. "They have taken away the key. I am a prisoner, signore."

Belli spoke for the first time. "Don't bother about a key. I'll find one."

"Behold," said Lucia, "how God provides! It is a miracle that you can do this."

To Andrea's astonishment, Belli flushed. "No, not a miracle," he muttered.

"Well, then," Orsini went on, "does Your Reverence recall the cypress tree across the lane from your garden? It must be visible above the wall."

"Yes," she nodded.

"And if a piece of linen or paper should be carried by the wind so as to catch in the branches opposite this house, Your Reverence could see it?"

"Surely, sir."

"Then, harken." Leaning forward, Andrea again lowered his voice. "We cannot hope to leave Viterbo on any day much before sunset and the closing of the city gates. We must count on darkness to help us across the plain in case of pursuit. When my friend and I are ready with our plans, Your Reverence will see a linen or paper clout tangled in the branches of the cypress. It will be a sign that we are waiting for you in the lane and that the garden gate is unlocked. Then join us at once. But look for this sign only toward the end of the afternoon."

"I understand," said Lucia. "I shall look for it. We must have faith that all will be well. God works with those who trust Him."

She got up. "I must leave you. It's the hour of vespers. We shall soon be meeting again. Sirs, I thank you and I shall pray God to reward you."

Belli's voice crackled suddenly in the quiet room. "Yes, pray for me," he burst out. "Blessed Lady, pray for me." His face twisted convulsively; his fists were clenched. He kneeled before her. "Lay your hand upon me. I am in need, in great need."

A lump rose in Andrea's throat. Instinctively he sank down beside the other. "And I," he murmured.

A remote bell sounded and then voices raised in a chant. But Lucia forgot vespers. Her face was transfigured by an expression of eagerness and love. She dropped to her knees in front of the two men.

"We shall pray together. But first look at me, so that I may know better how to pray."

Her eyes moved slowly from face to face. Andrea could hardly endure the calm, pitiful regard that seemed effortlessly to read him.

"My dear brother," she said at last to Belli, "you have let bitter pride stand between you and God, and between you and men. There is your torment. For God pays no heed to pride that demands or bitterness that rebels. And so, like a famished wolf, you rend yourself and hate God and man. You are a prisoner of self. I bid you slay yourself that you may be free in God."

"But you, my brother," she said to Andrea, "are in worse case. For you are one to whom much has been given, and you are false to the trust. You know that this is true, but you lie even to yourself. Woe unto you, hypocrite! But I say to you and to you" — the compelling eyes turned from Andrea to Belli — "that all things are possible to God, that the hunger of your sin is as nothing to the hunger of His love. . . . And now let us pray that the three of us may find deliverance from that foul self and may be made acceptable to Him."

She prayed silently, but Andrea was reminded of a flame, now sinking, now passionately rising in a current of air. It was significant that neither he nor Belli felt the slightest resentment at her analysis of them; nor were they aware of any spiritual patronage or, indeed, of personality, while she spoke. They would have maintained that an unearthly light appeared in her eyes, and that the voice they heard was not hers.

In the end, she rose and laid her frail hand on the head of each. It was so loving a touch that a glow of gratitude and devotion passed along Andrea's veins. When he and Belli looked up, she was gone; and they could hear her halting footstep gradually die away along the corridor.

In silence, they left the house, disappointed the garrulous watchman by only a few clipt words, and silently re-entered the inn. They did not refer to the episode, any more than they would have discussed what had passed in a confessional. If the words of Sister Lucia burned within them, they did not speak of it. They had come through a sort of Judgment Day; but they knew from sad experience that words do not change the set of the years, that they are at best seeds of change if they fall on proper soil. Tomorrow and yesterday are not apt to be very different, even though a saint has passed between them.

Only, after supper, Belli, in regard to nothing, exclaimed suddenly: "Look you, I can say this, at least, that, far gone as I am, I still know righteousness when I see it. I say *when*, for it's a rare bird in my experience. And I should hold it a mercy from God if I could die in Her Reverence's service or could sink my knife into anyone who slanders her."

He broke off, ashamed of his outburst, and shot a quick glance at Andrea. But the latter, staring at the tips of his fingers, did not smile. Oddly enough, he was thinking of Varano's remark that the mission to Viterbo might teach him more than he expected.

Finally he shrugged. "Well, Mario, what you need, I suppose, is a blank key, some wax, and a file. Don't forget oil. I shouldn't wonder if that garden lock shrieked like ten rats. Good thing there's no moon tonight. Need help?"

Belli shook his head. "Child's play."

"It's the first step," Andrea went on. "At least something to do. When you've made the key, we'll consider what comes next. I'll admit I don't know. It's a blind game."

CHAPTER XXX

EVEN next morning, when Belli displayed the result of his midnight activities — a key which, he reported, worked like butter — the game still looked blind.

The two men discussed it off and on during the day, while keeping up a pretense of visiting the sights of Viterbo. When all had been said, the obvious expedient of smuggling Sister Lucia out of town in disguise promised better than any other; but even so, it offered considerable risk. They observed that a sharp watch was being kept at the city gates upon all who went out as well as upon those who entered. Especially friars in cowls or people in any way muffled up were subject to scrutiny and sometimes to being halted. Probably this was no more than a police measure, the result of some recent robbery or other crime in the city; but it made the escape of so well known a person as Sister Lucia extremely difficult, no matter how she might be disguised.

"Look at these wine carts," suggested Belli, "or these carriers of goods. There's food for thought in *them*, Your Magnificence."

Andrea nodded. "You mean prevail on a carrier to replace some of his merchandise with Her Reverence? It's possible. But, by God, it would take fine handling! You'd have to sound out your man and make sure of him. A false step there would cook the goose. Then, too, in an open lane, by broad daylight, to bestow Her Sanctity in a cart or a hamper without being seen needs a miracle. However, the thing's worth considering. There's risk every way." He thought awhile, then added: "You know, I'm tempted to call on the Podestà."

"The Podestà!" Belli echoed in a tone of awe at mention of the Chief Magistrate. "I hope Your Lordship's well! What's the point? Ask him to let Her Reverence go?"

"Exactly — for a consideration."

"I see," nodded Belli. "But don't you imagine Captain Alessandro has tried that?"

"No doubt. But, learn that although all men are for sale, they don't nell themselves to all buyers. Perhaps you'll agree that I have a knack in such dealings, greater possibly than the Captain's. He'd visit the Podestà with a frank offer — so many broad ducats. Offensive to a man of honor. I shouldn't handle it that way."

"No," Belli agreed, "I'd take my oath you wouldn't. And I protest the word *knack* as an insult to Your Lordship's genius. You'd buy him with promises."

"Call it imagination," Andrea amended. "That's how most people are bought. . . . And yet," he went on less confidently, "I'll admit that turning to the Podestà is a bold measure that shouldn't be taken lightly. I must see him beforehand, smell out his weak points, if you take me; and that means a day or two."

Still undecided, they returned to their inn about the middle of the afternoon and sat down for refreshment under a small pergola on the sunny side of the courtyard. Through the latticework, they could watch the come and go of guests, the loading and unloading of pack animals in front of the stables, that opened upon the other side of the enclosed yard. What with patrons of the inn, mule boys, ostlers, and casual idlers around the central drinking trough, the place was fairly animated. Through an archway on the side opposite the pergola could be seen the movement of the Piazza San Tomaso.

"That's what I mean," observed Belli, pursuing his theory and nodding at a couple of new arrivals with their pack mules. "You see those hampers? A slender woman, like Her Blessed Reverence, would fit into one of them easy as a pigeon. No trouble to breathe through the wickerwork. Lay some goods on top of her — *et voilà*."

A portly, middle-aged man, dismounting from his mule, supervised the unloading of the animals. He was evidently a well-to-do linen merchant, probably from Mantua, who was overseeing the transport of his goods to Rome. Two muleteers worked at the hampers, unhooking them from the wooden pegs of the packsaddles, easing them to the ground, and then carrying them to an overnight storeroom adjoining the stables.

"Consider," Belli went on. "Here's a fellow undoubtedly from the north, with no ties in Viterbo, whose one aim is money. Seems to me a safer bet than your Podestà, and much less expensive. I'll wager Your Lordship could buy him for fifty ducats — plus a little imagination, as you call it."

Andrea hesitated. "Maybe you're right. At least, it won't hurt to get acquainted. We'll stroll over there and have a word with him."

Leaving the pergola and apparently sauntering, Orsini and Belli drifted across the courtyard and edged nearer to the merchant, who by now had finished bestowing his wares and had turned toward the main section of the inn.

195

"A fine day, sir," smiled Orsini.

To his amazement, the man's eyes widened, and snatching off his hat he bowed as low as his big stomach permitted.

"Your Illustrious Magnificence! Captain Orsini! What a joy to meet Your Lordship! I did not know that Your Grace had left Ferrara."

"Hush, man, for God's sake!" snapped Andrea.

But it was too late. The word *Ferrara* had already dropped like a live coal among brushwood. The heads of bystanders went up; their eyes focused on Andrea.

The merchant blinked. "Beg pardon, my lord. No offense. I don't understand. The last time I had the privilege of seeing Your Lordship, you were entering the Palace of San Francesco with the illustrious Don Alfonso. I had just sold the steward two dozen napkins — " Orsini's frantic winks and frowns began to register. "Hm-m. Ha. Excuse me, sir. How could I tell that you're incognito?"

Almost at once people began centering in on the merchant and Orsini. A voice said, "Ferrara?" Another said, "The gentleman's a Florentine." Another said, "Incognito! Hear that? I saw him yesterday coming out from . . ." Somebody called suddenly, "Dirty Este spy!"

But before the circle closed, Belli stepped back. With all eyes fixed on Andrea, no one saw him fading across the courtyard and under the eaves of the stable. He paused a moment on the threshold of the stable door, then disappeared into the darkness behind it. He could still see the group outside, however, with Orsini's head above the others.

A nasty business, thought Belli. Experience had taught him that getting stuck in a mob or in a bog was the same thing.

"Stand back, ape-face!" came the voice of Orsini. "You don't need to prove that you've eaten onions." The hearty, laughing tones dominated the crowd for a moment. "Friends of Viterbo, what's the pother about? Is it a crime for a Florentine to visit Ferrara — aye, or other cities? I'll be frank with you. I've even visited Milan. Does that make me a French spy, eh? And what do you mean with your *spies?* What reason have the Estes to send a spy here? It makes no sense. Come now! I'm asking for information."

Belli grinned to himself. Even at that distance, he could feel a slackening tension. Once give Andrea Orsini a chance to speak, and he could work magic. Several voices began explaining.

"Slowly, please," said Andrea. "Do I understand — is it possible that the lords of Este would attempt to carry off this venerable Sister? I comprehend your anger. I deeply share it."

"And didn't I tell you all that yesterday?" someone roared. "Why do you act as if you never heard it?"

Belli winced. It was the voice of the watchman.

"Ah, there you are!" returned Orsini, evading the question with the utmost cordiality. "My friend, explain to these people who I am."

"But — but — "

The watchman floundered. Belli cursed admiringly in the darkness of the stable.

"What's your real name?" shouted another voice. "I heard yesterday it was Salviati; today you're called Orsini. I happen to know that a Captain Orsini is high in the favor of Duke Ercole d'Este, that he's an officer of crossbowmen — "

"Like the damned robber Captain Alessandro," put in another.

Andrea laughed. "Now, now, sirs! Keep cool, I beg. Both names happen to be right. Allow me to present myself. Captain Orsini Salviati, a poor soldier of Florence, at your service."

A new voice from the edge of the now considerable crowd made itself heard.

"Don't let yourselves be bubbled, friends. I'm from Ancona. I passed through Città del Monte three days ago. They were talking of a Captain Orsini who had just visited there and who was sent from Ferrara by the illustrious Duke with no other purpose than to lay hold on some saint or other in Viterbo. I drop you the hint for what it's — "

The roar that went up in the courtyard meant blood. Instantly Belli's mind was made up. Reaching his horse's stall in several strides, he backed the animal out, caught up a pitchfork as the only available weapon, and swung himself on the horse's back. There was only one thing to do: charge the crowd, reach Andrea, give what help he could.

But on the point of emerging from the stable, he held up. Another sound mingled with the uproar, which his trained ear at once interpreted: a different type of yelling on the fringes of the mob toward the archway from the piazza, a sort of regularity in the scuffle. Then a new shouting began. "The watch!"

Belli dismounted and led his horse back to the stall. It was no part of his engagement to get arrested and jailed with his patron. That would help neither of them.

By the time he had tied up his horse and crept back for a peep into the courtyard, the tumult had died down. He could see Andrea, with a smear of blood on his face and with ruffled hair, surrounded by a group of men in half-armor, to whom he was pouring out his indignation.

The linen merchant had fared worse; he stood collapsed between a couple of archers. Meanwhile, the captain of the watch on horseback was half restraining, half pacifying the mob with promises of what would be done to the two spies when they had been brought to the castle.

With his usual acid smile, Belli peered out at the conclusion of the act. Andrea and the merchant, their arms and hands tied, were placed in the center of the guards and led off, shepherded by the mounted captain; while the entire rabble, gesticulating, yelling, and mud slinging, trooped along to see that justice was done. The din of the courtyard suddenly gave place to complete silence. Not a soul remained. Even the stablemen could not resist the enticement of that procession through town, of which the clamor still drifted back. As far as Belli could see, he was the only occupant of the immediate premises.

He gave an all-inclusive shrug. That was that. It behooved him now to consult his own safety and get out of Viterbo before the hunt began for him. To leave at once on horseback through the city gate was a possibility. Perhaps the news of the riot had not yet reached the gatemen. He gnawed at his forefinger undecidedly. Or perhaps it was better to slip down from the walls at some unguarded point and cut across country toward Rome. No, by God, he would make a dash for it! Once more he approached his horse's stall, with an eye on the saddle, hooked over a connecting bar. Then a footstep approaching the main door warned him; and, with a muttered oath, he had only time to slip into the stall and flatten himself between the side of it and the flank of his horse.

CHAPTER XXXI

IT was a furtive footstep that paused outside the stable. Then a man entered. Evidently with a view of assuring himself that the place was empty, he passed between the lines of stalls and even whistled a quiet tune as he went. Thereupon the footstep quickened. One of the pack animals was backed out of its stall and tethered. The man left the stable, but a minute later came lagging in again. This happened a couple of times.

Peeping around the edge of the stall toward the open doorway, Belli could now see what was going on. A mule was being fitted with a pack-saddle. Near by lay a couple of hampers and some bundles of goods, which had obviously been carried in from the adjacent storeroom, and which Belli recognized as part of the linen merchant's stock. He recognized, too, the fellow tugging at the saddle girth, though with his face turned attentively toward the door. It was one of the linen merchant's muleteers. With his master in the hands of the law and the stable temporarily vacant, the rogue was quick-witted enough to make the most of his chance to steal his master's goods.

Belli grimaced sourly to himself. The precious margin of time that permitted escape was shrinking. But at once the grin faded. An inspiring idea shot through his mind. *Vive dieu!* If he had been stupid enough not to think of it! Here was something better than a dash through the city gates or slithering down from the walls, something handed to him on a plate. *And that wasn't all!* The thought of his own escape suddenly receded. By God, what if, in spite of luck, in the teeth of failure, he could still carry out the mission!

Hungrily, intently, he peered around the corner of the stall. Within half a minute, he had made his plan. But he must have luck. If one of the stablemen returned too soon, the game was over. He listened for any approaching sound more fearfully even than the thief, panting and swinking at the loading of the mule.

By now the hampers were attached to the saddle, and the muleteer was tossing the corded bundles into them. This being done, they were not yet filled. Would the idiot risk his getaway for the sake of a few more goods? Ah, *Seigneur Dieu*, enlighten him! But greed got the best of it; the man slipped out. And in that instant Belli darted from his hiding place, and, silent as a bat, ensconced himself in the shadow of some bales of straw heaped up between the loaded mule and the alley door. At least he would be that much nearer the point of action.

Sweating and breathless, the muleteer came in struggling with a couple of additional bundles, clapped one of them into each of the hampers to equalize the weight, hooked down the covers, and, grasping the mule's leading rope, pulled the animal toward the rear door, which was fastened by a heavy sliding bar. Belli unsheathed his dagger, though with no intention of using the blade. He wanted no telltale blood in this operation. The man, having reached the door, turned his head for a last backward glance; but his scream of terror upon finding

Belli at his heels was cut off. The loaded hilt of the poniard crashed against the angle of his chin and crashed again on top of his head as he crumbled down.

"*Jusque-là, bien!*" thought Belli, resheathing the knife.

Then, in a fury of speed, he stripped off the man's rags and hauled the body behind the bales of straw. A minute later, he was out of his own clothes and authentically dressed as a muleteer, pendent wool stocking on his head, brogans on his feet, and indiscriminate tatters in between. His ugliness helped out the disguise still further. No one could possibly challenge his professional appearance.

Jerking back the bar of the door, he opened it and led the mule out into the lane, taking care to close the door again, with a stone propped against it. As for his recent victim, whether or not he had killed him, that trifle did not cross his mind. Everything up to this point had been preparatory; the real adventure was about to begin.

Following the lane a couple of hundred yards, he reached the back of the nuns' garden and stopped under the sentinel cypress which faced the garden gate. It was a warm afternoon, but Belli sweated more from nervousness than heat, as he dug a linen napkin out of one of the bundles in the hampers, wrapped it around a stone, and — with a final glance left and right — tossed it up into the prickly branches of the cypress. The maneuver worked; the white rectangle hung dangling. Then he slipped over to the gate, drew out the newly fabricated key from his belt pouch, and unlocked the door.

At this point, sheer anguish began. So far he had had only himself to consider; now everything depended on Sister Lucia. Would she notice the signal? Would she be able to get away through the garden even if she did notice it? Belli tried to close his mind to these questions, but it would have been easier to shut out the daylight. He occupied himself briefly in preparing the hamper nearest the gate to receive Lucia; opened a bundle and spread its contents over the bottom of the wickerwork to provide a cushion, concealed superfluous bundles among the high weeds lining the alley, opened up a last couple of packages to cover the nun when she was finally installed. After that there was nothing to do but wait.

A lizard, scuttling along the garden wall, sounded like a footstep. He started at a crumb of masonry that dropped to the ground. Moments seemed minutes, minutes hours. Looking back, it appeared an eternity since the altercation in the tavern courtyard had started; and yet he realized that it had been little more than a half hour. In his suspense, he leaned against the neck of the mule — all ears, all eyes — while every detail of the hot lane printed itself on his mind. But there was no stir, no footstep, on the other side of the garden door.

Belli growled an oath. Time was up. He must be on his way with the stolen mule and brazen it out at the city gate.

"I grieve to have kept you, my brother."

He had not seen the garden door open. For an instant, he even fancied that Sister Lucia appeared through the solid wall, so frail and white she seemed, so utterly ethereal.

"I waited only to pray," she went on, "that God would enlighten me in case it was wrong to leave. But He told me again that it is His will."

Yesterday's sense of awe once more dominated Belli, though he could not help wondering whether her prayers had not cost them the chance of escape.

"Where is the lord Orsini?" she added.

"He is delayed, Your Reverence. We must leave without him. We must hasten. There's very little time."

On pins and needles with suspense, Belli removed the cover of the hamper and in a few hurried phrases explained the plan of concealment, at the same time stooping to offer his hand as a step for Lucia's foot.

She gave one of her rare smiles that seemed to irradiate the space around her, like a patch of sunlight. "It reminds me of when I used to ride with *Mammina* as a small child. We had a mule named Alexander, a white mule, and the hamper I rode in was lined with silk, a little nest. I'm glad this one is larger."

"*Cré dieu!*" sweated Belli, working his hand up and down near her foot. "If Your Blessed Reverence will only hurry! We may be discovered at any moment — "

"Hush, Messere!" Lucia paid no attention to Belli's hand. "I know the French tongue and it is not right to take Our Father's name in vain as you just did. This is displeasing to Him, who is our Protector and only Help."

"I know," Belli groaned, with a glance up the lane. "I ask His forgiveness and Your Reverence's! But, *foi de gentilhomme*, if we don't get started — "

"There, there!" She laid her hand, light as a leaf, on his shoulder and smiled again. "My poor brother! You are fearful and anxious, but be at peace. I tell you to have no fear. . . . And now let us go."

With all the deliberation of a great lady mounting her horse, Lucia rested her foot in Belli's hand and a moment later was installed in the hamper, her glorious eyes looking up at him. He had an odd sense of ligtness and freedom — or was it a kind of blessed enchantment?

"If Your Reverence will recline," he said. "I must place these linen things over you." He hesitated. "Would it be too much — Might I ask — "

"What is it, Messere?"

"To kiss your hand? To crave a blessing?" Leaning forward, he touched her fingers on the edge of the hamper with his lips.

She made a light sign of the cross upon his forehead. Then, sinking down, she let him cover her with the linen. Over this finally he placed the wicker top.

But now every shadow of suspense had left him. He felt released — carried, as it were, on a serene, irresistible tide. People passed in the lane, as he led the mule toward the Porta San Pietro, but he had no fear of them. He knew that nothing could stop him on this journey. At the city gate, no one challenged him, and he took it almost for granted. Without hurrying, it seemed to him that the road beyond drifted past effortlessly, like a stream.

And gradually the gold of afternoon turned to the purple of evening. Then it had become night. But still there was no sound of horses' hoofs in pursuit. There could not be; God would not allow it. At a crossroads he turned and began the long swing north toward Narni.

An odd awareness crept over him. He, Mario Belli, assassin and traitor, had taken part in a miracle.

CHAPTER XXXII

THERE were times, like that afternoon, when Andrea himself forgot Orsini and reverted passionately to Zoppo. He was apt to do this when circumstances over which he had no control made a puppet of him. Probably the mob, with its stones and other less savory missiles, did not note the contrast between Andrea's language, en route to the castle, and his illustrious name. But when pieces of dung fouled his clothes and the fragment of a brick cut his face, he no longer personally cared what was noted. During the slow, turbulent scuffle from the southwest part of the town to the *rocca*, or castle, in the northeast, he found some consolation for the straps on his arms, the shower of refuse, and the prodding of his guards in the utter sincerity of Zoppo eloquence.

It was not until the exhausted watch had finally shaken off the mob on the drawbridge of the fortress and had taken refuge in the gray security of the courtyard beyond that Andrea resumed his adopted self.

"Do you know who I am?" he demanded, while the guard stood panting and cursing in the shadow of the keep, and the mounted captain got wearily off his horse.

"Orsini, aren't you?" returned the officer. "What of it? One can't spit without hitting an Orsini. My name happens to be Colonna, if you care to know, and there're plenty of us, too. But I take it you're not the Duke of Gravina, and I'm not the Head of my House either. So, pull in your chest."

"I repeat: do you know who I am?" Fortunately, being without a mirror, Andrea could not gauge the effect of the bombardment through which he had passed. It is difficult for anyone who looks as if he had been dragged from a sewer to achieve a majestic impression.

"I think so," returned the Captain. "You're a dirty agent sent here by the Estes to rob our city. . . . Very dirty," he repeated with a grin. "If I said filthy, it would be a compliment. . . . You've provoked a tumult here to the prejudice of our sovereign lord the Pope. That's enough for me to know and enough for you to answer." He pointed at Andrea and the collapsing linen merchant. "Set these men in irons and in keep until His Excellence, the Podestà, has leisure for them."

"God pity you!" Andrea observed. "I gave you your chance."

In spite of his appearance, the tone of voice had some effect.

"You did, eh?" said the Captain. "Thanks."

"Not at all. *Prego, signore.* If God has denied you wits, it can't be helped. Otherwise it might have occurred to you that Andrea Orsini ranks among the captains and friends of Cesare Borgia."

That was the name to conjure with, especially in Viterbo. As one of the Papal towns, its veneration extended to the gonfalonier of the Church. Or perhaps dread, rather than veneration, more aptly expressed the sentiment toward Cesare Borgia. Colonna cleared his throat and said, "Wait a moment," to the guards. Then he suddenly became very civil.

"Messer Andrea, you will excuse me, but I thought you were now in the service of Ferrara."

"One service does not exclude the other, I hope," replied Orsini.

"But these are matters," he added obliquely, "that are not discussed in courtyards."

"Hm-m, yes. Quite so. I beg pardon." Colonna lifted both hands in bewilderment. "Sir, I ask your advice, as one cavalier of another. What am I to do? How am I to know who you are? You change names faster than a flea jumps: Salviati one moment, Orsini the next; and Orsini Salviati in between. You are Florentine, Ferrarese, my lord Cesare's man — or what? You're a Proteus, sir; but I'm no Hercules. And I say again, what am I to do?"

"I shall tell you." Andrea had got his foot in the stirrup and would soon have circumstances in check. "It is true that you cannot be sure who I am, though you have my word for it. Therefore, I must be kept in confinement until the Podestà releases me. But, sir, as one cavalier should be helpful to another, you will speed my meeting with His Excellence and will enable me to appear before him in a state more fitted to my rank and House than the rabble have left me with. This is not asking too much of your courtesy and will earn my lasting friendship."

"Sir," bowed Colonna, impressed by Andrea's polished language, "you anticipate only what I would myself have suggested. If you will do me the honor to be confined in my quarters here, I shall send my servants to attend you and, meanwhile, report your case to the Podestà. . . . You, there," he directed one of the guards, "release this gentleman.". . . The straps dropped away. Andrea flexed his arms and rubbed them to set the blood in motion. "And now, sir," waved the Captain, "if I may conduct you."

A sudden bleat rose from the linen merchant, who had finally recovered his breath. "But what about me, Your Worship? Surely you'll let me go. I've been wrongfully dealt with, Your Worship."

Colonna frowned. "You'll be heard in due time. You break the peace and stir up riots. Justice must be served. Take him away, men, and lock him up as I told you. . . . My lord Orsini, at your service."

It was the way of the world. The two gentlemen walked off.

A half hour later, repaired and spruced up, Andrea was in some shape to meet the Podestà, His Excellence Julio Vettori, and he accompanied Captain Colonna through the windings of the castle to the Chief Magistrate's audience room. He reflected that all this mix-up was the result of following Belli's foolish suggestion regarding the linen merchant. His own scheme of approaching the Podestà had been much sounder and, if adopted, it would likely enough have solved the problem of Sister Lucia's escape with dignity and ease. But, by good luck, there was still time to attempt it now. It tickled his sense of irony that a riot and arrest should introduce him to the magistrate; but how much neater the stroke if he could turn such defeat into success!

Meanwhile, he wondered what Belli was doing? Having escaped the mob in the first place, it was not likely that he would be caught in Viterbo. At that moment probably he was clear of the town and heading for Rome. He knew that Andrea planned to put up at the palace of Monsignor Sandeo of Ferrara, and they would doubtless meet there. If Orsini could pull off this game with the Podestà, he looked forward to chaffing his ensign with that unexpected achievement.

But a remark of Captain Colonna's warned him that he ought not to count on too much too soon.

"My lord, far be it from me to pry into the reasons for your presence in Viterbo; but if, by any chance, the rabble were right in their suspicions of you, take care. Our Podestà is touchier on the point of Sister Lucia than a lion with a sore foot."

Andrea, walking at the other's side, slackened his pace. "What's wrong?"

"We've had too much of the Este arrogance, sir," retorted Colonna. "That's what's wrong. Too much of Captain Alessandro da Fiorano. Failing everything else, he even had the brass to offer His Excellency a round sum for handing our blessed saint over to him. I laugh. Sir, in this corrupt age, I tell you it's an honor to serve under Julio Vettori. The Holy Saint Peter himself is not more incorruptible. And try to buy *him* like a huckster! Faugh!"

"Exactly!" Andrea nodded. "Tut! Tut!"

While Colonna ran on, Orsini meditated. The incorruptibility of the Podestà was discouraging. These Viterbians were certainly in a fever.

"Julio Vettori," he interrupted finally. "I yearn to meet him. As a man of honor myself, I can understand his emotions at Messer Alessandro's offer. Has he been long in Viterbo?"

"Too long in view of his high merit," said Colonna, "though our city has greatly profited. To tell you the truth, sir, the Curia has not sufficiently recognized his abilities. A piece of luck for Viterbo, but disappointing for him."

"I can understand that, too," Andrea murmured, though a part of his mind quickened, like a hound that picks up the scent. "Alas, Captain Colonna! I say alas! How rarely does a good man receive his reward on earth! . . . Well, I take it this is the audience chamber."

A guard at the door stepped aside, revealing a long medieval room with heavy beams and deeply recessed windows. At the end of it, behind a table, sat a hawk-faced, purposeful-looking man in a dark robe and a black skullcap. As Andrea and the Captain approached, he kept a disconcerting, level eye on them, that struck Orsini as somehow theatrical. He had the face of a fanatic — sucked-in jaws, sensitive lips — a self-righteous but hungry expression. An expert in faces, Andrea, advancing, studied it with the sympathy of an artist and the coolness of a diplomat. He noticed, for one thing, that Messer Julio turned his head carelessly at last to look at the window. There was nothing to see there; the movement was unconscious, but it displayed a very fine profile.

"Your Excellence," said Colonna, "I have the honor of bringing before you Messer Andrea Orsini, the gentleman of whom I informed you. He was arrested on suspicion of practising in the interest of Ferrara for the removal of the venerable Sister Lucia from our city. His examination is in your hands."

The burning gaze of the Podestà struck vainly against Andrea's affable and half-deprecating smile.

"Do you admit this charge?" The voice was stern, resonant, studied.

Orsini made his most winning bow, a caress and adulation of arm and hand. "By the leave of Your Excellence, I can admit, at the moment, but the charge of selfish pleasure upon standing in the presence of a great man whom I have longed to see; selfish, indeed, as I conceive the annoyance that this occasion must cause him."

"I am not susceptible to flattery, Messer Andrea."

Again the scornful turning of the head; again the beautiful profile.

Andrea sighed. "Indeed, sir, I should be more than blind if I did not at once perceive that flattery would be only an affront to Julio Vettori. How often have I heard that said of you, my lord! — and no later than last week by the illustrious Duke Cesare himself."

"Duke Valentino?"

"Who else? When I had the honor of dining with him at Pesaro and receiving his commands."

"But then this charge, this accusation" — Vettori shot a glare at Colonna — "if you're in His Highness's service?"

"A mistake, sir," Andrea said generously, "an accident. As it happens, I am entrusted by the Duke with certain matters for the Pope's Holiness and am on my way to Rome. But, Your Excellence, in that connection, may I have a word with you privately? It is not that I distrust this noble gentleman, but the affair in question is only for your ears."

Colonna was already withdrawing. The door closed. At a wave from the Podestà, Andrea sat down facing him across the table. He noticed a further point — that the ring on Vettori's forefinger had a false stone.

By now he had sized up his man: poor, disappointed, proud of his honesty and his profile, acting a role that convinced both himself and his subordinates. Captain Alessandro ought to have offered him nothing or much more: that was the trouble.

But Andrea did not immediately launch upon the topic at hand. In reply to Vettori's questioning glance, he began to speak and then broke off. "My lord, by your favor, will you be good enough to turn your head a trifle? . . . Ah, there! Perfect! . . . May I ask whether you have ever had a medal struck to commemorate your term of office? . . . No? It's a pity, sir, a great pity. But forgive the interruption."

"I don't understand," said Vettori, trying not to look pleased.

"Of course not, my lord — I cry your pardon. It was only that, as an amateur of art, I reflected how wonderfully a medalist — say, Niccolò Fiorentino — would have portrayed you. It is rare that the features — brow, nose, and chin — are so remarkably, so expressively, proportioned. But again I ask your indulgence." Andrea turned businesslike. "The matter I hoped to discuss with you is this. Your Excellence is a statesman and will understand how confidentially I am speaking. I realize, too, that your distinguished probity deserves nothing less than complete frankness. To begin with, it is true that my visit to Viterbo is not unconnected with the holy Sister Lucia."

"But, sir — "

"One moment, if you please, and I shall explain."

Amazingly, Andrea told the truth for a while. Before the eyes of the unimportant provincial magistrate, he drew back the curtain of high intrigue: his mission to Ferrara, the desired alliance between the Houses of Borgia and Este, the approaching success. Julio Vettori, whose chief functions consisted in hanging malefactors and gathering taxes in a third-rate town, could not help being dazzled by the confidence reposed in him.

"Therefore, Your Excellence will perceive how it is that I happen to be serving the Duke of Ferrara with the complete approval of my Lord Valentino. And you will easily understand that, in the present posture of affairs, it is greatly to the interest of the said lord and of the Pope's Holiness to humor the illustrious Duke Ercole in respect to a matter so close to his heart as this of the venerable Lucia."

Vettori pursed his lips. He was attempting to look as important as the occasion demanded.

"All that may be true, sir, but what of Viterbo? The citizens will never consent to part with Her Reverence. She is their pride and the proof of Heaven's favor. Our city yields to none in loyalty to His Holiness, but it has its rights."

"Which a prudent Podestà could evade."

"Sir!" The Magistrate lifted his head, flashed his eyes, and looked like Cato. "I have given my oath to the city — *without* evasions."

"God bless you, my lord! I say no more then." And Andrea smiled.

There was a good deal in that smile to disquiet Vettori: Borgian displeasure, poverty, disgrace, perhaps worse. It is costly to play Cato.

"What do you mean by *evade?*" he hesitated.

"Nothing criminal, sir. You know that the General of Dominicans has ordered Lucia Brocadelli to Ferrara; you know that Her Reverence desires to obey. Is she to be kept a prisoner here? Has *she* no rights? When Your Excellence swore to uphold the laws of Viterbo, did you swear to uphold the injustice of its citizens? No, my lord. You would be justified in releasing Her Reverence despite the citizens. But that would cause turmoil. I suggest merely that you *arrange* her escape."

Vettori was not altogether a fool. "Well, then, let His Holiness make that suggestion by letter."

Orsini shook his head. "He is not apt to. He values the affections of the good people of Viterbo. The letter might miscarry. No, sir, you should make the decision on your own responsibility and earn the reputation of one who needs no orders to serve his prince. Besides," Andrea added, "you will earn more than that if you choose, the patronage of the House of Este. You are unaware how much the Duke of Ferrara admires you."

"*Me?*" Vettori forgot his role and gaped. "I have done nothing — "

"You have done everything to please so enlightened a statesman. You refused a bribe which the unfortunate Captain Alessandro had the temerity to offer you. My lord, you should have heard the commendation of Duke Ercole. 'There,' he said, 'is a magistrate after my own heart! There is the future Podestà of Ferrara!' "

Riches, honor, a great city — all of this showed in Vettori's face. Andrea knew that he had won the game.

"You almost persuade me — " began the Podestà.

A clamor of voices sounded outside the door. It swung open before a group of people.

"Your Excellence!"

"Now, by God," blazed Vettori, "what's the meaning of this! Do you break in on me unannounced?"

"But, my lord, you must hear. The blessed Lucia is gone. The ensign of this Orsini carried her off and half murdered this man in the doing of it."

Half-dressed in Belli's clothes, the muleteer, with a swollen jaw and a knob on his head, was pushed forward.

Vettori swung round on Andrea. "What do you call this?"

At that moment Orsini showed his true mettle. "A stroke of luck for Your Excellency," he answered, while his secret thought applauded, "Bravo, Mario Belli!"

CHAPTER XXXIII

ONLY the Podestà caught Andrea's last remark and the meaning look that accompanied it. The execrations of the group who had brought in the muleteer, coupled with the latter's laments and gesticulation, produced a hubbub that drowned out any single voice.

"*Silenzio!*" roared Vettori, his arms extended. "Will you be quiet? How can I judge of anything?" And, having reduced the tumult to a murmur, he pointed at the muleteer. "So then, you — what happened?"

Juggling lies and truth, the man got out an acceptable story. He had been fearful for his master's goods and had returned to the inn. Belli had attacked him in the storeroom, had carried him into the stable, had made off with his clothes and a mule load of linen.

"What has this to do with the reverend Lucia?" demanded Vettori.

A chorus took up the tale. Her Reverence gone. . . . Who but Belli could be guilty? . . . Linen found strewn in the lane outside the garden.

The Podestà once more turned on Andrea and met again an eloquent glance. "Are you responsible for this?"

"Responsible? Responsible that my ensign proved a rogue and stole some linen? Yes, and I shall pay the loss. But, Your Excellency, I ask you, what connection has this with the disappearance of that estimable Sister? I ask you, is it likely that a man fleeing with stolen goods, in fear of his life, should pause to carry off this saintly woman in a basket?

209

I beg you will reflect upon the absurdity of it. No, pursue the villain, retrieve the linen; but look elsewhere for the divine Lucia, whose loss to Viterbo I join you in lamenting."

A voice growled, "We aren't interested in the cursed linen; we want our saint."

The babble died down into silence. The bystanders exchanged uncertain looks.

Vettori nodded. Behind an expression of immediate concern, Andrea could read the shift of ulterior calculation in his eyes. "Captain Orsini speaks sense," he declared. "It's ridiculous to suppose that the rascal ensign has anything to do with the blessed Lucia. We have no time to scour the country for a thief, when our concern is for Her Reverence. My lord Orsini will make good the theft."

"Devil take it!" Andrea put in. "Couldn't there be some pursuit?"

The Podestà waved an impatient hand. He was playing his role perfectly. "We have no time. . . . Sirs," he went on to the group of citizens, "Sister Lucia must be found. Perhaps our fears are groundless. She may have left the convent merely to pay her devotions at some shrine. She may be still in Viterbo. Therefore, search the town, inquire at the city gates."

He paused a moment, his eyes on Orsini, as if this were his cue.

Andrea took it up at once. He knew the route that Belli would follow; they had discussed it thoroughly during the last two days: south from Viterbo, then due east to the hills, then north along the Flaminian Road to Narni. "But surely, my lord," he protested, "you'll send north along the Via Cassia. Isn't that the main road to Narni? If Her Blessed Reverence has left this city, wouldn't she travel that way? . . . A suggestion merely. Forgive my impertinence in offering it."

"I was about to order that very thing," said the Podestà. "Captain Colonna, you will take horsemen and ride north. Citizens of Viterbo, make diligent search within the walls. And now, dispatch, sirs, dispatch! Good evening, good evening." He waved them out and waited until the door was closed before asking Andrea, "What did you mean by *good luck?*"

Orsini bowed. "I hardly need to explain *that* to Your Excellency. Without trouble to you, with no breath upon your honor, my ensign has taken matters into his own hands. And I give you my word, he did it unknown to me. The risk is his; the credit will be yours."

"I'm afraid not," gloomed the Podestà.

It was necessary to conciliate Vettori a little longer. Andrea was not yet out of Viterbo. "Indeed yes, sir," he maintained. "You managed brilliantly — brilliantly. If you had raised a finger, Mario Belli and Her Reverence could have been taken."

"Remember, I ordered the pursuit."

"To be sure," Andrea nodded. "Nobody can reproach you. Most adroit; and I shall so report it to His Holiness and Duke Ercole."

The two men smiled at each other. After a while, the Podestà added: "Messer Andrea, I depend on you. Please present my humble respects to the illustrious Prince of Ferrara and press my cause with him. If he desires my services in the position you spoke of, I am at his bidding."

With much more earnestness than truth, Andrea answered: "Your Excellence can count on me. I am sure that Ferrara will rejoice in her new Podestà."

Then, as the fiction had served its purpose, he dismissed it from mind.

Next day the approach of sunset found him not far beyond Osteria Nuova on the slowly descending road to Rome. By the kind offices of the Podestà, he had recovered his horse and luggage from the inn, had hired a pack mule and driver for the last stretch of the journey, and, with a view to escaping any further display of public resentment, had been let out of Viterbo before dawn. By riding steadily, with only a break for dinner at Bracciano, he had covered most of the road to Rome and now could expect to enter the city before the closing of the gates. Indeed, he could see, or at least imagine, the phantom cluster of its towers on the horizon.

The weather had changed from the serene blue of yesterday to the overcast of autumn; and a wind, not yet cold but ominous of rain, wandered across the Campagna, bending the dry grasses by the road-side and sometimes wailing through patches of reeds. Far off, in desolate procession, the columns of the Trajan aqueduct led on, with their ruined arches, like a bridge from nowhere to nowhere. To the left, on a distant hill, appeared the ruins of ancient Veii; and scattered here and there were fragments of other ruins, long since nameless. Especially today, bereft of color under that lowering sky and haunted by the wind, the country seemed one vast burial plain sparsely covering the bones of a world. It had the damp smell of age, death, and abandonment.

By this hour, travel on the road had largely ceased; and for long stretches Andrea, followed by the muleteer, encountered no one. He could almost imagine himself at time's end, the last human survivor to look back across the ages and wonder at their futility.

In part, no doubt, for these reasons, he did not feel the exhilaration that the recent success in Viterbo justified — Duke Ercole pleased, another rung climbed. Personal schemes and petty achievements shrunk to nothing against the infinite negation of the Campagna. One of those moods over which he had no control, gray as the low-hanging sky, drained all color from life. A sense of lassitude and of self-scorn beset him, the sense, too, of spiritual hunger and of helplessness to satisfy it.

As the twilight darkened, he grew conscious of an illusion, that for a while faced him in whatever direction he turned. The two gray eyes of Sister Lucia, lovely and inexorable, hovered before him, gazed up from the earth, looked down from above. Even when he closed his own eyes, he could not escape them.

He crossed the Tiber at the Ponte Molle, where the great northern roads met, and joined the last stragglers hurrying toward the city gates. As the atmosphere of suburban Rome gradually closed in — the familiar dusty smell, the clatter of the wayside taverns — Andrea forgot his recent reflections. The spell of daily life reasserted itself. Tomorrow, he would wait on Pope Alexander, would present Alfonso d'Este's letter to Lucrezia, would catch up with the latest turn of affairs. But particularly he must be alert with regard to Camilla and Varano, when they arrived in Rome. He was convinced that the lord of Città del Monte would not otherwise leave it alive. Somehow, too, he must manage, while keeping his promise to Camilla, not to ruin his own career.

Entering by the Porta del Popolo, he crossed the then half-rural northern section of the city, threaded his way through the warren of narrow streets between hovels, palaces, and churches that sprawled along the Tiber, crossed the Ponte San Angelo, and so beyond into the Borgo, not far from the Vatican.

Monsignor Felino Sandeo of Ferrara received him at his palace with all honor and (having heard the report from Viterbo) with many congratulations.

It was here, two days later, that Mario Belli turned up, still wearing his stolen rags.

"Heart of gold!" cheered Andrea, greeting him. "Well done, Mario! Let me embrace thee! It's you who have won first prize in this affair. Is Her Reverence safely bestowed then at Narni?"

"Safe in the hands of Captain Alessandro," returned Belli. "By now, they'll have crossed the mountains. The bells of Ferrara will soon be ringing."

"A fine deed as ever was," Orsini declared. "And I bless the day you joined my service. The joke of it is that your plan and mine both worked, and each seconded the other." He briefly reviewed his dealings with the Podestà, while Belli pinched his chin.

In the end, the latter shrugged. "Yes, your plan or mine or another's. What need of plans in this case, when God opened the way? There's my opinion, Your Magnificence. But the wonder of the affair is that I had a part in it. What do you make of that?"

Andrea laughed. "What does one make of anything? . . . And what do you make of this?" He handed a heavy purse to Belli. "Your share, my friend."

To his blank amazement, the other returned it. "I've received my pay in full."

"From whom?"

"That's my secret."

"But still — " Andrea held out the purse again.

"No, my lord, keep it for another time, when I'm back at my old trade of serving Mammon. Today it would bring me bad luck." An odd, unexpected light showed for an instant in Belli's eyes, then vanished. He changed the subject. "And, speaking of luck, my humble congratulations! Is there no end to Your Lordship's good fortune?"

Still digesting the mystery of the purse, Andrea murmured, "How so?"

"Your great marriage. To be kin with dukes, cardinals, and popes."

"*Per Dio*, what do you mean?"

"What should I mean but your marriage with Her Ladyship, the divine Angela Borgia? Forgive me if I'm indiscreet."

Orsini stared. "Where did you pick up this nonsense?"

"Nonsense, my lord? *Cré dieu!* Call it what you please." Belli smiled indulgently.

"I asked where you heard this talk?"

Impressed by the look on Andrea's face, Belli turned serious. "From an acquaintance of mine, in a tavern, as I came back from Narni. One Simone Furia — or so he calls himself — a cavalier of my profession. We were at one time associated in the employ of the Marquis of Mantua. He is now in the service of Don Jofrè de Borgia-Lanzol, father of the lady Angela. When he learned that I was ensign to Your Lordship, he referred to the happy event I mentioned as having been recently decided. Naturally I held my tongue, for what do I know of Your Lordship's plans?"

"But for God's sake," Andrea burst out, "what babble! Madonna Angela was betrothed only two months ago to the young della Rovere."

"I alluded to that," Belli nodded, "and Messer Simone smiled. I imagine that either the betrothal or the young man will be suppressed, though, of course, Furia did not discuss it. I have never found him a babbler — quite the contrary. . . . So the news surprised you?"

"An absurdity!" Orsini declared.

But the rumor disquieted him. In his experience, there was seldom smoke without fire; and if a tight-lipped bravo in the service of Angela's father talked of such a marriage, there had been talk of it higher up. The thing was remotely possible. Andrea remembered his affair with Angela, her hot passion. Now his promised appointment to Città del Monte transformed the lover into a potential husband. If the Borgias proposed the marriage, how could he refuse it? Indeed, from the standpoint of ambition, he would be insane to refuse. And yet the thought of it cast a desolate shadow upon the future. Until that moment, he had never so completely realized his love for Camilla Baglione, nor to what extent his hopes centered in her. Now, at a breath, his whole card castle trembled.

"But, hark you," he added to Belli, "keep your ears open. Speak again with Messer Simone and fish up what you can. Fair weather or foul, it's the part of wisdom to be prepared."

PART THREE

Rome

CHAPTER XXXIV

SEATED at the writing desk in his cabinet on a late November afternoon, Rodrigo Borgia, better known to the world as Pope Alexander VI, drove an energetic pen across the sheet in front of him. The light from the courtyard, called "of the Parrot," fell but sparingly through the ground-floor windows and had been supplemented by a candelabra that cast its flickering upon his white skullcap and gray hair, mellowed his Olympian features, and twinkled on the heavy crucifix which dangled from the chain around his neck. He wrote impetuously, in the same fashion as he thought, the slender quill bending under the weight of his hand. At one point, it snapped and was cast down. Whereupon Asquino di Colloredo, the secretary, presented a sheaf of pens, from which His Holiness selected one, after pursing his lips and trying the nib on his forefinger. Then the headlong scribble was resumed.

Generally Asquino found it hard to believe that the Pope was approaching seventy. His sparkling eyes, fine color, erect bearing, the height, bulk, and force of him, implied twenty years less. Indeed, he seemed to be entering on a second youth. He abounded in vigor and animal spirits. Disguised as it was by courtly grace and charm of manner, a certain rankness, a brutal quality, exhaled from him. It was this, as well as the ox of the Borgia arms, which gave point to the recurring motif of the bull Apis that appeared in the glowing frescoes, with which the artist Pinturicchio had recently adorned the Papal apartments.

Having supplied a fresh quill, Asquino withdrew into the background, which he shared at the moment with Gabriellino, the Pope's clown, a gangling figure seated tailor-fashion in front of the fireplace. Familiarity with the Pontiff had not bred contempt on the part of such attendants as these. It takes philosophy to scorn a fine presence coupled

217

with ruthlessness and power. The buffoon and the secretary were not philosophers. In his jovial moods, they sunned themselves in their master's exuberant vitality; in his rages, they rounded their backs; but they were never quite so heedless as not to fear him.

They had best fear. Indiscreet or presumptuous servants in the Vatican had short lives. They had best not even speculate why, on this afternoon, His Holiness preferred to write a letter in his own hand to Duke Cesare rather than dictate it. Asquino and the fool knew many of the Pope's secrets — enough to prolong indefinitely the crop of lampoons that were chalked up at night through Rome — but they did not know most of them and found it prudent to be incurious. That deep affairs were in question when His Beatitude wrote *propria manu* to his elder son could be assumed. For the rest, it was wiser, like a pair of dogs, silent and vacant, to await the prince's pleasure.

In that word *prince* lay most of the difference between their conception of the Pope and that of earlier or later times. In him the Vicar of Christ had declined into a temporal sovereign. Alexander ruled over provinces and cities, had armies in his pay, contracted alliances with or against kings and emperors; the House of Borgia concerned him rather than the Household of Faith. Victim as well as exploiter of a relatively brief historical epoch, he was no more typical of the Papacy than is a fungus typical of the mighty oak to which it may be attached. Contemporary and modern Catholic historians of the Church have adequately condemned him. Sensual, shallow, and greedy, he merits no defense except as the creature of his times, which contributed to his sins and made them possible.

At the moment, Borgia found himself torn in two directions. He alternately chuckled and frowned as he wrote. Having been coaxed into a promise some minutes ago, he let his mind wander toward the fulfilling of it and away from the immediate task. But this business in the north had to be attended to. The letters that morning from his son had been discouraging, and a courier waited for the reply. The siege of Faenza lagged; a full-fledged assault had been turned back with loss; the mule-headed citizens of the town still clung to their young lord, Manfredi; it looked as if the place could not be carried before winter, perhaps not until spring. And, meanwhile, the crushing expense of maintaining the troops! Endless money! Did Cesare ever write him without demands for gold? Well, thank God for the revenues of the Jubilee Year! And there were still benefices or cardinals' hats to sell or fatted prelates to be squeezed. Beloved Cesare should have his gold and his kingdom. As to where the money came from, why, even the jokers took a tolerant view of it. A recent lampoon crossed the Pope's mind.

> *Alexander* [it went] *sells the keys and the altars and Christ —*
> *But fairly enough, for didn't he purchase them first?*

Having finished the most important part of the letter, Borgia added a few lines of random news:

> *We hear from our agent at Città del Monte that the illustrious Marc'*
> *Antonio Varano and his noble spouse are to visit Rome incognito for the*
> *pilgrimage. They will stop with the lord Fabrizio Colonna at Marino*
> *and will be guests here at the palace of the late Cardinal Savelli. This*
> *leads, of course, to certain reflections. Be assured that I shall have them*
> *committed to prison and Varano himself to the Tiber at the proper time.*
> *But it is possible that he may have moneys deposited in several hands,*
> *which he could be induced to bequeath to the Holy See upon his demise.*
> *Therefore, it would be undesirable that his death should come too soon*
> *before said persuasion could be applied. Your Signory will smile, as we do,*
> *at the simplicity of this lord in imagining that he could visit Rome — or*
> *make any move, for that matter — without our knowledge.*

The Pope chuckled at the quaintness of it, then added:

> *You have been informed, my son, that the Lady Angela, our kinswoman,*
> *is hot for this* novus homo *of yours, the versatile Andrea Orsini, and*
> *pleads to be wedded with him. To which we say: wherefore not? We want*
> *no dealings with that old Satan, the Cardinal Juliano, nor with any of*
> *the House of della Rovere, accursed spawn that must be destroyed. Damsel*
> *Angela's betrothal to the young Francesco cast dust in their eyes at the*
> *right time. Let it be set aside. Then, too, we are taken by this Orsini,*
> *who bids fair to become a man of weight. We should fix his loyalty by this*
> *marriage. But chiefly we favor the thing because it eases us in the matter*
> *of dowry such as the della Roveres expect. Messer Andrea would content*
> *himself with honor and the person of the lady. And so —*

He finished the letter with a flourish and a blessing; sealed, stamped it, and gave a puff of relief. Subconsciously he was never quite at his ease with Cesare, even at writing distance. The pale, cryptic face of the cherished son, hovering in his thoughts, provoked a shiver.

"Let this be carried at once," he directed Asquino. "I say, in haste. — And now, admit Captain Orsini. He should be waiting."

Summoned to the Vatican by a special messenger, Andrea indeed had been cooling his heels for some time in the Hall of the Liberal Arts adjacent to the Pope's cabinet. A detail of Swiss guardsmen, posted at the doors with their halberds, and a scattering of glum-looking churchmen, among them a bishop, waited in the handsome apartment with him. By now, he had had plenty of leisure to wonder why he had been called and to steel himself against surprise; for anything, in the case of His Holiness, was possible.

An anxious atmosphere pervaded the room, which remained silent, except for a whispered exchange now and then between a couple of priests. It was the kind of atmosphere to be found in a court before the judge hands down sentence, one that keeps people fidgeting and works on the kidneys. Especially the bishop looked harried; and he well might, thought Andrea, in view of his rich dress and the gorgeous amethyst ring which he kept twisting on his finger. Such peacocks were apt to lose their skins in the dungeons of St. Angelo to the profit of the Pope's war chest. When the bishop could stand it no longer and hurried out for a moment, everybody understood his predicament.

Shifting from foot to foot on the hard majolica pavement, Andrea diverted his mind to a study of the frescoes, which he had not yet had so favorable an occasion to inspect. They were unequal to those in the adjoining Sala dei Santi; but, even so, he found them admirable and had soon forgotten himself in artistic reverie. Even the pale autumn light and northern exposure did not wholly defeat the glorious colors, though it was a pity to waste such masterpieces on a ground-floor, courtyard apartment. The corresponding halls upstairs were better adapted; but, after all, the Borgia was no patron of art. As for the allegories of Grammar, Music, Geometry, and so on, Andrea half admired, half criticized. For the moment, he was no longer a courtier but the rival of Pinturicchio. The papal secretary's hand on his arm brought him back with a start from one world to the other.

"His Holiness desires your attendance, Captain Orsini."

He was conscious again of the beady-eyed priests, the impassive guardsmen and the nervous bishop; of the sidling, speculative glances that followed him as he crossed the threshold of the Pope's cabinet.

But here, whatever misgivings he might have had were at once dispelled by the Pontiff's high good humor. Roars of laughter greeted him.

Having moved to an armchair by the hearth, Alexander was engaged in watching his jester, Gabriellino, mimic one of the cardinals.

"*Ah, scimmione!*" laughed His Holiness. "You baboon!" Then, becoming aware of Andrea, he gave a final guffaw. "Be off now before you're the death of me. Here's a coin. No physic like a good laugh. Ho, ho! Begone. I've business with the noble Orsini. . . . You too," he nodded at Asquino. "I'll ring when you're needed."

The fool capered out, followed by the sedate secretary. Refreshed and still smiling, the Pope beckoned Andrea and advanced his foot slightly on the footstool for Orsini to kiss. Sinking to his knees, the latter pressed his lips upon the embroidered cross of Alexander's low-cut, red shoe, while the Pope raised a negligent finger in blessing. Then, at a word, Andrea rose again with consummate grace and stood attentive.

"We have news for you, Messere," said His Holiness. "It may be that the reward of your distinguished services in Ferrara is nearer than anyone could have supposed, aye, and a twofold reward at that. Let no one imagine that the illustrious Duke Valentino and I are unmindful patrons of merit such as yours. The report you gave us of your mission, the gratification expressed by Her Signory, Madonna Lucrezia, with respect to certain letters brought to her by you, have greatly pleased us. Therefore, we thank you, Messere, and are vigilant in your interests."

Whatever the Pope might be, he was a gracious speaker. His mellow voice and seraphic smile gave added luster to what he said. In reply, Andrea could only protest his small deserts and that to have won the approval of such a kind and triumphant princess was a reward in itself exceeding his dreams. But, for all that, he remained very much on guard. Experience warned him that smooth waters were dangerous and to beware of reefs. . . . "My fondest dreams," he repeated.

"I applaud your modesty," said the Pope, "as a foil to your worth; but that does not absolve us of our obligations. . . . And so, to the point. I believe you know that the Varani, your recent hosts, are to visit Rome. Most commendable of them as Christians. But — you will draw your own inferences."

Andrea's training stood him in good stead. He showed no surprise, although, now that the bolt had fallen, his blood ran cold. Varano's fate was sealed. The Pope had disclosed a great deal in a few words. Orsini had said nothing about his visit to Città del Monte. There was no reason he should, and apparently no umbrage had been taken at his silence. But he ought to have guessed that the Borgias kept a spy close to Varano.

"Inferences, hm-m," he muttered. "Yes. . . . I see that Your Beatitude has been kept well informed. Is it permitted to ask the name of Your Holiness's agent at Città del Monte?"

"Certainly. In fact you should know it, with a view to possible developments. Who but Galeazzo Branca, captain of Varano's guard?"

The red-faced man who had crowed so loud against Cesare Borgia. That, in itself, ought to have given Orsini the hint.

"An excellent choice," he remarked, his hands itching for the traitor's throat. "I thank Your Holiness for pointing him out to me. He shall be remembered. . . . And so I may infer — "

"Everything to your profit," interrupted the Pope. "But such matters are better not discussed." He gave a toss of the hand that closed the subject.

But, to Andrea, one point was clear. If he was to keep his promise to Camilla, he must get off a messenger at once with an imperative warning. On no condition must Varano enter Rome.

"I spoke of a twofold reward," the Pope continued.

"Your Apostolic Majesty overwhelms me," Andrea murmured, more alert than ever.

"What do you say to an alliance with our House?"

Orsini marshaled every faculty to meet the crisis. If he had not been somewhat prepared, he could not have managed so excellent a piece of acting: amazement, deprecation, humility. Even so, he had to play for time.

The Pope, beaming like a benevolent Jupiter, submerged him with the honor of Angela Borgia's hand, unveiled the glittering future, and quite understood that the recipient of such benefits could not adequately express his thanks.

As for Andrea, the conflict which had begun at Città del Monte and had continued subtly enough at Viterbo was now hemming him in. He could accept these rewards from the Pope only at the cost of relinquishing Camilla, of Varano's death, and of utter treachery. On those terms, the career which he had followed so long and at such effort was assured him. But, after all, there might be other terms, another approach. One did not throw over a career without exploring every alternative. He distrusted heroic decisions. The proper game was to close no doors, to wait and see, to use his wits. Meanwhile, he was beginning to wonder more and more about the effectiveness of treachery as a means to either political or personal success.

"I am unable to find words, Your Holiness . . ."

"Do not attempt it," Alexander nodded. "I am happy in your happiness, Messere. But, of course, your good fortune depends upon one member of our House, whose consent you must secure. I am merely the great-uncle of Her Ladyship. My nephew, her illustrious father, will give the final word."

Here was an unlooked-for respite. It might take several days to gain formal audience with Don Jofrè de Borgia-Lanzol. He might even be out of Rome.

"And I have the pleasure to inform you," went on His Holiness, "that the said lord now awaits your attendance close at hand in the Sala del Credo. He expects your coming." The Pope smiled again and rubbed his hands. "But have no fear, sir. I have every confidence in your diplomacy."

When Andrea had taken leave of the Pope with all due ceremony and had backed himself out of the room, the sharp-eyed priests in the antechamber could well imagine that it had gone hard with him. However, by the time he had passed the guards on the threshold of the neighboring Sala del Credo, he had repaired his smile and straightened his shoulders. Since he had no intention of marrying Angela, he might skillfully contrive to fail in his suit with her father.

The apartment was empty. . . .

No. At first, he had not seen the figure in the deep-set recess of the opposite window.

"Well, Messere," exclaimed a familiar voice, "does it take the Pope himself to bring you to me? How now, Andrea?"

And, stepping down from the embrasure, Angela Borgia held out both her hands.

CHAPTER XXXV

LAST summer, before the potent mysteries underlying Angela's silken gown had been revealed, Andrea had flamed at the touch of her. But now, as he covered his confusion by dropping to one knee and pressing his lips upon her jasmine-scented fingers, the earlier heat was gone.

He knew her too well. He had learned also that love has other, more enchanting facets than the obvious ones she presented. Not that she was no longer attractive — he had never seen her more ravishing than in this pale green *gamurra* edged with gold, that blended so perfectly with the spun gold of her hair — but there were no new charms in reserve. The mole above her garter was just as familiar to him as the exquisite plucked line of her eyebrows.

And yet policy required him to conceal his actual indifference and, when he spoke, to give his words an authentic ring.

"*Madonna bellissima*, what a surprise!"

Turning her hand, he kissed the palm of it — an old caress between them. She ran the fingers of her free hand through his hair, tilting up his face.

"*Sallo Iddio*, my Andrea, I've been missing you." Then, as he stood up, she added: "You were really surprised? His Holiness didn't betray me?"

"No, *mia cara*, by not so much as a hair. I expected your illustrious father. I found" — he paused a moment; the invitation in her eyes gave him his cue, and he met it appropriately — "your lips."

Above them, unseen, a secret panel in the wall slipped back, and a benevolent, handsome face looked down. The Pope nodded approvingly. He noted the hint of possession when Angela, slipping an arm around Orsini's waist, her head side-tilted upon his shoulder, drew him over to one of the deep window recesses. Alexander's lips moistened. He felt the righteous glow of a benefactor. Then, with a final nod, he closed the panel.

But the possessiveness on Angela's part, which had delighted the Pope, chilled Andrea. He stiffened inwardly as they walked toward the window alcove, and he seated himself opposite her.

"How now!" Angela pouted. "Here's a place beside me. Must you sit facing me, as if I had the pox? . . . So! That's better." He drew her convincingly against him in the circle of his arm. "Much better! Now we can talk. But tell me first why you have spent five days in Rome without waiting on me. Is that devotion?"

"Madonna, shall I be truthful?"

"If it's possible."

Andrea sighed. "The doubt grieves me. . . . Know, then, that I failed to present myself for two reasons. In the first place, clothes. I make my vow it took two days of brushing, scrubbing, airing, and perfuming before I had a stitch fit to wear. And even now I blush to approach Your Signory."

"*Sei matto!*" said Angela. "Pretexts."

"No, Madonna, consideration for you. But hardly had I freed myself from the smell and sweat of the journey when I was overwhelmed by the rumor of such honor that, even though just now confirmed by the Majesty of the Pope himself, I still dare not credit it."

Angela glowed. "What honor?" she murmured.

"If Your Signory doesn't know, far be it from me to give presumption a tongue. But if you know, you will understand the dilemma."

She drooped her eyelids. "Dilemma to be offered my hand? I should think that would bring you to me like a stooping falcon — that is, if you cared!"

"Cared! *Santa Maria!* But remember, it was only a rumor until now. In what guise could I wait upon you before I knew the truth? If I said too much or too little, I should be equally damned. I could only wait."

She nestled closer to him. The low cut of her bodice only half contained the insurgence of her breasts.

"Kiss me," she put in. "No one can kiss like you, Andrea. *Ah, carissimo . . . !*"

At that point it was easier to make a kiss more convincing than excuses.

She leaned back contented. The dull blur of sunset through the window accentuated both her charms and their limitations: the arrogant, full mouth that would sometime be only arrogant; the piquant curve of her cheeks, which did not need as yet the make-up that the light brought out too distinctly; the nose still pert rather than sharp; the nakedness of her depilated forehead; the swell of her thigh where the gown tightened.

"Well, I forgive you. So — you accept my hand?"

His dramatics satisfied even Angela's expectations. But meanwhile, back of them, Andrea's thought drifted a long way. He could not avoid comparisons between what she and Camilla represented. It was only a step from there to other reflections. He had been out of the Borgian milieu for some time. His recent interview with the Pope, this present tête-à-tête, brought home vividly the significance of the Borgian attitude in contrast with what had impressed him at Città del Monte. On one hand, ethical depravity and sensual grossness; on the other, honorable principles and refinement of manners. He found that the glamour of the future on Borgian terms had greatly faded since Venice, and that cynical enlightenment seemed less enlightened than he had once thought. What if it were possible to shift his career out of the Borgian orbit? But perhaps that was too late.

Angela misinterpreted his sigh.

"Yes," she declared. "We'll be very happy. It must mean a great deal to you to marry me. You had never looked so high, had you? But I'm like that, Andrea. I enjoy giving you everything. What sacrifice is too great for love?" Her broad thumbs cocked back. He thought of Camilla's slender hands. "Be sure I shall push your fortunes."

"My sovereign lady and patron!"

"If it could only be tomorrow!" She leaned her head against him. "This tiresome betrothal of mine with Francesco della Rovere! And you're still not lord of Città del Monte. Six months to wait — six months at least! Perdition!"

"Long, indeed, Madonna." It was a comfort to reflect that only the possession of Città del Monte made him eligible for this marriage.

"Yes, but for the best part of it we need not wait. When will you come to me, *caro?* You know the way." And, as he did not answer at once, she half lifted her head from his shoulder and repeated, "When?"

"I was thinking only that the way might not be so easy as last June."

This time Angela raised her head completely. "Why not, *per Dio?*"

"The honor you have just accorded me. To lovers, much is permitted; but, if it is understood that we are to marry, the same freedom might be ill-considered. I suggest merely." Once again he held her hand against his lips.

"Hm-m," she mused. The difficulty had not until now occurred to her. Everything got around in Rome. Their past love affair had called for tolerant winks; but, if she was to marry Andrea, decency required that from now until marriage he should not figure as her lover. Even fashionable license had its conventions. She admitted the force of the objection, but at the same time it nettled her, perhaps because she felt that he accepted it too readily. "I suppose you're right; but there are ways of managing — that is, if you choose."

"If I choose!"

He put enough conviction in his voice to reassure her. She brightened.

"For example. You've heard of the new statue dug up near Castel Gandolfo — haven't you? — an Apollo or Bacchus. Everybody's talking about it."

Andrea nodded. The discovery of an ancient masterpiece was a notable event. He recalled that this one had been found last week in the ruins of a villa of Domitian, and that the Savelli, who owned the place, had set it up in one of their villas at Castel Gandolfo. But what the newly recovered statue had to do with Angela's maneuvers escaped him.

"I'm burning to see it," she added. "Aren't you?"

"Most certainly."

"And so is Madonna Lucrezia. Suppose we made up a party for Castel Gandolfo — do you think it will rain tomorrow?"

The fog in Orsini's mind began to clear. He gazed out through the window at the blood-red disk of the sun setting in a bank of clouds on the rim of the Campagna. It boded foul weather.

"Perhaps not," he said dubiously.

"Well, then, tomorrow," she went on, "or the first fair day after that. We ride, a full party of us, to the hills, visit the lords Savelli, admire Bacchus or Apollo. Then I fall ill." Angela gave a radiant smile. "Touch of the heart. The Savelli are gallant hosts. We spend the night at the villa. And if you can't imagine the rest of it, I despair of you."

It did not take much imagination. Angela's waiting woman, Mona Tonia, was most resourceful and discreet. The corridors of a country manor lent themselves to secret flittings from room to room. The darkness and cold upland air were sharp spices to love.

"You see" — she gave a toss of the hands — "it's as easy as that. A fig for your caution! The devil's in it if we can't take our pleasure from time to time without scandal. Who will know except Tonia? And she copies the Sphinx. She remembers what happened to my last maid who babbled."

"What happened?" he asked absently, his mind on the weather and other postponements.

Angela shrugged. "Oh, something." Her smile hardened. "So, my Andrea, there you are. And Castel Gandolfo isn't the only place. We'll have fun. It's more amusing when it's not too easy." She leaned back with a deep breath. "Fun," she repeated. But perhaps she was not entirely assured. "Tell me again that you love me."

"The word is too faint, Madonna."

"For I love *you*," she put in with an odd intenseness, "and I do not trust you."

"Alas!"

"Alas, indeed, *mio diletto!* Be careful!" She menaced him with her forefinger. The playfulness did not wholly cover up a certain glint under it. "I say be careful. If I caught you tripping, don't expect me to fold my hands. *Ahi!* I pity the slut who poaches my game. As for you — " her eyes froze, then melted — "as for you . . ."

With a turn of the wrist, he unsheathed his dagger and presented the ivory hilt — a gallant gesture. They sat for a moment silent, the cool blade between them, while she fingered the carving.

Finally, she laughed. "Love's a mad thing, Messere. . . . But, now, this party of ours to Castel Gandolfo . . ."

Upon leaving the Vatican an hour later, Andrea lost no time in dispatching a messenger who would stop the Varani en route. He carried a letter, unsigned and written in suitably veiled language, warning them that under no circumstances should they enter Rome.

CHAPTER XXXVI

To ANDREA'S immense satisfaction, the rain began next day, continued the next and the next, and bade fair to usher in winter without permitting the excursion that Angela Borgia had proposed. Meanwhile, since his messenger to the Varani did not return, he could take it for granted that the former had been compelled to ride several days north — perhaps to Città del Monte itself — and that the old lord and Camilla had either not commenced their journey or had been spared all but a short stage of it.

As soon as he received definite news, he planned to write them in greater detail. As it was, he had a clear conscience regarding his promise to Camilla and could give full attention to his own concerns. Obviously, if he was to avoid further entanglement with the Borgian marriage, he must leave Rome. But, for that, orders were necessary either from Ferrara or from Duke Cesare, and he sent letters to both, expressing impatience at his inactivity and his desire to serve on some other mission or nearer to their persons.

Unfortunately, however, good weather returned after a week; Angela's summons came; and he found himself compelled to take part in Lucrezia Borgia's glittering cortege to the Alban Hills. Although pleasure was clearly the chief object of the ride, a certain archaeological flavor was afforded by the presence of the learned architect, Master

Bramante from Milan, a connoisseur of antiquities, who would give his appraisal of the newly found statue.

Under a cupola in the autumn-disheveled garden of the Savelli villa outside Castel Gandolfo, the re-emerged god looked down with an imperturbable smile upon the foolish costumes of the new age; upon hose and doublets, bell-shaped skirts, triangular bodices, slashed sleeves, flat caps, and plumed headpieces. His beautiful nakedness made sport of this complicated haberdashery and cheapened it. Or perhaps he did not survey the company at all, as beneath his notice, and gazed rather, with the contentment of an immortal released from darkness into sunlight, at the once familiar slopes of the hills and the caress of the sky.

Upon Andrea, the god's gracious detachment from the group that clustered around his pedestal made a disturbing impression. It was reality amid a flickering of shadows: it was timelessness unconcerned with the grimaces of time. Even Bramante's scholarly comments sounded flat, like the bleating of an old sheep.

"Look you, signori, this may well be a Hermes rather than either Apollo or Bacchus. The shape of the head suggests it, though one misses the staff and cap or other symbols. Yes, lords, in my humble opinion . . ."

What the devil difference did it make? thought Andrea. He preferred that the god should remain untagged with a name, more illusive and compelling because unknown. It would be a joy, if he had paints and canvas, so to portray the Spirit of Spring returning to earth. The same smile; this background of clean, washed sky —

"But, sirs," coughed Bramante, "we can be sure of one thing. Here's no Greek original. An excellent copy, indeed, but Roman — I should say not earlier than Domitian himself."

"Come, now, Master," protested Luca Savelli, the owner of the villa, who saw the worth of his find diminished, "I'll pray you to make no snap judgments."

The artist held his ground against Savelli's black stare. "My lord, I speak only of what any trained eye can see. Look you . . ." He plunged into technicalities.

Madonna Lucrezia Borgia, with a toss of the head and a flutter of her plumed hat, laughed away the dispute. "Passion of me, gentlemen! Bear in mind that what we women admire in a good lusty figure is not pedigree but points. And I vow that Messer Hermes has the wherewithal to endear himself to ladies." She lifted an eyebrow. "I refer to his charming smile, of course — nothing else."

Angela, not to be outdone, put in: "That's just the word for it. Is there a gallant here with one more charming? Let's see now."

And the gates of ribaldry were open. Everybody laughed. The gentlemen planted fists on hips and flung their heads back; the ladies' stays creaked.

"Let's hear from the Magnifico Orsini," Angela challenged. "Where are your wits today, Messere?"

He threw in a quip spicy enough to rouse another gale.

But at that moment, glancing beyond the others, he became aware, first, of a newcomer, Troilo Savelli from Rome, and, next, of two figures in traveling dress beside him. For an instant, their familiarity delayed recognition. The square-built man in an old-fashioned hat; the slender, russet-clad girl with the wide fur collar and small, flickering plume! Varano and Camilla!

He gazed at them, stupefied. Struck by his expression, Angela stopped laughing. "Eh?" she said, following his stare, and then stared herself as he brushed past her, threaded the group of their own party, and dropped to one knee before the new arrivals.

"Madonna Milla! Your Excellence!"

Troilo Savelli spoke quickly. "You must know, sir, that this lady and gentleman are traveling unofficially. They do not wish to be presented to the company at this time. Their purpose here is to view the statue and to greet my kinsman."

Red with embarrassment, Andrea was on his feet at once. "My unfortunate blunder," he murmured. "The surprise — I crave pardon."

But as he drew back, Camilla could not resist a flick at him. "There was moss on that joke of yours, Messere."

He did not smile. "It's imperative that I have a word in private with Your Signories before you leave."

They were standing in the background of the pergola and no one of the main party, gathered about the statue, could have caught the words. But Angela Borgia did not need to catch them. She could see; and, by virtue of the strange sixth sense which jealousy gives, she could interpret. That inclination of the head, a fraction lower than courtesy required; the expression in Andrea's eyes, the lines of his mouth — these were all warning signals, however much he tried to offset them with a blank face as he rejoined the group. Therefore, she showed nothing but admiration and kindly curiosity.

"Who was that exquisite signora? A stranger? How lovely she is! Where did you meet her?"

He shrugged. "I regret, Madonna. Hold me excused from questions. You have just seen me make an ass of myself. These illustrious lords are on pilgrimage and choose to remain private. So, what must I do but stick my thumb in!"

But already Varano's well-known face had been recognized by a couple of the gentlemen. The whisper passed: *Città del Monte . . . the young wife . . . she of Perugia.* It did not help Orsini in the eyes of Angela, who knew something about the original bargain with Duke Cesare. Here was the girl who had first been promised. Of course *that* was in the discard. Of course the chit could not be compared with Angela herself, nor such a marriage with the one now proposed. And yet the way he had greeted this Camilla! Was there something between them? Lucrezia Borgia, eying her cousin, smiled; and Angela's glance in reply showed nothing but amusement.

"Not very private, after all," she murmured to Andrea. "A lovely creature! Such a pity she married her grandfather. I've seldom been so taken with anyone on first sight. You never told me you were friends with her."

Andrea was aware of thin ice. "Friends, Madonna?"

"Yes, you seem well with her."

The company was drifting from the pergola to stroll out along the paths of the garden. Varano, Camilla, and their host, who had withdrawn until they could view the statue alone, were exchanging compliments with Luca Savelli. He bowed them into the pergola. Orsini managed not to look back, as he walked on by the side of Angela.

His brain spun around. What would happen, unless he could prevent the sword overhanging the Varani from falling? And that it otherwise would fall he had not the least doubt, from the Pope's cryptic remarks a week since.

"*Caro,*" asked Angela, "when do you think I should begin?"

"What, Madonna?"

"You know," she smiled.

"Ah, indeed. Your heart attack." He wished her at the devil. "It grieves me that you should even pretend to suffer; but, if it must be, I should advise just before we mount. The effect would be more startling." This would give him the utmost time possible to seek out Camilla. "Will you swoon?"

"Of course. And, if you stand by, you'll have the pleasure of unlacing me." She patted her reticule. "The face powder's here. I promise to look like a ghost. But you'll bring back the color later."

They were rejoining others of the party. It was the proper moment to detach himself casually. Camilla and Varano must not return to Rome. The Colonna Castle at Marino lay close at hand and would give them protection. This was their last opportunity for escape.

Andrea was on the point of excusing himself when Lucrezia Borgia's sweetly imperious voice called: "Here are the laggards! Come and give an account of yourselves." There was no getting away at the moment.

The group stood at the door of an arbor, where, in view of the fine day (no doubt the last before winter), a cloth had been spread for a brief collation alfresco. Servants in the Savelli livery passed goblets of wine, chestnut bread, fruit, and cakes. Far and wide below and in front stretched the panorama of the Campagna, an autumnal sea, with the blur of Rome on the horizon.

Andrea felt like a man with ants in his breeches. Time was passing. The Varani might leave without his seeing them.

And then his release came in a fashion too simple to have been expected. A servant appeared with the request of *a certain gentleman and lady* that they might have speech with him before they rode. It was as easy as that.

He found Camilla in the pergola under the smiling benediction of the god.

She gave him no time for a word. "You see before you the most excited lady in Italy — the most enchanted. How shall I say? I have no words — "

"What is it, Madonna?"

"Do you know what my lord has done? You couldn't guess. Never could you guess. I vow to you I said nothing, not one word to incline him. I merely worshiped this beautiful thing." She turned to the statue with a look of adoration. "Sir, my lord has purchased it. He is at this moment closing with Messer Luca. We are to have it at Città del Monte. We are to take it with us on our return. It will be an object of pilgrimage, I can tell you. Our little town will be famous for it." She stood looking up, enraptured. "You beautiful god! . . . Tell me, Messer Andrea, has any other woman such a husband as mine? That he should make this sacrifice without a word from me, because he knew what joy it would give me!"

"Munificent, indeed, Your Signory! . . . Could I have a word with the lord Varano at once?"

The light went out of her face. "Is something wrong? Tell me — "

"Yes." He lowered his voice. "Didn't you receive my message?"

"What message?" she faltered.

"Why, the one I sent you a week ago by a special rider. I felt certain it had reached you on the road."

Her eyes widened. "But, sir, we've been spending the past week at the castle of our friend, Fabrizio Colonna in Marino. We entered Rome only last night by the Porta San Sebastiano."

At once he understood what had happened. The Varani had circled Rome to the south by the time his messenger had left. Instead of entering the city by the northern gate, the Porta del Popolo, they had entered from the opposite direction. The messenger, not having met them, would no doubt have continued vainly on to Città del Monte.

"*Sangue di Dio!*" Andrea muttered.

"But tell me what's wrong!" she breathed.

"The Pope — You and my lord must not re-enter Rome . . ."

He heard a footstep at the door of the pergola and turned, expecting Varano. Instead, a dark, masked figure in riding boots confronted them. Masked; but anyone who had ever seen it would recognize that erect, graceful form, lithe as a panther, who strode forward. Even before the mask had been flicked off, Andrea knew who it was though he could hardly believe his eyes.

At the same moment, the implications of this arrival flashed through his mind.

It was Cesare Borgia.

CHAPTER XXXVII

LOWERING his mask, the Duke revealed another, more subtle mask: his inscrutable, handsome features, serene brow, and charming smile. He could turn on, in his magnificent eyes, whatever light he chose; tender, menacing, ardent, imperious. No one actually knew what went on behind this façade, what dark councils and daring plans; but it was not hard to guess that an utterly cold, perfectly tempered will supervised each change of expression. Andrea Orsini, who had long studied him, conjectured that the mainspring of Borgia's nature was an egotism so intense as to be almost passionless, except for scorn of scruples and shortsightedness.

At the moment, only graceful cordiality showed in the Duke's manner.

"Am I wrong in believing that this is the illustrious Signora of Città del Monte?" he bowed. "Report has not belied Your Excellence's charms nor the resemblance you bear to others of your glorious House. I shall relinquish to no man the honor of presenting me to the divine Camilla Baglione, but shall assure her myself that Cesare Borgia is her devoted admirer and servant."

No doubt Camilla had guessed who the new arrival was, but she looked whiter at the mention of his name. Andrea could read the trouble in her eyes, even while she answered the Duke's bow. It was a dreaded name in itself, apart from any personal reasons for fearing it. Here was a man accused, whether rightly or wrongly, of the most unnatural crimes; known for his ruthlessness and implacable ambition; impressive in his physical beauty and in the sense he gave of unlimited power.

She murmured something in reply. Andrea came to the rescue by exclaiming upon the Duke's unexpected return from the north. He said nothing of this still more amazing appearance at Castel Gandolfo. His pulses beat fast. What would happen next? He knew, of course, that Borgia would have a band of armed men with him. By now they had probably closed every approach to the villa. No doubt Varano's arrest and Camilla's would follow.

"A visit of a few days only, my good friend," said the Duke. "Affairs of moment that required attention. They'll not detain me long. And, hark you, Andrea, make no more of my presence here than you can help. There's no need that the stubborn burghers of Faenza should hear I have quit the siege even for a day." He turned again to Camilla. "And yet even business has its amenities, such as this fortunate meeting with Your Signory."

Her eyes were on the doorway. Andrea furtively wiped the nervous sweat from his palms. He reflected that perhaps Varano had already been seized.

Dropping back a step, Borgia considered the statue of Hermes. "*Bellissimo!*" he admired. "*Stupendo! Per l'anima mia*, our friend Luca has

234

found a marvel. My collection needs just such a thing, if he's willing to sell."

In order to say something, but almost unconscious of what she said and still glancing at the doorway, Camilla ventured that her husband had just purchased the statue for love of her. "But if Your Grandeur desires it . . ." Her voice trailed out.

At once all gallantry, Borgia made a sweeping movement of the hand. "Heaven forbid, Madonna. Your pleasure is my own, and I should vastly more enjoy the thought of your possessing this piece of art than to possess it myself."

Andrea clenched his teeth at this unnecessary irony. He thought of a thrush in the spell of a serpent.

"And I shall hope to congratulate my lord Varano," Borgia added, smiling.

As if in answer, a familiar, swinging footstep could be heard approaching outside. So the arrest had not yet taken place. Andrea felt a growing tension at the sound of the footsteps. Camilla's face brightened for a moment and then froze. Borgia half turned toward the door.

"All settled, *dolce vita*," announced Varano, entering. "Messer Luca wasn't too unreasonable, though he drives a shrewd — " Becoming aware of the Duke, he broke off. "By this light! The lord Valentino!"

But if Borgia's sudden appearance had had a Medusa effect on Orsini and Camilla, it produced none at all on Varano, except apparent pleasure. He advanced with outstretched arms.

"It's been a long time since I had the honor of saluting Your Glorious Excellence. *Buon pro a la Signoria vostra!* You were but a lad when I saw you last — and now you're the most triumphant captain of the age! My humble duty to Your Grace!"

"My second father!" replied Borgia warmly. This time a fervent light went on in his eyes. It transfigured his cold features, like a candle behind alabaster. "My very dear lord!"

Andrea found the scene almost physically painful. It grew worse, as the Duke explained that he had used the term *father* in all sincerity, since he had modeled his own military career upon that of Varano and (a skillful touch) upon the exploits of Varano's illustrious friend, the ever-lamented Duke of Urbino. But what was the reason for such cant? It did not even fit in with what Orsini knew of Borgia's methods. No one could use hypocrisy better than the Duke when it served his purpose, but he did not play a double game for fun. At that moment, he had only to spring the trap, denounce Varano on one count or another, and call in his men-at-arms. The present tactics were gratuitous and puerile.

However, Andrea had to admit that they were effective, at least in reassuring Camilla. Gradually the Duke's charm asserted itself. Her eyes cleared; the tenseness relaxed; she began to smile at his compliments to her and Varano.

"Nothing," urged Borgia, "would have so pleased the Pope's Holiness and me as to have welcomed Your Signories to Rome with all the honor due not only to the Houses of Varano and Baglione, but to your merits, my lord, as the loyal and valiant servant of the Holy Roman Church, that so highly esteems you. To no one else can the words of the glorious Apostle be applied so truly in this corrupt age as to you, who have finished your course and kept the faith."

An archangel could not have looked more devout. In spite of the raging cynicism he felt at the moment, Orsini found it a masterly performance. With every word and smile, the Duke more completely established himself in his victims' confidence.

"But you gave us no choice," Borgia went on. "Since it pleases you to visit Rome in a private capacity and in humble devotion to God, we can only respect so virtuous a decision. The Golden Rose, which I believe the Holiness of our Lord wishes to confer upon you, must be held over until the next, though, I hope, an early occasion. Meanwhile, if in any way His Holiness or I can serve you at this time, you have only to inform us."

Oil upon oil! So winning was the Duke's manner that Andrea caught himself almost believing him. But that would be a little naïve. In the first place, why was Borgia here? Certainly not to see a statue or for the sake of an outing with his sister. On a hurried visit to Rome, he had no time for such trifles. No, he had come to Castel Gandolfo because of the Varani. But he could have ordered their arrest without personally supervising it. . . .

Then, in a flash, Andrea believed that he had hit on an answer to the riddle. This very visit to Rome, this preoccupation with the Varani. Why? Certainly, to effect the imprisonment and death of the old lord, it was not necessary for the Duke to participate personally at all. The Pope had every means adequate for that purpose. Might it not be that Cesare, apprised of the Varani's coming to Rome and already fully engaged at Faenza, considered any action against them at this time as premature? Might it not be that he was in Rome not to arrest, but to protect, them? Theory, of course; but it accounted for these extraor-

236

dinary and otherwise unnecessary attentions he was showering upon them.

The Duke's next words fitted this view. "I understand that Your Excellences did not arrive here in company with my sister, the Princess of Salerno, and that you are returning at once to Rome with Troilo Savelli. In that case, let me crave the honor of escorting you as well. The Campagna is not altogether safe. Time presses too hard to allow me the leisure of waiting upon Madonna Lucrezia's pleasure party, and I should delight in further talk with Your Lordships. It is enough that I have had a glimpse of this fine work." He glanced casually at the statue. "A masterpiece! Madama, you are fortunate to possess it."

By now, the report of the great man's arrival had spread; and, by the law of magnetism which operates in human relations, everybody at the villa gravitated toward him. He gave Lucrezia and her party a brief but gracious audience on the garden path outside of the pergola, kissed his sister and Angela, exchanged civilities with the gentlemen.

But it concerned Andrea at the moment that Angela Borgia, having gazed in the direction of Varano and Camilla, who, together with Troilo Savelli, were waiting at the garden entrance of the villa, exchanged a slight arching of the eyebrows with Lucrezia; and it concerned him as well that the latter so easily accepted the Duke's immediate departure. She expressed only moderate surprise and asked no questions. As sharing in the Borgia mentality, both ladies instinctively knew that something was afoot. The studied blandness of their faces showed this, and the inscrutability of their eyes, when they glanced toward the Varani.

Alert to this, Andrea reflected that his analysis of the Duke's intentions might very well be wrong. Perhaps Cesare, informed of the Varani's excursion to Castel Gandolfo, wished merely to assure himself that this was not a pretext for flight and resolved to make certain that they re-entered Rome by closing the trap on them himself.

Adjourning the audience with a wave of the hand, Borgia remarked: "And so, friends, I take my leave at this time and bid you farewell. A pleasant ride back! . . . Messer Andrea, you'll oblige me, I hope, with your company, since we have matters to discuss. Come, we mustn't keep the illustrious cavaliers and the lady waiting any longer."

Angela Borgia plucked up spirit enough to put in: "The lord Orsini came as my escort, Cousin. Devil take me if I release him!"

Cesare gave a knowing smile. "See what honor she does you, Andrea. But I'll make your peace with her. . . . *Andiamo.*"

"You didn't listen, my lord," Angela dared, though keeping her voice on a light tone. "I said I would not release him. Pray you, favor me."

The smile vanished. "How now, madam!" His glance abolished her. "Farewell again, signori. My good Andrea — "

Angela's face looked ugly for an instant, and her lips thin. She flashed a sullen glance at the Duke, who had already forgotten her.

Accompanied by Andrea, he walked down the garden path to the villa and apologized to the Varani and the lord Savelli for detaining them.

But Orsini had come to a final decision. If the Duke planned treachery on the road, he would fight to the utmost, however vainly, in defense of his friends. This ride might very well mean the end not only of his career but of his life.

As Andrea had expected, the Duke's guard waited in the outer court, some twenty riders headed by their captain, Michelotto. Compared with these troopers, many of them Spanish adventurers, the handful of Varano's and Savelli's servants looked submerged. But perhaps, more than anything else, it was Michelotto's grim face that cast a sudden chill on Varano and Camilla. Without recognizing him as Borgia's hangman, the strangler of Lucrezia's husband, they could still see the professional bravo in every feature. Camilla looked a question at her husband, whose eyes evaded her, and then at Andrea, who became interested in adjusting his riding cloak.

"A fine-looking troop," remarked Varano, with professional interest, though his voice sounded drier.

"Good men, all," Borgia nodded. "Prudence compels me to ride well-attended in the Campagna." He took the place of the servant who had led forward Camilla's mule and insisted on holding her stirrup himself. Then, effortlessly, with the bravura of a master horseman, he vaulted to the saddle of the fine black that was held in readiness for him, and gathered up the reins. "By your leave, signori, we'll ride well in front of these others to avoid the spatter. It's a foul road at this season."

Andrea noted that Troilo Savelli's eyes shifted here and there desperately, and that he kept moistening his lips.

Down the muddy hill path to the plain and so — now on a stretch of ancient pavement, now slopping through miniature ponds across the flooded road — past fragments of half-buried ruins projecting from the earth, past an occasional goatherd with his flock, they followed the immemorial Appian Way, while the towers of Rome drew nearer and flushed to gold beneath the setting sun. At last, like a faint, approaching tide of sound, they could hear the throbbing of the vesper bells. But twilight was falling before they threaded, with a prolonged rattle of hoofs, the mold-damp arches of the city gate.

Borgia resumed the mask, which he frequently wore to avoid public recognition. Michelotto's troop had closed in.

Instinctively Andrea braced himself. But the Duke, who had displayed all his conversational powers during the ride, went on pleasantly discoursing of the new Rome which would some day emerge when the present divisions of Italy had been healed. Camilla, once more reassured, listened enthralled, as did Varano. With the same ease and capacity that distinguished him in everything, Borgia disclosed another facet of himself, the statesmanlike, creative imagination which was as much a part of him as were selfishness and ambition.

They were crossing the southern, sparsely inhabited section of Rome, a district of ruins and small gardens. On the left, shadowy in the half-light, towered the brickwork of the Baths of Caracalla. Here would be the place, Andrea decided, if treachery were planned. Aware of Michelotto close behind, he felt his back stiffen, and his knees tightened against the saddle. But the Duke, listening to a remark of Varano's, gave no signal.

The road edged a tangle of gardens, solitary at that hour, and again Orsini's eyes narrowed.

"It's strange to reflect," said Borgia, "that this was once the Circus Maximus."

They bore right, along the Palatine, toward the Colosseum, and the dank smell of the city began to close in. Surely, this haunted quarter, secretive and ill-famed, was the proper setting for one more act of violence.

Suddenly a troop of horsemen confronted them. They wore the Pope's colors. But, upon recognizing Cesare, they fell back, as if at a sign from him. Orsini drew a breath of relief. He had guessed right. The reason for the Duke's concern with the Varani was now clear; only his escort had prevented their arrest.

Not long afterwards, Andrea recognized the portico of the Savelli Palace. At a word from Troilo Savelli, who rode forward to announce himself, the gates swung open, torches flared, and the party rode into the courtyard. Renewed compliments followed, renewed offers of service on the part of Borgia, cordial farewells.

Andrea found himself bidding good-night to Camilla.

"You see, Signor Suspicion," she whispered, "there was nothing to fear."

Varano gave him a quizzical glance. It was too kindly to be mocking; but it recalled the conversation at Città del Monte and implied a mild derision.

Profoundly thoughtful, Orsini rode with the Duke to the latter's Palace of San Clemente close to St. Peter's. When they were alone in Borgia's cabinet, the Duke remarked:

"You seem pensive, Andrea."

"Only lost in admiration, Your Grace."

"Of what?"

"Your Lordship's subtlety."

"Oho! Unlike the Pope's Holiness, you perceive why, at this time, it is necessary to treat the Varani with all honor?"

"Yes. The time for the Marches has not yet come."

"Exactly. . . . Fill me a cup of wine there, and one for yourself. Now harken . . ."

CHAPTER XXXVIII

"THE obvious is always a deceitful temptation in practical affairs," Cesare Borgia went on. "The more apparent the advantage and the quicker the returns, the greater need there is to look beyond. By forgetting this primary rule, His Holiness, who acts on impulse, has put me to the trouble of so long a journey. I rode posthaste to Rome to prevent a blunder."

Relaxed in an armchair, his thumb and forefinger toying with the stem of a wine goblet on the small table beside him, his head against a cushion, and his still youthful beard tilted up, the Duke eyed Orsini with a mixture of cold annoyance and amusement. Although they were both of the same age, Andrea never thought of Borgia as young. A certain timeless quality in the Duke gave him an advantage over even much older men. Perhaps his rank had something to do with this, and the fact that he carried himself always like a great prince; but, for the most part, the impression of maturity he made was not due to externalities — it derived from a deeper, more mysterious source.

"The obvious line," he continued, "was to take advantage of the old fool Varano's simplicity in coming to Rome. That certainly was the tempting play, the one that, except for me, His Holiness would have adopted. *Domineddio!* What an error! The more dangerous because so obvious. . . . And why dangerous? I'm up to the hams at Faenza, with no troops to spare. Bologna needs watching and the Florentines. A six months' business, not to mention that I may be called on for the French *impresa* against Naples. In short, as you have observed, I have no time at present for the Marches. But is Città del Monte my first objective there? Of course not — a side issue. Camerino's the main point. And by dealing so blindly with old Varano, we give the alarm to his kinsmen of that city, give them time to recruit, time to fortify, time to intrigue. By taking Città del Monte now, we raise tenfold the cost of taking Camerino later." Borgia rapped his forehead impatiently with his knuckles. "Even though at one time we did invite Varano into the trap, it seems to me that His Holiness might have understood to what extent the long siege of Faenza alters matters."

Andrea nodded. The exhausting campaign in Romagna temporarily protected the cities of the Marches. And that fact, in turn, protected Varano and Camilla in Rome.

"Of course," Borgia conceded, "the Pope might have held his hand until he heard from me. But, knowing him, I could not be sure of this. I could not even be sure that he would heed my letters. He's apt to be headlong when it comes to plucking a fat pear. I could not gamble on a matter of such weight. Therefore, I wasted no time after the receipt of his letter telling of Varano's coming. . . . Violence to my lord and lady?" Cesare added, taking a sip of wine. "*Che poltroneria!* On the contrary, all honor, love, attentions, compliments. Let the report of our kindness spread through the Marches and lull everybody, until they wake up with our troopers inside their gates."

'The Duke continued his reflections at some length. But, though Andrea missed nothing of the discourse, his private thought followed a path which would have amazed Borgia if the latter could have read behind his schooled features. Unknown to himself, the impressions of the last two weeks and those of that afternoon had germinated in Orsini's mind, and they now rose to the surface of consciousness in the form of revolt.

241

Was this the man to found a new nation, this cold brain divorced from any heart? Compared with Varano, he seemed merely a clever schemer. Even his shrewdness in sparing his victims until a more convenient time denoted craft rather than statesmanship. Andrea could no longer believe that nations sprang from ruthless reason and ruthless force. At Città del Monte he had admired the strength that derived from something entirely different. No, Borgia was not the man.

And having reached this conclusion, he withdrew at that moment unofficially from Borgia's service. A career on the Duke's terms had no permanence and led nowhere except to self-loathing. Orsini's manifest interest now lay with Varano and Camilla, to protect them and their little state, to defeat Borgia, if possible. That to do this he would have to meet guile with guile did not trouble him in the least. He changed sides, and he would keep that change very secret; but he had not yet reached the point of changing his technique.

When the occasion offered, he took a first step in the new direction by begging leave to ask advice on a certain point.

"At your service," said Borgia, fingering the stem of his goblet, his eyes far off.

"I hardly know how to approach so delicate a subject, my lord. It involves Your Grandeur's cousin, my lady Angela."

The eyes drifted back and quickened. "So? I had almost forgot that we were to be related." A slight curl of the lips gave point to the Duke's indifference. "You'll recall that that was no part of our understanding. It has been injected since, and I wished to discuss it with you. But you were saying — ?"

"That the proposed marriage may be, alas, an example of the inadequate foresight which Your Signory condemns."

Andrea spoke the more boldly because of that chill hesitation in Borgia's manner. Apparently the Duke did not welcome the marriage too eagerly himself. But, for all that, it was a ticklish point to discuss. Whether Borgia favored it or not, Andrea must avoid the slightest indication that he was cool to so flattering an alliance.

"You interest me," said the Duke. "Pray explain. What has foresight to do with it?"

"In this respect, sir, that I was putting my obvious advantage, the great honor conferred upon me, and the attractions of the lady Angela, before Your Lordship's interests in the Marches. You were good enough at one time to suggest the possibility of a marriage with Camilla Baglione after her husband's demise — "

"Neatly turned," Cesare smiled, interrupting.

"But when," Andrea continued, "this other so much more gloriou. alternative was presented me by the Pope's Holiness himself, I forgot every other consideration than the divine beauty and virtues of Madonna Angela and the overwhelming honor of a connection with your House. My lord, I am only human. I was dazzled — "

"What other consideration?" snapped Borgia. "Spare the compliments. Come to my interests that you mentioned."

"Sir, on my way south, after parting from you at Pesaro, I naturally took the occasion to stop by at Città del Monte. It was important to examine the situation there. One thing in particular struck me: the blind love of the people for their lord, a love in which his wife shares. It's a stubborn, mountain people — "

"I see what you're getting at," Borgia nodded. "I've had the same cursed love to contend with at Faenza. You think that your marriage with the Baglione girl would sugar the pill of Varano's loss and of your replacing him. Am I right?"

Andrea looked hesitant. "I had not gone so far as to reach an opinion. The thought occurred to me merely with reference to Your Lordship's profound remarks upon looking beyond an immediate gain to its possible drawbacks. I mention it rather in the hope that Your Excellence will reject the idea as overcautious and fine-spun. Only my zeal for Your Lordship's interests . . ." He let his voice fade out.

Cesare eyed him with inscrutable gravity. "My poor Andrea!" he said. "I can easily understand how it is. Certes I appreciate your devotion at its true worth. But, *amico mio*, much as I grieve to disappoint you, it seems to me that the objection you raise to the marriage with my cousin is well taken."

Orsini's heart gave a leap. It strained his face at this point, but he managed to look still more dejected.

"Policy," Borgia went on, "must take precedence of love, as you'll admit. Better to hold Città del Monte easily by marrying the present Signora than to sit there on hot coals with my cousin. Your future career and my government in that province are best served if you win the love of the people."

Andrea fetched a sigh more eloquent than words. It struck him that the Duke's prompt acceptance of the suggestion was a little too prompt, as if he was glad that Orsini had spared him the task of raising other objections to the marriage with Angela and he was snatching at this one as a pretext.

"Your reasoning is entirely sound, my friend," Cesare insisted, "and it does credit to your political sense. Have no fear that you will lose by your sacrifice in this matter. Your services at Ferrara, your services to Duke Ercole in Viterbo" (a faint smile flitted across Borgia's lips), "merit the highest reward. Who knows but that later, when the Baglione lady has served her turn, a marriage with Angela Borgia or with some other of our House might be arranged? I shall bear it in mind. Meanwhile, thanks that you are so reasonable and accommodating."

Was there a faint frost of sarcasm about this? Andrea could not be sure. It seemed to him that he and the Duke were like two players, each perfectly aware of the other's role, but, by a tacit agreement, pretending innocence. For different reasons, it suited them both that the original bargain should stand. The duet was in perfect tune.

Andrea squared his shoulders. "May I crave Your Signory's good offices with my lady Angela, to inform her of my grief, to explain that it is only in Your Lordship's service and at your command that I relinquish so fair a dream?"

"Certainly." The other's attention wandered. He began twiddling the chain of the Order of St. Michael on his breast. "Don't be concerned. She'll understand. I'll make all plain. . . . And now, by your leave, we'll turn to something else." The Duke's abstraction vanished, and he leaned forward in his chair. "Or rather to the next move in your game. I have been considering where to employ you, now that your mission in Ferrara is so brilliantly completed. You could return there, of course, and in high favor because of the little saint from Viterbo; but that would be the waste of a valuable man. I had thought of a post for you in France or even in Spain, but your interests lie elsewhere."

"They lie where Your Signory directs," Andrea put in.

Cesare made acknowledgment with a wave of the hand. "Your loyalty is one of your more endearing qualities. However, I have always observed that men work best in those situations which frame with their own advantage as well as with that of their prince. In short, Andrea, I depend on you to open me up the Marches. As future lord of Città del Monte, you could not be given a more appropriate field."

Orsini asked for further particulars.

"If all goes well," said the Duke, "I shall be ready for that *impresa* this summer. But I do not wish to squander good troops on Città del Monte and Camerino, as I am forced to squander them now at Faenza. When the time comes, I shall expect their gates to open before me as did those of Pesaro and Rimini. That's *your* business: to oil me those gates, to win me over the people of those cities and of the whole *contrada*. At the same time, you'll be sinking your own roots in Città del Monte. As to methods and means, I leave that entirely to you. It would reflect on your intelligence if I did more than indicate the problem. Draw on me for whatever funds you need in the way of bribes and gifts. Naturally you'll begin by establishing yourself somehow at Città del Monte."

"Naturally," Andrea agreed.

"For one thing," Borgia suggested, "I could recall our agent, the worthy Galeazzo Branca. You could sue for his place as captain of my lord's guard; though I admit that some reason to explain why an officer of Ferrara should seek so petty a post remains to be found. . . . However," the Duke added cheerfully, "you've cracked harder nuts than that. I'm convinced you'll crack this one." A twinkle showed in his eyes. "You might ask the lady Camilla to help you. You seem on close terms with her to judge by the tête-à-tête I interrupted today at the villa."

Andrea's face revealed nothing.

The other laughed. "I can think of a worse assignment than to present old Varano with a pair of horns." The quiver of Borgia's lips indicated more than he expressed. "It should help you to forget your sacrifice of our cousin. . . . Yes, let Madonna Camilla find you a place at Città del Monte."

He got up, as if closing the interview; but when Orsini, cap in hand, was on the point of taking leave, the Duke detained him with a crook of the finger.

"By the way, I'm informed that you have a very capable man in your service, one Mario Belli, about whom my future brother-in-law, the Cardinal d'Este, had much — though little good — to relate when I last saw him. A bravo of repute, he told me, renegade from the French and once in the service of Mantua."

Wondering at the question, Andrea answered, "Yes, my ensign."

"Well then, look you, sir" — the Duke's manner had become opaque — "such capacities should be used. When you're once in Città del Monte, they could be used to your profit and my service. I take it this Mario is a subtle rascal who knows the less apparent ways of sending people to glory."

"Most probably, sir."

"Excellent! I shall leave it to your discretion. But you'll grant me that you can't make Camilla a wife until she's a widow, and that gates open easier when the warden's gone."

245

"True enough, Your Grace."

"No marks on the body, of course. No *proofs*, understand?"

"Quite, my lord."

Andrea exchanged a bland smile with the Duke — and consigned him to the devil.

CHAPTER XXXIX

LIKE a good steel blade, it was part of a bravo's functions to serve as a weapon not only of offense but of defense, to parry as well as to thrust, and to guard the life of his master when not employed against the life of his master's enemy. In the situation that faced Andrea at this point, he considered it wise to take counsel with Mario Belli, and to supply him with as many facts as might be needed for intelligent co-operation.

It was all very well for Duke Valentino to guarantee Angela Borgia's acceptance of the latest change of plan. Compelled by his fiat and subject to family policy, she would have to accept. But on the other hand, knowing her as he did, Andrea had grounds for uneasiness. There was that unlucky appearance of Camilla's at Castel Gandolfo, for example, and the quick flare-up of Angela's jealousy. If, by any chance, she suspected that Orsini favored this about-face from the marriage with her, let alone that he had connived at it, the effects would be startling. In any case, he could not consider his relations with her at an end because of a bare word from the Duke. There would have to be a meeting, protestations, fervent vows, convincing woe. It would take the best acting he could furnish. But, meanwhile, he wanted to make the most of the Varani's presence in Rome, both for personal reasons and to give an appearance of zeal in Borgia's interests.

All this promised a tangle that demanded special alertness. Therefore, it was desirable that Belli be warned and consulted.

Closeted next morning with his ensign in one of the rooms assigned him at the house of Monsignor Sandeo, he discussed the problem with unusual frankness, barring, of course, any hint of his secret desertion of

246

Borgia. While Andrea talked, Belli squinted at the ceiling or nipped thoughtfully at the side of his thumb. Now and then a glint of his eyes showed appreciation of some particular factor in the case.

"A nice little salad," he remarked, when Andrea leaned back with a final shrug and wave of the hands. "Trust women to complicate life! It's one of the few bounties I have to be thankful for that I've never been the object of female pursuit. *Le bon dieu m'en garde!* I sorrow for Your Magnificence."

"Keep your sorrow," returned Orsini, "I want your opinion."

"Of my lady Angela?" Belli showed his teeth. "You know her better than I; but, from all accounts, she's a woman of determination and great spirit. My colleague, Furia, whom I've been cultivating at Your Lordship's command, has apparently done some odd jobs for her in the past. He's a discreet man and, of course, would not own to as much. I read merely between the lines. However, he holds her in high admiration."

"Hm-m," pondered Andrea. "*There's* a testimonial! This same Furia's a useful connection. He's attached to her household?"

"Virtually. He serves her father, the lord Joffré de Borgia-Lanzol. Is in on the servants' gossip."

"You'll not omit to drop him a word about my grief at the loss of this marriage, I hope."

Belli looked injured. "Don't teach an old monkey to make a face," he muttered. "I'll do what I can in that direction and keep my ears open. But, when all's said, it's Your Lordship's management that will count for most. And the sooner we're out of Rome the better, in my opinion. The climate's sickly. When do we leave?"

"Not before my lord and lady Varano. They'll spend two weeks visiting the shrines."

"So be it," grunted Belli. "I should say a good deal depends on whether Madonna Angela invites Your Lordship to a rendezvous. If she does, no doubt you'll dandle her into good humor. The danger is if she does not. In that case, *garde à vous!* You'll eat nothing that I don't prepare under your own eyes. You'll go nowhere without me at your shoulder. And, signore, above all, don't be seen too much with the lady Camilla."

Orsini shook his head. "There's the hitch. I have to frequent her for every reason — as I explained."

"*De profundis,*" Belli murmured. "I'm an ignorant man, but I know that much Latin."

247

The day passed without word from Angela. Orsini could not be sure when or how Cesare Borgia would inform her of the latest decision, and until then his hands were tied; for it was essential that she should hear it first from the Duke. Until she had heard, he could neither call nor write. But in view of the late fiasco of their plans at the villa, it was significant that she made no move to communicate with him.

On the third day, being in attendance on Borgia at the Palace of San Clemente, he found occasion for a word in private, before the Duke left for his incessant business at the Vatican.

"But of course," returned Cesare. "She was duly instructed, and at once. She chafed a bit, as might be expected; but that's of no moment. The ladies of our House know their duty. Give it no thought. . . . How go the approaches to Città del Monte?"

That same noon, Orsini waited on Lucrezia Borgia in the hope of an interview with Angela, who acted as her cousin's chief lady of honor. But the call was in vain. It appeared that Angela suffered from a rheum she had taken on the outing to Castel Gandolfo and was confined to her apartment.

"Your Highness will assure her of my sorrow," entreated Andrea upon taking leave — "my sorrow about everything." He contrived to look the picture of misery. Since others were present, he could say nothing more.

Lucrezia did not miss the point. "I shall tell her, Messere. At the moment, she considers herself ill-used by fortune. But a rheum doesn't last forever. She'll be enchanted to know of your concern." The Princess's limpid blue eyes narrowed. "Perhaps you might wish to express it in a letter?"

Acting on this hint, Andrea wrote a fervent epistle that night. It abounded in despair, exclaimed at the cruelty of fate, and begged an interview. But although he had it carried to the Palace of Santa Maria in Portico by a sure hand, no answer was returned. And the days passed. Mario Belli supervised his patron's diet and dogged his footsteps.

Meanwhile, in heaven, the Recording Angel had the gratification of making several entries to the credit of Orsini and Belli. In other words, they went to church with impressive regularity, appearing now at St. Peter's, now at St. Paul's, or again at St. John Lateran or at Santa Maria Maggiore. Varano and Camilla, whom they were constantly encountering, expressed warm approval of their devotion, though Varano wore a broad grin and a humorous spark showed in Camilla's eyes.

"There's hope for the world, Messer Andrea," Varano would say, "when a *politico* like you and a blade like Ser Mario take to religion so heartily. It should be a reproof to scoffers. The wolf and the leopard, eh?" — he glanced at Camilla — "and a little child to lead them."

When, on Saturday, the relics of the glorious apostles, Saints Peter and Paul, were shown to the kneeling multitude in St. John Lateran; and when, on Sunday, Saint Veronica's handkerchief was exhibited at St. Peter's, Camilla remained aware of Orsini's dark-clad figure, gracefully bowed and flanked by Belli's sinister face, behind her. On Sunday, too, they received together the Papal benediction. Together, on Monday, they admired the bright new ceiling, donated by His Holiness, which had just been completed at Santa Maria Maggiore; and, drifting slowly with the crowd down one of the long naves of the basilica, they kneeled in reverence before the high altar and confession that contained fragments of Our Lord's cradle. Or, on Tuesday, in that most beautiful of churches, St. Paul Without the Walls, they worshiped, not far from each other, beside the tomb of the Apostle.

"It's a very miracle," teased Varano, "that, in such great throngs, we should so constantly be meeting. Except for the devotion evident on the faces of you gentlemen, I should be inclined to doubt the coincidence. I suppose there couldn't be any other reason for it except chance and your zeal toward the holy relics?"

Andrea lent himself to the other's chaffing. "Devotion and zeal are the only words for it, my lord. I have never felt more edified. As to the miracle you speak of, I consider it rather an instance of the involuntary attraction exerted by Your Signories. Or perhaps the stars have decreed that our paths lie together. A happy dispensation."

In the end, giving up pretense, they visited the shrines together: Varano and Camilla, not too solemn but wholly sincere in their religious purpose; Andrea intent on Camilla; and Belli at all times inscrutable but alert. Together with the Varani's attendants, they made a compact little cohort amid the swarm of Jubilee pilgrims. The number of these had a good deal declined from the two hundred thousand whom the Pope had blessed last Easter in St. Peter's Square; but there were still plenty to fill the churches and the narrow streets between. Belli's cool eye probed and appraised those who pressed closest to Andrea. It was a matter of pride with him that no one of his employers had ever been successfully attacked while under his guard. But though now and then a jostler shrank away from his stare, and though he occasionally noted

249

a fellow bravo in the crowd, nothing occurred to focus his suspicions during these days.

"Which doesn't mean, of course, that Your Lordship isn't being watched," he reminded Orsini. "If the lady in question is enough concerned, she'll know of every glance between you and Madama Camilla. As a tribute to Your Magnificence, we'll assume that she does."

But Angela's spies, if any there were, had little to report beyond the fact of Orsini's faithful attendance on the signori of Città del Monte.

"No, Messere," Camilla would say, when Andrea, walking by the side of her mule, launched out on a compliment, "no, Messere. Hold your tongue. I'm not in Rome to hear pretty speeches but to scrub my soul. Come with us, if you please, but leave the courtier behind. By God, it won't hurt you for a while to think less about this world." She turned to her husband. "Will it, my lord?"

The bluff old man, fingering his rosary, paused to smile. "There's a true sermon for you, Captain. Let your wits rest for this time and try to be a child again in prayer and in faith. It may profit you."

And, as a matter of fact, it did profit him. The artist in Andrea did justice to virtues which, as a practical man, it would have been foolish to copy. He had leisure for once to study Camilla and her husband from a detached point of view. With something like nostalgia, during the frequent masses and ceremonies at the shrines, or on the way between them, he turned his thought out to pasture in once-familiar fields.

If he should ever paint a Saint Longinus, for example, he must not forget Varano's wide mouth and leathern lips, which could hook down into a line as forbidding as the eye slit of a vizor or could relax in a smile innocent as a baby's; and he must not forget the humorously shrewd, straightforward eyes. The centurions of the Lord's host at Armageddon would look like that. Or, again, Varano would do for a model of the Good Samaritan, as Andrea watched him and Camilla visiting the sick at the hospital of Santo Spirito, where they stopped almost daily on their way from St. Peter's. "For how can you pray before the shrines," Varano insisted, "when you keep remembering the poor, naked lazars of this world and that you haven't lifted a finger to help them? Stick me such religion up your breech!" He was especially fond of old, derelict soldiers at the hospital; and Andrea, in his mental sketchbook, noted the light on their faces when Varano stopped beside them to chat a moment. What he said helped more than what he gave, though he always came away with a limp purse.

As for Camilla, Orsini could never quite decide what he would make of her on canvas. She did not remind him of any particular saint or of a saint at all. If he took her as model of the Blessed Lucy or Cecilia, he would have to dim out the lurking mischief in her eyes, lengthen her nose, develop her into more of a woman and less of a boy in skirts; and so nothing of her would be left. Her face would do better for one of the attendants of the Three Kings; clad in a gold-leaf doublet and crimson hose, holding a couple of hunting dogs on the leash. Or for Artemis. His fancy veered to Parnassus. He dreamed of scenes in the manner of Botticelli or of this new master, nicknamed Giorgione: of nymphs and Graces and piping fauns. He recalled the smiling god at Castel Gandolfo.

But once a startling idea presented itself. It was when a dirty little urchin of four or five got caught in the crush outside one of the churches, and Camilla, with whip and tongue, cleared space enough to fish the half-naked child out from surrounding legs and, holding him in her arms with a hand under his plump behind, quieted his panic. Then, getting out of him that he had strayed from a neighboring street to see the church procession, she had him set before her on her mule and so, with her escort, took him home. By Bacchus! Camilla at the moment suggested a new conception of Our Lady herself, a gay, youthful Madonna, as yet unpierced by the Seven Wounds. The thought became more compelling in Orsini's mind when Camilla returned the child to its distracted mother, a blowsy, disheveled woman, half in ecstasy at recovering her son, half abashed by the great signora looking down so friendly and compassionate from her mule. But it was not only a new artistic conception of Our Lady. To Andrea, it seemed illustrative of the Divine Mother's inclusiveness, that identified her with any type of womanly unselfishness — Artemis-Camilla's as well as another's.

On the way home that evening, Belli remarked, "A most enchanting signora!"

"*Per Dio*, yes!"

"I congratulate Your Magnificence."

"Not yet," smiled Andrea. And when the other kept silent he added, "Some day perhaps."

Darkness had fallen as they crossed the Tiber and followed the Borgo to Sandeo's house. Near the main door of it, they suddenly became aware of a masked woman accompanied by a lantern bearer.

"Messer Andrea Orsini?" she queried; and at once Andrea recognized the voice of Angela Borgia's waiting woman, Tonia.

"At your service, *mia bella*," he answered.

251

"A letter to Your Lordship," she said in a low voice. "Perhaps you'll read it by the light of this lantern and give me the answer. I see that you know who I am."

The brief note was unsigned, but it needed no signature. It was the curiously delayed summons which Andrea had been awaiting from Angela. If he would present himself that evening at a door he knew of, a certain lady would be glad of his attendance.

To receive the letter was a relief — it ended the uncertainty of the last few days — but after his recent preoccupation with the Varani, it found him less inclined than ever to the make-believe which the interview with Angela entailed. The circumstances, too — the damp cold of the autumn night, the wheeling shadows, the faceless waiting woman — did not conspire to lift his spirits. But there was only one answer he could give.

"Assure Madonna that her letter restores me to life." He kissed the paper. "Assure her of my attendance and perfect obedience."

CHAPTER XL

ACCOMPANIED by Mario Belli and several armed servants of Monsignor Sandeo, with a couple of linkboys in front, Andrea made his way through pitch-black streets toward the Palace of Santa Maria in Portico close to the Vatican. A cold mist, rising from the Tiber, struck like a damp cloth against the face and twisted itself into ghostly forms within the narrow zone of light cast by the torches. The party moved with caution, regardful of arcades along the house fronts or of narrow street openings; for, in Andrea's opinion, the receipt of Angela Borgia's letter gave no reason for too sanguine assumptions.

"If she had written me the first or second day after Castel Gandolfo," he remarked to Belli, "I should say nothing. But six days! And not a word in reply to my letter! It smells bad."

"She may have been ill," grinned Belli, "as Madama Lucrezia said."

"Do you believe that?"

"No. I admit it's rather more likely that a band of picked men, headed by my gossip Furia, are even now awaiting Your Worship somewhere en route to the lady's salon. At any rate, I'll stand to your shoulder to the very threshold; and I wish I had a post inside."

"Do you care that much?" said Orsini, with a sudden pulse of affection for his strange follower.

But Belli was not to be drawn. "I have my pride. I'll not be put under by Simone Furia."

However, precautions that evening proved unnecessary. For reasons of delicacy, the main party halted at some distance from the side door of the palace; and only Belli attended Andrea the rest of the way.

"Wait here," the latter directed. "It's good to play safe. But God knows how long it will take, Mario."

He could sense Belli's smirk through the darkness. "I quite understand. It's not the first time I've waited at a door while others cosseted upstairs with Venus. Take your time, my lord."

He chuckled at Andrea's glum oath and drew to one side, while his patron, using last summer's signal, rapped three times and again three times. The door opened, revealing a dim vestibule lighted only by a candle, which Angela's woman, Tonia, was protecting from the draft by her cupped hand.

"*Siate il benvenuto, signore,*" she murmured. "It's like old days, *nevvero?*" And, turning, she led down a familiar corridor to a sidestairs spiraling upward in the wall.

Every feature of the entrance, the thick smell of damp stone, the woman's lithe figure tripping in front of him, reminded Andrea of last June. Then, he had followed her in a fever of impatience. Now his task was to ape his former self, blow up the spark to a semblance of flame. The spirals of the stairway seemed steeper and harder to climb.

Here was the well-known door. He paused a moment, like an actor about to go on stage, setting his face, tuning himself to the right pitch.

"There we are, my lord." Tonia opened for him and then, remaining outside, closed the door when he entered.

Everything was as he remembered it: the tapestried arras covering the walls of the big room, the ineffectual flickering of pendent lamps, the black window recesses. He recalled, too, the stuffy odor of tapestry, mingled with perfume and the lingering smell of incense pastils. Nothing had changed except that, because of the cold, a lighted brazier stood near the cushioned *cassapanca* where Angela was seated, and that, instead of silk, she wore a dress of heavy, many-colored brocade.

253

And, just as in the past, she rose from the settle and moved toward him, with her hand outstretched to be kissed.

So familiar it was that he found it easier than he had expected to play the required role and, having kissed her hand, to gather her into his arms. Holding her close to him, he could also inform himself that she wore no stays, and this gave an indication of her attitude toward the evening.

"Ever most beautiful!" he complimented, surveying the gorgeous dress patterned in a broad leaf design of emerald, gold, and crimson. "With no reflection upon Your Ladyship's other gowns, this one, I vow, becomes you supremely. And of all the gracious ways in which Your Signory arranges her hair, I find none so perfect as this. *Mia cara*, you should never conceal the lines of your neck and the loveliest ear in the world."

She wore her hair drawn up under a small, jeweled toque on the back of her head, a device that emphasized the superb column of her throat and the curve of back and shoulders. It required no effort on his part to flatter her. The rich colors of her gown, the sparkle of her headdress against the spun gold of her hair, the mysterious darkness of her eyes, were only contributing elements to the impression she made of queenliness and youth. It crossed Andrea's mind that no higher tribute could be paid to Lucrezia Borgia's attractiveness than that she dared comparison with such a lady of honor.

Angela made a slight curtsy. "You know how I value the compliments of an artist, Messere." She was one of the few who were in the secret of that portrait of Lucrezia which Orsini had taken with him to Ferrara. He had also done another in pastels of Angela herself. In her eyes his skill was merely an entertaining accomplishment that savored nothing of the artisan. "When it comes to ladies' profiles," she added meaningly, "you speak as an expert, and I thank you."

Perhaps there was the faintest touch of dryness in her voice, a hint of the tone he had noticed at the Villa Savelli. But he could not tell: she, too, seemed to be making a conventional effort. And almost at once, having reseated herself on the cushions of the settle, she came to the point.

"And so, *mio caro*, it was nothing but a dream." Except for a sudden external tension along the throat, her manner was quiet enough. "I shall never let myself dream again."

He sank down on a hassock beside the bench and, taking her hand, held it between both of his. It had the touch of fever; he could almost sense the hot vibrations of her pulses. And at this contact with the reality of her passion, he felt ashamed of his own pretense, a surge of pity that was almost the equivalent of renewed passion in himself.

"Dream," she went on, "that a woman of our House could make her own life, marry at her pleasure, take a husband she loved. What nonsense! Poor, simpering puppets of women! Believe me, Cousin Cesare put an end to such fancies. I beg his pardon for being a goose. No more dreams!"

Since he could find nothing adequate to say, Andrea kept silent.

"So much for me!" she shrugged. "Who was I, says the Duke, to set myself above Madonna Lucrezia? Hasn't she done as she was bid all her life? And shall I forget my duty to God and family? I preached that to Lucrezia once when she was moping at Nepi. It's the way the world's made. . . . But you" — she snatched her hand away and her voice quickened " — I didn't gather from my lord Cesare that *you* rebelled, or spoke up for yourself, or appealed to His Holiness, who promised you my hand not two weeks since. 'No,' says he, 'Messer Andrea himself agrees that policy is best served by this other marriage, though he regrets the fact.' *Regrets!*" Angela repeated. "By God, he actually *regrets!*"

She paused in a hot silence. It was an attack that Andrea had feared. He brought his hand down on the hilt of his poniard. "*Regrets?* Am I to blame for the words of the Duke? If he gave Your Ladyship to think that my *regrets* were less than despair, desolation, anguish, he did me great wrong. I begged him to picture my grief to you. That he made light of it is the last stroke. *Iddio, aiutami!* But did my letter mean nothing? Must you heed the Duke's words rather than mine?"

He let his head sink and sat staring at the floor. She said nothing, but somehow he felt that he was making progress.

After a pause, he went on in a bleak voice. "You speak of women as puppets. But what of men? Do we marry whom we choose, do what we please — we, who are not great Princes, but only poor gentlemen faithful to our lords? Are we not governed by their policy? This other marriage you speak of agrees with the Duke's purposes. I gather that he would have opposed our marriage in any case. Do you really believe that I could defy my lord Cesare's command and appeal against it to the Pope? Surely not."

These were telling arguments. Her hand strayed back to his. "My poor Andrea!" she murmured.

He pressed his advantage. "Poor, indeed! There speaks *la mia dolcissima donna!*" He caught her fingers to his lips. "But cruel! So cruel! To

255

let me languish six days without a word! To make no answer to my letter!"

"Do you know why?" she interrupted.

"I burn to know."

"Listen, Messere." She leaned forward closer to him, one hand on his hair, toying with it. "I can tell time as well as another. I know when a thing's impossible and I can accept the fact. I don't say quietly. To the devil with Cousin Cesare, for that matter! But I accept it. There's no use kicking against the wind. Only I happen to love you." Her voice dropped suddenly and lingered on the words. "I love you more than anyone else. You are like wine in my blood. Your kisses are fire to me. Your thoughts carry me with them, dull as I am. Well, in short, I love you." She broke off for a moment, then added: "No reason to say how much or why. But too much to let another woman into my place. I say *my* place. Marry whom you have to — this Baglione chit, if that's the move — and I'll be married to whom they please. So much I accept. But not to be discarded by you in favor of someone else — not that. You languished these six days, as you put it, at the heels of Camilla Baglione."

Andrea gave a gesture of impatience. "The lord Cesare could have told you why I waited upon her."

"I could guess. I know how things are managed." Angela ruffled his hair. "But you can wait upon a lady in different ways. I had to find out your way of doing it with her."

Orsini glanced up at Angela with a suspense that he was careful to disguise. "Well?" he prompted.

She laughed "Well, I'm informed you had a dull time of it, my poor Andrea. Relics, hospitals, masses, and telling of beads in between. By God, I felt so sorry for you after three days that I almost relented. Still, with a fox like you, one can't be too sure. My people who watched you were well-nigh exhausted. I venture tonight's the first time you've relaxed in a week."

He laughed, too, and dropped his head on her lap. This was a relief which he had not deserved.

"Egad," he said truthfully, "Your Ladyship's right."

Leaning over, she kissed him and, straightening up, clapped her hands for Tonia. "We'll have wine, and then to bed. I hope you're in fettle, sir. I demand consolation for Castel Gandolfo. . . . By the way, have you seen the steps of the last pavane from France?"

While Tonia dressed a small table with marchpane, *pinocchiata*, and other confects, flanked by pitchers of malmsey and muscatel, Angela showed a figure or two of the latest court dance. She had the lightness and undulant grace of a cat, half expressing, half concealing, the superb body under the brocade. The steps were slow and stately; but her coquetry, as she danced, set him on fire. Watching and at last joining her in a measure, he had no trouble shutting his mind to everything but the present.

"Point your feet more," she instructed. "Bow from the hips . . . the right leg straighter. There, you have it. Perfect! I'd rather have you dance opposite me than any cavalier I know. You catch the spirit. I wish we had musicians here. Remember our dance at the Vatican last June . . ."

They tripped the length of the room together and stopped at the table. Tonia, like a discreet shadow, withdrew.

Sitting side by side on the cushioned bench along the table, they nibbled at the confects, drank and gossiped. Angela knew all the scandals. Her jokes were salty, and he had brought others as good from Ferrara. With every cup of wine, the talk grew spicier. They made a handsome contrast: the black and gold of his suit, the flaming colors of her gown; his dark, rugged features and her blondness; her sparkling headdress, the medal of Europa and the Bull in his cap.

"*You*, an artist," she chided at one point, "and no eye for a beautiful thing! You haven't once admired my new cup that Master Antonio da San Marino just finished for me. Here, look."

"No eye for a beautiful thing, indeed!" he returned, with a full stare at her. "When the moon's out, who sees the stars?" But, taking the gilded silver cup, he turned it about, studying the fine workmanship of the embossed figures.

They were excellently done in the classic manner: Silenus, a group of Maenads, Dionysus in his car about to carry off Ariadne; delightful composition and movement.

"*Maraviglioso!*" he approved. "A gem of a thing!"

"Yes. . . . See if you can find me on it."

Orsini again turned the cup and scrutinized the various figures. "Ha, *per Dio!*" He stopped at Ariadne. Only the back of the goddess and a quarter-face showed in the embossed relief, but the nude figure was unmistakable. "Happy Master Antonio! Is it possible that Your Ladyship modeled for him?"

"Not quite." Angela pretended to blush. "I gave him the sketch you made of me once as Leda. Remember? It furnished him with the neces-

257

sary lines, and he didn't need to know whose they were. . . . Don't stare so, Andrea. Give me back the cup."

She snatched it away from him with a clever imitation of embarrassment, contradicted by the flicker of a smile.

"Madonna, let me have it as a souvenir of tonight."

"Well, perhaps," she hesitated — "if you deserve it. We'll see." She sat twisting the cup a moment and smiling. "At least, I'll say I'm better turned than this slim jade." She pecked at the figure of one of the Maenads with her forefinger; the nail scratched against the metal. "We'll call her Camilla Baglione. See, there."

"Ah?" But what Andrea did not see was the covert glance she gave him as he followed the pointing of her finger and that she noted the stiffening of his lips. He took the trouble to add carelessly, "After this week at the shrines, you know I'd hardly think of her as a Maenad."

"*Caro mio*," laughed Angela, "don't let her gull you. I protest the simplicity of you men is beyond expression. A woman can look through a little *santarella* like that as if she were clear glass. Why, poor gentleman, when you marry her she'll plant horns on your head as fast as she has on her grandsire husband's. And that's a known scandal."

Andrea's smile was gone. "I hadn't heard of it," he said.

Angela leaned forward. "What! You haven't heard — Oh, my poor love! Well, it shows how little you fear the pox. I confess I knew only that this signora existed until the other day. But after seeing her at Castel Gandolfo, I made inquiries, and, Andrea *mio soavissimo*, what a report!"

The evening had changed suddenly. The zest was gone; the colors were crass. Angela, viewed through altered eyes, seemed all at once to Orsini merely vulgar. He had the feeling as if some loved thing of beauty, which he had reverenced as apart from his shabby round of experience, were being set up in the common pillory. Perhaps he had had a cup too much; but at all events this time his shrewdness failed him. He did not note the lurking gleam in Angela's eyes nor smell the trap.

"Report?" he echoed.

"Oh, aye, shocking. You know I'm not too squeamish; but, 'sbody, I vow it gagged me. After all, there are limits."

"No limits to scandal."

"Scandal, nothing. This came from a sure source, one who knew her in Perugia and then at Città del Monte." Angela was drawing a random shaft, but it struck home. Orsini thought of the Borgian secret agent at

258

Città del Monte, Captain Galeazzo Branca. Probably a man like that would shape reports to fit the wishes of his employers. . . . "Besides," continued Angela, "you'll admit that the Baglione blood is as rotten as any in Italy."

"No, I'll not admit it. They're fierce lords, but of great parts and magnificence."

"Pooh! Rascals of the first rank. But, in any case, this Camilla — listen — "

"No!"

"Why not?"

"By the Mass," seethed Andrea, "you know why not. Shall I listen to slander of a woman whom it is planned I shall marry?"

Angela looked amused. "Don't be such a delicate fool. It's unlike you, *caro*. If you must marry from policy, there's no profit in marrying blindfold. I love you too much to permit it. Forewarned is forearmed when you couple with certain women. Nay, listen — "

He could not help himself for a moment but sat inarticulate, while Angela, with a titter now and then, spread out her wares. It was a coarse age, and what she said kept within the generous limits of convention. He had laughed over similar gossip earlier; but applied to Camilla it seemed to him irredeemable blasphemy. While his hostess dropped one gross word after another from her smiling lips, he thought of Camilla during the past week, recalled glimpses of her at Città del Monte, at Ferrara: the youth and freshness of her, like a breath from the hills.

"So," rippled Angela, "I grieve for you, my poor Messere. If you must marry the bitch — "

"By God, madam — " he could hardly get the words out — "hold your tongue." Rage strangled him. "*Puttana sfacciata!*" he choked.

And at once her smiling mask dropped. Her eyes narrowed to slits. Her lips writhed and laid bare the teeth. She jeered at him. "So-ho, I got the truth out of you at last! Double-tongued ape! Mouthing your sorrow because you must marry *her! Gaglioffone!* Sneaking to the Duke, I warrant, with a fine little trick for casting me off!" — her hand vibrated against her breast — "me, Angela Borgia — me, I say — for a thin-flanked draggle-tail from the provinces. . . . And you love her! By God, you love her! Will you deny it?"

"I'd deny salvation first." He had thrown common sense to the wind. The woman facing him on the bench sickened him. Reckless of anything else, he must somehow shake off the degradation he felt to have

259

listened to her. "Love? Yes, if I dare speak of love for so exalted a lady. There's truth for you . . ."

He was conscious only of a movement too rapid to follow. Angela had snatched the poniard from his belt. He saw the flash of it, saw her contorted features, felt the searing pain as she plunged the knife under his arm. She screamed something. He half struggled to his feet. The room wheeled into a blur. Still cumbered by the bench, he staggered, clutched vainly at the table. Then the world went blank as he dropped to the floor.

CHAPTER XLI

For a long moment, Angela stood breathing hard, her face convulsed, staring down at Orsini's motionless form. His backward movement had freed the knife, which she still held with so rigid a grasp that the knuckles stood out. Then suddenly her expression changed. Her body went limp; the blood drained from her face. Reaching out an arm to the table for support, she became aware of the dagger and the running stains along it, gave a retch of nausea, opened her fingers with an effort and let the blade fall clattering among the confects.

"*Santa Maria!*" she whispered. "*Santa Maria!*"

A tightening of the throat, half sob, half spasm, gripped her. Then slowly, fearfully, her eyes wide, she crept forward and bent down over the prostrate body.

"No, Andrea. Listen. Listen, I tell you. I didn't mean — It isn't you I hate. It's she. *Caro!* Will you listen . . ."

She caught his shoulders between her hands, tried to lift them; the dull weight resisted her. But the touch of him released a paroxysm. "Andrea . . . Andrea . . . Andrea . . ." Her voice grew fainter. "Dead."

Her hand, which had rested for a moment on his right side, was wet. She stared at it. And then, as if aware for the first time of what had happened, her shock becoming panic, she screamed. The sound, shrilling up in the silence, frightened her of itself, and again she screamed.

"Tonia! Tonia!"

260

The woman found her leaning against the table, corpse-pale, eyes haunted, her headdress awry, a coil of hair hanging to her shoulder. At the moment, Angela's personal fear replaced any other concern. She gave the attendant no time even to exclaim or raise her hands.

"A quarrel," she whispered. "He insulted me. . . . He must be got out of here on the instant. The body can be left in the Piazza. That way nothing can be proved. It would cost my life, you understand, if news of this reaches the Duke. Besides, the scandal! Tonia, quick! Are there any of the lackeys we can trust?"

Catching her mistress's urgency, the woman stifled her own terror. "Old Giovanni, Antonello. They would let themselves be torn apart —"

"Fetch them."

"But Madonna, are you sure?"

"About what?"

Tonia's black eyes reconnoitered the body. "That he's dead."

"Hm-m," muttered Angela. It struck her suddenly that she was not sure; but she shrank from finding out. "You look."

The other, a peasant by birth, had no special qualms about dead men. In a straightforward fashion, she squatted down at Andrea's side, unlaced his doublet, ripped open his shirt, and laid her ear against his heart.

"Still alive," she reported after a moment, "though not for long, I wager."

"Alive!" Angela forgot her fears in temporary relief. "God grant — " But the tone faded out. "Alive," she repeated. "Well!"

She stared thoughtfully across the room. Tonia, getting up, awaited the decision. It was not hard to guess what was passing through her mistress's mind.

"If he lived, what then?" said Angela finally. "I vow I didn't mean — But this finishes it. He would never love me. I shall have a thousand masses said for him. Perhaps you'd better drop a hint to Giovanni. What do you think?"

"Was the wound deep?" asked Tonia.

"To the hilt."

"Then Your Signory needn't bother. He's close to the end. The night cold will finish him. But if he should live, Your Ladyship's safe enough. He'd keep quiet for the sake of his pride as well as his life."

"That's true," Angela nodded, "though a bad enemy."

The woman shrugged. "As Madonna pleases. Giovanni will handle him if you wish."

261

There was a long pause. Suddenly Angela burst out: "No! I'll not take that on my conscience. If you loved me, you'd see to it yourself without my knowledge. But it's the girl I hate. . . . The main thing is to get him away from here, and at once. Fetch the two lackeys. Bid them leave him in the Piazza San Pietro as I said. And, Tonia — " the woman would never forget Angela's face at that moment — "remember that if a word of this ever crosses your lips or theirs, it would be wiser to hang yourselves at once. Much wiser, Tonia! . . . One more thing. Have Simone Furia attend me tomorrow. There's business for him" — she clenched her hands — "with a pretty little lady. *Orsù*, hasten." But when the woman had hurried out, she stood forlornly looking down at Andrea's limp body. Then, breaking into tears, she crossed herself and left the room.

A quarter of an hour later, Mario Belli, half dozing in the shelter of a doorway across the alleylike street from the palace, was roused by the click of a latch opposite him and caught the flicker of a candle. In spite of the misty rain, he could make out, for an instant, two ghostly figures with a heavy burden between them. Then the candle vanished inside; the door closed; and he could see nothing; but he could hear the shuffle of footsteps heading for the near-by Piazza. This wanted looking into, for the burden could easily have been a man. He would soon find out; and, if the matter did not concern him, he would return to his doorway.

Helped by the mist, and an adept besides in the fine art of shadowing, Belli was soon at the heels of the two men, though he could see absolutely nothing in the pitch-blackness of the alley. However, their first words told him all he needed to know.

"A well-set-up bastard," one of them growled. "Glad we don't have to lug him to the river. Who is he?"

"Don't know," panted the other. "Some gallant of Madonna's. The less we know, the better. We'll hear tomorrow after he's been found. . . . Lower away, will you? The cursed plank cuts my hand."

They were struggling with an improvised litter, awkward to manage. Belli flattened himself against a wall while they caught their breath.

"'Sfoot! I'm not curious," went on the last voice. "This is one of the things it's healthier to forget, if you want to live. Remember what happened to Gianbattista the page who blabbed, though what he said was only a trifle? Madonna's a lady of character."

The other voice put in: "Mistress Tonia's another. What was that about settling this fellow when we get him to the Piazza?"

"Why, that a blow or two more would be worth a ducat to us and wouldn't be displeasing to Somebody."

Belli, who had assumed the worst, put two and two together. There was a faint chance, then. His hand stole to his knife and to his sword hilt, making sure that both weapons were loose.

"But I'm not in this alone, gossip," the voice continued. "You'll prick him if I do."

"Trust me for that."

"*Avanti*, then."

They raised the litter and shuffled on carefully over the slippery pavement. Soon a dim light somewhere in the distance and a sense of space showed that they had reached the Piazza.

"Not at this street opening," said one of the men. "He's not to be traced to the Palace, look you. We'll shift him to the left."

With Belli at their heels, they bore off in the direction of the main entrance to the Vatican.

"Now! Dump him off. Have you your knife ready?"

"*Who goes?*" roared Belli out of the darkness with all the authority of a watchman — and, considering the nearness to the Vatican, he might well have been a guard on patrol. "Stand and account for yourselves!"

The crash of the litter on the pavement and the racing of footsteps answered him. He had nothing more to fear from the two servants.

In a moment, he was bending over Andrea. "Your Magnificence! My lord!" His hand found Orsini's wrist, but he could detect no pulse beat. Then unexpectedly came a sigh and a faint groan. "*Pasque dieu!*" exclaimed Belli.

To render any aid in the blind night was impossible. Turning away, Belli stumbled toward the Vatican entrance a hundred paces distant and at length caught the glimmer of a light from the guardroom.

"Captain Orsini," he replied to the challenge of the Swiss sentry, "Duke Valentino's friend . . . out there . . . dying! He was set upon . . ."

The portal erupted with torches. Andrea was carried inside. During the next ten minutes, Belli spun a fine tale which here and there skirted the truth. It dealt with a jealous husband and an affair of gallantry that Swiss gentlemen would naturally refrain from asking too closely about. He begged now for a litter to convey His Magnificence to the house of Monsignor Sandeo. As the Swiss *cavalieri* would allow, it would cause less scandal if he died there.

"Damn all husbands!" exclaimed the Bernese ensign devoutly. "And God grant His Lordship an easy passing!"

But Belli's efforts were not over when he had finally got Andrea to bed in the Monsignor's house. He had to drive off the servants, who clustered about the doorway, and prevail on Sandeo himself to let him deal with the patient.

"He's in more need of the sacrament, my friend," said the priest, who was still in his nightcap.

"All in good time, Your Reverence. I'll but have a look at the wound, if you please."

"Are you a leech?"

"Aye, sir, of the first water. By Your Reverence's leave — "

He edged Sandeo from the room, bolted the door, and, having stripped Orsini to the waist, washed off his side with water from the ewer.

"A sucking wound," he muttered grimly, listening to the hiss of air mingled with blood that issued from the opening under Orsini's right armpit. "Not much to hope for. Touched in the lung, I'll warrant."

Tearing Andrea's shirt into long strips, he made a sort of tampon, pressed it hard against the wound, and bound it firmly in place with a bandage around the chest. Orsini, having recovered from the first shock of the blow, was by now half conscious and breathing fast. Belli shook his head as he felt the racing of the heart under his finger tips. "If fever sets in," he reflected, "good night to him."

The requirements of his profession had trained Belli to a practical knowledge of wounds that made him actually superior to the usual physician of that time. He had acquired, too, a distrust for the average leech that was based on observation. How many stout fellows with nothing more than trifling wounds he had seen fade out after the doctors had probed, plastered, and physicked them! On the other hand, it had struck him that others in a worse case, who had been forced to get along without medical aid, recovered. Why this was, he had no idea, when all the weight of authority and learning was on the side of the professionals; but, being a rationalist by nature, he adhered stubbornly to his own rough-and-ready practices.

When he had finished undressing Andrea and had got him between the sheets, he sat down by the bed, chin on fist, and waited. He must not wait too long; it would not do to let his patron die without extreme unction. As he sat there, with his thin, twitching smile and the narrow glinting of his eyes, he made the very picture of Satan ready to pounce on a newly released soul.

And at this point, Andrea's eyes struggled open, staring wildly at Belli.

"Where am I?" he gasped, for the collapse of his right lung and the attendant shift of the heart made breathing a burden.

Interpreting the confusion in his eyes and urging him not to speak, Belli explained what had happened. He noted that the bewilderment passed and that the patient gave no sign of delirium.

"So?" murmured Orsini at last. His expression supplemented the word.

Belli stood up. "So, Your Magnificence, we'll take no chances. I'm fetching a priest. After that" — he shrugged — "*on verra*."

Sandeo administered the last rites. Belli renewed his watching that grew more intent as the night dwindled. He had seen many a poor soul pass at the turn of the tide. But the critical hours went by; the room turned gray. "*Pardi*," thought the watcher admiringly, "he's run death a stiff course tonight. Who knows but he'll shake him off for this time?"

Getting up to replenish the coals in the brazier, Belli was startled by a faint voice and returned to the bedside.

"My lord?"

"You'll recall the Mona Costanza Zoppo I visited that night outside of Crespino?"

"Aye." Belli kept his voice casual. "The mother of your friend."

"The same. . . . Mario, I'd take it kindly of you if you could manage to let her know that — " The voice stumbled. "Say that the great lord who called on her — that I, in short . . ." Andrea could get no further.

"Remembered her, eh?" the other prompted.

"More than that. . . . Said she was right. She'll understand."

Orsini closed his eyes, but a moment later he half raised himself. "And Mario! By God, I'd forgotten! Mario!"

"At hand, sir. Will you be quiet! Do you want to kill yourself?"

"No matter! Look you — " Andrea forced the words out — "forget me. I count on you to guard Madonna Milla. It goes upon her life for the hatred the woman bears her. You understand? *Gran Dio!* And I'm helpless! Your word? Promise . . ."

"I'll do my best, sir."

"But hasten!" Andrea sank back into the semi-stupor of the earlier part of the night; but his lips kept mechanically repeating the word *hasten*, until it faded out like an echo.

Belli renewed the coals in the brazier. Then, standing at the foot of the bed, he squinted down at Orsini.

"A queer mixture," he mumbled under his breath. "Cursed queer! Peasant, fox, and lord. Now add in lover, with Mario Belli the defender of beautiful ladies!"

CHAPTER XLII

DESPITE Andrea's renewed injunctions to haste, when he had once more sufficiently rallied to make them, Mario Belli stoutly refused to leave his patron during the whole of that day.

"And if Your Magnificence," he said, "were in better shape to use your wits, it would be clear to you that you need mine, not only to save your life but to handle this affair. Who's to protect you from the cursed doctors that might be fetched in? They would infallibly clap a hot iron to the wound, and you would die of the shock. Who's to satisfy curious people with the right story? I don't think the Switzers will talk, since I put it to them as honorable rakes not to betray a fellow sinner. But it's impossible that Duke Cesare won't be informed and send here to inquire. Your Magnificence isn't up to your usual finesses at the moment. So here I stay on every account."

"And meanwhile," sweated Orsini, "the lady Milla — "

"Meanwhile nothing. Take thought, sir. I give you my word to protect this signora as best I may, but there must be some plan to follow. She'll not be attacked in the streets because of her servants and my lord Varano, not to speak of the public cry it would make, so she's safe for today at least."

"You might warn — " Andrea began.

"Tut!" said Belli. "Warn her or the lord Marc' Antonio that my lady Angela, having stabbed you, is now set to murder her rival? And what figure will you cut then with Madonna Camilla, or how will that further your schemes — provided you live to pursue 'em? You can only warn with the truth. No lie would wash."

Orsini gazed blankly at his ensign and made a helpless movement of his head on the bolster.

Belli grinned. "Rest easy. There's but one thing to do, and that can't be done till evening. Then I promise you to take it in hand. I'll look up my gossip Furia. It's ten to one he'll know if anything's afoot and have the management of it. Also, it's ten to one that the lady Angela would not take him into her confidence respecting last night. I'll engage that she's sworn Mona Tonia and the lackeys to a silence deep as the grave. *Ergo*, I may get Furia to talk. Then we'll know where we are."

Belli's premonitions regarding the need of his attendance proved more than warranted. Having got off a message to the Varani at Andrea's request, announcing his patron's unhappiness at being unable to attend them to the shrines because of an accident, he had to answer the questions of Varano's servant, dispatched at once to express his lord's sympathy and concern. Whereupon, Camilla and Varano, returning from St. Peter's, called in person and insisted on seeing the patient.

"I grieve to assure Your Signories," said Belli, blocking the way, "that my virtuous lord is even now on the turn between life and death. The agitation of seeing Your Excellences would be too much for him. I shall hasten to comfort him, however, with the report of your condescension."

"Between life and death?" Camilla repeated, her cheeks pale.

"Even so, Madonna."

She stood frozen, gazing at Belli, while Varano burst out, "But, man, what is this? Why should anyone attack an officer of Ferrara and a friend of the Duke Valentino? What enemies?"

Belli improvised. "Some ancient vendetta of the Regno. You will recall that the lord Orsini is from Naples. The ins and outs of it are, frankly, obscure to me, sir; and, indeed, what I tell you is only surmise, as we had no view of the assassins." He gave a spirited account of swordplay on the Piazza di San Pietro. "The long and the short of it is that my illustrious patron's in a grave way."

"If I could but tend him!" put in Camilla. "Believe me, kind Messere, I have some knowledge of wounds and the care of sick men from our broils in Perugia. A woman is handier with a pillow and quicker to feel what's wanted than a man. Tell me something I can do."

She touched Belli's sleeve eagerly. The Frenchman's bitter face relented. "Yes, Madonna — and the truth from me is no less the truth than from another — you can pray for him. I have a notion that the prayers of certain people count. But at this time the presence of Your Ladyship would put a strain of courtesy upon him beyond his strength. Later it would be a very cordial to him; now, if he works himself into a fever, he's through."

"Right!" Varano nodded. "The lung, eh? *Peste!* Well, I've seen a few who got by with such wounds. See that he's kept warm. A rheum would play the devil. And, look you, keep us informed. We'll call again. Tell him we're ordering special intercessions."

"Tell him we love him," said Camilla.

When they were gone, Belli drew a long breath. "I may be damned," he muttered in French, "but for your sake, lady, we'll put some water in the Borgian trollop's wine."

A clatter of hoofs stopped in front of Sandeo's house. A hush fell. An impressed servant, fluttering up, announced Duke Cesare himself.

Belli met the great man in the corridor. "One moment, Your Excellence."

"Eh?" Borgia stared at the interruption; then, struck by the other's appearance, he smiled. "Ensign Belli, isn't it?"

"Your Grandeur honors me."

"I don't know how much honor it is, but I've heard of you. Well, how's your master and what happened?"

Belli stuck carefully to the version he had given the Swiss guardsmen; and, as in their case, the Duke accepted it without question. But his eyes blazed.

"What's the cuckold's name? We'll teach him respect for my officers."

Belli shrugged. "Alas, sir, would that I knew it myself!"

"We'll find out, then, from Orsini."

"Impossible, Your Grace. I beg your indulgence."

He hurried on with an account of the wound and did so well that in the end Borgia withdrew, though not without promising that the Pope's physician, Messer Scipione himself, should take charge of the case.

This meant further diplomacy when the learned doctor arrived. But what with flattery and what with the collusion of Andrea, who flatly refused to be cauterized or plastered, the celebrated leech was got rid of and his array of costly medicines consigned to the chamber pot.

As a result of these efforts, Andrea remained undisturbed during the day; his breathing improved; no more than a trace of fever appeared; and Belli had the satisfaction of noting that the wound had closed.

Then, after nightfall, having left one of Sandeo's servants on guard in the sickroom, Belli set out in search of Simone Furia.

Not far from the Campo de' Fiori and the place of execution, in the densest section of Rome, the Tavern of the Cow provided a meeting place for ruffians of the more exclusive and respected sort. There the masters of dagger and ambush, the well-to-do bravos of cardinals and great noblemen, gathered to drink or dice or engage in professional talk and reminiscence. The Cow enjoyed a central position, on one hand convenient to the palaces where most of these gentlemen lived, and on the other to the Tiber, where dead bodies were usually disposed of. Its proximity to the gallows on the Campo de' Fiori offered another advantage, since throats got dry from the hullabaloo of a hanging or burning, and it was pleasant to discuss details afterwards. Here for a while on almost any night, when not professionally active, Simone Furia was apt to be found.

He belonged to the swank elite of his trade, on the score both of the illustrious House that employed him and of his own admirable record. A dozen murders of the first consequence were ascribed to him by colleagues, not to speak of minor, routine killings. And though doubtless the number was exaggerated as a result of his fame, he enjoyed the credit of them. Certainly he had prospered. Everybody knew that he owned a couple of vineyards and a couple of brothels within the city, as well as holdings in the Abruzzi, his native province. Speculations regarding his wealth ran as high as ten thousand ducats. For him, a special table at the Cow, the choicest wines, the most scrupulous attentions, were reserved. To him, the aspiring young bravos looked up as to a god; and a smile or a clap-on-shoulder from him was an accolade. But he kept his dignity, associating only with other Olympians like himself. That he and his compeers accepted Mario Belli on even terms spoke volumes for the latter's eminence and wide reputation.

"Gut'n Abend," said Belli to the German innkeeper, when he had exchanged the cold reek of the night outside for the warmer reek of cheese and sour wine within. "Is my good friend Furia about this evening, or any of the other cavaliers?"

The taverner beamed. *"Herr Gott!* Messer Mario, I call this an answer to prayer. *About,* you say? Aye, about my ears. It happens that none of the worshipful gentlemen save Messer Simone is with us tonight, and there he sits in the inner room, pining for company and dicing one hand against the other. He's been cursing me for keeping an unfashionable house, neglected by the gentility. As if *I* could help an off evening! You know how careful he is in his choice of companions. He'll be right glad to see you, Master. Have the goodness to follow me."

Accompanied by stares of awe from the throng of scoundrels who filled the taproom, Belli made his way between tables and benches toward the inner sanctum, with a patronizing nod to one or the other of the least obscure guests. These were the rank and file, who would have given their ears to be admitted to that inner room. A discreet whispering followed Belli: "he of Mantua and Venice . . . in the service of the lord Orsini . . . bold stroke at Viterbo . . . Holy Virgin, what a face! . . . they say he's the devil himself . . . none better . . ." The door closed on a babble of admiration.

"Cuds me!" exclaimed Furia, banging down his dicebox on the table and starting up. "Here's someone at last! Friend Mario and no other! I salute you! How now, bully! . . . Host, bring us muscadine and eggs. . . . Sit down, gossip, sit down!"

He was a broad-shouldered, squat man, swarthy as a Moor, with a profusion of coarse hair, cut in a bang. He wore his cap on one side, with a cock's feather projecting forward. A dangling earring, set with good stones, added another rakish touch, as did the jeweled hilt of his dagger and the heavy rings on his square, dirty fingers. A blow at one time had flattened the bridge of his nose and tilted the nostrils up, so that the two black holes of them were prominent features. Another blow, by depriving him of several upper front teeth, had left a convenient passage for his tongue, which he liked to thrust out and upward, when pointing a remark. He was about thirty, a venerable age in his profession.

"How's business?" asked Belli, having thrown off his cloak and clapped his sword beside the other's on the table.

"Looking up," returned Furia, with a gap-tooth smile. "And how's it with you, bully boy? I hear you drew short last night."

Belli disguised the suspense that this remark caused by a few oaths. "What did you hear?" he added.

"That your patron got his in the Piazza and skirts the grave today." Furia shot out his tongue. "*You*," he twitted, "with your brag that no one ever got next to a signor you had the guarding of! Ho, ho!"

Belli relaxed happily. His guess that Angela Borgia had kept her secret had been right. But he looked chagrined. "What would you have, brother? It happens to the best of us. The trouble is that Messer Andrea has no will to live. Since the marriage that you and I know of fell through, he's a reckless man. Witness last night. That he should risk his life for a jade he has no leaning to! *Mort dieu!* The muck of it!"

Furia grinned, like a man who could tell something if he chose, but he said only, "What's your lay if he croaks? Where next?"

"For a while," Belli answered, twitching his nose, "I shall take it easy. You won't believe it, but my illustrious patron has willed me the key to his strongbox, with all that it contains."

"*Ma che!*" interjected the other ironically, with a wink. "Very handsome of him! In that case, I'm sure he won't recover."

270

"You wrong me. I took occasion last night to inspect the contents, and, though it's substantial, I could make more out of my gentleman if he lives. Still, there's enough for a time, and I shall lean back. Enjoy life, what? A man of my worth has only to choose his employer, you understand."

"To be sure, to be sure."

"The Venetian Ambassador, perhaps," Belli deliberated. "Or the Cardinal Farnese. But I had a talk with Duke Cesare today and am definitely attracted."

Furia took this bravado for what it was worth — he would have talked the same way himself — but it nettled him, as Belli intended it should, that an outsider from the north should crow so boldly about choosing the greatest patron of all, greater than Furia's, for Jofrè de Borgia-Lanzol did not equal the Duke.

"Then we'd be colleagues," Furia observed with a certain stiffness.

"Yes, in a way," patronized the other. "You could call it that. In the sense of belonging to the same House — as we did in Mantua. Ah, Simone, those were the times!"

There was great subtlety in this. It implied an equality in Mantua that both knew had not existed. Belli stood much higher in the household of the Marquis than had Furia. It rankled with the latter, besides, that Belli, however much a renegade, had been born a nobleman.

"I've come up since then," Furia asserted.

"So you have, brother Simone. It's always a pleasure to see virtue rewarded. And, in my opinion, you'll go further yet. Harken. I'm inclined to favor you. If I take that post with the Duke, I'll see what can be done to make an opening for you."

"Thanks," grunted the bravo, "I can take care of myself by your leave. Since Mantua, I've had my finger in more big jobs than you, by the Mass; and some of them with the Duke! Don't peacock it over me, my boy."

"No offense, gossip."

"And none felt. But no one takes the wall of me, understand?"

Belli backed off. He did not wish to provoke a quarrel with Furia but to condition him for the next move, and he proceeded at once to smooth down the man's ruffled feathers. The eggs and muscadine being brought, he raised his cup.

"Here's merry days!"

"With a whistle!" said Furia, and the cloud passed.

But a little later Belli crept in again. "I'd have your opinion on a certain point, Simone."

"Your servant," belched Furia.

"Well then, look you, this marriage between Madonna Angela and my patron — it would have meant money to me in the long run, more pay and perquisites — I had counted on it. And where's the hitch? None but this little hussy of Città del Monte, as I see it. Some plan of the Duke's that my lord must fit in with. I speak in confidence, friend."

"Aha," said the other, as one who puts two and two together. "I begin to understand. . . . Well?"

"If she were removed, the course would be clear. I gathered as much from my lord himself. A hint only. Suppose, then, I took this job upon myself. There's the point."

"Humph!" grinned Furia. "Yes?"

"You'll admit it's a bold scheme," Belli swaggered. "Not many in our line would have thought of it." He paused, as if for admiration, and looked insufferably superior. "A master stroke, eh?"

Furia was close-mouthed; but his vanity had suffered, and it got the best of him.

"Stale fish," he retorted.

"*How!* Damn you, sir — "

"A little late, *padrino*, a little late." Furia waved his hand. "We work fast here in Rome."

"Take me with you," stared Belli. "What do you mean?"

"Why, friend, I'm a length ahead of you, that's all. It happens that the lady you speak of is my meat — and no later than tonight. Madonna Angela thought of your master stroke before you did, and the job's mine."

Belli gave a perfect imitation of a deflated boaster. "How?" he stammered. "How . . . ?"

"Because," crowed Furia, "it looks as if my lady Angela saw eye to eye with your patron in this matter. She called me in this morning, left the case in my hands. You can trot home and give your lord something to live for. He'll marry Madonna, if the Baglione girl's the only trouble. She's as good as out of the way now."

"*Tiens, tiens,*" Belli murmured respectfully. "Think of that! I salute you, brother Furia. Damme, I'm proud of your friendship. . . . Knife work?" he hinted.

"No, sir, the necklace." Thrusting a hand into his pouch, Furia drew out a strap, with iron attachments on one end, and tossed it onto the table. It was the familiar garrote, or strangling thong. "There it is. You notice I like 'em thin. They take hold quicker, and give a better torque from behind."

Belli examined and approved.

"Madonna suggested poison," sneered Furia. "It's always the first thought with a woman. Poison! 'Sblood! Leave that to mountebanks. Give me something direct, if you want results."

"Exactly," agreed the other. . . . "You have someone inside at the Savelli Palace, of course?"

"Planted him today," Furia nodded. "A new page. He'll bring me upstairs to the lady. I hear she sleeps alone."

He added some obscenity, and the Frenchman laughed.

One thing was clear: Furia must not reach the palace. And Belli could think of only one way to prevent him.

CHAPTER XLIII

ABOUT two in the morning, Andrea Orsini awakened to find his ensign, still muffled in hat and cloak, on the point of relieving Sandeo's man, who had been on watch by the bed. The flame of a candle magnified Belli's profile into a nightmare phantasm on the wall, and several moments passed until Orsini could disentangle shadow from substance. Then, with a start, he remembered what Belli's errand had been that evening. By this time, Sandeo's servant had slipped out.

"Well?" Andrea muttered.

Without replying, Belli divested himself of hat, sword, and mantle and, having poured some water into a basin, washed his hands. Then, walking over to the bed, he felt his patron's pulse and noted the moisture of the skin.

"No fever yet. That's good. How fares Your Lordship?"

"Better, I think. . . . What about Furia?"

Belli sat down in the bedside chair. "Well, we were right. He had received orders from my lady Angela, but I reasoned with him. He won't trouble Madonna Milla."

273

"How *reasoned?*"

"Why, sir, effectively. How shall I say? Personal motives that prevailed with him." Belli's lips twitched with their usual nervous smile. "I won't assert that the argument didn't grow warm at a point; but all was peace in the end. I even had this of him — as a souvenir."

He drew out a leather thong, dangling it in the candlelight.

Andrea, recognizing it, shuddered. "The devil!" he breathed. And, as the realization of what had happened stole over him, he felt a certain horror of Belli's shapely hand, holding the thing up between thumb and forefinger. "No other way of handling it?"

Belli shook his head. "Tonight or never; his life or hers."

"In secret, I hope?"

"As secret as a wet midnight and an empty street could make it."

"You think she's safe now?"

"For the time." Belli got up. "You must sleep, my lord, and I shall. I've had my ration for today. Take no thought."

He drew off his outer clothes and stretched out on a smaller bed that had been set up for him. After a time, Andrea, too weak for thinking, dropped back to sleep. But for an hour Belli continued to stare up at the ceiling.

It was not the thought of Furia, whom he had ambushed close to the Savelli Palace, that kept him awake. As far as the night's maneuver was concerned, he could flatter himself on a bold stroke, and that his hand had not lost its cunning. To strangle the man with his own garrote, after stunning him, was a bit of irony that appealed to the Frenchman's sense of humor. But Furia was not the only bravo in Rome whom Angela Borgia could call on. No doubt she would shrug over this first broken tool and select another. Belli could not defend Camilla Baglione from all the means at Angela's disposal. He could not even guess how the next blow would fall. Some other and some radical method of defense had to be found. He might deal with Angela herself . . . Belli squinted up through the darkness. Impossible, he decided. Or else . . .

Every cunning line of his face crept out. "Not bad," he pondered. "Why not play my own game, too, for a change? *Cré dieu,* we'll try it."

Then he fell asleep.

Amid the throng of prelates, ambassadors, courtiers, and the like, who waited in the anteroom or corridors of the Palace of San Clemente for the chance of a word with Cesare Borgia, Mario Belli cut an odd figure. The Duke, always impatient of talk, was a hard man to interview at any time, but especially so on a brief and unofficial visit such as he was now making in Rome. The usher, who took the names of callers and promised, though without committing himself, to bring them to Borgia's attention, raised contemptuous eyebrows at Belli's request. If prince and cardinal had little chance of the Duke's ear, what could this hideous ruffler expect? However, the name of Andrea Orsini, and the very fact that his ensign looked like an emissary from hell, impressed the official to such an extent that word was conveyed to His Excellency of this strange caller. It scandalized everybody that the Duke ordered Belli shown in at once: an example of social decline under the Borgian regime.

Occupied with correspondence, the Duke waved his secretary out and fixed a searching gaze on Belli.

"I hope you bring me no ill news of your master," he said.

"On the contrary, sir, he breathes easier and shows improvement."

"Excellent! . . . So I gather you didn't come here on the subject of his health. What then?"

"On an affair which, I believe, should be brought to Your Grandeur's attention, since my noble patron is unable to deal with it in person."

"You're sent by him?"

"No, my lord. I took the responsibility upon myself."

"Oho!" said Borgia. "That's interesting." His manner became suaver; he smiled graciously. Experience taught him that it was not only the big wheels, but the little cogs, that counted. One learned a good deal through humble channels. Besides, he had had his eye on Belli for various reasons. "You can be seated, Ser Mario."

Belli was aware of the scrutiny behind this politeness. He could feel the cool probing of the Duke's mind. But, for his part, he was also sizing up the Duke. Here was a personage very different from Ippolito d'Este. No saucy tricks would do in this case. He could pull no wool over those eyes. It was deadly serious. He found himself pitted against an intelligence and cunning superior to his own. This called for his utmost shrewdness.

"I thank Your Illustrious Signory. My lord, I am too conscious of the great affairs that wait upon Your Grace and of my own insignificance to crave for more than an answer to one simple question. That I ask it at all springs from a sense of duty, first to you, and second, to my patron. . . . Is it perhaps your will that the lady Camilla Baglione should not return to Città del Monte but should die here in Rome?"

275

If Belli expected a start of surprise, he was foiled. Duke Cesare merely looked amused. "An odd question. What leads you to think that it might be my will?"

"Because steps have been taken in that direction."

"And by whom?"

Here was the great risk that Belli could not avoid. He answered bluntly, "The lady Angela Borgia."

"Tut, tut," smiled the Duke, "you're babbling, my friend; you've been misinformed."

Belli made as if to get up. "That, my lord, is all I wished to hear. It is unnecessary for Your Grace to speak plainer in the matter. And so I humbly take my leave."

The other raised his hand. "One moment. You make serious charges against my illustrious kinswoman. I must ask on what grounds?"

"The statement," replied Belli, "of one too low for Your Lordship's notice, an acquaintance of mine in the service of Her Signory's father, the bravo Simone Furia."

"Yes, I knew him." The Duke's voice was coolly casual. "Found strangled this morning near the Torre delle Milizie. Very eminent in his line."

"Strangled?" Belli exclaimed. Probe as he pleased, Borgia could read only amazed shock on his caller's face. "And it was last night that we supped together. Ah, the uncertainty of life! Who could be guilty of it?"

"I wonder," said the Duke, his tawny eyes on Belli, "I wonder. . . . But what did the man say?"

This could be answered with the truth. Borgia listened with an air of detached amusement.

"Probably drunk," he observed at last. And with the very slightest emphasis, "*Don't* you agree?"

"Most probably, sir."

"You have no longer any belief — now that I have assured you of its absurdity — that my noble and virtuous cousin would be guilty of such wickedness, *have* you, Ser Mario?"

"None at all, my lord."

"That's well. I see that you're a man of discretion, and the discreet have long lives. No, you may comfort Messer Andrea — if he requires such comfort — with the truth that the lady Camilla is under my special protection in Rome, and that he need have no concern. . . . However, my dear Ser Mario, unnecessary as it proved to be, I am touched by

276

your zeal, by your initiative, and I propose to reward it. I like men
who, at the proper time, act on their own hand, without waiting for
orders. They are useful men." Reaching out, he tinkled a silver bell
on the desk beside him and directed the secretary who answered it to
fetch him a purse of two hundred ducats. When the money had been
brought, and the secretary had once more withdrawn, Borgia added,
"There you are."

It was a princely sum. A flush crept over Belli's sallow cheeks as he
slipped to one knee with expressions of devotion. He had spent too
long in the school of poverty not to be dazzled by two hundred gold
pieces.

"A trifle only," smiled the Duke; "but I don't believe that even my
enemies will deny that I'm a good paymaster to those who serve me
well. Say no more about it. Since your patron, the lord Orsini, is in
my employ, so are you also, I hope."

"Entirely, my lord."

Borgia let the other bask a moment in his good fortune. Then, more
graciously than ever, he added: "If so, there are two on whom I can
count in Città del Monte. Not that I distrust your good patron —
nay, be seated again, Ser Mario — but flesh is proverbially weak,
vicissitudes occur, and it is always well to take precautions — if you
follow me."

Belli nodded. He understood perfectly that he was being bought
and yet, spellbound by the other's personality, he felt helpless.

"I see that you do," continued Borgia, "because no one of your
intelligence could fail to perceive where his permanent interests lie.
Thus, if the lord Orsini remains faithful to my purposes, you would
continue to serve me by serving him. But if — *absit omen!* — he should
waver for any reason, you would still continue to serve me. I shall
expect you to act on your own initiative, as you have today. And,
believe me, in that case your fortune will be made, Ser Mario."

"I'm Your Grandeur's slave," Belli murmured.

"Not at all. You're my esteemed friend. . . . Look you" — the Duke
turned on a confidential light in his eyes — "I understand human
values. There're not many in your trade who are better than artisans.
This man Furia, for example. No more than a clever brute. You, sir,
are an artist. You delight and impress me. You have the touch of a
courtier, the breeding of a gentleman. You are apt for great enter-
prises. Do I not judge you favorably?"

"You overrate me a thousandfold, my lord."

"By no means. Let me ask you a question. Have you and Captain Orsini had any discussion as yet with regard to the prolonged life of Marc' Antonio Varano and the check it gives to my policies?"

"Not recently, sir. At one time we touched on the matter. It is probable that my lord has it in mind."

"He should have it very much in mind, Messer Mario." (Belli did not miss the subtle change of title.) "Very much in mind. You will keep it before him at Città del Monte. But be guided by him. He's a master of what is opportune. . . . Another question. Have you any reason to suppose that Captain Orsini might let sentiment — tenderness, perhaps, toward this lord — interfere with practical advantage? The human heart has queer lapses."

Belli hesitated. "No reason."

"Eh?" probed Borgia.

"None, sir. He's not of one piece, as you know, and is variously moved. But I would say that he is bound to Your Grandeur not only by personal attachment, but because of your ultimate plans for Italy, which it does not behoove me to mention. It would be odd if he let anything divert him from that purpose."

"*Benissimo!*" approved the Duke. "Yes, he's one of the few who have caught the dream. I love him for it. . . . So, there's nothing but good you can tell me of the lord Orsini?"

Again Belli hesitated. He thought of the night outside Crespino, of what he had glimpsed through the closed shutter of Mona Costanza's window. It was valuable knowledge. . . . "Nothing that concerns Your Highness's service."

Then he felt that the floor had dropped from under him, as Borgia smiled. "His ancestry perhaps?" Belli's face showed that the question had hit the mark. "Come, Messer Mario, you don't consider me so dull that I fail to investigate the past of my confidential servants. I know your ancestry, too, for that matter." He gave a short laugh. "And what of it? I judge men by their ability, not their birth. Let people call themselves what they please, as long as they serve me. Just as long as that, friend Mario. But knowledge can be used to bridle or spur with, if the need arises. I think you understand me."

It took an effort to digest this. So, the private intelligence which had given Belli a secret sense of power during the weeks since Crespino amounted to nothing; or rather the power it conferred lay not with him but with Borgia. At the moment Belli wanted nothing so much as to escape from the Duke's overpowering presence. He felt a curious horror of the beautiful, masklike face and of the masterful eyes that made free of the inmost recesses of his brain. Until now, he had supposed that he knew all the reaches of evil; but that had been evil conscious of itself and, therefore, implying the existence of good. In Borgia, he confronted an inhuman force, indifferent to good or evil, something that dissected and absorbed him, and against which he had no defense.

"Yes," he stammered. "I understand."

"You will perceive also," hinted Borgia, "the value of silence in this matter until such a time (and may that time never come!) as I shall give the word."

"Quite, Your Signory."

"Then, Messer Mario, I bid you good day. Commend me to your illustrious lord, whom I shall visit shortly. As for you, sir, persevere in the enlightened course you are now following, and you may count on my patronage. *A rivederci*."

Still dazed, Belli found himself in the street outside the palace. To collect his thoughts, he walked on for a while at random until stopped by the Tiber, where he paused to gaze at the traffic on the water and to spit reflectively from the parapet. On the whole, he could congratulate himself. He had secured Camilla Baglione from further danger while in Rome and had, thus, fulfilled his promise to Andrea. He had become richer by two hundred gold ducats and richer still in prospects. His future was assured. But so perverse is the human mind that he took little comfort from these considerations. He felt somehow bruised and degraded. Thus far, however much an outcast, he had managed to keep his own twisted integrity, a bitter independence. Being typically French, he was also typically an individualist. It seemed to him now that his inner citadel had been sold out, not because he had taken the Duke's money or accepted the Duke's proposals, but because he had been made to feel like a puppet in doing so. He had accepted them weakly, no longer his own master with a cynical tongue in his cheek, but as the inferior of a man who dominated him.

"This lord's the devil in person," he reflected, "and I'm compelled to serve him. We'll see. We'll see. . . ."

His thought turned to Andrea, as if in relief. "Caught in the same net," he pondered. "Walk straight, my nobleman, or you'll find yourself without name or coronet. But you're no fool, either. The Duke may not find it easy. We'll see about that, too. . . . Christ!" he muttered. "The silly game's not worth the candle. Why play it? For what stakes? A grave. The end of magnificence and signories." Oddly, he found himself remembering a mountain road up from Viterbo and a frail woman smiling down at him from her mule. "By God," he exclaimed under his breath, "those were the very words used by Her Reverence."

Meanwhile, in the Palace of San Clemente, prelates and noblemen waited in vain for a word with Cesare Borgia. To the surprise of his secretary, the Duke had departed by a side gate, with the object, he said, of calling upon his enchanting cousin, the lady Angela.

And later that day Madonna Angela's women whispered of some words that must have passed between their mistress and His Lordship, words that had left her white and chastened and terribly afraid.

CHAPTER XLIV

To THAT great physician, Messer Scipione, the Pope's own leech, was given the credit of Andrea Orsini's rapid recovery. It afforded a topic of gossip to polite Rome for some time. Nor did the famous doctor himself reject the acclaim that the cure brought him. Indeed, so far as he knew, his prescriptions had wrought the miracle. They consisted, it seemed, in a special and secret blending of potable gold, pearl, Egyptian mummy, and unicorn's horn, with a supplementary use of bezoar and of moss scraped from the skull of a criminal hanged in chains: in short, a most precious combination of universal curatives. Hereafter, any gentleman suffering from wounds would hope to avail himself of Messer Scipione's services, if he could afford them.

It would have been ungracious and impolitic had Andrea not added his own testimonial to this chorus of praise. Duke Valentino himself had paid for the costly medicines and was gratified by their success. That they had not been used had to be kept secret. But, with returning strength, Andrea renewed his acknowledgments to Mario Belli.

"By the Mass," he said. "I owe you my life, and that's flat. If I had taken to retching from the learned doctor's drugs, it would have opened my wound — then *addio!* But here's a strange thing. Are Pliny and Galen wrong, not to mention Friar Bacon or others? What of the art of medicine? If the sick can recover without drugs better than with them, it argues against the ancients. I'm bewildered, friend. Who doesn't know that mummy and unicorn have sovereign virtues?"

"I don't, for one," Belli grunted. "I know it's been *said* they have, which, by your leave, is something else. But I'm no clerk or scholar. Failing books, I've kept my eyes open; and what they tell me I'm apt to believe rather than the statements of other people, however ancient. Sir, the artists of the age, yourself among them, have not wrought great things by keeping their noses in books. They have used their own eyes and hands and have studied nature itself. The cure of the sick is no different, to my thinking; but it lags behind. Perhaps some-day people will learn more about it."

Always attracted by new ideas, Andrea pondered Belli's suggestion. He recalled having once heard someone quote Messer Leonardo of Florence to the same effect. Most interesting. He sighed at the short-ness of life and the fascination of the unknown.

"You're a strange man, Mario."

"Strange?" Belli lifted his eyebrows. "Yes, I take Your Lordship's meaning. Unexpected facets, eh? But then everybody's strange — even to himself."

"No, I was thinking of the night we met in Venice — "

"You should say *collided*, sir."

"As you please — and how, having failed to murder me then, you nurse me now."

"Am I not in your service?"

"Wages don't purchase devotion, Mario, or sleepless nights or the risk you took with Furia. The strangeness is in that."

"Pooh!" Belli looked as if he were chewing a bitter nut. "Devotion's a tall word. I made a bargain with Your Worship and take some pride in keeping it — what else? You saved my life in Ferrara, didn't you? So, tit for tat. Remember, I promised a warning when I quit you for another patron. There ends our contract. Devotion, bah!"

Andrea smiled. "So be it. . . . I remember, too, that you advised me twice on a certain night and both times well: first, to wear a trump-ery leaden medal on my cap, and next, to take you with me to Rome."

"I've the gift of second sight," grinned Belli.

"Apparently. And I'm still alive because of it — a right sound bargain for me."

Impenetrable as ever, the Frenchman gave his soundless laugh. "*Vive dieu!* I haven't done badly myself. It's been a privilege to share in Your Lordship's fortunes."

But whatever the value of Belli's services, Andrea's convalescence owed much to Camilla Baglione. During the last week of worship at the shrines, which fulfilled the terms of the Jubilee pilgrimage, she stopped at the house of Monsignor Sandeo every day after leaving St. Peter's. When the week had passed, she came more often and stayed longer. Always, of course, one of her women and often Varano accompanied her; but somehow their presence did not lessen the delight that her visits brought him. She had the gift of intimacy. Perched on a high stool at his bedside (for the armchair was too low) she sat clasping one knee, her little plumed hat at an angle, her piquant face now grave, now gay, as they talked; and she seemed to him the very incarnation of April. Whoever was present, she gave him the sense of sharing with her in some whimsical, airy secret that others could never guess. It affected him like music.

"You know, Donna Milla," he said, "with you here, it's hard to believe that we're only at the start of winter. I keep expecting spring sunlight through the windows and the singing of *ritornelli* in the streets.

> *Flower of the cane!* [he recited]
> *When in the vineyard all your beauties show,*
> *How the campagna lightens once again!*

She hummed in reply:

> *Flower of the clove!*
> *In days to come, when I am dead, I know*
> *You'll mourn this hour and call me your true love.*

"Yes, it will be long till spring. I hate rain and cold, frostbites, wool stockings, smell of charcoal. . . . But spring will come."

Often, during these days, they discussed art.

"You're an artist, Messere. . . . No, don't say you're not. I've heard the gossip here in Rome. They say you painted a portrait of Madonna Lucrezia, a marvelous thing. Why do you blush?"

"After all," he protested, "a gentleman doesn't — "

"Rubbish!" she put in. "You and your gentlemen! Your politics! Your wars! You know perfectly well that Giotto and Donatello, Bellini, Leonardo, Mantegna — how many more! — will be remembered and admired when you big signori are long since forgotten. I wonder at you."

This was all very well, he reflected, as long as she considered him a magnifico, at the top of fashion, with a great name, the confidant of dukes and cardinals. But what if she knew him as the son of blacksmith Zoppo? Not much glamour in that, artist or not.

"So, being an artist," she went on, "you must give me your advice about a pedestal for our lovely god of Castel Gandolfo. What sort of design? Where shall we place him? Not on the landing of the main stairs. Not in the state corridor. You know, I think he belongs in the same *stanza* with that beautiful Mantegna you sold me, at the opposite end. They express the same mood."

Andrea had to give his opinion, and this led further until he had betrayed a more intimate knowledge of the painter's craft than a dabbling gallant ought to possess. Whereupon, Camilla laughed at him; and so they had gained another congenial field of argument and conversation.

But whatever the topic, and even (as in the first days of his convalescence) when there was no topic at all, and Camilla merely sat by the bed or straightened the pillows or poured a cup of water, everything, in Andrea's eyes, took its color from her and became significant because of her. When she was gone, he recalled so vividly what she had said, how she had looked, that these memories filled the time until her next visit. In this fashion, day by day, he learned something of the strangeness of love, that utterly new world which was opening before him.

He had once assumed that love meant physical possession: the real object, however poeticized, was the satisfaction of sexual desire. He now discovered that love could exist without that satisfaction; indeed, that love such as he felt for Camilla depended on self-control. If he should forget this, love would perish. For it was precisely her loyalty to Varano and Andrea's growing affection for the old lord that distinguished and deepened their relationship. It seemed that none of the time-honored conventions applied in this case. Remembering how he had once planned Camilla's seduction as an incident to be taken for granted, Andrea sometimes smiled and sometimes marveled at his sophisticated ignorance of love only two months ago.

"Let's tell fortunes," Camilla proposed one morning, when she and Varano were calling. "My old nurse, Mona Anna, in Perugia, was a famous reader of palms, and she taught me all her skill. Give me your hand, Messere."

The touch of her fingers was enough to send a glow through him.

"Don't let her pull your leg, Captain," Varano chuckled, leaning forward in his chair. "That's one of her tricks. I remember the fortune she told me this summer: that I faced a loss of money in connection with some journey (meaning hers to Venice, of course), but that I was philosopher enough to accept it. *Per Dio*, nothing could have been truer. She took care of that."

"Hush!" said Camilla. "Don't distract me. This sublime art needs attention. It is *difficilissimo*." . . . She peered at Andrea's palm. . . . "Out and alas, by God!" she murmured. "What do I behold! Poor gentleman! Never have I seen such a hand! Is it not marvelous that we carry about a chart of life, written on our own skins, if we have only the wit to read? But such a thing as this — Husband, consider that love line!"

"What's wrong with it?" Varano grunted.

"The infidelities! Treasons! Broken hearts! False promises! At least a dozen to the inch. Ah, Captain Orsini, never show your hand to a woman who knows palmistry. You'll get nothing of her. How glad I am to have seen this! Forewarned, forearmed."

"But look further," Andrea urged. "Mark you how straight it runs from that point on. Not a quiver, by Bacchus! A remarkable line. Nay, magnificent's the only word."

She pursed her lips. "No, sir, it means lack of opportunity — nothing more. Perhaps a long sea voyage or a term in jail. I can't tell which."

"What of the life line?" Varano put in. "Trust a woman to concern herself first with love!"

Camilla shook her head. "Hair-raising, my lord. A terrible hand, as I said. Battles, dangers, escapes. My head swims. You see, it is all affected by Messer Andrea's character, which politeness forbids me to reveal."

"Not one good trait, Madonna?" Orsini pleaded. "Remember, I'm a sick man."

"Well, a few, sir. I won't deny that you have an engaging quality that leads one to forget other things. And you take full advantage of it. But on the whole, Magnifico, *on the whole* — " her eyes met his, and he fell deeper in love than before — "the less said the better. . . . But note this." The tip of her finger tickled his palm. "See how clearly your accident shows here. Almost a break in the line. And now look. It is very clear that you are going to receive advice from some friend. Unless you follow it, your game's up, Messere, quite up." . . . She glanced at Varano. . . . "Isn't that true, husband?"

"By the Mass, it is, for a change," the old lord agreed. "Tell me, Captain Orsini, does the service of Duke Ercole detain you in Rome?"

Andrea's heart gave a leap. It was obvious what Varano was leading up to. "No, my lord. Since Viterbo, I've done little more than represent His Excellence at the Vatican. I should be returning to Ferrara."

"Why, then, sir," returned Varano, "you'll take the road with us. To judge by this last attack, you'd do well to leave as soon as possible. We'll gladly wait until you're well enough to be carried in a horse litter. You'll break the journey at Città del Monte and stop with us until we release you."

"*Ecco!*" Camilla exclaimed. "There's the advice I foresaw in your hand. Don't say I'm not a fortuneteller."

Andrea hesitated politely. Varano did not know that at that moment he was acquiring a new captain of the guard. "How can I thank Your Signories for this kindness! But the pace of a litter would too much delay you."

"Not at all," said Camilla. "Remember, our beautiful god rides with us in an oxcart. Everything's settled. We'll hear no excuses. And, as my lord husband has just said, *until we release you.*"

"Then welcome so fair a prison!" he answered.

And now he could plan the future. Once established at Città del Monte, not only with Varano's but with Cesare Borgia's benediction, he would make the place so strong that when the time came to show the Duke his colors, it might be possible to negotiate favorable terms of surrender, a safe retreat for Varano and Camilla to Venice or Mantua, an exile which Orsini himself would share until fortune changed. More than ever he felt that it was only a question of how long Borgia's luck could hold. More than ever, appraising the political outlook, he considered the Duke a meteor, not a star. At any moment, the end might come. Meanwhile, it was sound strategy to keep in with Borgia and in touch with his plans as long as possible. To win against this unscrupulous Colossus meant that one could not be too scrupulous oneself. Even Mario Belli must not guess that Andrea had changed sides.

A memorable talk with Duke Cesare, before that prince returned to the siege of Faenza, reviewed the situation.

"You know," said Borgia, who called on the eve of his departure, "I have every confidence in your future. You're an able man, Andrea. By the Mass, you can turn even misfortune to profit. That was a brilliant device for getting yourself into Città del Monte. My compliments!"

285

Orsini thanked His Ducal Excellence and expressed the belief that, once in the town, his visit there could be prolonged.

"Not the shadow of a doubt," returned Cesare. "We'll recall our man, Branca, at once, and leave you his position to slip into. You'll withdraw from the service of Ferrara on one pretext or another. As an officer of Varano, you'll have ample scope not only in Città del Monte but throughout the Marches. By spring, that province should be ready to drop into my hand at the first twitch."

Andrea reflected that Camerino, ill-governed and restless, would drop easily in any case. He could, therefore, make a show of zeal to the Duke in that direction without injury to Varano.

"Your Lordship, then, counts surely upon this spring?"

"At present, yes. Of course you'll be kept informed. If you play the game to our expectation, you'll be signor of Città del Monte before summer. And that's not all." A far-off look showed in the Duke's eyes. "You'll not be left to sleep in a mountain signory. You'll be needed elsewhere." For a moment, Borgia seemed oblivious of the man in the bed. Names rose to his lips. "Urbino . . . Bologna . . . Ferrara practically ours . . . Siena . . . then Tuscany. I'll find means to buy off the French. The center of Italy from coast to coast. Then inevitably, Andrea, I say inevitably, by geographic attraction, the Milanese. Venice driven back to the sea. Let France or Spain hold Naples if it can. Years? Perhaps not so many if my fortune lasts."

If it does! thought Andrea. Once he would have vibrated to this vision. Now it seemed to him a mirage because of Borgia's insufficiency. Every name he mentioned meant one more treason, one more slaughter, one more compulsion.

The Duke shrugged himself out of his musing. "We're both young. I shall need someone like you, who knows my mind, who can keep his eyes on the ultimate goal, without being distracted by trivialities — in short, a statesman, such as you give promise of becoming. Who else but you? Not one of my cutthroat captains nor any of the churchmen neither. You're the man. Think, *amico mio*. Chief Minister of a new, great kingdom. Builder with me of an Italy, no longer the spoil and lickspittle of others, but strong and imperious. Keep that before you. What prize on earth could equal it?"

Here was Andrea's once-dreamed-of career presented to him on Borgia's own authority. Presented to him by a greater man, it would have been hard to reject the offer. As it was, he considered these dignities a basket of paste jewels. They were not worth one glance of scorn from Camilla's eyes.

"But don't flinch," Cesare added.

"Flinch? What's Your Lordship's meaning?"

"That greatness has its price, Andrea. To speak for myself, I'm prepared to pay it, let the gossips of history call me what they please. Are you?" . . . The feline eyes focused searchingly. . . . "If so, welcome to glory. If not —" A snap of the fingers completed the phrase. "But I depend on you." He got up from his chair. "Farewell, then! We'll not be meeting until you welcome me at Città del Monte in the spring."

Snow had already powdered the mountains when Varano's small cortege, emerging from the woods beyond Fabriano, caught the first glimpse of home against an olive-green sky. From his litter, Andrea watched the slow approach of walls and campaniles and the dominating mass of the castle palace. Peasants in gala dress streamed out from the countryside to greet their returning lords. In front, drawn by garlanded oxen, wreathed with laurel, and surrounded by pipers and dancers, the marble god of Castel Gandolfo smiled an inscrutable benediction. Andrea hailed it as a good omen.

PART FOUR

Città del Monte

CHAPTER XLV

But Borgia did not come in the spring. The valiant defense of Faenza, one of those unexpected instances of heroic devotion that so often upset the schedule of conquerors, detained him fuming until April. By that time other more urgent interests diverted him from the Marches. He must reach an understanding with Bologna and Florence, who were both under the protection of France and so, for the present, unassailable. But tiny Piombino on the coast of Tuscany could be plucked off as a future base of operations. And now June was here, and a mightier current than even Cesare's ambition cut across his plans. The French, his allies and patrons, pressed down from the north, demanding his aid against Naples and the Spanish tide invading that kingdom from the west. Personal conquests had once more to be postponed. He rode south with the French captains. The summer passed; another winter discouraged campaigning in the Apennines; the mountain cities of Urbino and the Marches remained at peace.

Thus Messer Gentile Filelfo, the sleek old humanist and palace librarian at Città del Monte, had continued leisure to view the world with scholarly detachment and to extend his chronicle of the city, which he had pottered over during the last thirty years. It embraced not only a record of local occurrences but such contemporary events as, filtering through the mountain passes, merited inclusion. He wrote impersonally, concerned with grammar rather than content. Between the sweet-smelling shelves of manuscripts that lined the library, lulled by the flutter of pigeons in the courtyard outside, it was all one to him whether he recorded a fall of snow or the fall of princes, provided his Latin cadences kept the proper beat. With no more philosophy than that of a silkworm spinning its cocoon, he at least supplied the jarring fractions of life with the common denominator of deft and virtuous syntax.

So, if the chronicle survived, his readers would learn that on January 10th in this year of Our Lord 1501, a two-headed calf was born at the *masseria* of Gianpagolo Ruffini of Fabriano to the amazement of the whole countryside; and, *item*, that Messer Galeazzo Branca, captain of the guard, this day took his leave of the illustrious Marc' Antonio Varano, being minded to try his fortune in the service of the illustrious Duke Cesare Borgia. "And there is no great sorrow at his departure, for he is a man given to drink and of an insolence displeasing to our master."

"*Item*. February 12th. Letters this day from Ferrara have released the noble Andrea Orsini, at his request, from his office in the guard of the exalted Duke Ercole d'Este, lord of that city. And said noble Andrea has been appointed captain at Città del Monte to fill the place of Galeazzo Branca, to the joy of court and town. Truly, the lord Orsini has made himself beloved by all for the courtesy of his manners, the magnificence of his parts, and the devotion he bears toward the ever renowned and venerable Marc' Antonio. Indeed, it is commonly reported that he has relinquished the greater post at Ferrara solely for our lord's sake, that he may, as a humble apprentice, study the virtues and form himself upon the model of so famous a captain, *qui omnes omnibus superavit.* . . . *Item*. In these days, the French Sickness afflicts many in our town with sores and boils, for which, we hear, a sovereign remedy is: quicksilver, 2 oz.; laurel and scorpion oil in quantity; old pork fat, 4 oz.; a half-bowl of vine ashes well-sifted, to form a salve for application morning and night. . . .

"*Item*. April 3rd. Madonna Alda, dwarf of our sovereign lady, was this day hurt by a fall from her donkey in the palace garden. The broken leg was set in splints by Messer Mario Belli, ensign to the lord Andrea, said ensign being, it appears, adept in the care of wounds and like diseases.

"*Item*. April 14th. On this St. Justin's Day, the illustrious Marc' Antonio Varano, our signor and father, has proclaimed, before nobility and people, in palace and market place, the most noble signora, Camilla degli Baglioni, his chaste and dutiful wife, to be his plenary heir with the title of *Prefettessa*, following his decease; said most noble signora to hold this vicariate of Città del Monte in the name and subject to the consent of the Pope's Holiness, to whom letters explanatory have been sent. And of His Beatitude's approval there is small doubt — nay, it has already been obtained — partly because of our illustrious signor's merits in the service of the Roman See, and partly because of the ill-will

His Holiness bears toward the Varani of Camerino, who might else lay claim to our city. And certain it is that nothing in many years has brought more happiness to the people than has this same blessed proclamation. For the said most noble lady Camilla is beloved second only to our lord himself, and if there are any who would not die to uphold her right, they had best keep silent. May God long preserve in health the good prince Marc' Antonio, *pater patriae!* But, as even he is mortal, the fears of commotion attending his decease have thus been quieted."

Messer Gentile rarely stirred from the tranquil library, except for meals or when called upon to read aloud to Varano one of His Lordship's favorite authors, Caesar or Livy. The report of events near and far, the echo of echoes, sank no deeper beneath the placid surface of his mind than autumn leaves drifting upon the palace fountain. Whatever came to him mellowed gently into Latin on smooth vellum: in June, the portrait that the lord Orsini had made of Camilla, *dominae nostrae,* a thing of exceeding beauty at which all marveled; in July the pillage of Capua by Cesare Borgia and the French, wherein the illustrious Duke distinguished himself *et animo et crudelitate;* in September, the formal announcement of Madonna Lucrezia's betrothal to Alfonso d'Este. ("And it is said His Holiness has agreed to a dowry of 100,000 ducats.") In December, Lucrezia's wedding by proxy to the glorious Don Alfonso, an affair so rich and brilliant that it lighted up Italy with a flush of gold and inspired even Filelfo to vividness.

Such entries are the dim material of history, little better than nothing compared with the throb and glow of life they represent. What could Messer Gentile guess, for example, of the raised eyebrows and puckered smiles in Ferrara that attended Andrea's letter of resignation from the Duke's service?

"What trick now?" sneered Ippolito d'Este, discussing the matter with his father.

The old Duke's lip curled. "That's for Varano to find out. Like Belshazzar, he's not skilled to read handwriting on the wall."

"You mean another Borgian snatch?"

"Obviously. No need to consult the stars when Andrea Orsini appears. He's the vancourier of things to come."

"Fortunate we got rid of him in time," observed the Cardinal, adding — "if we did."

This was in January, and there were still hopes of the French marriage.

293

"*If* we did," Ercole repeated in a flat voice. "I sometimes doubt it." He sighed. "An astute man. I'm sorry to lose touch with him. If he could have been won over sincerely to our interest, we could have used him."

"Judas!" Remembering Pomposa, Ippolito's hot face flushed. "Mountebank! I hope sometime to watch the hanging of him."

The Duke shrugged. "Who knows? . . . At least Ferrara's indebted to him for the saintly Lucia, our fairest flower. There's solid gain. Your virtues, Reverend Son, were no safeguard from the wrath of heaven." And after listening to the Cardinal's profane rejoinder, he nodded, "Yes, you speak to the point. I'm glad you confirm me."

And how pale a reflection, on Filelfo's page, of that exuberant St. Justin's Day! If everybody — including townsfolk, peasants, magistrates, clergy, and gentlemen — got tipsy, it was not alone on wine from the palace cellars. April had something to do with it, and the sweet air and the blue sky, the ringing of bells, beating of drums, thronging of colors, dancing in the streets. Love had most to do with it, proud love of the people for their homely old lord in his outmoded hat, for his scars and wrinkles, humility and valor; love of the girl beside him, gay, approachable and warm, their beautiful lady, who would sometime rule over them. Filelfo failed to mention that even he got tipsy and danced a *riddone* in the courtyard with Mona Tina from the country. She wore beautiful yellow slippers, cut low on the side and tied with laces. . . . This would not do for Latin.

Andrea Orsini danced with Camilla in the great palace hall to the admiration of the court. More clearly than anyone there, he understood why the Pope had so easily approved her succession. Since the Borgias could now anticipate Varano's secret murder, it was just as well for the little state to be governed temporarily by a puppet acceptable to its citizens. Orsini could be counted on to manage the Prefettessa in his own and Duke Cesare's interests, until, without friction and, indeed, with enthusiasm, the new government grew out of the old. As he danced, Andrea imagined the Duke's satisfaction.

"You look grave tonight, Messere," Camilla whispered. "Why are you sad?"

Their fingers touched; they bowed in perfect time; he forced a smile. They swept apart, then together. He answered, "An effect of the light, Madonna."

It was not yet time to tell her what he knew.

But shallowness was Filelfo's least fault. He did not even remark that men change with the seasons, that none of the events he recorded took place without affecting the people concerned in them. His characters remained as static as their titles: *glorious, noble, illustrious, renowned*, once and forever.

This plastic quality in human nature is often forgotten by greater historians than Messer Gentile. It is unlikely that the pillage, torture, and butchery of the population of Capua, which shocked the rest of the world, left no mark at all upon the illustrious Duke Valentino, who shared in it. It was impossible that the months at Città del Monte, the interaction of personalities, the small daily decisions, did not in some degree color the lives of everyone there. Why, even tiny Alda's broken leg had a greater effect on Mario Belli than as merely an occasion for showing his skill.

The bravo and the midget were drawn to each other by the common bond of singularity — Belli's ugliness and Alda's size — that set them apart from normal people. They shared, too, a tacit rebellion against the universe. In each other's company, they were off stage, no longer outsiders on the defensive, but snug in the comradeship of a point of view. Their attachment ripened during Alda's recovery from her accident. It often took a philosophic turn.

Seating himself beside her miniature couch and looming above her, like Atlas, Belli would forget his usual manner.

"How goes my princess?"

"Well enough, Dr. Mario," replied the always amazingly full voice that bore no relationship to Alda's tiny person; "but the worse that you've kept me waiting for you. . . . And yourself? Wicked as ever?"

"Can anyone tell," the Frenchman pondered, "how bad or good one is? The best person I've known, Her Holy Reverence Sister Lucia, of whom I've told you, considered herself the worst of sinners; and the sinners I've known had a comfortable opinion of themselves. I've seen a bad deed turn to good, and a good to bad. Probably we're all so vile in the eyes of God that small differences don't matter."

"So, you still believe in God, Messere?"

"*Mort dieu!*" exclaimed Belli, with no thought of irreverence. "I don't believe in anything else."

"Why? He makes no sense."

"For that very reason, Madonna. There's no comprehending Him. If we did, He wouldn't be God. Is He good? Not as we know goodness. Is He just or merciful? We've seen people more just or merciful than He. Well, then, is He evil? Not in our sense. A contradiction at every point, and, therefore, compelling belief."

"I ask again why?"

295

"Because, if our reason is all, then *nothing* makes sense."

"How did you learn this, sir?"

Belli cleared his throat. "From looking at the stars through a loophole in hell."

"I understand," Alda nodded. "Perhaps, if I were big, I wouldn't understand so much. That's worth remembering. . . . Well, Messer Mario, set me on your shoulder and let me look out with you sometimes."

So Belli, waiting to be used professionally in the murder of Varano, and accepting damnation as inherent in his lot, found moments of respite with little Alda. This might not alter his conduct; but it exposed him to sentiments inconsistent with his trade — by no means an unmixed blessing.

And so it was, too, with the noble Andrea Orsini, who, as time passed, figured more often in Filelfo's chronicle. For one thing, he had leisure to paint Camilla's portrait; and that involved a great deal more than Filelfo's entry implied.

It involved the mood and color of May, the ineffable blue of the sky arched by an open casement, the fragrance of blossoms wafted in from the near-by garden, the flute calls of birds, the recklessness of spring. It involved the enchantment of Beauty, now all the more compelling because of past hunger, and more imperious as a revelation of Love. It involved reawakening faculties, deepening perceptions, vistas of Arcady.

He painted her half in profile at the open window, against an outer background of space and air, with a cloudlike shadowing of far-off mountains. The soft gradations of blue and gold, the lift of line, tilt of her face, all tended skyward, with the joy of a falcon on the point of flight. Skyward, not heavenward. The drollery of her smile, the impishness of the Negro page looking up at her, had no pious implications. Youth on the wing, summer at the threshold, freshness and gaiety, were the themes of every brush stroke.

In spite of teasing, he would not let her see the painting until he had finished.

"How do I know what you're making of me, Messere? I'll wager it's a fine daub, and I'm wasting my time. Fish eyes! Straw hair! Goat face! I know you amateurs. *Santa Maria!* I'll have your blood if you make a witch of me! Just one little peep."

"Have patience, Madonna."

"Or suppose you really know how to paint. No one can tell with a joker like you. No liberties, sir! I'll keep my clothes on, if you please.

I don't want to be Susanna or a nymph, remember that. You'll keep me chaste, by God, or you'll swing for it. Better let me look."

"What if you turn out a saint," he asked, "with a nice gold rim around the head?"

Her face fell. "Please don't, Messere. Still, if that's the sort it is, I want my aureole cocked and gay. You know I never wear my hats straight. I wish I wasn't a saint, though," she added wistfully.

At last, after a sitting, when she did not expect it, he enclosed the portrait in an improvised frame. "Now, Madonna. I tremble at the verdict."

"*You mean I can look?*"

"I throw myself upon the mercy of Your Ladyship."

She crossed the room in a flash and stood before the painting, her lips parted and eyes wide.

After a moment, she said in a hushed voice, "Do I look like that?"

"You are disappointed."

"Disappointed! Dear heaven!" She caught her breath. "It's the way I should long to look. But it's not me, I'm sure."

"As I see you always."

"Then, Messere . . ." She turned her face toward him. He read a new, wondering light in her eyes. "Then I believe you for the first time, Andrea. I believe you love me."

He stood silent, his heart too full for words.

"I've been so mistaken," she went on in the same low voice. "I thought you were only a courtier, a maker of compliments; only a lord of ambitions and schemes and dark plans. Forgive me, Andrea. You haven't painted me there, I know, but your own spirit. Now I believe in you."

Suddenly embarrassed, she looked back to the portrait, then added in a different tone, "*Ave, Maestro!* No one in Italy can paint like you. And you have kept your light under a bushel! Shame upon you!"

She took to examining the canvas, now close and now drawing back. All at once, she stopped.

"Your brushwork is like that in the painting you sold me — Mantegna's — and the management of the light. Exactly the same. That illusion of space. Curious. . . . Messere!" She turned sharply upon him. "Tell me the truth. Was it Mantegna who painted that picture?"

Andrea flushed. "What an idea!" he stumbled. "Does Your Lady-ship — "

"Tell me the truth, I say!"

He made a helpless movement of the hands. "Shall I return the ring?"

He was amazed that she suddenly flung her arms about him and then as suddenly stepped back, laughing.

"Rogue! Cheat! And I was just saying that I believe in you! But never mind. Don't you know that you're greater than Mantegna? Have you other paintings to sell? I'd rather have yours than his a hundred times. As for this one" — her eyes embraced the portrait — "thank you, *Maestro caro*, for immortality."

If the assembled artists of Italy had handed him a crown, he could not have felt more dizzy with pride than at that moment.

So a year passed. A year gained. Borgia had not come; perhaps he would never come. But this was still too much to hope. The meteor, if such it was, burned ever brighter and angrier over Italy. Andrea, on one pretext or another, strengthened the defenses of Città del Monte and prepared for the storm.

CHAPTER XLVI

THEN, at a given hour, on a day of early March, time ceased its pleasant meandering and quickened to the speed of a millrace.

On the noon of that day, crossing the market square with Varano and Camilla, who had been inspecting the new orphanage at the Convent of Santa Chiara, Orsini had every reason to suppose that the hour would range itself with all the other gentle hours which had preceded it over the face of the *piazza* sundial. A light spring shower had just washed the plump faces of the cobblestones and left them glistening. Shadows and walls showed a tint of green. The sun was warm enough to suggest the coolness of surrounding arcades; and, more delicious than anything else, a gay little breeze, scaling the town walls, brought a fragrant message from the fields and hills beyond.

"Ha!" exclaimed Camilla, inhaling it. "Ha, signori! It's spring again! It's spring!"

The throng in the square, trooping around their lord and lady, caught up her words in a laughing crescendo. *"Primavera! Viva la primavera!"*

To the delight of the crowd, Varano flourished his hat above his head in reply and gave Camilla a hug.

So, leisurely, with nods and smiles, stopping to chat with one citizen or another — for in the small town everybody was known — they strolled back to the palace courtyard, where Messer Gentile stood blinking in the doorway of his library. Camilla shooed back some pigeons, too lazy to make way for her, and acknowledged the bows of several court gentlemen, who had just dismounted. The guards at the main door grounded their pikes. It was all exactly as it had been for the past twelve months. On such a day, the mere fact of living was delightful. Andrea admired Camilla's jaunty little figure tripping up the state stairway in front of them.

She turned her head. "Winter in your bones, signori?"

On the landing, a page dropped to one knee before Varano. "The noble Captain, Don Esteban Ramirez, has but now arrived on the part of His Excellence the Duke of Romagna." (It was Cesare Borgia's latest title.) "He craves audience with Your Signory."

And the decisive hour had struck.

Don Esteban, whom Varano, in company with Camilla and Orsini, at once received in the official salon, was one of the Spanish mercenaries who formed the core of Borgia's military staff. They had a bad name for cruelty and greed; but, as foreigners, without other attachments in Italy, they were the Duke's most dependable tools. Afflicted moderately with the pox, Ramirez had a bleak, citron-colored face, stony black eyes with pouches under them, and sparse, short hair invaded by two bald peaks. A half-healed sore disfigured the corner of his mouth. Having entered Borgia's service within the last year, he was unknown to Orsini.

"I salute Your Excellences," he said in a guttural Spanish-Italian. His abrupt bow and too casual tone were perhaps rather the effects of ill-breeding than of intention, but they implied no respect. "These letters from the Duke's Majesty" — he produced a sealed paper — "explain themselves. They require an immediate answer."

Varano's rugged face stiffened, and he thrust forward his lower jaw. His good humor did not extend to malaperts. With a glance of distaste at the Spaniard's black-rimmed fingernails, he accepted the letter. Then, breaking the seal and with a curt "Be seated, sir," he set himself to read.

Meanwhile, Ramirez let his eyes wander over the richly gilded room. They had the speculative glint of an expert's intent on an inventory. They valued the supposed Mantegna at one end of the salon and the marble Hermes at the other, checked up on tapestries, furniture, and candelabra, then fastened on Camilla. Although she was looking anxiously at Varano, she seemed half-aware of the man's scrutiny and, flinching, gave her gown a little twitch, as if to preserve it from something unclean. A pulse swelled in Orsini's temple. His hot gaze caught the Spaniard's attention, so that for a moment they sat, trying to stare each other down. Then Ramirez looked away with a sneer.

Varano cleared his throat. "I take it you are more than a messenger, sir; that you know the import of this letter?"

Don Esteban nodded. "I act as the Duke's representative. He has given me leave to resolve any doubts Your Excellence may have as to his meaning."

Again, Varano cleared his throat. Andrea was struck by an odd blankness in the usually forceful eyes and by Varano's effort to keep it from showing. "What doubts? Nothing could be plainer." He stared down at the sheet in his hand.

Camilla leaned forward. "But tell us, then. What is it, my lord? Or is it secret?"

"No. It appears that His Holiness has but now launched a Bull against my kinsmen of Camerino, depriving them of the vicariate and their estates. The Duke plans shortly to enforce the Pope's will upon them by arms. I am required to afford passage to his troops, furnish supplies, and levy a thousand men for his service. He assumes that I shall welcome this occasion to show my zeal. . . . That's the gist of it, Madonna."

Orsini smiled grimly at the old, obvious game. Put pressure on a man to do the impossible and take his refusal as a pretext for attack. After all, a pretext had to be trumped up, especially in view of the fulsome assurances which had been given to Varano. Of course Borgia knew that the old man would never consent to make war against his kinsmen. Relations were not close between Città del Monte and Camerino, but they had long been ruled by the same House; the fall of one meant the fall of both. Cesare's letter was merely an indirect declaration of war. It told Andrea that time was up.

Camilla burst out, "But surely, husband — " and stopped short.

Varano folded the letter thoughtfully, then stuck it in his belt. "I'll take counsel on this. It concerns others than me. Meanwhile, Señor

Captain, I commend you to the lord Orsini. Messer Andrea, I beg you will see to the gentleman's comfort and that he has every attention. You'll rejoin us at your leisure." Giving Camilla his arm, Varano left the room.

After a moment, the Spaniard turned to Andrea. "I have another letter, addressed to you."

Orsini nodded. "Yes, I expected one."

Taking the missive, which the other half flicked at him, he walked over to the window. He knew that this was an ultimatum to him, and that he could no longer put off showing the Duke where he stood. As it was, his ruse had worked better than he could have expected in the beginning. He had hoodwinked Borgia for a year, and the defenses of Città del Monte were in as good shape as they could be. On the other hand, his main gamble had failed: Cesare's success continued unabated; his miraculous luck in every undertaking still held.

Glancing past the conventional opening of the letter, Andrea read:

> *Though well pleased with your reports that the Marches in general should give us little difficulty, I look in vain for certain definite news from Città del Monte. I should have received this news long since. By now you should be lord* de facto *of that city, with the lady Prefettessa as your mouthpiece. But I am fobbed off with delays and excuses. Now, mark well, I expect to learn of a certain death within two weeks. Failing that, I shall know what to think of you and shall act accordingly. Are you a softhearted fool, or do you plan to overreach me? Clear up this doubt (which begins to disturb me) by doing as I require; for, either as fool or fox, you will profit little. I have high hopes of Andrea Orsini in the future. You know what career I offer you. But I —*

Andrea gave a sudden start. The paper shook in his fingers.

> *But I have no place for Zoppo the peasant. To him I offer exposure and a gibbet. . . .*

Orsini looked up blankly, unconscious even of Don Esteban's scrutiny. Though the Spaniard did not know what the letter contained, he could tell that it made unpleasant reading. Andrea did not see him. He was stunned by this utterly unexpected, devastating blow. His secret, which the confusion of war had first made possible, and which his brilliant effrontery through the years had safeguarded until he believed it impenetrable, was now, and had probably long been, at Borgia's mercy. And what mercy that was! The mercy of Satan!

He read on:

So, be advised. Deserve my favor and send me the news I crave. I say, within two weeks. If not, you will learn from the noble Camilla Baglione herself what value she attaches to a name.

No acting that Andrea had ever done cost him so much as at that moment to steady himself, pocket the letter, and meet Ramirez's unrevealing eyes.

"And now, sir, allow me to escort you to your room and to assure your comfort, as my lord directed. All my regrets to have kept you waiting."

The Spaniard accompanied Orsini upstairs to the guest-room wing of the palace, though loitering now and then to appraise some work of art or costly marble.

"A marvelous rich house," he murmured. "Varano and that old Duke of Urbino skimmed the cream off of Italy. It's been poor pickings since. A marvelous rich house."

Andrea could see that the man's covetous soul burned for the looting of it. It was hard to remain even coldly polite.

When he had got rid of Don Esteban, Orsini returned to his own room. The embers of an early morning fire still glowed on the hearth, and, drawing out Borgia's letter, he burned it carefully to the last fragment. The yellow flames reminded him of the Duke's thoughts, the flickering that went on behind that serene brow.

He had a decision to make, and he must make it quickly. Not that the threat of exposure, appalling as it was, tempted him for a moment to knuckle under to Borgia and to betray his friends. That thought was now still more appalling. The decision turned on whether he should remain at Città del Monte and face the ignominy of being revealed as an impostor, or whether he should take to flight, sink into obscurity, and begin life over again on different terms. The thought of the Varani's scorn and disappointment seemed more than he could bear. Nothing would be gained by this crucifixion of his pride. When he had once been exposed as a charlatan, his career at Città del Monte would be over. He could at least save himself the shame of a face-to-face denunciation.

So absorbed he was that he failed to note the footstep of Mario Belli, who entered from the adjoining room; and he glanced around startled when the latter gave a discreet cough.

302

"Well," remarked Belli, "I gather that orders have come." He did not add that this took no mind-reading, since Ramirez had given him a separate letter from the Duke. "I can well conceive Your Lordship's reluctance to act on them."

"Reluctance!" Andrea echoed. He had drifted so far downstream in the last hour that it took almost an effort to recall that, in Belli's eyes, he was still the Duke's man enjoined to carry out Varano's murder. The time had come to enlighten his ensign. "Reluctance, indeed!" he muttered, seating himself on a bench at one side of the hearth.

Belli sat down opposite him. The Frenchman knew well enough what threat the Duke's letter to Andrea had contained, but, since the secret of his patron's birth no longer belonged to him, he had better keep his knowledge of it to himself.

"Your Magnificence," said Belli, "has come to the parting of the ways, a vexing position, I admit, but sometimes unavoidable. On one side" (it was perhaps not without satire that he pointed into the blackened mouth of the hearth) "you have everything: love, wealth, position, fame. *Vive dieu!* Greatness, what? I'm dazzled to think of it. You've sweated for this, how many years?" Belli waved slightingly toward the emptiness of the room. "On the other side, you have nothing, perhaps worse than nothing."

"Honor," smiled Andrea, "decency, a clear conscience. Eh?"

The other looked grieved. "Such words from Your Lordship! A year ago, you would not have been troubled by petty abstractions. I marvel at you. You're not the man to flinch from the last hurdle — a small one after all. Nor does it sort with my devotion to let you ruin yourself." The wheedling craft in the Frenchman's face suddenly changed to boldness. "Have done with this. You need action. I've studied the business in hand at every point with a view to Your Worship's convenience."

About to interrupt, Andrea held his tongue. It was perhaps just as well to learn what the bravo had in mind.

"The lord Varano must die," Belli was saying, "in a way to rouse no suspicion. Moreover, the first attempt must not fail; for, if he escaped one accident to die presently in another, you would have talk. I submit that gunpowder is always dangerous, and that his custom of inspecting the powder room in the castle with the master armorer incurs a risk. A small conduit, or maybe a fault in the masonry, leads from said room to an old rubble heap outside. I discovered it by watching a rat and by taking measurements. A powder cask rests against it. Nothing could be easier than to slip through a match of sufficient charge. The place outside is shut off from view. He makes his rounds on Wednesdays — that is tomorrow — close upon nones; and I should hear his voice through the conduit. Then all we need is a tinderbox. The wreckage of the tower will bury any trace of the match. Afterwards, who could say what happened?" Belli smiled complacently and rubbed his hands. "I ask only a nod. Well, then?"

Before Andrea could speak, a knock sounded at the door.

"Yes?" called Orsini.

A servant answered. "Your Lordship is wanted by His Excellence in council. The town fathers have been summoned."

"I'll talk with you later," Andrea told Belli.

CHAPTER XLVII

THE Magistrates and leading citizens, together with such of the landed gentry as had been within immediate reach, were gathering when Andrea entered the dining hall of the palace, which served equally for purposes of large assembly. Boards, trestles, and benches had been removed, and only the dais with its two high-backed chairs remained. Upon these Varano and Camilla seated themselves, while Orsini, as captain of the guard, stood at Varano's right. Slightly below and in front of them (clergy and judges in the center, tradesfolk and gentlemen on either side) gathered a throng as representative of the signory as if its members had been chosen by ballot. The urgency of the summons prevented ceremonial dress. Several of the townsfolk — among others, Ser Mattia of the butchers' guild; Ser Fabio, master of the paper works; Pier Francesco Pulci, spokesman for the vintners — had arrived straight from their shops with bare arms and sweat stains on their faces. Suspense, combined with respect for Varano, imposed a nervous hush in the hall. From outside could be heard the murmurs and trooping of people beyond the palace gates.

Orsini noticed that Varano gave no evidence of the first dismay he had shown upon reading Borgia's letter. Calm and paternal as always, he sat overlooking the throng, though there was less humor in his dark, heavy-lidded eyes than usual. Camilla, too slender for her big chair, with the Baglione arms carved on its back above her head, looked as high-spirited as a little sparrow hawk. Her piquant nose, her red, jeweled cap, at a pert angle, challenged the world. It was at such times that the hot Perugian blood showed in her every glance and movement.

When Varano could see that those summoned had arrived, he lifted his hand for attention. His voice echoed through the hall.

"Signori, it is because I love my people and because I believe that you are fitted to express its will that I have called you thus in haste. Tidings of grave import to our city have but now reached me from the Duke of Romagna, gonfalonier of the Holy Roman Church. They concern the future of you all even more than they do mine, since my life draws to an end. Hear, then, what the Duke desires of us."

He gave a dispassionate summary of Borgia's letter, repeating the separate clauses of it, so that they might be clearly understood. With regard to the levy against Camerino, a fierce murmur ran through the audience.

"Such are the Duke's demands," Varano went on. "If we do not meet them, it is clear that Città del Monte will fall under the same condemnation as Camerino. But even if we do meet them, it is equally clear that the days of this signory are numbered. For none but the blind will fail to perceive that the Marches, together with the Romagna, are now to be gathered into one state subject to the Duke. The end, however, in my opinion, is not there. By every indication, the other states of Central Italy — yes, even Tuscany — will, in time, be added to the Duke's domain. At least, so I read the purpose of this prince."

The intent faces of the gathering reflected sullen agreement with Varano's view and an equal hostility to the program he outlined. For a moment, Andrea forgot his own concerns in the thought that here was a miniature and a test case of world issues: change and conservatism, ends and means.

Varano continued on that level. "Sirs, it may surprise you that I heartily favor the Duke's objective. As there can be no peace among individual men where there is no law, so there can be no peace among states who are subject to no law. Treaties are futile; our holy religion itself fails to secure peace. The curse of Italy — it may be of the world — is that cities and states acknowledge no law superior to themselves. For only where law is, there is peace. Thus, that the states of Italy should be brought together under one rule is in itself desirable and worthy of support."

Orsini was not the only one who hung attentively on the words of the old lord, nor was he the only one who admitted their truth.

"I speak of peace," Varano added, "not power, and therein lies my quarrel with Duke Cesare. For, gentlemen, if our states unite not for the sake of peace but to provide a conqueror with the greater means of war, what profit have we? We change bad for worse. My point is this: I distrust *the man*."

A murmur of assent arose from the listeners. It echoed the opinion of the age on Cesare Borgia.

Varano tapped the letter with his finger. "This gives the measure of him. In Rome, he loaded me with courtesies and praise; now that the time is ripe, he shows his whip. The subtlety was stupid; he could have spoken out. I pay no heed to rumors and scandal concerning him. This is proof enough.

"It may be urged that if I favor the end he seeks, I should support him; that treachery and craft in a good cause are justified. Not so. If good at times springs out of evil, to God's almighty dispensation, not to evil, be the praise. He makes man's villainy to serve Him: that is His perquisite. But let no man believe that he serves God by villainy. The kiss of Judas brought Our Blessed Lord to the Cross and, thus, salvation to mankind, yet Judas hanged himself."

Within the motionless exterior of Andrea Orsini, who stood, eyes front, legs firm, both hands on the pommel of his sword of office, burned a flame of joy. He was thankful that a man like Varano existed to speak such words; and doubly thankful that, by the mercy of God, he, Andrea, had been spared from playing the Judas role which had once been planned. Half-consciously, too, inspired by Varano's personality, he was reaching a decision with regard to himself.

"Signori," the old lord was saying, "my course is plain. I do not think that the Duke will accomplish his final purpose; first, because he inspires no confidence, but hostility, among the Italian states, and to found a nation requires the faith and love of men; second, because his power depends upon the life of the aged Pope. It may be that God's inscrutable will decrees his success. In that case, so be it. But honor as well as duty forbids me to give aid or comfort to a man whom I consider false and perjured. Therefore, I shall refuse to take arms against my own House or assist the Duke in this *impresa*. However, your case is different; and for that reason I have called you together."

It was now obvious in what direction Varano's remarks were tending, and Orsini felt a redoubled interest. He scanned the upturned faces of the assembly, as the other continued.

"I have no desire and no right to condemn my city and people to the miseries of war against their will. Indeed, I recommend your submission to the Duke, because it seems more than doubtful that this signory could resist his determined attack. I have had my share of sieges and invasions, and I know the cost of them. Let it be admitted also to Duke Cesare's credit that he deals gently with those cities that offer him no resistance. For this reason, I advise that you suffer Madama Camilla and me to withdraw to Venice, there to await the outcome of events, and that you make submission to the Duke."

After a moment of dazed silence, the throng burst into a rumble of opposition. Varano lifted his hand.

"You have heard my advice. This is no trivial matter to be settled on the spur of feeling. I know that you love me. But you love your wives and children, your homes and fields. Think of them. I say, think well. For, if you resolve on defense against the Duke, there will be fire, rape, pillage and massacre, whatever the outcome." He stood up. "You have leave to debate without my presence. If you choose to resist, I shall lead you and do all in my power to make good the defense. You know me well enough, signori, to believe that I still enjoy the trumpets of war. But once again I counsel submission. In any case, I shall accept your choice. . . . Come, Madonna, and you, Captain Orsini. We shall leave these gentlemen to deliberate."

Ser Fabio, master of the paper works, spoke up. "One moment, my lord. To what extent can our city withstand attack? We are most of us unlearned in arms. If there is no chance of defense, it is madness to thrust our heads into the noose."

Varano turned to Andrea. "Let Captain Orsini answer that question."

Andrea could feel Camilla's eyes on him. He knew what answer she wanted, the answer that any man of her hot-tempered House would make if he had only a bodkin to defend himself with. But he decided on frankness.

"Sirs, all depends on what force the Duke would send against us. The enemy could be held off for a time in the mountain passes. Our walls are strong. But if the Duke should throw in his full weight, I doubt whether Città del Monte could do more than Faenza."

"I thank Your Worship," said the craftsman noncommittally.

Whereupon, Varano, Camilla, and Orsini retired to the anteroom beyond the hall and closed the door upon a tumult of voices.

"I hope. I hope. I hope," repeated Camilla, her foot tapping nervously on the stone flagging. "Messer Andrea, you should have spoken more roundly. I all but took the word away from you. I'd have put heart into them."

"No need of that, *piccolina*," Varano returned. "It's not heart they lack. As for Captain Orsini, he spoke no less than the truth. It must be a tight pinch for you, sir."

"How so, my lord?"

"To take sides against your former patron. But don't be concerned. If the people elect for war, you are free to leave at once. I would not constrain you in any way."

Andrea shook his head. "The affection I bear Your Signory constrains me more than my commission. If my earlier service of the Duke renders me suspect here, that is another matter."

Varano clapped his big hand on Orsini's shoulder. "Suspect! Rubbish! Haven't I earned my hire on different sides in the old days without discredit? You ought to know that I don't deal in suspicions, Messere. If I ceased to consider you my friend, I should not keep you as my officer. Be assured of it."

It was hard waiting in the antechamber. Varano might urge submission, but Andrea could see that the old soldier's heart bled at the thought of tame exile in Venice, and that he secretly hoped his offer would not be accepted. He wandered here and there, and kept glancing at the closed door of the hall. Camilla stood in front of the hearth, her eyes also on the door. Equally impatient, Orsini fingered his sword, slipping it up and down in its scabbard. If Varano and Camilla went into exile, he would be able to withdraw at the same time. The Duke's exposé of him, when, or if, it came, would not find him with them and would lose much of its sting.

Minutes dragged by, perhaps fifteen of them, though the time seemed thrice as long. Then the door opened.

"May it please Your Signories," said Julio Rosselli, one of the town judges, "we have reached a decision. It was not difficult."

"And what — " Varano began but checked himself. Curiosity, however sharp, must wait on dignity. Giving his arm to Camilla, he entered the hall. They resumed their seats. Orsini again took his place beside them on the dais.

From the faces of the gathering, Andrea found it impossible to guess what the decision had been. The various expressions might mean anything. He tingled with suspense as Rosselli came forward to address Varano.

"Your Excellence," said the spokesman in a measured voice, "has deigned to take counsel with us touching the course to be followed in respect to certain demands by the Duke of Romagna. This was by no means required of Your Lordship, but it is one more instance of the fatherly love and care that has long sheltered us. In the name of all, I tender Your Signory our humble thanks."

"*Santa Maria!*" thought Andrea. "Get on with it!"

"We have duly considered the alternatives expressed by Your Signory, and we can find no words adequate to our gratitude that Your Lordship will embrace exile itself rather than subject this people to hardship and suffering."

Orsini's hope brightened; but a muscle stood out along Varano's jaw, and Camilla bit her lips.

"The people of Faenza," Rosselli continued, "paid a bitter price for their loyalty; the people of Capua suffered no less than the holy martyrs themselves. They upheld their honor. But is honor worth that cost?"

The speaker paused. The answer was so obviously no.

"We of the Mountain City," declared Rosselli, "maintain that it is."

A shout went up in the hall. Varano half rose to his feet, but controlling himself sank back again with shining eyes. Camilla brought her clenched hand down on the arm of her chair. "*Bravo, signori!*"

"Shall it be said in aftertime," Rosselli continued, "that, while others defied the power of Borgia and stood true to their allegiance, we meekly fixed his collar on our necks? No! Cry *Viva Monte! Viva Varano!* Cry *Viva Madonna Camilla . . .*"

A roar submerged the rest of the speech. Varano, standing on the edge of the dais, extended both arms in a general embrace. It was for him the greatest personal triumph of his long life; it was the highest tribute that could be offered to a ruler by his people. Faced by destruction, free to avoid it, Città del Monte chose rather to perish with its lord than to survive without him. Nor was it a tribute that he could decline without affronting its heroism. There were tears on Varano's cheeks as he stood there, tears on other faces.

Caught up in the surge of enthusiasm, Andrea forgot himself, or rather he rededicated himself. Loyalty, loyalty on every side of him, generous folly, reckless devotion, the freedom of self-giving. This was the great hour of the little state. He would not forfeit his share in it for fear of any disclosure that the Duke might make of him. He would not sneak away to save his pride. Let him be exposed; he would still beg to serve, however humbly.

As they left the hall, Camilla read a new expression in his face. They were alone for a moment.

"Andrea, how shall I forgive myself?"

"For what, Madonna?"

She stood facing him, her eyes and lips more lovely than he had ever seen them.

"For being afraid of you, as I told you once. I thought you were too clever to be loyal. Now, in our need, you stand by a desperate cause. My lord husband is old, and our defense will depend on you. But what return can we make except our love?"

"What good thing in earth or heaven do I want," he answered, "except your love and my lord's?"

"Here," she said, plucking off her crimson velvet cap, "here is my favor, Andrea. Will you wear it for me on your helmet?"

But she was gone before he could find his tongue. He stood holding the velvet in his hand. It was still warm from the touch of her hair.

Belli sat gnawing the side of his thumb when Andrea entered the room. Hunched on the settle beside the hearth, he resembled a giant spider transformed into a man, as he got to his feet.

"*Eh bien,* now that the cheering is over, I can have Your Lordship's decision on the plan I suggested. I take it the town defies Duke Cesare. But a keg of gunpowder will change that. . . . So then?"

"Listen, Mario." Andrea seated himself in an armchair and stretched out his legs. "It's time I explained matters. I left Duke Cesare's service — let's see — " he thought of that November evening in the Palace of San Clemente and added — "a year and a quarter ago."

"*Left his service?*" Belli exploded.

"Secretly, my friend. Unknown to him, look you — but quite definitely. Since that time, I have devoted myself in all ways to the interests of my lord Varano."

"Is Your Worship mad?"

"Possibly."

"But why? What reason on God's earth — "

"Explaining takes long. No doubt, you wouldn't believe me if I put it on the grounds of conscience. So I'll say this. To my thinking, our fine Duke's bubble has all but reached its span, and those who see their future in it will have smarting eyes. However, to be honest, that's not the prevailing reason."

"No," returned Belli, "you're moonstruck. Granted that Borgia rides to a fall, you'd still be further along afterwards than swinging on a gibbet here. Talk sense. You're not so mad that you believe this town can withstand the Duke?"

"Longer than he thinks, Mario, but not too long. I admit that."

"And afterwards?"

Orsini shrugged.

The other stood before him, fists on hips. "Do you mean that you're throwing away fortune, success, your life itself, for the sake of nothing, moonshine sentiments that no enlightened man takes seriously?"

"Not moonshine to me. Are you enlightened, Mario? What side will you be on?"

Belli stared, without answering. Then he muttered: "*Tiens, voilà le comble!* You had me completely fooled. I ought to have seen through the trick of those new defenses. All for the Duke's future service and advantage! A neat trick! . . . Is there nothing I can say will bring you to your senses?"

"Nothing."

"*Tiens, tiens,*" Belli repeated. He took a couple of turns through the room. As far as his grim face showed anything, it expressed wonder and an odd excitement. Then, stopping in front of Andrea, he made a formal bow. "Your Magnificence will recall the terms of our agreement, that I could withdraw from your service with due warning. I now feel obliged to take leave. I shall ride south with Don Esteban Ramirez tomorrow."

"To Borgia?"

"Yes."

If anything had been needed to drive home to Orsini the perils ahead of him, it was Belli's desertion.

"You do well," he said — "at least from your standpoint. In any case, I should not long be able to employ you. As it is, I remain in your debt for service I could never repay."

"*De rien.*" Belli gave an ironical wave of the hand. "So, for the moment, I bid Your Magnificence good day, while I look to my saddle-bags. I repeat, good day, *Your Magnificence.*"

It was always hard to interpret Belli's tone of voice. The repeated title had a queer emphasis, as if he intended a jibe or perhaps (but that was impossible) a compliment.

CHAPTER XLVIII

NEXT day Don Esteban Ramirez, having received Varano's letters to Duke Cesare, of which he could not help knowing the uncompromising contents, took sardonic leave and, accompanied by Mario Belli, faded into the distance toward Fabriano. Chancing to walk out on the parapet of the palace, facing west, Camilla and Orsini were for a time aware of them as moving dots along the highroad.

"There goes a man," observed Camilla of the Spaniard, "who gives me the gooseflesh. You know, I think he's somehow tangled in my life, like a bat that flies into a room, and can't be got rid of." She gave a little shiver and made horns with her fingers, as if to avert the evil eye. "Have you ever had that feeling about a person?"

"Yes," said Andrea, "about Mario Belli, since we first met. I don't believe I've seen the last of him. People, not ghosts, haunt our lives, Madonna."

By this time, the dots had become pin points on the road.

Camilla drew a deep breath. "The air seems lighter without those two ravens. Why do you grieve for Messer Mario?"

Andrea shook his head. "I suppose as one grieves for a bad habit."

"He's a strange man," Camilla pondered. "Sometimes I shudder at him, and again I almost love him. You know, I found little Alda in tears this morning because he was leaving. She had a dream last night. Something about her and Belli in a dark vault. But they could look up through an opening. Then that, too, was closed. She kept saying, 'He can never see the stars again.' I had much ado to comfort her. Poor little poppet!"

The road to Fabriano was vacant, except for a faint twinkle that might have been the reflection of a sun ray on Belli's cuirass. They gazed out at the pale green slopes of the valley, crowned by distant summits, and at the silver shimmer of olive groves. The tiny bell notes of a lark, circling above them, floated down.

The serenity of peace suggested its opposite. "How long," Camilla wondered, expressing the question that henceforth would absorb the thoughts of everyone in the valley, "how long do you think it will be before the Duke comes?"

"He will write first," Andrea returned grimly. "He will see what the

312

pen can do before he takes the sword." Orsini did not add that he already knew what Borgia's letter would contain in regard to him, and that he dreaded the thought of it. He had about ten days of his nobility left. It was hard to look beyond them.

"He'll waste his ink, then," said Camilla. "But when do you reckon he will march?"

"I should say in May or June. It's not easy to attempt the mountains before."

Her eyes rested again lovingly on the quiet fields, dotted here and there with oxen at the plow, on the far-off girdle of woodland.

"So little time, Andrea, such precious time, before all this is changed."

Precious indeed, he thought, and for him so little that it was numbered almost in hours.

He turned to her with the broad smile that she found so engaging. "Why, then, it's a brave day for a ride, Madama. I have to survey the road from Fabriano through the woods to see how an enemy might best be checked in that direction. Do you not feel inclined to favor me with your company for the outing? Say yes!"

"Yes. And I'll try my new jennet. He looks as promising a horse as any I've mounted. We'll meet in the courtyard."

While he waited for her with the couple of pages who would accompany them, Andrea thought whimsically about their odd relationship. In eighteen months his love for Camilla had passed only from April into May; it still retained its first springtime freshness. The straw fires of earlier conquests seemed dull by comparison. But how did she really feel toward him? It was the despair and peculiar charm of his position that he could not tell.

She soon appeared in a habit of hunting green, that accorded with the appointments of the spirited white hackney which one of the pages had been leading up and down. The horse was a recent acquisition from the famous stables of Mantua. Drawing on her gloves, Camilla inspected him with approval.

"I think the lord Marquis did well by us, Messere, don't you?"

"Most excellently well," Andrea assented. "I've never seen a finer gelding. He has every mark of speed, blood and bottom. What's his name?"

"Narciso," said Camilla. "Look how he arches his neck as if he were in front of a mirror."

"Instead of admiring Your Signory. An appropriate name, by Bacchus!"

She gathered up her skirts to mount. "Look you, Gian Maria," she said to one of the pages, "let the Magnifico be your model if you would thrive with the ladies. He never misses an occasion."

"And never hits the clout," Orsini added. "He thrives on cruelty. *Despero sed spero* is his device."

He stooped with his hand upturned for Camilla's foot. She rose effortlessly to the saddle. Narciso almost lifted the page from his feet as he reared.

"So-la, *amico!*" she laughed, gathering the reins.

Orsini mounted his barb, and the pages their hackneys. The little party rode out from the palace yard, rounded the inner front of the adjoining castle, plunged into the darkness of the city portal, and so out again, with the sweep of the valley in front of them.

"Breathe him," Andrea advised, as Camilla's horse fretted and shied against the curb. "Race you a mile for a ducat."

"The stake's too small."

"Well, then, if I lose, Madonna, make it a thousand against a kiss."

"Messer Confidence! I'll have your money."

She was off, like an arrow; but her smaller horse, swift as he was, could not outrun Andrea's barb. To keep the race even, Andrea secretly held back and let her ride abreast of him. Meanwhile, he enjoyed the picture she made: cheeks flushed, eyes intent, the green of her habit set off against the white of the horse or repeated in the medallions of his headstall and wide curb rein — a harmony of color. The bells on the bridle tinkled in rhythm. Her hair fanned back on either side of the peaked hunting hat.

Glancing sidewards at one point, she tossed her head. "Poor Messere! A thousand ducats! I won't let you off — not a quattrino. Ride, sir! Ride! I'm gaining on you."

"You haven't won yet, Donna Milla."

"*Badate!* I shall."

But, not far from the next milestone, he drew ahead and reached it in time to wheel, facing her as she came up.

"Traitor!" she protested. "*Briccone!* You weren't half trying! You led me on!"

"I claim the wager."

"I defy you!"

"Traitor yourself, Madonna."

"Woe's me! Draw close then. But I hate you." Her lips brushed his cheek. "Paid in full." A wave of color deepened the flush caused by the race, and she glanced away. Through the dust cloud left behind them on the road, they could hear the gallop of the pages' slower horses. Suddenly she smiled. "You're a sad rogue, Messere, as I've often told you."

Soon afterwards, they were in the pine-scented coolness of the woods.

From his saddle pouch, Andrea drew out a rough map of the terrain, which he had prepared earlier, and set about studying the vantage points on either side of the road; marking now one and now the other, with approximate distances between them. As Belli had observed on their first ride into the valley, it was a notable place for ambushes. The rocky knolls, the deep thickets, the winding character of the road, gave every advantage to defenders against a force attempting to advance from Fabriano. But it was slow work reconnoitering uphill, over rocks and through undergrowth, sometimes on horseback but usually afoot. They had also to guard against animals of the woods. Once they started a bear, and several times they made a detour to avoid herds of wild boar.

Camilla insisted on taking part in the whole survey. She listened absorbed to Andrea's strategy of defense, a series of strong points, each supplementing the next. They studied the map together, cheek to cheek.

"But, look you here," she objected, "they'll send out skirmishers to draw fire. They'll pick you off your ambushes one by one, as I see it."

"They'll draw fire well enough," he explained, "but not from the main points. We'll leave false ambushes to cloak the real ones. In that way, their scouts will report to our advantage. For, if the captains strike where the skirmishers noted resistance, the attack will fall on nothing, and they will be caught from flank or rear. Then, mark you, if they shift, they fall into another trap."

"*Per Dio!*" she admired. "You're an artist in everything."

"Everything has its art," he answered. "But the chief point in the art of war is trained troops. There's our weakness. Our strategy's sound enough, but Borgia can break these defenses, do what we may. Our chief concern is to do all that's possible."

They lunched on bread, cheese, and wine in a small glen beside a brook. Andrea wondered why the smudge on Camilla's nose and the broad scratch on one hand were so becoming. It was an interesting problem.

She asked suddenly: "Why don't you ever talk about the past, about your lord father and the signora, your mother? About when you were a boy in Naples? I'd love to hear. You've been everywhere and done so many things; but all you seem to care for is the present. Why?"

He put her off. "How can I help myself when I'm with you?"

She shrugged at the compliment. "Please tell me."

"Why, there's not much to tell." But he told her a great deal. Fiction was another of his arts. He brought the Mediterranean, which Camilla had never seen, before her: its haunted promontories; the lone profiles of its cypresses; the wanton luxuriance of its gardens; its golden haze of retrospect. He described the tournaments and pageantry of his imagined youth at the court of King Ferrante before the barbarous French invasion. He wove her an evanescent tapestry of words evoking the glamour of southern nights, the call of music across water, fragrance of orange groves, the indolent breathing of the sea. As he talked, the little glen became a balcony at Sorrento.

He outdid himself to make the story magnificent. If his borrowed trappings were so soon to be stripped off, he would make the utmost of them in the few days remaining. And like an inspired actor, who forgets reality in the gusto of his role, Andrea became a part of his own inventions.

"There you have it, Madonna — a dream, as I look back."

She laid her hand a moment on his. "What beauty! No wonder you're a great artist. What teachers in courtliness! No wonder you're an accomplished cavalier."

At that moment, he could not shut out the recollection of Braccioforte Zoppo at the anvil and of himself, half-naked, handling the tongs, and of the dung-heap outside the door.

"But being what you are, with such a past and such gifts, you risk your life for us."

"For you."

She stood up, leaving the implied question unanswered. When the survey was ended, they rode back together in the glory of the sunset. And, out of his small store, that day had been spent.

So the next day passed, and the next. The town began feverishly to make ready for defense. Recruits had to be mustered, equipment prepared, the walls inspected. Time melted away, and Orsini's pretended lordship was melting with it.

Another day and another to round out the week. Ten days now. Would there be another? Perhaps by some good chance —

Then Captain Don Esteban Ramirez arrived with the letter from Duke Cesare.

CHAPTER XLIX

This time the Spaniard was received not in the festal salon but in Varano's grim little cabinet, that Orsini remembered from his first visit to Città del Monte a year and a half ago. On that spot beside the chair, Camilla's telltale scarf had fallen. He could still see Varano cracking nuts, as he talked in front of the fire. Now, as then, the room's bare walls and scant furnishings reminded him of a place of judgment.

Camilla, who, as Varano's designated successor, had been increasingly called into conference on important matters during the past months, stood with her husband before the empty hearth. She gave Orsini a half-smile as he entered, and remarked, "You see, the bat returns."

He replied something, but his mind was in a tumult. She could not have helped being struck by his expression had not Varano put in, "What do you mean by that, Madonna?"

"My name for the Spanish hidalgo, husband."

"And a right proper one, by the Mass," he grunted. "We'll set him flitting back to Rome within the hour. He'll not nest here again for a night. . . . Let him be summoned."

The Spaniard stalked into the room and made an ironic bow to Varano.

"Your Excellency sees me again."

"As we were just observing," returned the other dryly. "A profound truth, Captain."

Ramirez's beady eyes were on Andrea, as he held the Duke's letter out to Varano. The leering knowledge they revealed was unmistakable; and he so enjoyed his triumph that he failed to resent the old lord's sarcasm. His demeanor struck even Varano, who drew back, leaving the letter extended in mid-air, until Ramirez, becoming conscious of it, gave him his attention again.

"How now, sir!" Varano rapped out. "Let me tell you that among civilized people it is considered proper to look at a gentleman when you are handing him a letter."

The Spaniard's face tensed, and his mouth hardened. "I beg pardon," he bristled. "For a moment I was thinking of something else. A fault, I confess. . . . But let me tell you, sir, that a cavalier of Spain

317

feels no need of being taught the customs of civilized people by any Italian, high or low."

An ominous pause followed. It occurred to Andrea that he had never seen Varano thoroughly angry before. The phenomenon was as startling as the sudden crouch and roar of a lion.

"I'll not bandy words with you, my cockerel. I admit that no one could teach you manners. But I can teach you humility. Mark you, now! One more glance from you that mislikes me, and I'll have you down beneath the castle to a place where meekness is taught gratis. Do you give yourself airs here as the Duke's messenger? Do you think that impresses me? Dispatch your business and be gone. But carefully, carefully."

He dropped into a hot, alert silence. Daunted, the Castilian held out the letter again.

Varano took it and turned away. Doubtless, at that moment, Don Esteban was absorbed in one passionate prayer. If the future would only grant it, he could die content.

But Andrea gave no thought to Ramirez. His eyes hung on Varano's face, as the old lord scanned the letter. At one point, the exclamation, "*Per Dio*, what's this?" denoted that he had reached the fatal point. And just as Orsini had expected, he saw amazement, scorn, indignation, and anger succeed each other in Varano's expression.

"Ha! By the saints!" muttered the latter, handing the sheet to Camilla. "Read this, Madonna."

And again Andrea had the torment of watching her face reveal the same anger and contempt. When she had finished she returned the letter to her husband in a cold silence.

Then, without a glance at Orsini, Varano addressed Don Esteban. "Hark you, there. Since you're Duke Cesare's representative, you can take him my verbal answer. He wants war. I expected it and I accept it. Let him win this signory if he can. He will find us ready. As for the part of his letter which relates to the captain of my guard, Messer Andrea Orsini, tell him this."

He stood for a moment, frowning, while Andrea braced himself.

"Tell him," boiled Varano, "that, in all my life, I have never seen more transparent knavery; that if I needed any further testimonial to the merits of the lord Orsini, this would furnish it. *A la fè di Dio*, it's well said that hunger drives the wolf out of the woods! Knowing our reliance upon this lord, as an approved captain of war, the Duke can think of no better way to weaken our defense than a trumpery story about him. He was no masquerading peasant when he served the Houses of Borgia and Este: *that* comes now." Varano turned to Andrea. "You'll laugh when you read this, Messere. . . . As for the Duke," he continued to Ramirez, "I learn this much from his rigmarole. If I had no doubt of Captain Orsini's loyalty before, I am certain of it now. Though I had formed my own judgment of his worth, I am glad to find that Cesare Borgia values him so highly as to vent jealousy and spite upon him. There's a sincere tribute at least."

At the moment, Andrea, half-dazed, could not adjust himself to what he heard. Expecting damnation, he was loaded with honor. His shrewdness, as well as the Duke's, had failed to foresee this fantastic turn, that when the denunciation was made, it might not be believed. He glanced half-fearfully at Camilla to see whether she shared Varano's conviction, and the glow on her face reassured him. The whole thing was a miracle.

But if Orsini struggled with amazement, Don Esteban looked stunned. That the infallible Duke, after playing the trump which he had so carefully held in reserve, should lose the trick seemed incredible.

"Do you mean, sir," Ramirez faltered — "does Your Excellence mean that you don't believe the statements of His Illustrious Highness?"

"Sir, I have been endeavoring to convey that idea. I rejoice that it begins to penetrate. If Duke Cesare wishes his statements to be credited, he should tune them to probability. *Santa Maria!* A peasant who leads the fashion at Rome and Ferrara! A peasant who shines in all the arts! A peasant who distinguishes himself as a captain of *condottas!* A peasant who defeats the great Bayard in single combat! If so, God send us a few more such peasants — "

"But, sir," groaned the Spaniard, "I beg you to reread my lord's letter. You will find there the names of the fellow's parents, the date of his birth, the pigsty he was born in — "

"*Silenzio!* I could dish you up a pedigree in five minutes to prove you're the son of a swineherd in Estremadura and with a good deal more likelihood — "

"Señor! The Casa Ramirez is as ancient as Varano."

"And the Casa Orsini is more ancient than either."

"But, my lord — "

"*Silenzio!* We've had enough of this. Tell the Duke, in short, that I reject his libels upon Captain Orsini. Let him publish them through Italy, if he pleases. But, in this signory, I shall hang any man who dares even so much as whisper them."

"And tell him from me," Camilla put in, "that his own birth does not permit him to challenge the birth of others. I consider it less noble than the lord Orsini's, and I defy him to prove the contrary."

She smiled warmly at Andrea. But on his side, it was not pleasant to reflect that he was allowing his friends to champion a lie, and that his enemy spoke the truth. And it was vastly worse to imagine the day when the bubble would be pricked, for he knew that he was enjoying a reprieve only at double cost later on. Or was he? A good deal could happen in war — death, for one thing. He must take his chance in that lottery. Meanwhile the Day of Judgment had been once more postponed.

Accepting defeat, Don Esteban took pains to keep his yellow countenance inscrutable. It consoled him to think of Borgia's rage and of the vengeance that would be exacted.

"I have carefully noted the words of Your Illustrious Signories," he said, "and I shall convey them to my lord's Grandeur. I shall give him also," he added, with a bow of mock respect to Camilla, "Your Ladyship's defiance. At some time, he may wish to supply the proof which Your Excellence desires. . . . And so, unless there is more that should be brought to His Grace's attention, I beg permission to take my leave."

"There's one thing more," said Varano. "After all, his letter deserves some tangible reply. Take him this."

Plucking out one of a pair of gauntlets, stuck in his belt, Varano tossed it to the Spaniard's feet.

Picking it up, Don Esteban pronounced: "I take up Your Excellence's gage in the name of my master, Cesare Borgia, Duke of Valentinois and Romagna, Prince of Andria and Venafro, lord of Piombino, who will use such measures in defense of his right as may seem good to him."

Then, with a bow no lower than his own safety required, Ramirez withdrew, his footsteps echoing down the corridor. The realization of the dragon's teeth which had been sown imposed a brief silence.

"And now," said Varano. "May God shield our just cause!"

CHAPTER L

TOWARD the middle of June, through the Porta del Popolo at Rome, the booming and rattle of drums, the continuing flourish of trumpets, beat time to the march of Duke Cesare's army heading north along the Via Flaminia. For the roads were dry, the snow on the Apennines had melted, the mountain torrents had shrunk, and cloudless skies announced the opening of the year's best season for war. The man hunt, that most enticing and venerable of sports, was on.

Here they came, in veteran, well-ordered ranks, splaying out a little when they had passed the arch of the gate tower, the Spanish mercenaries, the Miguels, Pedros, and Diegos, of Castile and Aragon. Bearded and swarthy, they made a fine show in red and yellow, the colors of the Duke. Their battered steel caps, the bucklers on their shoulders, caught the rays of the early sun. Their short swords swung in rhythm. Ranks of crossbowmen mingled with those of the plainer foot soldiers. For all of them, hungry winter was past. Before them lay infinite chances of loot to fill purses that dice and women had emptied. Ah, the brave day! The heartening thump of the drums!

And here came the flower and pride of the army, the mounted men-at-arms, a dazzling flow of horses and colors, lances and pennons, a rollicking of trumpets and rattle of hoofs. There was the banner of Duke Cesare with the Borgian Bull, and the banner, silver and red, of Francesco Orsini, the young Duke of Gravina, commanding the cavalry; and there, the ominous banner of Oliverotto da Fermo, bloodiest of *condottieri*. The gentlemen rode in velvets and cloth of gold, for it was not yet time to put on armor. Like the Spanish adventurers, though on a bigger scale, they too could look forward to plunder and ransoms. And they had honor to gain, besides, and the pleasant excitement of travel. Therefore, let the trumpets crow, like so many brazen chanticleers. Good hunting lay ahead.

And here came light cavalry with the mounted fusileers among them; and then the pikemen of Romagna, a couple of thousand strong, skirmishers and light infantry. And here lumbered the nutcrackers of war, the siege guns on their creaking wagons, eighteen horses to a gun. These were the tools that breached the walls of defiant cities and let in the attack. And now followed endless supplies: kegs of gunpowder worth three thousand ducats; stone cannon balls by the cartload; pack mules with the armor of the cavalry; oxen to be slaughtered; wine for the gentlemen; a hodgepodge of personal effects; a tattered rabble of servants and camp followers.

Soon, from Ponte Molle to Prima Porta rolled a column of dust alive with ghostly forms of men and horses, a long-drawn rumble dominated by the pulse beat of the drums.

But Duke Cesare did not ride with his troops. There were secret councils at the Vatican, last-minute decisions. Then, spurring hard with a few of his staff, he rejoined the army at Spoleto, and, halting a couple of days for further council, sent on the main body to Foligno at the junction of the Via Flaminia and the path (for it could hardly be called a road) across the mountains to Camerino.

It was overlooking this junction point that vedettes from Città del Monte anxiously observed the numbers and watched for the next movement of the enemy. If Cesare's forces turned to the right, it meant that Camerino was their first objective; if they pressed on north toward Gualdo, it denoted that they were aiming at Città del Monte. Or perhaps there would be a division of strength at this point, and a simultaneous attack would be launched against both places. Through the short summer night, on an adjoining hilltop, the vedettes, too tense to sleep, watched the campfires at Foligno. Then, shortly after dawn, they could see the bulk of the troops continue north along the Flaminian Road.

So that evening, the nineteenth of June, two spent horsemen reached Città del Monte with the tidings that by now the enemy's vanguard must be close to Fabriano, and that tomorrow or next day the first blow could be expected.

"Let it fall," said Varano. "Thanks to you, my son" — he glanced at Andrea — "we've kept our word with the Duke. He'll find us ready."

For, if Cesare Borgia had been active in preparations during the past three months, Città del Monte had not been idle during the past twelve. As far as the signory's scant means of defense were concerned, they had all been mobilized. This entailed the purchase of supplies from neutral but benevolent Urbino, the strengthening of the town's defenses, the establishment of scattered strong points for a delaying action between the frontiers and the town, the storing of food, the enlistment and training of recruits. Unlike the sister community of Camerino, divided in itself and more than half resentful of its ruling family, the Mountain City, rallying about its lord, bristled at every point.

Nor was diplomacy overlooked. An agreement had been reached with Duke Guidobaldo of Urbino, guaranteeing protection to those of Città del Monte who might seek refuge within his state: an inestimable comfort, if all else failed. Even once-friendly Ferrara had been approached; but although Andrea Orsini was careful to keep his name out of these negotiations, the request for supplies and eventually for asylum met a cool reception. The Estes were now under Borgia's thumb. Andrea had served the latter too well. Besides, the hatred of Madonna Angela, who was in Ferrara with her cousin Lucrezia, and Cardinal Ippolito's personal enmity made itself felt in the terms of refusal.

Still, all in all, what with the sympathy of Urbino and the military measures that had been taken, the little signory was as well prepared to resist attack as its resources permitted. And for this, Varano had exaggerated nothing in thanking Captain Orsini.

"By the Mass, *figliolo*," he said once, "if you, with your energy and parts, had a Pope and a King of France to back you, I vow you would accomplish more in the end than Cesare Borgia, for all his hubbub, is like to do. But history, in the main, is a dull record of second-rate men, who have been given luck and means denied to their betters."

Without question, these three months had been the happiest of Andrea's life. By his own merits, he had won a place in the signory second only to Varano himself. Recruiting and drilling the new levies, directing the work on the fortifications, lending a hand to it himself, exhorting, encouraging, advising, he was familiar to every man, woman, and child of the *contrada*. More and more often his name was coupled with Varano's in the shouts of the people, when he appeared with the old lord on public occasions. He discovered that life in an odd fashion does not permit a man to give something for nothing, but insists on repaying him unexpectedly and often richly. In the past, absorbed by his personal schemes, Andrea had had little experience of that unforeseen harvest.

Something of all this crossed his mind now at the eleventh hour, when the scouts, having given their report and received praise for their zeal, withdrew, leaving Varano, Camilla, and him alone. They had been enjoying the cool of the evening under the arcades that flanked one side of the palace garden; and for a time, after the two men had gone, no one spoke. The plash of the central fountain, the sleepy notes of doves settling to rest, the rustle of leaves stirred by a faint air from the hills, had all the serenity and sadness of farewell. Each of them knew that the past was ending tonight, and that, where war has swept, nothing is ever again the same.

At last Andrea, harking back to Varano's confident statement that the town was ready, muttered, "Yes, ready in everything but the main point, my lord, if those lads counted right."

Varano nodded, but shot him a warning glance, indicating Camilla. No use to bring up again the insoluble problem: how with fifty lances and eight hundred men, most of them green as salad, to resist Borgia's veterans outnumbering them five to one? That had been the crux from the beginning. Even the few ruffian mercenaries left unemployed by Borgia's agents and by the Franco-Spanish war then raging in Naples had refused to hire themselves out in so forlorn a cause. And, in view of their quality, Andrea had been glad of it. But the fact remained that peasants, ignorant of war, were no match for five times their number of trained troops, even if they fought on the defensive.

Camilla, catching her husband's signal to Andrea, laughed. "Will you cavaliers never remember that I was brought up in Perugia, where brawls, sieges, and forays are the bread of life? But suppose we haven't the numbers. I've heard my lord father say that one man fighting for his home is worth three men fighting for gold. I've never seen more promising lads than ours. They'll give a good account of themselves."

"They will that," Andrea agreed. But he remembered how often in war he had seen enthusiasm and courage broken by the wedge of disciplined experience. He had seen it at Forlì. It had happened last year at Faenza. . . . He stood up. "By your leave," he added to Varano, "I'll ride toward Fabriano and alert our outposts. It may be, too, that I can pick up news."

"*Or sia con Dio*," sighed the other. "I ought to ride with you, but it's better to coddle my strength against later."

"And farewell to that song from Naples you were going to give us," Camilla protested, with a glance at the lute tilted against a column of the arcade. "But go your ways, Andrea. The song must wait on war."

"No great loss for this time," he answered, refusing to leave on a serious note. "But war itself can wait a moment." He noticed the pale slip of the new moon, edging above the garden cedars. "Close your eyes, Madonna, and stand up."

"*Che cosa?*"

"Please! . . . There you are. Now look over your shoulder but don't speak."

For a long pause, she gazed up at the moon.

"Thanks, Messere. Do you believe in such wishes?"

"They're infallible, Donna Milla."

"God grant it!"

He raised her fingers to his lips, then bowed to Varano. "I'll report to Your Excellence on my return."

It was pleasant riding along the valley in the twilight. His mission, though necessary enough, did not chiefly preoccupy him. It served rather as a relief from the nervous suspense of waiting and furnished the occasion for one last glimpse of the valley at peace. He let his thoughts wander. What had Camilla wished for? Victory, of course. Alas, poor wish! But how strange were the processes that governed life! Take himself, for instance. A year ago, who could have imagined that he would discard his career, knowingly commit himself to destruction! For what? Vague imponderables impossible to express. Clearly men were ruled by the stars. And yet he could trace each step by decisions of his own. Was he then his own master, only more than a little mad? Or was there something else, other than the stars, more mysterious? If so, why then, anything — even victory — was possible.

The moon shone brighter now. Here was the milestone of his and Camilla's race three months ago. The sour-sweet smell of a farmhouse reached him as he passed. It was there that he and Camilla had once stopped for water when they were out hawking. The brown-armed woman who served them had reminded him of his mother. A curious longing for home suddenly beset him. Home!

He had entered the forest before he realized it; and from there on, dismounted for the most part, he occupied himself with the concealed outposts, who had been stationed to defend the road through the woods from Fabriano. Since news of the Borgian advance had reached them, he found them alert enough, indeed, too alert for his own safety. With crossbows cocked, they were ready to shoot at the first rustle. "By God," he kept warning after a few narrow escapes, "if you loose your bolts at a venture, you'll have none left for the enemy and will kill your friends besides. Steady! And make certain who you're aiming at."

But on the Fabriano side of the forest, as he was inspecting the last outpost and assuring himself that instructions were understood, he broke off in the middle of a phrase, while the men around him held their breaths. It was pitch-dark by this time, but the unmistakable click of shod hoofs on the near-by road denoted a party of riders not far from the ambush. At once the recruits blazed up with excitement and would have sent in a volley from their arbalests, if Andrea, at some risk, had not thrown himself in front of them. On second thought, it was incredible that enemy horsemen at that hour would venture through woods which they must know would be defended. But, of course, there were fools everywhere.

"Easy, now!" he whispered. "We'll have a look first. Follow me to the edge of the road. I'll hail them from there. Don't shoot till I tell you."

With the men at his heels, he stopped behind a roadside thicket and, waiting until the slow sound of hoofs was nearly abreast, thundered out, "*Alto là!* Who goes?"

"Friends," quavered a man's voice. The hoofs came to a stop. "Friends from Ferrara." The voice added in a lower key, "Holy Saints! I knew this would happen!"

Peering through the thicket, Andrea could make out a confused huddle of horses and riders, but with the long-eared profiles of a couple of mules in front. These, although he could not credit his eyes, seemed to be mounted by women. At least, the vague configuration of head-dresses and mantles gave that illusion.

"What names?" he demanded.

"The very holy and venerable Lucia da Narni," came the amazing answer, "with her attendants."

"What!"

"Even so, signore. And I beg safe conduct — "

In a flash, Andrea had leaped down to the road. "Your Holy Reverence!" he exclaimed, directing his voice impartially at the shadowy figures in front of him. "What new miracle is this? Perhaps you remember me, your servant, Andrea Orsini?"

Out of the darkness came the haunting voice he had last heard at Viterbo. "I have often prayed for you, Messere. I should never forget you." She added, apparently to the horseman who had spoken for the party: "You see, Giuseppe of little faith, that, where God leads, the gates open before you."

"But, Your Reverence," begged Andrea, "how does this happen . . .?"

"It's very simple. The Holy Saint Catherine, in a vision, told me that I must visit my mother and kinsmen at Narni before I take the last vows of reclusion; that this is a deed of love pleasing to Our Lord. Therefore, the good Duke of Ferrara, after much urging, at last consented to the journey and permitted Sister Felicia here to accompany me."

326

Andrea could not see, but he could feel, her eyes upon him, as she spoke. He felt them so intensely that his consciousness visualized them: magnificently clear, deep, untroubled.

"But since the Via Flaminia is blocked by an army, it seemed best to turn off to Fabriano and, once there, to spend a few days at Città del Monte until the men of violence are gone."

"Alas, Your Reverence!" he exclaimed. "This is no place for you. We are momently expecting Duke Cesare's attack. I marvel that you passed his troops at Fabriano."

"What troops, Messere? There are none there. His army is marching north."

Andrea could only gape. "North? But where?"

"A Spanish gentleman, who craved a blessing of me, spoke of Urbino."

This was a thunder stroke. "Urbino!" Orsini repeated. "But there's been no talk of war against Urbino . . ."

Then, in a flash of intuition, he guessed the truth. A surprise attack. Declarations of war meant nothing to Duke Cesare. Why should Urbino be left as a wedge between northern and southern Romagna? Why should it be left to give countenance and protection to Camerino and Città del Monte? Another snatch. Another of Borgia's inspired treacheries. With Urbino taken, the cities of the Marches had no further backing nor hope and could be reduced at leisure. That the scheme was masterly, Andrea had to admit, even though he detested its ruthlessness.

"Are you surprised," Suor Lucia observed, "at any trick of the devil? . . . Let us ride on, sir, if you will be good enough to attend us."

"But, Your Reverence, I warn you that the Duke will strike shortly, that you may be in danger here."

She was silent a moment. Andrea could feel a curious withdrawal, as if she were taking counsel with someone. Then she said: "It seems best that I should go to Città del Monte, if you permit."

"If *I* permit!" he returned gravely. "God knows, I'm unable to express the honor and comfort it will give us."

By this time, the men of the outpost had gathered on the road. Upon learning who the personage in the darkness was, they pressed around her, entreating a blessing, endeavoring to kiss the sweep of her mantle.

"Upon you, my brothers," she said, "may the Lord lift up His countenance and give you peace."

To Andrea, it seemed more like a dream than reality as he rode by the side of her mule toward the distant lights of the city. He felt once again the strange, impersonal domination which had overawed him in Viterbo. It was all the more impressive because it seemed distinct from Lucia Brocadelli herself, an emanation of something, of someone, else.

At one point, she asked after Mario Belli.

"He has left my service," Andrea said coldly. "I believe he is now with the Duke of Romagna."

She made no comment upon this for so long that Orsini expected none. Finally she said: "If you were with the Duke of Romagna, would you not need our prayers? I love and pity him, as one who has suffered much. Pray for him. I say, pray for him at the blessed mass, for he is in mortal peril."

That night from the palace to every corner of the town spread dismay and joy: dismay at the news of Urbino; joy at the assurance of God's favor and protection in the person of Sister Lucia.

CHAPTER LI

Soon, through the mountain passes, the reports of Cesare Borgia's latest and most daring conquest filtered in. Converging from north and south, his troops had occupied the unsuspecting duchy of Urbino overnight. Caught unawares, the invalid Duke Guidobaldo had hardly time to escape in disguise to Mantua. His fabulously rich palace, the library and art treasures so lovingly collected by his father, had been appropriated. His devoted people, powerless to strike a blow, could only stare confounded at the alien garrisons that held them in a steel grip. The whole operation was a marvel of timing and audacity.

It dazzled the Italian imagination, only too prone to admire brilliance and *brio*, however unscrupulous. From Niccolò Machiavelli, on a mission to Borgia from Florence, down to the pothouse politicos in a dozen states, everybody marveled at Duke Cesare's genius and invincible luck, the unfailing *fortuna* that surrounded him with a superstitious aura.

A few of course, Varano among them, refused to admit the splendor of his achievement. Apart from the desperate isolation of Città del Monte, now that the moral support of Urbino was gone, Varano felt personal grief at the fall of the duchy. He had spent his youth there at the court of the beloved Federigo. Together they had discussed the building of the now desolate palace. He knew every part of the domain as he knew his own signory and associated it with his most cherished memories. The news of the invasion left him stunned and vacant. It seemed to Andrea that he had aged ten years overnight.

"I grieved bitterly at the death of my friend," he said once in reference to Duke Federigo. "How bitterly! How foolishly! He died in the late summer of his life — far better so than to have known this evil winter. If we love those who die, we should not grieve but rejoice." And once, at some mention of Borgia's military skill, he burst out: "What skill? Call me skillful if I rob an enemy, who is on his guard; call me Judas if I rob a friend. It takes no talent to fall upon peaceful states and outrage human decency; it needs only a false heart."

People found it ominous that in this emergency Varano did not seek the advice of Master Paolo, his astrologer. Once he had consulted him on every point. Evidently now he either despaired of the future or took no interest in it. He preferred, instead, to talk with Sister Lucia about her mystical experiences, and he increased his daily devotions in the palace chapel.

"Why make a horoscope," he observed to Andrea Orsini, "when it is time to make one's soul?"

"But, my lord, a cheerful prediction would hearten the people."

"Then *you* look into it." Varano gave a wan smile. "I dare say the learned master will oblige you. He and the stars understand each other."

"I hope Your Excellence will not lose hope now, because of the Urbino news, when everything depends on your example. We're in no worse case than we were before, and the coming of Her Reverence has been a great boon."

The old man squared his shoulders. "Have no fear for my example, *figliolo*," he returned — "now less than ever. I owe these thieves a debt on the score of Urbino, and I plan to pay it. As for the stars, I'm weary of them and of the sun as well. But do you consult Master Paolo, if it will please the people."

With this end in view, Andrea called on the stargazer in the latter's room on the top floor of the palace and asked for a horoscope as to the outcome of the war.

The sage, a pinched and peevish old man, with a high regard for his own dignity, looked askance at Orsini. "His Excellence should visit me himself. I could have foretold to him the fall of Urbino and thus have spared him the shock. Does he believe that this girl from Narni, with her dreams and visions, will safeguard him from destiny which is written in the stars? Does he neglect my science for new infatuations? Alas, Messer Captain, these are the signs of age and decay. But if he commands a horoscope — "

"He assuredly does, sir," put in Andrea. "And let me add that, if it's a pleasant and lusty one fit to be published through the city, I'll throw in a purse of twenty ducats for your trouble."

The astrologer puffed out his cheeks. "A bribe, Captain? To me! As if I would falsify the edicts of heaven!"

"God forbid, Master. I meant only that my joy at good news would express itself tangibly. Forgive a slip of the tongue."

They understood each other. Master Paolo set up his astrolabe and took the altitude of the sun. He then consulted charts of the heavens with attention to the summer signs of the zodiac: Cancer, Leo, and Virgo. He studied the position of the planets, turned the pages of several tomes written in Hebrew characters, drew three concentric squares subdividing each other into isosceles triangles, jotted down figures, mumbled, nodded, and at long last made his report. It was so encouraging that it richly deserved twenty ducats, and Andrea lost no time circulating the news through town. The stars had declared for Città del Monte.

That Master Paolo shortly afterwards slipped out of the city and returned no more was possibly the truer horoscope, but it escaped public notice. Strong in the grace of God made manifest by Sister Lucia and assured of salvation by the planets themselves, the city could face oncoming war with a high heart.

For now that Urbino had been eliminated, Cesare Borgia lost none of the fine summer weather in delay. Within a week, the vanguard of his captain, the Duke of Gravina, reached Fabriano, and outpost skirmishing had begun.

It was at this time that Lucia da Narni, in spite of repeated conscientious warnings on the part of her hosts and in spite, too, of a peremptory message from Ercole d'Este of Ferrara, announced her decision to remain for a while at Città del Monte.

"It is God's will," she said, with her usual simple directness that implied certainty rather than an act of faith. "He told me this morning at mass that He needs me here to comfort this people and to bear witness of Him. Our Lord does not unfold His purpose in advance but leads me from day to day. No doubt it was partly for this reason that He told me in Ferrara to go to Narni. I shall know when He wills for me to continue that journey."

The dangers of a siege, the horrors of a city taken by storm, lay before her. But against this serene reliance upon something immeasurably more important than life and death, it seemed childish to urge the obvious objections.

"Then the gracious will of God be accepted," said Varano. "It is not for us to refuse His bounty."

"No," added Orsini, kindling at Lucia's faith, "nor the assurance of victory that Your Reverence brings us."

Something in the gray depths of her eyes smiled at him. "Ah, Messere of the world," she reproved. "I see you have made progress since our first meeting, but you have still far to go. I did not speak of victory but of comfort. Do not deceive the people, *fratello mio*, with the illusion that God wars upon one side or the other. You cannot know that, nor can I. He speaks to you and to your enemy alike. If you both obey Him, to both of you will be given victory."

The midget Alda, who had been standing beside Lucia's chair, gazing up, laid a tiny hand on her knee.

"Is it permitted me to ask Your Reverence a question?"

Lucia smiled down. "I shall answer it if I can, my sister."

"How does one learn to know the voice of God? How can you be sure He has spoken? Is it a gift to you, a miracle, like the blessed wounds in your hands and feet; or does it come by effort and practice?"

"Yes," put in Camilla, leaning forward, "tell us, if we are not too bold."

Suor Lucia was silent a moment, her bandaged hand resting on Alda's head. "Everything is a gift," she said at last timidly; "everything is a miracle. But the greatest of all miracles is love. I can only say that I love and that more and more I hear the voice of my Beloved."

The Duke of Gravina, having felt out the defenses of the woods, chose rather to thrust a column of heavy-armed lances through them along the road than to waste time and infantry in a foot-by-foot advance. The scheme was a good one, provided the cavalry, with a complement of archers, could hold the Città del Monte side of the forest against counterattack. In that case, the defense outposts in the woods were to a large extent cut off and caught between two sections of the invading forces. But if the lances, having penetrated the forest, failed to maintain their position and were thrown back, they ran the danger of considerable loss. On both sides, then, everything depended on the counterattack.

Warned by spies in Fabriano that Gravina planned to strike shortly after dawn, Varano and Andrea, with about fifty lances and a hundred crossbowmen, left Città del Monte the preceding night. Now that the time for action had come, the old lord seemed renewed, like a smolder-ing brand that bursts into a last flame. As he stood in full armor on the palace steps overlooking the torchlighted courtyard, while his lances, the gentlemen of the signory, already mounted, gathered in front of him, it was not hard to imagine the days of his victorious youth. Camilla, slender and erect, stood beside him in a robe of crimson velvet. The tossing flames of the torches kindled answering sparks in the jewels of her hair; gleamed red on the armor of riders and the bards of horses; showed colors of standards and pennons (the Mountain and Eagle of the city, the Falcon of Baglione); lighted up Varano's hawk face with a fierce glow.

"Signori," he said, "we'll drink a stirrup cup together, as has been my custom in other years before battle. . . . Pages, see to your office." And when salvers with goblets had been passed along the line of horse-men, he went on. "Sirs, what is it we drink here but the blood of our own land, drawn from our vineyards, warmed by the sunlight on our hills? May it lift up our hearts to the honor that awaits us tomorrow! We are, indeed, privileged. For what praise can be greater than of those who make good the defense of homeland and hearth, or, failing it, die in so just a cause? But we shall not fail. I tell you that tomorrow I shall lead you to victory. If our numbers are few, our fame shall be the higher. Let those who are old remember our deeds of the past and crown them with glory! You who are young win laurels tomorrow to lay on the tombs of your fathers! Strike with the knowledge that your loved ones pray for you. Let our rallying cries be *Monte!* and *Urbino!* And, in honor of my lady here" — he turned to Camilla — "cry *Baglione!* Cavaliers, I drink to victory!"

A thunderous shout greeted the pledge. Goblets were emptied. Varano's embrace half lifted Camilla from her feet. It was no time for tenderness; tradition forbade it. . . . "God speed you, sir!" "The saints keep you, *vita mia cara!*" . . . Then, taking his helmet from a squire, Varano lowered it upon his gorget. With the carved eagle of its crest, it added a half-foot to his height. A moment later, he sat, like a pillar of steel, on his completely armored war horse, Rinaldo, and raised his gauntlet in final salute. The line of the men-at-arms opened for him and for the bearer of the civic standard, then wheeled into ranks behind him.

Andrea, contriving to be last, lowered his lance to Camilla as he rode by. He wore her crimson cap on his helmet. She waved her hand. As he looked back from the gateway, the picture of her, standing motionless in the torchlight, stamped itself permanently on his mind. It preoccupied him during the five moonlit miles that separated the town from the forest, hovering vividly through the silhouettes of the lances against the sky.

CHAPTER LII

THE battle tactics that Varano, together with Orsini, had worked out depended on a dip of ground flanking the road at a short distance from the woods. It completely concealed the small body of horsemen and archers from anyone on the road and, because of the general upward slope of the valley on each side, it would remain unsuspected by strangers. The scheme was to allow Gravina's cavalry free passage through the forest in the hope that any vedettes he might send in front, upon finding no resistance in the woods where they expected it and upon seeing the road to the city apparently clear, would omit further reconnaissance and report back favorably to the main column. In that case, a surprise charge delivered on the enemy's flank, after he had emerged from the forest, would have a good chance of throwing him into disorder and perhaps into rout. Then, if he retreated back along the road to Fabriano, the woodland ambushes would open fire upon him and probably add to his confusion.

When the bowl-shaped hollow had been occupied, couriers were sent on to the resistance points in the forest with careful instructions. "If you're asked," said Andrea to the messengers before dismissing them, "why is it that no bolts are to be loosed at the men-at-arms as they advance, explain to our lads that little mischief can be done against armored horsemen who are riding at speed and in good order. If they fall back in a rout, it's a different story. We could have barricaded the road point by point; but in that case we should have lost this chance at the cavalry. Tell them that we're risking something to gain much."

And now followed a feverish period of waiting, which grew more tense as dawn approached. Long before it was necessary, saddle girths were tightened; horses were mounted; the lances formed in a single line for the charge; the archers were posted on the flanks and behind to support the attack and join in harassing the enemy's retreat. After that, there was nothing to do but sweat under heavy plate armor, talk in hushed voices, and squirm uncomfortably in the saddle, while the final hour of darkness dragged by.

Andrea found himself remembering the first time he had worn armor, the harness of a dead cavalier he had found in the wake of a skirmish, when he himself was no more than a camp follower of the French eight years ago. Instead of selling the equipment, he had put it on; had presented himself, according to a preconceived plan, to the French Captain d'Aubigny as a young Italian gentleman seeking honor, and the long impersonation had begun. At the moment, he had considered it a master stroke of cleverness. Now, at last, looking back, he admitted its stupidity. Out of that lie had grown the beanstalk up which he had clambered until its weedy support snapped under him. His mother, that night in the Crespino farmhouse, had shown that she knew more about the underpinning of the world than he.

At the hour before dawn, life reaches an ebb. Glancing on either side of him along the almost invisible, motionless line, Andrea imagined a squadron of ghosts that would fade at cockcrow. Would that they might, and he with them! It would save so much fever. As regarded himself, he had no illusions about the ultimate outcome of this war. He was merely doing the next thing next.

All at once he realized that the profile of young Ettore Leone next to him had become distinct, and he could see, as a paler darkness, the morning mist stirrup-high above the grass of the hollow. It would not be long now. A stir of suspense ran along the line. The sleepy horses raised their heads; and one of them neighed, bringing a sharp curse from his rider, for the whole success of the attack depended on silence, now that the enemy scouts would be probing through the woods in advance of the main column. The valley had become suddenly gray.

Then, far off at first and softened by the forest, came the sound of rapid hoofbeats. They drew nearer, burst into the open about five hundred yards distant, stopped. This was the crucial moment. Would the vedettes be satisfied with the empty road winding down the valley to Città del Monte? Or would they look closer at the meadows on either side? *Now*, if a horse should neigh or if any sound should reach them from the hollow, the element of surprise in the counterattack might be lost and, with it, any hope of success.

The hundred and fifty men held their breaths. One of the archers, who had been posted to observe the movements of the scouts through the tall wheat fringing the hollow, peered anxiously. Then he raised his arm in triumph. The galloping sound of hoofs was withdrawing into the forest. The vedettes had suspected nothing. Varano, at the center, leaned forward in his saddle, waved his hand, and shot a humorous grin along the line. Then, with a touch, he flicked down his vizor.

The steel ripple passed from horseman to horseman; faces disappeared, leaving to shield and crest the office of asserting individual identity; armor rattled, as the cavaliers shifted forward to brace their buttocks against the rear of the deep saddle and thus present a straight line of body and lance to the shock of impact; lances were laid in rest. There must be no warning sounds before the moment of attack; the charge, when delivered, must fall like a thunderbolt.

And now a stir became audible from the forest. It increased in volume, like an oncoming avalanche: the unmistakable sound of a large body of heavily armed riders, pounding nearer through the woods. When at last they emerged, it did not need the signals of the watching archers to warn that the van was there. A clamor of trumpets burst out, expressing triumph that the forest had been so easily passed and blaring defiance down the valley.

Again there was a moment of suspense for the men in the hollow. It might be that Gravina would halt his column on the hither side of the woods and make sure of his rear before advancing further. But it was almost unthinkable that a young and dashing captain, with a free road in front of him, would fail to take advantage of it and demonstrate under the very walls of Città del Monte. Besides, there were farmhouses to burn and supplies to be foraged. The doubt was soon over. Down the road came the trumpeters, followed by the rattle of hoofs and the clash of two hundred men in full armor.

Unable to see the approaching company because of the slope in front of them, Varano's tense troop could still follow the enemy's advance. Now the trumpeters had come abreast of the hollow and had passed beyond it. A fog of dust, rising from the near-by road, indicated that the main force was near. But still Varano waited. The plan was to strike only the center of the column in the hope of cutting it in two and thus blocking the escape of that half nearest the city. Everybody stared at the couple of archers who lay with their eyes just above the lip of the slope, calculating the exact moment. Finally one of them turned, pointed toward the road, and nodded.

"*Monte!*" roared Varano.

Driving in their spurs, the entire line of fifty lances scaled the slope that faced them. To the startled men-at-arms on the road, it must have seemed that they had sprung out of the earth.

"*Monte! Baglione!*"

On a hundred-yard front, they crashed down against the flank of the column.

In the few seconds of the charge, Andrea caught a glimpse of the extended procession of the enemy, an array of steel shot through with colors, and above it, the gaunt shafts of spears. Then his arm jerked backward at the impact of his lance point against the weight of a body. He was aware of an empty saddle; his horse crashed head-on against the riderless mount, overturned him, straddled the lashing hoofs, reared against a second horse, burst through the column, wheeled and plunged in again. A haze of dust; glimpses of faces not yet shut out behind vizors; a man trying to free his lance from the tangle of the melee; another laying about him with his mace; press of bodies; oaths, yells. Then Orsini was again in the open. He found his lance shattered almost to the vamplate, tossed away the stump, and drew his sword.

For the first time, he could notice the effect of the charge. The surprise had been complete. Forty of the enemy's men-at-arms had been unhorsed and lay dead or wounded; or, encumbered by their armor, were struggling helplessly among the trample on the road. They were the prey of the archers, who had now swarmed out, knife in hand, from the hollow. All semblance of order in the column was gone. Those nearest the forest were pelting back in that direction. Of the vanguard, some were racing panic-stricken across country without purpose except to get away; others — and the larger number — though still in confusion and tangled together, were making ready to defend themselves and attack in their turn. These numbered, perhaps, a hundred lances, twice Varano's force, and sufficient to annihilate it if they were given a breathing space in which to find themselves.

336

The turn of the battle depended on keeping them off balance. And there was not much time; for the trumpeter of the Duke of Gravina was blowing madly *To the Standard*, and ranks were beginning to form. "*Orso!*" came the shout. "*Duca!*" A *gonfaloniere* on a tall charger lifted the Duke's red and silver banner high above his head as a rallying point.

Fortunately Varano's lances had remembered their instructions to keep together after the charge, whatever the temptation of pursuit; and they were now closing in around their own standard. Through the dust, Andrea caught a glimpse of Varano's horse, Rinaldo, a huge black, rearing against the curb, while the old lord waved in his men for the next onslaught. A moment later Andrea was beside him.

"Well done!" boomed Varano's voice from his helmet. "Chevy the bastards! Form line on me, cavaliers! *Vittoria! Monte! Urbino!*"

He had retained his spear, and the sixteen-foot shaft, laid again in its rest, sank forward. Rinaldo, gathering his legs beneath him, catapulted into the mass of the enemy. A half length behind, Orsini, without a lance, jerked sidewards to avoid the point of the opposing horseman and, colliding cuirass to cuirass, hammered his shield against the man's vizor until they were swept apart.

Then consciousness, on one level, ceased. It became, instead, a race of impressions too rapid for thought. Choking dust, half-aimed blows, shocks hardly felt, a glimmering of disjointed fragments passing before the eye slits of the vizor, a frenzied whirlpool of sensation. And the dust cloud bellowed with the clanging of a hundred and fifty anvils, the trampling of a hundred and fifty horses; war cries, screams, vociferation. Strategy of any kind had no place in the hurly-burly. It was fighting reduced to its blindest elements.

Andrea found himself all at once in a steel smother where blows rained like a hailstorm. He glimpsed a cavalier in front of him without a shield, one hand on a flagstaff and brandishing a heavy sword in the other, while the folds of a red and silver standard drooped upon his helmet. He formed the center of a wedge plowing forward. The blazon on the shield of the horseman guarding him at the right showed a golden bear, the well-known arms of Gravina and of the Roman Orsini. Here, at the standard of the Duke, was the focal point of the fight.

Driving in his spurs, Andrea shouted and sprang forward. His horse, rearing, grappled with the Duke's charger, which had similarly reared; so that, for a moment, the two steeds were interlocked, while their riders lashed at each other on either side of the barbed necks. Then the

337

heavier weight of Gravina's mount had the best of it. Andrea's horse toppled, but, coming down to one side, kept his feet. For an instant the true and the false Orsinis were close together, unable to use their swords; a second later, they were separated in the press. But Andrea's attack had opened the wedge enough to give Varano an opening. Through the dust, Andrea could see him interlocked with the standard-bearer. Then the banner was down. A tangle of lances and horsemen drove in between, shutting out the sequel. But this meant victory. The shout rose higher. "*Monte! Monte!*"

There came a sudden thinning of the melee that Andrea was quick to recognize. The enemy had broken. Singly or in twos and threes, the men-at-arms spurred toward the refuge of the woods. Only a nucleus surrounding Gravina kept some show of order; but when it had cut through the thin line of assailants, it made good speed into the forest.

Now was the time for pursuit, to keep on the tails of the fugitives and give them no chance to rally. It might even be possible to stampede the infantry and baggage train at Fabriano. But at once Andrea checked his enthusiasm. The forces were not available. Of the fifty lances who had made the first charge, no more than thirty were left. They and the archers could do something; and the forest ambushes, who would now open with their crossbows, could harry the retreat still more; but all together they were still not enough to drive home the victory. The thought was maddening that, with just a few more men, Gravina's entire army might have been scattered.

However, there was room for nothing but rejoicing. The little company of fifty had routed four times its own number and had shamed Cesare Borgia's leading captain. It had delayed his advance for at least a week. The report of the fight would echo through Italy.

Raising his vizor, Andrea called to one of the archers. "You, there, make haste to the city and present our services to Madonna Camilla. Tell her the good news. Set the bells ringing. We'll be riding back within two hours." And he spurred hard after the other lances, who were pricking on the retreat.

For a short stretch, the road was cumbered with the dead or dying, riderless horses, broken lances and equipment — the wreckage of battle. Then followed pell-mell the surge of pursuit. In the forest, all was confusion. Some twelve or fifteen of Gravina's cavaliers, acting as a rear guard, counterattacked, then retreated, then charged again. They checked the pursuit of the lances but could not stop the infiltration of the archers on either side of the road. These now began fire with their crossbows and occasionally emptied a saddle. Ahead of the rear guard, deeper in the forest, was an individual scramble and *sauve qui peut*. The fleeing men-at-arms now found trees across the road which they had covered so easily an hour ago; and, attempting to avoid them, fell to grips with the ambushes. A long-drawn hubbub resounded through the woods. Andrea's system of outposts was justifying itself.

Then, at one point, Andrea, who was pressing the attack against the rear guard, came face to face with Mario Belli. The latter's vizor, dangling by a hinge, revealed his hungry wolf's face, squinting eyes, and cunning mouth. It had the effect of an apparition.

"Ha, Your Magnificence!" he fleered. "My compliments! But we'll be meeting again." He stared oddly a moment, not at Andrea. "By God, who are we to fight with ghosts! Look who you're riding with!" Then, wheeling his mount, he disappeared around a turn of the road.

Glancing to one side, Andrea noticed for the first time a riderless horse that had come abreast of him. Its great neck and shoulders, the design of the saddle, could not be mistaken. It was Varano's black stallion, Rinaldo — and on the near side, the housing was drenched with blood.

CHAPTER LIII

LEAVING the now halfhearted pursuit to maintain such pressure on the enemy's rear guard as it might, but with instructions to waste no men and to advance no further than the edge of the woods toward Fabriano, Andrea turned anxiously back along the road, still accompanied by the riderless war steed. The fact that Rinaldo and his own horse had been constantly together and had a mutual attraction for each other explained why the former, drifting with the current into the forest, had attached himself to Andrea. But for all that, it was eerie enough to be riding next to an empty saddle, as if a familiar but invisible presence were still beside him.

The premonition of disaster weighed upon Orsini. He could not shake it off by telling himself that more often than not, men were unhorsed and wounded without fatal consequences. He scanned the edges of the road fearfully; but it was not until he had reached the scene of the fight that he saw what he expected: a group of archers clustered around a prostrate figure. Their slack shoulders and bowed heads implied the worst, even before he came near enough to see their woebegone faces.

Swinging disconsolately from his saddle, Andrea drew close while the group opened before him.

Varano lay on his back, half-draped in the enemy standard whose broken staff had slipped from his outflung hand. Someone had taken off his helmet, uncovering the sparse gray hair and lined face that now looked parchment white. His eyes were closed. At first, Andrea did not see the wound on the right hip. It was the ugly oddness of something projecting from the upper thigh guard that caught his attention: the splintered stump of a broken lance. It meant death. He was dead . . .

"My lord! My father!" The words were an unconscious cry. Sinking to his knees beside the body, Andrea stretched out a hand toward Varano's face, remembered his steel gauntlet and shook it off, then laid his palm on the white forehead.

Possibly it was this, or the rattle of Orsini's armor, that roused him; but the old lord's eyes suddenly opened, and he looked up blankly. It was as if a death mask had come to life.

"How's this?" he muttered. "Where — " His eyes quickened, turned from Andrea to the circling faces of the archers. "So! . . . I remember." And, wincing with pain, he repeated, "So!"

"My dear lord!"

"How is it with the battle, Andrea?"

"Victory. Your Excellence was a true prophet last night. We've thrown them back to Fabriano. It's a passage of arms that will long be remembered to Your Signory's honor. I regret only" — Andrea steadied his voice — "this accident, this — "

"The pursuit?" Varano interrupted. "The dogs should be straitly followed. They should be given no pause." He twisted his head from side to side; his lips tensed. "They should be given no pause. . . ."

"As far as our numbers serve, we are at their traces, sir. Take no care. They'll be harried into camp, I promise. But it's Your Lordship now who needs — "

340

"What are you doing here, Messer Captain? You should be with the men." A bead of sweat crossed the old man's forehead; he clenched his hands. "God help me! I'm in great pain. Do not leave me alone, *figliolo*. Forgive the weakness." A remote expression crept into his eyes. "Hark you! My compliments to the lord Federigo. Tell him we have held this pass to the limit and our numbers fail. Let him bring up his *condotta*, or the day's lost. Tell him I long for the sight of his banner."

Then, to Andrea's relief, he sank back into unconsciousness.

Standing up, Orsini exchanged a desolate glance with the archers. "Lucio," he said to one of them, "take my horse and ride full speed to the city. Have a litter sent in all haste, together with Don Procopio, the chaplain, and my lord's apothecary. See that he brings opium. Tell Her Signory that — " He paused. "Do not tell her everything. Understand?"

"*Sì, signore.*"

When the man was gone, they set about giving Varano what easement they could: loosening the buckles of his armor, providing a cushioned saddle for his head, erecting a makeshift protection against the heat of the sun. It was, of course, impossible to remove the broken lance shaft from the wound: that would have caused agony and immediate death. The best hope was that he should not come out of his swoon.

Crouching at his side, Andrea fanned him with a cap borrowed from one of the archers. Little by little, day by day, insensibly, Varano, once only an obstacle to his plans, had become dearer to him than any friend. So the mysterious strategy of life had ordered it. Once — not long ago — he would have hailed this event as a stroke of good fortune. Now the sense of personal loss so much absorbed him that he did not even think of the past. He realized only, more and more with every moment, what the old man's loyal spirit and great heart had meant to him. He thought of them in terms of a departing glory that would leave him poor.

Roused by the sound of horses approaching from the city, he rose and walked forward to meet them. As he had expected, Camilla rode far ahead of the others. She had kept watch all night; for she still wore the crimson velvet of yesterday evening and had delayed only long enough to throw on a blue riding cloak.

She reined up beside him. "The man spoke of a slight wound," she said in a low voice. "Tell me the truth, Andrea."

"It is worse than that."

341

"You mean — " Her hand crept to her throat, but the steadiness of her eyes forbade him to soften what she would soon know.

"Not yet, but he will not outlive the day, Madonna."

She sat for a moment gazing into the distance. From far off, up the valley, came the murmur of bells. It was the city, still unconscious of its loss, ringing for victory.

"I forgot to silence them," she said.

Andrea half turned away. "They should not be silent. No, let His Lordship enter the city to the sound of bells and the salute of cannon. It is more fitting."

She drew herself up straighter in the saddle. "I shall give order for it. You're right. He shall be greeted like a conqueror, returning not only from this battle but from many victories."

Varano regained consciousness while he was being placed on the litter swung, back and front, between two horses. The opium was then administered, and he made his confession to Father Procopio. They were both of an age and had known the old times together. When he had finished, the priest broke into tears.

"How now!" said Varano. "What an ugly face you're making, old friend! We're neither of us handsome enough to give way to sorrow. We must put on our best fronts for this pageant. But if I'm to see the last of it, we'd best be starting."

With the operation of the drug, his pain lessened; and he lay with half-closed eyes as the little cortege wound slowly along the road. Now and then, he smiled up at Camilla and Orsini, who were riding on either side of the litter.

But when they were nearing the town, he spoke: "Not to the palace. Carry me before the choir steps of Santa Maria degli Angeli. Let me die there. It's according to a vow I made once."

And later, becoming aware of the tumult of the bells from every campanile in the town, he asked, "What festival is this? I have forgotten."

"The festival of the Battle of the Forest, my dear lord," Camilla answered steadily, "fought today, which shall be held henceforth in your honor."

He lay silent a moment. Then he said: "I am glad of this. It is a great happiness. I thank you for this thought of me, *Madonna mia cara*."

"It was Andrea's thought as well."

He turned his head to look up at Orsini. "My dear son."

342

And when the cannon roared a welcome from the castle, he raised his hand in answer.

They carried him up the narrow street from the city gate between lines of mourning people; Camilla and Orsini drew back so that he might be seen; and again and again he raised his hand. More than once, someone, pressing forward out of the crowd, kissed the edge of the cloak that had been spread over him; until at last he was the center of a throng — rich and poor, men and women, with children among them — accompanying the litter on either side, murmuring their grief and love, calling upon God and the saints to bless him. And so across the crowded *piazza* to the church steps, above which the great portals had been thrown open. Here the horses were taken out of the shafts, and the litter was raised high on the arms of archers, who carried it up the steps and into the cool dimness of the basilica. Then the bells of Santa Maria fell silent, and the doors were closed.

From where Varano lay, he could look up at the crucifix on the high altar before a time-darkened painting of the Assumption; and his eyes turned to it often before the end. But consciousness varied with dreams, so that he did not always recognize his old servants from the palace, who, one by one, kneeled beside him a moment to bid farewell. The past seemed rather to be reclaiming him in its infinite tranquillity. He was aware of long-lost, long-loved faces invisible to the others. He spoke with his sons who had died at Fornuovo; his face lighted up at the presence of his beloved captain, Duke Federigo. . . . "You have long delayed, my lord. But now all is well." . . . And others came out of the past, known only to him. He said once, "You are beautiful, my lady mother. I dreamed you were dead."

But he recognized Lucia da Narni and asked her to pray for him. "And Your Signory for me," she answered. "But in that land you will speak face to face."

As evening came on, tall candles were lighted near the dying man, glimmering points in the enveloping darkness. They softened the lines of Varano's face to a marble serenity, so that now and then he seemed to Andrea a sculptured figure, like those on the ancestral tombs in the side chapels. A drift of solemn thoughts, the effect of weariness and sorrow, crossed Orsini's mind. Or perhaps they were hauntings of the place itself, the shadows that gathered beyond the hypnotic gleam of the candles. He could almost see them, the dead lords of the House of Varano, rising from their stone couches to greet the last and greatest of their name and bid him welcome. What lay behind those tombs, what unimaginable world? Here tonight, it seemed to him that he stood on the threshold and could feel the vastness beyond the opening door.

A voice startled him, and he saw Varano's head stir on the pillow. "Am I alone? Who is here?"

Camilla, who was kneeling beside the couch, bent down. "Do you not see me, my lord, and Messer Andrea?"

"No, it is dark. Give me your hand, Madonna — and yours, my son."

His grasp was so weak that they could hardly feel the pressure of it.

"Be true to each other," he said. "You have been true to me. I have understood."

Life gathered in a last flame. He raised his head. "After war, peace. Open the gates!"

CHAPTER LIV

THE long defense of Città del Monte, which now began when the Duke of Gravina, having licked the wounds of his initial defeat, resumed the advance, and which lasted most of the summer, aroused the admiration of Italy. Struck by the figure of the young and beautiful Prefettessa, to whom the city remained devoted in spite of the death of its hereditary lord, people extolled the *virtù* of Camilla Baglione and wrote sonnets in her praise. On the other hand professional soldiers, like Borgia's captains, knew well enough who was responsible for strategy, trick, and daring that held the vastly superior forces of the attack at bay during two long months; and, among these, Andrea Orsini won universal respect. His reputation extended even to Naples, where the great Spanish master of war, Gonsalvo de Córdoba himself, expressed esteem; and where collectors of honor, such as Bayard, generously envied him.

This, in large part, offset the reports of his imposture circulated by Duke Cesare. It was an unscrupulous age more impressed by end

344

results than by methods and not too shocked by successful deviousness. If Andrea Zoppo, having taken the name of an extinct family, conducted himself not only well but gloriously, the original deception did not seem too important. No living House could resent it, and even the Count of Nola, his assumed ancestor, had not been disgraced by him. As far as the name *Orsini* went, it could almost be considered a pseudonym rather than a sham.

"*Fête dieu!*" exploded Bayard, when his rival sportsman, Jacques de Monteynart, twitted him with defeat at the hands of a peasant. "The devil of a lot that has to do with it! I was defeated by one of the leading victors in that Battle of the Forest, at which I would have given my eyeteeth to be present. I was defeated by the cavalier who now holds Città del Monte against ten times his strength and who has proved himself an eminent captain of war. If he's a peasant the more honor to him. I hope to renew my acquaintance with Monseigneur d'Orsini sometime when this business of Naples is over. Meanwhile, I consider him my friend. And if you, sir, have a mind to question the honor of that friendship on horse or on foot . . ."

Rumor had it that Duke Cesare's fierceness against Città del Monte was embittered not only by the length of the siege but by his failure to discredit the traitorous charlatan, Zoppo. People close to Borgia were careful to guard their tongues against a slip when they mentioned Andrea; but, for all that, the assumed name hung on. Against this, there was only one cure: a rope. For the fickle world finds nothing to admire in a peasant on the gibbet. Strict commands were given that Andrea should be taken alive at any cost, and a fat reward was offered to his captor.

Meanwhile, within the desperate circle of the town walls, little attention would have been paid to sonnets or compliments if any whisper of them had passed the cordon of troops around the city. Feverish effort alternated with the sleep of exhaustion. On the days that were free from attack, every minute had to be spent in repairing the damage of the last onslaught and the continuous damage of the bombardment, or in concerting measures for strengthening the defense and harassing the enemy. As Andrea pointed out, the text that it is more blessed to give than to receive had a special truth in this case.

At first the city had given richly. It cost Gravina a week and a hundred foot soldiers to secure the woods from Fabriano. Then, when at last the Borgian troops roared out into the valley to forage and plunder, they found it bare. Flocks and cattle had been driven into the

345

city; villas and farmhouses had been stripped of their contents; even the harvest had been cut green and left to rot. On meager rations carted in from the Via Flaminia, the enemy dug trenches around the irregular hill that gave the town its name, set up his cannon, selected the proper point to effect a breach in the walls, and summoned the town to surrender. Upon meeting a flat refusal, he opened fire. Now was the time to wreak vengeance for the Battle of the Forest, the later bloody advance, the spiteful stripping of the valley. Here (said the company commanders, whetting the appetite of their men) lay a town bursting with food, valuables, and women, garrisoned by no more than a handful of recruits, waiting to make the fortune of brave lads who had only to walk in when the cannon had forced a breach. So they cheered on the gunners and yelled at the first smack of a stone ball against the rampart.

But it was easier to shoot down than up. It seemed that the city was surprisingly equipped with falcons and culverins, which opened in their turn, with such effect that several batteries were knocked out and a couple of cannoneers killed. It took a little time to reorganize after this, and another day was lost. That night an amazing sortie from the town made matters worse. Through a secret exit, Andrea led his men in an attack on the trenches, spiked a number of the guns, blew up some kegs of precious powder, spread panic through the camp, and, except for the crippling lack of numbers, might have broken the siege then and there. By the time the cannon had been repaired or replaced, new supplies of powder brought in, and the gun positions strengthened, a second week passed.

Then, spurred on by devastating letters from Cesare Borgia, who was absorbed in the affairs of Urbino, the enemy resumed his battering of the walls to such good effect that he opened a section a hundred yards wide, filling the outer ditches, and the breach was deemed practicable. Led by a picked band of dismounted men-at-arms in full harness, the infantry surged uphill to the attack; passed through the rain of crossbow quarrels from the walls; climbed up through the rubble of the breach; faced the sulphur, quicklime, and boiling oil hurled down upon them from the ramparts on each side; kept on advancing; and finally encountered a hedge of eighteen-foot Swiss pikes, reinforced by Andrea and the armored gentry. Through this, hack and rage as they might, there was no passing. The ordeal exceeded human endurance. Reluctantly the trumpets sounded retreat. Scalded and burned, exhausted by effort, heat, and wounds, the column sagged back downhill, leaving its dead upon the slope.

Another assault next day met the same repulse. A second breach was effected to no purpose. Attacks with scaling ladders led to nothing, because of a lever device invented by Andrea that toppled the ladders back from the ramparts. Mines against the walls were countermined. And a month went by.

So far the city had had the best of it.

But such defense paid the price of inevitable erosion. Of the eight hundred original garrison, nearly a half were gone. Powder ran low. The breaches in the walls could not be adequately repaired. The summer drought cut down the water supply of the town wells. An epidemic of fever, not yet known as typhoid, spread through the city. The palace became a hospital. The hot, narrow streets, crowded with refugees from the entire *contrada*, stank of corruption and death.

There was only one chance to pray and fight for, that the siege might prove too costly and might be raised from sheer exhaustion. But, of this, hope faded with every week. On July 21st, Camerino had fallen to the Borgian *condottiere*, Oliverotto, aided by some of Gravina's forces; and the combined armies could now turn on Città del Monte. Duke Cesare's prestige was too much involved to accept defeat at the hands of so petty a state. Utterly alone and marked for destruction, the little city now fought on with the courage of despair.

It fought on for another month. Old men and even women filled the shrinking ranks of the garrison; women and children carried stone for the shattered walls. Andrea and Camilla multiplied themselves, appearing at all hours, here and there, encouraging, exhorting, directing. Andrea became as well-known to the besiegers as one of their own captains. Was there an attack, they could always be sure to find him at the breach, the red crest on his helmet, the borrowed blazon of his shield still proclaiming him Andrea Orsini. Was there a sortie, the same shield appeared in the van. They could see him on the walls, passing from post to post. With the professional admiration of the age for a good fighter, they praised his gallantry.

"By God," said the Duke of Gravina, "he can show those arms, if he pleases, as far as I'm concerned. He's won a right to them."

Now and then, from behind the walls, shouts reached the near-by enemy trenches: "*Viva la Prefettessa! Baglione!*" Curiosity about Camilla ran high in the camp. Don Esteban Ramirez and Mario Belli, who had known her, were plied with questions.

Hardly less celebrated on both sides was Sister Lucia da Narni. From the humblest foot soldier, Spaniard or Romagnolo, to the staff of Gravina himself, every one of the besieging forces knew that a saint of God visited in the town, and that it was doubtless her favor with heaven which foiled their attacks and kept them baking outside the walls. Messengers from the anxious Duke of Ferrara, seeking vainly to tempt her away from the perils of the city, were most welcome to the Borgians, who wished them success. As for the town population, it worshiped the gentle, mysterious figure of the nun, so constant in her attendance on the sick, so accessible to any need. In the frenzy and haste of the defense, she provided a small zone of peace and of divine leisure that seemed to have time for all. It was like the circle of light around a steadily burning candle. Anxiety and pain, the fear of death itself, faded before the compassionate serenity of her eyes. If no crude miracle protected the city, a subtle miracle was continuous there. To Sister Lucia, as much as to any other cause, could be attributed the steadfastness of the besieged.

At the end of August another all-out assault was delivered at two widely separated points of the walls. Spending the last of his reserves, the last of his gunpowder, the last ounce of endurance, Andrea succeeded once more in holding the breaches. But when the sullen enemy trumpets sounded retreat, and when the attacking surge fell back, he realized that the city was as good as taken. The next wave would infallibly sweep in. A city carried by a storm, especially after so long and bitter a resistance, could expect no mercy. It meant the slaughter of thousands, rape, torture, pillage. That was the law of war. No captain, however humane or respected, could deny this prize to his men.

"And so," announced Orsini, discussing the situation with Camilla, "it remains only to take measures for Your Ladyship's safety."

They were on the same balcony of the palace from which — it seemed long ago — they had looked out at the springtime valley on the day of Belli's departure. Now it lay beneath them, gutted by war and parched by summer, an unlovely stretch of desolation. Almost at their feet they could see the enemy's trenches, tents, and shelters, sprawling over a strip several hundred paces wide and disappearing around the hill. An angry hum rose from the camp which was digesting the latest repulse. For refreshment, Andrea had taken off his armor; but the stains and wear of it showed on the once impeccable doublet and hose, and his forehead was still ridged from the helmet. A late afternoon sun lingered above the western hills.

"What measures?" asked Camilla.

"I suggest this: that you make use of the secret exit from the castle

348

beneath the guardroom, the one that helped us in the first sortie. As you know, the shaft through the rock goes down thirty feet. From there, the tunnel brings you out at the ruined chapel yonder." He pointed to a skeleton shrine, half-demolished by a misdirected cannon ball. "I'm sure they haven't found the concealed opening behind the altar. When the city's taken, you'll wait in the tunnel until night. By that time, every one of these slaves will be pillaging within the walls, and the camp will be empty. You'll cross it in the darkness, press on to the forest, and spend the night there. The following night, you'll continue toward Perugia or, if it seems best, toward Mantua. We'll see to it that Your Ladyship has a sure guide and is properly attended."

"An excellent plan," she nodded. "You'll not be escorting me, then?"

He smiled. "No, by your leave — except in spirit, Donna Milla."

She caught the grimness of the double meaning under his light manner. "In other words, you intend to die here. It's not so very gallant to pack me off alone. Your plan of escape is excellent, as I said. Why not follow it yourself?"

"I hardly know why not." Sitting down on the stone bench that lined three sides of the balcony, he stretched his arms and legs to get rid of the dull ache in them. It seemed to him that the accumulated fatigue of the siege made itself felt all at once in his entire body. "Perhaps the scruple that having asked so much of my poor friends of the garrison, I ought at least to stand by them now. But I've never been scrupulous, Madonna — a sad rogue, as you've often told me — so probably the truth is — "

He paused so long that she prompted him. "What truth?"

"Why — that it's only a choice between endings, and one is better than another."

"I marvel at you, Andrea."

"No doubt."

She stamped her foot. "I don't mean that. I marvel that you think so ill of me."

"Of you?"

"That I, the Prefettessa of this signory, the wife of my lord Varano, should sneak off to beg for refuge, while you and others, my people — Messere, it was shameful of you!"

He roused himself to meet this objection which he had foreseen. "Listen, Donna Milla. Heroism is a shallow thing if it is not rooted in wisdom. When the city is taken, you will not die. If you remain here, Duke Cesare will use you to further his designs or to gratify his arro-

349

gance. In any case, he will take care that you are of no more use to this people. If you escape and are beyond his reach, the day may come when you will return to comfort and rule them. So, in their misery, you would leave them something to hope for. Would your remaining here help anyone? No, it would help us more to know that you are safe."

"Thanks for your wisdom," she smiled. "But I don't intend to be wise. I can only be what I am. Let's talk of something else, if you please."

He stood up. "Of me, then. I make bold to ask you to leave for my sake, though it is boldness, indeed, to dream that that might have weight with you beyond other things."

"Not so bold," she answered in the same half-ironic voice. "How could my leaving serve you?"

"In this way, Madonna. I should like to know at the end that my life had been to some purpose. As it is, I see my failure at every point: in art, in politics, in war. Unfulfilled promise, incomplete designs. And the book is closing. If, for my sake, you do what I ask, you would make me feel that at the chief point of all I have not failed — no, that I have fully attained. Because I'm asking so much of you, the proof would be the surer; my happiness would be the greater."

He had not planned to speak in this way. The decisive moment had come unexpectedly. But the issue was inevitable. Behind the sorrow at Varano's death, behind the constraint which their respect for him and sudden freedom itself imposed on them, behind the anxieties and labor of the siege, lay the suspense of what they knew must find expression — a demand, an answer.

She met it frankly. "I think you need no proof, my Andrea." Reaching up, she drew a finger along the red band left by the helmet on his forehead. "And I need none. It's been strange — hasn't it? — our long road together — and yet not together. Hard sometimes, but splendid. Our own road, not the usual one. By God, I would not change it for all I've read in the romances. Remember how my lord took our two hands there in the church and what he said?"

Their eyes met steadily. In them and in the consenting loveliness of her lips, he read the fulfillment of his utmost hope. Holding her for the first time in his arms, he felt the quintessence of life, as if all the senses had become one flame. Past and future were forgotten.

Then, as if he had been too long indulged, the incredible rapture faded into the realization that it was only a glimpse of happiness seen through a closing door. The promise could never be fulfilled. That he possessed it at all was a glory, and he would possess it until the end; but the end was close.

After a while, he said, "But you haven't yet promised to do what I ask, *mia cara.*"

"No," she smiled up at him, "your argument's gone. You asked me to prove that I love you. If you aren't sure of it now, I can't prove it by running away and living safely somewhere without you. *Tristarello!*" she added, raising a forefinger at him. "You're very plausible."

"Madonna, you don't understand. It's no time for joking."

"But I do understand, and I'm not joking." Her smile faded. "It's only that we'll finish the last mile of our road together." . . . She turned her head to listen. "Did you hear that?"

The sound of a trumpet, tempered by distance, came from the slope of the hill in front of the castle. It was impossible to see beyond the curving façade of palace and fortress; but any trained ear could interpret the signal.

Orsini exchanged a glance with Camilla. "Am I dreaming?" he said. "Are they asking for a parley?"

Since the first summons to surrender, there had been no communication between the town and the enemy. Gravina's repeated assaults had given no reason to believe that he would negotiate on any conditions, and Andrea did not wish to show weakness by courting a rebuff. If the Duke now sought a parley, it meant weakness of some kind on his side. It opened a small door of hope. Andrea's pulses beat faster, and he could see his own excitement reflected in Camilla's face. Perhaps the enemy's losses today had been just enough to turn the scale. It might be possible to secure honorable conditions that would spare the city and permit Camilla to leave with an escort, including Orsini himself. Perhaps even better terms might be had. Why not? Good fortune was seldom niggardly, and this was Andrea's lucky day. The happiness of a moment ago might be only a prelude to the Earthly Paradise. His imagination, constrained so long by the hopeless outlook of the siege, expanded like a genie released from a bottle.

"We'll go down and see what it is." He drew her to him with a new lightheartedness. "One more proof that you love me. One last kiss, Madonna; and, if haggling's the game, I promise you Gravina's a lost man. Our road may be longer than we thought, *anima mia.*"

But they had hardly reached the landing of the stairs when a page, racing up from below at top speed, panted out the news: officers from the Duke of Gravina, who begged leave to discuss certain matters of importance with Her Signory and asking safe-conduct with admittance to the castle.

"We'll receive them in the main room of the East Tower," directed Camilla.

"But hark you, Beppo," Orsini added to the page, "let these officers cool their heels awhile until order has been taken to receive them worthily. The guard of the castle must be doubled. The place must be swarming with pikemen. They can judge of our numbers from that!"

"Always the fox," Camilla smiled.

"Restored by this new turn." Andrea tossed back his head gaily. It was indeed his lucky day.

CHAPTER LV

In a subdued state of mind, Gravina's envoys were ushered into the square, dim, medieval room on the second floor of the East Tower. Roving glances had given them small comfort. To judge by the well-equipped and numerous guards they had seen, the garrison was still capable of prolonged defense; and they were utterly sick of this inglorious, cursed war, of the fruitless assaults, the meager rations, and other hardships of the camp. If they had known that the soldiers they saw were practically all of the able-bodied men available for the defense; and that, in order to make such a show, Andrea had stripped the walls of everyone except women and cripples, they would have felt happier. Orsini chuckled inwardly at their long faces and promised himself amusement when it came to beating down their terms.

But expectations proved too sanguine. It turned out that the Captains Fracassa and Naldo were not envoys at all in the sense that they had any authority to speak for their superiors. They offered terms, indeed, but very much as town criers proclaim news. And these terms were not even Gravina's: they were dictated by Cesare Borgia himself, at that moment returning south from a conference with the French

King in Milan. Andrea, who had looked forward to the excitement and finesses of a card game, found that the situation much more resembled chess. If he had had only Gravina to deal with, he might have put up a good show, even with his few pieces; but he had little chance against the astuteness of Borgia.

And yet, as Fracassa outlined the conditions, they seemed incredibly generous.

"Duke Cesare," said Fracassa, whom Orsini had long known as a typical hanger-on in the Vatican anterooms, "does not wish the destruction of those domains, which he is restoring to the jurisdiction of the Church. No one can deny that he has shown himself most loving to the cities and peoples which have yielded themselves to his mercy."

"Why shouldn't he?" put in Camilla. She was seated in a high-backed chair facing the two officers, while Andrea stood beside her. "It would be madness to burn a house which you're seizing for your own profit. But we'll not debate that, Messer Captain. Pray continue."

"Therefore," bowed Fracassa, "His Excellence makes certain proposals to Your Illustrious Signory, that he believes you will find to your advantage."

Camilla smiled. "One moment, sir. Is it too much to ask why he makes these proposals so late, after the death of my lord Varano and of hundreds on both sides, after the damage wrought by your army to this state?"

Orsini nodded approval of the question. It was sound tactics to drive home the point that the Duke, and not the city, was making the overtures; and that, except for the fierce resistance he had met, the enemy would have offered no conditions at all.

Fracassa reddened and cleared his throat; but Captain Naldo, a handsome young man, evidently much impressed by Camilla, burst out: "*Sacramento*, Your Ladyship! Why beat about the bush! Our compliments to Your Grace's divine valor, which equals if it does not surpass the goddess Bellona's herself. Your fame, most noble Madonna, adds glory to Italian arms and it shall ring through Europe. It would be futile to deny that the illustrious Duke of Romagna offers these terms as a tribute to Your Excellence's courage and great spirit, lest harm should come to you and, therewith, shame to Italian chivalry."

"Holy Mother!" exclaimed Camilla. "What eloquence! *Mille grazie, signore!*" She glanced up with a twinkle at Andrea. "You see how valorous I am, my lord Orsini, what a captain of war!"

353

The hint was too plain for the comfort of Fracassa and Naldo, who had thus far ignored Andrea as much as possible. They were in a tight place. It was perfectly proper, as gallant enemies, to extol the prowess of a lady; but woe to them if they accorded anything to peasant Zoppo!

"I have long marveled at Your Signory," Andrea returned gravely. "Captain Naldo understates the truth. . . . But what, then, are these terms?"

"First," said Fracassa, consulting a paper, which he tapped against his palm by way of emphasis, "in return for the surrender of the city, my lord Duke engages to restrain his soldiers from a sack and to take no vengeance on the people."

"Very good," Andrea interrupted; "but what security does he offer that, when the gates are opened, the soldiers can be restrained?"

"His illustrious word!" snapped the other. Then, meeting Orsini's skeptical gaze, Fracassa grumbled: "I suppose he would agree to quarter the troops at Fabriano. We've already said that he doesn't want this town destroyed."

"Ah! . . . Well, what next?"

"Second, my lord Duke engages to permit the right noble Madonna Camilla to depart freely with her personal attendants and sufficient escort for whatever destination she pleases; or else, to remain here with the title of *Prefettessa* and in all dignity, provided only that a captain appointed by my lord Duke and commanding a garrison in his pay shall remain to assist her in the government."

What a marvelous move! Andrea had to admire Cesare's cleverness in every implication of it. The Duke offered a choice between freedom and duty. He guessed shrewdly enough that Camilla's devotion to the people would compel her to remain at Città del Monte, even as a puppet, in the hope that she could be of some help to them. So the change of government would be easier and more acceptable. But if she chose otherwise, not much would be lost; and in either case his reputation for generosity would be established.

Clever indeed, and apparently magnanimous. Andrea could not have hoped for more. The amazement in Camilla's face reflected his own.

"Has this captain you mention been named as yet?" he asked.

"Not to my knowledge." Fracassa cleared his throat again, hesitated, and went on in a flat voice: "Third. The above terms shall be considered null and void unless Andrea Zoppo, calling himself Andrea

Orsini and acting at present as commander of the city garrison, be delivered alive into the hands of Duke Cesare's officers, or surrender himself to them, to be dealt with as His Excellence may determine."

It was precisely as if, somewhere in Andrea's mind, the voice of Cesare Borgia had spoken: "Check and mate!" He had the sinking feeling of a loser at chess whom a surprise play of his opponent leaves helpless. The issue could not be clearer: his life or the lives of thousands, including Camilla. There was not one possibility of escape.

The realization of this filled the moment of silence after Fracassa had finished.

Camilla sprang to her feet. "Never!" Her hands were clenched; her eyes blazed at the unfortunate captains, who could only gape while her anger lashed out at them. "*Giammai!*" she repeated. "*Al corpo del giusto Dio,* you are bold to offer your insults here! You sheep, whom the lord Orsini has beaten in open field, in your own camp, in the breaches of this city a score of times — you, who are not worth the scabbard of his sword, demand that he be given up to you! *Santa Maria! 'Calling* himself Andrea Orsini!' That you dare repeat this lie to me!"

She stopped for lack of breath; but her hot gaze was so intent that Fracassa shuffled back a step and muttered: "Cry you mercy, Madama. *We* do not demand. We express merely the Duke's terms. Your Signory will bear in mind that we have a safe-conduct."

"*Al diavolo col vostro salvocondotto!*"

"Nay, Madonna," Orsini put in, "these gentlemen must deliver their message."

She bit her lips. "Well, they've delivered it. Now let them trip back to the Duke with my answer. . . . Tell him that I shall set a torch to the palace and burn in the flames rather than accept the conditions he offers. Is that clear?"

Fracassa bowed and sighed. "To be frank, we had expected Your Ladyship's refusal, which does credit to your fame. But, because of it, many must suffer and die, and this good city must be laid waste. Your Excellence will understand that the letters of our illustrious lord, Duke Cesare, permit no compromise. He believes that, as far as Your Ladyship and the city itself are concerned, his terms are generous. But" — Fracassa glanced at Orsini — "he will make no concession regarding this gentleman."

"You have heard our answer," said Camilla.

"We have, indeed," shrugged the captain. "And therewith we humbly take our leave. But I am authorized to say that the terms we

355

have offered stand until day after tomorrow at sunrise. They will then be considered withdrawn, and we shall renew the attack."

It was very quiet in the room when the two officers had gone. The candles, which had been set on a table to eke out the scant light, burned yellower as day faded beyond the narrow windows.

"So much for that," Camilla said finally. "And we'll renew the defense."

He shook his head. "We cannot — as I told you an hour ago." Then, touched by her blank expression, he added: "But we're in no worse position than before this interview. In fact, we're the gainers by thirty-six hours; and in that time — "

He fell into a brown study, his gaze on the candles.

"What, then?" she urged after a moment.

"I must have talk with the Duke of Gravina." What Andrea had to do demanded skillful handling if it was to be done at all, and, though improvising for Camilla's benefit, he took care to give his words the ring of confidence and deliberation. "I knew him well at one time. He's a young man of parts. You see, Madonna, when negotiations have been opened, it's usually possible to continue them. They may talk of no compromise, but it's clearer than day that Gravina and Duke Cesare himself are tired of the siege and would gladly be done with it. That's proved by the terms we have been offered. As far as they know, we can fight on for another month. Well then, it's hard to believe that my arrest is worth that cost to them."

"This petty tyrant of a Borgia!" she exclaimed. "Why does he hate you so much, *caro?*"

It was on his tongue to tell her the truth, but he could not force out the words. Not now on this day when she had given him her love. Not now, in view of all that had happened: Varano's faith in him, his own achievements during the siege, the long pretense he had kept up. To tell her now that he had first come to Città del Monte as Borgia's agent, that the Duke's charges were true, while he had still lied about his birth — to tell her this now was impossible. And because of what lay ahead of him, it was needless. He knew perfectly that Borgia would not whittle down one phrase of the terms, as they applied to him. And death was bitter enough without the humiliation of Camilla's loathing. He clung to her belief in him with all his soul. He was no martyr to truth.

But half-truths were possible. "My lord Cesare," he said, "has some cause to believe that I am responsible for this long check to his troops.

He does not relish obstacles. It's a point of pride with him to be thorough with his enemies."

"What do you plan, then?" she faltered.

"I shall ask for a safe-conduct and talk matters over with the Duke of Gravina tomorrow morning."

"Is it safe, Andrea? When you're once in their hands, will they let you come back" — her lips trembled — "to me?"

"Perfectly safe." He kept the secret irony of what he had actually decided out of his voice. "I have every confidence in Francesco Orsini, as a man of honor."

"Because, if there's any doubt," she insisted, "I beg you not to go. I'm not afraid of death, only afraid of meeting it alone."

Taking both her hands, he held them to his lips, his eyes on hers. He did not trust himself to speak. Since deception had been his role so long, it was appropriate to end on that note. The acceptance of Borgia's terms had to come from him, and she must not know of it until it was irrevocable.

But that evening, in the palace garden, he found it difficult to keep the right pitch. The mood of finality and of never-more that haunted every moment had to be suppressed. He must somehow act assured of the future, when he knew that there was no future. The tone of farewell, the passionate rebellion of his body and spirit, must find no expression. He dared not let her suspect that this was the last night, the last of everything. His Italian temperament demanded the anodyne of the dramatic, but he had to refuse it.

Hardest of all were the few minutes that Sister Lucia da Narni spent with them before she returned to her constant attendance on the sick and wounded. Not that her presence discouraged the calm front he was trying to maintain; but that he feared her power of insight, which often enabled her to read a mind as if it were an open book. It seemed to him more than once that her eyes looked through him and understood. At one moment — probably the effect of his own imagination — he felt even a strange approval. But she said nothing.

Camilla had told her of Borgia's terms. "I know little about such things," the nun answered, "and I have no word from God to enlighten me now. Sometimes I wonder how much Our Lord cares about the cunning schemes of men, except that He cares for all His children. But I know this, that he who causes the suffering of others has more to fear than they; for death is not the worst of fears. Messer Andrea, when you see the Duke of Gravina tomorrow, remind him of this. Tell him

357

also from me that they who serve the Dragon shall be destroyed by the Dragon."

When she left them, Camilla said, "What if Gravina will make no concessions?"

"No doubt he will; but, if not, we must take what comes."

"And yet, we shall have tomorrow night."

"Of course."

She was silent a moment. "Then, tomorrow night, would it please you to ask Father Procopio to marry us?"

He was glad of the darkness. "If it would please me! Soul of my soul!"

In his arms, she looked up at him, trying valiantly to give her voice a touch of its usual lightness. "Because I long just once to snap my fingers at the stars."

Later, he spent what was left of the night over a letter. It was not long, but he found it hard to finish. In one place he wrote: "If you refuse to accept the Duke's terms now, that will not help me and will destroy this people who loves you." He made much of that point. Then he poured his heart out on the page and left it there.

When the letter had been sealed, he sat for a while gazing at the pale emptiness of the dawn. He felt no uplift at the thought of performing an unselfish act; nor did he pose to himself. He was simply a man taken in a trap. Since he must die in any case, it was better to purchase the lives of others by dying alone. That was the jist of it.

Having washed himself and put on his best suit of black and gold, he went over to the castle, where young Ettore Leone, who acted as his lieutenant, had held the night watch. It was now past sunrise.

"You will send out a flag at once to the Duke of Gravina," he said, "asking a safe-conduct for me. I have matters to treat of with His Lordship."

Not long afterwards, the messenger returned with the Duke's promise, and Andrea ordered his horse saddled.

"Messer Ettore," he remarked, "one never knows what may happen in these parleys. If I am not back in three hours, give this letter to Madonna and my loving thanks to all our comrades."

Leone stared, then he wrung Andrea's outstretched hand. "God keep Your Signory!"

From the castle yard, the palace was hidden by surrounding walls, but Andrea glanced in that direction and hesitated a moment. No, he had planned this early departure to avoid farewells which might have betrayed him. He would not change now.

Mounting his horse, he raised his hand in salute to Leone and the pikemen on guard.

"Open the gates," he commanded.

Varano's dying words crossed his mind as he rode out in view of the enemy camp.

They greeted him with respectful stares and a ruffle of drums, when he crossed the trenches. Here was the formidable captain, the hero of the siege, whom they had thus far seen only in armor in the thicket of battle. He made a fine figure on his tall horse, attired as if for court, a white plume and a gold medal on his velvet cap. A *gran signore*, whatever people might say about him. The soldiers who guided him to the Duke's tent looked proud of themselves.

Gravina stood in the opening of his pavilion.

"Ha, Andrea!" he called in greeting. "I'm glad to meet you again unarmed. *Sangue di Dio!* I thought once or twice lately you would be the death of me. Welcome! . . . But, Messere," he added in a lower voice, when Andrea had entered the tent, "I hope you don't expect an abatement in Duke Cesare's terms. Even you could not talk away one pen stroke."

Andrea shook his head. "I'm not concerned with that but with the fulfillment of the clauses regarding Madonna Camilla and the city. What's the warranty for the good faith of your master?"

Gravina shrugged. There was a growing coolness between Borgia and his *condottieri*, a coolness that would end four months later in the strangler's cord for Gravina himself. "Frankly, none," was the reply, "except his own advantage. I'll withdraw my companies as soon as the articles are signed. There'll be no sack. That much I can promise you. As to Madonna, you'll agree that he has nothing to gain and something to lose if he breaks his word."

Andrea thought for a moment. Then, drawing his sword, he presented it to Gravina. "So be it," he said.

CHAPTER LVI

TEN days later, Cesare Borgia, returning from the north, had finally leisure enough to inspect the newest of his conquests and diverted himself by a visit to Città del Monte. It was seldom that the pressure of affairs allowed him such amusement as this excursion offered: a pleasant ride down from Urbino, the appraisal of revenues from his lately acquired estates, and the sweet indulgence of personal venom. With regard to the last, he felt the happy anticipation of a man about to witness an unusual comedy. He looked forward to several gratifying scenes before it was over.

The aspect of the valley, trampled and defaced by the recent campaign, whetted his resentment against the stubbornness which had made such damage necessary. If he could have taken over the *contrada* without fighting, as he had originally planned, it would have meant thousands more in his treasury. And for this loss, one miscreant, now awaiting death in the castle dungeon at Città del Monte, was entirely to blame.

Nor did the remarks of Mario Belli, who had joined the ducal retinue at Fabriano and who gave a first-hand account of the two months' struggle, sweeten Cesare's temper. Here had taken place the bloody advance through the woods, which, thanks to Andrea's system of defenses, had cost so many days and lives. And here was the site of the Battle of the Forest, where the Duke stopped to view the dip of land which had concealed Varano's horsemen. "It is now established," said Belli, "that this excellent device was the invention of my lord Or——, I mean Zoppo. Most surely it accounted for the defeat which we sustained at that time."

"Very clever," Borgia agreed. "I shall remember it to his credit."

But the last straw was the appearance of the city walls, as the ducal party approached them. Dilapidated, breached in a half-dozen places, they looked far more like antique ruins than like fortifications which had withstood a considerable army less than two weeks ago.

"Do you mean to tell me," blazed Cesare, "that our captains weren't able to force an entrance into this splintered hulk of a town that a drove of donkeys could storm? How much gunpowder did the blockheads waste here? I'll warrant it runs to a mad figure. And yet they

360

did not walk in but urged me to offer terms! *Alla croce di Dio,* I'll learn the reason for this!"

Belli put on his most hangdog expression, which hardly disguised the glint of malice behind it. "By Your Signory's leave, the reason is not far to seek. Had Your Sublimity been present, no doubt we should have walked in behind your invincible banner. Failing that, we could only do our best, as the number of dead will testify. I ask humbly, were we matched with a man of flesh and bones? No, my lord, with an incarnate devil, shrewd as a fox, savage as a lion, ever on guard, ever prepared with a new stratagem. Sir, I consider my lord — I mean Zoppo — a captain of mark, such as I have never — "

"Hold your tongue!" Borgia's calm gave a hint of cracking. "I've heard enough of the fellow's tricks. They've had their day. The devil will be exorcised, friend Belli. He is under treatment now, for that matter, and I wager our good Ramirez has made him aware of his flesh and bones. Don Esteban's a competent exorcist."

The horsemen nearest the Duke laughed; Belli jerked back his head in silent appreciation of Borgia's humor. Ramirez, who had been appointed captain of the Spanish garrison at Città del Monte, had a sinister reputation.

To the boom of cannon and dipping of standards, Cesare now entered the castle portal of the city and, skirting the long range of buildings, rode into the palace courtyard, where a guard of Castilian mercenaries, headed by Don Esteban in person, was drawn up to receive him.

"And where," smiled the Duke, when he had mounted the broad inside stairway to the first landing, "is our beautiful hostess, the renowned Prefettessa? I should at least have expected the civility of a welcome. Far be it from me to await any special mark of courtesy; but, as her humblest admirer, I grieve to be ignored. Where is she, Esteban?"

They were standing within the threshold of the first long salon, which had not yet been thoroughly cleaned. It looked bare and impoverished. Of its ornaments, only the god of Castel Gandolfo remained in a kind of forlorn vacuum.

The Spaniard ran a tongue over his ulcerated lips. "If Your Highness pleases, I should like a word in private."

Cesare waved back the gentlemen of his suite and walked over to a window. "So, then?" he inquired.

"I am at a loss," said Ramirez, "to know how I should deal with Madonna. Of course I informed her of Your Grace's arrival and requested her attendance. More than this, I could not do without transgressing your instructions that she be treated with all respect. I beg to learn your will in the matter."

Borgia's serene face showed a touch of impatience. "Use your imagination, man. Is it for love of her that she's permitted to stop here with an empty title and empty powers? Hardly! But, first, so that you may rule this people through her to my profit; and, second, because it amuses me to skewer her on a gilded pin and watch her flutter. Respect is the gilding I mean. Treat her with all respect, of course, but see that she feels the pin. And, by the way, she's yours if you can win her. Does that mean anything to you?"

Ramirez bowed low. "How can I thank Your Grace! Such condescension! I am overwhelmed, dazzled — "

"You deserve my favor, Esteban. It pleases me to reward your services." The Duke nodded graciously; but it was probable that hatred rather than benevolence prompted him at the moment. By unleashing this pox-ridden brute on Camilla, he prolonged and embellished the whole comedy. "I'll be interested to see whether you can win her," he added.

"I flatter myself," smirked the other, "that it will be possible."

"But remember the gilding, my good Esteban. Nothing abrupt or uncourtly. I insist on that. We must live up to our engagements."

"I understand, my lord."

"Then prove it by fetching her down to dinner — *with all respect*. But now, something else." Cesare's glance quickened. "The man Zoppo — I trust you have left enough of him for our entertainment. There's no sport in flogging a dead horse."

Ramirez smirked again. "God forbid that I should rob Your Signory of a moment's satisfaction! I have merely induced in him a more plastic frame of mind, sensitive to impressions. Diet and the whip are rare softeners. You will find him twenty pounds lighter and somewhat discolored; but, as for life and limb, he is entirely at Your Lordship's disposal. These peasants are a tough breed."

"We'll make proof of that," said Borgia. "Have him brought to us at the end of dinner. It will amuse the company. I understand you were able to secure the witness I suggested."

"Everything's ready, sir."

"And make sure Madonna's there."

After finishing his toilet and changing to a court suit, Cesare spent the intervening hour in an inspection of the palace. Accompanied by the terrified major-domo, he descended to the library and cast an appreciative glance over the costly bindings and manuscripts. They would make a handsome addition to his own and the Vatican collection. Or perhaps it would be wiser to dispose of them. He reckoned the value at not less than twenty thousand ducats. Then he examined the silver and gold plate, used for official banquets, and appraised them at fifty thousand. Demanding an inventory of furniture and art pieces, he checked up here and there and stopped to admire some notable items.

"Her Signory," he observed to several gentlemen of his suite, who made the round with him, "will doubtless be glad to express her gratitude for our generous terms by presenting us with such trivial keepsakes as meet our fancy. Her position does not require an elaborate display. Messer Renato, take note of our selection."

But, as he selected everything of value, the note taking was not complicated.

Dinnertime found him once more in the great salon, where he paused before an empty space at the end, which had evidently held a painting.

"What was here?" he asked the major-domo.

"A most beautiful thing, my lord, representing 'The Triumph of Virtue,' by Mantegna. Madama purchased it in Venice."

"So? I admire Mantegna. Where is it now?"

"In Madama's own bedchamber, sir. She treasures the picture especially."

"Why, then, I must have a glimpse of it — even in so impregnable a place. Take note, Messer Renato."

And he sauntered on to view the marble god at the opposite end of the room. He knew that Varano had paid five thousand ducats for it. Too much, but it was at least worth three. Meanwhile, his Palace of San Clemente needed just such a statue. "Take note, Messer Renato."

At this point, attendants announced dinner.

"We are still awaiting the divine Camilla," Borgia explained to his suite, some fifteen or twenty cavaliers, who now stood assembled at a respectful distance. "Ah, the coquetry of ladies! Cold victuals mean nothing to them, if only their hair needs one more touch. But hunger in patience, signori, for nothing will change them."

Then, at a light sound beyond the threshold, he stepped forward, as Camilla, with two of her women, entered. The line of gentlemen bowed; the Duke put on his most charming smile. But a chill passed

363

through the company. Camilla and her ladies wore complete mourning without any ornaments. Their somber robes and wimples gave them the appearance of nuns. Borgia had overlooked this detail. For some obscure reason, it took the sparkle out of the entertainment. The cruel comedy he wanted, the jaunty touch, bade fair to look merely cheap and brutal.

Sensitive to nuances, he changed his manner from polite irony to menacing politeness. Reaching out for her hand and finding it withheld, he drew back with a cool nod.

"You have kept us waiting too long for your welcome, Madama."

"I do not welcome you," she returned. "Your Spanish captain compels me to attend you. What's Your Lordship's will?"

He saw at once that this was neither pride nor defiance but a sort of dull indifference beyond the reach of harshness or threat. He chose another technique.

"Alas! What do I hear! Is Your Signory ill? Forgive me." And receiving no answer except the same frozen stare, he added, "Is there anything I can do?"

"Yes, but you will not do it."

"Ask and find out."

"The life and freedom of Andrea Orsini."

"You mean the peasant who calls himself Orsini?"

"Your Lordship knows who I mean."

The Duke turned on a gentle light in his eyes, softened his smile, and looked the picture of compassion. It would have disarmed any doubter.

"Is that all?" he encouraged. "Would so trivial a thing restore you?"

Fired by a sudden hope, she sank to her knees. "Illustrious Lord, if you will grant him life and freedom, I will do anything. I will obey your least wish. I will thank you with every breath. Oh, good Your Excellence, be gracious to me!"

He let her kneel a moment and glanced above her head toward the listening group of gentlemen. His face expressed only pity; but somehow he contrived a hint of the burlesque, and they took their cue from that. Mario Belli jerked back his head.

"This is most touching," said Borgia gravely. "You would do anything I asked?"

"Indeed, sir."

"For instance, you would take off this ugly mourning that so ill becomes you?"

364

Sensing a grain of mockery in the smooth voice, Camilla shrank a little; but the hope he had given her was so precious that she dared not risk offending him. "If you desired it."

"And you would consider me your friend and protector?"

"Always, my lord."

"You would promise never to see this man again?"

"Yes, if I know he is free and safe."

"Most touching!" Cesare repeated. "I am deeply moved. But Your Excellence must not kneel." The rigid grip of his hand on either arm startled her. "It is I who should kneel to you, Madonna, to crave forgiveness if in any way, beyond the needs of war, I have distressed you. What you ask is by no means impossible. Shall we discuss it at the end of dinner? Meanwhile, I beg you will not be downcast. Grant me a truce till then." He smiled contagiously. "Is it a bargain?"

When so much depended on his whim, she could do nothing but return the shadow of a smile.

"*Ecco fatto!*" he laughed. "*Benissimo!* Accept my arm."

She hesitated but he drew her arm through his.

"There you are!" he continued. "Now we can dine with some pleasure. And I repeat," he added in a whisper, "do not be downcast. All will come right in the end. I promise you will be surprised."

She was surprised, and not unpleasantly, when they had taken their places in the dining hall, to find Mario Belli next her at table. It seemed clear that he enjoyed Borgia's favor and had come up in the world. His mantle and doublet were stitched with gold thread, and he had a new poniard with a massive gold hilt. The submerged nobleman in him showed nearer the surface. Except that he had gone over to the enemy (which, as a soldier of fortune, he had every right to do), Camilla bore him no grudge. His Judas face and leering manner had always repelled her; but, as compared with the other men at the table, he was at least familiar. She connected him with Andrea, who had always retained a fondness for him, and with a hundred episodes of the past.

The dinner two years ago, when Andrea had first visited Città del Monte, crossed her mind. Then Belli had sat in the lowest place; now he was at her side. And everything else had changed. The hall looked dingy and unkept. Some tapestries had broken from their hooks and sagged down along the naked stone behind them. The dais and L-shaped tables were replaced by a single board, crossing the end of the hall that stretched desolately away to the now empty hearth. All the well-known faces were gone. Then it had been evening, and the carved candelabra had added a festive glitter; now, in midafternoon, the soiled windows admitted a matter-of-fact daylight.

"Yes," grated Belli's voice on her left, "times have changed, Madama. It's a habit they have."

She looked around at him, startled. "Are you a mind reader, Messere?"

"No, but the remark fits the occasion, doesn't it? . . . By the way, how fares my *belle amie*, the Princess Alda? You may recall that she bore me company at table that first time — and often afterwards."

"She misses you, sir, and often speaks of you."

"Indeed?" Belli was silent a moment. Rolling a piece of bread into a pellet between his fingers, he flicked it across the table onto the floor. "Indeed? . . . And may I ask whether the holy Sister Lucia is still in the palace?"

Camilla nodded. "She leaves today. For my sake she remained after the siege. God bless her for it!"

Struck by the note of torment in her voice, Belli gave her an intent look, but he made no comment. "I must see Her Reverence," he said. "It may interest you to know that she and little Alda are the only women I have ever loved." But he accompanied the remark with so evil a grin that it meant nothing.

"Your Signory's not eating," observed Borgia on her right.

"I'd forgotten," she said timidly. "It seems that today I have no taste for food."

"Nonsense! Look — this capon. Not bad. Permit me to carve it for you."

Beneath his sharp knife and capable fingers, the flesh dropped neatly from the bones. She felt a sudden horror of his muscular, shapely hands. Such peculiar thoughts came to her these days, clammy gusts of faintness and sick fancies.

"There! Let that tempt you."

She nibbled a little to please him and he turned to dip his fingers into a bowl of rose water that a page presented. Then, playfully, he began chatting about his recent journey to Milan, the festivities in honor of King Louis, gossip of the French court. He had returned south by way of Ferrara. . . .

She tried to listen, nodding dutifully at the right time or murmuring a word of interest here and there. He must be kept in a good humor, despite the waves of faintness that passed over her and brought out a cold sweat. But now and then she realized that she had not heard what he said. She felt utterly helpless and alone, a mere girl, by the side of this masterful prince whom the whole world dreaded. Was it possible to believe that he would grant her prayer for Andrea? Sister Lucia had told her that God might grant it; and now, while Borgia's compelling voice ran on, she prayed silently, as how often during the past ten days. Somehow the worst of all was to know that Andrea was so near, separated from her by only a few walls, and that she could do nothing; to wonder how he fared, what had happened; and, when she begged for a word, to be met with the silence of the grave, as if he were already buried!

A laugh from Borgia startled her. "Penny for your thoughts, Madonna!"

"But, my lord," she stammered, "I was attending. The illness of your illustrious sister in Ferrara. I grieve to hear — "

"Nothing of the kind. I was talking about my cousin Angela and the effect of her charms on the princes of Este. Now, if I had been speaking of *something else*, I wager you would have caught every syllable."

"It's true that I'm concerned — "

Cesare's practised eye noted the corpse whiteness of her face against the black wimple. Catching up a goblet, he pressed it on her. "Here, drink this."

"No, my lord, thanks — "

"Drink, I tell you." Frightened by the yellow blaze of his eyes, she took a few swallows. The wine steadied her. "Better, eh?" he demanded. "Well, then, I won't keep Your Excellence on tenterhooks any longer. Let's discuss this affair you have so much at heart. But don't you think it would be well to invite Messer Andrea himself to table, while we finish the confects? After all, the talk concerns him."

"You mean, I can see him, my lord?"

"Of course. I promised you a surprise."

The color flooded back into her cheeks. "How can I thank Your Grace for this mercy! I have no words — "

Borgia smiled. "Do not speak of it. You confuse me."

He nodded to Ramirez, who got up from the table and left the room. Voices died out along the board.

But almost immediately the main door swung open. Camilla pictured the tall, graceful figure of Andrea in his dark dress approaching down the sweep of the hall. What she now saw bewildered her. A barelegged man in a peasant's smock, under a weight of chains, while guards on either side half supported him. His cadaverous cheeks were covered by a black stubble of beard; and his hair hung matted over his fore-head. Evidently he had been beaten, for she could see red weals on his bare shoulders and legs. Even the smock he wore was in tatters. She stared in wonder at Borgia. Then, looking back at the prisoner, she met his eyes.

It could not be true.

"Well," remarked the Duke, and his voice had turned cold, "here he is. What do you think of him?"

CHAPTER LVII

ANDREA had not foreseen this. The starvation, enforced sleeplessness, and beatings of the last ten days, to be followed by an ignoble death, were to be expected from Borgia's personal hatred, but this last refine-ment of cruelty defied calculation. During his misery and torments, Andrea had taken it for granted that physical pain, graduated perhaps to the most intense degree this side of coma, was to be his portion. But now, unprepared and physically weakened, he found himself exposed to another, still more devastating, form of suffering, that involved Camilla as well as himself. He was to be made the instrument of her humiliation.

He understood Borgia's purpose at once; but he had no defense against it, not even the physical defense of a voice. He had been de-prived of all but the absolute minimum of water, with the result that speech was extremely difficult. Even his eyes, unused to the light, could express little. Held in a bent position by the weight and arrangement of his chains, he now stood in front of Camilla, with only the table between them.

"I repeat," said the Duke, "what do you think of him?" Cesare swiveled his chair for a better view of Camilla's face. "For, mark you, I'm showing him out of masquerade. There he is, I say, in his native colors, those proper to his condition and birth. He's worn brocade and medals long enough. Do you see any marks of gentility about him now?"

Camilla tried to get up, but found herself too weak.

"No, Madonna!" Cesare's hand rested on her shoulder. "You'll stay here awhile. You need to be informed about the noble Captain Orsini-Zoppo. You might have spared yourself this lesson, but my statements were not enough. You challenged me — I remember your words — to prove that this slave's birth was less noble than mine. *Less noble than mine!*" His scornful amusement passed along the table and caught up answering smiles. "Well, it pleases me to accept the challenge. I don't make statements at random. But tell me. Your concern for the fellow is transparent enough. You expected to marry this peasant? Is that it?"

With an effort, she fought off her dizziness. "I do not need to answer you. But I am proud to answer this. I love and honor the lord Orsini. . . . Is there no one here who is man enough to take his part?"

"Hear that?" Borgia smiled. His glance roved from face to face and assured itself that all were duly amused. "Is there really no one who will stand forth? It's a noble chance, cavaliers. . . . But you see, Madonna, there is no one, and I don't wonder."

He emptied his goblet and then eyed Andrea. "Messer Rascal, aren't you touched that my lady speaks up so bravely for you? Why don't you thank her?"

Camilla saw a familiar flame leap up in Andrea's eyes. He looked at her when he answered. "I thank her with all my heart."

The Duke was highly entertained. The comedy so far could not have been improved. It was like watching a show, directing and taking a part in it at the same time.

He proceeded now to take part and addressed the audience. "You see, gentlemen, the lady has swallowed this cheat's hook to the gills. God knows how we can relieve her of it, but we must do our best. In spite of everything, she still considers him a gentleman of the House of Raimondo Orsini, Count of Nola. And yet there's something to be said for her: he had a glib tongue — before he lost his voice."

The remembered scent of pinewoods, a breath from the past, hovered through Camilla's mind. She recalled the little glen in the forest where she and Andrea had lunched and talked that day last spring when they had ridden out toward Fabriano. She recalled the Mediterranean world of beauty which he had spread before her. It had been so clearly a reflection of his own passion for beauty. And with this loved memory, Cesare Borgia's voice now mingled, blighting and cheapening it.

"We'll give him one more chance to be honest," the Duke added. "Friend Zoppo, your goose is cooked. Why not tell Her Excellence what a mountebank you've been?"

But it was too late for confessions, even if Andrea had had the strength to make them. In this antechamber of death, it no longer seemed to matter that he had once called himself a gentleman. At least he had been faithful in more important things. What concerned him now was Camilla's white face and the torment of his own thirst, as a page filled the Duke's cup.

After a moment, he said, "Her Excellence knows what I am."

"You see," Borgia shrugged. "With as many welts on his back as a tinker's donkey, the yokel clings to his titles. We'll have to find other means to squeeze the truth out of him. Or perhaps I'm wrong. He says that Madonna knows what he is. Maybe he told her in a fond moment. Well then, Your Ladyship, what is he?" And when Camilla did not answer, the Duke's hand closed on her wrist. "I expect a reply. The question is very simple. Who do you take him to be: Orsini or Zoppo?"

She endeavored vainly to free her arm.

"Eh?" he insisted.

She replied tonelessly: "Why not slander *me* with the report that I am not Camilla Baglione? My lord Orsini comes of a greater House than mine and greater than yours. Let it suffice you."

Leaning back in his chair, the Duke laughed, and the company echoed him. Mario Belli seemed particularly amused.

"Spoken like one of the Magnificent House!" Borgia chuckled. "I wish her cousin and my friend, Giampaolo Baglione, were present with us. He'd be flattered. . . . But now, signori, having done what I could for the lady and her swain, I owe something to my own reputation for truthfulness. We must get a confession from Zoppo, one way or another. Captain Ramirez, see to it."

Andrea summoned up what was left of his fortitude. If they would only give him a cup of water! If he could only rid himself for a moment of this torment in his mouth and throat!

"Water!" he begged.

Camilla sprang up, but Borgia again gripped her arm.

"Be seated, Madonna. Messer Mario, see that my lady keeps her chair." His eyes were on the main door of the hall, leading to the anteroom. "Hush!" he pointed. "Look."

Ramirez had come in with a tall, plainly dressed woman, who wore a blue scarf, peasant fashion, on her head. The room was so quiet that

Camilla could hear her ask: "Where is he?" The woman's eyes ranged along the table, then stopped on Andrea's bent figure in front of it between the two guards. With a low cry, she hurried forward to look at him more closely.

"Andrea!" The tremulous voice sounded distinct in the silence. "*Figliolo mio!* What have they done to you?"

Andrea forgot the grinning Duke, the hard faces. Consciousness narrowed to this unbelievable appearance.

"*Mammina mia!*"

"What have they done to you, my son?" she repeated. "They told me you were ill, that you wanted me. These chains, Andrea! The look of you!" She stopped; her eyes widened at the sight of his half-naked shoulders. "Merciful God! They have beaten you . . . Tell me. Can't you speak?"

"Give me water."

Turning from him, she snatched a goblet from the table and put it to his lips. "Here's wine. Drink. Drink slowly."

"Let her be," Cesare said to the guards.

When the goblet was empty, Andrea muttered, "God reward you, *cara.*"

"But what does it mean? Why are you a prisoner?"

Borgia's voice cut in. "You'll be informed in good time, woman. Meanwhile, I want a word from your son." His gaze shifted to Andrea. "We'll make sure of this. Tell us who the woman is. Maybe you'll deny knowing her, now that you have your wits about you again. Who is she?"

"My mother, Costanza Zoppo."

The end of the hunt. The fox cornered at last. And devils' horns could sound the mort. Andrea could not look at Camilla, but he met the Duke's gaze steadily.

Borgia turned in his chair. "Have I answered Your Signory's challenge?" he asked Camilla. "Are you satisfied?"

She looked up slowly from the table. "Yes."

"Have you nothing to say to your true love now? He'll be pleased with a word from you."

"Yes," she said again. Her face was deathly pale, but she had gained control of herself. She leaned forward. Something in her manner excluded the others, so that she and Andrea seemed alone. "Why was it necessary?" she said. "You, with your mind and art and valor — you, who are so great. I don't understand."

"Because I was a fool," he said. "I hope someday you will forgive me."

"Forgive?" she echoed. "Forgive?" Suddenly tears blinded her, and she covered her face with her hands.

"Bravo!" exclaimed Borgia, with mock enthusiasm. "Well done! It remains only for me to wind up the play. Mona Costanza here still does not seem to know what it's about. Learn, then, that this son of yours, who was in my service, posed as a great lord and has been uncovered. That makes him guilty enough. Worse still, he betrayed me. I sent him here in my pay to effect the peaceful surrender of this state to the authority of the Church. . . . Perhaps you didn't know *that* about him, either, Madonna Milla." But as she merely sat frozen, Borgia raised an eyebrow at Belli. "Messer Mario could inform you on that point."

"Could I not!" returned Belli, looking like Satan's uncle. "Could I not, indeed! As captain of the garrison, he might have turned over this city to Your Grace, without the loss of a single man, except perhaps the old lord Varano. Instead, he turned against Your Loving Highness, who until then had kindly ignored the stigma of his birth, forgot his loyalty to you and his own advantage — with what result? By God, the death of hundreds of Your Grace's troops, vast expense, and loss of future revenues. An adder warmed upon Your Lordship's generous heart. I have never seen a more notable treason."

Cesare gave the Frenchman a sharp glance, but he said: "There, sirs, you have it from one who knows. On every count, the charlatan peasant deserves death. My sentence, Andrea Zoppo, is that tomorrow you shall be exposed in a cage on the castle tower, there to remain as a spectacle and warning until your bones drop apart; and that tonight you be subjected to such torments as your crimes warrant."

A cold silence fell. It did not take much imagination to picture what was to happen.

Mona Costanza lifted her clasped hands toward Cesare.

"No, my lord, no! As you hope for God's mercy, be merciful . . ."

"Keep her quiet, Don Esteban!" Borgia flamed at the Spanish captain. "Remove her. She's served her purpose."

"Have pity!" she cried again. But her voice was stopped by the arm of one of the guards, and she was hurried from the hall.

The Duke glanced right and left along the table. He overlooked Camilla, who had turned on him with blazing eyes and who was on the point of speaking.

"May it please you, signori!" he laughed. "*È finita la commedia! Plaudite!*"

But he broke off in surprise as the figure of another woman appeared in front of him. Absorbed by what was taking place, no one had seen Lucia da Narni enter through an opening in the arras that communicated with one of the service doors. She had stood listening awhile unobserved at one side of the hall. Her dark dress and almost ethereal slenderness made her a part of the background. Still unnoticed, she had come forward while Borgia was announcing the close of his entertainment.

"I have a message for you," she said quietly.

He frowned at her, puzzled. Then, observing her bandaged hands, he inferred who she was and frowned in another fashion. "The Reverend Sister Lucia, I suppose? I've wanted to see you. It has been brought to my attention that during the siege you gave much comfort and encouragement to my enemies, and that you remained here in direct opposition to the desires of my ally and friend, the illustrious Ercole d'Este. A tripping nun who, instead of remaining in the cloister, busies herself with worldly affairs. What have you to say for yourself?"

"I have a message for you," she repeated.

The calm power of her eyes disconcerted him. He unleashed the lion power of his own to overbear it, but found himself blinking.

"Message from whom?" he snapped.

"From our Lord God."

At that moment, on the lips of anyone else, the words might have sounded childish or mawkish. Spoken by her, they had an unearthly ring that froze everyone, including Borgia, to a breathless attention.

Rallying, however, the Duke forced a smile. "I am honored that Almighty God condescends to address me, though I must take your word for it. What's the divine will?"

She answered in the same remote voice: "Our Lord has spoken to me. He bids me tell you that the man Andrea is now clear of guilt, and that the time of his death is not yet. Our Lord wills that he grow for a while in this world to the end that he may bear worthy fruit. You will give heed to this."

Borgia's smile widened. "Is that all? . . . Signori, it seems I was premature in requesting your applause. The comedy has an epilogue. . . . I ask Your Reverence again, is that all?"

"No. For I must tell you that, if you disobey the message I bring, you will die tonight. Therefore, take heed."

373

CHAPTER LVIII

WHATEVER he might be, Cesare Borgia was not a coward. In battle, in the chase, in the arena (where his heavy sword had been known to decapitate a bull at one stroke), in his political career, so often threatened by assassination, he showed constantly a cool head and a steel nerve. Moreover, he belonged to the enlightened select of the age, who had freed themselves from old wives' superstitions. With him, religion was a matter of convention or of expediency, which had no more effect on his personal outlook than the cut of his clothes.

But neither courage nor skepticism helped him at this point. He was faced by the fact — no less hard for being intangible — of spiritual force; or, if *spiritual* is the wrong word, by something akin to the force which a lion feels in the presence of its tamer. Absolute faith, absolute assurance, has the faculty of communicating its conviction, at least temporarily, to other minds. It was the power of Joan of Arc; it was the power of Lucia da Narni. Therefore, at the moment, not only the others at table, but Cesare Borgia himself, believed what Lucia said.

Only his pride would not accept it. "Look you," he retorted, "this man shall be executed as I have ordered. Meanwhile, you will be detained here. And if I live beyond tonight, I'll see that you fare like other pious impostors and false prophets — the little friar Girolamo, for instance, who was burned in Florence. Don't imagine that the Duke of Ferrara will protect you from the Holy Inquisition. He detests religious frauds as much as I do. . . . Take your eyes off me. It's a good thing I don't believe in witchcraft. Why do you stare at me like that?"

"I'm looking into your mind," she answered, "to see if I can find any light there."

The Duke kept his frozen smile. "Well, do you find any?"

"Yes, for you are not yet dead. The last taper burns low, but it has not yet been put out."

"Easy to say," he scoffed. "If you know so much, tell me what I'm thinking of at this moment."

"Of death. And that you find it hard to kick against the pricks."

In spite of himself, he blinked and looked away; but he could still see her eyes in his brain. "If it's the will of our Lord God, why doesn't He speak to me?"

374

"Because you could not hear Him."

Borgia struck the table with his clenched fist. "There you have it: always an *ipse dixit*. How can you be so sure? How do you know these things?"

"How does one know anything?" she answered in the same untroubled voice. "One knows, one believes, one doubts. *I* know." Her eyes had recaptured his and held them. "You know that what I have said is the truth. I cannot tell you how."

"Truth!" he sneered. "What is — " But the famous analogy struck him, and he broke off, confused. "Hark you, it shall be as I have ordered, truth or not."

She drew back a step. "I have given you the message, Cesare Borgia. I shall now take my leave."

"Not so fast." He stretched his arm out, as if to detain her. "Suppose I conceded something on this point — not that I shall, but for the sake of argument — would our Lord God, on His part, remember it to my credit and return a *quid pro quo?*" He deprecated the question with a laugh. "Tell me that."

She gazed back at him. "Little man, Our Lord does not bargain. I have told you His will. That is enough for you."

"Wait," he urged, fascinated in spite of himself. "One moment. You, who know the future, do you see anything there that concerns me — anything I should avoid, any measures I should take?"

"I do not know the future," she returned. "I am permitted now and then to see a foot ahead, not more. Avoid evil, work righteousness."

Then, turning, she walked with her quiet, lagging footstep down the hall and, drawing the arras apart, went out by the side door. It seemed to the company as if she had faded into the wall. She left a curious hush behind her.

When he spoke at last, Borgia's usually modulated voice sounded harsh and out of key. "God's Cross! There's impudence for you. They ought to keep madwomen locked up."

But no one answered. Glancing here and there, the Duke observed his own thought reflected on every face. Calling names did not alter one iota of the fact. His gentlemen knew and he knew that, if the prisoner's sentence were carried out, he, Cesare, Duke of Romagna, would die that night.

He was not a coward, but he was a realist. He did not want to die. On the other hand — almost as much — he did not want to lose face.

Down the board, one of the captains spoke. "Your Grandeur owes something to us who are in your service and to the states you now rule. This same Lucia da Narni bears the marks of Our Lord's sacred wounds, as has been duly verified by the Pope's own commission. She is known to have strange powers and visions. After all, Your Illustrious Signory need consider it no shame to yield on this point, if such is the will of God. Indeed, not to do so would reflect upon Your Excellence's Christian piety. The *gonfaloniere* of the Church should be the first to show devotion."

"There's something in that," nodded Cesare.

Another voice said: "In view of this traitor's crimes, some mitigation of his sentence would redound to Your Lordship's reputation for mercy. A good deal could be made of it."

"Mitigation, eh?" The Duke's face brightened. "That's true. The woman spoke merely of his life."

Other voices chimed in. It was obvious that the company would think none the less of him for obeying the divine mandate; on the contrary, it would consider defiance on his part irrational and foolhardy. This agreed with Borgia's own point of view.

"Signori," he said at last, "I defer to your judgment. Personally I view the Reverend Sister's message as so much twaddle, the fruit of a sick imagination. But let it never be said of me that I am wanting in reverence to our Lord God, who has so gloriously assisted and favored me. Nay, I would rather that this villain escaped something of his just deserts than that I should ever be accused of impiety. . . . So, then, you knave" — he shot a baffled glance at Andrea — "though I wager this is simply another of your tricks and that you and the nun shaped it up together, you can have your life. Go on growing, as Her Reverence puts it. But you'll grow underground in as tight a prison as Don Esteban can find for you, until you grow into the grave. Captain Ramirez, I hold you responsible."

A chair was pushed back, and Mario Belli sprang to his feet. He looked convulsed, his teeth showing between taut lips, his eyes squinting beneath their heavy brows, a swollen vein across his forehead. "*Que Votre Excellence me permette* — one word, Your Lordship!"

Cesare stared. "What's wrong, man?"

"I protest, Your Signory. When I see this obscenity traitor, this unspeakable Judas here — " Belli's outstretched arm and forefinger pointed at Andrea — "when I think of the mischief he has caused, the ingratitude he has shown to you, the cheats he has practised, and when I hear that he is only to be imprisoned for all this, it is more than I can swallow in silence. I take it that Madonna Camilla herself is outraged by such mildness. Is it not true, Madonna?"

Torn between hope and fear, and at the end of her endurance, Camilla could only flinch under the dreadful face peering down at her. "Are you mad?" she breathed.

"*Voilà, Messieurs!* She agrees with me," Belli continued. "The rogue deserves a hundred deaths. Your Lordship's first sentence was by far too merciful, though it had the merit of exposing him for the world to gape at. But since that is impossible — and I admit it would be folly to risk Your Blessed Signory's life in such a trivial cause — leave him to me. Not prison. I vow there's no prison on earth can hold such an eel. No, make the world his prison blacker than your darkest *trabocchetto* here. Blind him, I say, and turn him out. He's been partial to colors: let him enjoy them with empty sockets if he can. Let him paint pictures then! What punishment is it for a half-dead carcass to rot in prison? Who but a few will know then what has happened to the tinsel signor? What shame is that to him? No, set him on the road with his hag mother to lead him, and, from the Marches to the Veneto, let people admire the justice of Your Signory!"

If Sister Lucia had cast a spell, Mario Belli cast another of the opposite sort. As he spoke, his physical appearance seemed to change. He was no longer hideous, but hellish. The alarmed gentlemen at table witnessed a case of demonic possession. They swore afterwards that they saw the features of a human being blend with those of a fiend. His jeering voice chilled them. He mimicked the gropings of a blind man. He could make them feel the agony of blinding. As Andrea stared across at him, he could hardly recognize his former ensign. Sister Lucia's fears for Belli recurred to him. The balance between good and evil in the Frenchman no longer existed. All was evil. Camilla closed her eyes and sat struggling against nausea and faintness.

Only Cesare Borgia felt exhilarated. His imagination embroidered on Belli's suggestions, until he could see that this was exactly the vengeance he craved. It had the spice of mockery that he liked. While reducing Andrea to impotence, it made him a lifelong object lesson to other people of the Duke's wrath. Since the death penalty was forbidden, this was the next best thing. More deftly than lifelong imprisonment, it complied with Lucia da Narni's terms but left an ironic sting that helped to even scores with her.

"*Benissimo!*" Cesare exclaimed. "My estimable friend, you are a man in a thousand. Your loyalty to me and your resourcefulness alike do you credit. I accept your advice. Don Esteban, remove the prisoner. Have sharpened stakes prepared and look to it that the sentence is carried out within the hour. Then — "

"By your leave, sir," interrupted Belli. "I asked Your Grace to let me deal with him. What need is there of stakes when I have my two good thumbs?" He cocked them up at arm's length with a dreadful relish. "Gouging's the thing. And what need to remove him when I can pop you his eyes out here before this worshipful company? I have the trick of it. One of my former patrons, who shall be nameless, admired this skill in me above all else. I blinded him ten rogues in the prisons of Venice before he could say a paternoster. Look you, it's as easy as this." Reaching out, Belli plucked a large hothouse grape from a salver and held it up between thumb and forefinger. By a trick of suggestion, he gave it somehow the appearance of a naked human eyeball. "Then, look you, a pressure, and out squirts the jelly. No harder than that." He plopped it into his mouth and smacked his lips. Then, selecting several more grapes, he repeated the operation, rolling his eyes with a horrible drollery to watch the effect on the audience. Several gentlemen turned pale; others stared at the table.

"My invaluable Belli!" the Duke applauded. "That would be a show worth watching. I'm sure Madonna here would like to see how a cheating peasant's eyes look out of their sockets. Wouldn't you, Donna Milla? Don't play squeamish. I know you're curious. . . . Well, then, Messer Mario, if you'll oblige us, I'll be grateful to you — a hundred ducats an eye."

"They're not worth so much," returned Belli, his mouth still full. "For the hate I bear the whoreson, I'm privileged in the doing of it. Have him strapped to a chair in front of His Signory, Don Esteban."

It came to Andrea that this was the last time he would see light or color. From now on, sight would not exist for him except in memory. A minute or so until perpetual blackness. It was the panic horror of this rather than the agony of the blinding that appalled him. They were tying him to a chair; his chained hands and legs were helpless; he knew that any appeal for mercy would merely add to the Duke's satisfaction. He saw Belli swaggering his way behind the chairs of the gentlemen seated at Borgia's right and rounding that end of the table. He saw one or two of them shrink forward to avoid contact with the bravo. He saw the Duke's handsome, mocking face. Then he fixed his eyes on Camilla, who was looking down. That must be his last memory. No, Belli now stood between him and the table. He stared up into the leering inhuman face poised above him.

378

"Take a good look at me," cackled Belli. "It's the last thing you'll see. And now, my lords — " He spread his hands toward Andrea. To the latter's distempered view they seemed already stained with blood.

A voice at the table rapped out. "Look to Madonna. . . ." A stir followed, and the rasping of chairs on the stone flagging. . . . "Wine here! Stand back, give her air." And a curt command from Borgia, "Fetch her women."

Undeterred, Belli leaned down, his lips tight across the teeth. A whisper came from them, like the hissing of a cat.

"Now, Your Magnificence, do your part. Show that you can act or, by God, we're both lost. Scream, when I touch your eyes. Act the part, I say. Understand?"

"Proceed, Messer Mario," ordered the Duke.

"At Your Lordship's service."

Belli gave a cackle of laughter and brought his thumbs down on Andrea's eyes. "Now!" he hissed.

The scream that shivered through the hall was authentic enough to bring the sweat out on the faces of several gentlemen. It was repeated and repeated.

"A tough oyster, Your Highness," panted Belli. "But we've got the first of them out of its shell. Now, for the second."

The cries rose again, rasping the nerves of the men at table. Andrea could feel that his cheeks were wet.

"Keep your eyes screwed together," came the whisper.

Then Belli stepped back and turned toward Borgia. "Here's the pulp, if Your Sublimity wants it," he guffawed. "Here's a keepsake. The eyes of an artist! The eyes of a traitor! So be it to all Your Greatness's enemies! Look. They're pretty, aren't they?"

What Cesare saw was a bloody, gelatinous mass, half dripping from Belli's cupped hands.

"Faugh!" he said. "Take the carrion away. It sickens me."

But Belli was not to be restrained from his triumph. He walked grimacing along the tables, showing his trophies to the white-faced captains. Then, to the horror of all, he slipped the wet mass into his pocket. "I'll keep these souvenirs in alcohol for myself then," he grinned, and proceeded to wipe off his dripping hands on a kerchief.

That what he displayed was the chewed pulp of grapes mingled with blood from self-inflicted cuts on his thumbs would hardly have been believed if he had declared it.

379

Meanwhile, the wretched spectacle of Andrea fixed the attention of everyone. He sat writhing against his bonds, his head twisting from side to side, his face contracted and covered with blood.

"God pity him," muttered one of the cavaliers to a table companion. "He was a gallant soldier, whatever they may say of him."

"And now," directed Borgia, "hand him over to his mother and turn them out. I think he's had his fill of palaces; he can grope his way back into a hovel."

CHAPTER LIX

ON Mona Costanza's donkey, which had carried her all the way from Crespino, Andrea felt wretched enough to have pleased even Cesare Borgia, if that great man, already intent on other affairs, could have seen him. Although it was urgent to get beyond the Duke's reach and a change of whim as soon as possible, Andrea could hardly sit upright on the little animal, plodding slowly westward in the late afternoon sun. Except for the shoulder of Mona Costanza, who walked beside him, he could not have ridden at all. The starvation and torments he had suffered, followed by the recent ordeal in the palace hall, left him in a state of collapse, where he was barely conscious of more than the misery of weakness. He knew that somehow he was miraculously free and that Mario Belli, by a trick which he had been unable to follow, had saved him from blinding. He knew also that he must play the role of a blind man, even to his mother, until there was no longer any possibility of pursuit, in case a report of his true condition reached Borgia. Otherwise, he drifted along the road in a sort of vacancy.

Under these circumstances, there could be no thought of travel beyond the shortest distance required to find some hiding place. Mona Costanza mingled her encouragement to Andrea with very sober thoughts as to what would happen when he could go no further. The valley, devastated by the war, did not offer refuge, even if it had been safe to remain there; the forest, as she looked beyond, appeared still more inhospitable; and evening was coming on.

"We'll find something," she declared. "If the Lord God could deliver us out of the hands of that prince of demons, he can direct us to a night's lodging, yes, and a good one, too, where you can rest and eat, my poor Andrea. Then we'll go home. Then you'll belong to me again, and I can look after you!"

But her heart stood still when, at the edge of the woods, she heard hoofbeats along a side path and, immediately afterwards, saw a rider in the crimson and yellow colors of the Duke bearing down on them. Almost at once she recognized him as the officer who had bragged of blinding Andrea and had mocked at them in the palace courtyard. Now he was evidently bent on further mischief.

Fear for herself did not even occur to Mona Costanza, but fear for Andrea made her desperate. Snatching up two stones, she let fly at the man before he could swing from his horse, then followed it up with a second volley.

The rider threw up his arm against the missiles. "Hold!" he shouted. "Let be, for God's sake!"

And at that voice, Andrea called out, "Wait, *Mammina!* Take care! He's a friend."

"Friend?" seethed Mona Costanza. But, looking around, she let the stone which she had just picked up slip from her fingers. Andrea's eyes were wide open and he held out a hand to the enemy, who had now slipped from his horse and was advancing with a smile.

"Mario, how can I thank you?"

"A nice piece of legerdemain, wasn't it, Your Magnificence? That grape pulp wasn't a bad invention. How goes it, Your Lordship? When they turned you loose, I feared you would never reach the woods. But all's well now. Come, sir, you need food, and I've brought you a good ration of it."

With an arm about Andrea, Belli half lifted him from the donkey and was helping him to the side of the road when Mona Costanza recovered her voice.

"*Che bella tresca è questa?*" she demanded. "One moment your eyes are out, and the next they're in; one moment this man is a villain, and the next he's a Good Samaritan."

"It takes some explaining, Mother," said Andrea faintly. "We'll tell you as soon as we have breath. Meanwhile, this is my deliverer, Mario Belli."

The Frenchman bowed. "I can see where His Lordship's prowess comes from, Madam."

"Lordship?" echoed Andrea with a touch of bitterness.

Belli said nothing until he had helped Andrea to a little clearing veiled from the road by a fringe of bushes. Returning to his horse, he fetched a package of victuals and a couple of wine flasks, which had been strapped behind his saddle. Bread, cheese, and meat were spread out, and he warned Andrea to eat slowly. Then he said abruptly, "You'll always remain the lord Orsini to me, and I think you'll be known by that name to all men-of-arms in Italy."

Mona Costanza was looking at Andrea with shining eyes. "Who cares," she said, "as long as he can see! Ah, *figliolo*, what happiness! What unbelievable happiness!"

It was amazing that food could do so much in a short time. When he had finished, Andrea felt new strength in him.

"Won't you be missed at the palace, Mario?"

Belli shook his head. "I begged for this mission. I'm supposed to be chivying you along the road with the Duke's approval. But, for my sake, remain blind awhile, or it will mean a surer rope for me than the one you saved me from in Ferrara. I have to think of my career, after all" — Belli sniggered — "and yours."

"Mine?" echoed Andrea. "Oh, yes! My career!"

"Now, now Your Magnificence! Don't be depressed. Your career will recover. Why else do you think I deserted you last spring?"

"I'm not up to riddles, Mario."

"No riddle." The Frenchman laid a finger on one side of his nose. "A flair for my own advantage. How could I help you and myself by uselessly dying in Città del Monte? You were headed downhill on a runaway horse. But I could cushion your fall at the bottom by changing sides — and I can still help in the same way. Understand?"

A sudden light broke in Andrea's mind. "You mean that you went over to Borgia because — "

"But naturally. I have a fondness for Your Lordship. No, I'll be frank. I owe you more than I can ever repay."

"Owe me for what?"

"Sir, I detest fine sentiments, as you may have noticed. But I'll say this. Twice in my life I've observed that the devil does not have everything his own way in the world. To tell the truth, I owe most to the Reverend Sister Lucia. But when Your Lordship renounced everything you had treasured for the sake of conscience, I could have kissed your feet. It meant, look you, that even I might crawl out of hell at your heels. A new life, what? Well, there you have it."

382

Andrea shrugged. "You're a droll dog, Mario, as I've told you often. Talk of my masquerade! What of yours? By God, I'm a scab to you! . . . But I'd like to know this. What would have happened today if Sister Lucia had not spoken for me?"

It was a moment before Belli answered. "Oh — I had a card to play," he said absently. "However, I don't understand one thing. The marvel of it is how Her Blessed Reverence knew that I planned to kill Cesare Borgia tonight."

He sat pinching his chin. The little clearing had grown dark. An owl challenged somewhere. At last Belli looked up.

"They ought to be here," he remarked.

"Who?"

"It got about *indirectly* that Your Lordship would be needing a quiet place in the mountains for a while and that you would wait here. We can expect some guides presently. Remember, you're blind." Belli turned to Mona Costanza. "Madam, the lord Orsini is the hero of this *contrada*. The peasants would all die for him; and, indeed, many have died. . . . When you're in fettle again, Messere, I suppose you'll return to Crespino for a time."

"Forever!" Mona Costanza put in. "I'd like to see him wandering off again under whatever name! He'll stay at home and paint pictures to the glory of God, as he should have done long since."

"No!" Andrea exclaimed. He was gazing in the direction of the city. "No, in the end, to the glory of God, I'll return to Città del Monte. Do you think Madonna will forgive me or understand, Mario?"

"Suppose she doesn't?" returned the Frenchman.

Andrea nodded. "Yes, that isn't the point. May she never forgive me until I restore what has been taken from her! Perhaps then I'll have the right to ask her forgiveness. Meanwhile, she should leave the city — "

"How?" Belli interrupted.

"Why, the Duke offered her a choice of going or remaining."

"She chose to remain." Belli's voice sounded grim. "Now there is no choice. She's as much a prisoner as you were until today. But that's not the worst."

"What do you mean?"

"I mean she's been promised to Don Esteban Ramirez." Speechless with horror, Andrea could only stare at Belli's somber face, half-visible in the twilight. "Borgia hates her second only to you."

"But then . . ."

"*Why, then,*" snapped Belli, concern showing in the harshness of his voice, "there's not much time. She has a high spirit, but Esteban's an expert tamer. I tell you I don't like the pattern. Still, here's something for your comfort. The Duke's *condottieri* — Gravina, Oliverotto, Giampaolo Baglione, Vitellozzo, others — are chafing at the traces and may soon kick over them. They love Borgia no better than we do. If they stick together they might even pull down the Dragon. Keep clear of them, Messere, for the Duke knows their plans as well as they. But if they rise, he can do little at the moment. Then's your chance for a sudden snatch at Città del Monte. What you can do without funds or favor I don't know. But I'll keep you informed of what happens. If you can make an attempt, I'll join you, if for no better reason than that my neck won't be worth its skin when Borgia learns that I nibbled him with your blinding. At present your first need is to get back your strength."

Mona Costanza burst out: "Then, I'm not to have you, my son, after all this?" But she stopped abruptly. "No, it's different now. *You* are different. Do what you think right — with my blessing."

Andrea covered her hand with his. "That makes the difference, Mother. . . . But, Mario, when I think of Donna Milla alone in the palace with this Spanish butcher — is there nothing you can do?"

Belli shook his head. "Not much at this time. The Duke leaves tomorrow, and I must ride with him. However" — the Frenchman paused a moment — "perhaps, before leaving, I can do something."

A crackle of underbrush sounded not far away, and then the sound of footsteps.

"Here come your hosts, Messere. You'll be well hidden. Be sure to let me know where to reach you. And, by the way, you'll be needing travel money. I forgot to present this."

Andrea exclaimed at the weight of the purse that Belli thrust into his hand. "No, friend, it's too much."

"It's your own property."

"I don't understand."

Belli gave his silent laugh. "It's the price I had from the Duke for your two eyes."

CHAPTER LX

THAT Mario Belli, following his exploit of Andrea's blinding, was an object of dread and disgust to all but the most hardened of Duke Cesare's attendants showed that, after all, there are limits to human callousness. Never a popular character in the Duke's suite, he now moved in a vacuum, which only the fear he inspired kept from becoming personally dangerous. As for the few who remained of the old palace servants, they fled from him like the plague.

It therefore shocked several passers-by profoundly that, on the morning after the grim exhibition in the dining hall, Madonna's midget Alda was seen familiarly conversing with him in one of the deep window bays off the main corridor. She even sat on his knee and rested a hand on his shoulder. This was proof positive that dwarfs had no souls; or rather that they were incarnate imps of hell, who would naturally find the company of Satan congenial. What the two were discussing, no one had courage to eavesdrop. Those who saw them shuddered and slunk by.

But, if this was shocking, fortunately no one, an hour later, saw Belli glide into Alda's small room on the third floor and, after a short pause, enter Camilla's bedchamber beyond it. More horrifying still to any beholder would have been the spectacle of Belli on one knee beside Camilla's bed, her hand raised to his lips. Nervously unstrung since last evening, she now looked revived. Her eyes shone; she even smiled.

"I grieved to cause Your Ladyship this distress," he was saying, "but it was that or worse. It would have been the devil's own business to get him clear of prison in time before his health snapped, after their handling of him. But Your Excellence has much to forgive me."

"Tell me again how you did it," she urged. "Alda was too excited to make it clear."

The midget had climbed up on the bed by the special steps which were contrived for her and now sat in the curve of Camilla's arm. Both gazed eagerly at Belli; and while the Frenchman described in detail what had caused such horror yesterday, they glowed with pleasure.

Alda clapped her tiny hands. "Haven't I told you about Messer Mario, and you wouldn't believe me!"

"You're too good an actor for me, Messere," said Camilla. "That's the truth of it. . . . But you saw him last night. You spoke with him. Tell me . . ." She kept plying Belli with questions.

"And so," the latter concluded, "he lives only to help Your Signory out of these straits by any possible means. That's the gist of his message to Your Ladyship."

Now that her anxiety was past, Camilla looked thoughtful. "He shouldn't have lied to me, Messer Mario."

"No," Belli agreed.

"And I could never forgive him — never!"

"It isn't to be expected," Belli nodded. "I told him as much last night. Nevertheless, his whole concern is for Your Signory, as is mine."

"It's the other way round," she said. "He's the one to be concerned about. As for me, nothing more can happen. I shall stay here if I can be of some comfort to this people; if not, I shall return to Perugia. The Duke has paid off his grudge against me to the full — or so he thinks. Now he'll forget me."

Belli found himself in two minds. Evidently Camilla did not know Borgia's intentions. It was perhaps a mistake to alarm her beforehand, but she should be put on her guard. He decided to be frank.

"Your Ladyship is gravely in error if you consider the outlook as simple as that. I know for a truth that you will not be permitted to leave Città del Monte, and that Duke Cesare has promised your hand to Don Esteban Ramirez, if you can be persuaded to marry him."

To Belli's surprise Camilla laughed. "I was not so wrong about the bat, was I, Alda? I look forward to his courting. By God, he won't forget the reception he meets, friend Mario."

The Frenchman shook his head. She did not know the methods of people like Ramirez. She had never been subject to that continued cruelty which racks the mind rather than the body and which in time breaks even the strongest will. It was Belli's duty to enlighten her.

"I'm familiar with Don Esteban," he said gravely. "He will not kneel more than once nor accept more than one rebuff. He will give commands — "

"Let him!"

"No, you will *not* let him, Signora. The commands will not be for you but for those you love."

"I don't quite understand," she hesitated.

"Then, forgive me for plain speech. You have many here in the town or palace who are dear to you. Suppose one of them is stripped and tortured before your eyes, the release depending on a word from you — how long will you withhold that word?"

She lost color. "He would not. No one could be such a beast. Besides, he is subject to my orders by the terms of surrender."

"Be sure of one thing," Belli answered. "Those terms will be carried out only to the extent of Borgia's profit. When the Duke leaves today, Ramirez will be absolute master here, and he will do as he pleases. How can you prevent him? He is not a beast. He is much worse. With respect to cruelty, he has the cleverness of a madman. This is the reason for our concern, Madonna. And it is important that you see the case as it is."

Once again her coolness surprised him. It crossed his mind that, after all, the blood of generations of her fierce clan underlay the young, boyish face propped against the pillow. In the coming ordeal, courage would not fail her.

"Thanks," she said. "I think I see it. Have you any advice to give me?"

Belli outlined the plans he had discussed with Andrea, a *coup de main* at Città del Monte. This required preparations and a force of trained men, which would have to be raised elsewhere. The *contrada*, disarmed and drained by the war, could not furnish enough.

"The trouble is money," he fretted. "A few thousand ducats would make the difference. But rest easy on that score. I'll back Messer Andrea to contrive something when he's in fettle again. The main point — "

She had thrown back the covers and slipped out of bed, a graceful, loosely clad figure in her silken nightclothes. Flitting barefooted across the tiled floor to a panel of the wall, she pressed a spring that laid open a compartment. From this she drew a small gilded casket. Then, returning to bed, she poured out the contents of the box on the counterpane. "Would this help?"

"*Par tous les diables!*" exclaimed Belli.

Here was a pearl necklace wòrth two thousand ducats. He valued a ruby-studded bracelet at an even higher figure. That jeweled hairnet must be worth a fortune. Rings, bangles, trinkets of all sorts, brought up the figure, at a rapid calculation, to twenty, perhaps thirty, thousand ducats.

"*Par tous les saints!*" Belli gasped.

"Then it would help?"

"Madama, we have here the pay of a good Swiss company for as long as necessary."

"Then take it. You will see that Messer Andrea is supplied with funds."

Belli was staring at the treasure. "Does Duke Cesare know that this is in Your Signory's hands?"

387

Camilla tossed her head. "He sent me up our major-domo to require a list of my jewels. I told him that all had been spent on the war."

"Excellent!" approved the other. "That was a lie worthy of an angel. . . . But I'm a poor man. Do you trust me with such wealth? I don't know that I trust myself."

She turned to Alda. "Shall we trust him?"

The midget, who was sitting on the edge of the bed, stared up at Belli, like a kitten at a mastiff. "He'll not disappoint us."

"I promise nothing," said Belli. "If I can keep honest enough, I'll raise a loan on these gems, and they can be redeemed later. But all are not necessary." He selected some items and returned the others to the box. "Keep the most valuable of these about your person at all times, Madonna. And let no one know you have them. They can buy life or bring death."

He slipped his share of the jewels into an inner pocket of his doublet and stood pondering.

"This is all very well, but the chief hitch remains: how Your Ladyship will manage for the next month or two until plans are ready. Of course you're in mourning for your lord. You might dandle Ramirez with promises. But that game takes art that I'm not sure Your Innocence is up to. He has a keen eye and lickerish taste. If he accepted the promise, he'd want something on account and would force your hand. No — "

From old habit, Belli's lips twitched with their usual sly smirk, the point of his nose quivered, and his eyes pricked here and there under puckered lids. "Oho!" he muttered at last. "Maybe! . . . Hark you, Madama, I see it thus. You had a blow yesterday that unhinged your reason and leaves you mad. That's the answer. Your swooning at table prepared people for it. No one will be surprised when the rumor spreads that you are out of your senses and lunatic, what?"

Failing to catch Belli's point at once, Camilla bridled. "Lunatic yourself, Messere! And out of your own senses! I've never been saner."

"No, by the Mass," returned Belli, so pleased with his invention that he grinned like a hungry wolf, "Your Ladyship raves. When Don Esteban Ramirez appears, you will fail to recognize him. When he makes demands, you will babble. And so with everyone else, your women and servants — even with Princess Alda, unless you and she make certain you are alone and unwatched. There's not much Ramirez can do with madness, if Your Excellence follows me."

"I understand. By Bacchus, I wish I had your subtlety!"

388

He shook his head. "No, it's learned in too hard a school. . . . But as to this affair, mark well: you must not falter. It's odds that Ramirez will try gentleness at first. And so you will gain that much time. Then he'll turn harsh: you must endure it for fear of worse. He's no fool. You will be spied on secretly. Do not be taken off guard."

"I'll do my best," said Camilla. "If I can trick that villain, it's worth being chained up for. May I live to see him quartered!" She put on a vague look and plucked at the sheet. "*Illustrious Spaniard, my own poppet, pray dance me a pavane on the tightrope*. . . . How's that?"

"Good," Belli commented, "but satiric. He might get the point. I wish I could stay to deal with him, but the long game's better. He'll dance that pavane in the end. And now, Your Ladyship, I must take leave. The Duke rides at noon." The Frenchman's ugly features did not completely hide the gentleness that softened them for a moment. "God keep you, and you, my Princess."

"One moment," said Camilla. "I want a parting gift of you, sir."

"If a *poveretto* like me can supply it," he shrugged.

"I believe you can. I want a knife."

Belli's eyebrows went up. Then he nodded. With a movement so rapid that she could hardly follow it, he drew a small stiletto from a secret sheath under his left arm and held it out to her on his open palm.

"How's this? I've had luck with it more than once. Be careful how you handle it."

She tested the needle-sharp point and keen edge with her thumb. "Where are such things best carried?"

"For you, in the bodice, I think, or in the left sleeve, if you wear one that's full."

She smiled thoughtfully. "Thank you, Messer Mario. Now I feel safe."

This time it was he who misunderstood. "I wish that were enough to make you so."

"Quite safe," she repeated.

He gave her a quick glance. "Ah, I see. Yes, it will serve for that purpose — and all honor to Your Signory! But remember this, that a good many have chosen that safety too soon. Meanwhile, be sure that relief will come before the end of next month at latest."

He stooped over her hand and embraced little Alda. When the latter had made certain that the corridor was free, he slipped out and shortly afterward mingled with others of the Duke's retinue in the palace courtyard.

"A word with you," he said to Ramirez, who was waiting for Borgia to mount. "I have a fondness for Madonna's midget. She and I have much in common. It would go hard with anyone who mishandled her. Pass the word, Señor, if you will do me the service, for I mean it."

"I shall take her under my own protection," returned the Spaniard, with the readiness due to one whom the Duke favored. "Have no care."

"I thank Your Worship." Belli waited until Borgia had appeared and obeisances were over. Then he added in a voice loud enough for Cesare to hear: "The dwarf tells me that Madonna has lost her wits and is completely distracted. It shows what importance a woman attaches to her own opinion, and how hard she takes it to be proved wrong. The Duke's Signory will be amused."

"What's this?" Cesare demanded.

Belli repeated a supposed conversation with Alda, and smiled as if hugely entertained.

"Hm-m," said the Duke thoughtfully. "No doubt she will recover. Treat her with consideration, Don Esteban. And take heed that rumors of this do not circulate. There's enough malicious gossip about us without adding fuel to it. Express my loving farewells to Her Excellence and my hope for her speedy improvement. . . . By the way, you will see that the furniture and other goods from the palace are delivered to our agents upon request."

Once more, to the dipping of standards and salute of cannon, Duke Cesare rode through the city gates. His long train of followers, winding along the road, made a glittering contrast to the desolation of the valley. Radiantly handsome on his black charger, he rode in a nimbus of fortune and victory. On the whole, his visit to Città del Monte had answered expectations. Now other successes awaited him beyond the horizon.

Only Mario Belli looked back at the shattered town on the hill. It seemed to him a kind of mute confederate. He wondered grimly what it would have to show him at their next rendezvous.

PART FIVE

Conclusion

CHAPTER LXI

AT THE end of September and during the first ten days of October, 1502, a group of magnificent scoundrels assembled at La Magione, an Orsini fortress overlooking Lake Trasimene, to concert measures for the defense "of the liberties and peace of Italy." They were the chief captains and *condottieri* of Cesare Borgia, each one a petty despot in his own right, meeting with the representatives of other petty despots. Between them they disposed of some ten thousand mercenary troops, the major part of Borgia's army, and potentially they could raise as many more. There was Vitellozzo Vitelli, lord of Città di Castello, so pox-ridden that he had to be conveyed to the conference on a litter; and Oliverotto, who had murdered his way to the lordship of Fermo; and Giampaolo Baglione, tyrant of Perugia, with Gentile his brother; and Ermete Bentivoglio for his father, the ruler of Bologna; and Antonio da Venafro for Pandolfo Petrucci, the crafty first citizen of Siena; and Ottaviano Fregoso, for his uncle, the Duke of Urbino. Their host was Cardinal Gianbattista Orsini, together with other chiefs of the Orsini clan, among them Paolo and the young Duke of Gravina.

They were brought together by a common fear, which had long been latent but which now had risen to a point of panic. In Borgia's pay or hoodwinked by his diplomacy, they had contributed to the ruin of other lords, who, like them, were independent feudatories of the Church. One by one, the Riarii, Malatesta, Sforza, Manfredi, and Colonna had fallen, and now recently the Montefeltri of Urbino and the Varani of the Marches. But that was not all. Duke Cesare's next move threatened Bologna; the Pope raged openly against the House of Orsini; it looked as if Perugia and Siena were marked out for conquest, not to speak of such small lordships as Fermo and Città di Castello. Therefore, as Giampaolo Baglione put it, in order not to be devoured singly by the Dragon, they must act now and act together, like true and loyal brothers.

393

But fear is a poor cement of common action in any case. Among rogues and self-seekers, it is no cement at all. The amount of truth and loyalty at La Magione equaled only the breath contained in those two words. Everyone there present knew that the others were past masters of double-dealing and chicane. Everyone was prepared to treat with the enemy to his own advantage. Their cause had no motive beyond self-preservation: the defense of wolves against a tiger. United, they could overthrow Borgia. But they had no confidence in each other, and he had supreme confidence in himself.

Nevertheless, having signed a long agreement, they took the field, defeated Duke Cesare's Spanish captains in a pitched battle, and regained the Duchy of Urbino.

It was at this point that a masked gentleman presented himself one evening at the allied headquarters in the palace at Urbino, asked for an interview with Giampaolo Baglione, and sent up a note. What with the come and go of couriers, subalterns, and hangers-on, the gentleman himself attracted little notice. There were so many reasons for so many people to travel incognito during the confused state of affairs that a mask meant little or nothing. What impressed the attendant who took up the note was Baglione's amazement, and that he directed the caller to be shown at once to a private cabinet adjoining his main apartment. But though the servant, having performed this office, lingered near the door, he heard nothing through the heavy oak panels.

"*Al corpo di Dio*," exclaimed the *condottiere*, when he and the visitor were alone, "until you unmask, I'll not believe what's written here." And he glanced at the sheet in his hand. "Is this another trick of Borgia's, or what?" But when the newcomer undid the oblong of velvet from his face, Giampaolo gave a wondering whistle. "By the saints, it's true! Andrea Orsini himself! My illustrious friend, what miracle is this?"

Andrea swept off his cap in deference to so great a lord and, at the same time, assessed the implications of the greeting. Giampaolo Baglione was noted for his graciousness; but he did not need to use the word *illustrious*, and the ring of his voice expressed esteem as well as surprise. They had met frequently in the past, but Andrea did not remember that the head of the Magnificent House had ever called him *friend*.

"Pray be covered," Baglione waved. "You have much to explain, sir. The soldiery of Italy wept to learn that so valiant a captain had been deprived of his eyes and brought near to death by those Spanish *marrani*. I am glad to see that it was a rumor. But, considering the Borgia's rage against you, I don't understand how you made your peace with him."

"Neither rumor nor peace, Your Magnificence," Andrea smiled, "but, indeed, a miracle. My eyes were removed in the presence of the Duke himself, and he considers me blind as a bat. God knows I was tormented enough. However, Your Grace may have heard that the holy Sister Lucia da Narni was then present in Città del Monte; and that, in all truth, I owe her my life. Shall I say confidentially that a touch of her blessed hands, unknown to the Duke, was enough to restore my vision completely?"

They exchanged limpid glances of perfect understanding. Baglione did not have to be told that Borgia had been hoodwinked and that, for very good reasons, discretion was necessary.

"Marvelous!" he observed. "Marvelous! I take it that as yet you do not wish the report of the miracle to spread. When the time comes, it will greatly enhance the reputation of that holy Sister. I doubt if our Suor Colomba of Perugia could have done so much. . . . But now, as to you, my friend, how can I serve you? Let me add that I hope you will favor me by accepting a command in my *condotta*."

Andrea bowed. "Words fail me to express my gratitude for Your Lordship's condescension. However, at this time, as you know, I am in the service of Your Grace's kinswoman, the illustrious Signora of Città del Monte, and am, therefore, unable to take on another charge. It is about her that I crave a word with Your Excellence."

"But she — " The other broke off. . . . "Well, be seated, sir, be seated."

Andrea felt an odd plucking at the heart as he faced Baglione. The latter's delicate features and charm reminded him so much of Camilla, though the *condottiere's* tall stature and powerful build were entirely masculine. The same sparkle and lovable grace distinguished both of them. But Andrea did not let the family likeness mislead him. He knew well enough that the treachery, hardness, and cunning of this handsome nobleman equaled his graciousness.

"To be brief," he said, "the time is now plainly ripe for a stroke at Città del Monte, which will restore the signory to Madonna Camilla. Thanks to your victorious arms, the Duke can do nothing at present. Each one of his garrisons must depend on itself without hope of rein-forcement. I hear that the lord Oliverotto is even now invading the Marches in the direction of Camerino. This leaves Esteban Ramirez

395

entirely cut off. I come to hire men for the *impresa*, if Your Lordship has any to spare."

"Hire?" Baglione repeated. "I'll be glad to supply them gratis. Indeed, I plan to retake the Mountain City myself as soon as other affairs permit. Since I learn with sorrow that my well-beloved cousin is mad, no one has a better claim to the signory than I. It can be administered in her name — "

"There are grounds for belief," put in Andrea, "that Her Ladyship will recover."

Once again they exchanged glances, and Giampaolo looked chagrined. "Another of these miracles, eh?"

"Something like it."

"Ah, Messere," sighed the other, "your reputation for resourcefulness is well-founded. It's a pleasure to converse with you. One always learns something. . . . But as I said, when the campaign permits, I shall be glad to aid you."

Andrea shook his head. "No, my lord, I am seeking an independent *condotta* for Her Ladyship, and I must secure it at once while occasion favors. It occurred to me that Your Grace might have more troops on pay than the event requires and so would be willing to decrease your charge. Or it might be that some have reached the end of their term, and you do not wish to re-engage them."

"Troops cost money," Baglione objected. "Have you the funds?"

"They are available."

"Here?"

Andrea did not miss the note of eagerness in the other's voice. "God forbid, my lord. In a sure place and in good hands."

Baglione sighed again. "A small loan would have convenienced me — but let it pass. An independent *condotta*, you say? Does that mean that you do not wish to act in concert with me and my allies?"

"Let's put it differently, sir: not in concert but parallel with Your Mightiness. My success will help the general cause."

"You would find greater support if my cousin's name were among the parties to the agreement at La Magione."

Andrea hedged. "Madama's consent would have to be obtained, which is at present impossible. . . . Does Your Lordship know of any troops to be had? I'll need veterans."

Baglione reflected. "There're some Swiss, Jacob Meiss commanding. I find them too expensive, but keep them on to prevent Borgia from getting them. I know of nothing else."

396

Andrea snatched at the opportunity. He recalled the last time he had seen Meiss: two years ago on the Flaminian Road. Here were three hundred men of the best — enough for the attack he planned.

"I thank Your Lordship."

Baglione nodded affably, but he looked preoccupied. "You're quite welcome, sir, quite welcome. I'll even forgo the commission which I could justly claim for this service." (Rascal! thought Andrea. When I'm relieving him of expense and helping the war at the same time!) "But blood is thicker than water," Giampaolo went on, "and I'm devoted to my little cousin. So you have leave to arrange the affair with Meiss."

"Your Signory overwhelms me."

"In return, I'll ask you a favor." Baglione's absent expression vanished. "Tell me frankly why you hold aloof from us who signed the agreement at La Magione. You can be quite open. It concerns me more than you think to know the reason. Sir, I do not flatter you when I say that among all those who have served the Borgia, none have an equal credit with you for astuteness and foresight. . . . No, I mean it. . . . If you shun our alliance, it is not without cause."

Thinking fast, Andrea could see no objection to frankness. After all, Baglione probably took a skeptical view of the alliance himself.

"The cause," said Andrea, "is only that it seems more prudent for Città del Monte to rely on itself rather than to become involved in the maneuvers of others."

"Maneuvers, sir?"

"Your Grace knows well that Borgia's first move will be to open negotiations with the separate members of the alliance; that he will make promises, cajole, flatter, sow discord, stir up jealousy, now here, now there, with a view to splitting the force against him. And Your Grace must expect, as I do, that he will succeed. Always excepting Your Lordship, is there one of these illustrious captains who would not sell out the others to his own profit?"

"I thank you for your confidence in me, Messer Andrea. I fear there is some truth in what you say. Alas for the wickedness of men!"

"Therefore, my lord, I consider it safer to take and hold Città del Monte for the noble Prefettessa independently of others. If Duke Cesare can withstand Your Signories, I believe that he will leave us alone for a time, as not worth the cost of another siege, while more profitable aims call him elsewhere. And in the course of time, much can happen."

397

"I see," Baglione nodded.

"But, as one good turn deserves another," Andrea concluded, "and I am most grateful for the Swiss troops, let me caution Your Lordship on one point. The Duke will bait his hook with sweetness and promises. I dare predict that, within six weeks, he will have talked back what your alliance has gained. He will then arrange a loving meeting with his captains. My lord, do not attend it. I say, do not ever again put yourself within Borgia's power for whatever reason. He may forget benefits; he never forgets an injury. That much I know by hard experience."

Giampaolo laid an approving hand on his guest's knee. "I shall take your advice as if every syllable were gold, and I shall communicate it to the others. It may help to keep your prediction from coming true."

That Baglione henceforth played a lone hand and avoided the fate which overtook his confederates at Sinigaglia may have been owing in part to this conversation. At the moment, he wore the look of a man whose opinions have been confirmed by an authority, and his manner grew still more cordial.

"*Mio caro amico*," he went on, "you just said truly enough that one good turn deserves another, and I insist on one more from my side. I can think of nothing which would so run a nettle into Borgia's breech as that you would permit me to have you enrolled as an honorary citizen of Perugia under the name which you have made illustrious during the siege of Città del Monte. You will be known by it anyway to all gallant men. Zoppo will never stick. I beg the privilege for my city that it may be the first to inscribe you on its rolls as *Andrea Orsini, nobile*."

Andrea flushed with pleasure. During the last month, he had felt almost nameless. Now the name which he had borne so long was restored to him as his legitimate property certified to by an ancient and distinguished city. The ascription of nobility it carried meant little more than words, but words were all he needed. A new line of Orsini could date from that moment. And mingled with this satisfaction was joy at the thought of Borgia's rage when the time came to divulge the legal transfiguration of Zoppo.

"I shall have the *Priori* of Perugia send you a document signed and sealed," Baglione assured him, after Andrea had expressed his thanks. "And I shall do so at once both for love of you and for hatred of His Illustrious Obscenity, whom I pray to have sometime in *my* power. . . . No, I understand that for the moment you're blind and forgotten. Have no concern."

Andrea felt that he could count on Baglione's discretion. As to the Borgian spies, who were certainly present in the army of the allied captains, he would have to take his chance. Mario Belli, who was now with the Duke at Imola and with whom he maintained a secret correspondence by means of trustworthy messengers from the hill country around Città del Monte, had assured him that not a whisper of the revived Andrea had reached the ears of Cesare. In view of this, he was reasonably safe; since, after securing the Swiss, he could now plan for an almost immediate blow at Città del Monte. Beyond that, there was no need of secrecy.

Delighted with the success of his interview, he took leave of Baglione and did not forget to put on his mask at once in the outer corridor. It was empty, except for the servant who had escorted him up and who now respectfully accompanied him to the main entrance. He decided to seek out Jacob Meiss forthwith and come to an agreement about the Swiss company. When he had done this and dispatched a messenger to Belli with a summons to join him, he would have taken a long step forward.

A fragment of the past drifted before Andrea, while he was still in the thronged courtyard of the palace. The outer gates were suddenly blocked by the outriders of a great lord, and he at once identified the livery of Ippolito d'Este. Then appeared the splendid Cardinal himself, looking as much like a red-combed fighting cock as ever. His flame and show eclipsed the shorter figure on his right, just as the bulk of his hackney concealed his companion's mule. But when he dismounted, a thin smile crossed Orsini's lips, for the torchlight disclosed a lady, at that moment engaged in pushing back her riding hood. And by the saints, it was Angela Borgia! The light fell on her blond hair and handsome features, as the Cardinal held her stirrup. Slipping to the ground, she steadied herself a little longer than necessary against his shoulder. Andrea had not seen her since that unforgettable night almost two years ago in Rome. The smile froze to his lips.

The *condottiere* Vitellozzo Vitelli himself appeared in the doorway to welcome them. As a prince of the Church and of neutral Ferrara, Ippolito could pass through the lines of the allied captains. And who would be ungallant enough to halt the Lady of Honor of Alfonso d'Este's consort, even if her name was Borgia? After an interchange of courtesies with Vitellozzo, they disappeared into the palace.

From the talk around him, Andrea learned that Their Highnesses were on the way to Rome, and that Madonna Angela traveled under

399

the Cardinal's protection. This sounded plausible, but it struck Orsini that if he were one of the rebel captains, he would keep alert to the movements of Borgia's charming cousin. She might be of more than a little value to the Duke in different ways.

Meanwhile, Andrea himself was glad of his mask. Hatred, like love, has a sixth sense. If an inkling of him reached the ears of those two enemies, it might be fatal at the present boiling point of his plans. As it was, he did not need to fear. Let them ride on to Rome and out of his life — he hoped forever. They recalled a phase of himself which he had outgrown and liked to forget.

The Cardinal and Angela faded from his mind as he made his way through the troop-crowded streets of Urbino, intent on finding Jacob Meiss's quarters.

Fortunately for his self-confidence, he did not know that the servant who had ushered him up to Baglione's apartment and had attended his departure found occasion that evening to wait on Madonna Angela.

"The Duke rides," he murmured apropos of nothing, while handing her a salver of fruit.

"To Cesena," she answered, selecting a plum.

Whereupon the servant, having glanced about him, communicated an odd fact of such importance that Angela could hardly wait to discuss it a few minutes later with Cardinal Ippolito.

CHAPTER LXII

HAVING once more explained his escape from Borgia, and after some agreeable haggling, Andrea had no difficulty in reaching an agreement with Jacob Meiss for the hire of the Swiss company. Aside from his earlier reputation and their former acquaintance, Andrea stood high in the opinion of the Zurich captain on the score of his conduct during the recent siege. It would be an honor, said Meiss, to serve under so renowned a cavalier. In the end, Andrea agreed to pay five ducats per month per man, instead of the four now received from Baglione, with the pay of the officers on a correspondingly higher level. The contract stipulated an engagement of at least two months, with an option of renewal at the end of that time.

"And now," said Meiss, when Andrea had handed over a purse of five hundred ducats on account, "what are the plans?"

In reply, Orsini drew out a rough map of the *contrada* of Città del Monte and pricked off the desired operations with a pocket knife. From the Via Flaminia, the Swiss were to turn left north of Fabriano and in groups of three or four, guided by peasants of the district, were to make their way across country to a point in the hills above the city. Today was October 15th. Could the company assemble at this destination by the twenty-first?

Having twisted his beard and calculated, Meiss nodded. "*Ja wohl*. Our boys know how to march."

Well, then, on the evening of the twenty-second, after nightfall, they were to drop down to the valley at *this* point, five hundred yards to the west of the palace side of the walls, which was partially concealed by an unevenness in the slope. Here peasants would supply them with rough scaling ladders for the attack. At the showing of a lantern swung repeatedly from a window on the top floor of the palace, they were to press forward and storm the walls which guarded the palace on that side. Thence they were to make their way into the palace itself. However, no attack was to be launched unless the signal of the lantern appeared, since the Swiss effort was to be co-ordinated with a rising of the townsfolk, who would assail the palace and castle from the other direction. Andrea had maintained contact with the leading citizens and believed that everything was in readiness, but difficulties might arise which would make the showing of the light impossible. In that case, the Swiss were to retire after midnight and reassemble at the same place the following evening.

"Is it permitted to ask," put in Meiss, "where Your Worship will be engaged during this affair?"

"In the palace, my friend."

"But, *Donnerwett'*, how will you manage that?"

"Toward sundown on the twenty-second," explained Andrea briefly, "I expect to enter Città del Monte with a friend, who is well-considered by the Duke and by Don Esteban Ramirez. I shall be disguised as a physician sent to tend the Lady Camilla. From the inside, if all goes well, I can help both your attack and the assault of the townspeople. But wish me luck."

"By God, I do!" swore the other. "It's a slippery business. I wouldn't be in your shoes for a thousand ducats. What happens to the venture if you're discovered?"

"In that case, *amico mio*, the signal will be my body hung from the castle walls. If I'm taken, your engagement is over, and you can do what you please. You'll have received your two months' pay in advance before you leave the Flaminian Road."

Meiss shook his head and grunted. "*Gott sei Dank*, I'm a plain soldier! No tricks and disguises for me! I say again, I wouldn't be in your shoes for a fortune."

"I'd step out of them if I could," Andrea agreed, "but they're stuck fast, *lieber Herr*. . . . And now, tell me back those instructions, will you, to see that everything's understood."

When he had reviewed the plans thoroughly, Orsini left Meiss's quarters with certain misgivings. He felt that the Swiss captain was just a little too much of a plain soldier. He had the courage of a bear; he was staunch as a stone wall; he would execute orders at any cost to the last syllable. But when it came to a quick adjustment that called for imagination and dash, he was apt to be dull or confused. Andrea would have given anything if he could have found some officer of the more brilliant sort to act with Meiss in handling the attack; but he could think of no one in the army of the allied *condottieri* whom he dared trust with the secret of the enterprise. Better a dull man than a talker or knave. He would simply have to hope for the best, and that Meiss's wits would not be put to too great a strain.

On the way back to his lodgings at the inn, Andrea made a detour past the Church of San Francesco, where he gave alms to a beggar.

"Fabriano on the twenty-second," he murmured. "My regards to Messer Mario."

In return, the man, who was one of the peasants used for liaison with Città del Monte, slipped him a small piece of paper. "From the palace. . . . I'll carry the word to Messer Mario without fail."

Burning with impatience to read the message, the first he had had from Camilla during five long weeks, Andrea made what speed he could through the streets filled with soldiers of the allied captains, and at last reached his tavern. Having bolted the door of his room and lighted a candle, he unfolded the unsealed scrap of paper. But his face fell on discovering what appeared to be only three or four uncertain pen strokes wandering across the sheet. Then, holding the paper closer to the light, he saw that the strokes resolved themselves into writing so minute that at first he despaired of reading it. However, in the end, with infinite pains, he made out the following words:

> *Madonna has been removed from the palace to the West Tower of the castle. No one is allowed to see her, not even me. A woman has been brought from Rome to attend her. I believe the Spaniard suspects that she is not mad; for I have heard him say that, if she is not mad, he will make her so. Hasten! There is little time. This by the hand of Alda.*

With a sinking heart, Andrea stared at the fragment of paper. It confirmed the suspense he had been under day by day since that evening with Belli in the woods near Città del Monte. He knew, of course, the perils involved in Camilla's desire for gaining time with Ramirez. Now Alda's message hinted at the Spaniard's counterplay. If Camilla was mad, she would receive the treatment of mad people, the chains, starvation, and brutality meted out at that time to the insane. If she was not mad, this might compel her to give up her make-believe or precipitate something worse.

At such moments, Andrea's imagination became his enemy. Having burned the message, he strode up and down the room, forgetting even to remove his mask or outer cloak, a prey to pictures that his own mind conjured up. What was happening this very night behind the thick walls of that West Tower? "Little time." And he could do nothing to hasten relief. He must allow time for his summons to reach Belli at Imola and for Belli to rejoin him at Fabriano. He must allow time for the Swiss to cover the distance to Città del Monte. Premature action would gain nothing; on the contrary it would ruin everything. Up and down, up and down. Suppose, in the end, he reached the palace, only to find that he had come too late?

Tense as he was, the rattle of the door latch followed by a vigorous knock startled him like a gunshot. What did this mean? Except for Baglione and Meiss, he felt confident that no one knew of his presence in Urbino. He had paid the landlord in advance for his room. The knock sounded again, imperiously this time. With one hand on his poniard and every muscle taut, he walked over to the door and drew the bolt.

On the other side of the threshold, a tall, broad-shouldered figure, muffled in a cloak and with a broad velvet cap slanting across the face, confronted him in the semi-darkness.

"*Fête dieu!*" came a foreign voice in broken Italian. "What do you mean, sir, by taking my room and bolting the door against me? In a mask, too, eh? By God, I wonder if you've been rifling my bags."

"Nothing of the kind, sir," returned Andrea. "This is my room, and I'm no thief."

"By Saint John," the other retorted. "I say it's mine. Stand back! I'll have a look."

He pushed forward, gazed around, and then gave an embarrassed *humph!*

"Monsieur, I owe you all my excuses. I could have sworn that this was the room they showed me to this afternoon. But I recall now it may have been on the next floor. *Je suis navré, Monsieur*, to have disturbed you. Accept my apologies." A hint of eagerness crept into the voice. "Or if you feel that you must have satisfaction, in view of my very maladroit reference to the bags — and certainly you have cause for resentment — I am at your service."

For an instant the candlelight shone full on the intruder.

"*Per Dio!*" Andrea exclaimed. "It's the lord Bayard."

"Ha!" answered the latter, stepping back in surprise. "I'll not deny it. But you have the advantage of me."

Orsini closed the door. "When I had the pleasure, my lord, of exchanging a few thrusts with you in Ferrara, I was saved by the personal intervention of the blessed Saint George himself. Does that indicate who I am?"

To Andrea's chagrin, Bayard stiffened. "It does, indeed. Alas, I'm afraid it indicates that you're a rogue. The illustrious captain whom I at that time had the honor of crossing swords with is now dead, or, if he lives, he is in a poor case. He has been foully dealt with, to the sorrow of — Ho! By the saints!"

Andrea had removed his mask and now stood full in the candlelight.

"By the saints! By Saint Denis! By Saint Paul! What wonder is this? . . . It can't be true! . . . Monsieur d'Orsini, *mon ami*, let me embrace you!"

It took an hour and a pitcher of wine before conversation caught up with the present. To Andrea, Bayard's company was a blessed relief from the impotent anxiety into which Alda's message had plunged him. The personality of the French soldier radiated strength and confidence. His generous mouth, clear eyes, the somber velvet of his mantle, were all facets of an integrity that heartened Andrea a good deal more than the wine they drank. The invasion and defense of Città del Monte had to be fought over step by step, and Orsini's miraculous escape retold. Then, more briefly, the events in Naples and Apulia were touched on.

404

It appeared that Bayard was returning to the garrison he commanded at
Minervino, after carrying dispatches and a report to King Louis's
viceroy at Milan; and that, instead of following the usual route south,
he hoped to find a ship at Ancona that would take him along the
Adriatic coast to Bisceglie, an Apulian port then in French hands.

"Ancona?" Orsini repeated. "That means you'll be crossing the
Marches by way of Città del Monte."

"Even so," Bayard nodded. "And I shall not fail to study the scenes
of your exploits."

A sudden idea flashed in Andrea's mind. If he could persuade Bayard
to act with Meiss in the attack on the town, it would be an ideal solution
to the problem of leadership.

"Do you know," the Frenchman was asking, "whether the situation
at Città del Monte allows me to present myself before the noble lady
Camilla and offer her my homage?"

"Out and alas!" Andrea muttered. "Listen, Monseigneur." He gave
an account of Camilla's predicament that brought a flush to Bayard's
cheeks.

Clenching his fist on the table, the Chevalier burst out: *"Foi de
gentilhomme! I* have never heard the like. That this illustrious lady, *une
vraie perle dans ce monde,* should be so treated! Ha, the scoundrel! It
would be an exceptional act of merit to bring that *vilain bougre* of a
Spaniard to justice. . . . But speak on, speak on. What do you intend
to do?"

Andrea outlined his plans, while Bayard listened intently. Whereas
Meiss had viewed the attack on Città del Monte as a routine job, Andrea
could read in the Frenchman's eyes how vividly he pictured every
detail: scaling ladders, relative positions of outer walls to palace doors,
crowbars and axes to force an entrance, handling of men — all leading
up to the climax of fighting, which would sweep through the palace like
a flame. An occasional *Ha!* or *Fête dieu!* expressed his enthusiasm.

And at the end, Andrea did not even need to make the proposal he
was leading up to.

"Monsieur d'Orsini, *mon ami,*" exclaimed Bayard, "I demand a share
in this action. *Cré dieu!* Can you imagine me jogging on to Ancona
while this feat of arms goes forward and Madame de Baglione could
use my sword! No, Monsieur. Such occasions for honor are not so easy
to come by. The King's business will take no harm if I'm a day or so
late in returning to my garrison. I confess that it gives me some pause
to be associated with Marius de Montbel in view of his earlier record.

405

But the man deserves praise for his conduct toward you. And who am I to deny to another sinner what I crave from God for myself? . . . In short, sir, give me some part, however small, in this venture. If you will, I shall always hold myself indebted to you."

Andrea could only reach across the table and grasp Bayard's two hands. As far as the attack was concerned, he could now feel perfect confidence.

"The debt is mine, as you know," he said, "and a greater one than I can ever repay. Captain Meiss will be more than proud to have so famous an adjutant."

"Why, then," Bayard answered, filling a cup, "I pledge that triumphant lady, Madame de Baglione, to whom I vow loyal service. And I pledge no less the day, October 22nd, and happy arms!"

"Amen!" said Andrea.

CHAPTER LXIII

In the late afternoon of October 22nd, Mario Belli and Andrea rode down the valley highway toward Città del Monte. Belli, on a staunch little bay, was dressed in the red and yellow stripes of Borgia's army. By the occasional sullen peasant, he would be regarded simply as another of the Spanish vultures who had been tearing at the carcass of the signory. His horse and equipment contrasted with the slovenly mule, civilian gown, and cloth headpiece of his companion. Andrea had always been clever at disguises — a skill connected with his artistic talent — and, since everything depended on it, he had given special care to this one. Even the sharp-eyed Belli had not recognized him when they met at the tavern in Fabriano. The scraggly beard was not overdone, nor were the faint lines of face and forehead. His iron-gray hair looked dirty and matted, as became a man of learning. His eyelids betokened too much study. Every detail of the costume had been copied from the middle-aged Paduan professor of medicine whom he had known in his student days and whose name he had also borrowed.

Aware, too, that disguises are less convincing if they represent only a type, he had borrowed the professor's mannerisms and personality as well. Even his attendant, who followed with a donkey carrying luggage and professional equipment, and who had been recruited at Cagli, did not dream that his master was anyone else than a famous doctor.

"*Sang dieu!*" commented Belli, with an approving glance. "At least we don't have to worry about your looking the part. What an actor was lost in Your Lordship! " He paused reminiscently. "On the stage, I mean."

Andrea nodded. "Yes, I've been a fairly eminent actor elsewhere. So, please God this last role of mine may succeed! Perhaps, then, the others will be forgiven."

"Aye," Belli muttered, drawing his mantle close. And apropos of nothing, he added, "Devil take this gray day! It's hard to keep cheerful, isn't it?"

As they approached the city, it grew still harder. They rode, as it were, into an atmosphere charged with increasing suspense, of which the low sky and plaintive wind were the fitting symbols. Since Alda's message a week ago, not a trickle of news had leaked through the walls now fronting them on the distant hill. The peasant spies had reported new executions in the city and new atrocities of the Spanish garrison. The people, goaded to desperation, waited only the signal to rise. But as to what had happened in the palace and castle, not a word. The West Tower, blunt and stark on an angle of the walls, stood impassive as a Sphinx. Visible the entire length of the road, it constantly focused the eyes and thoughts of the two men.

But there was another point at the palace end of the long façade which claimed attention. "Those rooms with the turret, eh?" said Belli.

"Yes, Master Paolo the astrologer's. They were left empty after he deserted. And they're apt to be empty still because of their remoteness. You'll mark that a signal from the turret will be seen at the same time by the townsfolk and by Meiss's company on this side of the walls. Moreover, it could not easily be seen by anyone at a window of the palace. But the turret doesn't matter too much. If it's occupied, or you can't reach it, show the lantern anywhere from the upper level, first on one side and then the other."

"I'll do that," returned Belli, "if I'm on my two legs." He tapped a bulge in his saddlebags. "The lantern's here. . . . I wish Your Lordship's game was as simple. Have you any plans after reaching Madonna?"

"No, I'll improvise. Her protection's the first object. Then I may be able to cause a diversion that will help the attack. I don't know — if only some rumor of us hasn't reached Ramirez in the meantime! That's the main fear."

Belli nodded. "We'll have to take the chance, Messere. It's a tight boat that has no leaks. Engaging troops, guiding them through the mountains, keeping informed of doings in the city — so many men, so many mouths. But I think we're in time. At least, I'll vouch for it that the Duke suspected nothing when I left Imola. He thinks he sent me to Lombardy, as I told you."

"And I'm practically certain of Urbino," Andrea pondered. "I kept under cover in the daytime and wore a mask when I went abroad after dark."

They scanned the walls carefully as they drew closer. Since the end of the siege, enforced labor under Spanish taskmasters had done much to repair the breaches opened by Gravina's cannon, so that the ramparts made a far less ruinous impression than they had six weeks ago. Andrea's spies had informed him of this work, which, indeed, was extremely welcome in view of a possible renewed defense against Borgia in the future. Nor was it a surprise that Ramirez evidently kept a close watch, to judge by the steel caps visible on the walls. Not to have done so would have been inexcusable on the part of a captain isolated and threatened, like him, by the movements of the allied *condottieri*. This alertness made tonight's attempt more difficult, but it did not imply a suspicion of imminent attack.

"Foh!" exclaimed Andrea suddenly. "Look at that!" Until then, they had not noticed against the gray of the walls the long cords and the objects dangling at the end of them, a dozen or more. Around two of these, they could soon make out a fluttering of crows; and, with a veering of the wind, came the stench of death. . . . "Butcher and fool!" Andrea went on. "Does Ramirez think that he can hold down a countryside by those means?"

"Very obviously he does," grinned Belli, "and in the long run no doubt he'll pay for his narrowness of mind; but, for the short run, I hope *we* don't."

Under any circumstances, the grim line of corpses almost fringing the city gate would have cast a shadow upon the spirits of those entering; but in view of that night's enterprise and of the uncertainties involved in it, Andrea closed his mind to thoughts of ill-omen and kept his eyes straight ahead. One of those queer notions which assail the nerves at

408

certain times whispered to him that if he looked up and recognized the features of one of the hanged men — no doubt recent companions of his during the siege — it would be the token of his own death. But a perverse temptation almost forced him to look up, as he entered the city portal.

"Young Ettore Leone," murmured Belli, unrestrained by such qualms. "A brave lad."

The further end of the tower entrance was closed. While they waited for the doors to be opened, the wind moaned beneath the arches like an unquiet ghost.

They did not have long to wait. Belli had been recognized from the walls, and he was now respectfully greeted by the portal guards, who remembered him with awe if not affection. He presented Andrea as Master Felice Ambrosio of Padua, whom he was escorting to Città del Monte at the command of Duke Cesare to examine the Prefettessa.

To Orsini's immense relief, not a glint of suspicion showed in the eyes of the Spanish soldiers. One of them asked Belli how he had got through the lines of the allied captains in the Borgian uniform. "It's possible to change uniforms, *mio amigo*," Belli winked. Then, without further delay, the newcomers were permitted to ride on to the palace entrance.

Nor did Ramirez look any more on guard than usual when Andrea and Belli were conducted to Varano's erstwhile cabinet, which the Spaniard used as an office. He received Belli with the politeness due to a privileged cutthroat and accepted Doctor Ambrosio without demur.

"I fear that Your Erudition will find Madonna Camilla beyond cure," he remarked, with the usual unrevealing stare of his beady eyes. "Her condition grew so much worse that I have had to use rigorous measures and place her in confinement." He jerked his head toward the door communicating with the castle, which Andrea so well remembered from his first visit to Città del Monte. "She's in the West Tower. When Your Lordship has refreshed yourself from the journey, I shall be glad to conduct you."

At least, Camilla was alive. The worst fear had proved unfounded. What Ramirez meant by "rigorous measures" had yet to be learned; but on the face of it his statement merely confirmed Alda's message.

"Shall we say within an hour?" Don Esteban added. He beckoned to one of the soldiers, who had replaced the old palace servants. "Show this illustrious master up to his room, and attend him here again at his convenience. . . . Perhaps, Messer Mario, you'll afford me a few minutes' conversation. I'm starved for news, as you can readily imagine."

"I'll tell you what I know," Belli answered, taking a chair. "Of course the Duke keeps his plans to himself . . ."

Andrea followed the soldier with a much lighter heart than he had had for weeks. The chief danger, that Ramirez had somehow been warned against him, was past. He felt certain that nothing now could prevent the success of the enterprise. Action itself had no terrors; it was the suspense that had been hard.

Night was already falling. Within an hour the Swiss would march; within an hour and a half it would be possible for Belli to give the signal. The overcast sky would hasten darkness, and Bayard could be depended on not to lose a minute. Even the blustering wind, which had vexed the day, added another element of security to the night by deadening possible sounds, as the Swiss company took up its position. In short, everything — even the weather — was favorable. Andrea could well afford to congratulate himself on his luck.

He decided to spend the full hour, which Ramirez had accorded, in his room. He could count on Belli to decide on the proper moment for the signal after he had gone over to the castle.

Preceded by the soldier up the familiar stairway, Andrea felt appalled by the change in the palace. Everything movable had disappeared: the tapestries, carved chairs from Venice, urns and pedestals. Naked walls faced him at every turn. Even a pair of inlaid doors had been removed from one room, which now gaped open upon the corridor. He hardly recognized the chamber which had been assigned him. The sumptuous bed had been replaced by a soldier's pallet, the other rich furnishings, by a mean chair, a table and washstand. His bags, which had been brought up, made a forlorn huddle in the center of the tiled floor.

"I take it," he said to the soldier in the sepulchral voice of the real Ambrosio, "that His Sublimity, the Duke, must have speedily removed the contents of this palace as the spoils of war and of his valorous arms."

"Speedily's the word," nodded the other. "But everything's still corded and packed on the ground floor awaiting the Duke's convenience. No way of moving baggage on the roads these days, with Oliverotto to the south and Vitellozzo to the north."

"Unfortunate," boomed Andrea. He reflected happily that the Duke's convenience itself would wait a long time after tonight.

He pinched out a coin from his purse with stiff fingers and held it up before the soldier. "*Mio amico*, I gathered from the remarks of Don Esteban that supper would be served to me here. Am I right?"

"The order has been given, Master."

"Then kindly entreat Messer Mario, the companion of my journey, to allow me the pleasure of his company, when he has finished with your valiant captain. Eating alone is a grievous thing for the stomach."

"I'll tell him, Your Worship."

Having pocketed the coin, the soldier made off. But, though Andrea spent as much time as possible over his toilet, brushing his gown and washing his hands, and though he dawdled over the last morsel of the rough food that was brought him, Belli did not appear. There were many possible explanations for this. Belli might have been detained by Ramirez and did not consider it prudent to leave him. Or he might already have contrived to reach his post on the upper floor and could not be found. Andrea regretted now that he had sent for him. It was not essential that they should meet, but it would have been reassuring to exchange a final word.

The hour was now more than past. The soldier reappeared with the compliments of Don Esteban, who wondered whether the learned master at length felt inclined to rejoin him.

Andrea adjusted the folds of his gown. "Did you convey the message I entrusted you with?" he demanded pompously.

"Your Worship, I regret. The gentleman had quitted the Señor Captain when I went down. I searched everywhere but could not find him. Shall I return your benefaction?"

"No, my friend, keep it. A small matter."

Andrea smiled inwardly. It was as he had supposed. Belli had now reached the signal turret or some other location near it. Andrea himself should make haste to keep his appointment with Ramirez and so gain access to Camilla.

Behind the soldier, who now carried a torch, he followed the well-known corridor to the cabinet.

Don Esteban's voice reached him at the doorway. "*Por Dios*, Master, you've taken your own time. But come in, come in."

As he entered, a flame of red struck his eyes.

In front of the fire, nose in air and red hat at an angle, stood Ippolito d'Este. And in a chair near him, her blond head gracefully reclined against the cushion, sat Angela Borgia.

CHAPTER LXIV

AMAZEMENT and consternation did not prevent Andrea from reading the triumphant faces of the Cardinal and Angela. It was clear that they saw through his disguise perfectly. He knew at once that, by some incredible mischance, they had learned about him in Urbino. On the road south, they had evidently stopped off at Città del Monte to warn Ramirez. But if they knew that Andrea was not blind, they knew also that Belli had betrayed the Duke and could be regarded as a confederate of Orsini's. Worse still, Andrea realized why Belli had not answered his summons. He had no doubt been taken prisoner immediately. In consequence, there was no one to give the signal. The enterprise was nipped in the bud. At a stroke, success became disaster.

But even at this pinch, Andrea's self-control stood by him. He covered up with a grave bow and a rubbing of the hands. At the moment he could at least fool them into believing that he thought he was fooling them. That might lead them to show their game and give him another opening.

"So this is the illustrious doctor, Felice Ambrosio of Padua?" inquired Ippolito, with elaborate irony.

Angela arched her eyebrows.

"Even so, Your Eminence." Andrea's professorial voice betrayed no hint of strain. "The humblest follower of the immortal Galen. Is it not true that I have the privilege of standing before that sublime prince, the Most Reverend Cardinal d'Este?"

"The same," nodded the other. "You've seen me before, have you? What of Madonna here? Do you know her?"

Andrea looked embarrassed and shook his head. "It is an ignorance that covers me with confusion, reverend lord."

"I should think it might." Ippolito puffed out his cheeks. "Learn then that Madonna Angela is cousin to the renowned Duke who sent you on this mission."

Andrea scraped and bowed.

"I understand you're here to treat the mad Prefettessa," Ippolito added. "Behold how concerned Duke Cesare is for the health of his enemies. What Christian virtue!"

"And I'm curious to know," put in Angela, with a quiver of the lips, "what treatment Your Mastership will use."

"I shall hasten to inform Your Grace when I have once viewed my patient. *Diversi sunt imbecillitatis remedii,* as Galen puts it."

What was their game, Andrea wondered in desperation. Most probably they were having some minutes of sport with him before dropping their very thin mask.

But suddenly a remark from Don Esteban gave a new turn to things.

"Come then, Master, it's time you viewed the patient. Their Highnesses will be interested in your report. This way, if you please."

He walked over to the door connecting with the castle, while Andrea made elaborate bows before the Cardinal and Angela to gain time for thought. Why, if they knew who he was, did they permit him to visit Camilla? There was only one answer to that: they intended to overhear the interview. In the role of the physician, who believed that he was hoodwinking them, his value was twofold: he might reveal to Camilla what his plans had been; and, equally important, Ramirez might learn whether Camilla's insanity was real or feigned. Memory, at that moment, supplied Andrea with a detail that fitted this construction. He recalled a concealed opening behind one of the arches supporting the vault of the middle chamber in the West Tower, the one probably occupied by Camilla. No doubt Ramirez had used it to spy on her before this.

"Come, sir," fretted Don Esteban at the door.

Andrea walked over to the Spaniard. "I must see my illustrious patient alone," he said, testing his theory. "I must gain her confidence and hold her attention. Nothing so much distracts a person of weak wits as the presence of more than one visitor at a time."

"You'll be alone with her."

Andrea noticed an exchange of glances and believed that he had guessed right. Before he and Ramirez had traversed the length of the covered gallery leading into the castle, he heard the door open again behind them and a sound of cautious footsteps.

He thought furiously, vainly — and then caught at a sudden notion that occurred to him, as a faint hope. He would try it. There was no other finesse available — one last shift of the fox.

A vaulted corridor ended at the central section of the West Tower. Ramirez unlocked the door that opened into the tower itself, and Andrea noticed that he did not close it. At this point they stood on the landing of a stairway that served the rooms on different levels. Directly opposite was the strongly bolted door of the middle chamber. Ramirez crossed over to it, put down the lantern he had been carrying, and drew back the bolts with a harsh scraping of iron.

Orsini found it impossible to steady his nerves. The anxious uncertainty of the past weeks, which had centered in Camilla, was now about to be solved. Had she — imprisoned and mishandled — been able to play her role of madness without becoming submerged in it? Alda's message had hinted at that fear. The answer to this doubt lay on the other side of the iron-rimmed panels.

A brawny harridan of a woman, with disheveled black hair, faced them as Ramirez shoved the door open.

"How's Her Excellence?" he demanded.

"Wild as ever," returned the woman in a flat, matter-of-fact voice. "I'm quitting this job."

"Are you?" murmured Ramirez.

"Well, I mean — "

"Get down to the guardroom," he ordered, "and stay there till you're called. I've brought the learned Doctor Ambrosio from Padua to examine Her Signory. He wants to be alone with her."

"Let him take heed not to get too close," the woman advised. "She might fly at his throat. If her ravings are true, the magnificent Baglioni are all killers."

Out of the obscurity of the room came a trickle of laughter that stirred the roots of Andrea's hair.

"She's wakened," said the woman. "*Cospetto!* I'm glad to get off for a breath. I'll be crazy myself before I know it."

The laughter rose to a scream and suddenly stopped. Andrea's blood ran cold. He could make out a figure seated on a pallet at the end of the room and heard a tinkle of metal. Evidently Camilla was chained to that particular spot. He noted also that this was in the range of the concealed opening at the angle of the opposite arch. Anyone standing on the outer stairway several steps up would have a complete view of her.

"Do you want more light?" asked Ramirez.

"If possible."

Apparently there had been times when an outside watcher needed light, for heavy iron brackets on the walls were provided with thick candles. Andrea noticed that these were only at Camilla's end of the room.

With a taper kindled at the lantern, Ramirez now passed from bracket to bracket until the space surrounding Camilla was reasonably light. To an eavesdropper on the stairs it would give the effect of an illuminated alcove.

As the candle flames burned higher, Camilla could be seen kneeling on the pallet. She was dressed in a robe of tattered black velvet with loose sleeves. The contrast of this with the whiteness of her skin, and the effect of her hair tied in a plain knot behind her head, made an impression of almost painful slenderness. She looked like some glazed figurine that a touch would break. Babbling incoherent words, while Ramirez was lighting the candles, she crouched, when he came closer to her, like an animal about to spring. An iron girdle around her waist was connected by a light chain to a staple in the wall.

"You see how it is," remarked the Spaniard. "I wish you good luck with your treatment, learned sir. When you've finished, come down to the guardroom below. I'll wait for you there."

The closing of the door wakened hollow echoes under the vault.

Sick with distress, Andrea stood in front of the kneeling figure on the pallet. But in spite of misgivings he had to make one last attempt to save her and himself, desperate as it was. Facing her, he stood with his back to the listening post, which he had now every reason to hope was occupied.

Lowering his voice to a whisper, which could be heard only by Camilla, he said, "Donna Milla, if you can understand me, listen and do as I ask you. We are being watched and we can be overheard. Continue to act mad, no matter what I do or what happens, until I speak to you again in this same voice. But I'm afraid you don't understand," he added more to himself than her.

It seemed almost an echo of his whisper that came back to him. "Thank God!"

And at those two words, courage flowed through him again in a hot surge of joy. Now he could play this last hand as he had never played before!

He whispered: "*Per Dio, per Dio!* I'm restored to life. Do as I asked you, Madonna. Be as mad now as you please. *Ah, mia carissima donna!*"

Then he proceeded to transform himself. He plucked off his beard, shifted the hilt of a sword from back to front, tossed away his cloth headpiece, and shook the tangles from his hair.

"Behold, Madonna!" he said in a voice which he was sure would carry to any listeners. "You see, it was only a disguise. I'm here at last. In an hour you'll be safe."

A wild laugh answered him.

"No, Donna Milla," he went on in the same distinct tones, "you have no need to pretend any longer. I tell you, you're safe. Listen.

Mario Belli and I arrived here not much more than an hour ago. He stands well with Ramirez; and no one recognized me — not even the Cardinal Ippolito d'Este or Madonna Angela Borgia, who are stopping in the palace. Though I talked with them face to face, they had no idea that I was not Felice Ambrosio of Padua. Even you were deceived. . . . But listen. Belli and I are not alone. Captain Meiss and my lord Bayard of France are leading a force of Swiss against the walls at the next stroke of the clock. At the same time, the city will rise. The Spanish *marrani* will be caught between the two attacks. It should be within a half hour from now. If it had not been opportune tonight" — Andrea raised his voice slightly — "I say, if there had been any reason to hold back, I should have signaled by swinging a lantern from the upper turret at the north end of the palace. In that case, no attack would be made until tomorrow night. But there was no need to delay." (And now, he added to himself, God grant these rogues wit enough to get the point!) "I repeat there was no need to delay, Madonna."

He had played his last card. Perhaps, after all, no one was listening; or, if there was, perhaps the bait would not be taken.

True to her part, Camilla burst into laughter. The jeering echoes answered and left a silence, still more ominous, behind them.

CHAPTER LXV

THE problem was time. If the enemy had been duped into giving the signal, Andrea had to allow roughly a half hour between the showing of the lantern and the actual attack. The period might be less or it might be a trifle longer, depending on circumstances. Meanwhile, whether right or wrong, there was nothing for him to do but continue to act on the assumption of eavesdroppers behind that concealed opening. If this assumption was true, the two-edged usefulness of the listening post had not been exhausted. Provided Andrea's trick had worked, it would no doubt be Ramirez who would hurry off to give the signal, while Ippolito and Angela remained behind. They had still not learned whether Camilla was, or was not, insane. It was therefore good tactics to keep them in suspense about that as long as possible. Andrea must invent another subject to hold their interest. Probably Ramirez would return, and remarks could afterwards be addressed to him. The object was to keep all three of them absorbed and off guard in the event that the hoped-for attack took place.

But everything was theory and dark play and a very faint chance.

Andrea continued by pleading with Camilla in a distinct voice to drop the now unnecessary pretense of madness. "I implore Your Signory not to keep me in anxiety," he begged. "I know that you're merely feigning what was agreed upon. But why continue it, Madonna? You're too excellent an actress. You almost persuade me — No, I vow you don't, either. If you're pleased to amuse yourself, I'll admire your art." . . . He pretended to listen. . . . "The hour should strike any moment now. Then you'll hear a tumult."

He wondered if Ippolito and Angela were savoring the irony of this. Poor Orsini listening for the attack which would never come! And it would begin to look to them as if Camilla were actually mad. Another amusing touch.

Andrea laughed. "Speaking of the Cardinal and Madonna Angela, it's a sad case. You'll remember Don Giulio d'Este, my lord Cardinal's half-brother of sorts, the handsomest member of the House. And there's Don Ferrante, the second of Duke Ercole's sons. I heard recently from a sure source in Ferrara that the Cardinal thinks he absorbs Lady Angela's favors. But she's been heard to remark that the eyes alone of Don Giulio are more attractive than the Cardinal's whole person. And recently Don Ferrante supplied my informant with a glowing description of Madonna's intimate charms, which I'm sure he didn't obtain from the Cardinal."

Was this hitting the target, thought Andrea. It might be ungallant; but the gossip was authentic. One thing could be considered certain: if Ippolito was listening, he would continue to listen, and Angela to writhe.

In reply, Camilla babbled incoherently. But as if absorbed by his topic, Orsini went on to develop it. He had a full score to settle with Angela. He produced facts about her that only he knew; and, if he invented others, it was all for the sake of good measure. The subject led naturally to Duke Cesare, who considered Ippolito an ass and Don Alfonso a gull. If relations between Ferrara and the Borgias were strained after this, Orsini would not grieve.

Suddenly the great bell in the campanile of Santa Maria struck nine, though the tones, muffled by the walls of the tower, sounded far off. If Ramirez had returned, he ought to be receiving attention.

Andrea stopped in the middle of a sentence. "Did you hear that, Madonna? Now, very soon, will be the moment of triumph. Very soon you'll have this Spanish dog at your mercy, to repay him for his conduct to you and his outrages upon your people. I pray you to put off this role of madness, as no longer befitting." He paused. . . . "It can't be that I'm mistaken! It can't be that Your Signory is actually — "

A peal of hysterical laughter shivered up, reverberating under the arches.

He stepped back, as if horrified. But he felt that time was running out. He could not hold his supposed listeners much longer. Surely by now, if his trick had succeeded, the attack ought to begin. Straining his ears, he imagined that he heard a faint sound in the distance. He must take the risk that it was not imaginary.

"Now, Madonna!" he whispered.

In contrast, the normal tones of her voice were more startling than the former outbursts. "Thank you, Messer Andrea," she said, following his example by speaking louder than usual. "That such an actor as you should be deceived by my acting is the highest compliment. I couldn't resist the temptation of leading you on, even though I admit the joke was unseasonable. . . . But the attack you spoke of — how long are we to wait?"

He realized that this question was not intended only for the benefit of the listeners. A sickening awareness crept over him. The bells of the city ought to be stirring; the first mutter of the storm ought to be heard. There was only silence.

He forced himself to put on a bold front. "At any moment now, Your Signory. . . . Meanwhile, forgive me that I have not yet relieved you of this chain." And, stepping behind her, he pried open a link close to the girdle with the blade of his poniard. "Henceforth may you ever be free, Madonna, as the falcon of your House!"

At the same moment, the door was thrown open. Behind the three adversaries he had expected appeared a backing of armed men. In any case, he had not been wrong about the listening post.

The Cardinal's face was redder than his cloak. Angela Borgia, her head thrust forward and her lips drawn back, had suddenly lost her beauty. Only Ramirez, being what he was, appeared unchanged.

Vulgar, blatant, and passionate, their anger flooded in. But if the Cardinal glared at Orsini, he glowered at Angela. His voice interrupted the vitriol she was spitting.

"Hold your tongue," he thundered. "It seems to me you've used it enough, my tripping lady. If Giulio d'Este loses his beautiful eyes — and I think it's likely — he'll have you to thank. . . . Let me speak to this charlatan bastard." The Cardinal's agonized pride almost choked him as he flamed at Andrea. "So you expect Lord Bayard and the Swiss, eh?"

"Why not, Your Eminence?"

"Why not?" spluttered Ippolito. "Why not, you imbecile! You'll wait their coming till you hang! You talked a little too much. Your signal called off the attack."

Thank God! It was no longer a fancy — this deep murmur Andrea heard, and the far-off notes of a bell!

He threw back his head. "On the contrary, *your* signal called it on."

"What does the rascal mean?"

A sudden clangor answered Ippolito, a growing clangor that pierced the thick walls of the castle as the bells of the city rang the tocsin. The bell of Santa Maria, the bell of Santa Lucia, the bell of San Francesco, the bells of other saints of heaven. Faster and faster, like mad bronze pulses. Louder and louder, but not so loud as the roar from thousands of throats, the yell compounded of two words — "*Carne carne! Ammazza ammazza!*" — the death shout of a populace thirsty for blood.

The artist in Andrea subconsciously noted for future reference the faces that confronted him. They provided a study in deflation. Ippolito's crimson faded; his outstretched arm and eloquent hand drooped; his features slowly took on a look of aggrieved bewilderment. Angela, who had been white with anger, turned white with fear, somehow a different kind of white. For once, Ramirez's eyes showed a gleam of expression.

"*Por Dios!* The tocsin!" he exclaimed.

A new sound rose from the opposite direction, another sort of thunder, the familiar uproar of battle; then suddenly a *ta-ra-ta-ta-tà*, the crowing flourish of a French trumpeter. Bayard had gained the walls. A deep-throated bellowing rumbled for a moment. "*Schweiz! Zurich!*"

"You can hold the castle," Ippolito shouted. "That way, at least, they'll grant terms. Now it's massacre — "

Ramirez turned to the pikemen on the landing. "Bolt the doors," he commanded. "Have *Retreat to the Castle* sounded. Block off the . . ."

An imminent crash, like a thunder stroke, blotted out his voice. The tower rocked. Red fire leaped up for an instant outside the window openings. Stones volleyed against the walls. And almost before the boom of the explosion had died away rose the yell of the mob storming closer.

"The powder room!" shouted one of the pikemen. "Someone has touched it off. God help us! The crowd is in the courtyard."

Without warning, Ramirez struck. The glint of his poniard at Andrea's heart and his words came at the same moment. "*A muerte!*" he snarled.

The steel bent and snapped, leaving only a rent in Orsini's doublet, through which the chain mail showed. In the next instant Andrea had caught the Spaniard by the throat, following him, as he staggered backwards, until he was pinned to the wall.

"How foolish, Señor-r, to forget that a doctor, like me, wears an undershirt!"

"No!" choked Ramirez at the sight of Andrea's dagger. "No!"

"Christ!" exclaimed Este. "You there! Guards!" But glancing toward the doorway, he found the pikemen gone. Instead of them, he faced Mario Belli with a group of townsfolk behind him.

Alive to the situation, Belli, springing forward, grasped Andrea's arm. "That's too good for him, Your Magnificence. Here's a better way." And, turning to the men at the door, he called, "Enter, friends. We have a gift for you."

They were upon Ramirez like wolves. But, breaking from them, his mantle gone and his doublet half torn off, the Spaniard clung to Camilla's knees.

She drew back from him. "I see no mercy in protecting the wicked and forgetting the innocent. You owe more to this people than your life can balance, but at least you'll pay that to them. . . . Out with him!" she ordered. "Give him to the people!"

Half dragged, half carried, the wretch disappeared through the door. They could hear his cries on the stairs, his cries from the guardroom below, then only the roar of the mob.

CHAPTER LXVI

"I'LL explain when we have time," Belli was saying. "They had me in keep. It would have gone hard if Alda hadn't managed to slip me a file. I owe her everything. By the way, I ask you to appreciate the value of my former researches around the powder magazine. . . . But where's the Princess? I hope nothing — "

His eyes stopped on Camilla, who was holding the midget in her arms. The small head leaned against her cheek. The tiny hands smoothed her hair.

Through the outer door of the tower sounded the continuing fight in the palace, where the Spanish mercenaries were making a last stand.

"I'll join my lord Bayard and Captain Meiss," said Andrea. "Perhaps for reasons of delicacy, Mario, it would be well if you did not associate yourself with the Chevalier at this time — "

"I get the point," nodded Belli.

"Besides," Andrea added, "we need someone to guard these persons." His glance rested on Ippolito and Angela.

"Persons!" echoed the Cardinal, ruffling like an angry cock. "Let me remind you who I am."

"It's unnecessary, Your Eminence, I've been reminded of that for the last hour, though I don't believe we'd agree on the definition. However, we'll say, if you prefer, *to protect these honored guests*. It would be unhappy if the citizens of the town mistook you for enemies."

His eyes encountered Angela's. She stood woebegone against the wall, her clasped hands against her breast. In that attitude, it struck him that she would have served as the model of a Christian martyr.

Her expression brought a smile to the lips of Camilla, who, leaving Alda with Belli, had joined Andrea at the door.

"Have no fear, Madonna," she said. "Ride on to Rome tomorrow. I should never flatter you nor His Eminence with the title of enemy. You belong to those of whom the poet wrote: *look at them and pass by*. . . . Come, Andrea."

"But, Your Signory," he protested, "wait until — "

"This way, Andrea." And, crossing the landing, she went out into the darkness beyond it, while Orsini strode after her.

An hour later, when the tumult of battle in the palace had changed to the tumult of joy, Camilla stood on an improvised dais at the end of the great dining hall and looked down with flushed cheeks at the crowd who were cheering her. People of all kinds — men, women, and children, citizens still carrying their weapons, brawny Switzers in steel caps and up-to-date equipment — thronged the place to the doors. Everybody who had the good luck to force his way in was there. Torches, stuck into brackets, cast a flaring, agitated light over the mass of faces.

In her tattered gown, Camilla seemed the incarnation of the past months of war, hardship, defeat, and victory. On her right, as captain of the guard, stood Andrea Orsini, no less the object of acclaim than she. On her left, still in their armor, except for helmets, stood Jacob Meiss and Pierre de Bayard.

At moments, Andrea had almost the sensation of a dream. He felt as never before life's surge and change. Dreamlike, indeed!

He came to himself with a start at the sound of Camilla's voice. "Messere, I would speak to the people."

Raising his arms, he called: "Silence for Her Signory, the Prefettessa! Attention to the right noble Signora Camilla degli Baglioni!"

With her hands clenched at her sides and her head high, Camilla exerted herself to be heard in the farthest corner of the hall.

"Friends — for we have long been friends, in the brave days of peace when my lord the ever-beloved Varano lived; in the hard days of battle, when again and again your valor outmatched the number of our enemies; during these recent days of cruel tyranny; and now when we have thrown off that yoke — friends, shall I attempt to express the inexpressible? *Thanks* to you from me? The very word belittles your loyalty and courage and this night. No, rather, on our knees tomorrow in the Church of Santa Maria degli Angeli, let us render thanks to God's almighty Spirit who alone has given us love and courage. Thanks to *Him* only from us all! But tomorrow, while we hear the high *Te Deum*, let us remember to pray for His continued grace, that, if again our enemy assails us, we may still stand firm, repulse the assaults, make good our defense, until the day of lasting peace."

She paused a moment. Then, in the absolute silence of the hall, she turned to the Swiss captain and Bayard.

"Thanks, I have said, belong to God Himself. But it is only fitting that acknowledgment from our hearts should be made to these brave gentlemen without whose help tonight would have been impossible.

To you, signori, my gratitude and the lasting praises of this people. To you, Monseigneur de Bayard, that honor which you love and have so gloriously won. And to you both, with these poor tokens, my lasting affection."

She beckoned to the blackamoor Seraph, who, in a somewhat shabby turban, had been standing with Alda at one side of the dais, and who now strutted forward with a small casket. From this, she selected some jewels, which she presented to the two captains, while the hall roared its *vivas*. Meiss beamed and growled in the language of Zurich. Bayard turned red with embarrassment.

"*Fête dieu*, Madame! Your Signory makes much of little. I regret only that I could not serve you more or serve you longer. But I value this favor of yours as I value your high heart. And herewith I make my vow to wear it in your honor, when I next ride in tournament before the Most Christian King."

When the hubbub of applause had slackened, Camilla turned to Andrea.

"As for the lord Orsini," she continued with an odd inflection of voice, "since he has done no more than his duty as captain at Città del Monte, he deserves no special praise or reward, and I have none to offer him."

An immense gasp could be heard in the hall. The crowd stood thunderstruck. "*Ah, mais non, Madame!*" exclaimed Bayard.

"Except my hand," she added.

If there had been tumult before, it was nothing in comparison with what now shook the hall. *Vivas* for the new lord of Città del Monte! Outpourings of devotion! A carnival of joy! Wave upon wave.

Kneeling, Andrea pressed Camilla's hand to his lips. "I ought to have been warned by the wickedness in your eyes," he whispered, as he got up and stood at her side. "By God, Madonna, I think you'll play a joke on me at the very steps of the altar!"

"One moment," she said in return, and, raising her hand, brought the crowd at length to silence. "I have not finished my acknowledgments. There is one to whom I owe more than to any other except the lord Andrea himself. . . . Messer Mario" — she glanced down at Belli, who stood close to the dais — "you should be beside me here. No, I'll permit no modesty. Stand forward."

At the sight of the Borgian uniform, a stir passed through the crowd.

"I'm hardly dressed for the occasion," grinned Belli.

Once again Camilla's voice carried through the hall. When she had described Belli's services and how he had saved Andrea in this very place, the cheering broke out anew. In the end, she held the casket, with what remained of the jewels, out to him.

"Gift for gift," she smiled. "These in return for your knife."

To the amazement of everyone close by, Belli shook his head. "The only gift I desired in return for that, Madonna, was that you should not have to use it, and this has been gratefully received. More than that I cannot accept."

"What do you mean, Messere?"

"I mean that I am now taking service with a patron so jealous that it would offend him if I received these jewels from Your Signory. But, on second thought, if I could have the disposal of them, it would pleasure me much more than to take them for myself."

"They're yours, Messer Mario, to do with as you please."

"Then I shall pray you, Madama, to give them to Princess Alda as a token of my love. . . . Will Your Highness," he said to Alda, "not accept them from Her Excellence in my name?"

Hardly visible to the great majority in the hall, the tiny creature advanced with all the dignity of a queen, while people craned their necks to see what was happening. Having curtsied to Camilla, she turned to Belli. Her full voice, apparently from nowhere, set those in the rear elbowing and straining more than ever.

"*Mio caro, amico,* what do you mean by *another patron?* Isn't the lord Orsini patron enough?"

Andrea, who had been waiting on needles for a chance to speak, put in: "I ask that, too. *Santa Maria!* Are you deserting me again, now that we have stood out this storm together?"

"Even so, Your Magnificence." Belli pinched his chin and lifted an eyebrow. "I have a chance to better my condition, and, after all, a man must look out for himself."

"But, Messere," Camilla protested, "we would give you anything in our power."

"It would not be enough, Madama. I regret. My future patron is no less than a king. He has long promised me extravagant wages; but it's a dangerous service, and partly for that reason, partly because of affection for the lord Orsini, I have postponed accepting the offer. Recently, however, it was renewed by His Majesty's ambassador, and I can no longer afford to decline."

"What ambassador, in God's name?" Andrea burst out.

It was odd that Belli's face at that moment looked almost handsome.

424

"In God's name," he repeated, "Sister Lucia da Narni."

A hush fell on the group and spread through the crowd. Bayard, who had been muttering that he wouldn't be surprised if Marius de Montbel had taken service with the Grand Turk, crossed himself and made a vow of penance. Little Alda pressed her cheek against Belli's knee.

Andrea stared. "Are you serious, Mario?"

"Entirely, my lord. You will find me next in the disguise of a Franciscan."

"*You* a friar!"

"Call me that, if you please. But I shall still consider myself a bravo in the service of my patron." Stooping down, Belli lifted Alda to the crook of his arm. "Receive, little Princess, this parting gift from your friend, which Her Excellence has promised."

Alda held the casket gravely between her two hands. Then she returned it to Camilla.

"I am rich enough without jewels," she said, and her voice could be heard by everyone. "Are we not all rich tonight, signori? Let us go out and dance in the streets and look up at the stars!"

CHAPTER LXVII

TEN months later, on a September afternoon, the gondola of Messer Aldobrandino di Guidone, Ambassador of Ferrara to the Signory of Venice, glided leisurely along the Canale di San Marco toward the entrance of the Canal Grande. In the rays of the declining sun, the water, iridescent as Murano glass, reflected lengthening shadows of marble and gold as the gondola drew closer to the palace-fringed shore line. It was the hour of promenade and relaxation. Other gondolas, with boatmen in handsome liveries, floated by; and the Ambassador was able to point out many Venetian notables to the distinguished young visitor from Florence who had called on him with letters of introduction from Duke Ercole.

More benign and patriarchal with every passing year, Messer Aldobrandino felt thoroughly at peace in a diplomatic world whose values
he understood and approved of. He took comfort in the profundity of
his wisdom and delighted solemnly to display it to young men of promise
and station, who were beginning the career he had almost finished.
So, at ease on the cushions of the gondola, he mingled sage reflections
with the particulars of buildings and names of people. Since the young
gentleman was well-bred, docile, and eager, Aldobrandino rather
warmed to him, all the more as he represented a great banking house,
and the Ambassador had a lively veneration for money.

Entering the Grand Canal, he pointed to one of the Contarini palaces
on the left and to the Palazzo Giustiniani on the right, then to other
palaces. But a little further along, he held up his hand for the boatmen
to stop in front of a handsome façade facing west.

"This, young sir," he remarked, "should, I think, interest you as
much as any other *casa* in Venice. I speak not primarily of the noble
house itself, though the curious find much to admire in its elegant pro-
portions. I speak of it as the residence of one who should be the model
of aspiring youth, of those who, like yourself, aim at great things. Can
you guess who I mean?"

The visitor gazed at the carved shields flanking the door. "I see
the arms of Città del Monte, of Baglione, and of some other House,
which, I confess, I'm not familiar with." Then, excitedly, he added:
"Is it possible that Your Excellence refers to the celebrated Andrea
Orsini, hero of the Marches, now a chief captain of Venice — that
he lives in this very house?"

"None other," Aldobrandino nodded. "The palace was but recently
presented to him by the Signory after Borgia's fall. He ranks now as
Lieutenant General of the Republic."

"*Stupendo!*" marveled the other. "*Maraviglioso!* Then this is actually
his house! I have heard so much of him. The only lord of the Marches
who withstood Cesare Borgia to the end."

"Aye," spat Aldobrandino, as befitted a reference to the now discarded favorite of fortune. "The Dragon left Città del Monte alone
after it had been retaken by my lord Orsini. He had his bellyful of
fighting the first time and did not choose to break more fangs. He
thought that time would deal with it, but time dealt with *him*."

Across the minds of the Ambassador and his guest passed inevitably
some reflection of those events which had startled Italy some weeks before: the Pope's death, Cesare's illness which kept him powerless while

426

his enemies seized power, the dissolving of his dukedoms like cloud castles. But present success was more interesting than past failure.

"Does Your Excellence think," ventured the young Florentine, "that I might possibly have the honor of waiting upon this great captain before I leave Venice? Only a word or two. It would be something to tell at home. Or, at least, if I could but catch a glimpse of him — "

Aldobrandino regarded the other with approval and fingered his beard. "It pleases me," he observed, "to meet one of your generation who knows how to put his travels to profit and makes the most of opportunities. Knowing the right people is the keystone of success. I shall be glad to procure you an audience with the lord Orsini, who gives me the honor of his friendship." The Ambassador smiled complacently. "It may interest you to learn that I was one of his first benefactors and started him off on the career which he has so happily pursued."

"Really?" exclaimed the young man, deeply impressed. "Would it be indiscreet to ask the circumstances?"

"Please regard them as confidential. . . . The lord Orsini, at that time an officer of Duke Valentino's, was engaged in negotiating a matter of extreme delicacy with the illustrious princes of Ferrara. Becoming acquainted with him, while he was still in Venice, I at once perceived his exceptional merit and afforded him my protection. It was entirely due to my letters of recommendation that he succeeded in his mission at Ferrara — and so step by step to his present eminence."

The other abounded in admiration.

"And what eminence it is!" Aldobrandino continued. "Lord of a fine little state, one of the highest paid officers of Venice, respected by princes and kings (they say Pope Julius has offered him the Captain-Generalship of the Church), Magnifico of Magnificos, famed for his manners and address. And all of this from what source? A wayside farm in the Polesine. It illustrates the adage that the deeper the dung, the richer the rose. Who remembers the dung when the rose has blossomed? They say he's established his peasant mother in a fine property at Città del Monte and that she appears often at court there with all honor. . . . No, young Messere, I speak from long experience when I tell you that success covers all. Be a success and you can be anything else you like."

"I would gladly learn," hinted the Florentine, "what Your Sagacity considers the chief element in the success of this great man, if it is possible to define it."

"Brains!" Aldobrandino returned emphatically. "Foresight, quickness of wit, subtlety of judgment. Those who have dealt with him, as I have, will tell you that they have never met so wily a negotiator, one so fertile in plots and deceptions, and at the same time so adroit in concealing his craft under an open and smiling manner."

"Admirable!" sighed the other.

"Admirable, indeed," the Ambassador nodded. "Consider his dealings with the Borgia, who was himself a master of stratagems and deceits. At every point, Cesare drew short against my lord Orsini. To take only one example, the Duke endeavored to hook him with fine words after the revolt of the *condottieri*, promised him free pardon, high command, and everything possible. In reply, Captain Orsini, *while negotiating*, hired another company of Swiss and took every measure of defense. It is said that Giampaolo Baglione lives today because he followed this lord's advice. As you know, the others — Vitellozzo, Gravina, Oliverotto, Paolo Orsini — made friends with Borgia and were promptly strangled at Sinigaglia or elsewhere. No, young sir, I say again, pattern yourself upon Andrea Orsini if you would secure that place and consideration in the world to which, I believe, your parts entitle you."

"It shall be my chief aim," said the Florentine humbly. "I pray you will not forget to arrange the audience we mentioned."

"Have no fear," Aldobrandino assured him. And, nodding to the gondoliers, "Proceed," he directed.

Behind the light silk curtains that shut off the now direct rays of the sun from the *stanza* on the second floor, Camilla laughed.

"*Che cosa?*" asked Andrea, who was relaxing that afternoon with paints and brushes and stood balancing in front of an easel.

"Admirers of yours down there," she answered. "Some old gentleman talking about Orsini. The name rose like a fountain." Separating the curtains, she peered out at the departing gondola. "Someone of consequence. Good liveries. . . . Oh, I see now! The badge of Ferrara. It was Messer Aldobrandino di Guidone with a young man."

"The old owl!" grinned Andrea. "I told you how he hired Mario Belli to assassinate me that time. No? Surely I have. Well, it was like this."

Pausing now and then to add a few brush strokes, and complicating the description at one point by holding a brush in his mouth, Andrea gave an account of his first acquaintance with the Ambassador. Camilla cursed that dignitary in the very frank language of the age.

428

"Now he circles around me at all times," Orsini continued, "and flatters me on my success. Probably that was his theme outside there. I was tempted to tell him the other day, when we met in the Doge's anteroom, that the chief success I ever had was when I gave over the deceits and subtleties he credits me with. But I should gain nothing by that. He would only consider it another evidence of guile and flatter me the more." Andrea chuckled. "What would he think if he could see us now!"

It was fortunate, indeed, for Aldobrandino's peace of mind that he could not see them. The hero worship, too, of the young Florentine would have suffered damage. Andrea, in shirt and hose, a smudge of paint on his forehead, bore no resemblance to the ideal of a great captain, *gran signore*, and magnifico. As for Camilla — barefooted, barelegged, and but slantingly covered otherwise in a tunic, as a model for Artemis — the very suggestion of Aldobrandino's looking in was appalling.

She shuddered. "If he could see me now, by God, I'd faint. When can I put on some clothes, Messere? I tell you it isn't nice, even before my own husband, to flit about naked like this."

"You are not naked. I wish I could prevail on you to let me paint you as Aphrodite. And pray do not flit. Take up the position again, as if you were bending a bow. I must get the foreshortening of the right forearm. That's it!"

"What concerns *me*," flushed Camilla, "is the hindshortening of this tunic. You had it made that way on purpose. Another of your deceits. Messer Aldobrandino's right."

"You have an adorable hip. . . . A breast like Hebe's."

"Don't be indecent, Messere. Hurry! This is tiring."

"One moment, *cara*. Hold it." He worked feverishly. "Ah, *ecco!* There we have it. Rest."

She slipped around to look at the canvas. "What a virago you're making of me! Am I such a vixen as that?"

"Not always. Sometimes. Ha! Behold the turn of the thigh. Sound anatomy. It won't be bad at all when we've finished."

He did not miss the occasion to slip his arm around her waist.

"You know, I'm beginning to be jealous of your art."

He put down palette and brushes, lifted her suddenly in his arms and, walking over to a chair, set her on his knee.

"Jealous?"

"Yes."

He kissed her. Several minutes passed.

"Jealous?"

"Not quite so much." She swept back a lock of hair that had dropped over her face. "But still jealous."

"You'll take back that word tonight, Madonna. I vow you'll be sorry. . . . Meanwhile, listen. Never be jealous of what art I have. It is there I find you most. It is there I most realize you — more even than when I hold you in my arms. Then I can dream and ponder, remember and anticipate. Be jealous of these council rooms and camps, of wars and policies, of the empty world, which is empty because you are not with me. And yet not too jealous either, since these things whet my hunger to be with you again."

"But why not always," she urged, "when your engagement with Venice is out? Art is your signory, an unfading lordship. Why be concerned with these shifting sands of alliances and leagues and the rivalry of states? Return to Città del Monte; paint your pictures; govern our people. Love me, *caro*. I say, love me."

Leaning back, she laid her cheek against his, an arm around his neck.

"Think, Madonna," he said after a moment. "Do you mean it so? . . . Love, of course. Love for you always. Love for you everywhere! . . . But think. As the years pass, and I paint my pictures, linger with you, ride hunting, play master in our little court, while this great age of ours marches towards destiny and other men strive to the utmost, could it ever happen someday that the thought would cross your mind of a trifler grown soft and negligible? If we have sons, how will they think of me?"

"But art," she protested, "is your happiness, the expression of your inmost self."

He shook his head. "One expression only. Otherwise, I could never have left it all these years. I am not Botticelli nor Mantegna. Art is their one concern, and so they will always surpass me as artists. I am engrossed by many things and cannot be satisfied to have no part in them. That might have been once; I have grown out of it. You must take me as I am."

"Universal mind," she half teased him. "It's too late now to help taking you as you are." She sat up again. "But you're right, Andrea. When art becomes pastry, it's no diet for a man. Some men were born to grow fat; I'm glad you weren't. But you've let one secret out of the bag. You'll have to paint pictures now and then to prove that you love me."

"Provided you promise always to be the model."

She gave him a tap on the cheek. "Try taking another model! Try it, I say! Now that I know what models don't wear! Let me catch you with one of those baggages!"

"But I *must* do an Aphrodite or, at least, a Susanna. Every painter does."

"Why, then, I'll submit even to that. But no trollops! . . . Ah, *Andreuccio mio!* There you are again with your stratagems, hooking me into doing what you want! A sad rogue — "

Again several minutes passed.

She adjusted the tunic. "And I've never forgiven you for lying about your name. *Mai e poi mai!* Never! What a trick that was! So silly!"

This time it was he who brushed back the lock of hair under the fillet of Artemis.

"Most tricks are silly. I've learned that now, and it's more than Messer Aldobrandino will ever learn. The cleverest trick in the bag is truth. But you'll have to admit that Signora Zoppo isn't euphonious. If you don't forgive me, I'm going to call you that." His eyes wandered back to the painting. "The hip needs a touch or two. I must manage the light differently. Ah, Donna Milla, because I shall have to play soldier and *politico*, don't imagine that this sublime art of color and line does not remain my passion and despair. If I could but once attain to Mantegna's mastery! . . . Take up the position again, *mia cara*, for one little moment."

But Camilla had hardly resumed the pose of the goddess when a knock sounded at the door. Slipping over to it and keeping well out of sight, she peered around through a crack.

"Seraph, go away! Didn't I tell you that His Signory and I wish to be undisturbed! Do you want to be spanked?"

"No, Mistress, by God! I tell these two old gentlemen you busy. They say you send for them."

"What are their names?"

"They say they called Lorenzo da Pavia and Andrea Mantegna of Mantua."

"By the Mass!" exclaimed Orsini. "Mantegna! The Most Christian and the Catholic Kings together could not do us such honor by a visit! Hark'ee, Seraph," he called, "show these divine masters into the grand salon, have refreshments served them with all dispatch, tell them that Her Ladyship and I are hastening to welcome them and grieve for every moment they are kept waiting. . . . Madonna, why didn't you tell me you had sent for them?"

Camilla was already half out of the tunic and half into her stays. "I called at Lorenzo's shop to buy a viola," she hurried, "and he said (please draw me these laces, Andrea) — he said Mantegna would soon be in Venice. I said it would highly honor us if he brought us acquainted with this great master, and that at any time — Where's my *camicia?*"

Ten minutes later, Messer Aldobrandino and the young visitor from Florence would have found only what was to be expected in the appearance of His Illustrious Excellence Andrea Orsini and of the noble Signora Camilla Baglione. The stiffness of brocade and glitter of jewels accompanied them over to the grand salon, where deep bows and the most finished compliments were exchanged.

"It has been," said Andrea, "the enduring regret of my life that, among those luminaries of art which are the glory of Italy, I have thus far been denied the honor of paying homage to the greatest and most venerable of them all. You may, therefore, imagine, *Maestro illustrissimo*, with what devotion I cast myself at your feet. Your paintings have long been the object of my study and reverence. It is with the deepest emotion that I now can acclaim their creator."

Mantegna, who carried his seventy-two years well, replied with an allusion to Mars and Minerva, whom everyone hailed as the parents of His Renowned Signory, though it was equally evident that Apollo and the Muses had stood sponsors at his baptism.

After similar civilities to Master Lorenzo and proper rejoinders, the instrument maker referred to their meeting three years ago in his workshop. "I rejoice," he remarked to Camilla with a twinkle, "that Your Ladyship completely neglected all my warnings against this eminent gentleman and followed your own judgment. It proves once again how much wiser is the heart than the head and teaches me humility."

"I don't know about that," Andrea put in. "Your head was sound enough, Messer Lorenzo, and so were your warnings. I confess it in deep confidence. But I hope the heart was not too wrong either. Madama must speak for that."

Camilla looked doubtful. "Only the future can tell. I sometimes wonder. So don't be too humble for a while yet, Maestro. And that reminds me — that and the presence of this divine artist. Do you recall that His Lordship at that time sold me a painting, which he had stolen at Forlì, called 'The Triumph of Virtue'?"

"As if it were yesterday," Lorenzo nodded. "A lovely thing."

"And that you and he both considered it an unsigned work by this great master whom we are honored to welcome today?"

"Most certainly it was," said Lorenzo, combing his beard. "I hope nothing has happened to it."

"On the contrary," smiled Camilla. "It hangs in that small salon yonder." She turned to Mantegna. "I can never be parted from it, honored sir, and I brought it with me from Città del Monte. Would it please you to view it and affix your signature?"

"If it is mine, with pleasure, Madonna."

Andrea's cheeks burned. He could see the imp in Camilla's eyes and could do nothing. It was hardly the moment to confess his forgery. He must let her have her joke.

Leaning on his cane, Mantegna stumped into the adjoining room. His brows went up at sight of the painting. "Hm-m," he said, and "Ha!" To Andrea's relief, the face of the artist showed wonder and admiration. It showed also a trace of furtiveness. . . . "Unsigned, eh?"
. . . He stumped back and forth, inspecting the canvas at varying distances. His admiration grew, and, with it, the look of a man sorely tempted. "Ha!" he breathed again.

"Of course it's yours, isn't it, Maestro?" asked Camilla demurely.

Temptation had the best of it. "Of course, Your Excellency, of course. One of my more notable works. I was merely endeavoring to recall when I had painted it. My memory fails with the years . . ."

"Fly, Seraph!" Andrea whispered to the page. "Fly! Bring me here my palette and a brush."

Something in Orsini's voice propelled the boy on his way. He was back in a moment.

"Yes," said Mantegna, succumbing still further, "I've often wondered what had become of it. Odd I should have forgotten to sign a work of this importance. Absence of mind — " Mechanically, he hooked the palette on his thumb, mechanically mixed some colors, and painted in his *pinxit* a little larger than usual. "There, signori."

"You see," triumphed Lorenzo da Pavia.

"You see," Andrea winked at Camilla.

She looked up at him, her eyes deep with pride. "*You see!*"

* * * * * * *

433